Ruby looked at the huge stainless steel bowls full of cookie dough. It had taken them hours to mix. "We're not throwing it out, that's for sure. One of us has to stay here and bake and the other one has to go down and get a business license. Do you have any extra money?"

"Ruby, you know I don't have any money."

"You told me you and Hugo have a joint savings account. That means whatever is in that account is half yours. If you want to, you can draw out all the money; all you have to do is sign a withdrawal slip."

"Okay, I'll do it!" Dixie said in a shaky voice after a long moment of struggling with her fears.

After her friend had left, Ruby dropped her head into her hands. What right did she have to tell Dixie to steal from her husband? Ruby reached for the phone. Her heart pounded. Finally, Dixie's breathless voice came over the wire. "Don't do it, Dixie. Don't go to the bank. I'll think of something else. I'm sorry, Dixie. I had no right to put you in a position like that."

The rest of the day passed in a blur for Ruby. But the best _____ ____ happened was her realization that frie_____ _____ ___portant than material things, _____ ____ ___ _____ felt now as though _____ ___ ___ ___ ___ was carved in granit_

By Fern Michaels
Published by The Ballantine Publishing Group:

SEASONS OF HER LIFE

Fern Michaels

BALLANTINE BOOKS • NEW YORK

A Ballantine Book
Published by   e Ballantine Publishing Group
Copyright © 1994 by Fern Michaels, Inc.

All rights reserved under International and Pan-American Copyright Conventions. Published in the United States by The Ballantine Publishing Group, a division of Random House, Inc., New York, and simultaneously in Canada by Random House of Canada Limited, Toronto.

http://www.randomhouse.com

Library of Congress Catalog Card Number: 93-22134

ISBN 0-345-36591-7

Manufactured in the United States of America

First Hardcover Edition: April 1994
First Mass Market Edition: December 1994

OPM   28   27   26   25   24   23   22   21   20   19

*I'd like to dedicate this book
to someone I used to know.*

{{{{{{{{ PROLOGUE }}}}}}}}

The graduation dinner for Ruby Connors wasn't really a graduation dinner at all because George Connors, her father, demanded a six-course meal in their house seven days a week. Tonight the fare was fresh fruit, soup, salad, a fish mixture, roast chicken, stuffing, cranberry sauce, string beans and peas from the garden, mashed potatoes, gravy and homemade biscuits suitable for sopping up gravy, and a cake. It was a rich double-chocolate cake, three full layers, with nearly an inch of frosting between each layer. The top was full of swirls and little peaks with colored jimmies all over.

Grace was long and drawn out. Ruby wished her father would get on with it so she could attack her food, not because she wanted it, but because she had to eat it. At least four times a week she puked up her dinner. She watched, her face blank, when her father loaded up her plate. Already her younger sister, Opal, had tears in her eyes. Opal could never eat all her food and always had to sit at the table till eight o'clock, when her mother would take the plate and wrap it in waxed paper so it could be served to Opal for breakfast. George Connors called the heavy, horrible meals "providing for his family."

Opal Connors cried a lot, but not Ruby. Ruby had learned to do what she was told, for the most part; otherwise punishment was swift and terrible. Once she had spilled a handful of salt on the floor, and her father had forced her to lick it up. Often he had beaten her until she limped. If he found out she threw up after these heavy meals, he probably would tape her mouth shut.

Tomorrow would change all that. Tomorrow she was leaving this house and Barstow, Pennsylvania, and she was never coming back. Tomorrow she was going to Washington, D.C., to live with her older sister, Amber, and to work for the government.

Ruby watched as her father poured glasses of milk for her and

Opal. She hated drinking milk because it filled her up even more. This was her second glass, to be consumed with the cake. If only one of her parents would say something about her vale-dictory speech and graduating with honors, but she knew there would be no words of praise. There never were.

At least Grace Zachary, the Connors' next-door neighbor, had been there for her at the ceremony. Grace had sat with her hus-band, Paul, in the front row of the bleachers, smacking her hands together in applause after Ruby's speech and enthusiasti-cally poking her husband in the shoulder while he whistled be-tween his teeth and hooted, "Yay, Ruby!" How often Ruby wished they had been her parents instead of the ones she'd been given.

The moment Ruby finished her cake, she asked to be excused. George reached out, slapped his hand over her wrist, and said, "You sit there till your sister finishes her supper." Ruby's heart fluttered. Her eyes swiveled to her mother, who was staring at her own wedge of cake as if it were her enemy. Ruby sat back and folded her hands in her lap.

She had the ability, from long years of practice, to shift her mind into neutral when she had to. But the moment George Connors left the table to go out to the shed, she flew off her chair and scraped Opal's plate defiantly into the coal stove. She watched the banked coals spit and hiss before she stared down her mother.

"Eat the damn cake, Opal, and stop sniveling," she snapped, but not unkindly. To her mother she said, "I suppose you're go-ing to tell, like you always do." This time her voice *was* unkind. "This is as good a time as any to tell you I throw up these damn dinners almost every night. Tell him *that*, too," Ruby said, marching out of the room and upstairs. If she'd taken the time to look, she would have seen her mother's eyes fill with tears.

Ruby waited for her stomach to rumble and churn, then bee-lined for the bathroom and upchucked.

PART ONE

SPRING

{{{{{{{{{ CHAPTER ONE }}}}}}}}}

1950

Almost free. Almost.

Ruby Connors looked around her room for the last time. She was really leaving this house, this room, and if she had anything to say about it, she'd never come back. Her eyes fell on the white curtains hanging stiffly at the window, starched in sugar water and stretched on curtain stretchers. No more of that, Ruby thought gleefully. No more pinpricks. And no more white iron bed with its crazy quilt made by her mother with patches from her older sister's dresses. She hated the quilt, just as she hated Amber.

Someday she was going to have a pretty bedroom like the pictures in the Sears, Roebuck catalogue. She'd have a dressing table with a white organdy ruffle with curtains to match—and not the kind that had to be stretched, either. She'd have a meadow-green carpet and a real bedspread. Every table and corner would have plants and flowers, mostly daisies. On her dressing table would be silver frames with pictures, maybe of her dog or cat. Everything would be alive. Maybe she'd even put her picture of Johnny Ray in it, the one she'd sneaked out of a *Photoplay* magazine.

Ruby sat down on the edge of the bed, and the springs squeaked under her ninety pounds. The room was sweltering hot, even though it was only June. In the summer she baked alive, and in the winter she froze with cold drafts from the attic.

Almost free. Almost. "I'm leaving and I'm never coming back, nevernevernevernevernevernevernevernevernevernevernevernevernevernevernevernevernevernevernevernevernevernevernevernevernevernevernevernevernevernevernevernevernevernevernevernevernevernevernevernevernevernevernevernevernevernevernevernevernevernevernevernevernevernevernevernevernevernevernevernevernevernevernevernevernevernever," Ruby singsonged quietly.

Her suitcases were packed; she was wearing her sodality medal and the scapular that her mother always insisted on. Her dress wasn't new, but it wasn't as faded as her others and a ruffle had been added to cover the let-down hem. Her hairstyle, if it could be called a style, was a dutch boy with bangs. As soon as she could, she was going to get a permanent and some colored barrettes, maybe a ribbon or two if that's what the girls wore in Washington, D.C.

Ruby scuffed at the braided rug with her polished saddle shoe. The shoes were almost new, and so were her socks, but they smelled like No Worry. So did her underwear. If only she weren't so skinny and plain-looking. She was starting to worry now and have doubts. She *was* doing the right thing. There was no way she wanted to stay home and work in the shirt factory. She'd seen girls that graduated a year or two ahead of her getting off the bus at the railroad tracks with threads all over their clothes. They always looked so tired and listless. Her mother called the shirt factory a sweat box. Living with her older sister, Amber, was not going to be divinely wonderful, either. Amber was prissy and meticulous, and she was a liar. But it would be better than living here and working in the factory.

Ruby carried her suitcases out to the hall. Two hours to go. She put the rag rug back in place at the side of the bed. Two quick swipes and the quilt was wrinkle-free. She backed out of the room. Her hand stretched toward the door. If she closed it, she would no longer exist, she thought. Her parents would walk right past it and never think of her. If she left it open, they just might think, this is Ruby's room. *Maybe . . . could be . . . dumb thought, Ruby.* She pushed the door shut, a defiant look on her face.

The house was so quiet, Ruby thought as her saddle shoes snicked at the rubber treads on the stairs. Her mother, Irma, was probably on the back porch, shelling peas for dinner. Her father had gone uptown for the mail and to shop at the A&P because he said Irma didn't know how to shop and look for bargains. Opal was at catechism class. She was going to miss Opal. Out of necessity she and Opal had banded together against their parents and Amber. She'd promised to write to Opal, but to send the letters to her grandmother's house. Opal had promised never to show the letters to their parents. Opal was going to have a tough time with her gone.

In the wide center hallway, Ruby listened for any sound that might mean her father had returned. The screen door squeaked when she opened it and squeaked again when she closed it. She waited a moment on the front porch to see if she would be called back into the house. A bee buzzed about her knees. Ruby swatted it and killed it with her bare hand. Amber would have squeaked and gone white in the face the same way she'd always gotten white in the face when it was her turn to scrub the porch floor. Because of Amber's regular weekend illnesses, Ruby scrubbed this porch every Saturday for as long as she could remember. She would never again have to do it. Now it was Opal's turn.

Ruby ran, careful not to scuff her shoes, down the street, past the lumber mill, over the railroad tracks, past Riley's Monument Works, where her father worked. She raced past her uncle's garage, over the bridge and up the hill. The smell of stale beer from Bender's beer joint made her hold her breath as she careened around the corner that led to her grandmother's house.

A smile tugged at the corner of Ruby's mouth. She'd said good-bye to Bubba every day for the past two weeks, but when you weren't ever planning on coming back, you couldn't say good-bye often enough. Besides, she *needed* this last visit, this last good-bye.

Almost free. Almost.

Ruby took a moment to drink in the sight of her grandmother's house, to commit it to memory. It was a squat little house made from fieldstone with a matching wall. She'd never sit on that wall again, never lie under the old chestnut tree in the front yard. She loved the old chestnut and the way its branches hung down and covered her like a grand umbrella. She would forget the house she grew up in, but she would never forget this house. Never.

Inside, the kitchen was big and square with cabbage-rose wallpaper that sometimes made her dizzy, but her grandmother loved bright things. The windowsills and shelves held glossy green plants in colorful clay pots, and the room always smelled of cinnamon and orange. The curtains, as cheerful as the wallpaper, were made from linen and trimmed with inch-wide red rickrack, handsewn by her grandmother. They were changed twice a year, when the mullioned windows were washed. The crazy quilt linoleum on the floor was blinding. What she loved most, though, were the old-fashioned coal stove and the pots that constantly simmered with orange peels. It was a kitchen of pure love. This house was similar to her parents', having been built by the same lumber company, but love had made it into something very different. Love was something she was never going to be without again.

"Ruby, is that you?" her grandmother called from the back porch.

"It's me, Bubba," Ruby trilled as she made her way past the snowball bush, which was in full bloom. Once she'd picked a bouquet from it for her room, and her mother had thrown it out, saying she didn't want any bugs in the house. Later Ruby had pulled the wasted bouquet from the trash.

Ruby planted a noisy kiss on top of her grandmother's head. "Apple pie tonight, huh?" Her uncle John loved apple pie. Uncle Hank liked rhubarb. Ruby knew there would be two kinds of pie tonight. "I came to say good-bye again." Ruby laughed.

"I knew you'd come this morning." The old lady smiled in return. "You look pretty, Ruby. Did you have breakfast?" Ruby nodded. "Are you nervous about going on the train all the way to Washington?"

"No. Well, maybe a little. About Amber mostly. She's supposed to meet me, and she won't like that. But I bought a present for her last week at the company store, so she'll have to be nice to me. I'm going to do my best to get along with her." She could tell by the anxiety in her grandmother's eyes that she wasn't convincing her.

"You know, Bubba," Ruby went on, "I feel different ... inside ... I'm changing or else I already changed ... it's not just me going away, either. It's something else, something I can't explain. Maybe it's because I'm turning eighteen next month. But whatever it is, I think it means you don't have to worry about Amber and me. It's going to work out, it really is."

"I hope so," Mary Cozinsky mumbled under her breath. "You stand your ground with your sister, Ruby, and don't let her push you around."

"You're not going to worry about me, are you, Bubba?"

"Every single day until I know there's nothing to worry about. But I'm happy for you, too. Do you remember when we talked about the seasons in a woman's life? You're in the spring of your life, Ruby, the best time of all. Everything is still before you. It's your time to grow, to spread your wings, to turn into the wonderful woman I know you will become. By the time you reach the summer of your life, you'll be married with children of your own. I think by then you'll understand how the cycle works. Right now your head is so full of anticipation and excitement, it's hard for you to think about things like seasons."

Ruby wanted to tell her she understood perfectly, but then she would have to admit that she knew her beloved grandmother was at the end of the winter of her life. The thought, the words, were unbearable. Better to pretend she was excited. Better just to change the subject.

"I'm going to write to Opal and send the letters to your box number," she said. "Opal will read them to you. She's going to scrub your kitchen floor on Fridays, and on Wednesdays she'll go to the farm for your pot cheese. She'll pick the blueberries and help you make jelly whenever you're ready. She can iron real good, Bubba. She can do the Sunday shirts if you want her to. You can depend on Opal, Bubba, and I think you should keep her money the way you did for me. Pop will make her put it in the collection if you give it to her." Ruby's eyes snapped angrily. "Pop gave me my bill this morning. It's so much money. I have to pay rent, buy food, buy tokens for the bus, and a bunch of other stuff. I'll be an old woman before I pay it off. Your parents are supposed to give you a present when you graduate from high school. I didn't get a present. I got a bill for my keep and for all the money I put in the collection basket on Sunday. Eighteen years' worth! I figured it out, Bubba, it's ten cents for every Sunday Mass." Ruby cried heartbrokenly.

"How much does it all come to?" Mary asked quietly as she stroked Ruby's dark hair.

"Church is $93.60. The bill for my keep is six thousand." Ruby felt the tremor in her grandmother's body.

"I have a present for you, Ruby," the old lady crooned. "You have to stop crying now, or your eyes will be red and swollen when you get on the train. Smile for me, Ruby," she said in a quivering voice. Ruby wiped her eyes on the hem of the sweet-smelling apron her grandmother wore.

"A present?" Ruby's moist eyes glistened. "How big is it?"

"Very small, sweetie. I'm glad you have a pocket in your dress. This . . . present has to be a secret. You must promise me that you'll never tell Amber, even if she makes you so angry, you want to shout about it. And you must not tell your father. Not now anyway. Someday, perhaps, when you're secure and happy. Will you promise me, Ruby?"

"Oh, Bubba, you know I will. I never broke a promise. Not

a peep. Amber is the last person I'd spill my guts to, you know that."

Mary fumbled in the pocket of her apron and withdrew a rumpled-up ball of linen. Ruby knew what it was the moment she saw it. She gasped and the old lady's eyes twinkled. Ruby held her breath. It was years since her grandmother had shown her the prize that was wrapped so carefully in cotton and then again in the white handkerchief.

"The czarina's ring! Oh, oh, oh, it's more beautiful than the last time I saw it. Truly, you're giving it to me? I know you promised, but I thought you . . . you just wanted to make me feel good. What if someone steals it?" Ruby said, holding out her hand.

"It's your responsibility now, Ruby. It's up to you to make sure it's kept safe."

It was so heavy, but it felt good in the palm of her hand. The band was wide, reaching almost to her knuckle, where it crested into a cone-shaped pyramid of diamonds and rubies. Ruby sucked in her breath as she struggled to count the stones in the ring. "How many stones are there, Bubba?"

"Lord, child, I don't know."

"Do you think it's worth two hundred dollars?" Ruby asked naively. The old lady smiled secretly and nodded.

"I'll keep it safe, I swear I will. I won't ever wear it, I promise."

"You'd look kind of silly if you did." The old lady chuckled. "This ring is fit only for royalty. The president's wife doesn't have anything half as grand. Only you, Ruby."

When Ruby's grandfather had been alive, he would regale her with stories of the ring every Sunday after Mass. The more beer he drank, the wilder the stories became. To this day, neither Ruby nor her grandmother knew for certain if the czarina had bestowed the ring on her grandfather for a deed well done or if he stole it, like he said, as he was falling into his beer stupor that was permitted only on Sunday.

"I think she gave it to Grandpop because he was so young and dashing, a true cossack. Don't you, Bubba?"

Mary did not answer, but instead gave her a mysterious little smile, then handed over a small square of white paper. "There's a man's name here who lives in Washington, D.C. He will buy the ring if you ever want to sell it. Your grandfather was going to sell it before he died to make sure I was taken care of, but I wouldn't let him. He was so proud of that ring. Your uncle John and uncle Hank take care of me. Besides," she chuckled, "my fingers are all crooked. What do I need with a ring? It's yours, child. Although there's going to be a war around here when I die and your father finds out the ring is missing."

Ruby's eyes filled. She bundled up the ring and stuffed it into her pocket. "I can't wait till I'm eighteen," she said.

Mary smiled. "Hand me that apple bowl and don't go wishing your life away."

"Do you think anyone will ever love me besides you?" Ruby blurted out.

Mary pretended to think. "What I think is you're going to have beaux standing in line, waiting to take you to the picture shows."

Ruby giggled. "I'm so plain and ordinary. Maybe if I get a permanent. I'm going to get a tube of lipstick, too, and maybe some pearl earrings. I have thirty-four dollars I put away. Pop doesn't know I have it. I think it's enough for maybe two new dresses, shoes for work, and a brassiere," she said impishly. "I'll grow breasts, too, you wait and see. My hormones are just slow right now." The old lady laughed in delight at her granddaughter's gamine face.

"You better start home, Ruby, before George comes looking for you. Be a good girl now. I mean a proper young lady."

"I won't shame you, Bubba. Don't worry about me. Opal is going to take care of you, but I'm not coming back here, ever, even when ... you know ... I'm not!" Ruby said adamantly.

"Ruby, I know that. I don't want you coming back. I want you to remember me like this, not the way I'll look when I'm laid out in those purple dresses the undertakers put on you. That's why I gave you the ring now. There's nothing for you here, Ruby, so you stay away. Send me pictures. Amber sent me a postcard and said she had a camera."

"Boy, was Pop mad about that!" Ruby giggled. "She paid off her bill, so he could only holler at Mom. She sent pictures and Pop threw them in the stove. Said they were the devil's handiwork. It was a nice picture of Amber, too. She was sitting under the cherry blossom tree and had her legs crossed. Her skirt was up to here," she said, pointing to the middle of her thighs.

Ruby dropped to her knees. She looked earnestly into her

grandmother's face. "I don't think I'll ever love anyone as much as I love you. You've never said a cross word to me even if I deserved it. I'll think of you every day. I'll keep all my promises, and you'll never have to be ashamed of me. I'll remember you sitting here like this. When I'm old I'm going to peel apples just the way you do, all in one curl."

Ruby leaned closer and hugged her grandmother. "Are you sure," she said huskily, "that you don't mind if I don't come to your funeral?"

"I'll mind if you do come. If you do, you'll have to see your father. Make up your mind, Ruby."

"I'm not coming," Ruby said in a jittery-sounding voice.

"That's good. Now, get along," Mary said firmly.

Ruby kissed her grandmother one last time and raced off the porch and down the walkway to the street. She didn't want to think about the tears on her grandmother's cheeks.

Almost free. Almost.

Mary Cozinsky slumped back on the old wicker rocker. The dearest piece of her life was gone now. So many pieces were gone. She set the apple bowl on the floor and withdrew her rosary from her apron pocket. She raised her eyes upward and prayed, simple words from the heart. "Protect my little Ruby," she pleaded. "And, God, if you decide to send her father, my son George, to hell, I won't question your decision."

She'd known this day was coming; still, she wasn't prepared for the empty feeling, the devastating sense of loss. She'd given birth to seven children, and she loved them dearly, with the exception of George, but none of her own children touched her heart the way Ruby did. When Ruby was seven and permitted to cross the road and the railroad tracks, the child had begun visiting daily, sometimes twice. By the time Ruby was eight, she was tightly ensconced in the hearts of both her grandparents. When George objected, her husband had straightened him out in the blink of an eye. The handsome cossack had stepped on George the way he would have stepped on a pissant, telling him that Ruby was to visit whenever she wanted. George recognized the threat: either he allowed Ruby to visit or he would forfeit his share of any inheritance.

Still, Ruby paid for her visits in other ways: gross punishments, hand-me-downs, and the loss of her freedom. While the other children played and had fun, Ruby was reading scripture with a Nancy Drew book inside the Bible. The wiry little girl had cooked and cleaned, run errands, and lived in fear in that damnable cell she called a bedroom. Only at her grandparents' house could she be herself, and she blossomed under the umbrella of their love, willingly doing any of the chores asked of her. In the beginning, it was hard for Ruby to accept the rewards—a quarter here, a half-dollar there, wonderful desserts, the love of Sam, the old bloodhound who had died right after Ruby's twelfth birthday. It was an awful birthday for her that year. Just days before, George had told her she hadn't been named Ruby for a precious gem at all, but because she was red and ugly when she was born. Old Sam spent hours licking her tears. Her grandfather had to physically restrain her the day they buried the old hound, for she would have crawled into the special burying place along with him.

She had so much love, that little girl. Often, late at night, when Mikel had been so sick near the end, they would talk about Ruby and what would happen to her. Wanting to leave no stone unturned, Mikel summoned Ruby's mother, Irma, and spoke with her at length. Irma, in her squeaky voice, mumbled that she would never go against George, and Ruby would do as they said. After graduation she would go to Washington to live with Amber, and work. Although it hadn't been said aloud, it was understood that Ruby would begin paying her debt just the way Amber had paid hers. They'd offered, on the spot, to pay on Ruby's behalf, but Irma had squirmed in her chair, frantically shaking her head. From somewhere she summoned the gumption to ask what made Ruby so special to her in-laws. Mikel had looked at her with pity and told her to go home. The moment the screen door banged shut, Mikel asked for the czarina's ring and said, "This is to go to Ruby when you think it's time."

Two hours after Mikel's funeral, when the beer had flowed and the food was all eaten, George had asked Mary when she was going to sell the ring. She remembered her words as though she'd just uttered them. "You might think I'm a dumb Polack and your father was a dumb Russian, George, but you're wrong. Your father made a will and the ring is mine. I can do whatever I want with it." And then she blurted out without meaning to: "Ruby told us to make a will; she learned all about wills in school." The others, George's brothers and sisters, were all behind her chair in the kitchen, supporting her words, when George dragged a screaming, crying Ruby from the house. With Mikel gone, there wasn't a thing any of them could do. Ruby's punishment was compounded daily and ran for months at a time, but Ruby wrote notes that friends delivered and read to her grandmother after school.

Mary wiped her eyes with her apron. She smiled through her tears. She'd done the best she could for the child; the rest was up to Ruby. As long as she had the ring and her picture of Johnny Ray, Ruby would be fine. Her watery eyes took on a sparkle when she thought of Ruby's eighteenth birthday and what she could give to her. Money, of course. Hank and John would contribute, and she'd take all her change in the lard can to the bank. Maybe, just maybe, she could scrape up a hundred dollars. She smiled then, picturing the look on Ruby's face. She could buy all the things she wanted. A real pocketbook, some nylons, maybe some nail polish and new underwear. All the things a young girl would need when she lived and worked in the city.

As for George, Mary made a mental note to deduct $6,093.60 from his share of her estate.

There were so many things she'd never forgive her son for, though she knew there were reasons for the way he'd turned out, reasons almost too horrible to think about. In a town as small as Barstow, with only seven businesses on a small main street, a tiny high school, telephone party lines, conversations over clotheslines, wintertime quilting bees, and summertime garden clubs, there could be no secrets.

The gossip had filled in the details—an older boy had done terrible things to him, sexual things, all while a local tomboy named Bitsy Lucas stood by laughing and taunting and urging the older boy on. But Mary had seen the violation in his eyes the minute he had walked into the house, and he had never forgiven her for the insight. He'd been only eleven years old at the time, and she'd had to take him to the doctor's, so Mikel inevitably found out. From that day forward, father had looked at son with disgust in his eyes.

And from that day forward, whether because of Bitsy Lucas or herself Mary didn't know, George hated all women. He hated her the way he now hated Irma and even his own daughters.

The familiar pain was creeping around her chest again. That

old fool of a doctor had told her she shouldn't upset herself. She snorted. With George in the background, how could she be anything but upset? Obviously, a second rosary was called for. The comforting prayers calmed the pain in her chest almost immediately.

Ruby slowed her steps and shifted her mental gears the moment she crossed the railroad tracks. Her right hand was in the pocket of her dress, her fingers caressing the tightly wrapped ring. She hoped it didn't bulge too much. Her hand worked to flatten the linen handkerchief as much as she could. They'd just think she had a hanky wadded into a ball. She crossed the fingers of her left hand. Sometimes she thought her father had X-ray vision.

Skirting the gravel lot at the lumber mill, Ruby headed up the street to her house, knowing her parents would be on the porch, waiting for her. She wasn't late. In fact, she still had almost ten minutes before it would be time to leave for the train station. She sucked in her breath as she cut across the Zacharys' lawn next door. She stepped behind an ancient white pine and observed her parents for a minute. They were both tall, but there any similarity ended. Irma was incredibly thin with large, bony feet, red hands, and short fingernails. Her hair was a soft brown, the color of the spring wrens. Ruby was never sure what color her mother's eyes were because she rarely looked directly at her. Probably a greenish-brown. Hazel maybe. She had a warm smile though, particularly when Amber did something that pleased her. Overall, her mother was a tired, weary woman. She worked tirelessly, never sitting down for a cup of coffee or tea. She couldn't, Ruby thought, because George made her perform. The bathroom had to be scrubbed every day from top to bottom. The kitchen floor had to be scrubbed, too. Monday was wash day; Tuesday was ironing day; Wednesday was baking day; Thursday was for changing beds and window washing. Friday was clean-the-whole-house day, and Saturday was for scrubbing the porches, dusting the jars in the fruit cellar, and going to confession. If there were any free moments, they were spent at the sewing machine or mending by hand. Idle hands were the devil's work, her father said. If that was true—and Ruby didn't believe it was—then Irma Connors was damn near a saint. Right now her mother looked nervous, Ruby thought. She was always nervous when she was in her husband's company, always fearful she would say the wrong thing. Irma survived the only way she knew how, by obeying her husband and keeping quiet. Ruby's eyes darkened. Her father wasn't around *all* the time. There was time enough for an occasional hug or pat on the head or kind word, time her mother chose not to give her.

George was pacing on the porch, his face surly and mean. As far back as she could remember, he'd always looked just the way he looked now. Muscular and hard, long-legged in creased work pants, his shirt ironed to perfection. Her girlfriends thought him handsome; she thought him ugly, inside and out. He was strong and arrogant. Every day of her life she'd felt that strength and arrogance. Cold, piercing eyes were scanning the sidewalk, watching for her. Even from this distance Ruby could see how his lips thinned out. He was angry—at her, at life. Twice she'd seen those cold blue eyes become warm, and both times he'd been staring at Grace Zachary, their neighbor. He often said Grace was the devil's own disciple, in her scanty shorts and halter top. Her mother said she was trash. But nothing could make Ruby deny her affection for Grace, who called her honey and sweetie. She'd liked her even more the day she saw her stick out her tongue and make a face behind her father's back.

The Angelus rang. Noon. Ruby ran around the pine through the yard and along the side of the porch. She wouldn't be late until the last peal of the bell.

"You're late, girl!" George said harshly. Ruby lowered her gaze, staring at the cracks on the porch floor. Early on she'd learned never to look her father in the eye. "Where you been, girl?"

"I went over to Bubba's to say good-bye . . . sir."

George's eyes narrowed. "Your grandmother give you a going-away present?"

"No, sir." Ruby lied with a straight face. She crossed her fingers inside the pockets of her dress. Bubba hadn't given Amber anything when she went away, so there was no reason for her father to think this time would be any different. Because it was so important that he believe her, she raised her eyes and said, "She did give me a hanky because I started to cry."

She withdrew the square of white linen with the shirt-tail hem. Her heart took on an extra beat, but she didn't lower her gaze.

"Did you clean your room, girl?"

"Yes, sir. This morning."

"Did you pack your Bible?"

"Yes, sir. Last night." Before she got off the train at Union Station she was going to ditch the Bible. If Amber was dumb enough to ask her where it was, she'd lie and say someone on the train stole it. Girl. He'd never called her anything but girl. Was Ruby so hard to say? Or dear or honey? She risked a quick glance at her mother, who immediately looked away.

"Get your bags, and don't be slow about it. Close the door, and don't slam it. I'll bring the car up."

Ruby climbed the steps to the truck room, a lump in her throat. Close the door, and don't slam it. She'd like to slam the damn door so hard it fell off its hinges. They'd never think of her again until her payments started rolling in. Angrily, she pushed her suitcases down the hall to the top of the stairs. She closed the door quietly, and in a last fit of rebellion, she kicked both suitcases down the steps. They landed with a loud thud. Ruby clapped her hands and grinned, then went downstairs again. Her suitcases upended on the front porch, Ruby stared at her mother, willing her to say something, something kind, something personal. Even a look would do, Ruby thought desperately. She wanted to throw her arms around her mother and cry, but she didn't. You must love me a little bit, she thought, I'm your daughter. She cried silently, never taking her eyes from her mother's face. Hurry, Mom, he'll be here in a second, just a word, a look. Please, Mom. Oh, God, please say it. Now, now, before it's too late. Ruby didn't need to see her father's car come to a halt at the side of the house; she saw the relief in her mother's face.

"I think it's going to rain before long," Irma said loudly enough for George to hear.

"There won't be any rain today, woman," George said coldly.

Irma blinked and looked overhead at the dark gray clouds that would erupt shortly. "I'm sure you're right, George," she said.

Ruby carried her bags to the car. God, wasn't her mother even going to say good-bye?

"Say good-bye to your mother, girl," George ordered.

Without turning, Ruby mimicked her father, "Say good-bye to your mother, girl."

At the same moment the words tumbled from Ruby's mouth,

Opal skidded around the corner of the house screaming at the top of her lungs, "RubyRubyRuby! I thought I would miss you. I asked Sister Clementine to let me out a few minutes early. She said to say good-bye for her."

Ruby saw George's hand move, and Opal took the blow high on her cheekbone. His slap caught her full in the mouth, cutting off anything else she might say. Opal's eyes filled with tears. Ruby caught her sister close and whispered, "Don't you cry, don't you dare! That's what they want, especially *him*. Don't ever let them see you cry. Soon as we leave, go over to Bubba's. You can roll out the dough for the pies. She's waiting for you. I'm leaving that damn Bible on the train. Think about that to-night when you fall asleep. Go on now, get up on the porch and I'll wave to you."

Ruby rolled the window down, fixing her gaze on her mother. Irma looked away. Ruby waved at Opal, who was struggling not to cry.

Almost free. Almost.

Three hours into the trip, shortly before the train groaned to a stop in Harrisburg, Ruby finally felt confident enough to get up and go to the bathroom, knowing all eyes would be on her lurching walk to the end of the car. It wasn't so bad walking down the car because she was looking at the back of people's heads. Coming back they'd be staring at her. She knew she was dressed all wrong. Her hair was wrong, too. Even the saddle shoes were wrong. So was the sandwich and apple her mother had packed for her. She'd be damned if she'd eat the egg salad sandwich. That would be left behind with the Bible.

It took Ruby a full five minutes before she figured out how to flush the toilet, and when she did, she smiled from ear to ear. She had a lot to learn, so much was new to her: the train ride, the strange countryside, the washrooms, the colored people. How could she be so ignorant about these things and yet so smart in school? She *was* smart, too; she could take dictation faster than anyone else, faster than her teacher, Miss Pipas, and her typing was almost sixty words a minute with no mistakes. Miss Pipas said she was the best, the most accurate student she'd ever had.

Head high, aware of the stares she was receiving, Ruby marched back to her seat and sat down. Miss Pipas had tried, in her own way, to prepare Ruby for what she'd called the outside, but she hadn't paid that much attention. Now she wished she had listened more carefully.

Ruby looked at the backs of the passengers' heads, all curly hair set with Wave-Set. Even the men had some kind of stuff on their hair. There were young people her age on the train near the front of the car. They were having a grand old time, laughing and teasing one another. Ruby ached to join them, to be part of them for a little while. She settled deeper into her seat and watched the countryside through the window. The wheels clicked on the tracks seeming to say Amber, Amber, Amber.

Regardless of what she'd said to her grandmother, Ruby knew things would not go well with Amber. Amber didn't want her; Ruby had read the letter and heard her parents talking. The gist of that conversation was George telling Irma that if she, Ruby, didn't obey Amber, she would be sent home to work in the factory. "She'll listen or else," George growled. "You tell *your* daughter in your next letter that if she can't keep a tight rein on Ruby, I'll go down there and fetch them both back here." And he would do just that.

Not me! Ruby screamed silently. You'll never get me back here! What it all meant, Ruby decided, was she had to toe the line and do *exactly* what Amber said.

But God, how she hated Amber. All the reasons for her hatred rivered through her, leaving her weak and trembling. She thought about how, when she was five and her sister was eight, Amber had pushed her under the water in the field pond. The memory made her gasp; just as she had then. If it hadn't been for one of the older boys, who'd fished her out, she would have drowned. Amber didn't want to be saddled that day with a younger sister. She hadn't wanted to be saddled with her the day she left her with her foot caught in the railroad tracks to go on with her friends to play stickball. She'd been lucky that day, too, when an old miner worked diligently to free her foot, though she'd gotten a whipping for her torn shoe.

Ruby never understood Amber's hatred of her until her grandmother explained that Amber had always wanted to be an only child, as if that would make her loved and wanted.

That in part explained why Amber had always said she had been born an angel, complete with wings and halo. She said she was supposed to go back to heaven, but her wings had been injured on the trip down to earth. Arms had sprouted from the injured wings and their mother had found her in the nick of time. Ruby believed all this, but when she found the nerve to repeat the story to her beloved Bubba, the old lady had scoffed and told her it was a big lie. She smarted for over an hour at her own gullibility. For years she'd actually believed the terrible lie that her sister was somehow special, more deserving of love than she, Ruby. She'd gone home and stalked her older sister like an animal, catching up with her at the crick and beating her almost senseless. Amber had crawled home bawling and calling her a devil. For that Ruby had been whipped with a belt, banished to her room for five days, and told to read the Bible from cover to cover. At the end of the five days she'd read only twenty-three pages and was whipped again when she couldn't answer any of the questions her father asked her. The real punishment this time was far worse: she wasn't to go to her Bubba's for a month.

Ruby braced herself as the train came to a grinding, crunching halt in Harrisburg. Ahead, some girls were counting out money and buying pop and snacks. They wore earrings and charm bracelets and seersucker playsuits with matching sandals. She knew they were her age, possibly younger, but how sophisticated and confident they were. She'd bet the thirty-seven dollars in her suitcase that their parents, both of them, had kissed them good-bye at the train station. If she ever had children, she would smother them with love and affection.

Ruby morosely fished a dime out of her pocket for a bottle of Orange Nehi.

She set the bottle on the floor and reached overhead for her suitcase. This was the perfect time to fish out the Bible and slide it under the seat. She made a mental note to rip out the first page with her name on it. She didn't ever want to see the Bible again.

People were looking at her, but Ruby didn't care. None of them, she noticed, offered to help her with the smaller of the two cases. Lickety-split she had the Bible out, facedown on the seat. Stretching to her full height, she jammed the case into the overhead rack. She inched the book across the seat before she sat down.

She thought about the egg salad sandwich then as she watched the girls laughing and eating potato chips. She'd die before she did something to embarrass herself, and eating a homemade sandwich on the train was embarrassing. Besides, egg salad always smelled like her father's smelly underwear on wash day.

Ruby relaxed. The empty pop bottle was now safely under the seat along with the Bible and the egg salad sandwich. She leaned back and stared out the window. Gradually, the clickety-clack of the train wheels hypnotized her to sleep.

The girls in the front of the car squealed in glee when the train pulled into Union Station. Ruby found herself jolted forward and caught herself before she slid from the seat. To her horror the Bible and the egg salad sandwich slid out from under the seat. She bent over to look for the pop bottle and saw it three seats ahead. With the toe of her shoe she shoved the Bible and sandwich as far back as she could. She hoped the couple in the seat behind her hadn't seen the garbage she was leaving, but when the man offered to get her bags overhead, she realized they couldn't care less what she left behind.

With her suitcases banging against her shins, Ruby found her way to the end of the car and struggled down the three steps to the ground. It was dark and gloomy. As Ruby trudged along with the other travelers, she could hear over the hissing steam from the trains the young girls shrieking with laughter. She wondered what was so funny about lugging suitcases all this way.

The moment Ruby set foot on the concourse, she spotted Amber leaning nonchalantly against a wall. She set her suitcases down as she fought for a deep breath. She watched her sister for a full three minutes before she walked toward her. She looked almost elegant, Ruby thought, with her upswept hair and summer sundress. She thought her yellow sandals the most beautiful shoes she'd ever seen. Ruby felt ugly and angry at the same time.

If she smiles, things will be okay. If she doesn't smile . . .

"Amber, I'm here," Ruby said, setting down her suitcases. She stretched out her arms to hug her sister. Amber stepped back, her eyes snapping furiously.

"I've been waiting for almost an hour!" There was no smile. Ruby's arms fell to her sides.

"They had to add water or something in Harrisburg. I heard someone complain that we'd be late. It wasn't my fault, Amber," Ruby said quietly.

"I suppose it's mine. I had things I wanted to do today, and you've managed to foul things up as usual. Don't just stand there, pick up your bags and let's go."

"If you'd help and carry one of the bags, we could move faster," Ruby grumbled.

Amber stopped in mid-stride. Ruby, struggling to keep up with her long-legged sister, literally bowled her over. She found herself apologizing as she reached out to help Amber to her feet. "Get away from me. Now look what you did. The strap on my sandal broke. You're here five minutes and already everything is wrong. No one helped me when I had to come here. I had to find my own way."

Ruby sat down on one of her suitcases. Her eyes shot daggers at her sister. "I didn't ask you to pick me up. I'm not so stupid I can't find my own way. So leave. I don't need you."

"You're just what I need, Ruby. If I leave you, you'll call for a cop and God only knows what you'd say, not to mention calling home and telling them I deserted you."

"No, Amber, that's what you would do, not me," Ruby said softly.

"This is not going to work," Amber said.

"You're telling me," Ruby muttered. "Just see if I give you your present. When crows turn pink and grow a third leg, you'll get it."

"What did you say?" Amber demanded.

"I said"—Ruby enunciated each word slowly and distinctly— "I hate your guts."

Amber laughed, a fiendish sound in the hubbub following them out of the station. She continued to laugh as they boarded the bus that would take them to the YWCA.

{{{{{{{{ CHAPTER TWO }}}}}}}}

Amber watched her sister struggle with the two heavy bags. One of her friends, a farm girl from Iowa, was waiting in the lobby, which smelled of cinnamon and coffee. She hurried over to offer her help. Amber was at once solicitous of Ruby as she punched the elevator button. Ruby wanted to cry in relief at Ethel's wide, warm smile. She was sure her arms would fall from their sockets at any moment.

Amber held a key aloft. "You're in 809, eighth floor. I made up the bed. All you have to do is unpack. There's a Hot Shoppe around the corner if you're hungry. I'm charging you for this sandal," she hissed.

"Somehow I knew you would," Ruby said sweetly. "I can manage from here on in. Thanks, Ethel," she said warmly.

Ruby waited until the two girls were on the elevator before she fit the key into the lock. This was such an important moment in her life.

With tantalizing slowness Ruby turned the knob. She stepped over the threshold, her breath exploding in a loud sigh of pure happiness. Her own room!

It was little more than a cubicle, but it had a carpet, a twin bed with a plaid spread, and matching drapes on the single window. There was also a dresser with four drawers and a chair with a plaid cushion that matched neither the spread nor the drapes, but Ruby didn't care. A closet ran the width of the room and held an overhead shelf. The mirror was clear with no sign of the backing wearing off. There was only one door, and it had a lock. Privacy, peace, for the first time in her life.

The moment she locked the door, she whirled and danced a jig around the small room. Hers and hers alone. She was going to be sooooo happy in this room. There was no way Amber was going to spoil this for her.

After going down the hall and taking her very first shower, ever, Ruby went out to the Hot Shoppe around the corner for a bite to eat. Her hamburger was overcooked, her french fries were greasy, and her Coca-Cola was watered down, but to her, it was a better meal than her mother's best Sunday dinner. Afterward, she went home and slept peacefully, dreamlessly.

She spent the next day sightseeing. She went to the Shrine of the Immaculate Conception, in case her parents or Amber put her to the test about going to church. She swore to herself this would be the *last* time she went into a church. The rest of the day she spent wandering around Washington, stopping only to eat or rest. When she returned to the Y, it was dark, she was tired, and her sister Amber was waiting for her in the hallway.

"Where have you been all day?" Amber demanded.

"To church, where you should have been," Ruby said.

"Stop lying. You don't even know where the church is."

"It's at 1315 8th Avenue. Or haven't you found it yet?" Ruby replied sweetly. "What will Pop think when I tell him that?"

"You damn little snip. Just wait till I tell Pop how *you're* acting."

"I'll be glad to wait. And if you want to talk to me any further, we can do it in my room."

Amber strode down the hall and waited until Ruby opened the door. She sat in the only chair, leaving Ruby to perch on the bed.

"I paid your train fare here and a month's rent. I'm going to give you carfare and food money to last you for the month because I promised Mom I would help you out."

"Why don't you tell the truth, Amber? Pop told you you had to do it or you'd go back to Barstow."

"That's right, he did. He also said you were to give me your paychecks. You don't know the first thing about handling money."

"Maybe I don't, but you aren't going to teach me. I'll learn myself. There is no way, no way at all, that I am going to give you my paycheck."

Amber stirred uneasily in the chair. This was a Ruby she didn't know, one she didn't want to know. "Here's twenty-five dollars for food and carfare. You can pay me back out of your first week's salary. Tomorrow you can buy tokens. Be ready at seven-thirty. If you're late, I'll leave without you. You'll have to take a secretarial test and then be interviewed. I scheduled you for eight-thirty. By the way, I told them your shorthand was acceptable, so it had better be."

"I'll be ready. And don't worry about my shorthand. It's *more* than acceptable. So is my typing. Wouldn't it be something if I get a better job and make more money than you?"

Ruby loved the look *that* brought to her sister's face, but Amber had the last word as she sailed through the door.

"Sure. Then you'll pay off your bill to Pop that much quicker."

Ruby deflated immediately.

* * *

In the lobby on the following morning, Ruby had time for a quick cup of coffee and a cinnamon bun before Amber and Ethel walked out of the elevator. Ethel gave her a smile, and Ruby returned it. Amber glowered. Ruby trailed behind the two girls all the way to the bus stop, where they boarded the Ft. Meyers bus along with a stream of other girls, all on their way to the Navy Annex. From time to time Ruby noticed Ethel staring at her. She was probably wondering what was wrong between her and Amber.

At the Annex, also known as Federal Office Building No. 2, the girls parted. Amber motioned Ruby ahead of her to an office marked Personnel. "They're expecting you. You'll have to find your own way back."

"How about good luck or I'll see you later?" Ruby mumbled. Her sister looked so stylish in her seersucker summer suit and crisp white blouse. Her high heels were white and had open toes. Ruby wanted to snatch them right off her feet, that's how badly she wanted an identical pair. The seams in her stockings were just right. She even had a watch now, and a pin on the lapel of her suit. Ruby's heart thumped in her chest. Envy was a sin, her father said. She didn't believe anything he said, but her grandmother had said the same thing, so she had to believe it. "You look pretty, Amber, like the actresses in the magazines. I saw the suit you're wearing in *Photoplay*, only it was pink striped instead of blue."

Amber fixed her dark eyes on Ruby. "Get it through your head, Ruby, we are not going to be friends. You're a noose around my neck, and all the compliments in China aren't going to help either one of us. As for good luck, we each make our own. If you're as smart as you said last night, then you shouldn't have a problem."

Ruby's throat closed tight. She struggled with her thick tongue. "Go to hell, Amber," she said in a tight, squeaky voice, "and I hope you break your neck in those shoes!"

"You wait till I write home, Miss Dirtymouth," Amber spat out. Instantly her face changed as she smiled at a young man in a white sailor suit who nodded bashfully.

For an hour Ruby was challenged. She breezed through each test at top speed, knowing she was scoring perfect grades. The man administering the tests raised his eyes several times to look at the director as though to say once in a while you get a smart one. The moment she finished, she was ushered into a small waiting room to await her evaluation.

Ruby's heart thumped and bumped in her chest. Would she get the job? If perfect scores were the only criterion, yes, she would get the job. If appearance and clothes counted, the answer was no. She waited and watched the busy hallway as young women and Navy personnel walked back and forth. The girls were all dressed plainly but stylishly. She itched to head for the nearest store to spend her thirty-six dollars.

An hour later the personnel director, a middle-aged woman with graying hair, called her into her office. She had such a kind, gentle face, Ruby wanted to throw herself into her arms to be hugged. The woman smiled.

"You have a perfect score, Miss Connors. It's been a long time since I've seen anyone type so fast and so accurately. Your dictation is flawless, not one mistake. Everything was perfect. Are you available to start work this week?"

"Oh, yes, ma'am," Ruby said breathlessly.

"I have just the position for you. Captain Dennison is in need of a secretary. You can start on Wednesday."

Mabel McIntyre did something then that she'd never done before but knew she would never regret: she lied. "We sometimes give new girls an advance on their pay to help ease the transition from . . . from hometown to city life," she said. "Fifty dollars in your case, Miss Connors. You will come in here each payday and give me five dollars. Is that satisfactory?"

"Oh, yes, Miss McIntyre," Ruby said, her eyes full of unshed tears.

"Good, then it's settled. If you'll just wait here, I have to go to . . . to petty cash and get the money."

Mabel McIntyre walked down the hall to where some of her friends were working, and Ruby overheard her asking for all the available cash they had. Including her own ten, she managed to collect sixty-three dollars.

Back in her office she handed the money to Ruby. "It seems I've made a mistake. You're entitled to sixty-three dollars. Ah, Miss Connors, please don't . . . it wouldn't be wise—"

"I won't tell anyone," Ruby blurted out, knowing full well where the money came from.

"Then it's all settled. I'll look forward to seeing you on

Wednesday. Eight sharp. I'll take you around to Captain Dennison's office and personally introduce you. You'll like him, and I'm sure he's going to like you."

Ruby leaned across the desk to reach for the director's hand. Someday, perhaps, she could return the woman's generosity. Until then, she would pay her back five dollars each payday until the debt was cleared.

Ruby's first stop after returning to the Y was at Lerner's, where she carefully selected a partial wardrobe with the help of a young salesgirl. She explained her situation and the amount of money she had to spend.

"And now for the grand total!" the salesgirl said as she tallied up the price tags.

Ruby squeezed her eyes shut.

"You'll make it, kiddo. It's $84.50. Two of the skirts were on sale."

Ruby heaved a sigh of relief. "I can't thank you enough. Will you be here in October when I have to buy winter clothes?"

"Sure will. Christmastime, too. You just ask for Nola Quantrell. That's me. Good luck with the shoes. Try Henry's right down the block. They're reasonable."

Ruby walked on air all the way to Henry's. She bought a pair of high-heeled pumps almost like her sister's and a second pair in black. At the last minute, she impulsively bought a pair of yellow sandals.

Her last stop was the Super-X, where she spent the remainder of her money on a Toni home permanent, bobby pins, a wave set, two bars of soap, and a new tube of toothpaste. When she calculated the cost of her purchases, she went back to the cosmetics counter and bought a tube of Tangee lipstick and a can of Djerkist talcum powder.

Ruby felt every inch a queen as she walked back to the Y. Her spirits were so high that even Amber couldn't dampen them.

Jealousy blazed from Amber's eyes on Wednesday when Ruby fell into step in the flowered summer dress, complete with high-heeled shoes that she'd practiced walking in for hours, up and down the hall, and her new perm.

Amber was already angry that Ruby had been hired as a

GS-3, which meant that her salary was equal to her own. The new clothes made her even angrier.

"You better not tell me you used your food money on fancy clothes, because if you do, you'll starve before I give you another cent." Ruby knew she meant every word she said.

"Bubba gave me money for some new clothes before I left," Ruby lied with a straight face.

Amber snorted. "It figures."

So when they rode to the Annex in silence, Amber glowered, but Ruby smiled, and she was still smiling when she walked into Mabel McIntyre's office. She held her breath, waiting for the personnel director's reaction to her new look. Later she decided the director was too professional to allow more than a sparkle to show in her dark eyes.

Ruby Connors was on her way.

June crept to a close and July moved to the front with equally warm days and bright sunshine, enough to keep Ruby content in her new life. Her birthday passed uneventful with cards from her grandmother and Opal and a money order for one hundred dollars that she immediately turned over to Amber, canceling out her debt to her sister. When the unbearable dog days of August passed into oblivion, three things happened to Ruby Connors. She cemented her friendship with Nola Quantrell, the helpful young woman from Lerner's; Captain Dennison said she was ready to move to the Pentagon and showed her a job description she should put in for with a personal recommendation from him; and her sister decided it was time for them to move into an apartment with four other girls, claiming it would be less expensive.

"I don't understand," Nola Quantrell said over a cup of coffee. "How can your sister force you to move with her? and her friends? Don't let her do this to you, Ruby. When you confided in me, I wanted to go over to the Y and smash her face in. How do you stay sane?"

"Sometimes I wonder myself. Maybe it won't be so bad. If I move over to the Pentagon, I'll be working for an admiral and making a lot more money. I might even be able to save some money."

"But you'll be paying out more in rent, and she'll make you

send more home. It doesn't make sense. This is your chance to save some money and take some night classes with me."

"I can still do that, take the classes, I mean. Do you think you could get me a job at Lerner's on Saturday and maybe one night a week?"

Nola shook her head glumly. "You're dragging now, Ruby. How will you handle it all? You already put in too much overtime at the office. It's like you're damned if you do and damned if you don't."

"It's easier this time around." Ruby grinned. "I have you to bounce things off. Here's the list Amber stuck under my door this morning. I have to contribute to the food budget, the utilities, and the rent. I also have to do my share of the chores, and carfare is going to cost more. It comes to eighty dollars a month more, plus two hundred I'll have to borrow from Amber just to move. I called her office today and told her no. You know what she said? She's calling home tonight at nine o'clock. That means my father will get on the phone and tell me I either move with Amber or I go back home. He'll come and drag me home, Nola. He will!"

Nola leaned back and lit a cigarette.

Nola Quantrell was the fifth youngest in a family of eleven children, not counting the eight orphans her parents looked after. She had learned the meaning of standing up for herself by the age of six.

"Why don't you tell your father you can send more money home if you continue to live at the Y?" she suggested. "If he's so gung ho on your sending money, he might go for it. In my opinion, what he's doing is outright extortion."

Ruby snorted. "This is Amber's show; I'm just one of the bit players. I'll give it a try, but don't be surprised if I'm not around next week. God, I wish I were twenty-one."

Amber Connors' eyes spewed venom when Ruby walked through the lobby doors of the Y at five minutes past nine. Amber was dressed in a yellow playsuit with a wide green belt and matching sandals. An ornate green comb with a ticklish-looking feather was stuck in her hair at a crazy angle. Ruby almost laughed, but she didn't when she saw the hostility in her sister's eyes.

"I'm not moving," Ruby shot over her shoulder as she headed for the elevator.

"Don't tell me, tell Pop. If you aren't going, you better start to pack, because he'll be here on Sunday to pick you up."

Ruby jabbed the button on the elevator. "Stuff it, Amber, I'm not moving. You tell Pop." She entered the elevator, Amber on her heels. Ruby stared straight ahead, refusing to acknowledge her sister.

"You're really stupid, Ruby. You act as though this place is Shangri-la. It's the damn YWCA. An apartment will give us room to walk around; we can do our own cooking, have a re-frigerator. There's even a garden. You'll have your own room. What more do you want?"

"I want exactly what I have. I'm happy here. I can afford this. I don't need anything else, not right now. Find someone else."

"I can't find someone else. Pop said you were my responsibil-ity, and while I don't like it, there isn't much I can do about it. I don't want to go back to Barstow, and Pop will drag me back with you, so you might as well agree here and now."

"The way I see it, Amber, you're the only one who gains from this move. What's in it for me? Tell me one thing!"

"You little snot, you always spoil everything. I hated you the day you were born and I still hate you," Amber shouted. "I wish to God you were never born!"

Ruby's throat closed tight. From somewhere deep inside her she summoned her last bit of courage. "Ask me, Amber. Ask me to move, don't tell me. Don't threaten me. Tell me you can't swing it without me. Don't tell me any lies about what's best for me; it's what's best for you. Say it, Amber, say you need me and I'll give you my answer."

Amber's lips thinned out in anger, and her eyes narrowed. The words came out slowly. "Okay, I need you to make the move."

"Why?" Ruby demanded.

"I told you why."

"No, there's something else. I can see right through you, Am-ber."

"Everyone has a boyfriend. We can't bring men here, but there we'll have a parlor."

Ruby felt drunk with her advantage. *Get it all now, everything you want from her, because you won't get another chance.*

"Well, aren't you the sneaky one. I guess that means you already have a boyfriend. He must be deaf, dumb, and blind to like you."

"Well? Will you make the move with me?" Amber said as if she hadn't heard Ruby's insults.

Ruby pulled her suitcase from the top shelf of her closet. "I can be bought, Amber. If the price is too high, find yourself another sucker. What's his name?"

Amber responded automatically to the iron command in Ruby's voice, so like her father's. "Nangi Duenas . . ." The stricken look on her face delighted Ruby. She replaced the suitcase on the top shelf.

"That Filipino guy who has been hanging around the lobby?" Ruby whooped her victory. "A Filipino! That's a good one! That's the same as going with a colored fella. Oh, boy, Pop is going to yank you home for sure when he finds *that* out!"

Amber was on her then, pulling her hair, pinching and gouging wherever she could. Ruby pulled the green comb from Amber's hair, ripping it down her bare arm at the same time she brought up one long leg, locking Amber in a viselike hold. Her clenched fist shot upward, catching her sister full on the chin. Amber toppled to the floor, Ruby towering over her. She was pleased to see blood trickling down Amber's arm onto the wrinkled playsuit.

"Do you remember the time I beat the shit out of you over that angel business?" Ruby gasped. "I can do it again, right here and now. Nothing would give me more pleasure, but you know what, Amber, you aren't worth the effort. I'll move with you, but I'm not going to owe you a cent. You can put up my rent increase, and we'll go on from there. You are never saddling me with a debt again. Take it or leave it!"

"Pop was right. You have the devil in you. You'll pay for this, I swear you will," Amber gasped as she lurched to the door Ruby was holding open.

"So much for bravado," Ruby whimpered, falling onto the bed.

Ruby woke on Saturday morning believing it was going to be the best day of her life. She tingled, she glowed, and her summer-blue eyes sparkled. Today was not routine; today was different. She was going to buy a new dress just for this dance, and she was going to tell Amber flat-out she was going. Tell her, not ask her. Her first real show of independence. She had a bad moment when she realized she would have to dip into her food budget to buy the dress. So what if she ate crackers and tomato soup for a week? She wouldn't starve. Nobody starved.

Once again Nola's practiced eye ran over the racks of dresses, searching for just the right one for her friend, a dress that was daring and different. "Wait a minute, Ruby, there's a dress in the back on layaway. I know it's your size, but the girl never came back to pick it up. We were supposed to put it back on the floor yesterday, guess they forgot. It's ah . . . it's different. I'll get it."

It was different all right, Ruby thought in dismay, and absolutely the most gorgeous dress she'd ever seen, all colors of the rainbow with three inches of fringe around the skirt bottom. She could hardly wait to try it on. "It's . . . scandalous. My father would lay down and die if he saw me in this." Ruby gurgled.

"That would be one way of getting rid of him," Nola muttered under her breath.

"How much is it?" Ruby asked, pulling the dress over her head.

Nola peeked into the dressing room. This was the sticky part. "It's . . . it's nineteen dollars. The person who had it on layaway paid nine already, but she hasn't been back, so you can have it for ten dollars. That's a bargain, Ruby, you can't pass it up."

"Won't she want her money back?" Ruby called out as she smoothed the perfectly sized dress over her hips.

"No," Nola lied. "If layaways aren't picked up on schedule, the customer forfeits the money. It's your lucky day, Ruby."

Ruby's feet barely touched the ground as she walked back to the Y. Her hands were reverent when she hung the dress on its hanger. Where would she ever wear it again? It was unbelievably gorgeous, she thought, the color of a hundred Popsicles melting together.

Five hours later, her narrow face full of hostility, Amber Connors watched her sister sashay out of the lobby. Her eyes glinted angrily when Ethel commented on how pretty Ruby looked.

Ruby was a whirlwind as she made her way down the street. It was going to be a wonderful evening. She caught sight of the bus pulling to the curb. Nola would be getting off it. She raised her hand the minute she spotted her friend. Behind her was Nangi Duenas. A devil perched itself on Ruby's shoulder.

"Hello." She smiled. "I'm Amber's sister. She's waiting for you."

She was rewarded with a dazzling smile showing perfectly aligned teeth, but it was the approving look in the man's eyes that Ruby wanted to see.

Satisfied, she stood back to admire Nola, resplendent in a skin-tight lime-green dress with a vivid purple sash. She had a pretty, heart-shaped face, a clear complexion, and soft, dark eyes that she enhanced with mascara and a deep charcoal line at the base of her eyelashes. Tonight she wore a deep burgundy lipstick that looked almost purple, a perfect match for the vivid sash and huge purple earrings. She'd never seen Nola's hair curled and frizzed before. To Ruby's eye she looked exotic.

"Wait till all those marines from the Marine barracks get a load of us!" Nola laughed uproariously. "A friend of mine told me most of the girls wear these simple little dresses with Peter Pan collars, you know, all prim and proper. We, on the other hand, look . . . experienced . . . I mean, we look as if we've been to these dances before. Trust me when I tell you we are going to dance our feet off right up to our anklebones."

Excitement rivered through Ruby when they arrived at the dance. She'd never seen so many people in one place before. There had to be at least a thousand voices contributing to the sound coursing through the huge building.

In the lead, Nola shouldered her way through throngs of young men in military attire: sailors in immaculate white, young airmen in Santiago blue, soldiers in khaki, and marines in olive green. The young women were dressed mostly in starched crinolines, sundresses, and white gloves.

"Which floor do we want?" Nola shouted to be heard over the blaring band on the first floor. "There's a dance on seven, five, three, and this floor." Ruby pointed upward.

"We'll work our way down," Nola shouted a second time. "Get your money out." Ruby did as instructed. She paid her quarter and had her hand stamped. She made up her mind not to wash her hand for at least two days. She wanted to remember every little detail of this night.

The music thundered as the two girls fought their way through the crowds. Slightly ahead of her, Ruby saw a young

Marine lieutenant crush Nola against a wall. She was about to
elbow the young man in the ribs, when she saw Nola smile flir-
tatiously. Ruby hung back, bumping into a second young man,
a marine. His eyes seemed to apologize as he shouted into her
ear, "Andrew Blue. Would you like me to cut a path for you?"
Ruby nodded weakly, her eyes on Nola. Panic rushed through
her. They hadn't discussed the possibility of becoming separated.

Nola winked at Ruby as she clasped the lieutenant around the
waist and followed him.

"Good idea," Andrew shouted. "Grab hold, Miss Rainbow,
and we'll make it to seven or die in the effort." Without hesitation Ruby reached out.

Her father would call this place a hotbed of sin. Ruby laughed
aloud. Today she didn't care what her father would think.

Andrew was handsome, Ruby thought, tall and lean with
sandy hair cut very short. His uniform was immaculately
creased, his cap folded neatly in his belt. She'd had an impression of blue eyes full of humor and a wide grin. He jiggled his
hips in a rumba motion, which caused Ruby to burst out laughing. She knew he was grinning.

"We're here!" Nola bellowed over her shoulder to be heard
over the sounds of "Pennsylvania 6-5000." "This is seven.
Ohhh, listen to that band. Let's meet back here. I'm Nola, this
is Ruby, and this is Alex," she said, pointing to her partner.

"This is Andrew," Ruby laughed excitedly.

"Let's dance," Andrew said, motioning to the floor. "I love to
dance, do you?"

"Uh-huh," Ruby muttered, trying to remember Nola's instructions. Throw your hips out to the left, then to the right, then
swing around. Let your partner do the rest.

Andrew Blue was fun, Ruby decided two hours later as she
made her way to the closest wall. She was thirsty and had to
find a bathroom. Frantically, she looked around for Nola but
couldn't see her anywhere. Sensing her distress, Andrew said,
"Follow me, I know where *it* is."

Somewhere between the seventh and third floors Ruby lost
Andrew in a crush of sailors and giggling, laughing girls. Ohhh,
she was having such a wonderful time, and the fringed skirt felt
so delicious against her legs. She'd seen more than one girl look
at her dress enviously. She'd returned their looks smugly, mostly

because of the dress and partly because of the handsome lieutenant whirling her about.

The ladies' room yielded a long line that stretched into the
corridor. Patiently, Ruby waited her turn. She was jiggling from
one foot to the other when she looked around to meet a pair of
dark, amused eyes.

He was shorter than Andrew Blue by a good three inches with
brush-cut hair which was dark as ebony. He also had large ears.
Ruby wondered crazily if he could wiggle them. He wasn't
handsome, far from it, but his eyes drew Ruby, warm and brown
with a slight cast. Greek? He was suntanned. Or was his skin
this honey color because of his race? He must be Greek, Ruby
decided, although she'd never seen a live Greek in her life.

"If you're going, go," a girl in a blue dress bellowed in her
ear.

"What?"

"Are you in this line or what?" the girl bellowed again.

Calvin Santos laughed then, showing strong, even teeth. Ruby
blushed furiously when he said, "I know where there's another
one."

Ruby jiggled again, allowing the girl and two of her friends
to go ahead of her. She groaned and the young man smiled
again.

"Come on," he said, reaching for her arm. Ruby followed
blindly as he led her to a small corridor off the main lobby to
a door marked OFFICE STAFF. "Straight through there." He
grinned. "No lines, no waiting. I'm Calvin Santos," he said with
a low, sweeping bow.

"Ruby Connors," Ruby said nervously.

"I'll wait right here, Ruby Connors."

She stared up into the young man's warm, gentle eyes, and in
a heartbeat, Ruby Connors fell totally and completely in love.
"Wait here," Ruby whispered. "Please wait."

"Forever," he said softly.

"What did you say?"

"I said I'll wait forever. But it won't take you that long, will
it?"

"Five minutes," Ruby said, holding up her hand. "Three if no
one else is in there."

She was out in four, her seams straight, wearing fresh lipstick.

Calvin was leaning nonchalantly against the wall. For the first time Ruby realized he was wearing an Air Force uniform.

"You're the prettiest girl here," Calvin muttered. Ruby flushed. The only person who had ever said she was pretty was her grandmother. Was she supposed to say he was handsome? She had no idea about what to do. Somewhere she'd heard that a smile was universal. She smiled.

"Would you like a soft drink?" Calvin offered.

"I'd love one," Ruby said breathlessly. "But could we go outside to drink it? I can't breathe in here."

"Neither can I."

Ruby's heart skittered in her chest as she waited for Calvin to return. While she waited she ran scenarios over and over in her mind. Walking hand in hand with Calvin along the tidal basin, picnicking in Rock Creek Park; dancing . . . close, cheek to cheek. He was . . . so . . . so . . . ordinary. Yet he wasn't ordinary. She knew now, seeing him in a closer light, that he wasn't American. He wasn't Greek, either. She realized suddenly she didn't care *what* he was. The thought brought her up short. Was this the way Amber felt about Nangi Duenas? Not that that mattered, either. Calvin was a person just as she was; nothing else should be allowed to matter.

Outside in the warm air with the star-spangled night above them, the two young people walked and talked as they shared a frosty bottle of Coca-Cola. Ruby felt as though she'd known Calvin for years.

"You went to the Citadel. You're an officer!" Ruby said in awe. She was intimidated now, moving away from him slightly.

Calvin frowned, closing the distance between them. "Did I say something wrong?" he asked anxiously. He seemed almost apologetic when he added, "The Citadel is a wonderful school. I graduated with top honors."

Ruby moved again. Top honors. She was horrified. He added to her horror when he asked what school she attended.

"Penn State, Georgetown?" he teased.

The hatred Ruby felt for her parents at that moment welled up in her like a choking smoke. She should have gone to college, been given the chance, but oh, no, she had to pay back $6,100, more than an education cost. What was he going to think when he found out she was a government girl? Ruby clenched her teeth and said coldly, "Some of . . . of us aren't fortunate enough to be going to college. Thanks for the Coke. I think I better find my friend. Excuse me, Calvin." *Don't cry, Ruby, don't even let your eyes fill up. This is going to happen again and again. Get used to it.*

Stunned, Calvin watched her weave her way through the crowd. He wished he were taller so he could see where she was going. He knew he had to follow her *now* or he'd never find her again. He hadn't meant anything by his question. In Saipan all students went on to higher education. If he could have, he would have ripped out his tongue as he dashed after her. He could have sworn that she liked him, sworn that his ancestry didn't matter. He truly understood her sensitivity, for he, too, knew about hurts and slurs in a strange land. He had to tell her, but first he had to find her. Calvin's heart jolted in his chest when he realized Ruby was no longer in his line of vision. He swore then, ripe American cuss words he'd learned at the Citadel. It didn't make him feel better.

He ran, shouldering young officers and enlisted men out of his way, apologizing to the many young girls he jostled and shoved. He had to find her.

When he reached the fifth floor, his dark eyes scanned the whirling dancers, looking for a rainbow-colored dress. Already his crisp blue shirt was as limp as a rag, clinging to his body like a second skin. He swore again.

"You can say that again, bub," a sailor said out of the corner of his mouth.

He didn't spot her until he made his way back to the seventh floor. The band was playing "You Go to My Head." She was dancing with a Marine second lieutenant, smiling up at him as they glided about the crowded floor. The lieutenant was saying something that made her laugh. *He* wanted to make her laugh. But only for him.

He'd learned more than the English language since coming here five years before. He'd never practiced being obnoxious and usually he went out of his way to be accommodating. Tonight was different. Tonight he would damn well do what all these young men did—cut in on *his girl.* The huge clock on the far wall told him he had exactly five minutes before the last song.

Calvin pushed his way across the dance floor and tapped the lieutenant on the shoulder.

"Watch it, pal," Andrew muttered nastily.

"I believe this is our dance," Calvin said in his best courtly voice.

"I believe you're mistaken, buddy," Andrew snarled. "Buzz off."

In a wink Ruby found herself in Calvin's arms and was whisked across the floor, Andrew Blue in hot pursuit.

"I'll punch his lights out if he makes trouble," Calvin said hotly.

Ruby panicked. Two fellas fighting over her. She looked up in time to see a burly MP in Andrew's wake. "I'll meet you outside. Wait for me," Ruby yelled as she made her way back to Andrew Blue and the MP.

Calvin watched in delight as the Marine lieutenant was marched off the floor. She'd said she would meet him outside and to wait for her. "Forever," he muttered as he made his way to the overflowing stairwell.

He almost missed her, and he would have if a girl in a startling lime-green dress hadn't shouted her name. This time he didn't care whom he shoved and poked as he made his way to her side. "Quick, where do you live?" he shouted.

"The Y," Ruby yelled back.

"I'll come by at noon. Will you go out with me?" He waited for agonizing seconds while Ruby made up her mind. He let out his breath in a loud swoosh when she nodded.

"What was *that*?" Nola gurgled.

Ruby smiled. "*That* is my destiny. And I think he knows it."

"You look like you're in love." Nola laughed.

"So do you."

"I have a date tomorrow. Want to double?"

"Sure." A date. A real date. Ruby swooned.

Two things happened that Sunday morning. Ruby actually *saw* Amber and Nangi together, and Andrew Blue left a message in her mailbox saying he would stop by around twelve-thirty to take her out for a bite of lunch.

Later, Ruby swore to Nola that her heart stopped beating when she saw Amber and Nangi sitting in the lobby. Obviously, they were waiting for someone, possibly Ethel. Ruby watched and waited from the hallway, out of sight, for Calvin to appear.

He would be on time. Andrew would be early, she just knew it. Her intuition proved wrong. Andrew arrived at precisely noon.

Ruby watched in horror as Andrew walked up to her sister. Amber smiled and shook her head. What did *that* mean? A minute later Amber was on the elevator. Ruby backed farther into the hallway. Now what was she supposed to do? When in doubt, do nothing, an inner voice warned.

Amber was back five minutes later, walking toward Andrew. Ruby inched closer so she could hear what was being said. "She isn't here. She probably went to the late Mass. You can wait here or go to the Hot Shoppe for coffee." Go, leave, don't come back, Ruby prayed.

Then Ethel arrived, and the three of them left. Thank God. Where was Calvin? Where were Nola and Alex?

He was here. Today he was even more starched and pressed. Spiffy. He looked wonderful. Nola and Alex were so close behind Calvin, it appeared they arrived together. Quickly Ruby made the introductions, whisking her guests out the door so fast, they ran into one another.

"Let's go this way," Ruby dithered.

"Fine," Nola said, falling into step behind Ruby and Calvin. "Where are we going?"

"Why don't we . . . ah, go . . . to Mount Pleasant." She turned to Calvin. "I'm moving there to an apartment with my sister and several of her friends. I haven't seen the place. Would you mind? Then we can go to Rock Creek Park. Is that agreeable with you guys?" she asked nervously.

"It's okay with us," Alex and Nola chorused.

When Ruby looked over her shoulder for the third time, Calvin asked what she was looking for. "Do you think someone is following us?" he asked, looking over his own shoulder.

Truthful by nature, Ruby blurted out her concern.

"Did you make a date with him?" Calvin asked miserably.

"No!" Ruby exploded. "Why would I do that? I have a date with you."

"I just don't want to be hurt," he muttered. "It wouldn't be the first time."

"I don't want to be hurt either," she replied softly.

Misty blue eyes met misty brown eyes. Calvin reached for her hand. Ruby sighed happily.

When they reached Mount Pleasant, Ruby barely glanced at

the house on Kilbourne Place, where she would live. At the end of the street was a park where they could sit on the grass and talk. Maybe they could get ice cream or nuts. Something they could share. Ruby felt as if she were racing to the moon with Vaughn Monroe. She'd never been this happy. She had someone. At last.

"They seem to like each other," Calvin murmured, nodding in the direction of Nola and Alex, who were laughing and giggling.

They do seem to go together, Ruby thought, happy for her friend.

"Nola really loves clothes. She knows all about the latest fashions. She hopes to be a famous designer someday, and when I'm rich I'm going to be her best customer. She comes from a family of nineteen kids—some of them were adopted, of course—so she's been sewing and moving hemlines all her life. She's a wonderful friend," Ruby said. She felt as if she was babbling incoherently.

Calvin sat with his arms roped around his knees, staring at Ruby inscrutably.

"A penny for your thoughts." Ruby smiled.

"I was thinking about . . . actually I was wishing that I—"

"Felt more comfortable? I'm not real good at small talk, and to tell you the truth you're my first . . . my first real date. If there are rules . . . oh, heck, why don't we just make our own. Rules, that is . . . we're just two people . . . persons . . . I'm me and you're you, and you don't have to worry about what you are with me . . . by the way, what *are* you?"

Calvin's face became suddenly gloomy. "What do you think I am?" he hedged.

"At first I thought you might be Greek. Actually, I don't care. It's what's inside a person that counts. Does the question bother you?" Ruby asked quietly.

"Sometimes," Calvin said miserably. "I'm Filipino. I come from Saipan. I haven't been back in over five years." He watched Ruby carefully, as if for her reaction.

"That's terrible. Don't you miss your family? Do you write? Do you get homesick?"

Calvin laced his fingers tighter around his knees. "Yes, yes, and no," he said and then, in a tired, defeated voice, admitted to her that he would give up half his life if he could be a real, white American for just a little while. Just long enough to see what people's reaction to him would be. He looked away, his face miserable.

Ruby digested Calvin's confession and without a qualm launched into her own sorry past. When she was finished she reached over for Calvin's hand. "I guess this is what they mean when they say birds of a feather. Neither of us feels as if we quite fit in. Let's go for a walk, my rear end is getting damp from this grass."

Ruby stood. "I don't think we have to talk about this . . . ever again. I don't want to remember last month or last year. I bet if we walked around this park we'd come to a crick where we could stick our feet in and cool off."

"What's a crick?" Calvin asked, puzzled.

"City people call it a brook or stream. People in Pennsylvania call it a crick. It's water deep enough to stick your feet in. See you guys later," she called over her shoulder to Nola, who waved airily.

They walked along jauntily, hands swinging, laughing at everything and nothing.

She had someone.

And there was going to be hell to pay, one way or the other.

"Who gives a shit," she muttered.

"What did you say?"

"I said, shhh, look at the squirrel chasing his tail." Ruby grinned, and Calvin threw back his head and laughed.

The afternoon rushed to its conclusion. Ruby knew she should go back to the Y. Amber always checked on her at dinnertime, weekdays and weekends, but Amber had gone out with Ethel and Nangi. Calvin hadn't said anything about extending their afternoon into the evening.

"I have to go back now; it's almost suppertime."

"Oh," Calvin said forlornly.

"What are you going to do this evening?" Ruby asked quietly.

Calvin shrugged. "Read the Sunday paper, maybe go to a movie. Unless you want to go to one. Do you?" he asked hopefully.

"I was hoping you'd ask," Ruby said.

Back in Barstow, movies were forbidden. Sex, lust, and fifteen-cent admissions were Satan's handiwork to George Connors' way of thinking.

"*A Streetcar Named Desire* is playing on Fourteenth Street. In

the movie house by Dupont Circle *The African Queen* is playing. Which one do you want to see?" He squeezed her hand.
"Should we ask Nola and Alex if they want to go?"

Ruby's first thought was to say no. ~~She wanted to be with~~
Calvin alone, but when she was called to task for this day, she
might fare better if she could truthfully say she was with three
other people. "Not really, but I think it's the polite thing to do.
Do you mind?"

"If you don't mind, I don't mind," Calvin said agreeably. "We
should get something to eat first, though."

"Sure," Alex chimed in. "And what say we have dinner?
Horn and Hardart, on me. I just got paid." Nola squealed her
agreement.

Calvin looked at Ruby and caught her winking at Nola. He
wondered what that sly wink meant.

"Let's walk." Nola winced but agreed good-naturedly.

Walk they did.

Dinner was wonderful. Anything, Ruby decided, was wonderful if you were sharing it with friends. Later she couldn't remember what she ate.

She sucked in her breath and squeezed Nola's arm when
Marlon Brando pranced onto the screen. A definite hunk. She
loved it when he yelled, "Hey, Stella" and laughed aloud. But
what she liked even more was Calvin's arm around her shoulder,
just as Alex's arm was around Nola. Both girls sighed happily.

Outside the movie house they split up, Nola and Alex taking
the trolley, she and Calvin walking.

She wants to be alone with me, Calvin thought.

My feet hurt, Ruby thought, but she couldn't in good conscience let him spend any more money on her. She noticed that
he'd left the tip for the waitress, even though Alex paid for their
food. Somewhere along the way they must have come to an understanding, because there was no quibbling in regard to the bill
or the gratuity. Calvin wasn't a cheapskate. She felt pleased with
the thought. Oh, she had so much to write to her grandmother
about.

On the corner of F and Ninth streets, Ruby came to a halt
under a streetlamp. "I think I should go the rest of the way
alone. In case my sister is waiting in the lobby ... she's ...
sometimes she doesn't care where she is when she says something. I had a swell time tonight, Calvin. Did you?"

The night was soft and dark, the lamplight dim and intimate. A dog woofed softly in the darkness. "Don't the stars look like a giant blanket?" Ruby whispered.

"Yes," Calvin whispered back. "Will you go out with me again?"

"Sure. I've been wanting to go to the zoo ever since I got here. I could make us a picnic lunch. Saturday or Sunday?"

"Both," Calvin said, drawing in his breath, as if in anticipation of her answer. He looked as if he wanted to kiss her, but then panic came into his eyes, and he stepped back and jammed his hands into his pockets.

"Okay," Ruby said cheerfully. "I'll see you Saturday at the entrance to the zoo. Is noon okay?"

"Noon is fine. Good night, Ruby. I had a great time."

" 'Night, Calvin," Ruby said, striding off.

When Ruby was out of sight, Calvin looked around to get his bearings. He decided to walk for a while. He wanted to think about Ruby.

Yes, sir, he told himself, he'd had a great day. Ruby was his girl. She was. He whistled the melody of "Oh, You Beautiful Doll," and his feet picked up speed. He wanted to get back to the base and into bed so he could think about Ruby and what it would be like to kiss her . . . and . . . other things.

By the time Calvin reached the base he had himself convinced he was a "real" American. If he were otherwise, a girl like Ruby Connors wouldn't give him the time of day. Today was the closest he'd come to being one of the people he'd so envied all his life. Ruby's friends had acted as if he were one of them, and Ruby hadn't blinked when he confessed to being Filipino. Decades back in his ancestry was Samoan blood; the result was his height. He didn't look one bit like those pipsqueak, subservient little people who served as meticulous waiters and kitchen help to the military.

He had a girl now, a real live, walking, talking, smiling girl who liked to hold his hand, a girl who smiled with her eyes, a girl who *understood* him.

His girl.

Ruby walked into the Y with shining eyes. She stopped in her tracks, and her jaw dropped when she saw her sister sitting on one of the orange chairs under the window with Andrew Blue next to her. Amber was smiling and so was Andrew. Ruby's guts churned. When Amber put her mind to it, she could charm the feathers off a duck.

"Are you waiting for me?" Ruby asked coolly.

"Andrew's been waiting for you since noon," Amber said just as coolly before Andrew could open his mouth.

"Noon! Why? We didn't . . . that's ten hours," Ruby said in disbelief.

"Where were you, Ruby?" Amber asked sweetly.

Ruby wanted to tell her it was none of her damn business. "I went to the park with Nola and then we went to the movies. Today's Sunday, so I can do what I want. Where were you, Amber?" she asked just as sweetly.

Before Amber could answer, Andrew stepped forward. "I know we didn't have a date, and I suppose it was foolish of me to hang around all day, but I kind of hoped that you might like to go out. Look, I have to leave or I'll miss the last bus back to the base. How about next Saturday?"

"She'd love to go." Amber bubbled. "Ruby has no plans, do you, Ruby?"

"I'm sorry, Andrew, but I do have other plans. It really was . . . nice of you to come all the way up here and wait like you did." How miserable he looked. How clean and neat and pressed. So very tidy. He was fumbling nervously with his cap and trying to smile. "How about Sunday?" she blurted out.

"You got a date! How would you like to go to Glen Echo for the day?" Ruby nodded. "Great, I'll see you next Sunday. Let's go to church, breakfast, and then head out to the park. Eleven okay?" He turned to Amber, almost as an afterthought. "Do you want to come along?"

"No." Amber smiled. "I was there today. Thank you for asking, though."

The moment the door closed behind Andrew Blue, Amber reached for her sister's arm and dragged her to the elevator. "It's time you and I got a few things straight once and for all." She punched the button for Ruby's floor.

"Shove it, Amber, we straightened things out the day I beat the hell out of you in my room. Get off my back."

Amber shoved Ruby through the door as soon as it slid open, then followed her down the hall.

Ruby noticed that her sister stood by the door, ready to bolt if need be. She waited.

"One of the reasons we're moving out of here is because of you, Ruby. Pop said you can't be trusted. He called you a sneak and he knows you have . . . what he said was you had the makings of a . . . a tramp. I have to keep my eye on you, and I can't do it here with you on one floor and me on another. He's right, you can sneak out anytime you want. Like today," she spat out. "I have to call home tomorrow, and I'm not lying for you. And as to this friend of yours, Nola, she can't be very respectable if she works in Lerner's and lives by herself."

Instinct told Ruby that if she rose to Nola's defense, Amber would decide that Nola wasn't to be seen again. She remained tight-lipped, her eyes narrowing dangerously. Amber backed up a step.

"I've decided that Andrew Blue is acceptable. You can date him one day of the weekend. I'll tell Pop he's okay. He told me all about his family and they're good Christians. I saw your face when he said he'd take you to church. You're no good, Ruby. Pop is right; you're going to go to hell."

Ruby advanced a step and stiff-armed the door, preventing Amber from opening it. "You're right, I probably will go to hell, and you know why? I'm going to kill you, and then they'll put me in the electric chair, and I'll laugh all the way down. Make sure you tell Pop."

"I'm going to tell him everything. *Everything,*" Amber screeched. "Your mouth is like a sewer!"

To the best of Ruby's knowledge, she'd never openly said anything worse than *shit* or *damn.* Now she let loose. "Sewer! You want to hear sewer, Amber? I'll tell you what I've learned. Captain Dennison says *fuck* seventy times a day. *His* boss calls all women cunts. The enlisted men call everyone assholes, and Admiral Mallory thinks everyone walking the earth is a son of a bitch. That's how these Navy men talk. Be sure to tell Pop you subjected me to this. In fact, tell him anything you want, but you are *not* going to pick my dates. I'll go out next week with Andrew because he is nice and he did wait. Don't do it again. Because if you do, I'll snatch that little runt you're dating and I'll tell him all about you, starting with how dirty and sneaky you are." She was breathless when she finished.

"Do whatever you want," Amber seethed. "You're nothing but garbage. Human garbage."

Ruby's voice took on a singsong quality. "Garbage? I know a thing or two about garbage, Amber. Our father, the pillar of St. Barnabas, lusts after Grace Zachary. I saw him undress her with his eyes. Grace sticks her tongue out at him behind his back. Mom saw him do it, too. He's a goddamn lecher, and I'll bet you're just like him when nobody's looking."

"Filthy mouth. You wait. You just wait!" Amber seethed, and with that she was out the door.

Ruby's arm shot out for the door and slammed it. *Human garbage.* So that's what they thought of her. Her eyes burned. Her shoulders slumped. She didn't care if her father said it, but somehow the fact that her sister believed it ate at her soul. She couldn't say why, but it did.

Amber checked the handful of change before she laid it on the small metal shelf by the pay phone. She wondered vaguely if she would have to call home again tomorrow night. Her hand was poised to drop in the first dime, when she looked at her wrist. It wasn't eleven yet, so it was all right to call. Her parents went to bed at eleven. Nothing was allowed to interfere with her father's routine. According to Ruby, though, Grace Zachary interfered with ... something. She shook her head to clear her thoughts. Pop was right, Ruby had a dirty mind.

Until tonight, when Amber had to devote extra minutes to compose herself, she hadn't realized what a responsibility it was calling home every week. Mondays she always had a headache; sometimes they carried into Tuesday. She had a headache now. Damn Ruby.

She dutifully waited while the operator placed the call. She dropped her money into the slot, coin by coin. Although she always hoarded change all week for her duty call, so far she'd never talked for more than three minutes; more often than not, her father hung up after the first ninety seconds.

George always picked up the phone on the third ring. Up from the chair, across the living room, out to the hallway and the foot of the steps, sit down, pick up the phone. Right on schedule.

"George Connors." No hello, no greeting of any kind.

Amber worked a smile into her voice, hoping to hear it returned, even though she knew better. "Hello, Pop, it's Amber. How are you? How's Mom? This isn't too late, is it?"

"Not too late, daughter. Five minutes till it's time to go up-stairs. Your mother is fine." He never said how he was. He never asked how she was, either. Amber sucked in her breath and forced a smile. For whom she didn't know. Maybe herself.

"Pop, it's Ruby. She's doing terrible things. You . . . she cusses something fierce. She won't listen to me." Her voice was pleading. Again, for what she didn't know.

"I placed Ruby in your charge, daughter. Are you telling me now I made a mistake?" Not bothering to wait for her defense, he went on. "It's up to you to use a firm hand, a strong hand. Give her what-for every hour if she needs it. Maybe I made a mistake, sending you girls to the city." The implied threat was there, and Amber felt her knees weaken. "I have next weekend off. Your mother might like a ride down there. Is there anything else, daughter?"

"No, Pop."

"Then I'll say good night. Don't make this kind of call to me again unless you're ready to answer for your failure."

"I'm sorry, Pop," Amber whispered, but her father broke the connection. Amber looked at her watch. Two minutes and ten seconds. Why had she expected more? Daughter. He never even called her by name.

Amber backed away from the phone, inching her way to the orange-covered chairs. She'd just ratted on her sister and herself, too, for that matter. For what? What had she hoped to gain? A kind word? To be called by her name?

Amber's thoughts boiled. She didn't want to go back to Barstow. She didn't want to live in her parents' house, and she didn't want to work in the shirt factory. If her father decided to come here and yank both of them home, she knew she didn't have the guts to put up a fight. Ruby did, though. Ruby would fight to the death, and she'd made a deadly enemy of Ruby to-night. Even though she was twenty-one going on twenty-two, and of age, she knew she didn't have the nerve to cross her fa-ther. Ruby had guts. She'd thumb her nose at George and make him carry her, kicking and screaming, all the way back to Barstow, while she herself meekly climbed into the car and said, "Yes, sir, I'm happy to be going home, and sir, I'm sorry I failed you." A vision of Ruby thumbing her nose at their father brought a smile to her lips. She wished she could fall off the face of the earth into a deep hole that would truly route her to China. Her father would never find her in China.

A second vision of her father leering lasciviously at Grace Zachary made her want to vomit. All the neighbors looked at Grace in her shorts and skimpy halters. She wondered if her father ever saw her mother naked. Not likely, she decided. That was sinful, decadent, and wicked. It was a mystery how she'd ever been born. But then, she hadn't exactly been born. She'd come down as an angel. As long as she believed that, all the rest was bearable. This was simply temporary until . . . Until what, she asked herself wearily. Until what?

"Till marriage," she said aloud in the elevator. Nangi had spoken of marriage and going back home. He'd hinted, but he hadn't asked. His home was on the other side of the world. Her father couldn't touch her that far away. He'd also disown her. One of these days she was going to decide just how much that mattered to her.

The day was misty, overcast, with gray, plodding clouds circling overhead. Not a day for the zoo, Ruby decided when she bounded out of bed. Damn, the weather report predicted clear, sunny skies. Sunrise was a mere five minutes away. Ruby crossed her fingers. "Don't spoil my day," she murmured to the empty room.

Her eyes fell on the wicker picnic basket, compliments of Nola. She had hoped to go with Calvin to the park after the zoo. "I emptied out my sewing box and lined it with a dish towel. I won't be doing any sewing today," she'd said cheerfully. Nola had the answer to all her social problems. Now all she had to do was stop at the corner delicatessen and pick up ham and cheese sandwiches, Coca-Cola, hard-boiled eggs, and some peaches. Maybe a square of cheese for nibbling. It wouldn't hurt to get some potato chips, too.

She was flush, as Nola would say. With her paycheck yesterday Captain Dennison had given her a card with twenty-five dollars in it and a note saying she was the best secretary he'd ever had. He'd also wished her luck in her new job with Admiral Query, which she was to start on Monday. The moment she cashed her check at lunchtime, she'd gone to the personnel office and handed over her final payment to the director. She was now seven dollars ahead of the game and in debt to no one, a feeling she liked. The picnic would wipe out the seven dollars, but she didn't mind.

She should be thinking about her new job, planning her weekly wardrobe, and mapping out the way to the Pentagon, but that was pretty much a waste of time, as she would be moving in another week.

Ruby opened the window. Hot, humid air, thick as soup, rushed into the room. She closed the window just as fat raindrops began to fall. The leaves weren't moving. Her grandmother always said if you could see the underside of the leaves, there would be a storm, and that if rain fell in fat drops, it wouldn't last. Ruby crossed her fingers.

By the time she dressed and brushed her hair the rain had lessened and faint streaks of sunshine could be seen. She sighed happily. Somebody must be watching over her. Sunshine was important for this particular day.

Over a breakfast of coffee, juice, and toast at the Hot Shoppe, Ruby ran over the dialogue she would have with Amber on her return. Lie or not to lie? It all depended on Amber's mood. She dawdled over a second cup of coffee until it was nine-fifteen. Amber always got up at nine on weekends.

"You'd better not give me any grief, Amber," she muttered as she made her way back to the Y.

Ruby spotted her sister in a local coffee shop. She was alone with a copy of *Redbook* open in front of her. Amber looked up as Ruby came to her booth.

"You aren't going to spoil my day, are you, Ruby?" she snapped.

"No. You don't mind if I go to the zoo this afternoon, do you? And to the park for a picnic. Nola gave me this great basket."

Amber waited a long moment before she replied. When she spoke, she barely moved her lips. "Are you going with your friend?" The word *friend* sounded obscene coming from Amber.

Ruby nodded.

"You'll be back around suppertime?"

It was a question Ruby wasn't prepared for. She shrugged.

"Is that a yes or no?" Amber asked.

"I thought about going to the movies, the early show; it lets

out around nine. *The African Queen* is supposed to be good. I
can't get into any trouble at the movies, Amber."

Amber debated another full minute. The zoo was okay, a picnic was okay, and the movie . . . "You should start to make other
friends. I told you before, I don't like that skinny girl."

Here it comes, Ruby thought. She waited.

"When we move to Mount Pleasant, I don't want to see you
palling around with her."

Ruby would have agreed to anything just to get out of Amber's sight. She hadn't had to lie outright, either, which had to
mean Amber had plans of her own. From the looks of things,
Andrew Blue was going to give her more than one alibi.

How was she ever going to juggle things to keep everyone
happy? Ruby made a mental note to start writing things down,
and that thought reminded her to write to Opal and her grandmother.

Ruby left the Y at eleven o'clock to stop at a deli on Ninth
Street, where she filled Nola's sewing basket with a delectable
lunch. She dropped the two letters she'd written in a mailbox on
the way. She'd planned on walking to the zoo, but the basket
was heavier than she anticipated, so she turned right on Connecticut Avenue and boarded the trolley that would leave her off
at Woodley Road and the entrance to the zoo.

She felt wonderful. The sun was definitely out now, the sky
a rich blue with marshmallow clouds. She looked good, too, she
thought, in her pink-and-blue plaid playsuit. Nola had sewn
inch-wide white rick-rack around the legs, the collar, and pockets to give the outfit a touch of what she called Rubyism. She'd
even lent Ruby her white sandals, which she'd polished till they
looked almost new, and two combs for her hair.

Ruby craned her neck over the visiting throngs of tourists,
parents, toddlers, and infants in buggies. Ahead she could hear
the tinny music of an organ grinder. Thick, earthy, musty smells
assaulted her as she searched for a bench. She wished she had
sunglasses.

After what seemed a long time later, Ruby stopped an elderly
couple to ask the time. "One o'clock, dear," the white-haired
lady said gently. "Are you waiting for someone?"

Ruby flushed, and her gaze dropped to the picnic hamper.

"Perhaps your friend is waiting at one of the other entrances."

"Other entrance?" Ruby said blankly. "You mean there's more than one entrance?"

"Yes, child." With the help of her husband, the woman offered directions to Hawthorne and Cathedral. Ruby sprinted off, the picnic basket banging against her legs.

He had to be there. Surely he would wait. She felt stupid; she should have checked to see if there were other entrances. By now Calvin should have done the same thing. "He probably thinks I stood him up," Ruby muttered as she careened around a fat lady tottering after two dogs snarling in their leashes.

Ruby and Calvin spotted each other at the same time. The annoyance Ruby felt disappeared as soon as she saw the anxiety leave Calvin's face.

"I was waiting at the Woodley Road entrance," she said breathlessly. Her tone was sharper than she intended. He should have known about the entrances.

"I'm sorry. It never occurred to me that there might be more than one entrance. I've never been here. I thought that maybe you had decided today wasn't such a good idea after all." He was so apologetic, so . . . obsequious that Ruby's eyes sparkled with irritation.

"You aren't going to pull that . . . you're better than me routine, are you?" Ruby demanded. "You made a mistake and so did I. Let's forget it, okay?" she said.

Calvin reached down for Ruby's hand. "I would have come looking for you," he blurted out.

It was a lie, she decided. He would have waited till four o'clock in the hot sun because he couldn't bear to search Ruby out for fear she'd stood him up.

"When?" Ruby teased. "When would you have started looking? You know, Calvin, sometimes there are extenuating circumstances. For instance, if something came up, say I got sick or something. There is no way I can get in touch with you. I wouldn't know who to call to ask for you at the base."

"I know. I guess it's just hard for me to believe you . . . want to go out with me," Calvin said miserably, his grasp on her hand tighter.

For a fleeting instant Ruby felt as though she were the protector, motherly somehow, to this shy young man. To a degree she understood his feelings of insecurity; after all, who was more insecure than she was? She had to bring a smile to Calvin's face so their day wouldn't be ruined.

"I wish I had a camera so I could take your picture, Calvin."

"To remember me by?" Calvin asked, tight-lipped.

"No, well, yes, in a way. You see, I bought this photo album for my sister, but she was so nasty, I never gave it to her. Kind of silly, huh? Anyway, you look so handsome in your summer blues, I wanted you to be my first picture. If I had a camera."

"I have a camera. I'll bring it next time, okay?"

"I'll buy the film," Ruby volunteered. "We'll get two sets of prints, one for you, one for me."

"Sounds good. I'll bring it tomorrow. We're still on, aren't we?"

"Let's sit over here on this bench, Calvin. I have to talk to you about something. I don't want you to get upset or anything, but I know you will. At first I was going to make up a story, tell you a lie so I wouldn't hurt your feelings, but you're twenty-four years old," Ruby said as though that would make her explanation more tolerable. "Hold my hand and look at me while I explain. And don't be a shithead," she said, using one of Captain Dennison's favorite expressions.

Calvin listened, his face glum, as Ruby told him what she was going to do in order to keep seeing him. His expression told her he didn't like it, not one damn bit, but he nodded. "How often will you be seeing this guy?"

"As little as possible. Calvin, I don't want to go back home. I have to do this."

Calvin looked at her, saying nothing.

"Are you going to see . . . other girls?" Ruby asked hesitantly.

"Hell no. No one is breathing down my neck. I can do whatever I want. It's all right, Ruby, I understand."

"Listen, I've had enough of the zoo. Let's go to the park, I'm getting hungry."

His breath exploded in a loud sigh as he reached down to take Ruby's hand. When they reached the park, they found themselves among other couples with picnic baskets looking for a shady spot and privacy. Overhead, birds chittered and squirrels scampered. Ruby laughed and pointed at a baby squirrel that wasn't as fast on his feet as his companions. Calvin stopped and watched. He felt light-headed when Ruby leaned against his shoulder.

He was meticulous, Ruby noticed as he spread the blanket, careful to smooth the corners and wrinkles in the center. As Ruby set out the food, Calvin arranged it geometrically. She felt irritated and didn't know why. This was a picnic, not a military drill. Picnics were supposed to be fun, haphazard. Poor Calvin. She wondered what Calvin would do if ants invaded the blanket. Probably panic and shake out the blanket and find a different spot. She couldn't help but laugh at the thought.

An hour later, with no sign of ants, Ruby gathered up the crumbs from their sandwiches and set them on waxed paper at the edge of the blanket. "A detour of sorts." She giggled. When she turned to face Calvin he was leaning against the tree. Panic seized her. Where was she to sit? His broad back covered the tree trunk. She'd noticed other couples; sometimes the girl had her head in the guy's lap and sometimes the guy had his head in the girl's lap. Whichever way it went, she supposed she was safe.

Calvin motioned for her to sit next to him. He inched his arm up around her. She leaned against him.

Ruby's heart thumped in her chest. This was real . . . she was actually sitting with a guy whose arms were around her, and if she was any judge, he was going to kiss her any minute. She sensed that Calvin was no more experienced in the kissing department than she was, so they would probably make a mess of it, but that was okay. They would go slowly and learn together. She felt safe with him. Andrew Blue would touch, or try to, but not Calvin. Damn, she hated it when the marine crept into her thoughts. She snuggled closer, her eyes on the couple down the hill. Talk about a clinch. Mesmerized, she watched a flash of tawny legs as the girl moved and thrashed about on the blanket. The fella seemed to have four hands, and they were everywhere. She heard Calvin suck in his breath and realized his arm had tightened its hold. She burrowed deeper into his arms; strange feelings rushed through her, feelings she knew her father would call sinful.

Ruby raised her head. From this angle Calvin's eyes didn't seem so narrow, and they were definitely full of some feeling. The word *lust* ricocheted around her mind. What was he seeing in her eyes? She had no time to think about it because he was kissing her, his lips mashing her own, but he was off the mark by half an inch. Laughter bubbled in her throat, but died when his tongue parted her lips.

She pressed closer, twisting slightly so that their lips were even. Her arms reached out to circle his back, bringing her closer still. She tasted apple on his tongue.

Calvin's sudden yelp of surprise startled Ruby. Flushed, she reared back, aware that her hipbone was grinding into Calvin's groin. She was responsible for the hard bulge in his uniform trousers.

"Jesus," he groaned, and turned away from her.

"What's wrong?" Ruby demanded.

"There's nothing wrong," he said. "It's just that you're a good girl, and guys have ... what they do is they ... they muck around with girls who don't care. You care, I know you do. That marine you're going out with tomorrow is that kind of guy. I'm not."

"How do you know that?" Ruby demanded, not liking this turn in their conversation.

"I know, that's all. I bunk with guys like him. All they do is screw around and talk about their scores over breakfast, lunch, and dinner. They don't say nice things, either."

Ruby digested the information. Calvin respected her. That was good.

"I think we should kiss some more. Not right now or even today," Ruby said hesitantly, "but one of these days. How else will we get to know if we really do like one another?"

"I know now and I do like you. If I thought you could ever be serious about someone like me, I could even see us married someday. We'd have a girl who looks like you and a boy who looks like both of us."

Ruby stared intently into Calvin's eyes. "Why don't you want the boy to look like you? If we got married, I'd want him to look like you."

"I don't want him to go through what I've gone through. I don't want him to be different."

"I'd want him to look just like you," Ruby said softly, "and I'd make sure every day of his life that he knew he was the greatest person in the world. I could do it, too. My children are not going to be raised the way I was. I'm going to love them and do things with them, and I'm always going to listen when they tell me something. I'll never be too busy when they want to confide. I'll be their parent and their friend, too. I know I can do both. What kind of parent do you think you'll be?" she asked breathlessly.

"Strict."

"Not if you marry me," Ruby said blandly. "On the other hand, I might never get married."

Calvin's face fell. "Why?"

"For one thing, I don't ever want to have the kind of marriage my parents have. I think they hate each other. My grandparents had a wonderful marriage. They laughed a lot and touched one another. You have to love someone a lot to get married." She wondered what kind of marriage Calvin's parents had and if he would volunteer or confide in her. She waited, but he remained quiet and thoughtful.

Finally, instead of answering, Calvin leaned over and kissed her full on the lips. It was a sweet, gentle kiss that spoke of many things and promised even more.

When they moved apart, Ruby's eyes were shining. "I *liked* that," she said with no trace of embarrassment.

Calvin threw back his head and laughed so hard, tears came to his eyes. It was a moment Ruby treasured, and it stayed with her for the rest of her life.

"Come on, I'm taking you out to dinner, so put on your lipstick. Is there someplace we can ditch this picnic basket without going back to the Y?"

"Dinner? You mean in a big restaurant or the Hot Shoppe?"

"Hogates on the Potomac, Ninth and Maine Avenue. Southwest. Best seafood in town. I think you'll like it. Unless there's someplace else you'd rather go?"

"It's the company that counts, and if you're paying, it should be your choice." A dinner date. Wait till she told Nola and her grandmother. She didn't like fish all that much, but if Calvin did, she would learn to like it.

"How about Chinese food, then?" Calvin said, as if he couldn't make up his mind.

"If you really mean it, then I'd love to! I've never been to a Chinese restaurant. Are you sure?"

"Of course I'm sure. We'll go to the Dragon. Next week we can go someplace else."

When they were outside the Dragon, Ruby looked pointedly at the picnic basket. "I'll tell them we have our favorite cat in here," Calvin said, flipping the lid. "Or should I look the guy in the eye and stare him down and mumble something about military secrets?"

"I like the one with the cat." Ruby giggled. He had a sense of humor, too, Ruby thought happily. Damn, her world was so right, it was scary.

An elderly Chinese man with a long, straggly beard looked at the basket but made no comment. Calvin raised his eyes and Ruby giggled.

Ruby ordered chop suey and Calvin ordered chow mein. They ate from each other's plates and drank the entire pot of tea. The litchi nuts were sweet and wet. She loved them and ate six. Calvin ate two. They saved the fortune cookies till last.

"You read yours first, Calvin."

Calvin snapped open the crusty cookie and stared down at the message.

"Well, what does it say?" Ruby demanded excitedly.

Calvin cleared his throat twice. "It says, 'Your true love sits next to you.'" Calvin flushed, knowing his ears were as red as apples.

"That's so romantic." She broke her cookie open, certain it was going to echo Calvin's message. She read it twice and then a third time. "It says, 'You're almost there.' What do you suppose that means? Oh, well, I guess we shouldn't take this too seriously. Can I have yours? I'll paste them in my album."

She watched Calvin deflate before her eyes. He puffed up immediately when he realized Ruby was staring at him.

"I think," he said loftily, "there was a slight printing error."

"I think so, too," Ruby laughed as she pocketed both messages.

It was twenty minutes of nine when they parted, Ruby to the Y and Calvin, back to the base, as he had to go on duty at eleven. Ruby turned at the last minute and called, "I'll think about you tomorrow. If you want to call me at the Y tomorrow night, I'll be in the lobby at ten o'clock."

"I will," Calvin shouted.

The night was warm and comfortable, as warm and comfortable as having Ruby sitting next to him in the park. He craned his neck to see the millions of tiny stars overhead, knowing Ruby was probably looking at them just the way he was. Right now, this very second, he believed he could do anything, be anything he wanted if Ruby believed in him. It occurred to him that Ruby was a crutch to lean on. He slumped down on the seat. Ruby didn't need a crutch. Guts, she said. Ruby was tough where it counted, like some of the guys in his outfit. But she was soft, too, incredibly soft and gentle, and he loved her sense of humor. She'd made him laugh out loud. He couldn't remember when he'd laughed like that. Years and years ago. Far too long to be so serious and miserable. God, he was happy. Tomorrow night he would be even happier when he talked to Ruby at ten o'clock and she told him what a miserable time she had with the marine.

Calvin continued to watch the dark night through the bus windows as he plotted the marine's death in fifty different ways. Ruby was his, that's all there was to it. She'd even said she would think about him tomorrow.

Before going on duty, Calvin showered and dressed in a clean uniform. He was as meticulous with his dress as he was with everything in his life. He wanted no condemnations, no questioning glances. He wanted to blend in, to be unobtrusive yet noticed at the same time.

Satisfied with his appearance, he left his quarters and did double time to the office, where he would spend the next eight hours.

It wasn't until he was settled behind his desk that a terrible thought struck him. He couldn't be the rock, the stable force for Ruby that most men were for their girls, though only to himself would he admit that. In order to be that way he had to be in control of his own life, and he wasn't. What bothered him more was the realization that Ruby was her own rock. She didn't need his support. The thought that his girl didn't *need* him caused perspiration to bead on his forehead. Today she'd spent a lot of time bolstering his ego, and like a jellyfish, he'd let her. He'd needed her strength, her little pep talks. She made him feel like a real person, like a white person. It occurred to him at some point, when he was halfway through the duty rosters, that in a way he was using Ruby, but he pushed the thought so far back into his mind, he immediately forgot it.

The moment Ruby struggled to wakefulness, she knew it was going to be a miserable day. Her small room was filled with gloomy early morning shadows. She propped herself on her elbow and squinted to see through the slats of the opened venetian blind. Outside, the day looked gray. She listened intently for the sounds of birds but heard nothing.

She didn't want to get up, didn't want to meet Andrew Blue, or go to church. She wanted to lie in bed and think about Calvin. She felt warm all over when she remembered the way it felt to kiss him. She smiled at the memory of his red ears. Her breathing quickened when she recalled the frenzied couple down the hill from where they sat. She mouthed the word *sex* several times, then said it aloud. Her face grew warm.

Ruby burrowed her face into her pillow to stifle her laughter as she imagined herself and Calvin having sex. He was so meticulous, he would probably want to wear his spiffy, pressed uniform during the entire act. And even if he didn't, Calvin was as virginal as she was. The stupid leading the ignorant.

Andrew Blue, on the other hand, struck her as experienced. She knew that before the end of the day, he would try something with her. She wondered how she would handle him. She wanted to know how a man's hands would feel on her so she would know how to react when Calvin got around to it.

Calvin and Andrew. Andrew and Calvin. Calvin, Andrew, and Ruby. A triangle. She was part of a triangle. She stretched luxuriously, feeling wonderful, almost wicked. At least her thoughts were wicked. She imagined they were the kind of thoughts Grace Zachary would have.

It had been Grace who told Ruby about sex, and to this day, that little bit was all Ruby knew.

"Honey," Grace had said, "sex is as natural as eating breakfast. You know how you don't like oatmeal too much, but you can still eat it and feel full? Well, sex can be like that or it can be like this huge, scrumptious breakfast I always make for Paul on Sunday mornings: waffles with blueberry syrup, light scrambled eggs with the bacon just crispy enough, toast with homemade strawberry preserves and delicious yellow butter, fresh-squeezed orange juice and coffee that smells up the whole house. Sex for me and Paul is always like that," Grace said, her eyes lighting up with love for her husband.

"Everyone in town thought I was a tramp, some kind of wild slut because I liked to have a good time, but I was a virgin when I married Paul. The people in this town are house angels and street devils," she said sourly, "not that I give a hoot what they think about me. Me and Paul have a good marriage, probably one of the best in this stinking town. Do you understand what I just said, Ruby?"

"Pretty much. I guess it's not good to have sex before you get married, huh?"

"If you care about what people think, then the answer is no. If you're in love and don't care about what other people think, then go ahead. Life is too short to worry about other people."

Puzzled, Ruby said, "But you waited."

Grace laughed ruefully. "I came damn close, honey, any number of times, but something always held me back. I was in love. That's why I waited. There's a world of difference between lust and love, Ruby," Grace said gently.

Ruby thought Grace was pretty with her wild blond hair that resembled a bird's nest out of control. Her wide baby-blue eyes and sweet dimples complimented her glowing skin that she said she worked at twice a day with Porcelana and glycerine water. Her hands were soft, the fingers long and tapered with rosy red polish on the nails. Her toenails, too. Sinful, Ruby's father said.

Grace tilted her head to the side, her hands on her ample hips. "You thinking about taking the leap?" She grinned.

Ruby blushed. "Oh, no. I just . . . you know I need to . . . everyone should know . . . certain things. I asked Mom once, but she almost died."

"It figures," Grace said sourly. "What about your pa?"

Ruby snorted. "Can you picture me asking my father *anything*, Grace?"

"No, kid, I can't. When you get out of this burg, I better not ever catch you coming back, you hear me?"

"Don't worry, I'm never coming back. I'll send you a postcard, how's that, and if I ever find anyone to . . . to love or lust after, I'll write to you before I . . . I do anything."

Ruby wondered if it was time to write.

Andrew was in the lobby and so was Amber when Ruby stepped out of the elevator. This was one thing she was going to put a stop to. From now on, Andrew Blue had better not open his mouth where she was concerned to her sister.

Andrew was on his feet in a flash. "You look pretty, Ruby," he said.

"Are you ready?" she asked coolly as her eyes sought out her sister's. "We're going to church, now," she lied. She waited for some word from Amber but her sister remained quiet, although her eyes followed Ruby till she was through the door and outside in the pelting rain.

"Listen, Andrew, I don't feel like going to church, so I'm not. If you want to go, it's okay with me. I'll wait for you."

"Hell no. I just said that last week to get in good with your sister. I sized her up real quick."

"Well, obviously, you didn't come to *all* the right conclusions, so let me tell you a few things about Amber." She did. The lieutenant's mouth was hanging open when she finished. "So you see, Andrew, if you ever so much as speak with Amber about anything but the weather, I will never see you again. If you can't handle that, let me know now. I don't like it when people push me or make plans for me without my consent. That's something else I want you to remember."

Andrew stopped, his umbrella shielding both of them from the downpour. "Why do I have this feeling you don't care if you see me or not? Are you going out with me because of your sister, because of last week?"

Ruby looked into wistful brown eyes and was tempted right then to tell him the truth, but she didn't want to hurt his feelings. When in doubt, compromise.

"Sort of. Do you like it when people pressure you and make plans for you?"

"Is that what I'm doing? I'm sorry. I'm really sorry. Look, let's start all over. I know the rules now and I won't break them. Can we just spend the day together and have a good time?"

Ruby noticed a movement out of the corner of her eye, but when she turned, all she could see were lowered umbrellas as people walked up and down the busy avenue.

"Hook your arm in mine so you're closer under the umbrella." Andrew shouted to be heard over the rain.

Ruby laughed as she linked her arm in his, but not before her eyes raked the passersby a second time. She had a feeling she was being watched.

Breakfast was strawberries and waffles at the first Hot Shoppe they came to. Neither Andrew nor Ruby looked in the direction of the cathedral, where they were supposed to be attending Mass. They dawdled over a third cup of coffee. Ruby did, however, find herself glancing outside, through the sluicing rain.

Someone was standing across the street. She had the feeling he was watching her through the brightly lighted window.

Ruby turned to Andrew and smiled. "We should leave, people are waiting for our table. This is our third cup of coffee, Andrew."

Andrew shrugged. "So I'll leave the waitress a generous tip. Money talks. As for those other people, they should have gotten up as early as we did. I'm so comfortable, I could stay here all day."

"Well, we can't. We aren't going to Glen Echo, are we?"

"No, it'll be closed on a day like this. I thought we'd go to the Capital and see Johnny Ray. He's onstage. Do you like him?"

"You mean in person? Live? I have his picture. I can't believe this!" Ruby gushed.

Andrew laughed. "I guess that means I did something right. I bought the tickets from my buddy this morning. Seems his girl doesn't like Johnny Ray. Sixth row, middle of the aisle. They don't come any better than that," he said, delighted with Ruby's starry eyes.

"You look good enough to kiss . . . right here, in front of everyone. Dare me!" he said devilishly.

He would, Ruby thought, he wouldn't care who saw him kiss her. She felt as though she could kiss him, but she didn't want to, even for Johnny Ray. "What kind of girl do you think I am?" she said in a cool voice.

"I thought *all* girls liked to be kissed. Guess I was wrong. Let's forget it, okay?"

"Forgotten."

Ruby finished her coffee. Damn, now she was going to have to go to the bathroom six times. As she got to her feet, she again glanced outside. Her heart leapt into her mouth. She recognized the figure across the street: Calvin!

She watched a moment longer, her eyes squinting to see through the heavy downpour. The figure moved off, the umbrella shielding his face. Ruby sighed with relief as she made her way to the rest room. She had Calvin on her brain. If she didn't watch it, she'd be seeing him all over the place.

The moment Johnny Ray pranced off the stage, Andrew Blue grabbed Ruby and kissed her full on the mouth. It was a hard kiss, mashing really, his nose grinding into hers so she could barely breathe. There was nothing pleasant about the feeling at all. She told him so.

"That was just for starters. C'mere," he said, moving her gently so he could cup her face in his hands. He moved slowly and deliberately, his eyes locked on hers as his mouth sought her trembling lips. She was ready this time and waited for the tip of his tongue. Her eyes snapped open just as the lights came on. She still had the feeling she was being watched.

"Better?" Andrew said mockingly.

"Not much," Ruby said honestly. Andrew snorted, barely controlling his irritation.

It was after six when they walked out of the double-feature-plus-stage-show. Nervously, Ruby looked around, her eyes searching the moving umbrellas for a familiar face. It was still raining.

Farther down the block, his neck tucked into his raincoat, Calvin watched the couple. He'd been two rows behind Andrew and Ruby. If the person sitting in front of him hadn't been obese, he would have leapt over the seats and punched out the marine's lights. He knew it was wishful thinking on his part. No matter what he felt, he would never call attention to himself as long as he was wearing his uniform. He probably wouldn't do it any other time, either, he thought morosely. The bastard had kissed his girl. He wondered if Ruby was comparing the marine's kiss with his own and worried about her conclusions. "Shit!" he said.

They were probably going out to eat now. The damn marine would take her to some fancy restaurant and show off. He could feel his anger start to build, knowing he'd have to stand outside in the rain again, and he'd just about dried off. It never occurred to him to give up his surveillance and return to the base. Ruby was his girl, and no stupid marine was going to take her away from him.

"Would you like to try a French restaurant or go to a steak house?" Andrew asked Ruby. He sounded as if he was still smarting over her remark about his kiss.

Ruby pondered her choices. She'd never eaten French food.

She wondered if it was expensive. If it was and she didn't like it, she would have to eat it anyway, to justify the cost.

"Is it expensive?" she asked.

She watched surprise and worry cross the marine's face. "Look," she said, "I didn't mean that I want to go someplace expensive. I don't. I've never had French food, and if I don't like it . . ." She let the rest of what she was about to say hang in the air. Now he looked embarrassed, injured.

All about them rain fell, rolling off the umbrella like a miniature waterfall. Ruby rather liked the sight and said so. "Don't you? It's kind of romantic, walking in the rain."

Andrew gaped at her stupidly. "In a mist, not this downpour. My shoes are ruined and so are yours. My pants are soaking wet and this umbrella is starting to leak. I can't see one damn romantic thing about it."

Ruby's back stiffened. "You are absolutely right, Andrew. I'm soaked and you're soaked. What you should have done this morning was call and cancel our date. I think you're sorry you didn't, and so am I. So, if you don't mind, I am going back to the Y and change my clothes. Thank you for breakfast and the show. I enjoyed both tremendously, though I did *not* exactly enjoy your company. Good-bye," she said, and ran for the trolley pulling to a stop in the middle of the street.

As she dropped her token through the slot, she was aware of a blur of movement behind her. He damn well better not be following her. She turned, about to snarl something uncomplimentary, when she saw Calvin grinning from ear to ear.

"You were following me," she snarled. "All day, weren't you? I thought I saw you."

"Uh-huh," Calvin said happily. "I wanted to see you even if he was with you. Are you angry?"

"No." Ruby laughed. "He was a real wisenheimer. He can't kiss worth a darn, either. I suppose you saw that, too."

"Yep. I was tempted to deck the son of a gun."

Ruby was so pleased with Calvin's confession, she beamed. She linked her arm through his. "I'm soaked, you're soaked, what should we do?"

"Let's get off this stupid trolley and walk in the rain. Do you want my coat?" He hoped she'd say no. She did.

While Ruby and Calvin slogged their way through the city, laughing and giggling, stomping in puddles and splashing each other like children disobeying their parents, Andrew Blue was doing his own stomping and cursing in his quarters at the Marine barracks.

He snarled at the good-natured heckling he received when he squished and stomped his way to his locker.

"Lookee here," Mike Moss chortled, "the guy struck out. She must have been a bimbo. Ah, come on, Blue, tell us what happened."

"Yeah." Jack Davis grinned as he eyed the strip of paper pasted on Andrew Blue's locker door. A straight line of X's denoted Andrew's "scores" with girls. A second column, headed by a capital V, denoted Virgins. There were seven check marks and sixty-seven X's. A third column, headed SO for "strike outs," held no markings of any kind. All four men had a similar strip of paper, but none were as detailed as Andrew Blue's.

In a position to observe Andrew's eyes, Chris Pape nudged Brian Peters to cut short the heckling.

Andrew was down to his skivvies, reaching for his soap, when Mike Moss handed him a pencil. "There's a first time for everything, buddy, just put a big fat zero under the old SO and let's get this show on the road. We want to hear *all* about your day. Don't leave anything out."

"Buzz off, Moss, I'm not in the mood."

"Blue didn't get any pussy today, guys. Let's make him feel better. Somebody go get him an ice cream cone so he has something to lick." Brian laughed devilishly.

"I told you to knock it off," Andrew snarled. But he wasn't following the rules, rules he set up when the five of them started to bunk together. He knew he was going to have to say something, or they'd never get off his back. How in the fucking hell was he going to tell them the girl he picked up at the U.S.O. dance preferred a flip over him? And that's what he damn well was. A slant-eyed, fucking pineapple.

That would blow the whole contest. Not only would he look like a fool, he had a hundred bucks riding on the outcome. A hundred scores before they were transferred and ten virgins, zero on the strike outs. Shit!

Jesus Christ, who the hell was this Ruby Connors, anyway?

August waned and ushered in September's dry, sweet air. Ruby loved autumn. Back home the kids would be getting ready to return to school. Opal would be in the eighth grade this year with only four more years under George and Irma's roof.

Ruby was enrolled now in two classes at the Y on Tuesday and Wednesday evenings. She'd signed up for a business management course and an accounting class and was playing around with the idea of taking a real estate course. She had no idea what she would do with all this higher learning, as she called it, but it was something to do in the evenings besides sitting around her room and waiting for the weekends, when she could see Calvin.

She was in love with Calvin, although she'd never professed it openly. Calvin, on the other hand, talked of nothing else but his love for her. The time they spent together was unbearably sweet, and she hated to return to the Y when the evenings came to an end.

The new apartment was proving to be less of a hassle than Ruby had anticipated. The girls were nice and didn't bother her. What was even stranger was that Amber wasn't bothering her, either. Amber, Ruby thought, was in love, and love somehow magically dulled the edges of everything else. Or else Amber was afraid Ruby would tell George that Nangi was at the apartment almost every night. Once she'd seen Amber jam her hand into her pocket when she noticed Ruby looking at her. Ruby suspected that Nangi had given Amber a ring. She also suspected that Amber was having sex with Nangi. Nothing else could account for the sappy, drooly expression on her sister's face. For whatever had gotten Amber off her back, Ruby was truly grateful to Nangi.

Everything was so right for Ruby, it was scary. Everything except Andrew Blue.

She spent alternate Saturdays with Andrew and then switched to alternate Sundays to fit Calvin's schedule. Their dates were interesting, but nothing more. Andrew had roving hands. Twice she'd slapped him when his probing fingers had gone above her knee. He'd pouted and called her a tease and a flirt. She didn't care. He always came back. Kissing Andrew was like sucking on an egg. His hands weren't gentle, either, but hard and rough. And all he thought about was sex. Unfortunately, today was Sunday and Andrew's turn.

Ruby perched on the wall outside the house, waiting for him to announce their plans for the day.

Andrew threw his hands in the air. "Something special," he said, his eyes twinkling, "just for you. A real Washington party. You know the kind," he said authoritatively, "where they have all kinds of nibble food and lots and lots of stuff to drink. Beer, wine, gin—you name it. I think you're dressed okay." His critical eye didn't seem to agree with his words, Ruby thought. Whatever, it was a way to get through the day.

"I have to be back by six. It's my turn to cook dinner and I have to study for a test."

"Plenty of time." Andrew grinned happily.

"No funny stuff either, Andrew. I'm tired of fighting you off every time we go out. You do one thing out of the way this afternoon, and that's it, I won't see you anymore," Ruby said.

"Why do you keep seeing me, Ruby, if I offend you so much? I'm just a normal guy, and normal guys like to touch and feel and kiss. You're such a prude."

Ruby threw his question back at him, an uneasy feeling settling between her shoulder blades. "If *I'm* so different, why do you keep seeing me?"

"Okay, okay. You're nice, I like you."

She stared at him for a moment. He had surprised her, or at least his tone of voice had. He had actually sounded sincere. She wondered.

They walked hand in hand up Kilbourne Place to Mount Pleasant Avenue, where they turned on Meridian, following it to 14th Street, where they boarded a streetcar for downtown.

"Where exactly is the party?" Ruby asked.

"The Ambassador Hotel at Fourteenth and K. Have you ever been there?"

Ruby thought it a stupid question, but she shook her head. "Have you?"

"No, but I've heard a lot about it."

"Who's going to be there? Is it a big party?"

Andrew shrugged. "I guess we'll have to wait till we get there."

The lobby of the Ambassador hotel was beautifully decorated. Nola would say it was smart and tastefully furnished. She liked the seascapes and all the brass which was polished to a high sheen. The carpet felt as plush as feathers and cotton. She felt grand, elegant, walking with Andrew. Several couples turned to look at them, their gazes approving, but then, who could not look approvingly at Andrew, who was as handsome as sin. If she were in love with him, this would be so exciting, but since she wasn't, it was just a wonderful experience to cross the lobby and ride the elevator to the party.

But the moment Ruby saw Andrew fit the key into the lock, she knew he'd bamboozled her. There was no party. He had rented a room. Her eyes were furious as she blocked the doorway. So that's why people were watching her in the lobby. They knew. Why else would a serviceman be at this hotel? "Damn you, Andrew!" she exploded.

"Wait a minute, Ruby, I know what you think, and you're right, but only to a point. Yes, I had ulterior motives, and yes, I lied to you. I'm sorry. This is all paid for, so we might as well sit for a while and . . . talk. I know you're mad, but I'm mad, too. You're stringing me along and going out with that . . . that bird from the air force. That's not very nice," Andrew said.

Ruby was stunned. "I suppose next you're going to tell me you followed me." At his sheepish look, Ruby exploded a second time. "What a dirty, mean, sneaky thing to do. And here I thought you were so self-assured. You're just a stooge and I want to leave. Now!"   ·

"Ruby, wait, let me explain!"

"You can tell me in the elevator or outside, but not in this room. Don't you get it, Andrew?"

"I was just trying to one-up the pineapple."

"That's it! That's it!" Ruby screeched.

"For God's sake, lower your voice before they send up the house dick," Andrew ordered as he tried to muffle her screeches with his hand.

Ruby lashed out, driving her elbow into Andrew's stomach with all the force she could summon. She stomped on his foot twice before she spun away from him, her eyes furiously sparking. "Don't you ever lay a hand on me again. I'm going downstairs and . . . and reporting you to the desk manager, and when I'm done doing that, I'm going to call your C.O. and tell him how you got me here under false pretenses."

"Jesus Christ! Will you listen to me! I'm not going to do anything to you. You sound like a male cat the way you're wailing and carrying on. I never forced myself on a girl before, and I'm not about to start now." He made a mistake then by reaching for her arm. Ruby clenched her fist and hauled off and socked him in the nose, dead center. Blood spurted in every direction.

"That's for thinking I'm easy. You, Andrew, are a *cur!*" she said dramatically, and she sailed through the door.

Andrew Blue had made a bet with the guys at the barracks that today would be the day he nailed Ruby Connors, but now he cursed himself for going through with it. He had made an obsession of her, of the challenge she represented to him. No girl had ever turned him down before. And when he had followed her two Sundays ago, and he had seen her with that pineapple from the air force, he had told himself that this little hayseed from Pennsylvania was using him, Andrew Blue, to cover for her with her sister. He wasn't going to lose out to some flip with a little dick and no balls. That's when he'd become so enraged that he made the bet and marked the calendar.

Now he was sorry. He was sorry because when he'd told her she was nice and that he liked her, he had realized he was telling the truth. He did like her. She was real, genuine, honest. But his pride wouldn't allow him to lose the bet. He shook his head. Not only had he lost the bet, he'd probably lost her as well.

He wanted to run after her, to apologize, but he had to see to his nose before he ruined the fancy gold-threaded bedspread, not to mention his uniform. "Son of a bitch!" he snarled as he ran cold water on a snowy washcloth. Now what in the goddamn hell was he supposed to do? Sleep, of course, that's what most people did in a hotel. As he drifted into sleep, he wondered if he was falling in love with the smalltown hayseed named Ruby Connors.

Outside in the crisp afternoon air Ruby drew deep, gulping breaths as she walked to the nearest phone booth. She dropped in her dime and called Calvin, crossing her fingers that he was in his quarters. When she heard his voice, a sob caught in her throat. "I'm downtown. Can you meet me at the corner of Fourteenth and K?"

The catch in her voice alarmed Calvin. "Don't stand on the corner, look for a coffee shop or something. I'll be there in an hour. I'll find you," he said reassuringly.

An hour and ten minutes later, Calvin roared, "He did *what*!

Jesus, Ruby. Are you okay?" He put his arm tightly around her shoulders.

"Sure," she hiccoughed. "You should have seen the blood, Calvin. It was all over. What if I broke his nose?"

"I don't think you have to worry about that. Are you going to call his C.O.?" he asked with a frown.

"Maybe. I should. What do *you* think?"

"It will go on his record, and if *nothing* really happened, you don't want to cause trouble."

"Calvin, whose side are you on?" Ruby hiccoughed again.

"Yours, of course. It's just that there's a man's entire career at stake here. Look, don't mind me, I'm kind of blue today. No pun intended."

Ruby was immediately full of concern. "What's wrong?"

"I'm being transferred."

"Where? When?" Ruby demanded, suddenly frightened.

"Two weeks. Beale Air Force Base in California. I had a choice. California or Ladd Field in Alaska."

"California! That's . . . that's . . . so far away. Oh, Calvin," Ruby cried.

Calvin felt like crying himself. "Let's get married," he said desperately.

"Married!"

"Hitched. Yeah. Come with me to California. Don't you want to?"

Ruby wiped her eyes. Married. Marriage meant babies and . . . her father would have to sign a consent form, something she knew he would never do. "I'm underage, Calvin. My parents . . . my sister . . ."

"But you said they don't know about me. If you just . . . left, disappeared, leave a note behind so the police won't look for you . . . how could they find you? I can take care of you, Ruby. I'm going to be a general someday. We can live on the base. You could even work if you wanted to. For now we could get married by a justice of the peace, and when it's safe, we can be married in church. Don't you love me, Ruby?" he asked anxiously, his dark eyes full of concern.

"Of course I do. It's just that I never gave marriage much thought. I'm only eighteen and I haven't done anything yet. My parents . . . some way my father will find me. My God, he'll kill me."

"He can't do that if we're married. I'll take care of you, Ruby, I swear I will. Do you want to marry me? Just say yes or no. We'll work on the rest later."

Did she? He was waiting for her answer, his eyes pleading. Suddenly her legs felt like straw, her arms as limp as a rag doll's. The thought of Calvin going up against her father was a nightmare. If it were Andrew Blue squaring off against George Connors, she might have a chance, but not Calvin. The thought was so disloyal, she felt like crying. Poor Calvin.

But the moment Calvin's shoulders slumped and she read the rejection in his eyes, she answered, "Yes!"

Calvin looked deliriously happy.

With his arm around Ruby's trembling shoulders they walked up one street and down another, talking and planning until they completely lost their bearings. They walked on, not caring. After what seemed like hours later, they entered Rock Creek Park, Ruby's favorite place in all of Washington. At dusk their final plans were made.

"It's simple, Ruby. If we make it too complicated, something will foul up. Simple, cut and dried, that's how we do things in the military. Don't do anything out of the ordinary to make your sister suspicious. Write home to your grandmother, but don't say anything. I'll get you a ticket for California. You'll have to decide, though, if you want to go by train or fly. The trip will take almost a week on the train."

"Fly? In the air! Oh, Calvin, I've never been on a plane. I just know I'll get sick. Do you have that much money? Where will I stay?"

"I have enough money, and I'll find a boardinghouse or a Y, something. Just trust me, Ruby. Please."

"I do, Calvin . . . this is so sudden . . . my job . . . what if I ever need a reference? How can I leave Admiral Query in the lurch?"

"Okay, okay. Give your notice. The admiral isn't going to call your family. You'll be safe on that score. All your expenses are covered at the apartment until the first of October, right?" Ruby nodded. "Good, then it's their problem, not yours. Are you sure you can handle all of this, Ruby?"

"Yes. I've done pretty good so far with Andrew and you. I . . . I can do it, Calvin," Ruby said nervously. Married? Oh, God!

"I think it will be best if you come to California a week after I leave. I'll need at least a week to scout out the area and get a place for you. I . . . I might have a problem with my C.O. and chaplin, but there's this guy in my outfit who . . . well, what he did was he forged his girl's parents' names on the consent form. No one ever found out. He's white, though, so I . . . there might be a problem, you have to be aware of that, Ruby."

Ruby bristled. "Calvin, I wish you wouldn't keep referring to me and your buddies as white. It always sounds like you think you're colored, and you're not. You're Asian."

"Dammit, Ruby, I'm different no matter how you say it." He put his hand next to hers. "What color are you and what color am I?"

Ruby giggled. "I'm off-white and you're off-tan. Your skin is the color of honey or light coffee. Colored people are brown. You aren't colored, Calvin."

"Okay, you win for now," he said, sounding completely unconvinced. "We might not be able to get married right away with all the red tape. It might take a month or so. Is that okay?"

Ruby nodded, although the worms were back in her stomach. "What about your family, Calvin? What are you going to tell them?"

"After we get married, I'll send them a picture of us. They'll like you, and I know they'll get used to the idea, but not right away. My mother is a sweet, kind lady and she only wants me to be happy. They're very simple people, Ruby," he said shyly.

"I'll love them, Calvin. I'll write to them every week, the way I do my grandmother. Someday we'll all get to meet one another. Your family, I mean. I don't ever want you to meet my parents. *That's* something you have to understand."

"Okay, it's a deal. Do you think we missed anything?"

Ruby wiggled her fingers in front of his nose. "No engagement ring." Calvin's face went blank. Ruby almost wept. "It isn't important, I have something better." She told him about the czarina's ring. "I want to wear it when we get married. We'll tell everyone it's my engagement ring, okay?"

"If that's what you want, Ruby, it's okay with me. Someday, though, I'll get you a real engagement ring. I promise."

"Are you going to wear a wedding band?" Ruby asked.

"You'd damn well better believe I'm going to wear one. I was hoping you'd want me to wear one."

"You're damn right. I don't want one of those blond California girls trying to snatch you away from me."

"I love you, Ruby," Calvin said in a shaky voice.

Ruby's voice was just as shaky when she uttered the same declaration, because she didn't know if the words were true. Then, a second later, she was more certain of it than anything in her life. She loved Calvin Santos, heart and soul. Any doubts, any insecurities she had felt, disappeared in the warm evening air.

Calvin seemed to sense the change in her. "You weren't sure, were you, till just this minute?"

"How did you know?"

"I just knew. I guess you can say we're on the same wavelength. It's going to be perfect, Ruby, at least as perfect as I can make it."

"I'll make it just as perfect for you, too, Calvin," Ruby said happily.

"Then nothing can possibly go wrong," Calvin said.

Ruby shivered in the dark night. Calvin was wrong, of course. Nothing was perfect. But she wasn't going to think about that tonight. God, she could hardly wait to call Grace and tell her. And Nola would absolutely wet her pants at the news. Ruby laughed joyously, and Calvin kissed her. Then he promised her the world.

The evening was so beautiful, star-spangled, Ruby thought as she walked from her accounting class at the Y to the trolley that would take her home to Mount Pleasant.

Autumn here in Washington seemed different somehow from autumn in Pennsylvania. Here the air was thicker, the leaves changing earlier. She was wearing a sweater, a bargain Nola had found. She didn't really need it this evening, but she liked to wear it cape-style over her shoulders. There were so many things she liked, things she would be giving up. Her fledgling independence for one thing, and the apartment, not to mention Nola and a few of her office friends. She liked Washington and wanted to be around to see the cherry blossoms in the spring. She wanted to continue her classes, too. She was doing so well, and she liked the instructor. In fact, she loved everything about her life. She adored Admiral Query and couldn't wait to go to work in the morning. But she loved Calvin more. She would do anything for Calvin.

She really did want to marry Calvin, she told herself. It was normal for her to be jittery and anxious. Nola said she had to go with her feelings. Ruby frowned as the trolley ground to a halt. She'd expected Nola to be delighted with her news, and she had been, to a point, but her eyes were clouded with worry. The worry, however, Ruby found out later wasn't for her, but for herself. Nola was pregnant and Alex, her boyfriend, had left four weeks earlier, transferred to someplace in the Midwest.

"I'm going back home, Ruby. If I'm lucky, my parents will take me in and help me. I'll find some kind of job. I'll clean houses and take in ironing if I have to."

"What about your career?" Ruby asked, dumbfounded.

Nola snorted. "A pipe dream, Ruby. A baby is reality. I don't have any choices. Maybe someday. Oh, hey, look, here's the sketch I made of the dress for the Harvest Ball. Sorry you won't be going. If you're getting married, you might want to have a dress made some day for a special occasion. I took the liberty of signing it. Swear on . . . on your grandmother that if you ever have the dress made it will be sky blue, brilliant and dazzling."

"Do you have enough money to get home?" Ruby asked.

Nola shrugged.

"I have twenty-some dollars. Call it a loan if you're too proud to take it. Nola, what if . . . what if your parents . . ."

"My parents love me. They'll be disappointed for a few months, but they love kids, and a brand-new baby . . . well, my mother will just love it to death."

"Did you tell Alex? Does he know? How could he leave like that with you . . . it's his flesh and blood."

"He shipped out before I found out for certain. Anyway, Alex is a free spirit. He doesn't want to be tied down to a wife and kid. I'm on my own, Ruby. I don't want you worrying about me, you have enough on your mind as it is. I'm leaving on Saturday. Everything is packed. Oh, Ruby, I hate going home with my tail between my legs. I made such grand promises and now I can't deliver." Nola cried. "All my dreams down the drain."

Ruby hugged her. "Let's spend Friday evening together, just you and me. I'll cancel my date with Calvin, but on Saturday we'll take you to the bus station. I want to see you off. I probably won't see you for a very long time."

"We'll probably never see each other again," Nola wailed.

"Of course we will. You're going to be rich and famous someday, so you can track me down. Just call the base locator and give Calvin's name, rank, and service number. You'll find me."

Nola scribbled her parents' address on Ruby's notebook. "Oh, Ruby, I am going to miss you so much. Let's write, okay? And keep on writing. Friends tend to lose touch," Nola said tearfully. "I don't want that to happen."

"I won't *let* that happen, Nola," Ruby said vehemently.

"Are you happy, Ruby?" Nola asked wistfully.

"I love Calvin." Ruby was surprised at the stubborn tone in her own voice. "The truth is, I'm scared. Nola, I'm giving up everything. I gave my notice to Admiral Query today, and I started to cry. He gave me his handkerchief and I kept right on blubbering. I . . . I told him the truth and . . . and he said I was too young to get married. His wife is taking me to lunch tomorrow to try to talk me out of it. I have to be polite and go. I lied and told my boss my parents were signing the consent forms. I had this feeling . . . still have it . . . that he might call them and . . . God, he could say anything. I think it was a mistake to tell him, but I couldn't leave him in the lurch. He's been so good to me. I just feel it in my gut, Nola, he's going to call them. He's so upright and old-fashioned."

"Well, then tomorrow you'll have to convince Mrs. Query that isn't a good idea," Nola said with a hint of impatience. "I'm sorry, but I'm real tired, Ruby. I've been on my feet all day, and my ankles are swollen. Let's call it a day. I'll meet you Friday after work and you can tell me what happened. Where?"

"A dive, someplace where we can both enjoy it because I have this feeling . . . what I mean is . . . our lives are changing and we should *really* enjoy ourselves. How about McGyver's on Sixteenth? We'll get ourselves dolled up enough to look twenty-one. Maybe we'll get served."

Admiral Query poked his head out of his office. Ruby almost giggled aloud when he jerked it back immediately. Like a turtle, she thought. He could have buzzed her, called out to her, but he said he preferred personal contact.

Ruby got up and reached for her steno pad. "Do you want to dictate a letter, Admiral?"

"No, Ruby, I want to talk to you. Do you think you could imagine me as a kindly uncle for just a few minutes?"

Puzzled, Ruby nodded. "Is something wrong?"

"I don't know, Ruby. I'm concerned you might be making a serious mistake. You're so young, child, you have your whole life ahead of you. Getting married is very serious decision. Children come along and money isn't plentiful. You have to struggle and you get short-tempered. You'll be moving around a lot, unable to put down roots. Your children will be constantly leaving friends behind. Have you thought all this through, Ruby?" Query said fretfully.

"Yes, sir, I have. Are you really worried about me, Admiral Query?"

"Hell, yes, I'm worried. If I had a daughter, I'd be saying these same things to her. Besides, I don't want to lose you. You're the best secretary I ever had. Still, if this is what you really want, then I won't interfere. I know I said it might be a good idea to speak with your parents, but that was . . . that was something I said in the heat of the moment. Out of concern. I want you to believe that."

"I do, Admiral, and I'm going to miss you, too. I'll write. Will you write back?" Ruby smiled.

"If they send me someone who knows how to type, I will. Even if they don't, I'll take pen in hand myself," he chuckled.

"I'll look forward to your letters, Admiral."

"It will give me something to do. They're getting ready to put me out to pasture, you know. They think I'm too old. Retirement. My wife thinks I'm looking forward to it. She's dead wrong about that," he grumbled good-naturedly.

He was such a kind, gentle man, Ruby thought. So gallant and courtly. The word *old-fashioned* sprung to mind. Mrs. Query had told her once, when she had stopped by to take the admiral to lunch, that she'd never seen him without a tie, except when he went to bed. She told her other wonderful things about her husband and the way he treated the men under him. He never asked them to do anything he wouldn't do himself, Mrs. Query said proudly. And he was a real family man with a great respect for women. He didn't believe in divorce, and nothing made him angrier than spousal abuse.

"You're wool-gathering, Ruby," the admiral said tartly.

"I guess I was, I'm sorry. I was remembering what your wife said about you the second or third time I met her."

"I'll bet she could find only good things to say, am I right?"

"Wonderful things, Admiral Query. And I believe that she *is* looking forward to your retirement, even if you're not. It will be nice for you both. You can travel together and do things as a couple. I think she's lonely, Admiral."

"You do, do you?"

"She told me so."

"Then why didn't she tell me?"

"I think she did, sir, but you didn't hear her."

"It's amazing, Ruby, how you managed to turn this conversation around to me and my wife. We need to get back to the matter at hand. I want to hear from you that you love this young man heart and soul, and I won't interfere. You need to be sure, Ruby. Having a family is a sacred trust."

Ruby smiled. "I'm sure, Admiral Query and . . . *my* family will be sacred. I know you've been polite about not asking me about my family back home, and I appreciate it. It wasn't . . . my parents don't have the same kind of marriage you and Mrs. Query have. My father . . . well, my father . . . is . . . he isn't . . ."

Query was off the chair before Ruby could finish talking. He wrapped the young girl in his arms. "I think I understand. But the words needed to be said. If there's ever anything I or Mrs. Query can do, you have only to call on us. I want your promise that you will, Ruby."

Ruby wiped her eyes. "I promise."

"Now, freshen up and get ready to meet Mrs. Query for lunch. I have it on good authority she's taking you to a wonderful restaurant. I'll tell her myself we settled this little matter between us. She was worried about you being so far from home and all. Now, scat. Oh, do we have any licorice?"

"Yes, but Mrs. Query said I wasn't supposed to let you eat it," Ruby giggled.

"We won't tell her. Fetch it, Ruby."

"One stick or two?"

"Two, of course. And one for later." He bowed, a courtly gesture that made Ruby giggle even more. "War is hell," he muttered as she closed the office door behind her.

Ruby's relief was so great that she felt light-headed. Everything was going to be okay.

Friday night didn't prove the wonderful evening Ruby had planned. "We're like two wet blankets," she said as she sipped her cherry phosphate.

"I'm sorry, Ruby, I get morning sickness that carries into the afternoon and evening. All damn day," she said tiredly. "I can't eat anything. But you go ahead."

"I'm not really hungry, either," Ruby mumbled.

"God, Ruby, what if I get sick on the bus tomorrow," Nola said listlessly. "Where do you throw up on a bus?"

"You open the window and stick your head out. What else can you do? Calvin's going to meet us at the bus station. Here," she said, slipping twenty-seven dollars across the table, "I wish it were more."

Nola's eyes filled. "Ruby, how can I take this?"

"You just take it, that's how. I want you to have it, Nola. Now c'mon, let's get out of here."

Ruby felt magnanimous when she paid the check. Nola was going to need every cent she could get her hands on. She wished she could look into the future to see if her friend would be all right, but she canceled the wish immediately. Nola would make it. She had pluck and grit, and she was smart. She also had a wonderful, loving family. She would be just fine.

The following morning Calvin and Ruby watched as Nola boarded the bus that would take her to Michigan. Tears ran down both girls' cheeks as they hugged each other, promising to write and keep in touch.

"Be sure you let me know if it's a girl or a boy so I can send something in the right color."

Ruby cried then as she'd never cried in her life, and the tears were still streaming down her cheeks when the bus pulled away from the underground lot out into the bright September sunshine.

"Don't cry, Ruby. You act as if she's dead," Calvin said. "She's going away, that's all. You can write to her every day. You'll find a way to get together again someday." His tone was almost petulant when he added, "I didn't know you felt so strongly about her."

"She's my friend, Calvin. She helped me. Really helped me. I'm not even going to try to explain." She whirled to face

Calvin. "On the other hand," she said, blowing her nose lustily, "maybe I should explain."

Ruby pocketed her handkerchief. "Andrew Blue teases me about being a hayseed, a hick from the sticks. I guess I am. I'm a small-town girl in a very big city. I came here, knowing my sister hates me, without a friend in the world. I had no job, and I looked like I just fell off the hay wagon. Nola made it possible for me to look like I knew how to dress as well as everyone else. My sister didn't help me, or even care. But if I needed a quarter and Nola didn't have it, she would borrow it from someone to give me. That's the kind of person she is. Now she's gone, and I feel bad. You have to care about people, Calvin, or you're nothing but a robot. Sometimes I'd like to see you display a little emotion without fear of . . . forget it."

Calvin stumbled over a culvert but righted himself. He looked chastised. "I can be your best friend, Ruby."

Ruby threw her arms around him. "You are, Calvin, but you're a guy. Nola is a girl, and that's different."

Then it occurred to her that Calvin worried that she was wrinkling his tie and shirt collar, because he nodded and patted her on the head clumsily, then he tried to inch away. Poor Calvin. But couldn't he understand? She had lost something when Nola left, something irreplaceable.

When she found herself in front of the house she lived in, she hardly noticed the girls sitting on the stone wall. She thought she mumbled something as she made her way up the concrete steps. She barely glanced into the living room, where Amber was sitting with Nangi.

Inside her room she threw herself on the bed, buried her face in her pillow, and howled her grief at Nola's departure. Or was her grief misdirected? She didn't know and didn't care.

After a while, Ruby dragged herself off the bed to the bathroom. Her eyes were puffy and red. She made a face at herself. She looked so ugly, *how* could Calvin love her? *Why* did he love her? Before she knew what was happening she heard herself answering her own question. "Because he needs my strength. I'm stronger and tougher than he is. I mother him and pat him on the back and tell him he's wonderful. That's why."

Ruby sat down on the edge of the bathtub and dropped her head into her hands.

"But does Calvin love you? Does he really love you the way Paul Zachary loves Grace?" she asked herself.

"He says he does," Ruby murmured fretfully.

"Do you believe him?" the voice pressed.

"He wouldn't lie about that."

"What about you, Ruby? Do you love Calvin?"

"Of course I do. I wouldn't marry him if I didn't love him."

"Sure you would," the voice needled. "You'll do anything to get away from your parents. Anything."

Ruby snorted. "I'm already away and I'm happy here. I don't have to get married to get away."

"Sure, sure," the voice whispered, "but if you're married, your father can't snatch you away and take you back. He still holds that power over you as long as you're here . . . anywhere. Admit it, you're fascinated with Calvin's culture, with him. You like playing the strong one, the one who can make it all come out right. You like taking care of him. You like pretending he's your brother, your father, your youngest uncle. You like it that he's gone to college even though it made you feel inferior at first, and you like it that he's a snappy lieutenant without a lick of common sense. That's where you excel, Ruby. Do you want to go through life nurturing a misfit? Do you want to go through life picking him up and dusting him off every time his feelings are hurt? He's a weak sister, Ruby."

"Shut up!" Ruby said through clenched teeth. "Just shut the hell up!"

"Okay, I'll shut up," the voice whispered, "but not until you tell me why. Why do you love him? Or like him? Or feel sorry for him? Just tell me why."

"I like the way he makes me feel wanted. I feel good when he reaches out to touch me. He's gentle and kind. When my father's hand came out, he used it to slap me. I love Calvin and I'm going to marry him. Now leave me alone, I'm going to bed."

The following day, Ruby cut her lunch hour short to return to her desk and write a letter to Grace Zachary, which she slipped into the outgoing mail. She looked at the office clock and decided she had time to write to Opal and her grandmother as well. A newsy letter to Opal full of trivia and lightness, but nothing about Calvin. That would be too much of a risk.

At four o'clock the phone on her desk rang. "Admiral Query's line," she said in her professional office voice.

"Ruby, this is Calvin." Ruby's heart thumped, certain he was calling to tell her he had changed his mind. It irritated her that he always announced himself so formally. "Listen, sweetheart"—and that was another thing she hated, being called sweetheart; she had a name, didn't she? "I don't know how this happened, but I won't be going on the MATS flight to California. I'm to take a commercial flight, so I can go with you. I know the plan was for you to leave a week after me, but this is better. I have enough money for you to stay in a hotel for a week. It's wonderful, isn't it, Ruby? Just five more days. I wanted to talk with you before I got your ticket. It's okay, isn't it?" he asked uncertainly.

For a moment Ruby couldn't breathe. "Uh-huh," she mumbled.

"I get it," Calvin said happily, "your boss is close by. I'll see you tomorrow night."

Ruby nodded, forgetting Calvin couldn't see her. "Okay." Five days. One hundred and twenty hours. Seven thousand two hundred minutes. Forty-three thousand—"Five days!" she yelped.

Admiral Query stuck his bald head out of the office. "Is something wrong, Ruby?"

"No, sir. I just made a mistake. I'll fix it. I hate it when I make a mistake," she mumbled.

"No one is perfect, Ruby, not even me," the admiral said.

Ruby had hardly returned to her notepad when the phone rang at her elbow. Her voice sounded angry when she said, "Admiral Query's line."

"Ruby," the voice said briskly, "I'm calling to ask if you and your friend would like to double date tonight?"

"I'm sorry, Andrew, but Nola went back to Michigan. I can meet you for coffee after work or for a bite to eat. If you want to."

"Sure I do. Don't you have a class or something?"

"Not tonight."

"How come you're being so agreeable?" Andrew asked suspiciously. "You should be really ticked off at me."

"I was, but I'm not anymore. Listen, this isn't my personal

line. I can meet you at Sadie's on K at five-thirty, or is that too early?"

"Make it six and it's a date. Did you get my flowers and candy?"

"Yes. Thank you. I accept your apology. You didn't have to do that, Andrew." A third voice came on the line, listened a second or two, and then said, "Congratulations, young man. If you don't make this girl happy, you'll have to answer to me. War is hell, but then, you birds in the Air Force know all about that. Admiral Clark Query signing off for the U.S. Navy."

"What the hell . . ."

"I have to go now. I'll see you at six, Andrew," Ruby said, her voice shrill with panic.

Now she would have to tell him. Andrew was a wild card. What would he do with the information?

Oh, God.

Andrew Blue walked into Sadie's, a deli bar, at fifteen minutes to six. He'd managed to hitch a ride into town with a major headed to Arlington. A cab brought him the rest of the way to Sadie's door. He was so hot under the collar, he thought he would explode. All he'd done the whole afternoon was think about Admiral Clark Query's words. He didn't need to be a genius to understand what the old geezer said. Ruby was planning on marrying the flip and the squid knew all about it. If he hadn't called, he probably never would have found out. Well, by God, now he knew. The question was, what was he going to do about it, if anything? Did he really care enough to kick up a fuss? The flip seemed to have the advantage and was running fast in the outside lane. Shit, he didn't know he had to qualify. If he'd known, he would have given it everything he had. He knew how to win. His coach in junior high school had told him there were two kinds of people in the world: winners and losers. Which did he want to be? He had been a winner all the way, in every sport in junior high, high school, and at Annapolis. All-star material from the git-go. His parents had been so proud of him, especially his old man, who, until then, hardly knew what his name was. Yeah, his old man was proud, even prouder, if that was possible, when he came out of Annapolis a commissioned officer. His mother had cried, but his old man clapped him on the back and said "A second looey" out of the corner of his mouth, like James Cagney. His mother would like Ruby and Ruby would like her. Not that it made a difference one way or the other.

"A beer," Andrew said to the hovering waitress. "I'm waiting for my girl." He flushed when the waitress smirked, but he stared her down. He did think of Ruby as his girl.

He wished now he'd asked Ruby questions about the flip, but with his ego at stake, he hadn't dared. What exactly was he up against? Just how great was this air force pogue? He'd looked like a twit, like one of those pansy guys who danced in a leotard. What could Ruby possibly see in someone like that? How could she prefer a pineapple to him? Jesus, he was six-two and packed one hundred and seventy pounds on his frame, all pure, hard muscle. It must have been the marriage proposal that did the trick.

Andrew groaned. Marriage. If the flip offered marriage, then he had to do the same thing and hope for the best. You just never knew about females.

But did he want to win Ruby enough for the big one? Runny-nosed kids, smelly diapers, animals, overcooked dinners, and *no more freedom*? If he decided to go for it, what the fuck would he be winning? He might be in love, but so what? That didn't mean he had to go and get married.

Andrew drained his second glass of beer just as Ruby walked through the door. He hailed the waitress by snapping his fingers. "Double time," he said loudly enough to be heard at the next three tables, all seated civilians.

Andrew smiled warmly and sized Ruby up. Just how good an officer's wife would she make? With a little work she could definitely be an asset. She was pretty, not beautiful, but she had stunning eyes with thick lashes. Bedroom eyes. He liked that. Today her color was high and it wasn't from makeup. She wore a crisp white blouse with a small black velvet ribbon under the collar. After a full day of work, the blouse had barely a wrinkle. He liked her hands with their shiny white nails. He wondered how she typed and how good she was. He asked, not because he really cared, but more to have something to say.

Ruby smiled, but it was a forced smile. "Around sixty words a minute. Without mistakes. Can you type?"

Andrew leaned back in his chair. "As a matter of fact, I can. This may surprise you, but I can knit, too. The coach of my high school football team made all the players learn to knit. It develops the hand muscles. Since I was the quarterback and handled the ball, it was important. I made an afghan once. My mother keeps it over the back of the chair she sits on."

"What color is it?"

"Color?" Andrew asked stupidly. He had to think. "Green and yellow. Is it important?"

"No. It was something to say. You never talked much about yourself."

"Marines are like that. We're private people," he said, puffing out his chest.

"Do you read?"

"Everything I can get my hands on."

"I wish I'd known all this about you before."

"All you had to do was ask," Andrew said softly. "I figured if I started telling you all kinds of things, you'd think I was bragging. I wanted you to like me for myself."

"How could I do that, Andrew, if I didn't know you? These past months you were like a cardboard figure to me. Even now, all I really know about you is that you like to read, you can knit, and you have fresh hands. Not much after you've been seeing someone for a couple of months."

"How much do you know about that bird in the air force?" he asked sourly.

"Enough. He took the time to let me get to know him."

"You weren't interested in me. You told me so yourself. You even admitted that you used me to see him. How do you suppose I felt when . . . that was a real cheap trick, Ruby," Andrew said piously.

Ruby blushed. "I know and I'm sorry. It's just that my sister . . ."

"Speaking of your sister. I think I saw her the other day. She works at the Pentagon with you, doesn't she? I had to go over there for my C.O. She didn't see me, though." *Get it now, Blue, otherwise it's a lost cause.* The guys said to go through the sister.

"Amber works at the Navy Annex."

Andrew motioned to the waitress. This time he didn't snap his fingers. "We'll have two shrimp salad sandwiches, two orders of potato salad, and some cole slaw. I'll have another beer and the young lady will have a ginger ale." She was dismissed the moment his gaze returned to Ruby. She looked surprised. Maybe he shouldn't have ordered for her. Don't lose the initiative now, he told himself.

Andrew assumed a calculated pose of hurtful bewilderment. "I saw you first, Ruby. That should count for something. Is it my fault you had to go to the bathroom and met this other . . . guy? I told you I was active in sports in school. Well, at the end of every game you had a winning score and at the end of the season you went on to participate in the finals or playoffs. If you won, you got a prize. That's how I thought of you, Ruby. You were going to be my prize. I was playing the game the only way I knew how. I've been with a lot of girls, but I'm the first to admit I don't know anything about them. Sure, I've played bedsheet roulette, all guys do, but it doesn't mean anything." He leaned back to better observe the conflicting emotions play across the girl's face. Blue, you are a ring-tailed son of a bitch, he complimented himself.

Ruby seemed at a loss for words. Andrew leaned across the table and took her hands in his. Ruby jerked backward and yanked her hands free. Andrew's eyes turned sad and woebegone. "I'm really a nice guy. My parents think I'm one of a kind. I'm nice to little kids and dogs. I used to be a Boy Scout." Christ, she wasn't responding to anything he was saying. "You must have liked me a little to go out with me even if . . . it was to cover up for that . . . other guy. How much do you know about him, Ruby? And, yeah, I got the drift of what your boss was saying. When's the wedding?" he asked softly.

"It's none of your business, Andrew," Ruby said miserably.

"It is my business. Everything is fair in love and war."

"You don't know anything about me. You can't be in love with me," Ruby said tightly.

"That's true, I don't know nearly enough about you. I didn't want to go too fast, to rush you. I didn't want to take advantage of you, and for God's sake, don't throw that hotel in my face. That's what made me realize you were . . . worth fighting for, worth waiting for. Ah, Ruby, rethink what you're planning on doing. Don't go off half-cocked and make the biggest mistake of your life. If you won't tell me when, it must be soon."

"I'm leaving in five days. Now, you can go to my sister and tell her all about it. That's your plan, isn't it? It isn't going to work. I've made up my mind and if you do anything to interfere, I'll hate you forever. And if you care about me like you say you do, then you should want to see me happy. Look, I don't care for shrimp salad, and cole slaw isn't on my favorite-food list. It would have been nice if you consulted me before ordering." Ruby fished around in her purse for change and laid a dollar and ten cents on the table. "Good-bye, Andrew."

"She dumped you, huh?" the gum-chewing waitress snickered. "You spit-and-polish marines are all alike. I could have told you she was going to do that the minute you ordered her food. I seen it in her face." She slapped the check on the table and sashayed to her post.

Fall back and regroup, Andrew cautioned himself. He still had five days.

Ruby didn't know if she was angry or elated as she stepped onto the trolley and dropped in her token. She settled back and rode through two full stops before she hopped off and crossed the center island to wait for a trolley that would take her back to Sadie's.

She was impatient, tapping her foot on the hard concrete as her eyes scanned the knots of people out for an evening stroll. Somehow she had to find Andrew. She crossed her fingers the way she had when she was little and expecting the worst. What would she do if he was gone? He hadn't looked angry. On the contrary, he'd looked rather smug. And that could mean only one thing. He was going to go to her sister. Why would he do such a thing? Just to make trouble? She suspected he'd given her a real con job, telling her he considered her a prize, but it was nice to hear. Worth waiting for. And worth causing trouble for?

Ten minutes later Ruby smoothed her skirt and shook her shoulders to try to relax before she entered Sadie's. She decided to look into the window before she entered the crowded deli-bar unescorted. Her heart thumped crazily in her chest as she pressed her face up close to the frosted glass. Then her breath exploded in a loud hiss. Andrew was inside, laughing with three girls. Andrew chose that moment to lift his head. She swore she saw him mouth the words "Oh, shit" before she turned and ran. She hopped onto a trolley, bound for God only knew where. She dropped a third token, grabbed a transfer, and staggered to the back, where she sat next to an elderly man carrying on a conversation with himself. She joined in, muttering to herself. It wasn't until she reached Dupont Circle that she realized the man was conversing with his dead wife.

Andrew Blue's face was disdainful as he went through the cafeteria line at the Navy Annex. In his crisp marine uniform he stood out like a pimple on a debutante's nose. Not that he gave a damn. He was there on what he called a bullshit mission, and he could sling it with the best of his superiors. He knew he was being a real prick, but he didn't give a damn about that, either.

It was five minutes till noon, the hour when most secretaries took their lunch. He scanned the food trays and decided on ham and cheese and iced tea. He didn't want any messy lunch staring him in the face when he spoke to Amber Connors.

He'd gotten there just in time to grab a table for four all to himself. The swabbies were eyeing him and probably wondering what he was doing there. "Bullshit, men, pure bullshit," he muttered, sinking his teeth into the dry-looking sandwich, his eyes glued to the entrance.

Three minutes later Amber Connors walked through the door with her friend ... Edna ... Ellie ... something like that. No, Ethel. That was it. He waited as they chose their lunch, and when they came toward his table, he stood, his bearing Marine Corps all the way. He knew the swabbies' eyes were on his six-foot-two frame, as well they should have been. By God, the Corps *did* turn out a superior individual.

"Miss Connors," he said just loud enough for Amber to hear. He motioned to his table in the rapidly filling dining room. Amber's face broke into a simpering smile.

He was courtly and gracious when he pulled the chairs from the table and held them for the girls. "Fancy meeting you here. And I thought I was going to have to eat alone."

"What brings you to the Annex, Andrew?" Amber asked, shaking her napkin free and settling it on her lap. Remembering her manners, she said, "You met Ethel, didn't you?"

"Yes, and the pleasure was all mine," he said. His smile, warm and wide, seemed to embrace both girls. Amber preened, and Ethel flushed.

They talked about the weather, the seasons of the year, the approaching holidays. It was an awkward conversation, but Andrew adroitly managed to turn the conversation around to himself and Ruby.

"I really liked her and I'm going to miss her," he said with just the right amount of regret in his voice.

Amber picked at her salad. "Oh, are you being transferred?" She didn't sound as though she cared one way or the other.

Andrew wagged his finger under her nose. "Aren't you the sly one." Amber smiled, as if it were a compliment. Another hayseed. "No, I'm referring to Ruby. Are you standing up for her? Gee, did I say something wrong? You being her sister and all. I just assumed . . . guess I put my foot in it, huh?"

Ethel stopped chewing.

"What are you talking about?" Amber demanded, laying her fork across the plate.

"C'mon, Miss Connors, don't put me on the spot like this. I'm sorry if I said something that . . . look, I'm sorry," he said, gathering up his plate and napkin. "I've got the general's staff car, and he's going to need it. Gotta go. It was real nice seeing you again. Guess we won't be seeing each other again."

"Wait," Amber said, panic in her voice. "Explain what you just said."

"Look, I'm out of line here. With Ruby getting married to-morrow, I just thought you would . . . Look, I really didn't mean to upset you. These things happen in families all the time." He was babbling now, something he was real good at when it came to females. Girls loved to think they were throwing him for a loop. He smiled uneasily, shifting from one foot to the other. He noticed that Ethel still wasn't chewing. Amber's face grew red with anger.

Over his shoulder, sotto voce, Andrew said, "Give my best to Ruby and tell her I hope she's happy with that . . . that . . . Fil-ipino, or whatever he is."

"Filipino?" Amber gasped. "Come back here, Andrew," she ordered tightly.

"Can't, Miss Connors, I'm late now. I hate to say this, but the gentleman in me has to. The best man won, and it wasn't me."

Amber watched him leave, as did every other secretary in the dining room.

Ethel resumed chewing, but her eyes were lowered.

Amber took one deep breath and then another. Ruby was getting married tomorrow! It had to be some kind of joke, but the marine hadn't looked as if he was joking.

"My God!" was all she could say.

"Wouldn't Ruby—"

"No, she wouldn't," Amber snapped. "She was always a sneak. She must be planning on running off. Right under my nose! I have to go now, Ethel. I have to call home. No, I can't do that, either. My father won't be home till four o'clock, and I can't tell my mother something like this."

"Amber, wait," Ethel pleaded. "Why do you have to tell them? Obviously, Ruby is trying to keep it a secret. If she's in love, why can't you let her be happy? If she was my sister, I wouldn't tell. I think you should mind your own business."

"Ruby is my business," Amber spat out.

"Not really. She's doing just fine on her own. I remember when she got here in June. She was like both of us when we arrived. Now she has a better job than both of us put together. She's going to school at night. She's got some nice clothes and . . . Amber, she's trying to be happy like the rest of us."

Amber pushed her tray away. "You don't understand, Ethel. My father—"

"I've pretty much figured it out about him on my own. You're over twenty-one now, and there's nothing he can do to you. Before you decide to fink on Ruby, you better look at what you're doing yourself. Nangi is . . . well, you know what he is. You can't be this unfair." Ethel stuck a forkful of lettuce in her mouth and chewed methodically, but her eyes remained on Amber. "Forget what this Andrew Blue said."

Amber leaned back in her chair. Nobody wanted to hurt Ruby. Why was that? If she listened to Ethel, she would be defying her father. He would hate her, blame her. Probably disown her. In her mind she wasn't sure if her father didn't hate her already, the way he hated Ruby, and her mother, and probably Opal, too. Maybe he hated all women. Damn, how had Ruby managed to pull this off? Without Andrew she still wouldn't know. Part of her had to admire her sister's deviousness and subterfuge. And there was something else to consider. If her sister really did run off and get married, she would be someone else's problem from now on.

Amber gathered up her tray and smiled down at her friend, her *only* friend. "Andrew who?"

Ethel laughed and followed her from the dining room.

{{{{{{{{{ CHAPTER THREE }}}}}}}}}

With the mail clutched tightly in her fist and her book bag thumping against her slender thighs, Opal Connors raced to her grandmother's after school. Ohhh, she could hardly wait to read her sister's letter. Her grandmother had gotten one as well. She would be so happy to hear from Ruby.

Her mood sobered. She should write to Ruby. She should tell Ruby about how hard it was becoming for their grandmother to breathe. She should tell her that the doctor came by every other day, sometimes every day, and about all the pills she had to take. Her uncle Hank always looked scared now when he looked at his mother, and Uncle John stayed real close to home. They hardly ever left the house these days.

Her own routine had changed too. Every day before school, she would skip over to the little fieldstone house to pick up the grocery list to drop off at the company store. She'd pick up the groceries and lug them home on her lunch hour, fix her grandmother a sandwich or a bowl of soup, and then go back to school.

After school she would pick up the mail from the box at the post office, return to the little house, start supper, do a few odd chores, and then run home to do her own chores. She'd return again after supper to do the dishes for her grandmother and fold the laundry. She was doing many of the things Ruby used to do. Ruby had also ironed, though, and she had scrubbed and hung out laundry. In the summer she had even mowed the lawn if her uncles worked double shifts. Opal wondered how her sister did it all.

Opal was always so tired and cranky, but maybe that was because she was keeping the state of her grandmother's health from her sister. Keeping secrets made her dizzy. She wished she could complain to someone about how tired she was. She wished she had time to jump rope and play marbles and jacks with the other kids.

Opal was breathless when she banged the kitchen screen door. "I'm here, Bubba, and there's a letter from Ruby. Bubbaaaaa."

"Shhh, Opal," Mrs. Matia, her grandmother's neighbor, said, placing her index finger to her lips. "Your grandmother is in bed. She . . . your grandmother's had a stroke."

"What's a stroke?"

"Why it's a . . . it's not important for you to know. She's very sick, Opal, so you should go home now and don't caterwaul like that again. You hear me, Opal?"

"Yes, ma'am," Opal whispered. "Is my grandmother going to die?"

"More than likely," Mrs. Matia said briskly. "You best tell your ma and pa. Go on now."

Opal looked at the letters in her hand. Should she leave them for her uncles? Or should she take them with her so she could read them tonight in her room? Opal waged a battle with herself until her forehead beaded with sweat. She *wanted* to read the letters. She decided she would keep her own and leave her grandmother's.

"Mrs. Matia, will you take this letter to my grandmother's room? My uncles will read it to her later. Ruby's letters always make Bubba feel better."

"I'll take it up and you tell your pa it isn't right for neighbors to be seeing to a person's own mother. You tell him to send your ma over here. I have my own family to take care of. Mind me, Opal, and do as I say."

"Yes, ma'am," Opal said, stuffing Ruby's letter into her history book.

Tears were dribbling down Opal's cheeks when she came to the monument works. She'd never stopped there, not once, neither had Ruby or Amber. She climbed the two steps that led to the front office of Mr. Riley's business. No one was there. Hesitantly, she pushed at the door leading to a cavernous room beyond. Sounds of chisels hitting stone grated on her ears.

Opal stared at her father's broad back and muscular arms as he hammered his chisel into a large piece of marble. Would he do Bubba's stone?

She waited for a lull of sound and said "Pop" in a squeaky voice. George Connors turned, his eyes full of something that scared Opal half to death. "Mrs. Matia said I should tell you . . . Bubba had a . . . a stroke and she's most likely to die. She said to tell you it isn't right for neighbors to take care of Bubba and you should send Mom over." Opal turned and ran. She knew she'd get whipped for daring to enter her father's place of work, but now she didn't care because later she would have Ruby's letter to read. She could read it all night long, over and over.

Opal cut through the backyards and ran headlong into Grace Zachary, who was pulling weeds from her flower border.

"Whoa, Opal." She laughed. "Oh, honey, what's the matter?" she asked as she noticed the tears falling down the little girl's cheeks.

Opal blurted out the past hour's happening, ending with "I know he's going to whip me. Mrs. Matia said to do it. My pop always said you have to mind your elders. It was important to tell him, wasn't it, Mrs. Zachary?"

"Of course," Grace crooned, gathering the little girl in her arms. "Look, sweetie, I know this isn't going to sound . . . I mean you might not understand, but someday you will. Nothing is forever. Pretty soon you'll be as big as Ruby, and you'll go away. In the meantime you have to make the best of things. If you ever need someone to talk to, come right on over. Scoot now, go in the back door and you can be up in your room when your pa gets to the house. Hurry, Opal," Grace said anxiously.

Wiping her eyes, Opal ran.

Opal felt like a trapped animal as she crouched at the top of the steps. Was she going to get a whipping or not? If she was, she wished her father would do it and get it over with. He should have come after her by now, but maybe her grandmother's stroke was worrying him. She made a face. Nothing worried her father.

She strained to hear her parents' voices. She wished her mother would speak louder. All she could detect from her father's voice was anger. If that was the case, then her mother wasn't talking at all.

Suddenly the voices were nearer, in the hall. They were heading for the stairs. Opal inched her way into her room on her backside so as not to make a sound. She heard her mother say, "I'll change my dress."

"No need for that. A dying woman isn't going to care what

you're wearing. You walk fast, woman, before that busybody starts telling tales about us."

Opal hunkered down over her history book. Wasn't he going? Bubba was *his* mother.

"If ... if your mother should ask ... what should I say, George?"

"She won't be doing any asking," George said firmly. "You see if you can find that ring before my brothers get home. This is the perfect time to search for it. There's no one to stop you. I don't expect you to come back empty-handed."

They were on the steps now. Why had they come upstairs? Opal wondered. Of course. Her mother had come up for her shoes. At this time of day her feet were always swollen and pink. Opal knew it must have been painful to squeeze her shoes on, and now she had to walk all the way over to her grandmother's. She wanted to cry for her mother, but Ruby had said not to cry. No, she had said not to *let them see you cry*, but when she remembered that, she didn't feel like crying anymore. All she felt was relief that she didn't get a whipping.

Opal ran to the window and saw her father striding down the street, way ahead of her mother, who was walking slowly, almost limping. He wasn't going to Bubba's house, he was going back to Riley's Monument Works.

A delighted giggle burst from Opal's mouth. She danced around her room. She was all alone in the house for the first time in her life. She could do anything she wanted, say anything she wanted, even cuss if she wanted to. Not that she would. She realized in dismay that there wasn't a thing she wanted to do in *this* house. Not a single thing except to read Ruby's letter and her library book. Maybe she'd answer the letter, too, but where would she get a stamp? Her grandmother had always provided the stamps. Maybe Mrs. Zachary would lend her one.

Mary Cozinsky knew she was dying. What she couldn't understand was why it was taking so long. She wanted to get on with it and join Mikel. She had so much to tell him. While she couldn't talk now, she knew she'd be able to talk once she got to heaven. God would see to that.

It was so hard to breathe, and she knew there was something wrong with the left side of her face and neck. She couldn't move her left arm or leg. It was time to let go, to leave this earth. She wouldn't be sorry to go. If she had any regret, it would be that she wouldn't see Ruby and Opal again. Opal had been here today, but she hadn't come upstairs. Adelaide Matia had seen to that, the old sour face.

She had no idea what time it was. Her vision was so blurred she could barely see, not that there was anything to look at. She was alone. The doctor had come and gone, and her sons would be here before long. They would call her daughters, and they would come, too. Ruby wouldn't come, though. She was never going to see Ruby again.

Now what had she been thinking? There was something wrong with her brain. One minute she could think clearly and the next she couldn't.

There was noise in the room. Her breathing. No, steps. The doctor then or Adelaide Matia. The voice, though, didn't belong to Adelaide but to . . . dear God, Irma, her daughter-in-law. She was babbling something Mary didn't want to hear, not from Irma, not from George. Was George in the room? She didn't want George in her room. George who? Irma who? She was choking, trying to cough.

"Let me help you," a gentle voice said. Strong hands tried to pull her upright, to brace the pillows behind her head. Who was it?

"That should help you a little. I would have come sooner, but I didn't know," the gentle voice was saying. "They shouldn't have left you here by yourself. What kind of doctor would leave you like this?"

Mary felt something cool on her face. She sensed a certain trembling, agitation, in the soft ministrations. The pain in her chest was like the heat of a branding iron. It wouldn't go away. If only she could see . . . the gentle voice was whispering now. Again she sensed movement, the covers being straightened, the coolness again. "I'm sure your daughters will be here before long. Hank and John will come, too."

Irma wished then that she'd spent more time with George's mother, but there was no time in her day for a trip over here, and George . . . with his estrangement, she knew she wasn't welcome. She liked Mary Cozinsky even though she knew the old lady thought her weak and ineffectual. Amber told her once that her mother-in-law called her a doormat. She was, she couldn't argue the point. She was worse, she was practically a slave to her husband. To be otherwise would incur his wrath, and she'd had to experience that only three times never to let it happen again. He'd dragged her to the cellar and beat her unconscious and she couldn't even remember why, what she'd done to warrant such a vicious attack. He'd left her there with her neatly lined jars of pickles and peaches. She remembered coming to with the smell of coal dust in her nostrils. She was lying on the earthen floor in the root cellar, her clothes torn and ragged. He'd beaten her with his wide three-inch work belt, the buckle gouging her back, her breasts, her thighs. All places where it wouldn't show. What could she have done that was so terrible? She should have gone to a doctor, knew she needed a doctor, but then the whole town would have known what happened. The beating was terrible, but what was worse was having to sleep that same night with the man who beat her. Amber was five, Ruby two that day, neither one in school.

That night, long after George had emptied himself into her, she realized he was capable of beating her children senseless. Whatever she had to do, whatever she had to become to prevent that from happening, she would. And, of course, she prayed, daily, hourly, as she went about her housework. She'd shed enough tears to form a lake, but nothing changed. Pure and simple, she was afraid, afraid of showing affection to her children, for if she did, George would ... she didn't know what he would do, but he would do something. Kill them maybe. She couldn't risk the lives of her little jewels. How she loved them. They were more precious than the czarina's ring she was supposed to be searching for. Well, she wasn't going to do it. She wouldn't steal from a dying woman. Not for George, not even for her children. And if she had to suffer a beating, she would.

Irma pulled her chair closer to the bed and positioned it so she could see the hallway through the open door. She reached for her mother-in-law's hand and started to talk, not knowing, not caring if the old lady could hear her or not. She was finally going to purge herself. She was realistic enough to know it would help for the moment, but as soon as she went home, everything would be the same.

* * *

Mary lay helpless, listening to the garbled words that made no sense to her. All she heard was sound, but she was still aware of the gentleness.

It was so dark in the room and the gentle voice was fading away. Her chest felt like a giant balloon about to pop from too much air. She had one split second of lucidness. Mikel was waiting for her, but he wanted her to do something. What? He was trying to tell her, but the golden light behind him was so bright, she could hardly see him. He was pointing to something. She wanted to go to him, to the bright light where there would be no pain. She wanted to join her cossack and ride across the steppe again, where they would join all those who had gone before them. What? she screamed silently. What do I have to do before I can cross over? The letters, of course, Mikel was pointing to the pile of letters on her dresser. She struggled then, in that split second, to make her deformed mouth work, to say the words to the gentle voice. They catapulted from her lips in an explosion of garbled sound. "Ruby's letters!" She left then, a young girl dancing her way to the golden light and Mikel's arms.

Irma bounded from the chair, her swollen feet almost giving out under her. She grabbed the edge of the dresser and saw the pile of letters. Her eyes swiveled to the bed. Tears streamed down her cheeks. She made the sign of the cross. Gently, she closed the wide, staring eyes. She had to call the priest. She should have done it before, done it sooner. George would never forgive her. None of his brothers and sisters would forgive her. For so long she'd obeyed orders without questioning them. She never thought for herself, never exercised her mind in any way. Mary had ordered her with her last words. How clear they'd been. Ruby's letters. She tottered to the dresser and picked them up. So many. Where in the world was she to hide them? Where? She wanted to read them, all of them, more than anything in the world. Maybe if she kept just one, the last one, the one on top. She had to hide the rest, though, before they came. She had to call the priest, too. In her frenzy she leaned over and blessed her mother-in-law, knowing it wasn't the same, but still she did it.

As fast as her swollen feet could walk, Irma made her way down the hall to the staircase. Pain shot up her legs, but she didn't stop. Her hands gripped the banister for support. She fumbled with the phone and dialed the rectory. In a trembling voice she reported Mary's death. Next she called George, who listened to her shaking voice. When she finished he demanded to know if she found the ring.

"It's not in her room. Mrs. Matia was here for a while and I couldn't look. I'll look now until Father Flavian gets here."

She had to hurry. George had long legs; he'd be there in a few minutes. She had to hide the letters. She finally wadded them into the back of the walnut radio. No one would be playing it for a while, not with a death in the family. The top letter, the one she kept, she folded into a neat square and slipped it into the pocket of her dress. If only she could take off her shoes. She couldn't, not with the priest coming. Someone had to call the undertaker, but who? She didn't think it was her place. Or was it? She didn't know anything anymore. She hobbled up the steps, stopping to stare at her reflection in the gilt-edged mirror. How awful she looked. So plain and dowdy. She'd been pretty once with a nice complexion. Almost as pretty as her three jewels. Opal was going to be a beauty someday. Amber would be pretty, too, once she learned how to be happy. Ruby's face swam into focus. Ruby would be pretty once she got rid of the anger and hurt. "I did it so you could all survive," she whispered as she made her way down the hall to the big sunny bedroom where her mother-in-law lay at peace. If she had a choice, right now, this very instant, she would choose to follow Mary Cozinsky to that place from which there was no return.

She wondered why she had married George Cozinsky. He wasn't George Connors when she married him. That had come later. Why had she been so stupid? She should have seen, sensed, that he was like a devil, but she hadn't. He was handsome, charming, and such a churchgoing Christian, her parents had been delighted. "A good man," they said over and over, until she began to believe them. Her friends all thought he was a good catch; she did, too. He was confident, arrogant, and seemed to want to please her. They picnicked, canoed, took long walks, and held hands in the movie house. He said he loved her and wanted to marry her. She walked on air. All her friends were so jealous.

Her parents had given her a wonderful wedding. They got so many presents. They went to Niagara Falls for their honeymoon, or nightmare as she now thought of it. She'd found out on those terrible seven days just how brutal George Cozinsky was. In bed. The rest of the time he was almost as bad. Two weeks after their marriage he changed their name. The whole town, including her parents, had whispered about that for months. He'd even been considerate of her, but he never listened to anything she had to say. The consideration stopped when her parents died. An only child, she'd inherited the house they now lived in and four thousand dollars, after the funeral expenses were paid, of which she'd never seen a penny. To this day she had no idea what happened to the money. If only she had it now, she would leave. She knew she was lying to herself. Where would she go, what would she do? Four thousand dollars wouldn't last forever. Amber and Ruby certainly wouldn't take her. How could they? First they had to forgive her, and they might never do that. Then there was Opal. She couldn't leave Opal.

In the mirror Irma could see Father Flavian at the foot of the steps. "Please, Father, come up. It was so sudden. I wish I had called you sooner, but . . ."

"Don't fret, Irma. It's done. I'm certain the Lord has her in His arms even as we speak. Mary was a good woman and the Lord is forgiving."

Irma waited in the hall, unable to watch the priest. She felt faint and needed the support of the sturdy banister. She looked around to see what was so special about this house that all her children loved. She wanted to believe it was the house and not the woman she called her mother-in-law.

She turned to see George's brothers, Hank and John, walk through the door. Their eyes pleaded with her. She shook her head ever so slightly. As they passed her at the top of the stairs, she saw their eyes fill with tears. Seconds later, George walked through the door. It was all she could do not to put her hand into her pocket. How cold and unrelenting his eyes were, she thought as he passed her. There was no sign of a tear. She hadn't expected any.

"I'll see myself out, Irma, don't bother coming down," the priest said. Irma nodded gratefully.

"I didn't call the undertaker," she said, addressing the three brothers. "I thought . . ."

"You always think the wrong thing, Irma," George said harshly. "Call him now."

"No, Irma! George is the oldest, let him do it," Hank said coolly. "He expects all the privileges of the oldest, so let him earn them." He moved an inch or so in George's direction, his brother behind him. They were as tall and as muscular as George, and younger by ten years. If they had a mind to, they could wipe the floor with him. A long time ago Irma learned that George was good only at bullying women. She watched him stalk off. She would pay for Hank's intervention, but she didn't care.

They were so handsome, Irma thought, look-alikes of George, but these two young men had feelings, feelings they weren't afraid to show.

"I was holding her hand, talking to her . . . and . . . and . . . she . . . went to sleep. I came as soon as Opal told us. I wish there was something I could do."

"Did she . . . did she say anything?" Hank, the youngest, asked.

Irma licked her dry lips as she looked over her shoulder.

"She . . . said . . . very clearly . . . Ruby's letters. That's all. They were on the dresser. I . . . I stuffed them behind the radio downstairs. I . . . I kept one, the one on top," Irma said in a low whisper, her back to George. Both young men nodded.

"I'll get your mother ready. Show me where her things are. I imagine the undertaker will be here soon."

"All her things are in that dresser. Her good church dress is hanging in the closet. She made us all swear we wouldn't deck her out in one of those purple things the undertakers put on everyone. We have to get washed up. We'll use the bathroom downstairs. My God, Irma, what's the matter with your feet?" John asked, horror in his voice.

"It's nothing. They swell up around this time of day. At home I usually wear slippers, but I had to walk over here."

John's eyes popped. "Like that! Didn't George drive you?"

"No, I didn't. I was at work the way you were. Don't worry about my wife's feet," George said coldly.

"Someone should," Hank said, pushing Irma gently to the only chair in the room. "John, get Ma's slippers for Irma." He tugged on the leather shoes until Irma thought she would scream. Free of the confining leather, her feet seemed to swell even more. She tried to fight the tears in her eyes but failed. Oh, she was going to pay dearly for this, too. "Jesus," both brothers said in awe as they stared at Irma's feet. Even George wore a stunned look. "You sit there, Irma, we'll get cleaned up, and we'll wash up Ma. You can't do it. We'll drive you home." Irma didn't demur. There was no sense to it.

"You're a very stupid woman, Irma," George said coldly. "I thought you had more sense." The look of disgust on her husband's face frightened her.

Opal cowered at the top of the steps. Something terrible was going to happen. She'd watched her mother get out of Uncle Hank's car. She could hardly walk. She lay down flat on her belly so she could see through the spindles on the staircase. Her eyes filled with tears when she saw her father punch her mother, who was staggering across the room. She leaned closer to the first step, craning her neck to see better. She wished she hadn't when she heard the cellar door open and then watched as her father pulled his belt free of the loops on his pants. So far, the only sound she heard was a grunt. She turned, crablike, and crawled to her room, where she buried her face in the pillow.

In the cellar Irma cowered on the floor. Her voice was a hoarse croak. "Why are you doing this, George? What did I do?"

"You made a horse's ass out of me in front of my brothers with your stupid feet. By tomorrow every woman and man in this town will be talking about us, saying I prevented you from going to a doctor and my brothers had to take care of you. Every one of our neighbors saw you get out of the car. And you didn't get the ring like I told you. You're just like your daughters, you never do what you're told." He slapped out at one of the cellar beams with the belt. It was so loud, to Irma it sounded like thunder.

She inched along to get away from her husband. He reached down and grabbed hold of her shapeless dress, dragging her to her feet. His hold was secure, otherwise she would have toppled to the floor. He ripped her dress, the thin material giving way until the fabric snagged on the huge patch pocket. George gave a tug and the dress ripped to the hem line, where it snagged again. Irma's eyes rolled back in her head when she saw Ruby's letter, folded so neatly, fall to the floor. George let go of her so suddenly that she fell backward and struck her head on the sauerkraut barrel.

Irma would have thought it impossible for her husband to be angrier than he had already been, but now his face grew so contorted that his eyes seemed to pop from their sockets, and his handsome face became ugly and infused with purplish-pink. Huge veins swelled on the sides of his neck. Dear God, what had Ruby written in the letter?

"Get up, Irma!" George raged. "You weren't going to give it to me, were you?"

Irma tottered, but stood her ground. He would beat her if she lied, and he would beat her if she told the truth. "No, I wasn't going to give it to you."

The blow to the side of her head was so hard, so fierce, she knew her eardrum was ruptured. She fell and made no move to get up.

George dropped to his haunches and waved the letter under his wife's nose. "I'm going to read this to you, Irma," he said softly. Irma shriveled inside herself. She didn't know which was worse, his loud rage or this quiet, ominous tone.

Dear Bubba,

I'm writing this at work on my lunch hour. I just wrote to Opal and Mrs. Zachary. Today isn't real busy here at the office.

Listen to my news. I can tell you because I know this secret is safe with you. Opal will never tell. I'll skin her alive if she does. I'm leaving on Tuesday for California with Calvin Santos. We'll get married as soon as we can, probably a week or so. I really am excited. No one knows but you, not even Amber. Calvin is the guy I told you about from Saipan. He's so much better-looking than Nangi, the Filipino Amber is dating. I'm sure Amber and Nangi are in love, they look so sappy together.

We planned everything down to the last detail so nothing can go wrong. Calvin is fantastic when it comes to details. The best part is that Pop can stick his damn bill where the sun doesn't shine. I'm not starting off my married life owing a bill for something I shouldn't have to pay. I think you were right when you said Pop is sick in his head. I don't care if he is my father. You know I hate his guts. That's so terrible to say, but it's true and I don't care anymore.

I had to dump Andrew. I feel bad about that, though he really wasn't all that nice. He was so fresh, always trying to feel me up. Calvin isn't like that. He respects two things—me and his uniform. Isn't that a hoot, Bubba?

Well, I should get back to work. My boss will be here any minute now, and as of this second I'm on government time. I know you want me to be happy and I am. This is what I want. Can you believe I'm getting married!!!!!

Opal said you weren't feeling too good, but that was all she said in the last letter. I hope you're feeling better. Make sure you take those pills for your blood pressure. I'll write to you as soon as I get to California. It will be my first trip on an airplane. I can hardly wait.

Opal, this message is for you. Make sure you tear up this letter as soon as you finish reading it to Bubba, and don't write to me here. Wait for my next letter.

I love you both. Tell Uncle John and Uncle Hank I said hello and that I miss them. I miss you, too.

Love and kisses,
Ruby

"Did you hear this letter from *your* daughter, Irma? Did you hear every word?" George demanded in a voice so cold and tight-sounding, Irma shivered from the blast of his breath.

Irma inched back, struggling to a sitting position. "There's nothing you can do now," she whimpered.

"Yes, there is," he said in his strange, cold voice. His work boot with the reinforced toe lashed out, kicking her full in the ribs. Irma fainted and still he kept kicking her. A long time later, she didn't know how long, she heard a voice calling her name and then strong arms were carrying her upstairs. She heard Opal crying and Grace Zachary cursing. Paul must be carrying her. Someone was making strange mewling sounds. She had to talk, to say something. For Opal.

"Paul," she whispered, "take me upstairs. Grace and Opal can . . . help me. Please. If I need a doctor, have him come here. Please, Paul."

"Do what she says, Paul." It was Grace's voice. "If you try to put her in the car, you might hurt her more. Opal, call the doctor and tell him . . . tell him your mother fell down the cellar steps. Hurry, honey."

* * *

In the Connors house, Grace waited while Opal washed her face and brushed her teeth. Doctor Ashley had just gone. It would be a long, uphill battle, he had said, but Irma would recover fully if she looked after herself. Despite his assurances, however, Opal looked frightened. Maybe she'd want to talk, Grace thought.

"I have to say my prayers, Grace. You don't mind, do you?"

"Heck, no. I'd blister your hiney if you didn't." Grace giggled. She listened with tears in her eyes as Opal went through her long list of God-blesses, ending with "I know You need Bubba, and I think it's okay that You decided to let Ruby get married." She made the sign of the cross and hopped into bed.

"Is Mom okay, Mrs. Zachary? She won't die, will she?"

"Your mom is okay. I mean, she's going to be okay in a while, but she has to stay in bed. I guess your father will have to take off work and see to her. Your mom says he's gone to Washington, so I expect he'll be back tomorrow. Don't worry. I'll sit here with you till you fall asleep."

"Tomorrow is my birthday," Opal said sleepily. "Bubba bought me a present last week. I don't care about the present, really I don't, but I wonder what it is. What do you think it is, Mrs. Zachary?" she asked sleepily.

Jeez, what did she know about grandmother presents? She shifted her mental gears and remembered what she'd wished for on her younger birthdays. There was a smile in her voice when she replied, "Probably a golden unicorn with a big diamond on the end of his horn. Maybe a string of rubies around his neck and, oh, let's see, maybe emeralds on his back hooves and opals, real opals on his front hooves." It was make-believe, and Opal knew it was make-believe. The smile on the girl's face almost broke Grace's heart. What was a crumby carnival locket compared to a golden unicorn?

It was late when Grace finally stirred herself to leave Opal's room. She tiptoed down the hall to check on Irma before going home. "Thank you, Grace," Irma whispered.

"My pleasure," Grace said softly. "I'll be back in the morning to make breakfast and see Opal off to school."

The lights burned in the Zachary kitchen all night. The radio played softly, the kitchen was fragrant and warm. Grace and Paul sat at the kitchen table, drinking coffee and holding hands. At four o'clock the three-tiered cake was cool enough to frost with thick, creamy icing. Paul stuck hard-candy rosebuds into the cake and attached pink candles.

"There, what do you think?" Grace asked a moment later when she fastened the large red bow to the tiny box.

"I think it beats a goddamn unicorn is what I think." Paul laughed. "Let's take it up now and put it on the kitchen table. I'll carry the cake and you fetch the present and some pop."

"For breakfast?"

"What the hell kind of party will it be if you don't drink pop with the cake? You gotta do it early, because old George might make it back by noon."

Like giggling children they walked through the yard to the Connorses' back porch. Grace opened the door quietly and held it for Paul so he didn't mess the thick icing. He set it in the middle of the table. Grace laid the small present next to it. The pop was set on the shelf in the refrigerator—four bottles, one each for Opal, Irma, Grace, and Paul.

They held on to each other as they made their way home. Grace slipped on the wet grass, pulling Paul down with her. They rolled down the little incline, their arms around each other, until they came to a stop on their own property. "What d'ya say, honey, we've done it everywhere else, why not here?"

"If you don't mind getting your ass wet, neither do I!" Grace said, rolling her panties down over her hips.

Their lovemaking was sweet and tender, their caresses sure and deft. They were never more one than now. Spent, they lay cradled in one another's arms. They spoke softly in hushed whispers about getting up, bathing, and going to the party.

Paul rolled over and came to his feet. "I'll start the tub," he said softly.

It was ten minutes of seven and the occupants of the house on Kilbourne Place were scurrying around, dressing and waiting their turn for the bathroom. Ruby was still in her pajamas, telling Ethel she could go ahead of her because she wasn't going to work today. "I have such bad cramps I can hardly stand up." Ethel smiled and thanked her for her turn. Ruby walked toward the kitchen for her coffee and bowl of cereal.

When the doorbell rang, bedlam broke out in the apartment. Ethel ran down the hall, with Ruby right behind her. Doors opened, bathrobed figures, their hair full of curlers, careened behind Ruby and Ethel. A ringing doorbell meant company, and all personal belongings had to be moved or shoved into a closet. Ruby picked up her manicure set and nail polish and stuffed an afghan under her arm. Ethel heaved the metal free-standing hairdryer over on its side and stashed it behind the sofa. Jane plumped the pillows as she pushed day-old newspapers under the same couch with her foot. Amber confiscated two Coca-Cola bottles and three teacups and paper napkins and ran to the kitchen with them. Anna straightened the magazines on the table as she kicked the wastebasket into the closet. Sally stuffed two unmatched socks in her robe pocket as she picked up slippers and a pair of shoes for two left feet.

"Three minutes!" Ethel chortled. "We're getting better each time we do this." Her face was so gleeful, Ruby laughed.

They were getting better. In the beginning their routine was like something hatched from a bad egg, but now everything was so smooth, it was almost effortless.

It was fun living with this bunch of girls, although only Ethel and Amber were close friends. The other four girls and Ruby all had outside friendships and didn't pal around together. That's why it worked, Ruby decided. They were considerate of one another, and each knew that if she didn't carry her share of the load, she would have to move.

"This place is like a zoo in August," Anna grumbled good-naturedly.

From her bedroom doorway Amber called out. "Is anyone expecting a caller this early?" A chorus of nos from every direction was her answer. She carefully avoided looking at her sister. "Then I'm not going down to answer it," she muttered.

The doorbell rang again. And again.

"Whoever it is probably has the wrong house," one of the girls called from the back of the apartment.

The bell continued to ring until Amber went to the living room window. By craning her neck she could see the tall figure standing by the door. She swayed dizzily.

Amber ran down the hall, her eyes wide with shock. "Ruby," she said, "Pop is at the front door. He knows! My God, Ruby, he knows. I swear to God I didn't tell. Ask Ethel. I didn't, Ruby!"

Ruby's face drained. Amber was too panic-stricken to be lying. My God, what was she going to do? "Maybe something happened at home and he came down to get us," Ruby said miserably. "How long are we going to let him stay out there? I bet he drove all night and has been watching the house. He knows we haven't left yet," Ruby said, trying to be logical as her mind raced.

"Hide, Ruby. I'll . . . I'll tell him you left last night. Ruby, I don't want to go home. Neither do you. What are we going to do?"

"Face him. *You* don't have to go, you're twenty-one. I'll tell you something else. I'm not going, either!" She buttoned the top button of her pajamas and walked down the hall.

"Ruby, wait," she called. "Please, just wait a minute. You don't understand. If we don't go, he'll . . . Mom will . . . Ruby, listen to me, you were too little, but I remember . . . my God, I remember." She told her then what she remembered about that awful day. Ruby's jaw dropped as she listened. The horror on her sister's face told her it was true.

The phone rang. One of the girls picked it up and called out to Ruby. "It's someone named Grace Zachary."

Amber leaned against the wall, her face a mask of fright. My God, Nangi was coming to give her a ride to work. "Oh, God," she dithered.

"Amber, come here. Hey, everybody, don't go out yet, that's our father ringing the bell, and he's a real . . . prick," Ruby said nastily. "Amber, you better come here and listen to this." Both girls leaned their heads together with the phone between them. Their faces were blank when Ruby replaced the receiver. Both girls ran to the living room window.

"My God, he looks so normal," Ruby cried. "Bubba's dead and he's here." She wondered if he was going to demand the ring back. Today was Opal's birthday.

"Nangi is getting out of the car, Amber. Amber, look at me. Did you hear? Nangi is getting out of the car, and holy shit, there's Andrew Blue. Amber, for God's sake, say something. You have to help me."

"What? What can we do?" Amber wailed.

"Offhand I'd say this is the time to use your guts. The longer he stands out there, the worse it's going to be. The girls have to go to work. What's it going to be, Amber?"

"Let him in," Amber croaked.

The girls, Ethel in the lead, walked down the steps. She

opened the door. The girls filed out; Andrew, Nangi, and George Connors stood aside and then climbed single-file up the stairs.

They gathered in the living room. Nangi, horrified, took up his position next to Amber. Andrew stood in the center of the room, every bit as tall as George and every bit as muscular.

How clean-cut he looked, Ruby thought. How normal and handsome. His fists, Ruby saw, were clenched. Right then she wished he would lay her father out cold. They all waited.

"Get your things and be quick about it!" George ordered. Amber automatically started to rise. Ruby moved swiftly behind her chair and forced her back. She was happy to see Nangi grasp Amber's shoulder.

"No. We're not going," Ruby croaked.

"Don't sass me, girl. I said get your things. Who is that nigger?" he demanded of Nangi.

"He's not a nigger," Ruby defended. "You can't make Amber go, she's twenty-one. And I'm not going because I damn well don't want to. We know what you did to Mom. Amber told me what you did to her a long time ago. Grace called us. You broke Mom's ribs and punctured her lung. She can't move and something's wrong with her ear. If we go with you, you'll do the same to us."

"I told you girls to get your things. I won't tell you again. If you want, I'll fetch the police. Now, you give me the name of that boy you're planning on running off with. Now, girl. Don't try my patience."

Andrew Blue moved to stand next to Ruby.

George's eyes narrowed. "I was testing you, girl. I have it right here," he said, pulling Ruby's letter to her grandmother out of his pocket. "Calvin Santos, another one of *those*," he said, jerking his head in Nangi's direction.

George backed up toward the telephone. He picked it up slowly, his eyes on the little group. They listened as he asked the operator to put him through to Andrews Air Force Base. He gave his name, the address on Kilbourne Place. He asked in a cold, brittle voice to be connected to Lieutenant Calvin Santos's commanding officer.

Ruby felt herself sway sickeningly. Calvin's worst fear was coming to pass, and she was helpless to do anything. "Forgive me, Calvin," she murmured under her breath. In desperation she locked her eyes with Andrew and mouthed the words "Do something. Help me." Her shoulders slumped. Andrew Blue's face was a study in horror. Her head jerked when she heard her father's belligerent, angry voice identify himself to the faceless voice on the other end of the phone.

"I want something done and I want it done now. Your man is planning to abduct my daughter and run away with her to California. She's underage. You take care of him and I'll take care of mine, you hear me? I don't want excuses and sorry explanations. I'll press charges if I have to. And I expect a full written report sent to me at my home in Pennsylvania." He rattled off his home address, his eyes murderous as he stared at his two daughters. "I don't mean next week or the week after that. I mean tomorrow."

Ruby cringed when her father slammed the receiver back into the cradle. He turned to Andrew.

"Who are you?" he demanded.

Andrew sprang to Ruby's defense. "Me, sir? I come by in the mornings to take out the trash, and before you can ask, I'm over twenty-one and my superior is a full-fledged four-star general who pounds guys like you to shit, so if you have any ideas about reporting me, think again. And I don't have a name." Ruby's shoulders straightened. George stepped back. Ruby knew no one had ever spoken to him like this. His forte was bullying women. He'd been careful all his life to avoid confrontations with male counterparts.

"I think you should leave, sir," Andrew said coolly.

"Yes," Nangi put in in a soft, cultured voice. "I think you should do exactly what the lieutenant said. I am well versed in the martial arts, and I can kill you with one blow."

Ruby's mouth dropped open, so did Andrew's. Amber reached up to grasp Nangi's hand in her own.

Ruby inched closer to Andrew, she didn't know why.

Nangi ran with the ball. "I'm planning on marrying your daughter."

"She deserves you," George snarled. "She never was any good. As for you," he said, addressing Ruby, but he didn't get a chance to finish.

"I'm no good, either. I know. I hope you're happy now that you ruined my life. I won't go with you. I'm never going back there. And if you beat Mom again, I'm calling the sheriff. Grace and Paul know what you did. They'll tell. So will Opal. I'm not afraid of you anymore, and let me tell you what you can do with that money you say I owe you. Stick it up your ass! The way I look at it, you owe Amber six thousand bucks, and somehow, I'll find a way to get it out of you. It might take me the rest of my life, but I'll do it." Ruby knew, for all her defiance, that she would have packed her bags and gone if it weren't for Andrew and Nangi. So would Amber. My God, she was free. They both were finally free.

"The door, sir," Andrew said respectfully, holding it wide open. Ruby wanted to laugh, but she cried instead. Hard, dry sobs racked her body and tears flowed down her cheeks. Amber was crying just as hard against Nangi's chest.

The four of them huddled by the front door, their faces pressed against the wide pane of glass.

"Look how tall he is," Amber said tearfully. "He's not even looking back at us. Oh, God, we don't have a father anymore," she wailed. "Ruby, let's call him back. He's our father!"

Ruby felt her shoulders sag as she watched George open the car door. He settled his long legs beneath the steering wheel before he pulled the door shut. "Now he'll look at us. He knows we're here. He knows we're watching. He thinks we're going to run out. No, he doesn't think that at all. He's disowned us. He's going to drive away."

"Ruby, we're never going to see him again," Amber wailed.

Ruby worked her thick tongue around the inside of her mouth. She thought it strange that she had no saliva. "I know," she whispered. Her hand twitched as she reached out to Amber. "We're free," she croaked. "We never have to worry about him again."

"What about Mom? Ruby, what about Mom?"

"I don't know, Amber."

"Lieutenant, I would be very pleased to buy you breakfast if you have no other plans," Nangi said quietly as he ushered the girls back into the house. "In the meantime, my girl ... and yours ... can compose themselves."

Andrew looked at the dapper little Filipino and grinned. "What the hell, if you're paying, I'm game."

Ruby cried for her grandmother, and for Opal, and for Calvin. His career, and their future together, were ruined.

Amber cried for herself and for her mother.

"I'm going to get dressed and go to Sacred Heart. We're too late for morning Mass, but we ... I can say a rosary. Do you want to go, Amber?" She nodded miserably.

They walked down the hall together. "That's some guy you got there, Amber. Can he really kill with a kick or a smack?" Ruby said just to hear her own voice.

"Yeah," Amber said proudly. "You know, Ruby, Andrew is ... maybe you can make something out of him. That other guy ... I'm sorry. I guess it wasn't meant to be."

"Do you have any idea how I feel right now? Any idea at all?"

"No," Amber whispered.

"Then let me tell you. I feel completely empty. Bubba's gone, Pop's gone, and now Calvin's gone. Even if I could make things right, it's too late for me to go to the airport. I'd never get there in time. The plane is probably leaving right now."

"Tomorrow, Ruby, tomorrow you can make phone calls. Tomorrow you can make things right with Calvin. If he's half as smart as Nangi, you'll be able to fix it up with him. Why, he'll probably call *you* when he gets to California. It will all work out."

"No, he won't call, Amber. I know Calvin. He's thinking I deserted him. He's thinking he's not good enough for me. I don't know why he feels that way, but he does. And now his career is wrecked because of me. There's no way I can ever make this right."

Her step faltered. Amber reached out to steady her.

"What is it?" Amber asked, full of concern.

"I was thinking about Bubba," she said, and then her voice cracked so that she couldn't speak. Her grandmother's death was so devastating, she couldn't bring herself to talk about it.

"Listen, Ruby, that sounded real good ... what you said about not paying your debt, but it wasn't very realistic," Amber said to her. "If you don't pay, it will go real hard on Mom. Do you want that on your conscience?"

"I want to know how you managed to pay off yours, Amber," Ruby said, testing her voice a second time.

"Nangi loaned me the money."

"Why didn't you tell me about that?" Ruby demanded, knowing Amber spoke the truth about the debt. "I should have been told."

"Why, Ruby? Would you have done anything differently? It served no purpose. He's gone now. We can do whatever we feel like doing."

"Yeah, now, when it's too late." God, she was never going to see her grandmother, never feel her arms, those wonderful protecting arms. Never see the apple peel in one piece again. Never sit on the back porch again. When it was her choice not to return, she'd been able to come to terms with it, but now it was different. She wouldn't be allowed to return. It was all lost to her, just the way Calvin was lost to her.

"Mom . . ." Amber said tentatively.

"What about her?" Ruby asked coldly. She wondered what her uncles would do with her grandmother's wicker chair on the back porch.

"She . . ."

"She what? She didn't give a damn about us. Especially me. She didn't even say good-bye to me. She never patted me on the head, never kissed me good night. She never even told me what to do when I got my period. Bubba had to . . . to show me how to fasten the sanitary belt. I should have known about boys, how to act, what to do, and I didn't. Mothers are supposed to be your friend. If there's one thing I learned, it's that you have to have guts to survive. Mom doesn't have any. She should have called the sheriff the first time."

"The town, the gossip . . . Pop . . ."

"Bullshit, Amber," Ruby snarled. "You believe whatever you want to believe and I'll believe what I want. I wonder if they'll dress her in one of those awful purple dresses." She realized she would never know. She also realized there would be no more letters from Opal. Wet, hot tears pricked at her eyelids as she closed the door to her room, closing Amber out of her life.

Calvin Santos's eyes scanned the busy concourse. His watch told him Ruby was late—by five minutes. They'd synchronized their E.T.A.'s right down to the last second, military style. He'd allowed for grumpy cab drivers, morning traffic, Ruby's busy bathroom, and the weather. He'd even allowed two full minutes in case Ruby decided to eat toast or cereal instead of waiting to have coffee and danish in the coffee shop.

Something was wrong.

Calvin started to sweat when he looked at his watch.

Somehow she'd found out he was distantly related to Nangi Duenas. He should have told her. For the life of him, he didn't know why he hadn't. Maybe Nangi had told him not to, he simply couldn't remember. He'd been so stupid to tell Nangi what he was planning, but his cousin had sworn on the name of his father, his uncle, and every priest he could remember that he wouldn't tell Amber. Maybe Ruby overheard Amber and Nangi talking. Ruby would consider keeping a secret of that nature from her unforgivable. He knew he was lying to himself. He'd deliberately not told Ruby because he thought Nangi could feed him information, via Amber, about Andrew Blue. Damn!

Ruby changed her mind for her own reasons. If he had to decide what to believe right this second, it would be that Ruby changed her mind because he wasn't good enough for her. It had nothing to do with Nangi. In his gut he knew his cousin wouldn't betray him. He looked at his watch again. If he called, he'd hear the words. . . . Once words were said aloud, they couldn't be taken back. He simply could not handle that kind of rejection, that's all there was to it.

A squadron of bees swarmed inside Calvin's head, a battalion of them in his stomach. He felt dizzy, disoriented. When his vision cleared, he was certain all the busy travelers were staring at him. He had to do something. He blew his noise in a white handkerchief that smelled of Clorox.

He had been so sure she would come. So certain. He felt like crying. He loved her. He *really* did. He'd told Nangi so, and Nangi in turn had said he loved Amber. They were going to marry in the spring. He'd felt so damn good when he told his secret, and Nangi had slapped him on the back and said something about still waters and then called him a son of a gun. He'd felt so damn good thinking he belonged at last.

It had all been a lie. Ruby didn't want him. He simply wasn't good enough for her. The hell with it. If she *did* want him, she'd have to do the calling. He wasn't sticking his neck out again to get it chopped off.

Calvin ached for his loss. He shackled his defense, this time more securely. He'd never trust anybody again. He sealed off the place in his heart allotted to Ruby Connors. At least she would always be with him there.

* * *

George's voice was so normal sounding, Irma cringed against the pillows. He'd gotten home a short while ago, just in time to speak to Dr. Ashley, who had been on his way out. She couldn't hear what they had said.

"Do you need anything, Irma?" She shook her head. "Where's Opal?"

Irma licked her lips, made dry by the medication she'd been taking. "Your brother came over to get her. She couldn't do anything for me, so I told her to go. Grace Zachary came over to help."

George replied in the same agreeable tone, "If she's needed over there, you were right to send her. Don't want that Zachary woman here, though. What happens in my house is none of her business. You hear me? Now, if you don't need anything, I'm going to sharpen the lawn mower and then mow the lawn before it rains."

Irma tried to dig her body deeper into the bedding. "The girls . . ." she whispered.

"Ruby won't be getting married anytime in the near future. They're bad seeds, Irma, they take after you. They've taken up with foreigners that look like niggers. Fil-yip-pinos. One of the little bastards informed me he's marrying *your* oldest daughter. I called the other one's commanding officer and told him what-for. Then I disowned both of them. They won't be coming for their grandmother's funeral, and they'll never darken this door-step again. We have only one daughter now." It was all said so matter-of-factly, Irma knew it was true. "None of you women are any good. Underneath, you're all like that one who lives next door. Filth, garbage. You all want the same thing, don't you?"

Irma closed her eyes. She wished she could die that very moment. When she opened them again, she stared through the window at the dismal gray day to where her husband was standing inside the shed, sharpening the lawn mower. This was normal, she'd seen him do the same thing hundreds of times from the kitchen window. If she didn't think about her daughters, she wouldn't cry. She continued to watch her husband while she thought of all the letters Ruby had written to her grandmother. She wondered what was in them. Bits and pieces of her daughter's new life that she wanted to share with her grandmother and Opal. Opal had never once let on that she'd heard from Ruby. Why, Irma wondered, was God punishing her like this?

Irma was shaken from her dark thoughts, when she noticed her husband do something strange. He threw the blades to the lawn mower onto his workbench. He smoothed back his hair and jerked up his trousers. Her hand flew to her mouth. She watched him walk out of the shed and cross the lawn, still in her line of vision, toward the Zacharys' property. As far as she knew, he'd never stepped foot on their property, but he was stepping on it now, walking toward the back porch, where he would be cut off from her line of vision. She knew where he was going and what he was going to do. She screamed as loud as her dry throat would allow, but there was no one to hear her.

The moment Grace heard steps on the back porch, she turned from the stove, where she was cooking up the last of the autumn grapes for winter jelly, a radiant smile on her face. When she saw that it wasn't Paul, her hand, holding a wooden spoon, froze in midair. Her first thought was that Irma had taken a turn for the worse; her second was that George had found the frivolous locket she'd given Opal and had come to return it. Then she looked into his eyes, and she knew at once exactly why he was there.

Grace backed up as she brandished the wooden spoon, grape jelly dripping to the floor. "I want you to leave my house, George. I want you to leave *now*! Paul will be home any second. He'll kill you, George. I know he will." God, Paul took the dog to the store with him. She was trapped and she knew it. To fight or not to fight. If she fought him, he might do to her what he'd done to his wife. She couldn't just stand there and let him . . . she couldn't.

"Slut!" George hissed. "Jezebel! Tramp!"

"Why are you here if I'm all those things?" Grace demanded, trying to reach the drainboard and the butcher knife. She'd whack off his fucking balls. Too late. George read her intent. He reached out and ripped the criss-cross straps of her halter-style sundress, exposing her breasts. Grace shrieked as she tried to cover her breasts with her arms, one hand still clutching the wooden spoon. Grape jelly trickled down between her breasts. She was more vulnerable this way, she realized, and as she moved backward, searching for something to fight with, she tripped over the step stool she'd used to get the paraffin from the top shelf.

He was on her then, ripping her sundress and red panties from her buttocks. With one arm he pinned her to the floor, while with the other hand he fumbled with his belt buckle.

Grace struggled, even though she knew it was futile. She couldn't give in to this bastard without a fight. The more she resisted, the more incensed he became.

He was like some hungry, frenzied animal as he drove into her, pawing and gouging her breasts, and when he'd had enough of them, he gripped her buttocks, cruelly kneading them. "This will teach you to mind your own business, you little tramp."

She whimpered, soft cries of pain. He continued to thrust and thrash as he tensed and then seemed to relax. In one terrifying moment she thought they were fused together, that he would die atop her and she would never be free of him.

His own noises registered with hers, animal sounds, panting, groaning. When he uttered his last piglike squeal of excitement, Grace knew it was finally over. She rolled away and crawled to the doorway. He was on his knees, trying to pull up his pants with one hand while with the other he balanced himself.

Holding on to the door frame, Grace noticed the sound of her jelly bubbling in the enamel pot. It was the last of the autumn grapes, the best of the season. Paul's favorite. She wiped her eyes with the back of her arm. She wouldn't wait for Paul to kill him.

She moved so fast, she almost slipped as she reached for the bubbling pot of jelly. She blistered her hands, blisters she didn't feel. He was up now, on his feet, but not steady. She pitched the still-bubbling jelly at him, catching him directly in the stomach and groin. His yowl of pain brought a grimace to her face, but she didn't stop. She grabbed the frying pan from the drainboard and brought it down on his head in a mighty thrust. Still not satisfied with her retaliation, she dumped hot, melting paraffin all over him.

Grace was panting, her fear gone now that she was in control. She wondered again if this animal would die in her kitchen. "You want to play with the big dogs, Mr. Connors, then you better learn to piss in the tall grass," she spat out. "Get out of my kitchen, and don't you ever come back. You're an animal, but I took care of that, didn't I, Georgie," Grace cried hysterically. "You won't ever, ever be able to do it again."

She watched through her tears as George struggled to get to the door. In her life she'd never seen such dead, evil eyes. She heard him fall down the back steps, heard his curses. She laughed, the sound strange and alien to her ears, then she sat down on the floor and cried, her toes digging and smearing into the rapidly cooling jelly.

What had just happened . . . had happened only if she . . . allowed herself to think about it. It would kill Paul. And Paul would kill George if she told him. Paul would go to jail and her life would be ruined. The town gossip would be that Grace had been asking for it.

She couldn't burden Paul with this. He'd never feel the same about her. Even if he said it didn't matter, it would. Nothing would ever be the same. She loved Paul too much to shame him.

"It never happened," Grace said over and over as she cleaned the kitchen and the back steps. They'd have to live with the grape stains. As long as Paul didn't know, she could live with anything.

Dr. John Ashley was just about to close his office when the telephone rang. He listened, his jaw going slack, then a smile spread across his face. "I'll be right there. Imagine that," he muttered, "George Connors making grape jelly." Everyone in the world knew men didn't belong in the kitchen. And then a second call came from Grace Zachary as he was walking through the door. She'd burned her hands on a pot. He told her he'd be there shortly.

Somehow John Ashley had lived through seventy years of life without swearing. A casual damn didn't count. "I'll be a son of a bitch," he muttered as he shuffled out to his ancient car. Who should he see to first—Grace or George? He cackled when he made the decision to see Grace. He wheezed and sneezed his way through town in his rickety car, wiping his old watery eyes from time to time.

George Connors did not attend the rosary being said for his mother that night, nor did he attend the funeral three days later. He was in the hospital with a team of doctors, none of them specialists, who were trying to treat his burns and reconstruct his penis.

One month later, the head of the nonspecialized surgical team looked at his colleagues and said, "I say we let him piss through a tube and call it a day." They all agreed. "Put him in a private room. I think he's going to want to be alone."

Count your blessings, Ruby Connors. Every day if necessary. Pep talks were good, important to one's well-being.

She missed Nola and Calvin, but she didn't cry anymore. She didn't cry for her grandmother either. She'd made the commitment to get on with her life and not look back the day after her father's unexpected visit. "Everything," she said aloud, "is a learning experience."

Ruby stared at herself in the long mirror attached to the back of her bedroom door. "I think, Ruby, you grew up, overnight." She leaned closer to the mirror. "Yep, you did. Now it's time to move on." She whirled around to face the calendar on the narrow wall behind her. "Time to move on," she said again.

The summer of her life beckoned. She smiled. She took a tentative step, then another. "Now it's my time. I'm ready," she said softly. "Oh, yes," she said again and again, "I'm ready."

Ruby Connors walked into the summer of her life with her shoulders straight and her head high.

PART TWO

SUMMER

CHAPTER FOUR

1953

Ruby Connors stared up at the house numbers on the tree-lined street. It was a nice neighborhood, close to the stores on 14th Street, but she didn't like the house or the neighborhood as much as she liked the old brick three-story on Kilbourne Place. She did like the front porch at 1454 Monroe Avenue, though, and spent the warm summer evenings sitting with the own-ers, Rena and Bruno, on old wicker chairs, discussing anything and everything. Still, it wasn't the same. Nothing was the same anymore.

For a moment the seven steps leading to the wide front porch seemed insurmountable. She squared her shoulders and walked up, careful to stay on the narrow unpainted portion. She found herself smiling at the hand-painted sign Bruno had erected: STEY OF PENT. He meant stay off the paint, but she wasn't going to mention his spelling to him. Bruno was proud of his limited En-glish. How was it possible, she wondered, that strangers could come to this land and immediately buy a house, collect rent, and live comfortably? Financially, she was in just about the same po-sition she had been in two years earlier, when Amber had mar-ried Nangi and moved to Saipan. Bruno and Rena had been here only eighteen months, and already they owned two houses and worked two jobs each. Which just went to prove you could do whatever you wanted if you worked at it.

The screen door banged behind Ruby. The hallway leading to the second floor was cool and dim. As always. Her hands traced the brilliant zigzag lightning bolts on the wallpaper that seemed to propel one upward at a faster than normal rate of speed. Rena liked brilliant colors in her attire as well as her decor. Ruby smiled as she always did at the vivid crimson, black, purple, and yellow lightning bolts. To her left, the white stairway gleamed with glossy white paint. It was Bruno's job to paint and Rena's to decorate.

The hallway was narrow, much like the one on Kilbourne Place, and Rena had carried the lightning-bolt pattern all the way through. It would, she thought, make the girls move faster up and down the hall and into the bathroom. Rena didn't like anyone to dilly-dally because she herself was always in constant motion. She often reminded Ruby of a shark, with the way she was never still, but there the similarity ended. Rena looked like a precocious chipmunk with her plumped-out cheeks and dark, inquisitive eyes.

It was a pleasant place, and she had her own room. She'd deliberately chosen the smallest so she wouldn't have to share. Her roommates were all new, and while they got along, they weren't friends. Ruby preferred it that way. Friends, real friends, like Nola, caused heartache.

Ruby kicked off her shoes and flopped down on the bed. For some reason, she wanted to cry, to bawl her head off, to kick and scream, to rail and rant. It would be childish and immature, but that's how she felt. Her eye flew to the calendar tacked to the back of her door. It had been two years ago today that she was supposed to have left with Calvin to get married. *Oh, Calvin, where are you?* Tears stung her eyes. She wiped them angrily. Damn you, Calvin, you never called; you didn't so much as send a postcard. If you *really* loved me, you would have given me a chance to explain.

Ruby sat up on the bed and crossed her legs, Indian fashion. It wasn't quite true that she wasn't any better off than she had been two years before. She had inherited three thousand dollars from her grandmother's estate. Her father hadn't been able to take that away from her. He'd tried, but her grandmother or her uncles had seen to it that the money was put in trust for her until she was twenty-one. She'd seen a copy of the will. The lawyer had forwarded it. Amber and Opal had each received a hundred dollars, and according to the will, her father's share of the estate was a little over five hundred dollars, because her debt had been wiped clean. Legally.

Boy, had she bawled that day. Free and clear for all of ten minutes. Some contrary streak in her, some honorable seed somewhere in her being, insisted a debt was a debt and she would honor it, so she kept sending her money home on the first of the month. In a way, she supposed she was rich, certainly better off than her roommates, better off than Amber or Opal. She had the money and the czarina's ring, a steady job, and a roof over her head. She was independent. And so damn lonely, but by her own choice. Maybe tonight she would splurge and call Nola and ask how her godchild was. She hadn't heard from her old friend in four months, and she was starting to worry. Yes, she'd call later. Nola would lift her spirits and tell her about the baby and the other orphans. Tears pricked her eyes again. God, why couldn't she be happy? *Calvin Santos, I hate your guts.* She sniffed miserably. *Why couldn't you believe and trust in me? You didn't know me at all, you miserable . . . you miserable . . . you . . . you . . .*

Ruby blew her nose twice. Her grandmother would have told her to pull up her socks, get moving, and don't look back. "Dammit, today I'm entitled to look back," she muttered. She bent over and gave her imaginary socks a hitch before she headed for the living room to call Nola. She needed a friend now, not at eleven o'clock, when the rates were cheaper.

Little fingers of fear fluttered in Ruby's chest when she heard Mrs. Quantrell's tired voice on the other end of the line. The tiny little flutters took wing and exploded when she was told that Nola had taken the baby to Europe.

"Europe!" Ruby squeaked her dismay. "Why? What happened? When did she leave?"

The tired woman explained that Mr. Quantrell had contacted the Air Force and tracked down Alex, who had then come to Vermont and married Nola. He had taken her off to Germany, his next billet.

"It happened so quick, we barely had time to get things together for them. I'm sure she'll write to you, Ruby."

The storm in Ruby's chest quieted. "Was . . . is she happy, Mrs. Quantrell?"

"I think so, child. The baby needs his father's name, and Alex, well, he seemed . . . fatherhood is difficult." Her voice brightened suddenly and sounded just like Nola's when she said, "She'll be able to visit all the famous houses of fashion and get a feel for it all over again. She was very happy about visiting France. Do you want me to tell her anything when I write to her?"

Of course she had at least two hundred things she wanted to

tell Nola, but this wasn't the time. "Tell her . . . tell her to be happy and not to forget me. Good-bye, Mrs. Quantrell." Ruby cried then. She knew as sure as she knew she had to breathe to stay alive that like all the others she'd come to love, Nola was lost to her.

"Ruby, Ruby," a soft, accented voice called softly. "Oh, honey, you're crying. What's wrong?" Rena, her landlady, asked as she swooped down on the girl like a protective mother bird.

Ruby sobbed and cried, hiccoughed and blubbered as she confided in the tiny woman with the kind eyes and soothing voice. She poured out her heart the way she would have to Grace Zachary.

Rena Musad was Egyptian. Today she was attired in an emerald-colored Indian sari with matching sandals and feathered headband. Jewelry clanked and rattled on her thin arms. She was beautiful and exotic, Ruby thought as she dried her eyes. At first glance she appeared fragile, breakable, until you looked into her licorice-colored eyes and saw the strength in them, the strength Bruno drew upon twenty-four hours a day. Rena was a driving force, one to be reckoned with. She was thirty-five, slender as a reed, and weighed no more than eighty-five pounds.

She listened now, her dark eyes sad yet stormy as Ruby unburdened herself, then businesslike when Ruby mentioned the three thousand dollars. Ruby hiccoughed for the last time, and Rena clapped her hands in delight. "You silly little pigeon, you must make that money work for you. From what you've told me, your grandmother did her best to make things secure for you. I think that you should buy some property. We will discuss it with Bruno. Shame on you, Ruby. You are such a smart girl, why didn't you think of this yourself?"

"I did. Today, as a matter of fact. That's why I called Nola. I was going to offer to help her, you know, give her a stake of some kind, but she's gone. You coming up here must be some kind of divine providence, don't you think?"

Rena had no idea what divine providence meant. The eight bracelets on both arms tinkled as she waved the mail under Ruby's nose. "You have two letters from that marine who keeps writing to you. While you read them I am going downstairs to fix Bruno his supper and talk to him. I will call the man who sold us this house and the two others we own. He is honest and will work for you, Ruby." She added, "I will take thirty-five dollars as a commission if things work out."

Ruby found herself nodding dumbly. Rena tapped her foot happily. It was then she saw the diamond imbedded in Rena's big toenail and the three gold ankle bracelets studded with rubies. Her jaw dropped.

"I believe in carrying my wealth with me. As much as I love Bruno, he is becoming Americanized. One cannot trust men. Ever. Remember that. Also remember that all your property is to remain in your name alone. I will be back later."

"Rena . . . wait, what do you mean? Is your property in your name? Doesn't Bruno object?"

"On an hourly basis, but if he wants to share my bed, he does as I wish. As I said, he is becoming Americanized, but he still has much of our culture in him. What's mine is mine, and what's ours is mine, too. It's just as well. Bruno has no head for business." She laughed merrily as she tinkled and clanked her way down the staircase to her first-floor apartment.

Ruby sat for a long time, digesting Rena's words, though as much to put off opening Andrew Blue's letters than anything else. She leaned back in her chair and stared about the oversize living room. It was comfortable, bright with color, thanks to Rena. Her roommates loved it; she did, too, when it came right down to it. The large, overstuffed sofa was covered in lemon-yellow chintz with meadow-green trim. The carpet was apple green, one shade deeper than the trim on the sofa and matching chair. Two cherry-red wingback chairs graced the farthest corner with a lampshade covered in sheer lemon-colored chiffon. At night it was warm and cozy with the light shining on the vibrant-colored furniture. The furniture was all cheap, Ruby knew. The covers had been made by Rena on her treadle Singer, but it didn't matter. Nola would approve. The house was clean, bright, and neat.

Ruby was opening the first letter from Andrew when two of her roommates came in from work. They greeted one another before the taller one announced that she had a date and asked if could she use the living room. Ruby nodded absently and made her way to her bedroom to be alone.

Andrew's first letter wasn't long, a page and a half. Ruby smiled as she read it, and then went on to the second. Andrew was witty, she had to give him that. In her own way, she treasured his letters because they reminded her that someone knew and cared she was alive.

Andrew had come to Washington twice in the past year and a half to see her. Secretly, she believed he'd had business to handle for his commanding officer at the Pentagon and she had been an afterthought, but it was nice to hear he had come all the way from North Carolina just to see her, even if it wasn't true. Now he was saying he wanted to visit again in a few weeks. *Oh, Calvin, where are you?*

As always, the girls sat down together for dinner. Afterward, clean-up took exactly twelve minutes. It was Ruby's job to sweep the floor and take the trash downstairs to the alley, where Rena had a special can for their apartment. It was painted yellow with harlequin designs in flashy green and purple. It was blinding to the eye and could be seen all the way down the alley behind the house. At Christmastime Rena tied the trash can in silver and red and left a case of beer for the trash collectors. Ruby grinned as she forced the lid on the dent-free can. The painted can was the only one without a mark or dent of any kind. She herself had seen the trash collectors snort and make snide remarks about the colorful container, but she noticed that they handled it just short of reverently.

The smile stayed with Ruby as she started for the back stairway. She was halfway to the landing when Rena called her.

Ruby blinked when she entered the landlady's kitchen. It reminded her of the fireman's carnival back in Barstow. There were so many doodads, knickknacks, pictures, figurines, and calendars, it had a dizzying effect.

Bruno was seated at the table, eating alone, his plate on a piece of brown wrapping paper. Rena always served Bruno alone because she said she couldn't stand the way he dripped, slurped, and burped his way through a meal, and why should her dinner be spoiled? Ruby thought Bruno was a sweetheart for the way he tolerated Rena, who, in her opinion, was the Americanized one, not Bruno.

He grinned, revealing white teeth as he stuffed his mouth with a greasy concoction of grape leaves and a rice filling. Once Ruby had eaten one of Rena's delectable dinners and had paid for it with a raging case of diarrhea.

Bruno was a short man, not much taller than his diminutive

wife, but he was round all over. He wore his shiny bald head like a king with a crown. His eyes were dark, like dessert dishes of chocolate pudding, and they always twinkled, even when he was upset with Rena, which was most of the time. He wasn't a pretty man, Ruby decided, with his dimples, his hawkish nose, and a chin that met folds of fat underneath. But his hands fascinated Ruby; they were big as ham hocks, with fingers like sausages. She liked Bruno.

"Sit, sit," Rena said as she moved about the kitchen, pouring more lemonade for Bruno and snatching his plates away as soon as he finished. His bread plate and salad bowl were already in soapy water. Ruby perched on the edge of a chrome chair covered in raspberry-colored plastic. She waited, declining a glass of lemonade, which Rena had set before her on a napkin.

"I have written here everything—the name of the man who sold us our houses, information from the bank where we have our mortgage, everything you need to know. Tomorrow at five-thirty he will meet us to see two houses. Bruno has agreed to"— she pursed her rosebud mouth into a small round O—"do whatever renovations need to be done, for a very small fee. We must help one another, and I," she said dramatically, "will help you decorate. Again for a very small fee. What do you think, Ruby? A grand idea?"

"It's so sudden." Ruby gasped. "I sort of like the idea of having money in the bank. I just . . . what I mean is I haven't thought . . . I suppose it's a good idea, but maybe just one house, not two."

"Nonsense. You must make that money work for you. If you charge enough rent, you can have what my man with the numbers calls cash flow, and before you know it, you will replace the money you used for the down payment. You must do this, Ruby. Next year the houses will cost more and the year after they will cost still more." Rena's bracelets tinkled as she waved her arms about to make her point. Ruby noticed Bruno shaking his head up and down in agreement. Bruno was not stupid, even though Rena implied that he was.

"Two!" Rena said firmly. "You are living very nicely in my house and making ends meet and still saving a few dollars after you meet all your bills. Two!" she repeated.

"Who knows? The houses may not even need repair or decorating." Her bangles tinkled and clinked. "You will post notices where you work, and before you can blink, you will have tenants like yourself. I will allow you to copy my lease, for a small fee."

Bruno belched and rubbed his round stomach. He struggled off the plastic chair and bowed low before his wife. "It was an excellent meal, my little dove." Rena giggled when he brought her hand to his lips and kissed it noisily. "Ah, another new ring. Wonderful! And how much did this one cost?"

Rena simpered, her cheeks puffing out. If Ruby hadn't known better, she would have thought the tiny woman had a toothache. She stifled a smile when she heard Rena say, "We can live two years off the sale price, should I decide to sell it."

"Tomorrow you must get a matching one for the other hand, my dove."

Rena was moving again, cleaning the shiny raspberry tabletop, whisking the greasy brown paper into the trash. The moment the dishes were in the sudsy water, she clapped her hands; the bracelets chimed and tinkled melodiously.

"Shoo, shoo," she said. "I must start to think about a suitable wallpaper for Ruby's new houses."

Ruby waved halfheartedly and climbed the stairs to her own kitchen. She felt weak with the decisions Rena was making for her. She wished she had someone to talk it all over with. Perhaps Andrew when he came to Washington, but that was still a few weeks off. She wondered if she could stall. She also wondered if it was wise to tell Andrew. Probably not. She wished she'd taken the real estate course she decided against a year ago. Maybe it wasn't too late. She could go to the library and see what they had. Anything of importance could be found in a library. And there was no time like the present.

Ruby was back in her room by nine forty-five with a load of books the librarian had recommended. Ruby found herself staring at them and then at the two letters from Andrew Blue. Should she write to him or read the books? She was always annoyed with herself when she had to make a decision concerning Andrew, even if it just meant writing a letter.

Ruby's eyes swiveled to the calendar behind her door. Her thoughts again went back to Calvin. It shouldn't hurt this much, not after all this time. She buried her face in the pillow. "You should have died, Calvin, then I could come to terms with it the way I did when my grandmother died," she whimpered. "Death is final ... this ... this thing between us ... it's still there, it won't go away. Someplace, somewhere, you're as alive as I am, but we might as well be dead."

Ruby threw Andrew Blue's letters across the room and pushed the stack of library books to the floor.

In a flash she was off the bed and rummaging in her bottom dresser, where she kept her mementos of Calvin. In a minute she had the cards, notes, and pictures in the wastepaper basket. So little to show for such an intense relationship.

Dry-eyed, Ruby carried out the trash for a second time that evening. "Now you're dead, Calvin," Ruby muttered as she fit the colorful lid back on the trash can. "You're really dead!"

Back in her room, Ruby sat down and wrote a cheerful letter to Andrew Blue, so unlike her cut-and-dried polite previous responses.

When she read the letter over before sealing the envelope, she added a postscript saying that she was looking forward to his visit and would plan something for the weekend. Not sex, she added in a second postscript. She mailed the letter on her way to work the following morning.

After work Ruby met Rena and Hal Murdock on the corner of 31st and P streets. Hal, Ruby decided ten minutes later, was the closest thing to a greased pig she'd ever seen. He talked out of the side of his mouth in a language Ruby didn't understand even though she knew he was speaking English. She didn't like him, and what surprised her even more was that Rena didn't seem to like him, either. Obviously, Rena had read the same library book she had, the one that said it isn't necessary to like one's real estate agent as long as he gets his customer a good deal.

An hour later Ruby had seen Hal's two offerings, one a three-bedroom house on O Street with a finished basement and a walled-in courtyard. The second house was a building on Poplar Street that had been converted into a two-family house. Ruby's eyes sparkled, as did Rena's, when she thought about the rent she could charge. Hal's eyes gleamed and his capped teeth sparkled like a barracuda's.

Back in Hal's office, which was little more than a dingy storefront, Ruby looked at the sheaf of papers she was handed and told to read over. She looked helplessly at Rena.

"Tomorrow will be soon enough. We must look these over

and have Miss Connors's attorney scrutinize them. Not that you would ever do anything wrong. A precaution, you understand."

Hal said he did, but he seemed jittery to Ruby, and that made her suspicious.

"You might as well tell me now what's wrong with the house on Poplar Street," Ruby said. "That's the one you whisked us out of so quickly. And you didn't have the key to the basement. I find that rather strange."

"The basement floods when it rains," Hal said out of the corner of his mouth. "I don't have a key. There's water damage."

"Then the price should reflect what it's going to cost for repairs, assuming I intend to buy," Ruby said. "Why don't you talk to both owners tomorrow and see if you can't come up with a more reasonable price. If we can't come to terms on Poplar Street, then I won't be wanting the other one on O Street. Tomorrow we can ... huddle, here at your office. Same time. Thank you for showing us around."

On the trolley Rena looked at Ruby and laughed. "Huddle? What does that mean? Where did you learn to be so ... forceful? I think, Ruby, you are going to get the houses at a lot less than we anticipated. Your offer is low, but sound. I was so green when we bought our first one. We actually paid the asking price. I'll never do that again. All you need is a sump pump, and Bruno can do that for you—for a small fee. I'm thrilled for you, Ruby. It's wonderful to be a property owner, but also a little work. We will make a notation, in small print, on the rental lease that the tenants are responsible for *everything*."

Ruby gaped. "Everything?"

"Everything." Rena was as smug as a cat catching her first mouse. "Ah, I see you didn't read the lease *you* signed. You must make that a rule in life, Ruby, never sign your name to anything you disagree with or don't understand. Always have a good attorney in the background, even if it costs more than you want to pay. In order to make money, you must spend money ... wisely and with a clear head."

"I'll remember that," Ruby muttered, wondering what else was in the lease she hadn't bothered to read.

In the days to come, Ruby alternated between fits of elation and spasms of depression, which led to bouts of abject fear. Her sleep was invaded by demons named Hal, Rena, and Bruno. Was she doing the right thing? After she had asked herself for the hundredth time if her grandmother would approve of what she was doing with her inheritance, she finally decided to go through with the real estate deal. She would certainly be no poorer, and if things got sticky or messy, she would sell the czarina's ring and hope for the best.

Yesterday, after work, during a raging thunderstorm, she'd signed on the proverbial dotted line. Acceptance of her final offer was just a formality, Hal said. She was putting a thousand dollars down on each house, and if the bank approved her mortgage application at four percent, she would be an official property owner in forty-five days. She'd done her best to estimate hidden costs, Rena's fees, and closing costs. If she was lucky, she'd squeak by without touching her two-hundred-thirty-three-dollar savings account.

Two days ago, when it looked as if the sales would go through, Ruby posted a notice on the bulletin board at work. So far this evening she'd had eight calls from parties interested in renting. She'd probably get another dozen before the week was over. What she had to concern herself with now was Rena's nickel-and-diming her to death.

She was uneasy, but in her gut Ruby knew the tension she was feeling had little to do with her property. Andrew Blue would arrive tomorrow. Or was it tonight? She couldn't remember exactly. All she knew was she had a date for brunch tomorrow with the handsome marine, and she wasn't sure how she *really* felt about Andrew Blue now that she'd officially pronounced Calvin Santos dead. "Be up, Ruby, act positive, give Andrew a fair chance. You're twenty-one now, time to get your personal life in order. Time to think about *not* becoming an old maid." Andrew had hung in there for two years, and so had she. That had to mean something. Especially now that she had finally put Calvin completely in the past.

Today she'd bought a new dress. Consciously or unconsciously, she bought it for Andrew. That was a start in the right direction. Tomorrow she would be cheerful, happy, and accommodating to him. She would tell him she was happy to see him, delighted to be in his company and she would let him know she was amenable to seeing him more often. And from now on she would change the tone of her letters. As of tomorrow she and Andrew would be what the girls in the house called a thing. She was settling, something she promised herself she would never do, but time and life didn't stand still for a Calvin Santos and a Ruby Connors.

Ruby cried herself to sleep.

Andrew Blue spat on the rag in his hand and applied it to the already-high shine on his shoes. He was so clean, neat, and pressed that his appearance screamed Marine Corps. Spit and polish, piss and vinegar, and damn proud of it.

He was ready for his date with Ruby Connors. She was the one thing he hadn't come to terms with since his transfer to Camp Lejune. He'd used leave time to come to Washington at his own expense to see her. For the life of him, he could never explain to himself why he had kept up his correspondence with her. At one point he'd actually thought he was in love with her, but he wasn't. He did feel something, though. Otherwise, why would he have kept writing to her every ten days? And what the hell did she write back? Words, just goddamn words with no meaning. The sun is shining ... Admiral Query said this or that ... my landlady got another diamond today ... there's a storm due tomorrow ... bullshit. He wanted more, something personal.

Ruby was still a hick from the sticks, but the last time he'd seen her, he'd been surprised at her appearance. She'd always been exceptionally neat and clean, but she was now dressed better; she'd put on a few pounds in all the right places, and she had a new hairstyle that was very becoming. She even wore earrings, little gold things that kind of swung from her ears. As they said in the Corps, Ruby was put together. He approved and he was not unaware of the stares he received from other guys when she was with him. She still wasn't beautiful, but there was something about Ruby ... he wanted her ... had never stopped wanting her.

Maybe this trip would be different. The tone of her last letter had left him puzzled. If was almost as if someone else had written it. He remembered laughing over several lines. Maybe the little hick was finally over the flip and that business with her bastard father. Now, *that* was something. He wanted to know more about that day, but Ruby refused to offer explanations, and finally he had to accept that he would probably never know what was behind that visit from her father.

His return to Washington this weekend was not strictly to see Ruby. It was the first step in a campaign. If, his colonel told him, he were married, he had a good chance of moving up in rank, so long as he played ball and kept his nose clean. For "favors rendered," he would be grateful enough to pass along Andrew's name with his own personal recommendation. He had enough ears at his disposal to make good on his promise.

Andrew's stomach churned when he thought about the "favors rendered" part of the deal. If caught, his ass would be out of the Corps, and he'd get a dishonorable discharge. Whoever would have thought a colonel in the Corps on his way to being a brigadier general would have a passion for nubile young girls? Andrew had been revolted, but in true Corps fashion had kept his mouth shut. If he wanted to be honest with himself, he knew the main reason he hadn't turned his back on the colonel was that he would move up in rank that much faster. In the military, one hand washed the other. Everything was politics, playing the game to win.

Still, Andrew hated what he was doing for his colonel. This move and promotion, if it ever materialized, would get him out of the colonel's clutches. He had to make it work, had to zero in on Ruby and go on from there.

On his way from Quantico, in a friend's car that he'd managed to appropriate with an appropriate line of bullshit, he wondered what Ruby would say if she knew how he was advancing his career. He also wondered if she would be impressed with his speedy promotion to captain in a year or so. It wasn't till he drove across the 14th Street Bridge that he admitted to himself that no matter what he did, he would never impress Ruby Connors. He wondered why that was.

He should have made some lasting friendships in the Corps by now, but he hadn't. He could go to the Officers' Club with the guys, have a drink or a beer, but it never went beyond that. He was a loner. Ruby could change that. Ruby would make friends with other officers' wives and they'd cultivate a circle of friends that would make him appear stable. Marriage. Andrew snorted derisively. A kid would clinch everything. A big step, but he was ready for it. His career demanded it. If Ruby would just cooperate, they could be married by the end of the year and get a good tax deduction. Thanksgiving or Christmas. For sure, he'd never be able to forget an anniversary.

Andrew tooled along, enjoying the major's car. Marriage would necessitate a vehicle of some kind, a clunker, a rattletrap, something for Ruby to drive. Of course, Ruby didn't know how to drive, which meant he'd have to teach her.

Jesus! He was acting and thinking as if marriage were in the works. Ruby could still dash it all with one word. *No!*

He turned onto Monroe, and his bright blue eyes, behind dark glasses, searched for house numbers. He saw her the same moment he saw the brass numerals attached to the white column atop the banister. She was rocking in a wicker chair and wore the same kind of sunglasses he wore. A chill washed over him. His hands grew sweaty on the steering wheel. This was the way Ruby would look when she got old. She'd sit placidly and rock in a chair on the front porch. His mouth suddenly went dry, and it became hard to swallow. How badly do you want to be a captain and how bad do you want to get away from Colonel Lackland? "Damn bad," he mumbled as he pulled the car to the curb.

The moment Andrew reached the rocking chair, he lifted Ruby bodily out of it. "Don't ever let me see you rocking in a chair again until you're ninety-three years old." He smiled, but there was no humor in his voice.

Ruby laughed. "It's so nice to see you again, Andrew. I've been looking forward to your visit. How long will you be here?"

Andrew sucked in his breath. Nice to see me? he thought. This was a new Ruby, a very new Ruby. "Till eleven o'clock Sunday night. If you're amenable and don't have anything else to do, we can cover a lot of ground between now and then. Sixty dollars' worth." He grinned. "I've been saving up to show you a good time." Actually he'd won forty-six dollars in a crap game two days before. As far as lies went, it was a small one; he had saved the money for two days.

"Where did you get the car?" Ruby asked happily. She was almost giddy as she settled herself.

Andrew threw back his head and laughed. "There's a long story to how I got this car, and I'm not sure I won't end up in the stockade when I return it. It belongs to a major at Quantico. I wanted this weekend to be special, so I sort of . . . what I did was . . . hell, I stole it, is what it boils down to. I did fill out some papers . . . maybe they'll pass muster if the major doesn't have anything to do this weekend. On the other hand, if he, too, had some kind of date planned, it's safe to say my ass is grass. Let's not think about it."

Ruby giggled. "I've never been in jail before."

"Me, either." Andrew grinned.

Fourteen hours later, Andrew steered the Nash to the curb outside the house on Monroe Street.

"I had a great time, Ruby," Andrew said softly as he leaned closer to her. He'd expected her to move away, but she didn't. He was puzzled at the change in Ruby.

"I did, too, Andrew. You can be a lot of fun when you aren't being overbearing and pushy. Don't go getting any ideas now, either. But if you want to kiss me good night, that's okay."

"Who said I wanted to kiss you?" Andrew teased.

Six months ago Ruby would have been flustered by the remark. Now all she did was shrug. "Your loss, Lieutenant," she said airily as she made a move to get out of the car.

"Hey, hold on here," Andrew drawled. "I always walk my dates to the door, and that's where I kiss them. I don't mess around in car seats. When are you going to get it through your head that I'm not the kind of guy you think I am?"

Ruby smiled in the darkness. "Right now, Andrew," she said, leaning over and kissing him full on the mouth. She was out of the car in a flash and halfway up the steps before Andrew stopped groaning. He tried to flatten his instant erection. His long legs propelled him up the steps, where he caught Ruby by the door. "You're a tease, Ruby," he said irritably.

Ruby threw up her hands. "I don't understand, Andrew. Do you want to kiss me or not?"

"Goddammit, Ruby, for two years you've held me at arm's length, and now all of a sudden you're giving off signals."

"Oh, shut up, Andrew, and kiss me good night!" Ruby ordered. He did and Ruby swayed. She told him she wanted to kiss him again.

Something surged in Andrew, but he pushed her away. "Not on your life, Ruby. First thing you know you'll have me on that rocking chair and you'll be on my lap and then . . . oh, no. I'm leaving you here safe and sound, the way my mother taught me to do. I have to hit the road. I'll see you tomorrow bright and early. Get yourself all Mickey Madooded, and we'll go on from there."

"Huh? What's Mickey Madooded?"

"An old Indiana saying. Get dressed up, spiffed up, you know . . ." he said, taking the steps two at a time. "See you tomorrow."

Mickey Madooded! Ruby giggled all the way up the steps to her apartment.

At six o'clock the following evening, over a candlelight dinner that he had just enough money to pay for, Andrew asked Ruby to marry him. Ruby didn't blink, didn't simper, didn't look away or pretend to be flustered. She thought about how much fun they'd had the day before. She thought about how good it felt to have someone. She thought about how satisfying it was not to think about Calvin. She looked at Andrew across the tip of the candle flame and said in a normal-sounding voice, "It sounds like a good idea."

"Huh? Does . . . does that mean yes?"

Ruby nodded.

Andrew looked like he'd been kicked in the gut, but he still smiled.

She smiled back. He looked ill. She felt ill. She wanted to run screaming from the restaurant.

"When?" she asked in a matter-of-fact voice.

Andrew shrugged. "Isn't it up to the girl?" he said in an identical-sounding matter-of-fact voice.

It was Ruby's turn to shrug. "I don't have anyone to invite except my roommates and landlords."

"I don't know anyone here anymore. Why don't I leave all that up to you? We should do it before the end of the year, though. Is that okay?"

"Sure." Anytime before the end of the year meant she could settle on the two houses and make arrangements for Rena to take over as manager. Forty-five days till she closed. A few days to get her clothes together and give Rena notice. Time to give the girls a chance to find a new roommate.

"Where will we live?"

"I'm waiting for orders. Don't worry, I'll see to housing wherever I land. Military housing isn't the greatest, but it will do for now. I have some money saved, not much, but it will see us through. If we get married by a justice of the peace, we can save on a wedding. We can honeymoon for a weekend and go away somewhere later. I guess we'll need money for furniture, that kind of thing." Ruby nodded. "Do you mind not having an engagement ring?" Ruby shook her head. "I'll get you one later," he promised. Two years ago he could have won all kinds of diamond rings from busted romances in a crap game. Now the girls were getting smarter; they kept their rings. He hadn't seen one in the pot for a very long time.

"Are you going to . . . will you wear a wedding band?" Ruby asked nervously. He damn well better, she thought.

"Hell yes. I want the whole damn Corps to know I'm married." It sounded like a lie to Ruby, but she didn't say anything.

"Let's get out of here," Andrew said. "It's a special night. We should spend some time alone."

The candles on the table were at the halfway mark now. Ruby stared across at Andrew. She wanted to remember this evening. I should take a souvenir, she thought. A matchbook, something. It occurred to her to blow out the candle and stick it in her purse, but she didn't realize she had spoken her thoughts aloud until Andrew snuffed out the candle with his bare fingers and handed it to her. "It's romantic of you to keep it. I'll take the matchbook."

He plastered a wide smile on his face and rose to help Ruby from her chair.

Andrew settled behind the wheel of the major's car. "How about a walk around the tidal basin? It's a nice night, too nice to spend driving around, unless you'd rather take in a movie?"

"I'd like that," Ruby said shyly. Shouldn't they be talking about the wedding, or making plans, or holding hands or . . . or something? She should be sitting closer to him instead of leaning up against the door. Maybe with her hand on his thigh. Something intimate, either by gesture or word.

"Do you like autumn, Andrew?"

"Yeah. I think it's my favorite time of year."

"It's mine, too. I love walking down Rhode Island Avenue under the tunnel of trees in the fall. It's so gorgeous, it takes my breath away. I'm going to miss Washington," she said with a catch in her voice.

"It's just a place, Ruby. It's not like it's home."

"To me it is. My home was . . . not like other people's. I've made this place mine. I really will miss it."

"The military is a great life. You'll make all kinds of friends. It's always new and exciting. And there's a real camaraderie among Marine families. It's great!"

"I know it is," she said, convinced he had just given her a line of bull. "Do you want to talk about . . . about setting the date? We really should discuss a few things. Like, are we going to have children right away or wait? Will I be able to get a job? I assume we're going to need money for furniture and things. You know, Andrew, I've been on my own for the past few years. I like controlling my own money and not having to ask . . . will I have to do that with you? I've read some stories in magazines where the wife gets an allowance from her husband but has to tell him what she does with the money. We have to talk about my . . . about the money I still owe my father. It's my debt, my only debt, but I have to pay it, so I guess I'll have to work. Do you have any objections?"

"Jesus Christ, yes! What do you mean, you have to keep paying it? I thought when he left that day, you said you *weren't* going to pay it."

Ruby didn't like the hard edge that had crept into his voice. "Yes, I did say that, but it's a debt . . . sort of a debt of honor on my part. If I don't pay it, that makes me no better than him. If this is going to cause trouble between us, now is the time to say so."

Andrew clenched his teeth. "How much do you send every month?"

"Ten dollars a week. Forty dollars a month except the months that have five weeks. I've hardly made a dent in the total. So far I've paid off only twelve hundred dollars. It's going to take a very long time. I don't expect you to pay it. I will. Just don't ask me or expect me to renege on it, because I won't."

"Let me ask you a question, Ruby. What if we had only fifty dollars to get by on for the month after the bills are paid, even with you working. Would you still send it?"

"I don't know, Andrew. Maybe half and do without something else. I *have* to pay it. I know you don't understand, and that's all right. I want it out in the open and I don't want us quarreling about it later." This was the time she should tell him about the two properties. Now, she should tell him now, so his face would relax. He looked so angry, so upset. Her shoulders squared stubbornly, but she didn't confide. The houses were *hers*, negotiated for before Andrew asked her to marry him. Surely there would be enough left of the rent to pay her debt, even if she didn't work.

"You handle it, Ruby," he said, rolling up the window of the car. "It's your problem. Mine is that I'm starting to worry about the major's car. I might be able to get a flight out if I can hitch a ride over to Andrews." He reached across to take her hand. He squeezed it and said, "Would you mind if I took you back?"

Ruby moved closer, her shoulder touching Andrew's.

"Not at all," she said softly. "It's been a wonderful weekend and you have a long trip ahead of you. Sunday nights I have a lot of things to do to prepare for the week. I might do some studying," she said lamely. This was a fizzle as far as romance went. She felt as though she had a pile of rocks in her stomach. Something was wrong. Andrew looked as if he felt it, too.

"Are you sure you want to get married?" Ruby blurted out.

Andrew almost ran the car off the road with the question. "Now, why are you asking me such a ridiculous question?" he barked in annoyance.

"Because," Ruby said in a matching tone, "you don't seem too happy. In fact, all of this seems a little too cut and dried. I . . . neither one of us is smiling, we're not making plans, we're not excited . . . you didn't say you love me. Why do you want to marry me?"

Andrew's face drained of color. "Hey, look, Ruby, I've never asked anyone to marry me before. If there are rules and guide-lines, I don't know them. You want me to . . . act like the guy you *think* I am and rip your clothes off and say all kinds of stupid things, okay. I can pull the car over and do it. The reason I'm acting so . . . reserved is because I don't trust myself. I wouldn't ask you to marry me if I didn't love you. I'm asking you to share my life; I'm promising to take care of you for the rest of yours. All that goes with marriage. I know there's going to be as much bad as good, and we'll fight and all that, but I knew when I met you at the YWCA that you were the girl for me. That was two and a half years ago, and here I am. What more do you want?"

Ruby felt the wet prickle of tears against her eyelids. It

sounded good. But they were words with . . . no feeling. Just words. "Okay," she said quietly.

"Feel better now?" Ruby shook her head, afraid if she spoke he would know how close she was to bawling.

"Listen, I'll try and get back up here in a few weeks, and we'll make all kinds of plans. I'll have more information by then on my transfer. I think we're both overwhelmed right now. And by the way, I don't recall hearing you say you love me, either," Andrew said peevishly.

Ruby turned his own words around and said, "I wouldn't agree to marry you if I didn't." It was such a monstrous lie, she almost choked. She would never love anyone again. Never ever.

Andrew looked uneasy. He squeezed Ruby's hand and shouted so loud, Ruby jumped. "We're getting goddamn married! Holy shit!"

Ruby giggled and he grinned, as if he knew it was what she wanted to hear.

Ruby doubled over laughing when Andrew started to sing "From the halls of Montezuma," the "Marine Hymn." Ruby joined in, her voice clear and loud, unlike his boisterous off-key singing. Like two schoolchildren caught doing something wrong, they cut off the words as Andrew drew the car to a halt in front of Ruby's apartment.

Andrew was out of the car in a second, rushing around to open the door for Ruby. He bowed low and gallantly, and offered her his arm. Giggling, they raced up the steps to the front porch, where Andrew immediately took her in his arms and kissed her resoundingly. Ruby was breathless when he released her minutes later. Andrew, Ruby saw with delight, was breathing like a long-distance runner.

"You're something, Ruby Connors," Andrew muttered as he backed away from her. "I . . . I'll call or write . . . you, ah, you aren't going anywhere in the next few weeks, are you?"

"Uh-uh." Ruby smiled in the darkness. "It was a nice weekend, Andrew. I guess I'll see you . . . whenever you get back."

"You bet," Andrew said, backing down the steps. Twice he almost lost his balance, but righted himself at the last second, to Ruby's amusement.

"Good night," he called softly.

" 'Night, Andrew."

Inside her room with the door closed tightly, Ruby swayed

dizzily. She'd just committed herself to marriage to a man she didn't love. She thought about her mother for a moment. If there was a time for a girl to talk to her mother, this was it. If only Nola was here. Right now she'd even settle for Amber. God, she must be nuts.

Ruby's aloneness depressed her. She should have made more of an effort to develop some friendships. She should have gone to more dances, even if she'd had to go alone, but instead she had burrowed in, like a mole.

Ruby had been the exception to most of the girls she knew in Washington. All the girls talked about in the cafeteria was how close they were to nailing some guy at the altar. Now she was just like them: about to get married for all the wrong reasons. She wished she knew what the statistics were for girls who married just for the sake of marrying. How many of those unions survived?

Damn you to hell, Calvin, this is your fault. Marriage was for a lifetime. Religion forbade a divorce. For better or worse. For richer or poorer. In sickness and health. Ruby whimpered as she dropped to her knees to open her bottom dresser drawer. She'd put the only birthday card she'd received this year in the drawer. From Amber. She'd been surprised until she opened it and realized why bitchy Amber sent it. Inside was a note saying Calvin had been in Saipan and had not asked about her at all. After his visit home, he had been transferred to the Mediterranean. Amber also said she was pregnant and expected to give birth sometime in early December. On a separate slip of paper was a list of things she could use for the baby.

Ruby rocked back and forth on her heels, crying. Amber having a baby. Amber married. It was more than Ruby could bear. "It's not fair. If even Amber can be happy and loved, why can't I? What did I do wrong?" The Mediterranean was on the other side of the world.

Ruby slammed the drawer shut. She wanted to throw the card into the wastebasket, but she didn't. It was the only thing Amber had ever given her. She'd send a present to the baby and sign the card Aunt Ruby. The thought brought a smile to her face. Aunt Ruby Blue, that's how she would sign it. Ruby Blue. Aunt Ruby. She loved the sound of the title.

She tried to sleep but couldn't. Twice she got up to go to the bathroom. When the clock on her dresser read midnight, she was still tossing and turning, and she knew why.

Ruby crawled from her bed and wrapped her housecoat about her trembling body. She was quiet as she tiptoed out to the kitchen and the back door. She was extra quiet as she made her way down the wooden stairs to the backyard. She found her way to the trash can and inched off the lid. The can was empty. Her mementos of Calvin were gone.

Tears streaming down her cheeks, she trudged to the back porch, where she sat down on the steps, barely noticing the chilly night. She cried, hiccoughing and sobbing, wiping her eyes and nose on the sleeve of her housecoat.

What seemed like an eternity later, Ruby heard Rena come up behind her. She cried harder. She hugged her knees to herself.

"Shhh," Rena crooned as she sat down next to Ruby. "If you want to talk about it, I'm a good listener."

Ruby told her about Andrew's proposal, her feelings, and the way she'd discarded the mementos of Calvin. She continued to cry. She wanted a mother, *needed* a mother.

"So you still love the young man. One never forgets one's first love. I understand," Rena said softly. "I think I can help a little. Excuse me, Ruby, I'll be right back." Minutes later, Rena returned with a small parcel. "I believe this belongs to you. As a rule, I do not go through trash cans, but I saw you that night. You looked so sad, so I said to myself, I should check what it was you were throwing away. Now I am glad I did. You aren't ready to let go of this young man. Tomorrow you must do everything in your power to find him. You cannot marry the marine until there is no more hope. You understand me, Ruby?" Ruby nodded miserably.

"He's on the other side of the world. If I couldn't get to him when he was in California, how will I be able to find him in the Mediterranean?"

"You work for the navy, Ruby. Surely there is someone who can help you. There are records."

"Every time I love something or someone, it's taken away from me. It happened with Calvin and it happened with Bubba. I *like* Andrew. I can see myself married to him and raising a family. And if I never love him, at least I'll know he won't be taken away from me," Ruby blubbered.

Recognizing that she was a poor substitute for a mother, Rena said, "Tomorrow morning before you leave for work, I want you to call your mother. Regardless of the differences between you, I'm sure she will have good answers for you. A mother shares with her daughter. Promise me you'll call her," Rena said quietly.

Ruby nodded glumly. Rena didn't know her mother. It was worth a try, though. She'd agree to anything as long as it wiped away this sick feeling that was engulfing her.

Rena stood up briskly. "Now it is time to go to bed. I am so cold, my teeth are chattering. Come along, Ruby, tomorrow you have a busy day. Hopefully, it will end the way you want it to. Shoo," she said, waving her hands as though she were chasing pesky chickens.

Ruby clutched the parcel in her hands as she climbed wearily to the second floor. She wasn't going to look at the contents; just having them back in her possession was enough.

As Ruby snuggled down to sleep, she realized she'd resurrected Calvin Santos from the dead.

The following morning Ruby waited until all the girls left before she walked down the hall to the living room. She was going to call her mother. She settled herself on the lemon-colored sofa and looked at the hands on her watch. Her father left for work at seven o'clock. She would wait fifteen minutes, time enough for her mother to clear the breakfast table. Opal would still be upstairs, getting ready for school. The minutes crawled by, the hands on her Timex barely moving. She was trembling violently when she had the operator place the call. The phone rang seven times before her mother picked it up. Ruby had to clear her throat twice before she could get the words out.

"Mom, it's Ruby. I need to talk to you. Please, don't hang up. Just listen. Pop, is gone, so there's no reason you can't talk to me." But there was. There was Millie, the operator, who was probably listening in. Her mother knew it, too. It was a shitty idea to call. "Mom, I'm getting married. Sometime in December. I wanted you to know. I called to ask you something. I wouldn't have called, but this is very important to me. Did you love Pop when you married him? I feel something for Andrew, but it isn't what I felt for Calvin. Pop ruined that for me. Will what happened to you . . . will that happen to me if I marry Andrew? Mom, say something, please, for God's sake, I'm your daughter, I have no one else to talk to. Look, I know you're afraid . . . get out of there, take Opal with you. Uncle John will take care of you ... Mom, are you there? Damn you, I bet you don't even know Amber's going to have a baby. Well, she is, in December. Mom, is it going to kill you if you talk to me? Mom, please, just this once, help me." When there was no reply she said, "Bubba was right, you are a gutless wonder. I hope I never turn out like you. If I do, I'll kill myself. Good-bye, Mom." She slammed down the phone.

Not a word. She hadn't said a word other than hello. Perhaps she'd hung up and Ruby had been talking to an empty line.

A sick feeling settled in Ruby's stomach. The feeling was so strong, she clamped her hand over her mouth. What if chatterbox Millie spread the word, and her father found out and beat her mother again? God, Ruby, that was the stupidest thing you ever did. She wanted to cry, to rant and rave, to kick and smash something. She couldn't do any of those things, so she loaded an extra measure of guilt on her shoulders. She felt weighed down by it as she walked to the bus stop.

She was on her own the way she'd always been. She'd make her own decisions, right or wrong, and live with them. *Until death do us part.* Her own personal death sentence, if she went through with her marriage to Andrew.

Ruby worked liked a beaver all morning to clear her desk. At eleven o'clock she asked Admiral Query if she could take an extended lunch hour. Forty-five minutes later Ruby was at the Navy Annex, remembering the first day she'd come here with Amber. She wondered if the few people she'd taken the time to know were still there. Government personnel seemed to stay in their jobs till they retired or died. It wasn't a happy thought.

Mabel McIntyre's eyes sparkled when Ruby introduced herself. "Do you remember me, Miss McIntyre?"

The personnel director smiled and nodded. "Very well, Ruby. You don't mind if I call you Ruby, do you?" Her bright eyes took in Ruby's glen plaid suit and tailored white blouse. "I hope you're here to ask for a job."

"I'm afraid not. I did ... I want to ask a favor of you, Miss McIntyre. If you ... can't or if it's against the ... I don't want to cause a problem, it's just ... this is so important to me, and I didn't ... I ... I need to locate someone in the air force. Can you help me?" Ruby blurted out, her face changing color and her eyes filling.

Mabel's pink cheeks puffed out, and her springy gray curls seemed to stand at attention. She was heavier, Ruby thought, but she still had the kindest face she'd ever seen. Her eyes, though, bothered Ruby; they were full of pity. She's disappointed in me, Ruby thought in dismay. She watched as the director searched for a pencil.

"Name, rank, and serial number," she said briskly. Ruby rattled them off.

"This ... Miss McIntyre, this isn't what you think ... what I mean is, I don't know what you're thinking, but if I were in your position, I would be thinking ... it's not like that ... I need to get in touch with Lieutenant Santos before I get married."

"For a prospective bride, you don't look real happy," Mabel said bluntly.

Ruby nodded. "I guess I'm still in a daze. It just happened ... Andrew proposed last night, and I ... I'm ... I said yes, but ..."

"You want to be sure. I understand, Ruby. Look, I'll do my best. Is it all right to call you at the office?" Ruby nodded and wrote down the number and extension.

"I should have this information by noon tomorrow. Is that soon enough?"

"That's fine. I won't tell anyone about this," Ruby said quietly. ·

"I won't tell anyone, either," Mabel said softly. "Let's just call it our little secret, okay?"

"Thanks, Miss McIntyre, I really appreciate what you're doing for me. If I can ever do anything for you, just ask."

"Be happy, Ruby." Mabel leaned across her desk. "Take a good look at me. I've been in this job so long, I'm part of the furnishings. I'm an old maid waiting to collect my pension. All I have to show for my life is a small apartment in Arlington and two old tomcats. I let the right man get away from me once because I thought ... there was something better around the corner. There wasn't. Go after what you want and don't be afraid. My advice to you, my dear, is to follow your heart, cornball as it sounds."

* * *

Somehow, Ruby managed to get through the rest of the day and the next morning, until Mabel McIntyre called her at two P.M.

Ruby held her breath as she scribbled frantically, taking down every single word the personnel director uttered.

Mabel McIntyre's voice lowered to a bare whisper. "Ruby, why don't you think of a reason to call Clark Air Force Base? Doesn't the old reprobate still play chess? Tell him there's an officer there who is a champion chess player, or make up some story. You'll have to be devious, can you do that? Lord, I don't believe I'm telling you this. Whatever you do, good luck," the personnel director said, breaking the connection.

In longhand Ruby transcribed the squiggly notes. Calvin Santos was stationed at Clark Air Force Base in the Philippines, recently transferred from Germany, and would be transferred again very shortly to Yokota Air Force Base in Japan. The last transcribed squiggly marks were the main telephone number for Clark.

A quick glance at the maritime chart pasted on the pull-out tray of her desk told her she would have to wait till, at the very least, seven o'clock to call the Philippines because they were twelve hours behind the eastern United States.

Ruby's thoughts were frenzied as she contemplated how she could call Clark, using the military line on her desk. If she got caught, she could get fired. Instinct told her to be bold and brazen and just do it and suffer the consequences. Logic that wasn't working at full capacity warned her to go slow and create a cover story for the phone call.

God, why was she going through this? Where's your pride?

"I don't have any," she whispered, "when it comes to Calvin." Two and a half years is a long time. *He could have gotten in touch with you if he wanted to. His career is more important than you are,* her conscience needled. *There's no way you can justify his silence where you're concerned. You're making a fool of yourself.* "I have to try. Circumstances . . . maybe something . . . his commanding officer must have scared him with my father's threat. Once more, just once more. If I can't get through this time, then . . . then I'll forget him once and for all. Marriage is too big a step to take . . . I have to be sure, really sure," Ruby whispered.

The cover story, the lie, when she came up with it ten minutes later, was almost foolproof, Ruby thought.

For weeks now the admiral had been dithering about an up-coming chess game between himself and a Marine Corps general who, according to the admiral, was a top-notch player.

Ruby poked her head in the door of the admiral's office. "Sir, I just thought of something. It might help you next week in your chess game. A friend of mine told me there's a lieutenant stationed at Clark Air Force Base in the Philippines who is a cracker-jack chess player. Apparently he hates the army and the marines but is partial to the navy. Maybe he knows something about this general's game. I've heard he's played half the brass in all four services. I could call him after seven and see if he can help. I don't mind staying late."

"Damn good idea, Ruby. What would I do without you? I was just saying to Mrs. Query last night that without you I couldn't keep it all together. Run it up the flagpole, Ruby."

"Yes, sir," Ruby lied.

It wasn't until the admiral left for his barber that Ruby realized she'd boxed herself into a corner. When no Air Force chess player surfaced, how was she going to explain it to the admiral? Lord, what if he decided to call Clark himself and asked her for the name of the fictitious chess player? If there was one thing the admiral took seriously, it was his chess game. Ruby groaned.

Precisely at six o'clock, her heart hammering in her chest, Ruby dialed the Pentagon operator and placed her call. While she waited for the call to go through, she sucked on a long peel of orange rind. When a voice with a southern drawl came on the line, Ruby almost fainted.

"Clark Air Force Base, Airman Cummings speaking."

Ruby's voice turned brisk and professional. "This is Admiral Query's office in the Pentagon, Airman. The admiral would like to speak with Lieutenant Calvin Santos."

The airman snapped to full alert at the mention of the admiral's name. "I'll have to put you on hold, ma'am, till I see if I can locate the lieutenant. It's only six A.M here," he said.

"Admiral Query says the military rises at five. Do your best, Airman."

Ruby waited, her forehead beaded with sweat, for five minutes, and then another five minutes crawled by until the southern-sounding voice came on the line. Ruby's heart thumped wildly.

"Lieutenant Santos is stateside, ma'am. Would you care to leave a message?"

"Stateside! You mean here in the States?" Ruby squealed, forgetting she was in a professional call. "Where stateside?" she managed to croak.

"I have no idea, ma'am," the airman responded.

"Airman, that is not a response Admiral Query will accept. I suggest you run that one up the flagpole again and find out exactly where he is. I'll hold."

"Ma'am, that means I have to wake the lieutenant's commanding officer," the airman said hesitantly.

"I see your quandary, Airman. Perhaps it should be Admiral Query himself who wakes the lieutenant's commanding officer. The admiral doesn't much care for grunts, shavetails and pissants, Airman," Ruby said coolly.

Ruby smiled when she heard the airman groan. "My ass is going to be in a sling. Major Oliver said he wasn't to be awakened unless the base was on fire. Sorry, ma'am, I forgot I was talking to a lady. I'll get him on the horn, hold on."

Ruby wondered idly what the navy did to civilian employees who used their boss's name under false pretenses. She waited, her fingers drumming on the desk. She was so close to finding Calvin. Stateside. She could call him, offer to visit. Her heart soared. Finally.

"Major Oliver," a voice barked. Ruby went through her spiel a second time. She only half heard the major's comment about goddamn Navy fish who thought they ran the world. "Lieutenant Santos is on leave. He checked out a week ago and went stateside."

Ruby's hackles rose. "I know that, Major, so does the admiral. Admiral Query wants to know *exactly* where Lieutenant Santos is stateside."

"Charleston Air Base in South Carolina. He checked in on arrival. He may have left an address. Will that be all, miss?"

"Yes. Thank you, Major." Ruby thought she heard a chuckle on the other end of the phone.

Ruby hugged her shorthand notes to her chest, a look of pure bliss on her face. Calvin was here in the States, in South Carolina. Should she call now or wait till morning? Lightheaded with the thought, she leaned back in her chair, forcing herself to take deep breaths. She felt as though she'd just awakened from a deep sleep.

There was a sparkle in Ruby's eyes and a breathless lilt in her voice when she placed the second call. Still using Admiral Query's name, she waited while the airman in Charleston checked his records. The sparkle left her eyes instantly, and her voice turned flat when the faceless voice said, "Lieutenant Santos checked in a week ago today before going on leave. He's not required to list his final destination, ma'am. He will be in the state of South Carolina, that's all I can tell you. Does the admiral want to leave a message for Lieutenant Santos?"

In the same flat-sounding voice, Ruby said yes and left her office number.

Ruby gathered up her notes, folding them neatly before stuffing them into her purse.

All the way home on the bus Ruby told herself over and over, if it's meant to be, it will be. Her gut told her it would not be, that Calvin would not forgive her and was still probably blaming her for the trouble her father caused him with his commanding officer. *You could have written me a letter, Calvin, a note, something to tell me you didn't hate me.*

It wasn't until she was in her room with the door closed that she realized she was making a fool of her herself. She had to make a decision now and stick to it. She wasn't being fair to Andrew. She'd accepted his proposal and, he, she thought, had every right to believe she was making plans to go through with the wedding. And, she told herself, she didn't believe for one minute that Charleston didn't know where Calvin was, even though she'd backed down and accepted the airman's explanation.

A sick feeling settled in the pit of Ruby's stomach. The simple fact, and one she'd better come to terms with, was she was not going to hear from Calvin Santos. She'd hurt him too deeply, and because of who he was, he was not going to risk being hurt again. *Damn you, Calvin, damn you to hell!* Ruby cried silently. *Why couldn't you trust me? Why?*

The days dragged on, one after the other, and somehow Ruby managed to get through them, all the while keeping her eye on the calendar. On the last day of Calvin's leave Ruby deliberately called Holy Trinity Church and made arrangements to be married on December 10, at three o'clock in the afternoon. On the evening of the same day she called Andrew to ask if the time and place were agreeable. He said his three-day leave was confirmed. They talked a few minutes longer with Andrew promising to write that evening. Ruby smiled for the benefit of the girls in the living room. They were happy for her and possibly a little envious. She'd asked Rena to be her matron of honor, and she'd agreed.

Tomorrow Calvin would be back in the Philippines. Actually, with the time difference, it was already tomorrow at Clark Air Force Base. It was entirely possible that Calvin had her message in his hand even now, that moment. It seemed like months ago that she'd left the message for him. One good thing had come out of her deviousness. She'd gone to the library and taken a book out on the art of chess playing. Novice and as inexpert as he was, her boss had grabbed at the moves she'd written down for his benefit. He'd won his game with the Marine general and believed implicitly that Ruby's call to the Philippines had saved his neck. He'd even given her a bouquet of roses for her desk in thanks.

Ruby lay awake all night, her thoughts chaotic. She thought about Barstow and her parents, about Opal, wondering how she was doing, about Amber and Nangi and the new baby who would make such a wonderful Christmas for them. That was what she wanted, a real family with a Christmas tree, a place where she was always welcome.

It was five in the morning when she crept down the hall to the bathroom to get ready for work. The stress she'd put herself through these past weeks was evident. She looked haggard and drawn with dark shadows under her eyes. She was indeed a pitiful sight for a prospective bride.

The day seemed endless, the minutes and seconds crawling by so slowly that Ruby's skin itched from frustration. Each time the phone rang she drew a deep breath to compose herself before answering. Instead of going to lunch in the cafeteria, she asked one of the girls in the next office to bring her a sandwich, which she looked at but didn't eat. She was too fearful of leaving the office in case Calvin called.

Ruby was still at her desk at six o'clock. She was rearranging the files at six-thirty. At seven o'clock she retyped a personal letter for the admiral that had eleven mistakes on the first page.

She crumpled it into a ball and tossed it into the wastebasket. At seven-thirty she covered her typewriter and blew imaginary dust off her desk. She ran a comb through her hair, put on fresh lipstick, and powdered her nose.

Calvin should have called. The twelve-hour difference made the time seven-fifty. Perhaps he remembered Admiral Query was her boss and knew the call was from her. But did he dare not respond to an admiral's call? Calvin was so persnickety about things that could do damage to his career.

It was two minutes till eight when Ruby, her shoulders slumping, her steps dragging, closed the office behind her. A lump the size of a golf ball was lodged in her throat. Her eyes burned as she stepped into the elevator. If the door hadn't closed with such a loud swoosh and clatter, she would have heard the phone on her desk ring. It rang eighteen times before it turned silent.

Ruby walked into the night, grateful for the darkness that cloaked her shame. What a fool she was.

The next day she sent a postcard to her parents, informing them of her upcoming marriage. Tears rolled down her cheeks when she dropped the card in the mailbox. "Please, Mom, be happy for me. Think about me sometime. If you can't do that, stiffen your backbone and give Pop what-for."

George Connors threw the mail on the kitchen table. His eyes dared his wife to pick it up. She didn't. She kept on peeling the potatoes in front of her.

"Did you talk to the new neighbors, Irma?"

"No, George. I did hear them complaining about the grape stains on the back steps and on the kitchen linoleum. I was shaking the dust mop, that's how I heard them. They said they were going to sand the steps and replace the linoleum."

"Is it worn out?" George asked.

"I don't know, George."

"I'll be going back to work next week. My disability has run out. They need me down at the monument works."

"I'm sure they do, George. Mr. Riley said you were the best stonecutter he ever saw."

George Connors' eyes narrowed. "How do you know that, Irma?"

"You told me that, George."

"Ruby Connors is getting married, Irma. To a marine. She sent a card."

"Do you approve, George?"

"Don't approve or disapprove. I don't have a daughter named Ruby anymore. Opal is getting sassy, Irma."

"I'll talk to her, George."

"There's a letter on the table addressed to you from Grace Zachary, Irma."

The paring knife slipped and Irma gouged her thumb. "Did you read it, George?"

"No, I thought you should read it to me. Maybe we should just tear it up and not bother to read it. Why would she be writing to you?"

Irma watched a trickle of blood form on a potato. She picked up the paring knife and held it firmly in her hand. She raised her head. "Maybe she can't hold in her secret anymore. Maybe she wants to tell me how you raped her and she's the one who doused you with the grape jelly. Did you know Amber had a baby, George?"

"You get yourself upstairs and wash out your mouth with soap, Irma. Now."

"I don't feel like it. Don't raise your hand to me. If you do, I'll kill you when you're asleep. Do you want carrots or peas?"

"Both," George said, moving closer to the table. "What did you say?"

"I said I would kill you if you raised your hand to me again. I will, too. Your brothers will be on my side. So will this whole town if I tell them what you've done to all of us. You're a devil, George."

George's hand snaked out to grasp his wife's arm, but Irma was too quick for him. The paring knife was clutched in her hand, the blade pointing straight at George. With the kitchen chair in front of her she brandished the knife like a sword. "I mean it, George. Now, I want you to go and change your underwear. You smell like pissy-pants. Your tube must be clogged again. I'm going to read my mail. I wish Grace had killed you. I prayed all night that you would die. I promised myself I would kill you. Sometime. I don't know when. Maybe next week. Maybe tomorrow. I think you should move into Ruby's room. Yes, you should move into Ruby's room . . . Georgie. Go on, Georgie, don't stand there, looking at me like that. You brought shame on this house. Shame on you, Georgie," Irma said, wagging her finger in his direction. "Shame, shame, shame."

Even though the humidity was near the eighty-percent mark, Clark Air Force Base hummed with activity. Calvin Santos bristled with something akin to electricity. In his hand were two messages. When he first saw them and realized their implication, the blood rushed to his head. He remembered the major, but that's all he remembered. Now he was remembering how he'd done his best to call her once before, only Ruby wasn't in the office and the admiral had taken the call. He shouted his message as loud as he could, but the admiral, who Ruby had once said was hard of hearing, didn't seem to be getting it. He'd called a second and third time and didn't fare any better. He'd written two letters and sent them to the house on Kilbourne Place, but they'd come back to him with a stamp on both of them saying the addressee had moved. He'd sent one letter to the Navy Annex, but it had also been returned. He assumed Ruby no longer worked for the government. A month to the day of his arrival at Beale he'd been transferred to Germany. He'd made one last desperate try and sent a letter to Ruby's home in Barstow, hoping against hope that her parents would forward it. His thinking was, if Ruby moved, she'd moved up to a better job. There was always the goddamn time difference no matter where he was. What he didn't understand then and still didn't understand and would probably never come to terms with was why Ruby hadn't left a forwarding address. By sheer luck he'd remembered the name of the town where Nola grew up and sent a letter to her for Ruby's address. That letter and the one he'd sent to Barstow had not been returned to him.

Now, after all this time, Ruby had managed to track him down. *Now, when it was too late.* His stomach heaved and he felt another head rush.

Calvin placed his call, his knuckles white on the receiver. How was he going to tell Ruby he was married? He still didn't believe it himself. Actually, he didn't want to believe it. While he waited for the call to go through he thought about his new wife.

Eve Baylor was seven years his senior and hailed from Charleston, South Carolina. He'd met her at the Officers' Club in Charleston. He'd been drawn to her because she looked as unhappy as he felt. He'd been cautious, though, waiting to see if her plain, schoolmarmish appearance appealed to any of the other officers. It took all of thirty minutes to screw up the courage to walk over to her table, certain he would be rebuffed for his efforts. She'd accepted his offer to buy her a drink. She'd been polite, nothing more. An hour into a strained conversation, she had said she hated men, and Calvin had responded by saying he hated women. Neither discussed the reasons for their feelings.

A friendship of sorts blossomed based on mutual loneliness. She was a teacher and had a manner of speaking that irritated Calvin. She was also bossy, dictatorial, and manipulative, but Calvin didn't care; she was someone to spend his lonely hours with. He thought of her as a friend, and, as such, wanted to tell her about Ruby, but something always held him back. He never felt the urge to kiss her or hold her hand in a romantic way. Secretly, he thought her a cold fish and pitied the poor guy who eventually got her into his bed. He'd tried to be open with her, telling her stories about his fellow officers and a few off-color jokes, but she didn't respond the way he hoped she would. He came to the conclusion she was frigid and a prude as well. She was also a Southern Baptist, and that bothered him. When it came right down to it, everything about her bothered him.

As the months wore on, however, Calvin found himself getting used to her sharp tongue, her mannerisms, and way of doing things. He felt comfortable with Eve because he didn't care. It was that simple.

The Sunday she invited him to her parents' home for dinner was an experience he would never forget.

He'd taken the military bus from the base and got off in the Battery section and walked the four short blocks to Eve's house. His first sight of Eve's home left him gasping. It was beautiful with its wrap-around porch and stained glass windows. The azaleas and oaks surrounding the house had to be at least a hundred years old. He couldn't begin to imagine what it would have been like to grow up in a house as wonderful as this one. He was so overcome with longing and the need to belong, he didn't notice the chipped and missing cobblestones in the walkway or the rotting, peeling paint on the veranda or the dry rot in the porch floor. His gaze was so taken with the upper portion of the stained glass windows, he missed their rotting frames.

The doorbell was in the shape of a brass key. He turned it clockwise, blinking. It sounded like a dirge. He stared around the wide veranda with its ancient wicker furniture and wondered if the furniture was safe to sit on.

The massive oak door groaned as it opened, and Eve ushered him into the house which smelled of eucalyptus, cat urine, and the kind of liniment he rubbed on his aching legs after a hike. The smell was so overpowering, he started to breathe through his mouth.

Heat poured out of registers in the floor, and he noticed a raging fire in the massive fieldstone fireplace. The urge to bolt was strong, but he planted his feet solidly on the dull oak floor while he waited for Eve to introduce him to her family.

He'd assumed that Eve had told them about him, so he wasn't prepared for their gaping expressions at the sight of him. Her father, stone-faced, didn't offer his hand in greeting. Calvin did his best to stare him down but was unsuccessful. A retired colonel, he still favored his brush cut. Formidable, Calvin thought, and bigoted. He shook his head in something Calvin interpreted as disgust.

Eve's mother was an older version of Eve. Straight-backed, every hair in place, her face and neck powdered, with the fine granules lying in her deep wrinkles. Calvin wondered crazily if she was wearing a mask. She was dressed in an outdated, faded purple dress with a high neckline and wore a cameo brooch that called attention to her stringy neck. Austere, Calvin decided when her face remained cool and unwelcoming. She had the coldest eyes Calvin had ever seen.

The sister, Bea, was older than Eve and looked so much like her, they could have passed for twins. There was no welcoming smile on her face, either.

The introductions over, Eve led him into the front parlor, where the fire raged. She motioned for him to sit down and offered him a glass of wine, which he spilled when a huge black cat leapt onto his shoulder. Irene, Eve's mother, clucked her tongue in disapproval before she ordered Bea to "see to this mess." Eve refilled his glass while Timothy, her father, kept shaking his head. He wasn't passing muster, of that Calvin was sure.

The silence was so uncomfortable, it was deadly. Eve did nothing to break the silence, sitting with her ankles crossed and her hands folded in her lap as Bea trooped into the room with a bucket and a basket of rags and wiped the spill.

Minutes later, at some prearranged silent signal, the family rose and walked single file into the dining room, which was dark and dreary.

The room had a musty, unused smell, but even here he could smell the cat urine and liniment. No attempt had been made to wipe the dust from the mahogany sideboard or from the immense crystal chandelier hanging over the middle of the table. His visit was an inconvenience, and no attempt had been made to impress him. Eve pointed to a seat next to hers. He was about to hold the chair for her, when she sat down and pulled it closer to the table.

Calvin risked a glance at Irene as she said grace. Her thin lips barely moved. The words said she was thanking God for the food they were about to eat, but the tone was sharp and belligerent, as though she didn't want to share it with their guest. Without thinking, Calvin blessed himself and was rewarded with three piercing stares of disapproval. He knew, even though he couldn't see Eve's eyes, that they looked the same. *What in the goddamn hell was he doing here?*

"We don't talk during our meal," Timothy Baylor said in a voice choked with rage. Eve, Calvin knew, was going to be the recipient of that rage the minute he left.

After dinner, when he stepped into the bathroom, he heard the three women talking about him in the kitchen, their words carrying distinctly through the heat register. He listened, his shoulders slumping. The sisters were calling each other old maids.

"If he's the best you can do, then you deserve him. You're shaming us. He's the same as a nigger!" the mother said coldly. "Your father almost had a stroke. You had no right to bring someone like that into this house. Your granddaddy had slaves who were as dark as he is. You have no shame, Eve, none at all. The neighbors saw him coming here, what will they think of us?"

Calvin's face flamed. He sat down on the toilet to stop the trembling in his legs. He didn't realize he was holding his breath until he let it out with a loud swoosh. The least Eve could have done was defend him. For Christ's sake, they were friends, nothing more. What kind of people were the Baylors? *What kind of person was Eve?*

Calvin's hand was on the doorknob when he heard Bea cry, "I had a chance to get married, but you and father didn't like Jason because he had a lame leg. You said he wasn't an asset to this family. Now he has a family of his own, he built his own house, and is vice president of the Charleston Bank. You ruined my life!"

"That will be enough from you, missy," Irene said sharply. "You can't be blaming your father and me because you don't have husbands. Neither one of you can hold a real man."

Calvin slammed the bathroom door behind him and stormed out of the house. He was on the cobblestones before he realized Eve was following him.

"Are we still going to the movies on Wednesday?"

Calvin swiveled on his heel. "I thought we were friends, for God's sake. Why did you do this to me? If this is southern hospitality, you can keep it!"

"You didn't answer me, Calvin. Are we going to the movies on Wednesday or not?"

"Why? Do you have dates lined up around the corner?" Calvin snarled.

"Is that a yes or a no?" Eve demanded.

"I'm going. If you want to go, meet me outside the theater." What the hell else could he say?

The months that followed were much the same. Twice more he went to the Baylor house and couldn't explain why he tortured himself. The day Timothy Baylor called him "boy" as though he were addressing a slave he knew he would never fit in. He told Eve he never wanted to go back.

"Then don't," she said.

Three months later, on a warm Saturday afternoon at a sidewalk cafe, Calvin said he was being sent to the Philippines. "I'm going on a temporary basis and will return in six weeks and then go back for my hitch. I leave on Monday. And, as soon as we finish our coffee I have to leave. If you want, I'll write." He stared across at Eve. He still didn't know this strange woman sitting across from him. He referred to her as a friend, but so far they'd not shared anything more than dinner, a cup of coffee, or a movie. Maybe if she were prettier, a little younger, or if she had a sense of humor, he would have made more of an effort. If he had to sum up their strange relationship, he would say they were two lonely people who shared time together once in a while. He wondered if he would miss her, if he would mind being alone again in a strange country. Then he did something he thought himself incapable of doing, something so insane he wanted to rip out his tongue the minute the words left his mouth. He said, "Do you want to get married?"

There was no smile on Eve's plain face, no light of excitement in her eyes the way there had been when he had asked Ruby the same thing. She seemed to be weighing his question, mulling it over in her mind as though she weren't sure of what he said. "I don't have anything else to do. I guess it's a good idea."

"You do!" Calvin gasped in surprise. "I . . . I thought . . . what you said was . . . you hated men. I'm a man." Jesus, had he really said that aloud?

"You said you hated women. At least we have that in common. I'm not getting any younger," she said bluntly. "I would like to have a child. You don't seem to fare too well in the female department, so if I'm willing to accept you as you are, then you can accept me."

"Your family . . ." Calvin said desperately.

"You won't be here, so why worry about them? Their attitudes are their problems, not yours. They're never going to accept you; you have to understand that."

Calvin's heart pounded in his chest. He had to get out of this. "Why don't we wait till I come back? This way we'll both have time to think about it. It's a serious step, and I don't want to alienate you from your family. As you said, I have trouble meeting women, and as your mother said in the kitchen, you don't do well in hanging on to a man." This last was said with bitterness, although he felt contrite when he saw Eve flinch.

If there was one thing Eve Baylor dreaded more than anything in the world, it was becoming an old maid. In the South, a woman didn't count for anything unless she had a *Mrs.* in front of her name. A husband and a child made her respectable.

"I don't need time to think, Calvin. If you're serious, then I'm serious. We can decide right now before you leave. You'll want me to convert to Catholicism, won't you?" Calvin nodded weakly. "Then I can take instructions while you're away. When you return, we can get married quietly in your priest's house, not the church, because my family will throw a fit. I might not even tell them I'm converting until ... until I'm an actual Catholic. The question is, Calvin, are you serious?"

Calvin cleared his throat. Now his honor was at stake. By one careless, impulsive move, his whole life was changing right before his eyes. Was he serious? Hell no, he wasn't. The only problem was, he didn't know how to get out of the mess he'd just stuck both feet into without seeming an out-and-out skunk. "I suppose I'm as serious as you are."

"I guess it's settled, then. I'll make the arrangements when I go to the church to sign up for the conversion program, or whatever you call it. I'll write you."

"How can you do that when you don't have my address?"

"I'll have to wait to hear from you, and then I'll write. Do you feel all right, Calvin? You look a little pale."

"No, I'm fine. I have a lot on my mind."

"Is there anything you want to talk about? Anything you want to share with me, secrets you want to unburden?" Eve asked suddenly.

"Should there be? I don't seem to recall you sharing any with me. I *do* recall hearing your mother say there was a long string of men before me. Do you want to talk about *that*?"

"No, I don't. We'll start fresh. Your business is yours and mine is mine. One thing, though, Calvin, I want your word that you will never be unfaithful to me. I want your word as an officer and a gentleman."

Calvin shrugged. "You have it. What about you, do I have your word?"

"You don't have to worry about me, Calvin. I really do hate men. So if you ever shame me, I'll make your life miserable until the day you die."

Calvin shivered in the warm sun. "Since I really do hate women, I don't think that's going to be much of a problem."

As good as his word, he'd returned to Charleston in six weeks and married Eve at four o'clock on a Saturday afternoon. The church secretary was Eve's matron of honor and his best man was the janitor. Eve's sister and parents did not attend the wedding. Calvin considered their absence a blessing.

An hour after the wedding they drove in Eve's rattletrap car to Columbia for their honeymoon, a honeymoon that was a total disaster as far as Calvin was concerned. His face and ears turned

various shades of red as he remembered the shame and humili-
ation of his wedding night.

Anxious, yet excited, he didn't bother to remove his pajamas
and undershorts that he'd bought for his honeymoon. He was
light-headed with anticipation as he rolled on top of Eve and
ejaculated almost immediately. He reared back, his head snapping at an awkward angle when Eve screeched, "I thought you
knew what to do!"

In his shame and dizziness he forgot to be a gentleman. "I
didn't know you were so damn knowledgeable. I thought you
were a virgin!" he accused.

Eve jerked away from her new husband. "I didn't think *you*
were a virgin. Men your age aren't suppose to be virgins," Eve
said, her voice dripping venom. "If you were wearing any more
clothes, you'd be outfitted for a ski team."

"Don't talk about what I'm wearing, look at yourself. New
brides usually wear silky, slinky nightgowns. You look like an
old woman in those pajamas, and you have on a bra and under-
pants, Jesus, how was I supposed . . . this is our goddamn wedding night." Embarrassment and anger drove him on. "I couldn't
even find your . . . oh, shit!"

"You found it and shot off as soon as you did. What about
me? Slam, bam, thank you, ma'am," Eve said, rolling over on
her side of the bed.

"You mean I was *in*!" Calvin said stupidly. A split second
later he wanted to bite off his tongue when Eve rolled back over
and slapped him in the face.

"Are you saying I'm so *big* you got . . . you didn't . . . oh,
you hateful bastard. You're too *small* is more like it!"

Calvin recoiled. It was the final insult to his heritage and his
manhood. He wanted to reach out and strangle his new wife. His
manhood demanded he retaliate. "As compared to who!" he
barked. "How many, Eve, how many before me? Give me numbers and measurements. Now I know why you hate men," he
ground on. "And I was the fool who married you! Well, we can
change that real quick. When we get back to Charleston, we'll
file for divorce! You're just a damn dried-up old maid." If he'd
thought for days and weeks, he couldn't have come up with anything that would hurt Eve more. He saw the tears in her eyes
and the way she cowered up close to the headboard of the bed.
She'd struck the first blow, why shouldn't he retaliate?

Divorced on her honeymoon! She'd never live it down and would be the laughingstock of Charleston. Dumped on her honeymoon by a damn ... damn foreigner! She couldn't let that happen. Her parents ... her friends ... this was no time for stupid pride. In a voice she hardly recognized as her own she set about trying to make things right.

"Calvin, we're both upset. Things ... we said things we didn't mean, at least I did. I'm sorry. It's just that ... we each expected ... certain things ... we should have talked, shared our thoughts and what it was we expected ... I'll take half the blame for that. Going against my parents ... it's been traumatic for me ... here in the South, women are brought up differently ... what I said was hateful and I'm sorry. I'm willing to put this evening behind us and do my best to make up for your ... disappointment." She risked a glance at him, then threw in the clunker. "I changed my religion for you, and you know the Catholic Church forbids divorce. I changed my religion, Calvin. I don't know too many women who would do that for the man they marry." His countenance remained stony. "Let's get it all out in the open, Calvin, You are different. You're not white and I am. You're from a different culture, a different land. That's one of the things we should have discussed. We can't pretend you're the same as me because you're not. I accept you, and you'll have to accept me. I want to try again. Not right away. Tomorrow will do or the day after. It's up to you."

If she'd smiled or softened her voice, Calvin might have believed her. He capitulated only because he knew he'd be excommunicated from the church if he filed for divorce. He nodded, not trusting himself to speak. Their eyes locked. Eve was the first to break eye contact.

Calvin straightened the covers on his side of the bed and prepared for sleep. He didn't think about the past hour and his wife's pleadings. Instead, he thought about Ruby Connors and how their wedding night would have been.

Five days later Calvin boarded the plane for the Philippines, leaving behind his new wife, who would join him in a month's time.

Marrying Eve Baylor was the biggest mistake of his life. He knew it, and so did Eve.

Calvin was jolted back to the present when the operator told him there was no answer at the Pentagon. He wiped the sweat dripping into his eyes. Of course there was no answer at the Pentagon, it was after eight in the evening. Ruby worked late once in a while, but usually not past seven. The operator was asking him if he wanted to leave a message. "No, I'll call later."

Calvin stared at the black telephone for a full five minutes. He could call this evening when he was off duty if he wanted to. What good would it do? Calling now had been purely reflexive. Later he would have to really think about everything. What was that old saying? Let sleeping dogs lie. Calling Ruby now would serve no purpose. He was a married man and had given up his right to pursue happiness. "I'm sorry, Ruby," he murmured, "so very sorry."

The days were all the same now, Ruby thought as she window-shopped on 14th Street for her trousseau. It was going to be skimpy at best: a few new items of underwear, a nightgown that was sinfully sheer and wickedly expensive. When she'd tried on the sheer black froth of lace, she'd blushed from head to toe. She'd showed it to Rena the day she bought it. The little woman had clapped her hands gleefully and said it was exquisitely decadent.

Her roommates were giving her a shower and inviting some of the girls from work, along with Rena. She knew she'd get presents and had tactfully tried to mention little things she thought she might need, though nothing expensive, as all the girls lived on strict budgets.

She stopped to peer into a shop window at a dress she thought might be appropriate for her wedding. It was outrageously expensive, well beyond her budget. She smiled at her reflection in the plate-glass window. She knew exactly what Nola would say. Go buy a basic beige dress and do the trim yourself. Ruby stared at the creation in the window and mentally calculated the cost of the seed pearls, the lace, and the tiny pearl-covered buttons. She could probably buy all that for two dollars, maybe three. Of course she'd be blind by the time she finished sewing all of them onto her dress, providing she could find a dress.

She wanted her wedding to be the best she could make it, and for all intents and purposes it was measuring up very well. Rena had agreed to hold the small reception in her living room, which would comfortably take care of her dozen guests. Her roommates agreed to chip in and make a wide variety of finger foods. Rena offered to buy the champagne, and Bruno had beamed with approval. Tight as she was with a dollar, Ruby was a little surprised at Rena's generosity. She also wondered if she would be slapped with a small fee at some point.

Ruby's thoughts turned to her real estate project as she meandered down 14th Street, her eyes alert for a beige dress. In just three days she would close the deal on both houses. So far, no hidden costs had sprung up to haunt her. She'd paid her overseas call to Saipan, managed to buy the few items for her trousseau, and still had seventy dollars in the bank. All of Rena's little fees were also taken care of. She had renters who would take possession two days after the closing. It had all gone so smoothly, she was hardly aware of what was going on.

Rena had asked her where she planned to keep the deeds to the property and if she didn't plan to include her soon-to-be husband. "And how do you plan to pay your mortgage and collect the rent?" the little woman asked curiously. It was decided finally that for a small fee, Rena would collect the rents and deposit the money into a checking account in Ruby's name. For an additional fee she would make monthly withdrawals and pay the mortgage in cash. This last had been tricky, but the bank manager had gone along with the plan once he realized Ruby was moving out of state. For yet another small fee and a supply of stamps and envelopes, Rena had agreed to send on receipts once things were settled down and operational. Minus all of Rena's fees, the mortgage, and the utility bills, Ruby was left with sixty dollars a month.

Once Ruby had it all down securely in her mind, she made a special trip to the bank and spoke to the manager herself. She asked to have forty dollars sent to her parents on the first of the month. The remaining twenty dollars would be left to accumulate in her small savings account. She felt pleased with herself when she walked out of the bank. She wasn't going to take anything from Andrew's pay. And what she was doing was fair. Anything that happened up to the day she became Mrs. Andrew Blue was none of Andrew's business. Rena agreed. So did the bank manager.

Ruby was so intent on her thoughts, she almost missed the dress in the window of a shop called Helen's Apparel. Even through the window Ruby knew the dress was so cheap it would probably fall apart if she washed it. It was eight dollars and ninety-nine cents. It was, however, the exact style she'd been looking for: an empire waist and a skirt that flared, but not too much. She closed her eyes and tried to picture how it would look with pearls and buttons. If she didn't overdo it, the way Nola said most designers did, she would have a creation worthy of a wedding.

Inside the store, Ruby ran her fingers over the inch and a half of the hemline of the dress. The weight of the beads would pull the skirt down, tightening the loose weave. If she sewed a rim of grosgrain ribbon around the neck, it wouldn't drag down the bodice. She could do the same with the cuffs on the sleeves. She was pleased to find out the dress was on sale, with a dollar off. And she knew just what she was going to do with the dollar she saved. Nola said if one needed a decoration for one's head that was pure fluff, all one had to do was buy an embroidery hoop and fasten feathers, ribbons, and beads to it. A small veil of beige net would be perfect. If she was right in her calculations, her wedding outfit was going to cost no more than twelve dollars.

Walking out of the store, Ruby muttered, "Oh, Nola, I learned so much from you. I know you'd be proud of me, the way I've pulled things together lately." Ruby sighed heavily as she started toward home.

The settlement of Ruby's two properties took ninety minutes. Afterward, she left her lawyer's office with two sets of keys and two checks, totaling one hundred seventy-eight dollars, for the difference in the utility bills and insurance premiums. She stopped by a locksmith and had three sets of keys made, one for Rena, one for the bank, and one for herself. From there she went to the bank and handed over the packet of papers the attorney had given her. She smiled shakily when the bank officer congratulated and welcomed her as a new customer.

As she made her way down Pennsylvania Avenue, Ruby became aware that feathery flakes of snow were dusting her navy blue coat. She'd always loved snow, but now she prayed for it to turn to rain. If it snowed, she'd either have to shovel the steps, walkway, and sidewalks or pay Rena's husband to do it. God, she hadn't thought about that before. Neither had she thought about leaf raking and lawn mowing. Another fee.

"Oh, shit!" she said succinctly.

Ruby hunched into her wool coat as she pulled the scarf from around her neck and tied it on her head. Her step quickened till she was almost running. Thank God Admiral Query had given her the afternoon off, otherwise she would be paying Rena to wait for the furniture to arrive from the thrift shop.

She was on Poplar now, a half block from *her* house. She ran, her eyes sparkling, till she reached the steps. It was hers. The first real thing she ever owned. Slowly, to draw out the moment, Ruby fit the key in the lock and turned the knob at the same time. She stepped over the threshold, her eyes drinking in the sight of the empty rooms yawning ahead of her. The moment the door closed, she clapped her hands in delight and then proceeded to dance around the living room.

"My God!" she chortled happily. "This is mine! It's really mine!" She threw back her head and laughed. "Not bad for a dumb bunny from nowhere!" She continued to laugh as she walked through the rooms, mentally arranging them with furniture.

Ruby sobered. If only there was someone to share this with. Andrew's name crept to the edge of her tongue. No, not Andrew. Amber? Amber would turn up her nose and say something awful. Nola would like it of course. Or Calvin. Opal would love it. In just two more years Opal would be ready to leave Barstow. If she came to Washington, she could live here. "And I won't charge her rent, either!" Ruby chortled. It was all working out so wonderfully, thanks to her grandmother.

Ruby ran about the house then, turning on all the lights and running the water from all the faucets. She flushed both toilets just to hear the water gurgle in the pipes. She thought it was the most wonderful sound in the world.

"God, I just can't believe this!" Ruby squealed, dancing around the empty rooms. She'd never really had a secret before, certainly not of this magnitude.

Twenty minutes later a huge yellow truck with the words THRIFT CENTER printed in bright red pulled to the curb. It took exactly an hour for the furniture to be placed around the house. Tonight she was going to sleep in her very own house.

"I'll meet you at the house on O Street," she told the driver of the truck. She loved the feeling that coursed through her when she locked the door of her first house. No one was going to take this away from her. No one.

Ruby was a little kid again as she ran and skipped her way to the two-story brick house on O Street. She looked over her shoulder to see the huge yellow truck lumbering around the corner. Her feet picked up speed. She had to get there first to open the door for her own private moment. She ran faster. The door opened quickly and easily. She barreled through the rooms, turning on the lights and faucets as she'd done in the other house. She bolted up the stairs just as the truck driver killed the engine of his truck. Lickety-split she turned on the lights, ran the water, and flushed the toilet before she ran down the steps to open the door at the first peal of the bell.

It was dark when Ruby handed the truck driver a five-dollar bill for setting up the beds in both houses.

She was in business.

The days moved quickly now and the weather turned bitterly cold as Ruby drew closer to her wedding day.

Andrew Blue arrived in Washington D.C. on Friday afternoon, the day before his wedding. Rena and Bruno graciously allowed him the use of their spare bedroom, for a small fee. Ruby almost blurted out the story of all their fees, knowing Andrew would throw back his head and laugh. Her eyes widened at how close she'd come to babbling her secret.

Ruby watched her intended out of the corner of her eye as he joked and laughed with her landlady and roommates. He was so handsome, he took her breath away. Marine Corps spit and polish all the way. Admiral Query said marines were full of piss and vinegar, more piss than vinegar. Ruby was never sure if it was a compliment or not. She giggled suddenly when she thought about her roommates' plan to sing the "Marine Hymn" instead of "Here Comes the Bride" after the ceremony. She realized she'd never seen Andrew in anything other than his sharply creased uniform. She wondered crazily if he was hairy.

She felt his eyes on her, measuring her somehow. She smiled, wondering if she passed his scrutiny. When he grinned, she knew that whatever it was he'd been thinking was okay. He gave her a thumbs-up. She burst out laughing and ran to him and hugged him impulsively. At first he reeled back in surprise, but then his hold on her tightened. He looked down at her. Now it was her turn to be shocked. His eyes were *warm, caring*. He seemed almost to fall backward when Ruby winked seductively and whispered, "Only twenty-three more hours."

"Shameless hussy," he managed to croak. Then, as if to cover whatever feelings were rushing through him, he held up his arms and shouted, "Dinner's on me!"

Dinner was delightful, and Andrew proved himself a gracious, witty host. By the end of the evening Rena was flirting with him, and Ruby's roommates were staring at her enviously. Bruno, who understood his wife perfectly, was flirting with his tenants, one at a time. Ruby watched the goings-on with amusement and decided as they left the restaurant that she'd made a good catch.

Back at the house on Monroe Street, Rena waited while Andrew pecked Ruby on the cheek before she dragged him inside, clucking her tongue in disapproval. "No more. You don't see the bride now till tomorrow." To reinforce her statement, Rena grabbed Andrew by the arm and literally lifted him off his feet.

Andrew's excitement was at an all-time high as he entered Rena's guest room. He backed up a step and then another for a better overall look at the long, narrow room. "Jesus," he muttered. He felt himself snapping to attention and felt as though he should recite the Pledge of Allegiance at the same time. Cautiously, he stepped in and looked around. Red, white, and blue. Over the bed, which was covered with a replica of the flag, was a mural of the original flag with thirteen stars. Two little tables at the sides of the bed were covered with red cloths with the same thirteen stars appliqued around the hem, while the lampshades were dressed in blue with stars around the top and bottom of the shade. On the white wicker dresser was a matching striped scarf with tassled fringes in red, white, and blue. The rest of the room was similarly decorated. Andrew saluted smartly, then covered his mouth so he wouldn't laugh aloud.

Once the room was dark, he stripped down to his underwear and crawled under the quilt. At this time tomorrow he would have a wife and her name would be Ruby Blue. As he drifted into a restless sleep, he wondered if he would fall in love with Ruby at some point in their marriage. He decided, as he reached out to sleep, that Ruby loved enough for the both of them, and what he felt didn't really matter. He was giving her his name.

He would provide for her and give her all the children she
wanted. What else could she possibly wish for?

Ruby paced her room, her eyes on her packed bags and her
wedding dress hanging on the back of the door. It was already
her wedding day. If she wanted to, if she *really* needed to cut
and run, right now, this very minute, she could. She could go to
one of her houses and sleep. No one but Rena would suspect
where she was, and she wouldn't tell. Smothering panic ripped
through her and left her gasping for breath. She knew she
wouldn't leave; she'd made a commitment to Andrew, and she
would go through with her marriage. In time she would fall in
love with him. She'd made a mental pledge to herself that she
would be the best wife she knew how to be.

What she was going through now, she told herself, was what
all brides went through: prewedding jitters.

It was going to be a nice wedding. Simple, but nice. Her wedding cake, baked by Rena—for a small fee—was gorgeous. It
even had a little plastic bride and groom on the top. Bruno
agreed to take pictures with her Brownie Hawkeye. Ruby would
have them developed when they moved into their quarters at
Camp Lejune.

Her eyes went to the small pile of gifts, by the closet door,
that Rena was going to package and send on. She'd been
stunned at the elegant bed ensemble from Admiral Query and
his wife, which had arrived by mail from Woodward and
Lothrop just yesterday. Mabel McIntyre sent a gift, beautiful
crystal candle holders. She'd cried when she thanked the older
woman and hugged her so tightly, the personnel director
squealed for mercy. But the present she loved most came from
Nola's mother.

Ruby dropped to her knees and opened the carton and started
to cry. Inside was a homemade, worn quilt for a twin bed. Mrs.
Quantrell had written a note saying that Nola had made the quilt
out of patches from all the children's worn-out clothing. She had
embroidered a name on each little patch. Mrs. Quantrell had
gone on to say she knew Nola would want Ruby to have it for
her first child's bed. She'd also warned Ruby to wash the quilt
gently because the patches were already threadbare. Ruby loved
it on sight. Her fingers traced the delicate stitches, wondering
which name was that of a blood sibling and which belonged to

one of the orphans. Not that it mattered. It was something to think about because it brought Nola closer.

Ruby wiped her tears with the back of her hand. So much of the material was from flour sacks, the kind her grandmother used to have. Her grandmother had made aprons and dishtowels from the sacks.

She'd shown the gifts to Andrew and when he saw the quilt he'd said, "What the hell kind of present is that? It's worn out, for God's sake." Men, men like Andrew, simply didn't understand. Calvin would have, though, Calvin understood about family. Ruby's eyes filled a second time. Damn, she had to stop this or her eyes would be red and puffy for the wedding. In the new life she was starting there was no room for maudlin sentimentality.

Ruby repacked the quilt and then crawled into bed. She stared at the thin beam of moonlight on the ceiling. She was still awake when the new sun crept over the horizon, but she didn't get out of bed. Eventually, she dozed, then awoke at twelve-thirty. Her head felt clotted with memories. Her nose was stuffed up, and she felt like she was coming down with a cold.

She was on her way to the bathroom when Rena came down the hall with the mail. "There's a letter for you, Ruby, from your sister." Ruby reached for it. How like Amber to spoil her day. She was tempted to trash the letter but decided to read it while the tub filled.

Dear Ruby,

The crib came last week. It's nice. Nangi put it together today. I haven't done anything in the way of decorating because I don't know if I should do blue or pink.

Shopping over here isn't like it is back in the States. They don't have any of the things we take for granted, but now that I have the catalogue, I can order what I want. Thanks for sending it.

I got your letter saying you're marrying Andrew Blue. I hope you're in love with him, Ruby, because if you aren't, your marriage won't have a chance of surviving. Not that you ever listened to me.

Nangi received a card, actually it was a wedding announcement, from his cousin, Calvin. He got married last month to some southern woman who is older than he is. Maybe she's one of those southern belles. He's in the Philippines, and she's going to join him pretty soon.

See, Ruby, he didn't love you. If he did, he wouldn't have gotten married. Obviously, you didn't love him, either, or you wouldn't be marrying Andrew. Anyway, here's a picture of Calvin and his new bride; he sent us two of them. Personally, I think she looks like a withered-up old maid. Nangi said she could pass for Calvin's mother.

I would have sent you a wedding present, but there isn't anything here worth sending. Tell me what you would like, and I'll send it from the catalogue.

Send me your new address so I can let you know when the baby arrives.

Your sister,
Amber

Ruby folded the letter and stuck it in the envelope. She carried the picture that had dropped to the floor over to the sink, where she turned on the overhead light to see it better. She stared at the picture for a long time before she tore it into little pieces and flushed it down the toilet.

Ruby bathed, dressed, walked, talked, and she even smiled and giggled when it was called for. Only Rena seemed aware that anything was wrong, but tactfully, she said nothing. From time to time she patted Ruby on the arm or shoulder in a maternal way.

Outside the rectory, Ruby's and Andrew's guests threw rice as they burst into a lusty, off-key rendition of the "Marine Hymn." Ruby smiled and ducked her head the way all new brides do to avoid the pelting rice. Andrew laughed uproariously. Bruno snapped his pictures as Ruby kept smiling.

Mr. and Mrs. Andrew Blue posed for what Bruno said was the picture they should enlarge and call their official wedding photo.

"Let the champagne flow!" Bruno then ordered as he uncorked one of the two bottles his thrifty wife had provided. He himself had bought four more, just in case. Besides, he knew Rena would find a way to pay for it without upsetting their budget. This was a party, and he loved parties.

Andrew danced and flirted with all the girls right under

Ruby's nose. Ruby, in turn, danced with Bruno until she was dizzy. The finger foods were devoured, the cake sliced and eaten, the presents opened, and the champagne bottles emptied.

Rena pronounced the reception over at seven o'clock.

"Line up, ladies, so Ruby can throw her bouquet," she ordered briskly as she took her place in the line with the laughing, giggling girls. It was no surprise to anyone when she jumped the highest and outmaneuvered the girls to catch the limp bouquet of white roses. "I guess this means I will divorce Bruno and remarry," she chortled. "What do you think of that, Andrew?" she asked coyly.

"I don't believe in divorce," Andrew said curtly.

"That's a pity," Rena said blandly. "How does Ruby feel about it?"

Andrew had to admit he didn't know. Ruby was true blue, for better or worse, he thought. He shrugged.

"Ah, I think, Andrew, that it might behoove you to find that out. Why do I have the feeling you don't know too much about our little Ruby?"

"I know enough," Andrew said, irritated at the conversation.

"In a marriage, Lieutenant, one cannot assume nor can one presume. Remember, I am the one who said this to you. Now," she said, clapping her hands, her dozen or so bracelets tinkling merrily, "how did you like your wedding? I myself think it was wonderful."

"Yes, it was wonderful and Ruby and I both thank you. We'll always remember what you've done for us."

Mr. and Mrs. Andrew Blue waved good-bye to their guests as they stepped into a waiting taxi that would take them to the honeymoon suite Andrew had engaged at the Ambassador hotel, where they would share a honeymoon supper before they embarked on the intimacy their marriage license said was now proper.

In the taxi Andrew held Ruby's hand and nuzzled her neck. She blushed furiously. "I can do this, I can do anything to you I want; we're married now," Andrew whispered in her ear.

Ruby smiled and whispered back, "Only if I allow it."

Andrew reared back, his eyes suddenly suspicious. "What's that supposed to mean?"

Ruby smiled again. "It means I'm a person, not a thing. We

might be married, but you don't own me. Don't ever forget that, Andrew."

Rena's words ricocheted in Andrew's ears. There was more to this new bride of his than he suspected. Much more. He had to defend the silly amorous statement he'd just made. "Look, I didn't mean . . . you took it . . . the wrong way. We're married, we can do whatever we want now."

"We, Andrew. You and I. Two people. That means we both have to agree on things. Do you understand?"

"What I think is we should continue this discussion at the hotel."

Ruby smiled and nodded, but there was something about her smile that didn't sit right with Andrew.

"What's wrong, Ruby? I know something's bothering you. Last night you were fine. Today . . . today you're different. Do you think we made a mistake? You can tell me. Maybe if we talk about it, whatever it is won't seem so bad."

"I'm sorry, I didn't know it showed. I tried . . . I didn't want it to interfere with our wedding. It's a family thing, I had a letter from Amber today, that's all. I apologize." She squeezed his arm and placed her head on his shoulder.

"That's better," Andrew said, rubbing his hand up and down her thigh.

"We're here!" Andrew said suddenly.

Ruby sat up straight, her half-closed eyes popping open and into awareness. Already? In another few minutes, or as soon as Andrew registered and their bags were taken to the room, she would be alone with her new husband in the honeymoon suite. She swallowed past the lump in her throat.

The moment the door closed behind the bellboy, Andrew drew Ruby close to him and leered at her. "Should we wait for dinner or . . . go to bed now?"

"Didn't . . . I thought you said you ordered dinner. I'm hungry. I was so jittery back at the house, I didn't eat anything. I didn't see you eat anything, either." God, was that desperate sound in her voice real?

"You're nervous, aren't you?" Andrew said calmly.

Why shouldn't he sound calm? Ruby wondered. He did this all the time; he had years of experience while she was . . . new and inexperienced.

"Yes. As a matter of fact, I'm very nervous, and I'm not ready . . . I'm really not ready for . . . *that* . . . yet," she said in a voice so loud, her words bounced off the walls.

"Okay, I can handle that. Let's call down for dinner, and while they're getting it ready, we can unpack and drink some of this wine that came with the room. We can sit and talk. Did I tell you how pretty you looked? You look pretty now, too, but when you came out in that fancy dress, I almost keeled over. Bet that little number set you back a pretty penny, huh?"

"Yep, it wiped out my bank account." Ruby giggled.

"Listen, when you get around to having the pictures developed, I want one for my desk at work and one for my wallet. You're going to get that one outside the church blown up for our apartment, aren't you?"

Ruby was touched. She nodded. Somehow it was the last thing she'd expected Andrew to say. "I wish Nola could have been at the wedding," Ruby said wistfully.

"Listen, Ruby, I'm sorry as hell about that business with the quilt. I didn't understand. But how do you expect me to understand if you don't confide and share with me? You go getting hopping mad, and I don't even know what it's all about. You might not believe me, but I'm just as sentimental as the next guy."

"Andrew?"

"Yeah?"

"You didn't carry me over the threshold."

For a moment he looked crestfallen. "I didn't forget," he finally said, his voice injured-sounding. "This is a hotel, not where we're going to live. This doesn't count, Ruby. For God's sake, do you think I'd forget something that important?"

It sounded good, Ruby decided. And he looked sincere. But he also looked quite miserable. "Well, I would have preferred you to do it here," Ruby said, speaking her mind. "It's all right, it's too late now."

"Oh, shit, Ruby, are you going to let this spoil our evening?" Andrew asked in the same injured tone.

"No."

"No? That's it?"

"You asked me a question and I answered it. Do you want a litany or what?" Ruby asked testily, but then she dropped to her

knees to feel the thick, dove-gray carpet. She *was* spoiling the
evening, and that she did not want to do.

"I never saw a carpet like this. It's so deep and springy." She
kicked off her shoes and giggled. "This is wonderful. Everything
is so pretty. I guess the honeymoon suite is special, huh?"

"I paid enough for this damn room, it better be special," Andrew muttered under his breath.

Ruby looked around the room. It *was* stunning. Satin bedspread done in shades of mauve and pearl-gray, one shade
lighter than the carpet; mauve drapes; two chairs covered in a
nubby material that matched the streaky pattern of the spread
and drapes but were boldly striped; a dresser made of a light
wood; a huge mirror, directly in line with the double bed.
Ruby's eyes widened in alarm. She could see Andrew's reflection in the mirror as he watched her. She whirled around, a
smile on her face, the same strained smile she'd worn all day.

She peered down at the shiny black telephone without the circle of numbers she was used to. Andrew picked up the receiver
and made the final arrangements for their wedding supper.

"What say we have our own private toast?" he said when he
had hung up. "The ones back at your landlady's didn't count.
We're alone now." He uncorked the bottle with ease. Bruno had
struggled and struggled and somehow pushed the cork down into
the champagne bottle. She'd seen the shock of disgust on Andrew's face. She wondered if he always did everything so perfectly. The thought annoyed her, but the smile stayed on her
face.

"To us!"

Ruby drank the bubbly in a gulp and held out her glass for a
refill. Andrew's eyes widened in surprise. "I think you're supposed to sip it," he murmured.

"Why?" Ruby drained the second glass. "Who said so?"

"Well ... I ... if it's a good champagne, you're suppose to
savor it. How the hell should I know who said it? Some wine
connoisseur, I suppose."

"If you don't know for certain, you shouldn't say anything. It
sounds like you don't like the way I drink wine," Ruby said,
enunciating each word carefully. "I like to drink it all at one
time. I taste it that way. I guess marines don't know everything
after all."

Andrew looked as though he'd been stepped on. "I never said I know everything," he said huffily.

This time Ruby filled her own glass, but she didn't drink it right away. She wondered if her eyes were as glassy as they felt. Apparently, one shouldn't drink champagne on an empty stomach. She watched her husband shift from one foot to the other uneasily. She pointed to the chair across from her. Andrew plopped down, his gaze narrowing as he finished his wine in one swallow.

"Tell me about our new apartment. Is it nice? Did you meet the neighbors? What kind of furniture did you get? How many rooms does it have?"

"Wouldn't you rather wait and see it? I don't know anything about decorating. There's furniture and stuff. It has three rooms and a bathroom, and a fourth room that's too small for anything but storage."

"We don't have anything to store," Ruby said.

Exasperated, Andrew threw his hands in the air. "Then we'll leave it empty. Does it matter, Ruby?"

Ruby drained her glass. "It matters if we're paying for a room we don't need. Or didn't you think about that? I thought marines were smart."

"Do you have something against marines all of a sudden? I don't get it."

Ruby ignored his question. "We should have music. Why didn't you think of that, Andrew? So far, this isn't"—she waved the towel about—"very romantic. You aren't really romantic, are you? Music would have been nice."

"That's it, Ruby, I've had it!" Andrew blustered. "This is our goddamn wedding night, and so far all you've done is drink and pick me apart. If you think you made a mistake marrying me, I can take you back to Monroe Street right now. Make up your damn mind."

Ruby made an effort to straighten her shoulders. "I-made-a-commitment-and-I'm-a-Catholic! I-don't-know-if-I-made-a-mistake-or-not. It's-too-late-now. It's-too-late! Toolatetoolate-toolatetoolatetoolate."

Andrew looked as if he wanted to shake the living hell out of his wife, but the waiter knocked on the door with their wedding supper. He seethed and fumed as the man set out dishes and napkins and twirled the second champagne bottle in a chilled bucket filled with shaved ice. His tasks finished, he discreetly withdrew, closing the door quietly behind him.

Food, Ruby thought sickly. She was reminded of home as she weaved her way to the table.

"I'll serve," Andrew said briskly.

He ladled out glazed carrots, tiny green peas, and small white potatoes garnished with little green speckles of mint. The two pink succulent slices of prime rib were thin and delectable. He buttered a roll and presented it to Ruby with a flourish.

As Andrew was about to seat himself, Ruby wagged her finger playfully. "Didn't you forget something, Andrew?" She held her wineglass aloft.

"You've had enough," Andrew said testily.

Ruby continued to hold her glass under his nose. "That may be true, but I still want more. On the other hand, maybe you haven't had enough. You don't really care, now, do you? I certainly don't. So, if you don't really care and I don't care, will you pour the damn wine and let me enjoy my wedding supper? I hope you aren't going to turn into one of those husbands who spoils everything. I've had enough of that in my life. I think you should know that," Ruby muttered as her husband sloshed wine into her glass, which she immediately drank. She asked for a refill.

Andrew sat down and proceeded to jab and stab the food on his plate. Ruby tried to pierce a carrot with her heavy silver fork, but after missing several times, she dropped the fork and picked up a soup spoon. She giggled when she saw the appalled look on her husband's face.

"I should take your picture right now, I really should," Andrew said sourly. "How's this going to look to our children someday?"

"Someday is a long time away. I'll tell them the truth. What will you tell them, Andrew?"

"What are you talking about?" Andrew asked irritably.

Ruby tried to widen her eyes, but they kept drooping. "Truth is truth. Isn't that what the Marines Corps is all about? Honor, justice, semper . . . whatever . . . I'm going to be sick . . ." she muttered, lurching off her chair.

"Son of a bitch!" Andrew groaned as he leapt off his chair to drag his new wife to the bathroom. He dropped to his knees and held his wife's head while she emptied her stomach. Between her retching, she kept saying over and over, "I'm sorry, you don't understand; I'm so sorry, you just don't understand." Then she leaned back on her heels and stared at Andrew with tear-filled eyes. "I didn't think it was going to hurt this much. I'm sorry, I'm really sorry." She was far from sober; even so, she knew she was saying too much. If she'd had the strength, she would have run and hidden somewhere to cover her shame.

Andrew picked her up and laid her on the bed, then returned to the bathroom for a washcloth. He wiped her face gently as he crooned soft words. "I'm sorry, too, Ruby. I should have been more aware of what you were feeling. It's okay. Go to sleep and tomorrow we'll talk. We have to talk, I see that now. I'll sleep on the chair or the floor; it doesn't matter."

Ruby struggled to a sitting position and held out her arms. Tears streamed down her face. She wanted to say something, needed to . . . do what? "I'm sorry . . . there's no way you can understand . . . I wanted . . . I tried . . . it just hurts so muuuuch."

Andrew sat on the side of the bed for a long time, his wife cradled in his arms. From time to time he brushed her hair with his chin. He liked the clean, sweet smell of her. A surge of protectiveness rushed through him. How vulnerable she was now, asleep like this. Rather like an infant or a puppy. He didn't know what it was exactly that he was feeling for this young girl in his arms, but it was something he wanted to think about. He moved carefully then, not wanting to wake her. He managed to lay her back on the pillow. He leaned over and kissed her on the cheek. He hadn't noticed the dark smudges under her eyes before. Something stabbed at his heart. How pale and fragile she looked and that look in her eyes before . . . he kissed her other cheek, then he covered her with a soft pink blanket from the closet.

Throughout the long night Andrew watched over his sleeping wife. Each time she moaned or moved, he was off his chair in an instant, rushing to the bed to smooth the hair back from her brow or to pat her gently on the shoulder. He wished he knew what was wrong so he could try to make it right.

A long time later Andrew shifted his gaze from his sleeping wife to the gray dawn creeping through the window like a ghost struggling to come alive. He should shower now and change into a clean uniform. His watch told him they had four hours be-

fore they boarded their flight to North Carolina. He wondered
uneasily if he would be traveling alone. The thought bothered
him, and he didn't know why. He'd told himself over and over
that he could take marriage or leave it. But he needed Ruby.
That knowledge felt strange; he'd never needed anyone before,
and he'd die before he'd admit it to another soul. A marine
didn't need anyone but himself, right? It was bullshit, and he
knew it.

Three hours before flight time on the following morning, Andrew and Ruby were seated in the hotel dining room with a
huge silver pot of coffee in front of them. Ruby, badly hung
over, spoke. "Andrew, I'm sorry about last night. I don't know
why I ... did ... acted the way I did. I'll try to make it up to
you."

Andrew poured the coffee with a steady hand. "Put a lot of
sugar and cream in it," he said in a fatherly tone. "It's okay."

"No, it isn't okay. Why didn't you stop me from drinking so
much wine? I'm not used to drinking, and I hadn't eaten anything. I ruined everything."

"I did try to stop you, but you insisted. I suppose I could have
administered an uppercut, but that's not my style. We need to
talk, though. You acted as if our wedding was all a mistake. Do
you still feel that way? If you do, we can eat our breakfast and
then I'll take you back to Monroe Street. You can file for an an-
nulment. You said a lot of things I didn't understand, but the
rule of thumb is, when a person is drunk, he says what he
means."

"What did I say?" Ruby whispered.

"You really went to town on me, both personally and as a marine. You kept saying I didn't understand and that you were
sorry. And then you said something I still can't figure out. You
said it wasn't supposed to hurt so much. Would you mind explaining that to me?"

Ruby sipped her coffee. She willed it to stay in her stomach.

"I'm sorry, Andrew, I don't remember. I can't even begin to
imagine what I meant. I suppose I was apologizing for drinking
so much. What started me off?" she asked hesitantly.

Andrew grinned. "I know exactly what happened and I'm taking the blame. I forgot to carry you over the threshold, and you
let me have it with both barrels. It went downhill from there. So,

if anyone is sorry, it's me. Which brings me back to what I said in the beginning; if you think we made a mistake, it's not too late to rectify it."

"It wasn't your fault, Andrew. We're both sorry. No, I don't want to back out. If . . . if you feel it's a mistake . . ."

"Hell, no. There is one thing, though, Ruby, I want your promise that you won't say degrading things about the marines or the Corps. It's not just me that's an officer, *we're* an officer. You're an extension of me, and what you do and say reflects on me. You have to understand that."

"Of course. Last night was . . . it's over. You don't have to worry about me." An extension of him? She wasn't sure she liked that at all.

Seated by the window, because Andrew preferred being by the aisle, Ruby fastened her seat belt. Her heart thumped to a cadence that would have pleased any drill instructor. She planted her feet firmly on the floor of the plane, knowing she would brake with her feet and then sprag, a term the children of Barstow used when they were going downhill too fast in a wagon.

Ruby looked around. No one appeared as frightened as she was. Weary travelers, military personnel, and even small children were settling themselves as though going for a Sunday outing. Mind over matter, she told herself.

"Think about how much faster we're going to arrive by flying versus taking a bus or a train. If you relax, you'll enjoy the flight," Andrew said, an authoritative tone in his voice which Ruby found herself resenting.

"You know, Andrew, it's okay for me to be anxious and nervous. I've never flown before. It's not as if I'm whining or complaining. I'm trying to make the best of this. There are times when . . . like now, when I have to handle it in my own way, and I will handle this fear."

"I'm only trying to help. That's what husbands are for. Of course, I'm not really your husband . . . in the true sense of the word," he whispered. "I hope tonight will be better."

"I'm sure it will be," Ruby said quietly.

Amazing. I'm still alive, Ruby thought as she walked down the steps of the plane.

"Wait by the door, Ruby, while I get the bags. We'll take a cab to the base. This is our last leg, and then we'll be in our new home."

Ruby's stomach lurched as she walked to the door of the airport. Everyone seemed to be wearing smiles, happy that they were there meeting people—parents, grandparents, and friends. An elderly lady smiled at Ruby as she dragged her heavy case through the door. Ruby rushed to hold the door and offered to carry the bag to the curb. She smiled then, a smile that embraced the woman like a warm spring day.

"Thank you, my dear, it was kind of you to help me."

"Can you manage now?" Ruby asked anxiously. The woman nodded.

Andrew came up behind Ruby and hissed in her ear, "I thought I told you to stay by the door. Inside doesn't mean out here helping some decrepit old lady who should have someone else helping her, not you. I told you, Ruby, you wear my rank the same as I do, remember that!"

"Are you telling me you wouldn't have helped that old lady?" Ruby snapped in return.

"Oh, for Christ's sake. Forget it, just forget it, Ruby."

"No, I won't. Do you want to fight right here? If you do, I'm ready. I don't like your attitude, Andrew. You have no compassion, and I'm beginning to wonder if you have any feelings."

"People are staring at us, Ruby. I don't like that. I'm wearing my uniform and my rank, and like I told you, you're wearing them, too, but yours are invisible."

Ruby deflated under Andrew's tongue-lashing. She waved to the old lady, her own face miserable, her eyes hot and prickly.

The taxi ride to the base was made in silence. Andrew sat, stone-faced, the palms of his hands flat on his knees. Ruby cowered in the corner, her stomach railing its distress. The drumbeat in her head seemed to be increasing its tempo. She wanted to remember this ride, to watch the miles go by. She wanted all these memories to stitch into what she called her memory sampler so that someday she could tell her children how it was. All she could see was a blur of trees and a flat highway and the back of the cab driver's head. She felt like a sick, wounded puppy. A sick, wounded puppy who needed love and compassion and a kind word.

What seemed like a long time later, Ruby felt herself being jolted forward when the taxi driver pulled up to the gate. Andrew showed his pass and the corporal on duty saluted smartly. Ruby blinked at her husband's snappy return salute. She wondered if she was supposed to salute, since she was wearing her husband's rank. She didn't realize she'd voiced the thought aloud until Andrew muttered, "That's the dumbest thing I ever heard come out of your mouth, Ruby." The look of pure disgust was almost more than Ruby could bear. She shriveled into herself.

Nothing in the world could have prepared Ruby for her first sight of her new home. The sick feeling in the pit of her stomach rushed upward so fast, she had to clamp her hand over her mouth. Andrew strode forward, but she hung back, trying to take in the line of mean-looking apartments that were stuck together. She looked for trees; there were none. The few shrubs around were straggly and unkempt, nothing more than naked sticks waving in the wind. Her eye fell on a rusty red scooter minus its front wheel on the front lawn. A few feet away were equally rusty roller skates, long forgotten, as though their owner departed and didn't care if they were left behind.

"Are you planning on standing out here all day?" Andrew called over his shoulder. "I thought you wanted me to carry you over the threshold!"

Ruby's feet moved of their own volition. She thought she saw a curtain move in the apartment next to theirs. She wanted to cry.

Ruby watched as Andrew thrust open the door. He dumped the bags and whirled to pick her up. The next thing she knew, she was inside a square box of a room. The door closed with a loud bang, and she was on her feet almost immediately. She looked around, her eyes registering disbelief at what she saw. Andrew appeared oblivious as he bent down for the bags he carried into what she surmised was the bedroom.

Ruby fought the scream building in her throat. She couldn't live here. She didn't *want* to live here. Not in this ugly, mean-looking place. The windows were bare and so dirty it was impossible to see the outside world through them. There was no sign of a broom or dustpan.

Ruby turned to see the kitchen. It was as ugly as the rest of the apartment. As first glance the stove looked hopeless. She knew the refrigerator was supposed to be white—they didn't come in any other color—but it looked more like it was yellow and gray. She slammed the door so hard, the window rattled.

Linoleum that defied any color description caught in Ruby's heel. She stumbled and then righted herself without touching anything. She looked down and gasped. The floor covering was cracked and bubbled with large chunks missing in the middle. Crayon marks in the form of a hopscotch pattern graced the floor. With her foot, Ruby pried open the sink door and ran screaming when a family of rodents ran for cover. Shivering uncontrollably, Ruby ran straight into her husband's arms. "Mice!" she gasped. "A whole family of them!"

"We'll set some traps. Listen, Ruby, I have to check in. I'll be back in a couple of hours. Why don't you see what you can do with this place? Housing must have screwed up. The apartments are always spotless." His tone was cheerful when he said, "Fix it up like you did the other places you lived. You girls know how to do that. I'll see you in a little while. I'll bring something to eat so you won't have to worry about dinner."

Ruby's eyes were wild as she watched her husband leave. Fix it up! How? Dear God, tell me how.

Her answer arrived twenty minutes later in the form of her next-door neighbor.

Ruby flew to the door, thinking, praying, that it was Andrew returning to help her. When she saw the smiling face of her neighbor, the tears that had been held in check spilled over.

The woman held out her arms and Ruby fell into them, sobbing and sniffling. "I'm sorry." She gulped. "This is an awful way to meet someone for the first time. It's just that this . . . this . . ."

"Is so overwhelming." Her neighbor laughed then, a sound of pure mirth. "Actually, it's downright disgusting," she said, looking around. "You got here before the cleaning crew. Not to worry. Soap and water, some paint, and it will be fine. Trust me." She smiled. "I'm Dixie Sinclaire, and I know you must be Mrs. Blue. My husband said he'd heard you just got married." It was all said in one breath.

Ruby grinned, feeling better immediately. She liked her new neighbor.

She was plump but not fat, and she had the most cheerful countenance Ruby had ever seen. Her eyes sparkled and her crisp, dark curls crowned her round head like a halo. She was pretty, her flashing smile her best feature; it warmed and welcomed at the same time. When she talked, her hands moved constantly to accentuate or make her point. She was smaller than Ruby, coming only to her shoulder.

"Well," she said matter-of-factly, "I guess we better get started, and the sooner you get out of those fancy duds, the quicker we'll get this place into shape. While you change, I'll get the rest of the girls. By dinnertime, this place will be spick-and-span. We have this routine we go through when a new wife comes on base. We pool our talents, and when your husband arrives, he thinks you did it all. That makes for happiness. Of course, this place is a bit worse than the usual. See you in a few minutes."

There were five of them all together. They arrived with buckets, brooms, soap, and cleanser. Two huge trash cans stood in the middle of the floor and were filled almost immediately. Inside of ten minutes Ruby saw that Dixie was a human dynamo as she directed, ordered, and pointed, never missing a beat in her own chores. "View this as the ultimate challenge!" she crowed over and over as she sloshed hot soapy water on the buckling kitchen floor.

Ruby beamed from ear to ear. What a wonderful bunch of women. Not only were they helping her, they were using their own soap products and offering to lend her anything she needed until things were made right. Ruby accepted graciously when she was told by a redhead named Monica that in two weeks she'd be doing the same thing for a new family moving in four doors away.

"We have to band together," Christine said happily. "We baby-sit and shop for one another. It's the only way we can function in the military chaos. It's our job to make things easy for our husbands."

"What do they do," Ruby asked curiously, "while we're doing all this?"

The girls stopped as one and stared at Ruby. She sensed she'd made a gigantic mistake. "What I mean is, what . . . how do . . ."

Dixie rushed into the impending breach. "What they do is play cards, drink martinis and beer, and take us for granted. Of course, they appreciate us, if that's what you're asking. It's an unwritten thing, if you know what I mean. They're officers!" she said, trying to make her point, her arms waving wildly.

"I'm new at this. I don't know anyone who is married to someone in the military, so if I foul up, bring me up short. I don't want to do anything to embarrass my husband or you girls. I see where I'm going to need a lot of help," Ruby said ruefully.

"That's what we're here for. Ruby, you will make friends in the service that you will have all your life. Sometimes we're better than a blood family. If your man is in for the long haul and gets transferred tomorrow, say, why, who knows? Six years down the road you might meet one of us at some other base. It's like that. Look, you'll get used to it. We have some real nice parties, especially over the holidays, and in the spring and summer we have cookouts. Sometimes it's wonderful, sometimes it's damn near perfection."

"And other times it's devastating, like when you get transferred and have to leave friends and go through this all over again," said the young woman named Christine. "Tomorrow we'll requisition new linoleum for you. And a paint job. But that doesn't mean it will happen in the next few days.

"Jane," Christine said happily, "knows how to make slipcovers and she's taught us all how to put on the cording. This . . . this furniture that came over on the ark is going to look brand-new once we get chintz covers on it. Inside of a couple of weeks this little place will be homey and comfortable. Trust us. Oh, Monica is a real whiz when it comes to drapes and curtains. We pooled our money and bought a secondhand sewing machine."

Ruby felt better immediately.

"One good thing," Dixie said, beaming, "is that our whole row of apartments gets the morning sun in the kitchen. It's so nice to have breakfast and to kaffeeklatch in a sunny kitchen."

Three hours later, Sue, a sunny blonde from Orlando, Florida, said, "Welcome to Camp Lejune, Ruby Blue!"

The girls, all around Ruby's age, hugged her, promising to be lifelong friends.

"Thank you. I'm glad to be here." Ruby realized she meant every word. She was startled a second later when the phone shrilled to life. She looked at the girls, her jaw dropping as they broke into peals of laughter.

"Bet you didn't even know you had a phone, huh?" Monica chortled. Ruby shook her head.

"Well, you do. It's the first thing that happens in housing. An officer needs to have a phone. Since you're new, I'd say it must be your husband." Ruby rushed to pick it up. She almost laughed aloud when the girls raised their fingers to their lips to signal secrecy.

"What am I doing? Uh, I'm . . . cleaning. Two more hours? No, that's not a problem. Sandwiches will be fine, Andrew. Okay, I'll see you in two hours."

Dixie clapped her hands gleefully. "Good, now we can adjourn to my place for coffee. And you are not having sandwiches for dinner. We have enough dishes for you and we've already cooked your dinner. I made bread early this morning, so you get homemade bread from me. Monica made a salad. Her salads have everything, even tiny bits of real crisp bacon. Christine made a meat loaf and the gravy is to die for. Sue made you an apple pie, and Gertie made her string-bean dish with almonds and batter-dipped onions and also the scalloped potatoes. We chipped in for a bottle of wine, very domestic, but still good. Did I forget anything?" she asked the small group.

Ruby swallowed past the lump in her throat, her eyes swimming in tears. "I don't know how to thank you. Without you, this all would have been a real disaster. I think . . . no, I *know* I'm going to love it here," she said sincerely.

While the girls gathered up their cleaning tools and supplies, Dixie took Ruby aside. "I think we're going to be good friends, Ruby. I don't know why, but I think we're both cut from the same bolt of cloth, as my mother would say."

Ruby hugged Dixie. "Yes, we're going to be wonderful friends."

Ruby had the table set, the meat loaf warming in the clean oven, and the salad and vegetables in the refrigerator. The tidy, neat bedroom was made up with linens and scented candles the girls had brought. The radio was plugged in and playing softly. She felt a small thrill of excitement as she stripped off her work clothes and put on a fresh dress. Later she'd take a bath so she'd be fresh and clean for . . . for her first experience with . . . sex.

She poked around the kitchen for another ten minutes before Andrew walked through the door.

"Whew!" he said, slapping at his head. "I knew you were good, but I didn't know you were a miracle worker. This is great, Ruby. How'd you do it all? Is that supper I smell? C'mon, how'd you do it?"

"The neighbors! They were wonderful, Andrew. I could never have done it myself. In a few days I'll have this place as nice as theirs. It's meat loaf and a lot of good things. Apple pie, too."

"Guess we won't be needing these," he said, tossing a paper bag with sandwiches on the counter. -

"I'll eat them for lunch tomorrow." Ruby laughed. "I feel better, and I had coffee with the girls and Dixie in her kitchen."

Andrew grinned from ear to ear. His tie was off now, his jacket folded neatly over the back of the chair. Ruby thought he never looked more handsome than at this moment. She felt stirrings she'd felt only with Calvin.

Andrew drew Ruby into the circle of his arms and leaned down, kissing her lightly. "I like to unwind when I get off duty, and what that means to you is I want my slippers, a drink, and a cigarette. If you can't handle that, now is the time to tell me." There was such a teasing note in his voice, Ruby felt giddy.

"I can handle it, sir." Ruby saluted almost as smartly as her husband saluted the guard at the gate house.

"No wine for you, though," Andrew muttered under his breath as he placed the wine bottle between his legs to uncork it.

Dinner was electric. Everything that was said, every look, every gesture, took on a sexual connotation. By the time it was over and the wine bottle empty, Ruby felt ready to burst. Andrew himself was unable to sit still long enough to read the newspaper he'd brought home with him. He listened to the tap water run in the kitchen sink, the clink of dishes and silver, and Ruby's steps on the creaky linoleum. He wanted her and he wanted her *now*.

"That's it, Ruby. You can do the dishes tomorrow. It's time for other things," he said. Ruby whirled, her hands full of soapsuds.

"I'd . . . I'd like to take a bath. Actually, I need to take a bath with all the cleaning I did today. Do you want to take one, too? You can do that while I . . . while I finish the dishes. You always said you have a five o'clock shadow, maybe you want to . . . to shave." She was babbling and Andrew was grinning.

"I'll go first, and you're right, I do have a stubble. Ten minutes is all I'll need." He was leering at her.

"That's ... that's fine. I can be finished here, and I can take a bath in ten minutes, too. Five if you fill the tub when you're finished." That sounded good. Agreeable even. Maybe *cooperative* was a better word. A nervous giggle erupted suddenly that Ruby wiped away with her soapy hand.

Fifteen minutes later Ruby stood in the tiny bathroom dressed in her sheer nightie, every nerve in her body twanging. Her hand on the doorknob was shaking so badly, she had to clasp her free hand on top to make the knob turn. He was going to see through the gossamer web of the gown; he was going to touch her in all—She jerked at the door so hard, she was literally thrown off balance, the sheer nightie swishing its own tune as it whirled about her. This was it. There was no way to back out now, even if she wanted to.

A habit of long standing made her switch off the overhead light as she walked into the bedroom.

"C'mere, Ruby," Andrew said softly as he moved over to make room for her. She slid into the bed and immediately pulled up the covers. She could feel his nakedness against the thin material of her gown. It seemed to sear and scorch her, even though she was shivering. Part of her wanted him to just *do it* and get it over with so she could think about it and make plans to do it better the next time. The other part of her wanted to feel, to savor, to enjoy. She buried her head in the crook of Andrew's arm and nuzzled against him. She squeezed her eyes shut when she felt his erection against her thigh. She wanted to yelp, to leap from the bed. She nuzzled deeper, aware of Andrew's tight hold on her. She wasn't going anywhere.

He was talking, whispering actually, words that she had to strain to hear: how sweet and clean she smelled, how pretty she was, how gorgeous her nightgown was, and what it did to him when he saw her coming into the room.

He was touching her, running his fingers through her hair, nuzzling the back of her neck while his leg delicately hiked the sheer fabric of her gown up to her thighs.

His tongue was ... everywhere and somehow she wasn't in the crook of his arm anymore. The straps of her gown were off her shoulders, her breasts exposed. She was supposed to do something, react, but how? Her eyes snapped open when she felt

the gown being pulled over her head. Now, now was when she
could cooperate; she was almost sure this was the time. In a
squeaky voice she barely recognized as her own she said,
"Okay, I'm ready."

"For what?" Andrew laughed.

"To do it!"

"It doesn't work like that," Andrew whispered huskily. "It
works like this." Ruby lay perfectly still while he showed her.

"Ooohhh, do that again," she gasped, forgetting how uptight
she'd just been. "Hmmmmnn," she moaned as one shapely leg
moved to lock itself around Andrew's muscular leg.

He murmured against her mouth, not wanting to break contact
between them. He lifted her chin, bringing his mouth to hers,
drawing from her a kiss that was hesitant and poignant.

"I want to love you. I only want to love you," he whispered,
gently, almost protectively.

Ruby heard the words from a great distance and felt their im-
pact. She wondered if he really did love her or he meant he
wanted to make love. Suddenly, she didn't care, because her
need for him sang in her blood, and she was helpless to deny
herself the strength of his arms and the feel of his body. Running her fingers into his wealth of sandy hair, she initiated an intimate kiss, exploring the recesses of his sweet, wine-scented
mouth, wordlessly telling him that if he would have her, then he
must take her.

"Did you hear what I said, Ruby?"

"Yes, yes I heard," she whispered, searching the soft interior
of his lips, pressing herself against him in welcome.

Andrew's breath caught in his throat. He whipped back the
covers, aware of her fiery gaze as it slid along his body. She was
heavy-lidded and excited with passion, her mouth parting with
invitation. He heard her quick, indrawn breath as his eyes traveled the length of her silky body. She moaned again and again
as his masculinity pressed hard into the softness of her lower
belly, and his hands caressed the smooth roundness of her bottom.

She was overwhelmed by the sensation of lying naked in her
husband's arms. Her hands caressed the play of muscles on his
back. Her thighs pressed against him, marveling at the lean, hard
strength of him. She could hear and feel the thudding of his
heart.

His mouth captured hers hungrily, desperately. Their hands explored each other, his softly caressing, discovering each sweet curve and hollow.

Andrew shifted so that he was lying beside her. He leaned over to kiss her neck, tasting the delicate scent of her earlobe, the gently curving sweep of her throat down to the valley between her breasts. His hunger found the complexities of her, the slimness of her waist, the turn of her hip, the rising fullness of her breasts. His lips lingered where he could find and give pleasure.

Ruby bent and twisted in his arms, yielding up to him and aiding him in his discoveries. Her hands found the smoothness of his back, the hardness of his firm arms, the softness of his chest hair. She tenderly nipped at the slope between shoulder and neck, burrowing downward to the hollow under his arm. She was headily aware of the quiver of delight that rippled through him.

Andrew's hands worshipped her, his lips adored her, carrying her into a world beyond reality to a place of passion and desire known only to lovers. His arms encircled her, drawing her tightly against him, reveling in the soft yielding of each curve against his solid length.

She wove her hands through his sandy hair, pulling him down to her breast, arching her back, and murmuring a whispered entreaty. He lavished kisses on her breasts, his tongue trailing little circles around the crest before taking the tip full into his mouth. He heard her gasp, felt the writhing of her hips against him. She opened her legs, trapping his thigh between them, clenching rhythmically against it.

In the dim bedroom light her skin took on a sheen, pale ivory against the burnished gold of the bedcovers. She twisted her head away from him, her lips parted, the tip of her tongue visible as it pointed outward, as though tasting a rare delicacy.

Her mouth tempted him, invited his kiss, the explorations of his tongue. She returned his kisses, opening her lips, inviting him to enter. Straining against him, her body rose and fell, desperately seeking to fill their mutual need.

Andrew turned over on his back, bringing her with him, his thickly muscled thigh still locked between hers. She lifted herself, tipping her head backward, offering him the hollow at the base of her throat and the fullness of her breasts. She brushed against the column of his neck, the ridge of his shoulders, arching upward again to increase the pressure of his thigh against her center. Her nipples grazed the fine furring on his chest and roused an exquisite tension in her lower belly.

His skin seemed to come alive beneath her touch and her lips, and she was ever more aware of his throbbing expectancy, hard and hungry between them. Her eyes met his as he gazed up at her; she saw his lips tighten in a grimace of constraint as he fought to bridle his passion. Following her instincts, seeking only to satisfy their mounting passions, she straddled him, using her hand to bring him into her, gasping at the first slice of pain and then recovering quickly as his sheath filled her and created a new and different pain and hunger deep within. Supporting herself on her knees, she rode him, moving against him, bringing him together with her to the height of their desires. Her eyes were locked on his face, and he gazed up at her with wonder. He could see the astonishment in her eyes and noted the intake of her breath. His hands held her hips, directing her in her motions, lifting her haunches to help her find the friction between them that she craved. Her hair fell over her brow, and there was a feline litheness to her body, slender and strong, supple and graceful. She rotated against him, drawing the hunger and tenseness from his loins. Her body was offered to his hands, and she brought her hungry mouth to his. Together they found what they sought, each sharing with the other, knowing that only in each other would they find everything they would ever need.

A gentle wind beat against the sparkling clean bedroom windows, seeming to isolate the lovers from the world outside as they lay in each other's arms, breaths warm and humid against each other's face. Andrew smoothed the golden curls back from Ruby's face, burying his lips into the back of her neck. She sighed, relaxed, in his arms. As he drifted into sleep, he muttered, "I'll be goddamned, who would have thought it?"

Ruby lay awake all night, staring at the ceiling. She stirred once to turn off the lamp. How was it possible, she wondered, that she could do what she'd done and not be totally, completely in love? And she'd enjoyed it. Remember that, Ruby. You enjoyed it, and wanted more. Right now, this very second, she wanted to do it all again, to feel that wonderful exhilarating burst of fireworks deep within her.

Shortly before dawn she dozed, content with her new life. If it was all one had, then one had to be content. To be otherwise would be foolish. "I'm going to be the best wife a military man ever had," she vowed sleepily.

The following weeks were blissful for Ruby. Her days were spent working on the apartment with her new friends, shopping at the commissary, cooking economical, nutritious meals, and making love twice a day with her husband.

The small apartment took on a life of its own as slipcovers were fitted snugly on the old worn-out furniture, the bare wood floors were waxed with six coats of beeswax, which was buffed every afternoon before Andrew returned home. Each corner, each windowsill, held a starter plant in a baby-food jar. Gertie proved how adept she was with a screwdriver and hammer when she installed plywood shelves in the kitchen. They were painted white and now held every herb imaginable. Ruby nurtured them lovingly, longing for the day when she could pluck off a leaf or stem for a recipe. By serving Andrew hamburger twenty-eight different ways for a month, she'd managed to scrape up the money for material for drapes for all the windows. The soft earth tones of the nubby material brought a warmth and coziness to the ratty apartment she hadn't thought possible. Even Andrew commented on how pretty the room looked. Her own kitchen now had curtains, bright yellow and green checks, with wide sashes and ruffles that hid the rotting wood of the window frames. At the same store where she purchased the material for the drapes and slipcovers, she bought a gunnysack full of rags and odd lengths of material and was now hooking her own kitchen rug to cover the new but ugly kitchen linoleum.

The two cabinets over the kitchen sink held what the girls called the makings for cheap dinners. Rice, pasta, packaged gravies and sauces that gave just the right dash to a dollar meal. She learned that if she made a hearty soup, she could get by for a week with a rich dessert and thick sandwiches. Leftovers were a challenge, with a prize given each month to the wife who came up with the most ingenious ways of serving a meal that didn't smack of leftovers with a capital L. The prizes were small and handmade, usually nothing more than a square of net filled with dried leaves or pine needles and tied with a length of satin ribbon. Ruby intended to win one. She had cooked a concoction of leftover brussels sprouts in cream of mushroom soup, which she ladled over leftover meat loaf crumbled on the bottom of a casserole dish. Parmesan cheese was sprinkled on each layer. Andrew raved over it the first time and had two helpings. When she doctored it up a second time with a shredded cheese topping, browning it until it was crisp, he ate three helpings. The final consensus, according to Andrew, was that it looked awful but tasted wonderful.

The day Ruby prepared the casserole for the girls' end-of-the-month recipe test, she could barely contain herself. She wanted the little net bag of dried flower leaves so badly, she thought she would burst. And she won it. The moment it was in her hands, she raced to her apartment and placed it in her underwear drawer, but not before she danced a little jig around the small bedroom. She belonged. They liked her.

Dixie proved her best friend, possibly because she lived next door and was always available with a smile and her sense of humor, which never changed.

Ruby was curious about one thing. She had noticed that the plump girl limped slightly. She hoped that someday they would be close enough as friends for the girl to confide. As it was, Ruby was startled when Dixie told her she'd been married for seven years and was actually twenty-eight years old.

Ruby had noticed the sly looks some of the other girls directed Dixie's way. It was as though they knew a secret concerning Dixie but wouldn't share it with her.

Ruby's curiosity came to a head the week before Christmas, when a small white engraved invitation arrived in the mail from Captain Everly's wife for a trim-a-tree luncheon. She immediately ran next door, but Dixie didn't answer. She knocked a second time and then called out. She walked around to the kitchen door and was surprised to see that all the curtains were drawn in the back as well as the front. She rushed back to her apartment to call her friend, but again there was no answer. She waited an hour before she tried again, with the same results. When she couldn't stand the worry she was feeling another minute, she put on her coat and walked down to Christine's apartment and explained the situation, the invitation still in her hand. When Christine wouldn't look her in the eye, she knew something was wrong.

"For God's sake, Christine, tell her," Monica shouted from the kitchen, where she was lacing boughs of evergreen together to make a garland.

"Tell me what?" Ruby demanded.

"I guess you'll find out soon enough," Christine muttered as she heated the coffee on the stove. "Look, we don't talk about it, okay? It's . . . it's really none of our business, and all we can do is be here when Dixie needs us. By now you must know we don't stick our noses into each other's private business unless asked."

Ruby's heart thudded. Dixie must be sick and didn't want anyone fussing over her. "You've said a lot of words, but you haven't said what the problem is. Maybe I can help."

"You'd better not," Christine said sourly. "Hugo doesn't like it when people interfere in his and Dixie's business. Our husbands don't like it, either." Her plain face screwed itself into miserable lines as she poured out coffee. Christine was fond of saying her coffee was like Missippi mud. Ruby thought it was strong enough to curl a person's hair, but she drank it anyway. She brought the cup to her lips, her eyes on the two women who refused to meet her gaze.

"Is she dying, is she seriously ill?" Ruby asked in a trembling voice.

"Of course not," Christine barked, her lips drawing into a thin, tight line.

"Then, what is it, for God's sake?"

Monica threw the garland she was working on to the floor. "All right, already. We know . . . we suspect, I should say, that Hugo slaps Dixie around. In places where it doesn't show. That's how she got her limp. There's nothing we can do but be Dixie's friend. When . . . when Hugo does that to her, we don't see her for a few days. She kind of holes up and closes the drapes. We knock on the door and call, probably just the way you did, and then we come home. At least she knows we aren't . . . ignoring her. He's a real . . . prick!" Monica said vehemently.

Ruby's stomach roiled. She set the cup of muddy coffee on the table before she gripped the edges to steady herself. "My . . . father . . . beat my mother," Ruby said in a strangled voice.

"I knew we shouldn't have told her," Christine said, putting her arms around Ruby's shaking shoulders. "Take deep breaths, Ruby. Please, don't let Dixie know you know. She has so much pride. If she thought any of us knew, she'd never be able to face us. You have to promise."

Ruby nodded shakily. She shivered, but not with cold, all the

way back to her apartment. She had to keep busy, to try not to
think about her friend. A cake, she would bake a cake for Andrew, chocolate and gooey, just the way he liked it. If she sliced
the layers in two, she could spread chocolate pudding in between and then make a powdered sugar frosting mixed with the
leftover pudding. That's it Ruby, bake a cake. Keep your hands
busy.

If she could put Dixie out of her mind, she still couldn't help
but think about Hugo Sinclaire. She'd met him, of course, on
more than one occasion, and hadn't liked him at all. Andrew
didn't like him, either, but wouldn't down the lieutenant the way
he did most people he didn't like. It probably had something to
do with Hugo being a fellow marine.

For some reason, Ruby thought as she creamed the butter and
flour against the sides of the bowl, she never thought of Hugo
as the violent type. Obnoxious, foul-mouthed, and arrogant, yes.
How had she missed that other streak in him? She thought about
how normal her own father looked, and she slapped the wooden
spoon against the thick bowl in frustration.

Ruby searched in her utensil drawer for an egg beater, wondering why someone hadn't complained to Hugo's commanding
officer about the way he treated his wife. Her mouth worked itself into a grimace. Because it isn't anyone's business, that's
why. Why had her mother kept her beatings secret? Was it because nothing could be done? Was it because of shame and
weakness? Or was it because other people didn't want to become involved? She wished she knew. She didn't know what
she could do, but, by God, she would do something. At least she
would make the effort. She knew in her heart that if she brought
the matter up to Dixie, their friendship would end and Dixie
would deny the story she'd just heard. But somehow she would
find a way.

The egg beater whirred to life. In her mind Ruby was pulver-
izing Hugo Sinclaire to a pulp. Her mind whirled and twirled as
fast as the beater in her hands. If there were only someone to
talk to, someone to discuss this with in the hope of coming up
with some sort of solution to Dixie's problems. Andrew, of
course. Andrew was the only person she could discuss it with.
The beater stilled.

Ruby scraped the cake batter into the tin and slid it into the
oven. She looked at the clock. If she hurried, she had enough

time to take a quick bath, get herself powdered and perfumed before Andrew walked in the door. If there was one thing Ruby learned in the few weeks of her married life, it was that she could get Andrew to smile and do just about anything if she made wicked bedroom promises and honored them. Above and beyond the call of duty. For Dixie, she would do whatever it took.

When Andrew walked into the fragrant kitchen an hour later, he found his wife frosting a still-warm cake that smelled almost as good as she did. His eyebrows shot up. He nuzzled her sweet-smelling neck.

"If you're really good, Andrew, I'll let you lick the beater and bowl," Ruby gurgled.

"Before or after I lick . . . other things?" Andrew leered.

"Take your choice," Ruby said boldly. "But can we make it later? There's something I want to talk to you about." She reached for the invitation to Alice Everly's Christmas party. Andrew's eyesbrows shot up a second time.

"Make sure you dress properly. Don't upstage her. Remember your rank."

"I know that, Andrew. I've done everything you said, and more. I've spread myself so thin, there are days when I barely make it back here to have supper on time. Captain Alice has me working on her newsletter, she appointed me recording secretary for her charity drive, and yesterday she called to *tell* me, Andrew, not *ask* me, to recruit the other wives for a used-clothing drive, and in between all that she has me collecting used toys for her Christmas party. You don't have to worry about me embarrassing you."

"You just did," Andrew said tartly. "You called the captain's wife Captain Alice. Why can't you just call her Mrs. Everly? What if you slip and that captain bit comes out? How's that going to look?"

"Shitty. I'm not stupid, Andrew. Look, she's using me to make herself look good to Major Carter's wife. And Major Carter's wife uses Alice to make herself look good to Colonel Moses's wife, who, in turn, knocks herself out to make sure she performs for General Frankel's wife. I know how it works."

"Are you complaining?" Andrew asked testily.

"Yes. But only to you. You're my husband, Andrew. Why shouldn't I complain to you? I listen to your problems, and sometimes I come up with a solution for you. Right now I am experiencing a problem. So I need you to listen. Sit down, I'll get you a beer and your slippers. Please, Andrew, this is important to me."

"Okay, okay, but this better not be heavy-duty stuff."

Ruby's stomach fluttered. Andrew was not in a good mood. Perhaps this wasn't the time to mention Dixie at all. She could make up some problem and hope for the best, but she knew she wouldn't do that. Dixie was too important to her.

Ruby curled up on the floor by Andrew's slippered feet, her arms wrapped around her knees. She watched her husband's face darken, whiten, and then turn unbelievably angry as she told him what was on her mind.

"Let me see if I understand this," he said slowly, his eyes dark and angry. "You're saying Hugo slaps his wife around. You want to do something about it, and if you do that, I become involved. It will be all over this base an hour after you interfere. True or not, it will go on Hugo's record, and while I don't have any affection for the bastard, I can't see a man's career being ruined for something you stupid women *think* is going on. Did you hear the things you just said, Ruby? Have you given any thought to the repercussions? I forbid, I absolutely forbid you to become involved."

Ruby's eyes sparked dangerously. She uncurled herself from her position at Andrew's feet and stood over him. She made a mental note of the look of discomfort on his face. So, Admiral Query had been right. He had once told her that people sitting were at a disadvantage when someone towered over them. She pressed her advantage.

"Doesn't it count that a young woman is crippled because of her husband? She has to live the rest of her life like that. No man has a right to do something like that, and I don't care if he's a marine or not!"

"So what if he cuffs her around a little? She probably deserves it. You can't prove he made her a cripple, for Christ's sake. This is not your business and it definitely is not mine. Drop it, Ruby. Right now!"

Ruby leaned over Andrew. "And if I don't?" she asked softly. "Will you use your fists on me, Andrew? Will you slap me around because you think I deserve to be slapped around? If you *do* think like that, you are in for a shock, because I will give you back as good as I get."

Andrew blinked. "You're paranoid, Ruby. You're relating all of this to your parents. I can understand that, but this is different. We're talking about causing trouble and ruining Hugo's career, as well as my own. Let them handle their own business. If Dixie wanted to, she would have done something about it."

Andrew was on his feet now, towering over his wife. "Another thing, Mrs. Blue, if I feel like slapping you, I will. That's my prerogative. I'm your husband. I'm not saying I would do that, I'm just saying I could," Andrew said belligerently.

Ruby's voice turned dangerously cold. "If you *ever* raise your hand to me, justified or not, it will be the last thing you ever do to me."

"And just what do you think you can do?" Andrew blustered.

"Leave. After I turn you in to your commanding officer."

Andrew snorted. It was obvious he didn't like this conversation at all, just as it was obvious he believed every word his wife said. "Where do you think you'd go?"

A secretive smile played around the corners of Ruby's mouth as she thought of her two properties back in Georgetown. Now she knew for certain that she'd made the right decision not to tell her husband.

"I have any number of places I could go. All that's important for you to know is that I *would* leave. When it comes to guts, I have just as much as you marines. You can't intimidate me, so don't try."

For an answer, Andrew stormed into the kitchen, picked up the frosted cake, and threw it against the refrigerator. Then he kicked off his slippers, picked up his shoes and coat, and marched out of the apartment, slamming the door so hard, Ruby thought it would fall off the hinges.

"Damn you, Andrew," Ruby blubbered as she set about cleaning up the mess he'd created. Did he actually believe he had the right to slap her around? Had she gotten herself into the same situation her mother had?

Ruby ate her solitary dinner with a book from the base library propped up against the sugar bowl. Her eyes kept going to the clock on the kitchen wall. She continued to sit long after the kitchen was cleaned. She drank two cups of tea and ate nine cookies and a banana. Lately, her appetite had been awesome.

At ten o'clock she undressed and put on her robe. She settled herself in the living room with her book to wait for her husband. This wasn't over yet, she thought.

But it was. Andrew returned at six minutes to midnight completely drunk, a silly smile pasted on his face. To her knowledge, he'd never been this drunk. Her conscience pricked her, but she ignored it and continued to read the same page she'd been reading for the past two hours.

"C'mon, honey, let's make up and go to bed. I wanna make love to you." He grinned.

"You're blitzed, Andrew. And it's no way to solve a problem. We have to talk it through, but now isn't the time. I'll help you," she said, offering her arm.

"Don't need your damn help," Andrew snarled, staggering toward the bedroom.

She should have let well enough alone, but she didn't. "You know, Andrew, you're always worried about the impression you make. What if someone saw you in this condition? How's that going to look? People will say I'm married to a drunk, a carouser. Remember, I wear your rank. I don't like seeing you in this condition."

"Tough," Andrew snarled again. "Get in the damn bed!"

Thirty minutes later Ruby was crying into her pillow and Andrew was snoring lustily. He'd practically raped her, and she'd lain there, letting him abuse her in his drunken anger. He'd used her. He'd abused her both physically and verbally.

Their first fight. Fights always had winners and losers, and she knew she was the loser for all her defiance. She continued to cry softly into her pillow.

In the morning she feigned sleep and didn't wake to prepare Andrew's breakfast. It was the only thing she could think of to assert herself. She half expected her husband to shake her awake, but he didn't. And he didn't kiss her good-bye when he left. *His* show of defiance.

It was eight-thirty when Ruby climbed from the bed, and even then she wished she hadn't. She made it to the bathroom just in time to relieve herself of all the food she'd eaten the night before. She returned to the bathroom five more times. Each attack of vomiting was more severe than the last. By noon she was so miserable, she wanted to cry. She had to get dressed and walk across the base to the Officers' Club for a meeting on the clothing drive, a meeting that Alice Everly said she must attend. After that she had to make her way to one of the other girls' apartments to help wrap Christmas toys the club collected for the poor children in town. She wasn't sure, but she thought she had a third event scheduled: the food-collection committee for the local church group.

She should call Alice Everly and cancel. She was sick. She wasn't sure what was worse, being sick or listening to the deadly silence on Alice's end of the wire. Like it or not, she had to show up.

Ruby felt as though she'd been through a hurricane when she returned home at five-thirty. Dixie's apartment was dark, she noticed, while her own was bright and cheerful with the colored Christmas lights winking around the door. The urge to rush up to Dixie's door and kick it was so strong, she ground her heels into the patch of ground next to the walk. A scrawny cat skittered past her, hissing disapproval that she stood in his way.

The cold, crisp air felt good even though she was shivering. She knew she should go indoors, all she was doing was postponing the moment she had to face Andrew. He'd be testy over the fact that supper wasn't ready, even though she'd left him a note on the kitchen table explaining all she'd had to do. He was fond of saying, "Fit it in, but don't make me suffer." As yet, she hadn't figured out how she was supposed to handle it all.

Ruby jerked to awareness when she heard steps behind her. She whirled in time to see Hugo Sinclaire coming up the walkway. When he was within a foot of her, she moved closer to her own walkway.

"I suppose you're the ghost of Christmas past," Hugo said cheerfully. "How are you, Ruby? I haven't seen you for a while. Getting ready for Christmas, I see," he said, pointing to the colored lights around the door.

"Where's Dixie?" Ruby asked, her teeth chattering with cold. "The house is all dark."

"She probably has one of her migraines. Light bothers her eyes," he grumbled good-naturedly.

"She didn't answer the door yesterday," Ruby grated.

"She does that when she gets an attack."

"She never said anything about migraines to me," Ruby said coolly.

"Does that mean you girls tell each other all your little secrets? Is nothing private?" His tone had changed subtly, and Ruby knew he was staring at her in the darkness.

"If you have a secret, I think it's safe to say it's still a secret. Dixie isn't exactly a confiding person." She turned toward her door and then called over her shoulder, "By the way, Hugo, night before last I heard your radio when I was in my kitchen. That was some program you had on. I tried to get it on our radio but couldn't get a clear station." Chew on that, she thought nastily as she opened the door to her apartment. It was a bluff, but let him wonder.

"I'm home," she said listlessly.

"It's about time," Andrew said cheerfully from the doorway in the kitchen. He wore an apron and was smacking his hands together gleefully. "I, madam, have prepared a culinary delight to tickle you from top to bottom. Actually, what I did was take everything in the fridge and mix it together with scrambled eggs. It looks like shit, but I put enough spices in it to give it this . . . different taste. I made some tea for you, and I picked up a . . . chocolate cake from the commissary . . . for the one I ruined last night. I'm sorry, Ruby, I really am. About everything. I had no right to . . . tell me you aren't angry."

"I'm not angry, Andrew. Just disappointed. Thanks for making dinner. I didn't think things would take so long, but Mrs. Everly had her own way of doing things, and she made a point of saying officers' wives, as a rule, don't serve dinner till eight or so because it's more stylish and cosmopolitan, whatever that means."

"She said that?"

"Yes, she did. She said only peons eat at six or five or even seven. I think she meant lieutenants. Do you want to wait till eight to eat from now on?" she asked, knowing he would say yes.

"Sure, why not. I can have a snack when I get in. Listen, how about us taking in a movie tomorrow?"

"How can we do that if we're going to eat at eight, and I have a meeting for the food drive? Christmas is only a few days away, and Mrs. Everly has my time booked solid. I suppose I could get out of it if I had to. Besides, Andrew, I think I'm coming down with some kind of bug."

"Probably the same one Dixie has," Andrew said cheerfully. "We'll go after Christmas. You do what you have to do, and I'll make dinner. It's the least I can do. After dinner I want you to go to bed and snuggle up with one of your books. I'll clear up here. I don't want you sick for our first Christmas, and Alice Everly will never forgive me if you're too sick to carry your share of the load."

Ruby held back the sharp return that was on the edge of her tongue when she sat down at the table.

The food on her plate looked appetizing enough. It even had a sprig of parsley on the side with a curl of orange carrot. She smiled her appreciation to her husband. "It's not bad."

"Ruby, last night I said a lot of things and so did you. I went off half-cocked and got drunk and ... wasn't very gentlemanly when I got home. Can we forget it and start over?"

There were so many things she wanted to say. She knew what the rules were now, so there was little point in saying anything. She nodded.

They made love twice that night and once again in the morning. Ruby made a pretense of enjoying the coupling and faked orgasm all three times.

Somehow Ruby managed to get through the holidays and the round of partying that went with the busy season. The Christmas she'd expected didn't happen at all. She blamed her lack of holiday spirit on her tiredness, on Andrew's attitude, and on Dixie's absence at all the festive parties.

It was two days after New Year's when Dixie knocked on Ruby's front door, a plate of holiday cookies in her hand and a small gift-wrapped box in her pocket. She looked the same, Ruby thought as she hugged her warmly and invited her into the kitchen. She immediately put on coffee, and as the first delectable aroma wafted through the kitchen, she bolted to the bathroom. When she returned Dixie was smiling.

"When are you due?" she asked warmly.

"For what?" Ruby asked stupidly.

"You know, the baby. Isn't it wonderful? I'm pregnant, too. I just found out a week before Christmas. Then I came down with this horrendous migraine, the worst I've ever had. I mean I was literally laid up all through the holidays. Hugo didn't want to go to all those parties, but I pushed him out the door. He had to go. You know how it is. Did you make your appointment yet? If not, let's go together."

Ruby's head whirled in time with her stomach. My God, she was stupid. As the coffee perked, she walked over to the calendar and flipped the pages back to November. With her finger she counted off the days. How could she have been so unbelievably stupid? "Oh, God," she groaned. "If you hadn't come over here, Dixie, I'd still be thinking I had some kind of flu or something. I'm pregnant!" she yelped.

"You didn't know? Well, congratulations!" Dixie laughed. "I hope this one takes. I've had three miscarriages. What do you want, a boy or a girl?"

Taken off guard with Dixie's words, Ruby blurted out, "A boy. But a girl would be nice. Oh, I don't care." Later she would add up the times and remember each and every word Dixie said.

"Is Hugo happy about it?"

"Very happy. The other three times we were transferred, and I miscarried as soon as we got settled. It must have been the moves. They're never pleasant, with all that bending and lifting. It doesn't look like we'll be transferred this time, though. I'm keeping my fingers crossed. I'd like a boy, but it doesn't really matter, as long as the baby is healthy."

"How come you guys keep transferring? Everyone else seems planted for at least a year, mostly two from what I can gather."

Dixie shrugged her shoulders helplessly. "You get orders and you leave, it's that simple. We've moved a total of seven times in eight years. You learn to live with it." Ruby found her friend's words strange. She kept quiet, but there was something very wrong here.

"Let's go for a walk," Dixie said. "It's so crisp and clear outside, it will do both of us a world of good. I've been feeling real pukey lately, and you look like you could use some color in your cheeks."

Dixie went next door to get her coat.

"A baby," she said to herself in hushed tones as soon as she was alone. "Andrew's and my baby."

She wondered if Andrew would be pleased or unhappy with the news. She admitted to herself that she didn't know. When should she tell him? Tonight, or wait till she'd seen the base doctor? She made the decision to wait until she'd gotten the doctor's confirmation.

They walked until there was color in Dixie's cheeks and she complained she couldn't go another step. Ruby looked around for a place to sit, but there was none. "Do you think you can make it back? You can lean on me. I'm sorry, Dixie, I didn't realize we'd come this far."

"It's okay, I'll make it, we just have to walk slow. I hate it when this pesky leg of mine gives out like this."

"How'd it happen, Dixie?" Ruby asked bluntly.

Ruby could feel her friend stiffen. "It was the darnedest thing. I fell off the kitchen chair and fractured my hip. I guess you could call it a freak accident. I thought I just hurt it and didn't go to the doctor right away, and when I did it was . . . well, this is the result. Don't feel sorry for me, Ruby, I hate it when people pity me."

Ruby managed to look properly horrified at the statement. "I wasn't . . . I'm not. The only reason I said anything was it's my fault we came so far and put you through the long walk back." Fell off the chair, my foot, she thought. More like she was pushed off and denied medical treatment.

There was a hard little edge to Dixie's voice when she said, "I hope we get to stay here for a while now that I have you for a friend."

"Being pregnant at the same time will make us closer than ever. You have to teach me how to knit, Dixie. You're so good at crocheting and all that stuff. We can make little sweaters, booties, and hats. Oh, Dixie, we'll have such a good time. As long as you're feeling well. How often do you get those migraine headaches?" Ruby blurted out.

Dixie blinked. "Ah . . . well, it all depends on . . . the weather mostly," she said weakly. "Sometimes if I eat too many sweets one will . . . hit me." She was talking too fast and not meeting Ruby's gaze. "Or, when I get my period . . . guess I won't have to worry about that now."

"No, I mean, do they come once a month, every six weeks, every three months? My old boss at the Pentagon used to get them every two weeks."

Dixie cringed. "Why are you asking me all these questions? If you really need to know, I'd say . . . every six weeks or so."

"Next time you get one, you let me know, and I won't bang on your door or ring your phone off the hook," Ruby said cheerfully. "That must drive you batty."

"I didn't mean to be sharp with you, Ruby, I'm just tired."

"We'll be home soon. I'll make us a nice cup of tea, and we'll both feel better. Boy, I wish I could afford a car."

"Me, too. Things would be a lot easier."

"Isn't there anything to do around here to earn extra money?"

Dixie shook her head. "Even if there were, our husbands wouldn't let us take a job. Hugo simply would not permit it. Officers' wives don't work, didn't Andrew tell you that?"

Ruby shook her head. "I hate penny-pinching," she said. "When I was on my own I did it, but it didn't seem so bad somehow. Now I have to worry about Andrew and pretty soon a baby. I just thought there would be more money at the end of the month."

"It's a vicious circle, Ruby. The only way you get more money is if you move up in rank. But then you have to entertain more, dress better, buy better cuts of meat, so it goes that way. We chose this life, so we're stuck with it."

"Maybe, maybe not. I'm going to give this some thought. There has to be a way to make money that our husbands won't object to. Even if they do, so what? Money in the bank and steak on the table has to count."

"I can't help you, Ruby. Hugo is adamant on my not working. Lord, we're home. I can't wait to sit down. I think my feet are frozen. Ruby, don't stir up a hornet's nest, okay?"

"Okay," Ruby said agreeably. She had no intention of doing any such thing.

During the following days Ruby felt the effects of her pregnancy more and more. Her bouts with morning sickness, afternoon sickness, and evening sickness abated during the first week in February, to her relief, but her weight started to drop, and when she went to the base clinic she was stunned to see that she weighed only ninety-one pounds. She looked awful, tired and pale, with horrible half moons under her eyes that no amount of powder could erase. Andrew, while not alarmed, had commented more than once on what he called her scarecrow appearance. Dixie, on the other hand, positively glowed with good health. Her hair was thick and lustrous, and her eyes sparkled with happiness. She suffered no sickness of any kind and ate more than her husband. In the fourth month of her pregnancy she'd already gained eleven pounds; Ruby, approaching her third month, had lost seven. Dixie was so deliriously happy that Ruby found herself envying the lame girl.

Both girls walked out of the clinic, Dixie with a bottle of vitamins and Ruby with the doctor's confirmation that she was pregnant. It was February 13, the day before Valentine's Day.

"What are you wearing to the dance tomorrow?" Ruby asked as they walked along at a slow pace.

Dixie laughed. "Nothing fits. Monica gave me a maternity top that's red and white, kind of in the spirit of the day, if you know what I mean. It seems kind of foolish to start wearing maternity clothes already. People will think I'm showing off my condition." She giggled. "Oh, Ruby, I am going to love this baby so much. I'm going to rock it and sing to it and kiss and hug it as much as I can. I already love it," she said, patting her stomach. "I asked Hugo if we could put the crib in our room, but he thinks the baby should have its own room, so I'm trying to get a picture in my mind of how I can fix up that little cubicle next to our room as a nursery. It's not as big as the room you have, but then, this little fella will need only a crib and a small dresser. I've never been so happy. You feel that way, too, don't you?"

"I guess so," Ruby said listlessly. "Maybe if I weren't so wrung out, I'd be as excited as you are."

"You *do* look tired, Ruby. I think you should go home and put your feet up and relax a little. I'll get you a cup of tea and some of the spiced cookies I made yesterday. Now that your stomach is settling down, you're going to have to build your strength back up. A banana, too," she said in a motherly tone.

"Okay. Tea and cookies and a banana. Sounds great."

"A nap might not be such a bad idea, either," Dixie said as she bustled about Ruby's kitchen.

"Stop being so bossy," Ruby grumbled. "Besides, I have to write a letter to Admiral and Mrs. Query. Did I tell you they're coming to North Carolina ten days from now? They have a house in Chapel Hill, and Admiral Query knows General Frankel. They're going to play golf and chess. We're supposed to have dinner together. Here. Can you just picture that? General Frankel and his wife are coming, too. I tried to get out of it, but I couldn't. I'm afraid to tell Andrew. I'll have to serve a roast or a turkey or something. I think that's what's been making me so irritable and sick. I don't have the right kind of dishes or a fancy tablecloth or anything like that. I know how terrible I look and I'm pregnant. It's awful," Ruby groaned.

Dixie placed the cup of tea on a little table next to Ruby's chair. "Listen to me, Ruby. Both of those muckety-mucks were once exactly where Andrew is. Their wives were where you are. They won't have forgotten that. The fact that they *want* to come here has to mean they haven't forgotten. I bet anything they're all looking forward to it, and if you want my advice, I wouldn't worry about a roast or a turkey or anything expensive like that. You serve them that mess that won you the best leftover prize. Wine is cheap enough, so that's no problem. If you try to be something you're not, they'll see right through you. The admiral and his wife like *you.* You be yourself and nothing will go wrong. Trust me, Ruby. Now, while you're resting, I'll call around and see what I can find in the way of a tablecloth that isn't patched and see if anyone has a matching set of dishes and glassware. Don't worry about cleaning before they come. We'll all pitch in. Everything is under control!" Dixie said gleefully.

By nightfall the word was over the entire base that the Blues were entertaining flag officers in their apartment. When the word filtered down to Andrew, he covered his shock well and raced to the nearest pay phone to call Ruby, who didn't deny the story.

"Jesus Christ, Ruby, you could have told me!" Andrew blustered. "Where are we going to get the money to take them to dinner?"

"I'm cooking, Andrew. My brussels sprout casserole, the one that won the prize. I'll even make garlic bread. Wine is all we have to buy. The admiral invited himself. He also invited the general. Do you know how to say no to a general? Well? I thought not. But don't worry. The Querys are very nice people. It's going to be fine," Ruby said in a shaky voice.

"Yeah, just fine. Do you have any idea of what I'm in for here now that that story is out?" Andrew muttered.

"The bottom line, as you tell me all the time, Andrew, is they all wish they were standing in your shoes. If it will make you feel any better, tell them, and this is the truth, that the admiral and his wife are *my* friends. Of course, if you want to feather your own nest, say they're friends of yours, too. I have to go now, Andrew. Mrs. Everly asked me to call her, and I'm late now. I'll see you when you get home, okay?" Ruby could hear her husband muttering as she hung up the phone.

Ruby slept, her body finally relaxed. She was still sleeping when Andrew walked through the door at five-thirty. His first anxious thought when he saw Ruby was that something was wrong. Ruby never napped. She didn't have time. It must be the business with the admiral and general coming to dinner. Now that he was over the shock, he felt rather proud that his wife had a flag officer for a friend. There was no way the dinner party could hurt him. If anything, it might help him.

Ruby woke when she heard the soft tinkle of silver and china in the kitchen. "Andrew, is that you?"

"It is, unless you're secretly entertaining some other guy I don't know about. I tried to be quiet."

Ruby yawned. "I can't believe I fell asleep. It's just that I've . . . Andrew, would you please come here? There's something I have to tell you."

"You mean there's more?" he asked in mock horror.

"There's more. I went to the doctor today. I'm pregnant. I hope you aren't upset."

Andrew dropped to his haunches. "A kid! Yours and mine! Jesus! A kid! That means I'll be a father and you'll be a mother. We'll be goddamn parents. Holy shit!"

"Does that mean you aren't upset?" Ruby laughed.

"Hell, yes. I mean, no, I'm not upset. We're going to have to juggle and shift and economize, but we can do it. So that's what's been wrong with you. Are you okay? What did the doctor say?"

"He said I had to put on some weight but not to go over twenty pounds. I've lost seven or eight, so I can put on twenty-eight, I guess. I actually feel better than I have in weeks. He said he thinks the morning sickness is over. I hope so anyway."

"Do you think it'll be a boy?" Andrew asked boyishly.

"If it isn't a girl, it's gonna be a boy. There's only two kinds."

He was delighted, Ruby thought in relief. Thank God. Now all she had to do was work up her own enthusiasm.

"Are you happy, Ruby?"

"Of course I'm happy. Our very own little person. As soon as I start to feel really good, I'll get into the swing of things. I believe there's some sort of protocol for pregnant women."

"Can I tell everyone tomorrow?"

"I'll shake you out of your shoes if you don't." Ruby laughed.

"That means you're going to have to take it easy. I'll send a memo, through channels, to Mrs. Everly that you're on hold for the next nine months. No one is going to expect you to do anything unless you absolutely want to, and that goes for me, too. C'mere, honey."

Ruby slipped to the floor and snuggled into her husband's arms. They talked, for hours, about everything and anything. They touched and kissed and whispered. They giggled and laughed like small children. They rolled about on the floor, tickling each other, calling out baby names with gusto. They didn't make love, there was no need to. They were closer in spirit than they'd ever been.

When they were in bed, a long time later, curled together, she felt a lone tear roll out of the corner of her eye. She wiped it with the edge of the pillowslip. It had to be a tear of happiness.

It took exactly six days for Ruby's appetite to improve, and then there was no stopping her. She ate everything in sight, and when she ran out of food she mooched from Dixie, who was only too happy to accommodate her. The other girls brought over plates of cookies, brownies, and dried fruits, as well as assorted candies and jars of pickles. Ruby ate it all. She was one pound short of her normal weight the day of her dinner party.

The Querys and Frankels were due to arrive at seven. Women crowded in, carrying pails, mops, and brooms. Ruby was reminded of her first day on Iwo Jima Circle. By noon, when the girls took their first break, the small apartment not only gleamed, it sparkled and smelled pleasantly of lemon polish and ever so faintly of pine oil.

"Right before your guests are due to arrive, put these orange peels and this cinnamon stick over the pilot light and the whole place will smell as if you've been in the kitchen for hours." Sue grinned. "I saved the kids' orange peels this morning."

"Look what I came up with," Monica said, coming through the door along with a furious gust of wind. She held a square, silver-plated chafing dish complete with a candle. "I," she said proudly, "got this from Dolly Nevins, who got it from Sheila, who lives on Montezuma Drive, who got it at a swap meet. She said a retired colonel's wife donated it before they mustered out. It's absolutely perfect for your table, dead center after you remove the centerpiece. What do you think, Ruby?"

"It's perfect." Ruby beamed nervously. "I'm so jittery."

"Ruby, you are the belle of the base. Everyone is talking about this dinner, and it goes without saying we're all very, very jealous. It's the coup of a lifetime. Tomorrow you'll be famous. Hey, where's Dixie?"

Ruby's heart fluttered. Until this moment, with all the hectic preparations and cleaning she hadn't noticed her friend's absence. She looked around and saw the girls were all tactfully busying themselves. "I . . . she probably . . . you know, those migraines. I guess they're pretty terrible." She busied herself filling the teakettle and managed to spill half the water over the waxed floor. Christine rushed to wipe it up, their eyes meeting miserably.

With a catch in her voice Monica whispered, "Oh, well, you'll have a lot to talk about when . . . when she's up and about."

Ruby self-consciously turned the conversation to her own pregnancy and the way she was going to use the storeroom as a nursery.

By the end of the afternoon, the apartment was sparkling and a gorgeous table had been set with silver and china that belonged to some of the other women.

"You girls are something else," Ruby said, feeling an attack of giddiness.

"You wait till it's your turn," Gertie called over her shoulder as she swept through the door, the other girls behind her. "Good luck, Ruby. Call us as soon as they leave, okay? Secondhand will be almost as good as being here. Remember everything, every word, every gesture. We all want to know how to behave if we ever get the chance to do this."

"I won't forget a thing," Ruby promised as she dipped and swirled the Crisco can in soapy water, Dixie's contribution to the evening.

By five-thirty the ice bucket was full of ice, the casserole ready, and the oven lit. She'd already bathed so that Andrew could take his time shaving and dressing.

Ruby burst out laughing when her husband walked through the door. She'd never seen him in a dither, but he was in one now as he rushed about mumbling and fretting that he couldn't see his face in his shiny shoes. Ruby rushed to dab a smear of Vaseline over the highly polished shoes.

"Now, where the hell did you learn that?" Andrew demanded.

"One of the girls." Ruby giggled. "I keep telling you we have our own methods of keeping you guys on top."

Andrew hopped into the kitchen on one foot. His face was so miserable that Ruby took pity on him when he confided he was nervous. "Sitting at our table with two flags. It blows my mind, Ruby. Are you really sure that . . . that mess you're serving is good enough?"

"Will you relax, Andrew, you're making *me* nervous. Do I look all right?"

"Beautiful. I mean that, honey. You look great. This past week or so you've really snapped back to your old self. Are you . . . should I mention that you're pregnant?"

"I don't think you'll have to. They'll know. The wives, I mean."

"Ruby, how can you be so goddamn calm? I can't even sit down till they get here, or the crease in my pants will come out."

"No, it won't," Ruby said confidently, remembering they were fresh from the dry cleaner. "Trust me."

"I did, and look who's coming to dinner," he bellowed.

Ruby laughed.

The Frankels arrived in a staff car minutes after the Querys. There were kisses and hugs, handshakes and booming laughter that could be heard two doors away.

General Frankel, Ruby decided immediately, was an austere man. He had a ruddy complexion, which made his full head of white hair gleam like a halo. His eyes were green as grass.

The introductions over, the small group settled in and started a round of "do you remember when?" There was a lot of laughter, and after a while Ruby began to realize that these important people felt at ease in her home. They were friendly and outgoing, putting both her and Andrew at ease.

"Come over here, honey," Janet Query said, motioning to a place on the sofa between her and the general's wife. "Now, tell us, you didn't go out of your way for us, did you? We remember what it was like being a lieutenant's wife, and believe you me, the pay was a lot less back then."

Ruby smiled. "Actually, Mrs. Query, I was going to make a fancy dinner, but it wasn't in our budget, so what you're getting is my prize-winning casserole." There was no note of apology in her voice. Arlene Frankel nodded approvingly.

"They're still doing that, eh? I won a prize for an ungodly concoction using beef jerky, but it was only third prize. I wasn't much of a cook in those days. What did you win, my dear?"

"Would you like to see it?" Ruby asked eagerly.

She was back in a second with the little net bag that both women oohed and aahed over.

"You know, Ruby, I've been meaning to write and tell you that the admiral was absolutely lost without you once you left," Mrs. Query said. "He had six secretaries from the time you left until he retired on the first of the year, and he was always such a grouchy bear when he came home at night. You spoiled that man, you really did. It was his idea to visit you. Not that I didn't want to," she said hastily. "He wanted to be sure you were all right and that the Marine Corps was taking care of his girl. They are, aren't they, Arlene?" she said pointedly.

Ruby held her breath. How was the general's wife going to answer that?

"Edward, is the Marine Corps taking care of Mrs. Blue?" Mrs. Frankel called across the room. Janet Query winked at Ruby, who sat bug-eyed, waiting for the general's reply.

"Hell, Arlene, I don't know. Young man, is the Corps taking care of the two of you?" the general boomed.

"Ah, yes, sir, General," Andrew said in a shocked voice.

"Good. That's what I like to hear," the general replied.

"When is your baby due, Ruby?" Arlene Frankel asked, as if that had been the subject of the conversation all along.

Startled, Ruby blurted out, "Not for six months."

"That's wonderful." Janet Query beamed.

"I'll expect a cigar, Lieutenant," General Frankel boomed.

"Yes, sir," Andrew said dutifully.

"You'll send us an announcement, Ruby?" Janet asked.

"Actually, Mrs. Query, I was going to ask you and the admiral if you would . . . what I was going . . . do you think . . . ?"

"We'd love to." Janet laughed. "Clark has never been a godfather before."

"Thank you, sir," Andrew said huskily.

"My pleasure, young man."

When they sat down to dinner, Ruby was given compliment after compliment about her casserole, and everything seemed to go smoothly until, toward the end the kitchen wall suddenly came to life with violent thumping and a muffled scream from the other side.

Ruby's head jerked upright till she was staring into her husband's piercing gaze. She chewed on her lip when Andrew said the people next door were fond of playing their radio rather loudly. Admiral Query stared across the table at his hostess. She knew he didn't believe a word of Andrew's explanation.

"Wonderful dinner, Ruby," he said, obviously trying to ease her mind. "What's for dessert?"

"Clark!" his wife chided.

Ruby laughed, but the sound was hollow. "I made a chocolate cake filled with pudding and marshmallow and nuts. You . . . you freeze it and then slice it like a log cake. We have some . . . canned fruit if you think that's too rich." Her ear was cocked toward the wall, but she couldn't help it.

Janet Query noticed her distraction. Her own soft gray eyes were full of concern when she asked lightly, "Who lives next door, Ruby?"

"Which side?" Ruby asked tightly.

Janet pointed to the kitchen wall. Ruby felt like jumping out of her skin. She slammed the refrigerator door too hard and felt the bottles and cans bang against the door.

"Hugo Sinclaire and his wife," Andrew said quickly. "Her name's Dixie, isn't it, Ruby?"

"Yes, Dixie. She's pregnant, too." She turned then to reach for the cake plates from the shelf above her head.

"Nice people. Everyone is nice around here. They've made us feel at home. Ruby and Dixie are fast friends, aren't you, Ruby?"

"Yes. Yes, we are," Ruby said, slicing the cake in equal portions. "The coffee will be ready in a minute," she said in a choked voice.

"I know Hugo," General Frankel said thoughtfully. "Outstanding officer, and he's up for promotion."

Admiral Query swiveled in his chair. "Ruby, is anything wrong?"

"Wrong? Oh, no, Admiral Query. I think I ate too much, that's all. I'm going to pass on this cake. Sweets are my downfall," she said lightly. She knew she wasn't fooling her old boss, but it was the best she could do. Andrew was going to take a fit later when their guests left, she thought uneasily.

"I put chicory in the coffee, Admiral. I think it's just the way you like it," Ruby said, offering him the cake plate. She poured the fragrant coffee with a trembling hand.

Admiral Query met the general's eyes. There were no obvious nods, no words to indicate either man was aware that something was suddenly not quite right in the Blue household.

"This is wonderful, Ruby," the admiral said enthusiastically. "Give my wife this recipe, too."

The dinner conversation seemed to accelerate, to the point that Ruby thought she would scream. Her ears were so tuned to the back kitchen wall, she found herself staring at it, willing the occupants to keep quiet.

There were no coffee refills, no second helpings of cake. The men excused themselves while their wives volunteered to clean up the dishes, over Ruby's protests.

"If you're going to smoke that smelly cigar, Clark, you go outside," Janet Query ordered in a voice that matched her husband's when he issued a direct order to a subordinate.

"Your pipe isn't exempt, Ed." Arlene smiled. "Ruby's pregnant and smoke will make her sick. Go along now, this is women's work."

"Thank God," Clark Query muttered as he reached for his overcoat.

"Lieutenant, you're free to join us. I need to stretch my legs. A walk around this little area will bring back some fond memories. Of course, if you'd rather stay here with your wife while our wives play housemaid, we'll understand." The general's voice clearly indicated Andrew should favor the latter suggestion, which he did.

Outside in the crisp February air, Ed Frankel turned to his old friend. "Spit it out, Clark, what's going on?"

"Shit, Ed, I don't know. Something in the apartment next door. Maybe you didn't pick up on it because you don't know Ruby the way I do. Her husband was aware, too; things changed when that commotion started in the apartment next to theirs. I heard a scream and it didn't come from a radio. Sounded to me like someone got slammed against a wall."

"Jesus, Clark, are you suggesting we . . . spy on the Blues' neighbors?"

"We're out for an after-dinner stroll. Send your driver for

your pipe tobacco. Tell him you forgot it. Jesus, since when does the navy have to do your thinking?" It was an old argument between them. The general bristled but walked over to his staff car and issued the order.

"Now what?" he barked.

"Now we walk. If you wear glasses, this is the time to put them on." Query fitted his own wire rims over his ears that for the most part he was too vain to wear. The dark world burst into sharp focus as he stared at the apartment next to the Blues. The drapes were pulled, but cracks of light shone around the edges. The drapes on the Blues' front windows were also drawn against the dark night. It was entirely possible, Query thought, to get mixed up and knock on the wrong door when they returned from their stroll. He voiced the thought to his friend.

"Even a grunt wouldn't do something that stupid," Frankel grumbled.

"Right, but who's going to question *you*?"

"I know what you're thinking. This could be serious."

"Only if you act on it or bring it to a head. Ruby said the woman was pregnant. What if he's beating her up in there? Would you want that on your conscience? If this was my command, that bastard's ass would be out of here so fast, his head would be rotating on his shoulders. If I'm wrong, and I hope I am, no harm will be done."

"Has it occurred to you, Clark, that maybe it *was* a damned radio? Even in the military, a man's home is his castle, and what goes on—"

"Bullshit, Ed! We have our share of screwballs in the military. I've lived my life paying attention to my hunches; so have you, unless you've changed over the years. There's trouble there, pure and simple. It's your call; this is your turf. I'll not say another word."

General Frankel puffed on his pipe. "My problem is that Sinclaire is up for promotion. I've already written a glowing fitness report on him, based on his commanding officer's recommendation. If you're right about him, I'm going to have to spend a lot of time covering my ass."

"I know, Ed. I said, it's your call."

Five minutes later they were back at their starting point. Query moved in the direction of the Blues' apartment when the door next door burst open. Hugo Sinclaire froze, the open door yawning behind him. General Frankel moved quickly for a man his age and snapped a smart salute which Hugo Sinclaire had no choice but to return, which prevented him from immediately closing the door.

Both older men looked past him to the crumpled form on the floor outlined in the light of the doorway. "Nice evening, Lieutenant," Frankel said briskly, moving toward the Blues' walkway. "I used to live here myself," he shot over his shoulder. He heard rather than saw the door close. Neither officer spoke when they returned to the Blues' living room.

The Blues' guests stayed on an extra thirty minutes before they called it a night.

"Remember, now, Ruby, we want to know as soon as the baby arrives," Janet Query said, hugging Ruby. She whispered against Ruby's ear. "Everything is going to be fine. Trust us." Ruby completely misunderstood the admiral's wife.

"I'll call you in a day or so and have you join my expectant mothers' class, Ruby. I think you might like sharing this precious time with other mothers to be," Arlene Frankel said.

"Thank you, Mrs. Frankel, I'd like that. Is there room for my friend Dixie?"

"Why certainly," Arlene Frankel said without a moment's hesitation.

Ruby was returning from the commissary two days later, her arms full of groceries, when she saw the moving van pull away from the apartment next to hers. She set her grocery bags down and ran to the curb, demanding to know where the Sinclaires were.

"Gone. We got our orders to pick up late yesterday."

"But . . . you mean they're *gone*?"

"Sweetie, they ain't·in there, if that's what you're asking me. We're moving this stuff to the Mojave Desert."

"You're what?" Ruby wailed.

"Look, sweet thing, I'd like to sit here and talk to you, but we have a lot of miles to cover, and this stuff has to be there when the Sinclaires sit down. You know how it works. Look on the bright side, you're going to get a new neighbor."

Ruby walked over to the Sinclaires' apartment and opened the door. Her steps echoed as she moved from room to room. Tears gathered in her eyes. On a wall of the little cubicle Dixie had planned on turning into a nursery there marched nursery-rhyme decals. Her fingers traced over a smiling Peter Pan.

Dixie hadn't said good-bye. Ruby sniffed and blew her nose. Why? Maybe her friend had left a note under her door. She ran to her own apartment, forgetting the groceries sitting on the walk. She sobbed in disappointment when she found no note.

She remembered the grocery sacks and carried them into the house. She was still sobbing as she put the food staples on the shelf above the sink. She stopped only long enough to call the girls. When she hung up after her last call, she sensed that something was wrong. All the girls knew that Dixie and Hugo had left. They knew and hadn't said anything.

Gone.

She was still crying, curled into the corner of the sofa when Andrew came in from work. She hadn't bothered to turn on any lights and had made no attempt to start supper.

"She didn't even say good-bye, Andrew. How could she do that to me?" Ruby said, beating her clenched fists into the cushions. "Did you know, Andrew? If you did and didn't tell me, I'll never forgive you. All the girls knew; they said their husbands told them. Tell me the truth!" Ruby wailed.

"Ruby, I swear I didn't know. I *heard* that Hugo put in for an immediate transfer, but the way the Corps works, it usually takes weeks. I was going to tell you this evening. The story I got, which is probably fifth hand at best, is Hugo put in for the transfer, because he found out he was passed over.

"Honey, I know you feel bad. I hate to say this, but I did try to warn you not to get involved. Dixie wasn't the person you thought she was. If she cared about you as a friend, she wouldn't have left like that. How the hell long does it take to make a phone call or scribble a note and slip it under the door?"

"It's not just Dixie. The girls are all acting very coolly toward me these past days. Everything has changed, and not for the better. And don't tell me that I'm imagining things. And as far as Dixie goes, I believe her damn husband wouldn't let her say good-bye. If he was such a sure thing, and everyone says he was, how come he didn't make it?"

"Who knows," Andrew said. "He could have farted wrong."

CHAPTER FIVE

Ruby opened the front door of her apartment, then quickly closed it. There was no way she was going to walk against the buffeting wind all the way across the base. March, she thought ruefully, was roaring like the proverbial lion. It wasn't cold, though, so that was a blessing. Spring, she knew, hovered just around the corner. Yesterday she'd seen tiny little purple crocuses poking their heads up in the Sinclaires' straggly winterized garden. Only it wasn't the Sinclaires' garden anymore. Now a family named Galen lived in the rooms Dixie had decorated.

Penny Galen had her own car, a cream-colored DeSoto, and right off that set her above Ruby and the other girls. She also had stylish clothes and expensive shoes and handbags. Her two children, ages four and six, looked like little models from the Sears, Roebuck catalogue. Their furniture was expensive: a pale blue brocaded sofa with matching chairs in plum and pale blue. Grand was the term the girls used to describe the contents of the Galen household.

Penny Galen favored inch-long fingernails, highly polished to match her pedicured toenails. She went into New Bern to have them done once a week, along with her beehive hairdo, which was bleached a sinful white. Monica said the shade was called platinum. Christine wondered out loud how she wiped her rear end with her long nails. Monica said she was so perfumed and powdered, she left a trail all over the base. Penny Galen was not one of them. She made her point the day they descended on her and offered to help her clean her apartment. "I," she said regally, "have help." The help was a middle-aged Polish woman from New Bern who arrived on Tuesdays and Saturdays to polish and scrub. Penny Galen was an only child and a military brat who had lived all over the world. She let it be known from the first that her daddy was a full colonel and had pull. Dave, her husband, wasn't going to fiddle-shit around, trying to make points with low-ranking officers. The girls blushed and flushed and backed out Penny Galen's door, vowing never to return. Gertie, in a fit of pique, said snidely that General Frankel and Admiral Query were personal friends of the Blues and dined there frequently. Ruby wanted to slap Gertie when she saw the speculative look on Penny's face. She did not need a friend like Penny Galen.

Later, when she had time to think about the incident, she decided Gertie's motives were suspicious. All the old camaraderie was gone. Oh, the girls still included her in their kaffeeklatches and luncheons and do-good affairs, but it wasn't the same. It seemed to Ruby that they were constantly on guard and watched their tongues the way they watched their household money. It had almost reached the point where Ruby wanted to say the hell with it all and stay in her apartment by herself to read or clean. She was on edge all the time and so lonely; she found herself crying for no reason at all. The doctor said that crying was normal, that pregnancy affected each woman differently.

Andrew volunteered the information that Dave Galen was a stuffed shirt with delusions of military grandeur.

"Don't get involved," he warned Ruby in the same tone of voice he'd warned her about Dixie. But this time Ruby agreed.

"Andrew, she calls and knocks on the door, and I don't answer. What else can I do?"

"Tell her, point-blank. Why should you have to hide out or avoid the phone?"

"It's not that easy, Andrew. You've drummed into my head that I have to wear your rank and make nice because we never know when we're going to come up against them. You said we shouldn't make enemies."

"Do what you want, Ruby, but always remember the Sinclaires. That's all going to bounce back on us someday. I feel it in my gut. I'm not exactly popular at headquarters these days."

Ruby stared at her husband. He was blaming her. She felt miserable.

"I know it's all my fault," she said, though she didn't believe it for a second. She would never believe she had done anything wrong with regard to Dixie and Hugo, but if it made Andrew feel better to believe she had, so be it.

The succeeding days crawled by, each lonelier than the day before. She marked off days on the calendar with a red pencil, she didn't know why. She was gaining an alarming amount of weight, but she didn't stop eating the rich butter cookies and equally rich chocolate cakes she was addicted to. When she wasn't eating cookies and cake, she was making fudge, pounds of it, which she devoured in an evening.

The days were warmer now, and April showers had dampened the hard earth around the complex, making it suitable for planting flowers. This she did at dusk, when she knew Penny Galen was inside her apartment, serving a gourmet dinner to her family. She still met with the girls once or twice a week, even though she felt like an outsider. So many times she wanted to ask them what she'd done to make them change their attitude toward her, but she knew that if she did, they would tell her it was her imagination.

All the girls talked about these days was the promotion board's decision, which would be coming out shortly. Kent Aldridge's wife was so certain her husband was going to make rank, she had a party planned for the day of confirmation. There was nothing shy about Evelyn Aldridge. Kent deserved it, she said over and over. Hugo Sinclaire was never mentioned. Ruby was to bring a nine-bean salad to the dinner party.

Ruby felt the girls were envious of her relationship with General Frankel's wife, which had grown closer during the expectant mothers' class. The class had led to a friendly tea, a trip to the commissary with Arlene Frankel, and once in a while a ride home in the general's staff car. The general's wife was even giving her driving lessons. The day Penny Galen saw her getting out of the car, Ruby felt like thumbing her nose at the snobbish young woman. Instead, she'd nodded curtly and dashed into her apartment.

Today, Arlene Frankel had taken her aside and asked if something was wrong. Ruby hadn't meant to say anything, but the words tumbled out. She confessed her rapid weight gain, the other girls' coolness to her, Penny Galen's determination to invade her privacy, and the real gut-wrenching hurt of Dixie's departure without so much as a good-bye, drop dead, or see you in ten or twenty years.

The older woman's eyes saddened. "Ruby, my dear, life in the military isn't always easy, as I'm sure you've found out. But you're tough, Ruby, Janet and Clark told me that. You can make it. You've got it all going for you. Face the problems with courage, and if there's an unexpected boost along the way, accept it. As for your friend Dixie, it's her loss that she didn't consider you friend enough to say good-bye. Don't look back, my dear, only forward. Be prepared and remember your priorities. However, if you like, I can find out where the Sinclaires were transferred, should you want to write your friend."

Ruby's shoulders straightened. "No, thank you, Mrs. Frankel. It's better this way."

Arlene Frankel smiled. "Good girl, Ruby. That's exactly what I would have said. It's almost time for you to start dinner, so I'll have my driver take you home. If you have any problems, I want you to feel free to call me. Don't worry about the rank thing. Promise me."

Ruby nodded. She now had a mentor.

The fifteenth of April dawned clear and bright, although the weatherman promised rain by evening. It was warm, almost balmy, Ruby thought as she set about preparing the nine-bean salad for Kent Aldridge's promotion party. While the party was pot luck, it was being held at the Officers' Club. For the past two days she'd made congratulation banners and posters but had turned the ladder-climbing over to the other girls.

Ruby snapped the airtight lid on the Tupperware container, then burped it. Done. Now all she had to do was walk over to the commissary for milk and bread and she had the rest of the day to herself.

Ruby ran a brush through her short curly hair and was about to walk out the door when the phone rang.

"Ruby?"

Annoyed, Ruby snapped, "Andrew, who else do you think is going to answer our phone? Of course it's me. What's wrong?" she asked uneasily.

"Listen, I want you to meet me right now. Walk over to the commissary, and I'll be waiting outside. Now, Ruby!"

There was something in Andrew's voice she'd never heard before. "I'm leaving right now, as a matter of fact. It's going to take me at least fifteen minutes."

"Don't stop to talk to anyone, okay?"

"Okay, okay. If you hang up, I can leave." She was out the

door a second later and halfway down Iwo Jima Circle when Penny Galen pulled to the other side of the street. She lowered the window. "I'm going to the commissary, do you want a ride?" Ruby debated a fraction of a second and then nodded when she remembered how worried and anxious Andrew sounded.

"I guess you're all ready for the Aldridges' celebration this evening," Penny said in what Ruby called her uppity tone.

"I made my bean salad this morning, so I guess that means I'm ready. It was nice of you to offer me a lift. I'm meeting Andrew."

"You should have a car, Ruby. However, since you don't, I can drive you to Mrs. Frankel's for your classes. All you have to do is ask, Ruby."

Ruby bit down on her tongue. Sure, so you can horn in and make trouble, Ruby thought nastily. She forced a smile to her lips. "I need the exercise. It's good for me to walk. Thanks for the offer, though."

"I could pick you up after the class. You're probably tired from all that exercising. I can call Mrs. Frankel and drive the girls home. It's no bother at all."

"I don't think she'd like that, Penny. Mrs. Frankel is adamant that we do all the walking we can. Listen, I'll think about it. Maybe in my ninth month, when I start to wobble. Oh, look, there's Andrew. Thanks for the ride, Penny."

Ruby's heart thudded in her chest when she saw the high color in her husband's face. "C'mon, over here, where no one can hear us." Ruby's heart thudded a second time.

"The shit hit the fan, Ruby. I got the promotion, not Kent Aldridge. Jesus, Ruby, do you know how this looks?"

"We're having nine-bean salad for dinner," Ruby said stupidly. She felt her tongue grow thick in her mouth. "What about the party for Kent?"

"I don't give a shit about Kent's party. There's more. Are you ready to hear it?" Ruby could feel herself start to tremble. She nodded.

"I'm being assigned as Frankel's aide. The guy who has been with him for years is retiring the first of May. Frankel is going to Korea and I go too. Ruby, for Christ's sake, are you listening to me? See what having friends in high places does?"

"Let me get this straight, Andrew. Are you *blaming* me for

this promotion? If you are, you can stop right now. If you don't want it, give it back. Tell them you like what you do. I don't believe this. You made me come all the way over here so you could blame me? Stuff it, Andrew." Ruby turned and walked away. "If you want breakfast in the morning, you better get some milk and bread. I'm going home."

"Ruby, wait. Look, I'm not blaming you. But it's already all over the whole fucking base that I aced out Hugo and put a whammy on Kent all because of *your* supposed connections. And the kicker is, I have to go to Korea without you. You're going to be here by yourself. You'll be alone when you have the baby. Jesus, Ruby, think about *that*."

"When it comes right down to it, Andrew, even if you were here, I'd still be alone when I had the baby. You'd just be standing outside the delivery room, waiting to hear if it was a boy or a girl. I think I can handle it, *Captain* Blue." She whipped off a smart salute.

Andrew grinned from ear to ear. His blue eyes sparkled as he snapped off a return salute. "You're the first person to call me that. I gotta get back. Are you okay?"

"Right as rain, Captain. I'll see you at dinner. Remember, we're having nine-bean salad. Don't forget the milk and bread."

"Ruby, you're right here. Go in and get it."

"No. I have to think about all this. I don't want to run into anyone who might have heard. I want to be the one who decides how to handle this. Congratulations, Andrew. I know *we're* going to enjoy our new rank." Her husband laughed heartily.

The moment Andrew turned to walk back to headquarters, Ruby sobered. "Oh, shit!" she muttered. "Now what do I do? Do I call the girls, or do I sit tight and wait to see if they call me?"

Back in her apartment she alternated between looking at the Tupperware bowl of salad and the phone, willing it to ring. She knew it wouldn't, but she hoped.

Andrew was going to Korea and leaving her behind. She hadn't asked him for how long. Did he even know? Mrs. Frankel would. Was she supposed to call her and thank her? Maybe Mrs. Frankel would call and congratulate her. That sounded more reasonable. Andrew going off and leaving her. There was no doubt in her mind that she would survive, but she was going to be so lonely. So very lonely. Surely the tour wouldn't be for more than a year. A year was only twelve months, and she would have the baby to keep her busy during the last part. Maybe it wouldn't be so bad after all. Babies were demanding. This was going to take some getting used to. She continued to eye the silent black phone. If it did ring now, it wouldn't be pleasant. The caller would be harsh and bitter. She whipped the receiver off the hook and laid it down.

Ruby sat down at the kitchen table. The hardest thing would be trying to act as if nothing had changed. *She* was the same; *she* hadn't changed. "Well, I'm not going to hide out, that's for sure!" Ruby muttered.

She picked up the receiver of the squat black phone and dialed Evelyn Aldridge's phone number.

The phone rang seven times before Evelyn picked it up. She'd been crying, that much Ruby could tell from the raspy tone in her voice. Her hand gripped the receiver more tightly.

"Evelyn, this is Ruby. Please don't hang up. Look, Andrew didn't even know he was on the selection list. We all thought, Andrew included, that Kent was a shoo-in."

"That's all very easy for you to say, Ruby Blue, but we all know why those . . . those flags had dinner at your place. You're a regular little smarty-pants, aren't you? I could have done without this phone call, Ruby. You just called to rub my nose in it. Well, you succeeded. I could hardly hold my head up when I went to the Officers' Club to take down the decorations. Nobody trusts you, Ruby Blue. Nobody. And here's something that should put you and that husband of yours in a really good mood: Dixie Sinclaire lost her baby a few days ago. Chew on that, Ruby, while you and your husband are celebrating the promotion that should have been my husband's. Don't call me again, okay?"

"No, I won't bother you again, Evelyn," Ruby whispered as she replaced the receiver in the cradle. Dixie lost her baby. How did they know? Tears burned her eyes. The tears overflowed, followed by great choking sobs that ripped at Ruby's insides.

"What's wrong with me?" Ruby cried. "Am I really no good, the way my father said? Why me, why me, why me?"

Andrew sat at the bar in the Officers' Club, his long legs tucked in the rungs of the barstool, with his commanding officer, Lieutenant Colonel Lackland. It had been his colonel's invitation and one he couldn't refuse. He was drinking scotch straight up, as was the colonel.

This little private celebration was deliberately timed, he realized now, to coincide with the girls' dismantling the party decorations. Lackland was a first-rate bastard and proud of it.

"How does it feel, Blue?" Lackland asked out of the corner of his mouth.

There was no point in pretending he didn't understand what his commanding officer was referring to. "Not bad, sir. I joined up to see the world." A tiny voice warned him not to give Lackland anything to come back at him with. He was finally getting away from the son of a bitch, and if he had his way, he'd never think about what he'd done for him as long as he lived. He realized at that moment just how lucky he really was, thanks to Ruby. He grinned from ear to ear.

"Thanks for the drink."

"You'll never make full bird, Captain," Karl Lackland said out of the corner of his mouth. "I'll see to it personally."

Andrew swung around on the barstool. "Wanna bet? My diary for yours, if I make it before you do. I have this infallible memory, probably the same kind you have, *sir*."

Andrew was on his feet, towering over his commanding officer. He leaned over, and with a grin on his face for the benefit of the others in the bar, he whispered in Lackland's ear, "When it gets lonely in that godforsaken country and the general wants to make small talk, this whole thing will make for interesting conversation. What that means, exactly, is don't fuck with me, because if you do, you won't like the results. You're the one with the problem, not me. On second thought, I'll pay for my own drink," he said, slapping two bills on the bar.

Conversation at the bar dropped to a low hum and then ceased altogether when Andrew strode out of the Officers' Club. His fellow officers were now ripping him up one side and down the other, Andrew decided as he set out on foot to walk across the base to housing. As if he gave a good rat's ass.

He walked slowly, his thoughts on the faraway land called Korea. At least he wouldn't have to worry about getting his ass shot off. Being aide to Brigadier General Frankel would ensure that. Frankel had a long way to go in the military, and the smart money said he'd go the distance. His own rank, if he proved indispensable to his commanding officer, would rise right along with the general's. He was actually looking forward to Korea and a bachelor existence again. Of late, Ruby had been smothering him. Her world was so boring, it irritated him. The baby did please him, but what pleased him even more was he wouldn't be around to see his wife grow fat and bloated. He hated it when she got up five times a night to go to the bathroom. He hated the sour look on her face when she got heartburn and bouts of vomiting. He'd be away during the baby's sleepless nights. He wouldn't have to watch his wife pull out her tit to feed the baby. He personally thought it a disgusting practice, but Ruby was adamant about breastfeeding. Let her; he wouldn't have to see it. By the time he got back, the kid would be a little person, not a blob that demanded twenty-four-hour care.

It pleased Andrew that he was leaving behind a pregnant wife. She wouldn't be attractive to any of the free-swinging bachelors on base, and after she had the baby, she'd be too busy to even think about playing around.

His long-legged stride lost some of its momentum, however, when he realized he might miss Ruby. It was nice going to bed with her knowing she was his and he could do anything he wanted. Ruby was more than agreeable to sex in any position at any time of the day or night. Perhaps she was too agreeable. She got up when he did, made him breakfast, kept the apartment sparkling clean, and prepared dinners that were nutritious as well as inexpensive. Evenings, curled together on the sagging couch, were spent for the most part with his head in her lap or hers in his while they read silently or aloud to one another. He might miss that and he might miss the evening strolls they took together. But he doubted he would miss her enough to be miserable over it.

Andrew's stride quickened when the row housing came into view. He jammed his hands into his pockets and started to whistle. His good mood stayed with him until he opened the door and found his wife bawling her head off on the couch. His stomach churned. Christ, how he hated weepy, whiny females.

He squared his shoulders and sat down by her, his arms drawing her to him. He wouldn't have to put up with this all that much longer. Today he could be charitable.

"Nothing can be that bad," he said soothingly.

"Dixie lost the baby." Ruby hiccoughed.

"*That's* why you're crying?"

"Evelyn Aldridge told me. She sounded as if it were my fault. I never should have called her, but I wanted to do what was right so it wouldn't bounce back on you. I'll never do that again! I don't care what any of them do or think. I don't care," she said, enunciating each word carefully.

Jesus, he was glad he was going to be leaving this petty bullshit behind. "C'mon, give me a smile. Listen, it's possible there's something ... wrong with Dixie, you know, in her insides, that makes it impossible to carry a baby. It's not our fault, and I don't ever want you to take the blame for something like that."

Ruby's head jerked upward. She wasn't blaming herself, he thought, she was blaming *him*. She untangled herself and stood up.

"What's for dinner?"

"Nine-bean salad," Ruby said shortly.

"That's it? I didn't know there were nine different kinds of beans," Andrew muttered as he made his way to the bathroom to shower and change.

Ruby was approaching her sixth month of pregnancy when her husband said good-bye to her at their front door. She was dry-eyed, and there was a tremor running through her body that she couldn't explain.

"I'll miss you, Ruby. I'll write. Probably not often, but I will write. That's a promise."

"I'll write twice a week," Ruby promised.

"The minute you have the baby, have the doctor call the communications office, and they'll get word to me right away. I set it all up already. You won't forget to do that, will you?"

"That's very unlikely, Andrew. Did you remember to take the box of cigars?"

"First thing that went into my bag. The second thing was your picture." It was the truth.

The general's staff car pulled to the curb. The driver, a fresh-scrubbed lance corporal, jumped out and saluted crisply. Andrew snapped off one in return, and the enlisted man hustled to load Andrew's bags in the trunk.

"Stay right here," Andrew said softly to Ruby. "I want to remember you here like this. I'll miss you." He kissed her lightly on the cheek.

"Write," Andrew shouted.

"I will," Ruby shouted from the doorway.

Ruby watched the khaki-colored car with its single flag flying in the warm air until it was out of sight.

The apartment was quiet, except for the softly playing radio. It played all the time, but Ruby didn't actually hear it. She walked around the apartment. The breakfast dishes were still on the table. Last night's newspapers littered the living room floor. The bed was unmade and Andrew's wet towel hung over the bathroom door. It would take her an hour, perhaps a little longer, to tidy the apartment unless she wanted to scour the bathroom, which her husband left filthy.

Without stopping to think, Ruby pulled a bright yellow scrub bucket from the narrow linen closet and filled it with water. Forty-five minutes later there was no sign that a man had ever used the bathroom. "And it's going to stay this way for the next year," Ruby muttered.

In the kitchen she turned up the radio two decibels. Now she could at least hear the music and commentaries.

"Long live Ruby Blue," she said, holding her cold coffee cup aloft. "I promise to miss you, Andrew, at least once a day. I also promise to think about you every day. Occasionally, I promise to dream about you, and I will write faithfully. In short, I will keep our home fires burning." What more could anyone expect of her? What more could she expect of herself?

{{{{{{{{ CHAPTER SIX }}}}}}}}

As spring rolled into summer, Ruby summed up the time as whizzing by. She watched the trees dress themselves in full regalia as though to shade the tender, budding flowers she planted in front and back of her dreary apartment. The sun shone more brightly, she thought, now that Andrew was gone. One warm, sunny day melted into another. She was happy. She did miss Andrew, but not to the point of crying about it. She kept her word and wrote long, witty letters twice a week and received one in return every three weeks.

She read incessantly—novels, biographies, and every book on child care the library had to offer. When she wasn't reading, she did her stint for the Captains' Wives' Brigade, as it was known to all those who participated, willingly or unwillingly. She learned quickly that she could beg off anything by pleading swollen feet, nausea, or pounding headaches. All ailments were forgivable in her delicate condition. Mostly, she did paperwork, mailings, filing, and a limited amount of bookkeeping, all projects she could do in the evening when she was alone.

She ate well, perhaps too well. By her seventh month she'd gained forty-two pounds. She put herself on a diet, for the baby's sake, and started to eat more nutritious foods, although on Sundays she splurged and ate an entire pound of homemade fudge.

Nearly everything Ruby did was for the baby's sake. Be it a boy or a girl she carried deep in her belly, this baby would be hers alone by right of birth. It would always be a part of her and it would never want to leave her. Never, ever.

In addition to writing letters to Andrew, she often spent time writing to Nola's mother, Mabel McIntyre, and Janet Query. She also wrote letters to her sisters, but she never mailed them. In the evenings, when it was cool, she worked in the spare room that was to be the nursery. Now she was hand-painting nursery rhymes on a three-foot-high border that circled the small room, as Dixie had done. She'd already bought a used crib and rocking chair, and had stripped off their thick coats of paint, then primed them and added a sparkling white patina. Tonight she was going to sit in the rocking chair and sew the binding on a crib quilt she'd made by hand. It had taken her two full weeks to paint the walls and ceiling because her arms ached and she tired easily, but it was finished now. In the center of the room was a rug she'd braided that was so colorful, she wondered if it would keep the baby awake. She'd taken pot luck when she bought the bag of rags and had no choice but to use them. Once she finished the quilt she had only to mend the tears in the curtains she'd bought at a moving sale. The room would be finished in time for the baby's arrival.

At first, she'd wanted to put the crib in her own bedroom, but when she had mentioned it to Andrew, he'd written back so quickly, she'd been stunned. No, no, no, he'd written. Babies need their own rooms, and I do not, I repeat, Ruby, I do not want the kid in our room. She'd thought about it a lot and finally decided Andrew had a point. She would sleep in the baby's room on a quilt, but just in the beginning, until she was certain he would be all right throughout the night. Besides, she would have to nurse him, and what if she didn't hear his tiny cries? It was settled. What Andrew didn't know wouldn't hurt him. By the time Andrew returned home, she'd be back in their room.

Since Andrew had gone, she'd managed to save one hundred twenty-five dollars, and she wanted to buy herself a car now that she had her driver's license so she would be able to get around after the baby arrived. The only problem was she knew nothing about cars other than that they ran on gas. She'd written Admiral Query and asked him how she should go about buying a car and what it was she should look for. Instead of answering her letter, he arrived in person a week later and took her to Havelock, where she purchased a Ford that the salesman said was driven only to church on Sunday. A Baptist church, he'd clarified. The admiral had looked under the hood and pronounced that it looked as if what the salesman said was true. He himself had changed the oil, filled the tires with air, and washed the car before he said it was fit for her to sit in. Sit in it she did, sometimes for as long as an hour or until her belly got in the way of the steering wheel. Of late, Admiral Query had acted almost like a father to her. One of these days she had to think of something nice to do for him and his wife.

The car would open up the world to her. She could drive around and see things she'd only been hearing about. She could picnic with the baby in the spring and do just about anything she felt like doing. There were days now, Ruby thought, when she felt as if she lived in a cocoon. Still, she was enjoying her life and her second shot at independence. And she wasn't faltering, except that she occasionally found herself thinking of Calvin. She wondered where he was and what he was doing. Amber hadn't written for so long, and the last letter had no news of him. She daydreamed about what she imagined she had missed by not marrying him. She knew she had to, as Andrew would say, put a lid on it. She thought it harmless enough in the beginning, but as the days rolled along, she found herself carrying on imaginary conversations with him. She knew she had to stop before she started to lose touch with reality. Once again, by sheer will alone, she buried Calvin Santos deep in the recesses of her mind.

She was waiting. It seemed to Ruby that all her life, until now, had been spent waiting for one thing or another.

Ruby sat on her canvas chair with her feet propped on a wooden crate. Overhead, a mass of gray-black clouds scudded back and forth in an angry formation, as though they couldn't make up their mind which way to go. In the distance she could hear an ominous roll of thunder. A storm, one the radio said was to be the worst of the summer, was due to pelt the area with heavy rain by late afternoon. The brisk breeze gave way to a strong wind. A vicious bolt of lightning ripped across the sky, directly in Ruby's line of vision, but she didn't move until she saw a third bolt streak down to the open field to the left of the base. She thought she could smell the scorched earth and burnt grass. The area was too open for her to be comfortable outdoors now. Inside, she could curl up on the sofa and open the drapes if she wanted to watch the onslaught that was due any second. Obviously the weatherman was off schedule. It was just a little past noon.

Ruby walked around to the front of the apartment. She thought she heard Penny Galen's car, which meant she would have Ruby's mail, something she volunteered to deliver now that she was in her last days of her pregnancy.

"There you are! I was just going to knock on your door. You do have a load of mail today, Ruby," Penny said, handing over occupant letters and requests for donations that came in crisp, crackly envelopes. Penny had just had her hair done, Ruby decided, and the strong wind was making more of a mess of it. Secretly, she would have given up her Sunday fudge allotment to know how any beautician could allow a girl as pretty as Penny to walk out of her salon looking as if she'd stuck both thumbs in a light socket.

"You better get indoors before this wind ruins your do," Ruby said hastily. "Thanks for bringing my mail."

"Ruby, are you okay? I know you have only a few days to go. You have my phone number, don't you? Dave or I will be glad to take you to the hospital when it's time." She sounded so sincere that Ruby nodded.

It was dark as the inside of a vault now, Ruby thought as she hurried up the walk to her apartment. Inside, she turned on all the lights and opened the drapes. The weatherman might be early, but he was right about the intensity of the storm. She was glad that she lived in the concrete housing unit. The rain, when it came, slashed and tore at the windows, pounding down on her walkway with such force, Ruby cowered deep into her corner of the sofa. Five minutes later the power went off and she was up again, looking for candles. The letters she'd been holding dropped to the floor. She hissed in irritation as she set the candle on the end table. There was no way she could bend over, and if she did, she might not be able to get back up. She felt like a baby walrus as she struggled to flip the letters, one by one, with the tip of her shoe so that she could bend sideways to pick them up.

What seemed like a long time later, Ruby flopped down on the couch, her breathing ragged, her stomach cramping with her struggles. Penny was right, she did have a lot of mail. Her eyes widened when she saw Amber's return address had changed. She smiled at the name Mabel McIntyre on the second. She felt faint when she saw Opal's name on the third; Ruby opened it.

Opal's letter was a single page, expertly typed. The return address was for an apartment on Connecticut Avenue in Washington, D. C.

Dear Ruby,

I couldn't believe it when I met Mrs. McIntyre and she asked me if I was related to you and Amber. She gave me your address. Gosh, Ruby, I thought I'd never hear from you again. And you're married. I'm real happy for you. I almost took a fit right there in front of her when she told me Amber had a baby and that you're expecting one, too. I was an aunt and didn't even know it. I hope you're happy, Ruby. I know Amber isn't; she doesn't know how to be happy. She wrote home a lot at first, but Pop sent the letters back. After a couple of months, she stopped writing. Please write and tell me how she is and if she had a boy or a girl.

Grace Zachary and Paul moved to Pittsburgh. He got a promotion and a new store. People said she was pregnant when she left, but maybe that was just a rumor. People never said nice things about the Zacharys. I loved them both. Grace helped Mom a lot. Me, too.

Mom is okay. What that means is she's Mom. I think she had tears in her eyes the day I left, but they might have been my own. She didn't kiss me good-bye or anything, and Pop, he just dumped me on the train and walked away. I don't miss either one of them, and for sure I don't miss Barstow.

I lived at the YWCA like you did for a while and then I moved into this apartment with four other girls. Ruby, it is so wild, I can't tell you. It's so much fun. We're all slobs, and none of us can cook worth a darn, but we're surviving just fine.

I think I sort of have a boyfriend. My boss is a major, and his brother is at Annapolis, and he came down over the 4th of July and he introduced me. His name is Bill Barton and he's a third classman. He writes to me and everything. He looks real spiffy in his dress uniform. Boy, is he a good kisser. Midshipmen call their dates drags. Did you ever hear of anything so silly? I like him a lot.

I don't think there's any way you could know about Pop's accident, so I'll tell you. Maybe you aren't interested and don't care, but I have to fill up this page. That day he came back from Washington a couple of years ago was when it happened. Mom said he went over to help Grace do something, and this big pot of grape jelly fell off the stove, right down his stomach and between his legs. Lordy, lordy, lordy. He was in the hospital for a long time and had some kind of operation that didn't work. He has to wear some kind of gadget to pee. No one told me this. I saw Mom cleaning it one day and put two and two together. He walks kind of funny, too. He's still mean and nasty. Sometimes weeks went by and he wouldn't say two words. Bet you don't care about any of this.

There was holy hell to pay when Bubba's will was read. In her will she said your debt was wiped clean, but I know you still send your money. I pay mine, too. I'm not going back, not even for Christmas. I'm going to send Mom a present but I'm not buying one for Pop.

Uncle John and Hank really missed you. I went over on the sneak to say good-bye. It doesn't seem the same without Bubba. Uncle Hank said they're thinking about selling the house. Won't that be awful?

That's my news, Ruby. Oh, how I missed you when you left. I think I cried every night. I did what you did and ditched my Bible on the train. You want to hear something real kooky? I even miss Amber.

Please write to me and let's not lose track of each other. If you have Amber's address, send it to me so I can write to her. We only have each other. I want to know I have two sisters and where they are. I love you, Ruby, and I think about you every day.

Your sister,
Opal

Ruby wiped her eyes with the back of her hand. "I've missed you, too, Opal," she whispered. "Someday I'll tell you how much."

Ruby folded the short note and returned it to the envelope. She couldn't help but wonder if Opal had been the recipient of the "petty cash award." Opal would have mentioned it. She laughed then until she had to hold her stomach—Opal involved with a midshipman who was a great kisser.

Mabel McIntyre's letter was a paragraph saying she'd taken the liberty of giving Ruby's address to Opal and expressed the hope that it was the right thing to do. She said she was looking forward to cooler weather and to drop her a line and to be sure to let her know when the baby arrives.

The envelope from Amber was like a lead weight in her hand. Perhaps she shouldn't open it. On the other hand, there might be a picture of Amber's little girl inside. She only had one other picture of her niece, one taken at the baby's christening, but the infant had so many clothes on, it was impossible to see anything but the tiny pinched face, so like Amber's.

She squirmed about on the couch, trying to get comfortable, but the nagging cramping in her stomach was getting worse. If she lay flat, she'd get heartburn. If she stood up, her back would ache. If she kept on sitting the way she was, she wouldn't be able to straighten up. "Damn, Ruby, just be still and open the stupid letter," she muttered to herself.

Outside, the storm raged, but Ruby was oblivious of it as she read.

Dear Ruby,

Nangi has prodded me for weeks now, asking if I've answered your last letter. He really gets after me when I don't do things as quick as he thinks I should.

In my last letter to you I asked you what you thought of the name I gave the baby, and you didn't respond. I think Angela is a lovely name, and, of course, we call her Angel. You're still thinking like you did when we lived in Barstow. That's behind us now. Grow up, Ruby. If you didn't like the name, you should have said so.

Our weather has been warm and sunny, but we have days when it literally steams. I keep the baby in a diaper and that's all. She has prickly heat, but baby powder helps.

I had a letter from Ethel, and she said to tell you congratulations on your marriage. She said Andrew was a handsome devil and hopes you are happy. She's getting married in October to a farmer from Montana.

Nangi had a letter from Calvin, and he sent a picture of his new son. I'm sending it in this letter, but send it back. Nangi is forever pasting pictures in albums. He's so family-oriented, he makes me want to scream sometimes. Anyway, about Calvin, I know you're just dying to know what he's up to. He is up, I can tell you that. He's probably flying by now. You know, one of those hotshot glamour boys. He said in his letter he had no intention of spending his career shuffling papers in some dull administration job, so he put in for flight school and I guess he was accepted. Nangi was vague on the details. I think the reason he did it was because the promotions in administration are about nonexistent. Nangi is very proud of him. He didn't ask about you. He said his wife is a good mother. If you ask me, she looks like his grandmother. Calvin's, not the kid's.

I'm pregnant again. At first I couldn't believe it. Nangi is so happy. He wants nine kids, his own baseball team. He's so silly.

I don't have any more news now. Things are quiet over here, not like back home.

Don't forget to write when you have the baby, and be sure to send a picture so Nangi can paste it in his book. I have to go now. Angel's crying for her afternoon juice.

Your sister,
Amber

Ruby held the pictures near the candle flame. Angel was a cherub of a baby with licorice-dark hair. She was too fat and had a double chin. Ruby frowned. Amber and Nangi were both slight and slim. The little girl resembled a roly-poly ball. Cute, she decided. She sucked in her breath before she held up the other picture. The child looked to be about two months old. He wasn't sweet at all, and he didn't look particularly clean. She stared at the picture for a long time, wondering why the infant's hair grew straight in the air like a porcupine's. He had Calvin's eyes. Calvin's dark hair. He looked to be long rather than round, covered as he was in a long dress that was rolled up at the sleeves. She saw one tiny foot peeking out from under the hem. Calvin's baby. For one brief second she felt smug at the baby's appearance, then shame rippled through her.

The blind love and loyalty she felt for Calvin surfaced. "I'm sure he's a beautiful baby, Calvin, and I'm sure you love him dearly," Ruby whispered. Tears of frustration burned her eyes. She had to stop dwelling on Calvin and his new family. Amber wasn't worth thinking about. Amber was still as bitchy as ever.

It was time to put a new candle in the holder, but Ruby was reluctant to move from the nest she'd created in the corner of the couch. She realized she felt awful. She should have walked today, at least up and down the street. Lack of exercise must be the reason for the crampiness she was experiencing. Maybe she should eat something. The candle was starting to sputter, the acrid smell of the smoke circled her.

She struggled to her feet and then swayed. She felt light-headed, disoriented. As she wobbled to the bathroom, she took care to shield the flame. If it went out, she'd be in total darkness and she wasn't exactly sure-footed these days. She was hiking up her skirt when she felt a rush of warm wetness down her leg, soaking the anklets she wore. "Oh, shit," she muttered. The explosive words extinguished the candle flame. The urge to urinate was still strong, but light was of more importance. She squished her way to the kitchen for a candle, which she slipped into a cup. She looked down at her wet socks and sandals. It was at that precise instant that she knew what she'd experienced in the bathroom was her water breaking. "Oh, shit," she mumbled again, making her way to the living room and the telephone. She stiffened. The phone was dead. Her eyes swiveled to the front window and the storm lashing outside. Panic rivered through her as she broke out in a cold sweat. Now what was she supposed to do? Pictures she'd seen in *National Geographic* flashed in front of her. Women working in fields stopping only long enough to drop their babies, tie the cord, and resume working. She shuddered.

Ruby tried then to remember every single thing her doctor had said, but there had been nothing about home delivery or delivering one's own baby.

"Andrew, I should kill you. I didn't bargain for this. What am I supposed to do?" she wailed. "Oh, God, oh, God," she bleated as she beat one clenched fist into the other. Did she dare try to go next door to the Galens and hope they could get her to the hospital?

Did she dare? Her answer arrived a split second later when an explosion rocked her kitchen in the form of a tree branch crashing through the rotted window frame. She yelped in terror, tripped, and righted herself. She was petrified now as a violent spasm wrapped itself around her belly. Labor. She unclenched her teeth and drew in a deep breath when a second vise cramped her belly. She could feel perspiration dripping down her neck and between her breasts. For the first time in her life, Ruby was unable to think clearly. Should she clean the puddle in the bathroom or should she try to board up the kitchen window? Should she lay down, or sit down, or was it better to stand? If her life depended on it, which seemed to be her present problem, she couldn't remember a single thing she'd learned in the expectant mothers' class. Fear held her immobile. Her hands cupped her stomach. Her eyes rolled back in her head when a streak of lightning zapped across the sky. Thunder rolled, rain slashed and battered against the windows like a hungry monster's claws. Her stomach again contracted painfully. She should be timing the pains, but in order to do that she would have to move or carry the candle to her bedroom, where her clock sat on the night table. Her Timex watch was on the same little table. She hadn't been wearing it these past few weeks because the band was too tight.

The painful contractions abated as quickly as they'd started. Ruby drew in a deep breath. A reprieve, but for how long? She had to do something.

Duck fashion, she waddled to the bedroom for her watch, holding the candle high above her head. She felt like crying. She'd never been this helpless, even back in Barstow when her father was ripping into her for one thing or another. She'd had a will then, her mind and her thought processes, not to mention her Bubba, who always made things right. There was always a bright light at the end of the long tunnels of her life, but not now. Now she couldn't think beyond what was happening to her. Having a baby was far different from enduring a punishment. She needed help and she needed it soon. She tried the phone again. The lines must be down all over the base, and housing wouldn't be a first priority for the electricians and telephone men. Housing would be the last thing to be repaired. She had to accept that fact and decide what to do.

Outside, the storm continued. The decibel level of its cacophony was so high that Ruby clamped her hands over her ears. It was worse than any nightmare she'd ever endured.

Above the sound of the storm Ruby thought she heard the squawking static of her husband's battery-operated radio. She trundled into the kitchen with the intention of placing the radio on the back of the stove with the volume on high in the hope the Galens would notice and come to check on her. She wasn't even sure if Penny or her husband were home. Somehow she'd lost all track of time. On other evenings she'd heard the rambunctious Galen children riding their tricycles into the walls or screaming at the top of their lungs. The radio squawked and then quieted. The batteries must have given out, Ruby thought in despair.

For the first time, Ruby was aware of the water on the kitchen floor. Angrily, her fist lashed out at the wall. How in the name of God was she to clean up the water and have a baby at the same time? "I hate you, Andrew Blue, for doing this to me. I wasn't ready to have a baby. Now that the time is here, where are you? I need helllllp," she yowled. "I hate you for this. I do, dammit. What if I botch it up? Oh, God, oh, God."

Ruby sloshed her way to the shallow closet that served as a pantry and reached for the broom. She banged on the kitchen wall until the plaster crumbled, with no results. Crying hysterically, she went into her bedroom and started to bang on the far wall that was opposite the Simses' kitchen, the way her kitchen was opposite the Galens'. She gave up after a few minutes when she remembered that Don Sims was on temporary duty and his wife, Bernice, was staying with friends.

The storm continued to snarl angrily as Ruby did her best to stuff towels and pillows into the openings next to the monstrous tree branch that was taking up half her kitchen. Her effort so depleted her energies that afterward she made her way back to the living room and literally fell onto the sofa. She had to think, to plan, and to do that she needed a clear head.

First babies could come anytime, usually late. Labor could be long or mercifully short. If hers proved long, she at least had a chance of getting help, since the storm couldn't last forever. If it was short, she was on her own.

"Someday I'm going to think about this and laugh," Ruby said through clenched teeth. *Someday, someday, someday. This is now, Ruby Blue, and you aren't going to get a second chance. When this baby is ready to come, it's going to come.*

Her head cleared, her eyes narrowed, and her face turned grim. She searched for the last candles she had carried to the bedroom. She managed to light them all. On her second trip to the kitchen and hall closet she pulled every towel she had left and a bundle of sheets to be spread on her bed. From the bathroom she filled a basin of water and set it on the night table. She found her scissors, which she would use to cut the umbilical cord.

She swayed dizzily when she felt the pain start to ripple and then build in intensity. Somehow she managed to peel off her sodden shoes and socks. Her skirt, slip, and panties were next. She crawled on top of the bed, moaning and crying. She knew she should be counting, clocking the pains and breathing properly and panting, but there was no one to coach her, no one to help her along. There wasn't going to be anyone to bathe her forehead, to smooth back her hair, to hold her hand. "I hate you, Andrew, I hate you. It wasn't supposed to be like this," she mewled.

In the midst of a contraction that was so severe it took Ruby's breath away, she realized she was supposed to be shaved. She laughed so she wouldn't cry.

At three minutes after five in the morning, as the last of the storm abated, an exhausted but exultant Ruby Blue gave birth to a seven-pound fourteen-ounce baby girl, whom she immediately named Martha Mary Blue after her grandmother.

Andrew Blue was groaning and moaning—in delight at what the diminutive Korean girl was doing to him. "You like, G.I. American Joe? I do more, you see. You lay still and I will make you one happy G.I." Andrew moaned again, this time in pure ecstasy.

Her name was Soong Lee, and she was sixteen years old. Her brother, who was seventeen and a half, sold her to Andrew two weeks after his arrival in Korea. The price was twenty-five dollars a month and two cartons of Lucky Strike cigarettes.

Soong Lee washed and ironed Andrew's uniforms, polished his shoes, tidied his quarters, cooked, and gave back rubs when she wasn't, as Andrew put it, in the sack with him. She was so experienced in the art of lovemaking, she boggled Andrew's mind. Compared to Soong Lee, Ruby was a drag.

She was a sprite, a naked, tawny sprite with soft, velvety eyes. She did such wonderful things to him, he didn't want her to stop, not ever. She was taking him to planes and plateaus he'd never dreamed possible. Her fingers, her tongue, her long, coal-black hair worked such incredible magic, he could only gasp in delight and say, again and again, "Don't stop. If you ever do this with anyone else, I'll kill you." He meant every word. But she did stop, her velvety eyes imploring him.

"Me brudder say you pay more or I go. You American G.I. have much dollars. I too good for you, G.I."

Andrew lost his erection. "We made a deal. If he tries any funny stuff, I'll whip his skinny little ass. You tell him that for me."

"No say. Me brudder, he boss. He say, I do. American G.I.'s killed our mudder and fodder. Kim say you pay. You no pay, me leave."

"How much?" Andrew snapped.

"Three cartons of cigarette. Thirty dollar. Not much to G.I. Velly important to Kim. You pay?" she asked anxiously.

Andrew grinned. What the hell. "If I pay, what will you do for me?"

She showed him. Then she showed him again and again.

The moment Andrew crumpled into an exhausted sleep, Soong Lee was off the bed in a flash. Her velvety eyes were mean and contemptuous as she stared down at the naked man. "You motherfucking G.I.," she snarled. In a matter of seconds she was dressed in loose trousers and a pullover khaki T-shirt that she fitted into the loose band of her trousers. She had exactly three, maybe four hours to do the same thing to some other motherfucking G.I. and be back in time to see the stupid American wake up.

Ruby was sitting in the rocking chair with her new baby when the MPs entered her apartment from the rear, calling out to her. She had finally managed to get through on the phone. In seconds mother and baby were whisked to the hospital, where the doctor pronounced them both fit and in good health. It was suggested by the doctor that the baby remain in a pediatric isolation unit since she'd been exposed to so many germs and bacteria. Ruby didn't argue. All she wanted was a bath, sleep, and to know Andrew was notified that he had a brand-new daughter. Unfortunately, it took a full two days before her husband was informed. Priorities, the doctor was told.

When Ruby woke after a refreshing twelve-hour sleep, she was stunned to see the flowers, cards, and baby gifts that filled her room. She burst into tears and was still crying when the general's wife arrived carrying a gift-wrapped box and a teddy bear.

Arlene Frankel wrapped the weary girl in her arms, crooning softly as she stroked Ruby's matted hair. "I've seen her, Ruby. She is absolutely gorgeous. They let me peek at her. They've isolated her for the time being, and the nurse on duty told me you can see her when you feel like walking down the hall. She's beautiful. Ruby, I'm so sorry that things happened . . . it was an act of God. I was beside myself when I heard. I want you to know I don't know if I could have done what you did. Your husband is going to be so proud of you, so very proud. And before I forget, your apartment window is being repaired. You poor thing, you must have been frightened out of your wits."

Ruby sniffled. How wonderful it felt to be held in someone's arms, to be made a fuss over, to have them care. "I can't breastfeed," Ruby said ruefully. "The doctor said under the circumstances he didn't think it was wise."

"Bottles are so much easier. Carnation milk, Karo syrup, and boiled water, that's what your little darling is drinking right now. She guzzled the whole four ounces. They told me you did it all perfectly. I still can't get over it. Tonight I'm writing to the general, and I'm going to tell him what a little soldier you are. Oh, oh, here comes your nurse. I do believe it's bath time. Rest, Ruby, and I'll stop by tomorrow."

The second day of her stay was taken up with reports on Martha's milk consumption. "She can't get enough," one nurse said. Another said, "She burps like a six-month-old." Another said she sucked her thumb. The night nurse said she slept like an angel. Ruby preened and couldn't wait to hold her new daughter.

Ruby spent the third day writing notes to her friends. The letter she wanted to write to Andrew would have to wait till she got home so she could give him firsthand news. He would want to know every little detail, and she needed the privacy of her bedroom to write about all that she'd gone through and about the miracle of their daughter.

On the fourth day, Ruby's release was signed by Arlene Frankel. Her driver carried all the gifts and flowers to the car and took them to her apartment first, then came back for Ruby and the baby.

Arlene stayed just long enough to see that the baby and Ruby were comfortable. "Ruby, I took the liberty of sending over two cases of canned milk and some syrup for you. I see a dozen bottles on your kitchen table and the bottle pot for sterilizing. I can do that if you want, but I'll understand if you want to do it yourself."

"I do, Mrs. Frankel. I want to do everything. I want to learn to take care of this baby. She's mine, I . . . I feel like God did something special for me. I can't explain it. Thank you, thank you for everything."

The moment the door closed behind the general's wife, Ruby raced to the crib and picked up her sleeping baby. She kissed the downy head over and over. An hour later she placed her daughter in the crib, and with a speed she didn't know she possessed, she washed and boiled the bottles and made enough formula for two days. The minute the bottles were set in the cooling rack, she ran back to the baby and picked her up. She rocked her contentedly until she squirmed and let out a high-pitched wail for food.

"You're mine, all mine," Ruby whispered softly. "I'll never leave you. I'll take care of you until the day I die. I'm going to be so good to you. I love you so, little Martha. And I know you will never leave me. I'm going to be the best mother in the whole world. I want you to love me the way I love you. No one in this whole world will ever love you the way I love you, even if you marry, I'll always love you more."

The baby finished her bottle and burped, a healthy sound that made Ruby laugh. She nestled her back into the crook of her arm, rocking contentedly.

Ruby was happier than she'd ever been in her life.

Andrew Blue slogged his way through the mud, the torrential rain sloughing off his back like a waterfall. He hated this goddamn, godforsaken place. He was hot and he itched everywhere. He also suspected he had a good case of the crabs. That meant turpentine treatments. Right now he hated everything and anything that fell in his line of vision. He probably even hated Soong Lee. He should kill her, but he couldn't prove she'd given him the crabs. All he'd done for the past four months was fuck his brains out. Jesus, he itched.

He slammed the door of his quarters, stiff-arming Soong Lee, who was ripping at her clothing. Disgust showed on his face for a moment, and then he felt the beginning of an erection. That, coupled with the itch, sent him to the bed, where he pulled Soong Lee down on top of him. "Make it go away," he moaned.

Out of the corner of his eye he saw the pink slip on the stand next to his bed. He reached for it, bringing it closer to his face. "Hot damn!" he muttered as he ejaculated into Soong Lee's mouth.

{{{{{{{{{ CHAPTER SEVEN }}}}}}}}}

*Four weeks before Martha's first birthday, Andrew was sched-*uled to return to the States along with General Frankel. A leave in Hawaii, both officers' new billet.

He'd return to Hawaii like a prodigal son, and Ruby would greet him with the kid, and they'd be one happy family. His face furrowed into deep lines when he pulled the stack of letters from his footlocker. There had to be at least two hundred of them. Ruby had been as good as her word, writing two, sometimes three letters a week, each of them as long as four or five pages. All were full of boring events: the weather, the kid's sniffles and bottle consumption. If he lived to be a hundred, he'd never forget the blow-by-blow account of Martha's arrival, and what she'd gone through. He'd skimmed through much of the long missive, and when he got to the part about how hard it was to push the afterbirth out, he'd crumpled the letter. She didn't have to tell him all that shit. Like he really wanted to know about the bloody towels, lumps of blood that looked like slabs of liver, and tree limbs in the kitchen window.

Andrew looked at the blank paper in front of him. So what's new, Blue? Ruby complained that he never told her anything in his letters, and that they were too short. Their daughter, she said, was going to think her father didn't care about her. Andrew grimaced. He could just see Ruby reading his one-page letters to the kid and clucking her tongue. Shit!

An hour later he was finished with his letter. As usual, it said nothing of any importance. He missed her, was eager to see Martha and to hold her. He told her how hot it was and how he would bring her and Martha gifts from Korea. He was saving his leave so they could spend every hour, every second of the day together when he returned. He said he couldn't wait to put his arms around her. He signed it, as always, "Love, Andrew."

Andrew tossed the letter into the outgoing mail tray and promptly forgot about it.

His thoughts turned to the dry month he'd had since Soong Lee took off on him in the middle of the night when he said there was no way he was taking responsibility for the kid she was carrying. He'd cuffed her good on the side of the head and told her what she could do with her pimp brother. He hadn't seen her or her brother since.

Andrew whistled all the way to the motor pool and the jeep that was his for the asking. He liked driving the general's jeep with the single-star flag at attention. In another year there would be two stars on the general's flag and there would be maple leaves on his collar. All he had to do to get those leaves was continue to be indispensable to his general and somehow erase the doubt he'd been reading in his eyes. Pearl Harbor would do it. Once he returned to his little family, he'd be a model husband. Until then . . .

The week before Martha's birthday, Ruby received a letter from her husband saying his tour was being extended for another few months. He was being assigned to the Korean Military Group (KMG) as an adviser to the Korean Marines. He had volunteered, he said, because he knew it was what the general expected. There's going to be a screwup in orders, so just ride with it. You'll love our new billet, he'd added along with a line of exclamation marks to prove his point.

Ruby read the letter aloud to her eleven-month-old daughter, whose attention was riveted on a stack of brightly colored blocks. The moment they toppled, she crawled to her mother to rebuild them. Ruby smiled indulgently and rebuilt them carefully, reciting each color and shape. Martha clapped her hands and knocked them over a second time.

Later, when Martha was tired of blocks and wind-up toys, Ruby put her down for a nap, a full bottle clutched in her chubby fists, the handmade quilt tucked close to her face. Ruby smiled, her eyes full of love.

She was reading Andrew's letter a second time when a knock sounded on her front door. Thinking it was one of her friends, Ruby called out, "Come in."

"Corporal Wagoner," the young man said removing his cap.

"Are you Mrs. Ruby Blue?" Ruby nodded. "I have a message for you from headquarters, ma'am."

"Thank you, Corporal."

A message for her. Her hand started to shake as she read it. It was from Andrew, but had been copied out by someone in the communications office. It was cut and dried. Ruby blinked, first in surprise and then in anger.

"It isn't fair," she muttered. "First the baby and now this."

This meant Andrew's tour had been extended for an extra six months, not the three or four he'd mentioned in his letter. She, however, was to go ahead and move to their new location. In exactly one week, on Martha's birthday. "And just how am I supposed to do that, Andrew?" she said sourly. He'd said there would be a foulup. She didn't even know where the new location was. She knew a moment later when she flipped the page. "Hawaii! What about my car! Where am I supposed to get the money for all this?" she demanded.

Arlene Frankel hadn't said a word about her husband's tour being extended. Right now she was in Hawaii, meeting her husband, who was on leave. Was the general going back to Korea, or was Andrew left behind to clear things up?

Five days! It's impossible. Besides, she'd planned a birthday party for Martha. The Querys were coming. "Damn you, Andrew. I can't believe this all happened at the last minute, because if that was the case, I'm sure Mrs. Frankel would have told me," she muttered.

Ruby panicked then, much the way she had the day of Martha's birth when the awful storm hit. When she arrived in Hawaii, where would she live? Nothing was said about military housing, so that meant they would have to live off the base and pay out more money for expenses. Hawaii might be a transfer dream, but reality was something else. If there was a foulup in orders, she could end up living on the street. She'd heard horror stories about military screwups.

Ruby picked up the phone. In a brisk, professional voice she hadn't used since working for Admiral Query, she explained her circumstances and at the same time expressed her displeasure at having only seven days' notice to move lock, stock, and barrel with a year-old baby in what was obviously an error. "And what about my car, sir? What am I supposed to do with it?" She listened, not liking anything she heard. She was tempted to tell the captain what she thought of his explanations and then tell him to go to hell. She bit down on her tongue when he said, "Mrs. Blue, you are a military wife and as such you are expected to fall in and do as ordered."

Right then, that very second, Ruby knew she could pack up and walk out and return to Washington, D.C. She'd had just about enough of the Marine Corps and its gung-ho officers with their rules and regulations.

In the same brisk voice Ruby said, "Give me the bottom line, Captain." She listened, her eyes widening with shock as the captain's voice droned to an end.

"Well, that's all fine, well, and good, Captain, but I find it totally unacceptable. What that means is, it isn't good enough. There's been a mistake and my husband's tour has been extended. You'll have to do better than that, or I'm not going. I can be out of here in seven days, that's no problem. I'll be driving to Washington, D.C., where I know I can find a place to live. I'll leave it up to you to explain the circumstances to my husband and General Frankel. Thank you for your time, Captain." Ruby slammed the phone down so hard, Andrew's favorite ashtray crashed to the floor and shattered.

Colonel Oliver Peters expelled his breath in a loud swoosh and swore loud and long. Eyebrows shot up, grins stretched from ear to ear, and guffaws rang out.

"She's the one who delivered her own baby. Yeah, she's Frankel's pet. Has her own car. You bet your ass she'll drive to D.C. Totally unacceptable, eh? Not good enough. Screwup in orders. She was probably right. The goddamn marines never did anything right. The lady has guts. What are you going to do, Captain? Her old man is Frankel's aide, better not forget it. She sure isn't."

"I don't make the rules, gentlemen, I obey them just the way you do."

"Pass the buck," a brash major chortled.

"For Christ's sake, Ollie, pull some strings. It's done all the time. She's right, it's goddamn unfair, and she's probably right, it is a mistake in orders," another marine colonel said quietly.

"Look, I'll do my best, but I'm not making any promises. Orders are orders."

"I wouldn't drag my ass on this," the colonel said lightly. "All she has to do is pack her duds, put the baby in the car, and do exactly what she said she's going to do. She could be doing it as we speak."

Peters slapped his fist down on his desk. "If she does, she doesn't belong in the fucking military. How's that grab you?"

"Obviously, she's already arrived at that conclusion," the shy second lieutenant muttered.

"I gotta check this out. And don't even think about leaving this room. You're so goddamn eager to help, you can do it all if I get approval upstairs. This is a fucking first, I can tell you that. Who the hell is this Ruby Blue anyway?" the captain snarled.

"I do believe, sir, she's the one who . . . ah, entertained the two flags a year or so ago and then her old man got his promotion. Just like that!" the colonel said, snapping his fingers.

"Oh, shit!" Peters said, stomping from the room.

At seven minutes past seven, on his way to his quarters, Colonel Peters rapped on Ruby's screen door. He blinked when she opened the door, a sleepy golden-haired child in her arms. She looked ordinary enough. The kid was cute, too. "Yes," she said in a puzzled voice.

"I believe we spoke earlier, Mrs. Blue. I'm Colonel Peters. I believe we can accommodate you, Mrs. Blue. If new orders come through later, you'll be ahead of the game. One of my men will bring over your airline tickets tomorrow. Someone will meet you in Oahu and take you to Pearl. We'll have housing for you on base. Your car will be shipped, but you'll arrive before it does. You're not to pack anything except yours and the child's personal belongings. Professional movers will crate everything. If any of your property is damaged in transit, you'll file a claim and will be compensated. You've got top priority, Mrs. Blue. General Frankel's furnishings and yours will be shipped at the same time. We don't anticipate you . . . ah, roughing it for more than twenty-four hours. Is this acceptable, Mrs. Blue?"

"Why . . . yes . . . but I don't . . . yes, sir, it is acceptable. Thank you."

"My pleasure, Mrs. Blue."

"Pussies, my ass," he muttered as he slid into his brand-new car that he'd spent three full months wheeling and dealing over.

CHAPTER EIGHT

Ruby settled into her new quarters that this time were so clean, she gasped aloud. She wondered if it had anything to do with her husband being a captain or if it was because she'd asserted herself for the first time.

The first thing she did on settling in was write to Opal, Amber, and the bank in Washington. The second thing she did was rent a post office box so her mail from the bank would be safe.

She hadn't called the Frankels because she didn't want to interfere with their vacation. She was dying to hear firsthand news of her husband, but she would be stepping out of bounds if she did that. Sooner or later, providing Mrs. Frankel knew she was here, there would be a phone call or a note dropped off by one of their stewards.

She'd signed in on schedule, suffered through the obligatory luncheon, complete with plumeria lei, and ignored all other offers. She had a baby who needed her. She was polite but firm when she declined the invitations to teas and get-togethers. She wanted to explore this magnificent island and learn all about the people. She loved the beach with its sparkling blue water, and so did Martha. She spent long days in the sun with her daughter, frolicking in the water and building sand castles. She was having the time of her life.

A month to the day of her arrival there was a knock on her door. Ruby looked sleepily at the small clock on her night table. Who would knock this early? Barefooted, tying the belt of her robe, she made her way to the door, muttering about inconsiderate people waking up other people. Her eyes widened in shock when she recognized the housing officer. Her heart started to thump, knowing she wasn't going to like what she heard.

"Ma'am, you're going to have to vacate these premises by noon today. According to this," he said, flashing what looked like an order done in triplicate, "you don't belong here. There was a mistake in billeting. I'm sorry, but there's nothing I can do. This unit has been reserved for a colonel and his family. The housing office screwed up and misassigned Captain Blue to field grade quarters and only now found the mistake."

"I don't understand. I can't possibly move, I have a baby. I have nowhere to go. I. used all my money for this move, and my husband's allotment hasn't caught up with me. How can you do this to me? I can't possibly move my furniture. . . ."

"Ma'am, I'm just delivering your orders; you do as you're told just the way I do. Noon. I'm sorry for any inconvenience this may cause you." A second later he turned on his heel smartly and walked away.

Ruby slammed the door. Martha let out a wail that sent chills up Ruby's spine. "My God, this can't be happening!" she bleated. For the first time since Martha's birth, Ruby ignored her daughter as she frantically dialed the base housing number. Thirty minutes later she knew she had no choice but to move. Where, she didn't know.

Blind panic rushed through her. She had exactly twenty-three dollars and forty-seven cents to her name. She'd just paid the rent yesterday. Any hopes of getting that back anytime soon were nonexistent. The paperwork alone would take months. She'd stocked the refrigerator two days ago. What was she to do with the food? It would spoil in the heat without refrigeration.

In a trance she dressed herself and Martha. She forgot to wash her face and brush her teeth. Like a robot she pulled clothes from drawers and packed them any old way, staggering under their weight as she carried them to her car, Martha tugging on her skirt as she went along.

An hour into her packing her tears gave way to scorching anger. How could they do this to her? It wasn't right and it wasn't fair. Her slim body was rigid with fury as she carried the last of her belongings to the car. She had to leave the furniture, her cooking utensils, and Martha's toys behind. Her car trunk was full, as was the backseat. There was just enough room inside for her and Martha.

If she had to leave, she would leave, but not before she said what she had to say. She drove then, carefully, her eyes glittering with fury, her knuckles white on the steering wheel, to the housing office. She stormed in, Martha in her arms, and let loose with a volley of criticism so sharp, the men stood at attention. She ended her tirade with "And you call yourself marines! You should be ashamed of yourselves. Since none of you obviously has the brains to feel shame, I'll feel it for you. I am ashamed! You should all go to hell!" To drive her point home, she took her military pass and her PX card and ripped them into pieces, letting them drop to the floor. "This is what I think of the Marine Corps!" She stomped from the room, Martha whimpering in her arms.

Ruby drove through the gate like a tornado. Didn't anyone care? "Andrew, I hate you. I know the military can screw up, but somehow, some way, I feel in my gut this is all your fault. I should have heard from Mrs. Frankel by now. The fact that I haven't makes me suspicious . . . of you." She was crying again. How could she blame Andrew, who was in Korea? He was as much a victim as she was. It was the Corps, the damn Corps that was doing this to her.

She'd been intending to go into town, and here she was at the beach. She felt stupid, unable to think clearly. They were homeless, courtesy of the Marine Corps. She was helping Martha from the car, half in a daze. The little girl was squealing her pleasure as she tottered toward the sandy strip of beach on shaky legs.

While Martha ripped into the sand with a plastic shovel, Ruby sat with her head between her hands, crying. She had to get hold of herself and start to think about what she was going to do. Sleep on the beach, in the car? Martha was on whole milk now, how would she keep it cool?

It was all a mistake. Sooner or later it would be rectified. On the other hand, perhaps it wouldn't be resolved until Andrew returned, whenever that was. Would the Frankels wonder about her? She wished now she'd been friendlier with the other wives and had gone to their damn teas and luncheons, but that meant paying a baby-sitter, and she had no money for such luxuries. But would those persnickety wives have helped her? She doubted it. She knew now the girls from Iwo Jima Circle were unique, possibly because they were low in rank and just starting the climb. No matter what they said, she knew the camaraderie was a façade, a myth they all wanted to believe in to make life in the military bearable. It was me, me, me all the way. Where was that "we take care of our own" spirit? It was all bullshit.

Pure bullshit. Like a drum roll, her grandmother's words thundered in her ears. "The only person you can depend on is yourself."

Ruby's eyes filled again. She wiped them on the sleeve of her blouse. She couldn't keep sitting there, she had to do something.

Martha kicked and screamed as Ruby scraped the sand from her bare feet and carried her back to the car. She was still screaming when Ruby thrust the car into gear and headed back to Nimitz Highway. She would go to Waikiki and stop at the first church she came to. Surely, the good fathers would help her. Her shoulders slumped when she remembered how she'd all but renounced God. The memory of leaving her Bible on the train flashed before her. If she was going to be punished for it, this would be the time.

Martha was asleep now, sucking on her thumb, her blanket clutched under her chin. Poor . . . homeless baby.

Ruby pulled up short when she saw the white steeple looming ahead of her. She gritted her teeth as she read ST. ANDREW'S CATHEDRAL. It was an Episcopal church, but she didn't care. It must be an omen, some sort of sign she should stop there.

She'd driven a long way, it seemed. She vaguely remembered driving through Waikiki. Everything was such a blur. She knew she had to get her wits about her or she and Martha really would end up sleeping on the beach.

She hated to wake the child, but she had no other choice. Fortunately, the baby whimpered once and then nuzzled her head on Ruby's shoulder. Martha was getting heavy, Ruby thought in dismay. She had to do something decisive now, like put one foot in front of the other and walk around to the priory at the back of the church.

Ruby's face was flushed with the heat and the weight of the child in her arms. Her eyes were pleading when the man in the clerical collar approached her. "Father, I need help," she whispered.

Father Joachim led Ruby to a chair and offered to take the sleeping child. Ruby shook her head. "She'll wake up and start to cry. Strange places frighten her." She told him about her morning and going to the beach and driving around until she came to his church. She ended with "It won't do any good to go back and plead or fight. The mixup will eventually be straightened out, but in the meantime, I need a place for Martha. You have to help me, Father. I don't know what else to do. If you let me make a long distance call, I can call my bank in Washington and have them send me some money; it won't be much, but I can give it to you until the . . . the paperwork is straightened out. By that time Andrew's allotment should be here. Will you help me?" she asked breathlessly.

He had such kind eyes and such work-worn hands, Ruby thought. He seemed gentle, and when he smiled, the dim, paneled room seemed lighter somehow.

"Of course, child. We have a small building for visitors. You're welcome to stay as long as you like. But you must share the responsibilities, the cooking and the cleaning. We have several elderly people in need of care. I think that angel you're holding will be just the thing to perk them up. You can think of it as having a half-dozen grandparents for the little one."

Ruby's eyes closed in relief. "How much will it cost, Father?"

"In dollars and cents? Nothing. In emotion and physical work, quite a lot." His eyes twinkled merrily. "I think you're up to it. You see, I have several rather well-to-do parishioners who are generous with their donations. Perhaps someday when you are well off, you'll remember St. Andrew's."

"I will, Father, I swear I will. I don't mean I *swear* . . . what I mean is, I'll promise."

"Then, Ruby Blue, I accept your promise. To me," he said, his eyes twinkling again, "a promise is more binding than a legal contract. If you're up to it, I'll show you the way. It's no more than a block or so by city standards. I'll have someone drive your car around later."

It was a long building almost obscured by lush plumeria and huge banyan trees. Diamond-shaped windows and a heavy oak door gave it a fairytale quality. Everywhere, as far as she could see, were well-tended flowers and blooming hibiscus. The grass was trimmed and more green than a meadow of emeralds. A dog woofed softly.

The priest smiled. "That's Joshua, the guardian of this little establishment. Unfortunately, he is old, but he's particularly fond of children."

The building on the inside was as inviting as the outside. It was larger than she thought, with a kitchen, a sitting room, and three dormitory-style bedrooms with cots and dressers. However, there was only one bathroom. The priest apologized.

It was colorful with framed prints on the wall, obviously hung by some previous guests. The furniture was wicker with faded flowered cushions. A monstrous radio stood in the corner. Lamps made from shells and glass jars adorned all the little tables. On the tile floor straw mats formed a checkerboard pattern. The kitchen was modern and clean, as was the bathroom. There was even a service area that held a wringer washing machine. Two taut clotheslines stretched across the length of the backyard. To Ruby it was a palace.

"Come along, Mrs. Blue, and I'll introduce you to your roommates. They usually sit outdoors at this time of day with a glass of pineapple juice they make themselves."

Joshua, the taffy-colored springer spaniel, trotted over to Ruby and sniffed at her feet. Dark, liquid-brown eyes stared up at her. She hunched over and scratched the dog's silky ears.

The garden, Ruby decided, had to be the most beautiful spot on earth, at least the most beautiful that she'd ever seen. The colors of the brilliant, fragrant flowers seemed to explode about her. She inhaled deeply, savoring their exotic scents. The garden was walled in with decorative whitewashed cinder blocks, a perfect backdrop for the equally white trellises and climbing vines. The women, she noted, wore brightly colored, long dresses and sandals; the three men wore loose cotton trousers and flowered shirts. They were all elderly. It was hard to imagine them working as hard as they would need to to maintain the building and grounds.

They were smiling at her now and she smiled in return. One lady, who looked to be in her eighties, was holding out a glass of pineapple juice. Another held out her arms to take Martha. Still another motioned her, with a wide smile, to take her place at the table. Father Joachim urged her forward. "For a little while, this will be your family, my dear," he said, beaming.

"Father, how can these people do all the work required to maintain the grounds and house? When people reach their age, they shouldn't have to work like this."

"I couldn't agree with you more, but these people, as you call them, refuse to take charity. They're proud. When they can no longer contribute, they leave, it's that simple."

Shocked, Ruby asked, "But where do they go?"

Father Joachim shrugged. "I don't know, and the others won't tell. Most of them," he said, lowering his voice, "die here, peacefully in their sleep."

Suddenly, Ruby felt Martha leave her arms. Instinctively, she reacted and would have prevented the woman named Mattie from taking her child but for the pressure on her arm from the pastor. Martha squirmed and whimpered and then laughed as Mattie chucked her under the chin. The others crowded around, but not close enough to frighten the child. Joshua woofed his approval and immediately set about licking one of Martha's pudgy legs. The child giggled as she tried to touch the dog's lapping tongue.

"I think," the pastor said in an approving voice, "that Joshua has finally found a friend. He, too, is displaced. I found him half starved and wounded several years ago. I suppose you could say he's our mascot as well as our protector. He won't harm the child, so have no fear."

Ruby didn't really want the tart pineapple juice, but she drank it anyway. There was no way she was going to offend these smiling people.

"I'll leave you now. I have duties that require my attention. If you need me, send Joshua. All you have to say is 'Fetch Father Joachim.' Believe it or not, he understands."

"Father ... how can I ..."

"Shhh, child, it's not necessary. I'm just glad you found us. If you ever want to talk, come over to the priory after supper. I'm always available."

Ruby took her place at the table. Mattie held out her hand and Ruby grasped it. Nelie, a twin of Mattie, looked to be the same age, her hands gnarled and bent with what Ruby assumed was arthritis. Rosie was perhaps a few years younger than Mattie and Nelie. She smiled, her two gold front teeth gleaming in the afternoon sun. Ruby smiled self-consciously when Martha tried to reach for the artificial teeth. Rosie laughed uproariously. Martha was enjoying herself. The men, as old as the women, were grinning and clapping their hands. Simon, who was bent-over and had skin the color of a brown nut, said in a squeaky voice that Martha loved, "Hello, little one." Kalo, who said he was the youngest at seventy-nine, clapped his hands in delight. It was obvious that Kalo was retarded, but he pointed to the neatly trimmed flower beds to indicate he was responsible for their perfection. In a rush, he left his chair, and a few moments later his arms were full of plumeria. He held them out to indicate they were for Ruby, and then transferred them to Nelie, who immediately started to make a lei for her. Peter, a white-haired, toothless man, bowed formally and said, "May I hold your child?"

Ruby nodded.

"His family was killed when the Japanese bombed Pearl Harbor," Mattie said quietly. "He loves children, we all do. But none of us has a family. Perhaps you will allow us to love this child as a granddaughter."

"Can I be your granddaughter, too?" Ruby asked in a choked voice.

They looked at one another uncertainly.

Ruby waved her hands to encompass Martha. "Both of us could use grandparents. Even after we leave. I'll come back and bring Martha. I promise."

"You will come back?"

Ruby nodded, tears brimming in her eyes. She propped her elbows on the table, her gaze gentle, a smile on her lips. The Corps had fouled up, and she'd landed right side up. Until matters were straightened out, she couldn't think of a better place to be. In the end, her grandmother had always said, things worked out for the best. This was the best.

In the days to come Ruby worked from sunup to sundown, cleaning, scrubbing, doing laundry, ironing, and cooking, while the grandmothers and grandfathers looked after her daughter. Often she would find herself drifting into sleep at the supper table. Kalo, who sat next to her, nudged her and grinned, motioning to her fork. The others smiled indulgently. In the beginning they'd protested when she took over their chores, but when she explained she had to do it or leave, they gladly relinquished their duties in favor of baby-sitting. More than once Nelie or Rosie helped her to her cot, where she slept deeply and dreamlessly. She belonged, and so did her daughter, and that was all she cared about. Once a week Ruby called the base housing officer to see if the mistake in her housing assignment had been rectified. The answer was always the same.

She thought about driving out to the base to inquire for her mail, but some instinct told her any mail addressed to her previous address would have been marked Return to Sender, so she didn't bother to make the long drive. Besides, she had too much work to do and no extra money for gas.

Her intentions, when she first arrived, were to write to everyone and tell them where she was, but at the end of the day she was too weary to do anything but sleep. She had written one letter to Andrew, giving him her address in care of St. Andrew's. She hoped he would be pleased that she had ended up in such a place.

The day Ruby counted the change in her purse and found only two dollars, she realized she'd been at St. Andrew's for six full weeks. She couldn't put off calling the bank in Washington any longer. The two dollars would go toward paying for the phone call. She'd mentally chided herself for not calling sooner. When Martha took her afternoon nap, she would walk to the avenue and search for a phone booth. She realized suddenly, with the time difference, that she'd have to make the call early in the morning, as the bank closed at two o'clock. Tomorrow would be soon enough, she decided. She could set the breakfast table after supper was cleared away and make dough for cinnamon buns before she went to bed. If she cut the pineapple and made the breakfast juice, she wouldn't be shirking her duty. As long as she was going to the avenue, she would write to Andrew and mail the letter along the way. It was also time to make another call to the base.

Ruby stared down at the basket of ironing at her feet. Just yesterday Peter had complained that his pants were too stiff. The grandparents didn't like starch, she had to remember that. No one had ironed prior to her arrival, but they oohed and aahed over neatly hung long dresses and pressed shirts and trousers. Secretly, Ruby suspected they thought her efforts foolish. The heat and humidity, in an hour's time, left all the garments limp and wrinkled. She didn't care. It was part of her work schedule.

There wasn't a lot Ruby Blue cared about these days.

The following morning, while the dew still sparkled on the grass, Ruby trudged to the avenue in search of a phone booth, the change from her purse clutched in her hand. On waking, she'd decided to try to make the call collect and person-to-person to save the two dollars if possible.

Ten minutes later Ruby walked away in a daze. There was only nine dollars in her account. Two sump pumps had to be purchased for the house on Poplar Street because of heavy rainfall. A new refrigerator had to be purchased when the one on O Street started to smoke and couldn't be repaired. A section of the fence on Poplar Street had gone down from the same spell of rainy weather and had to be reinforced. Two of the back steps on O Street had to be replaced or the insurance company wouldn't renew the insurance policy. Bruno hadn't been able to do any of the work because he'd been diagnosed with a hernia, and the doctor had forbidden any type of manual labor. She'd wanted to ask for a loan, but she was too proud. She couldn't call Rena either. She had enough on her mind with Bruno. She figured she was ahead of the game, since the bank accepted her collect call.

Halfway down the street she stopped and returned to the phone booth. She dropped in her dime and dialed the familiar number of the housing office. Nothing had changed, and there was no mail waiting for her. She'd wasted her dime. Now she had only a dollar and ninety cents left.

She had to put a good face on things. The grandparents reacted to her mood changes. If she was simply tired or weary, they clucked their tongues and tried to help in little ways, smiles on their faces. Three days ago Rosie had seen her counting her small hoard of change. She'd watched when she handed the money over to the milkman for Martha's milk. They knew somehow that she was worried, and in turn, their own faces showed anxiety.

Today was laundry day. The pile of sheets staring her in the face made Ruby want to cry. She had to bake, too. Tuesday was always her busiest day.

Perhaps if she'd been more alert and less tired she would have noted that Kalo had absented himself the past few days right after lunch. She should have noted the pleased, secretive looks on the other grandparents' faces, but she'd missed that, too. Martha had been fretful, that she'd noticed, probably because her last stubborn tooth refused to come through her gums.

Ruby wiped her tears as she folded the last of the sheets. After dinner she would make up the beds, give Martha her bath, and turn in early. She was somewhat tired physically, but mentally she was totally exhausted. She was close now to being destitute, which meant not being able to provide for her daughter. The fact that she'd managed, up till now, to buy her child's milk, made her circumstances bearable. She knew, without a doubt, that Father Joachim would add another quart of milk to the priory bill, but she couldn't bring herself to ask. She was

Martha's mother, and milk was her responsibility. She'd already had to give up Martha's vitamins, and she herself needed new shoes.

The table was set with the flowers Martha picked each afternoon; Ruby always put them on the table in a low bowl of water. She loved seeing Martha clap her hands and say "flowers." Tonight there was stew made with lamb that was cooked until it fell apart, suitable for old gums. The grandparents loved to sop fresh bread in the thick gravy. Even Martha liked sucking on the bread crust.

Ruby squared her shoulders and did her best to carry on a cheerful conversation. She knew she wasn't carrying it off when Peter arose and carried the plates to the sink. The others were still sitting, which was unusual, since there was no dessert on baking day. Something was going on, she decided when she noticed the smug looks on the faces around the table. She waited, certain they were going to tell her a story about what Martha and Joshua had done that afternoon. She always giggled and clapped her hands for Martha's benefit.

"We have a present for you, Miss Ruby," Rosie said, her gold teeth sparkling. "Kalo, give the present to Miss Ruby."

Kalo rose from the table to walk around to her seat. He smiled, his eyes alight with mischief as he dug into his pockets for a small burlap sack he'd fashioned himself. It clanked softly when he placed it on the table where her plate had been. She looked at the old man, pure delight on her face. "For me?" He grinned. They all grinned. Even Martha had stopped banging her spoon on the table at this strange happening. She was certain the bag was full of lucky stones. She'd told Kalo how she'd fished for them in the crick back in Barstow. Every day he'd come to her with a pebble of sorts, and even though they weren't real lucky stones, she said they were. He now had a pile of them big enough to fill a grocery bag.

Ruby dumped the contents of the bag on the table and burst into tears.

"For Martha's milk," Simon said happily. "Now you stay longer."

"Is honest money," Peter said happily. "No charity. Gift for Martha."

"We old, not dumb. We see you count money," Mattie said in

her best English. "Enough for gas, too. You take us for ride to beach so we walk in water."

Ruby blew her nose. "Yes, more than enough, but I don't understand. Where did you get this?" she said, pointing to the mound of coins and crumpled dollar bills.

"We made leis and straw dolls. Kalo took them to Waikiki and sold them to tourists. Honest money. Is all yours, Miss Ruby," Nelie said happily.

"But how did he get there? It's so far," Ruby said, aghast.

"He walked," Rosie said importantly.

Ruby burst into tears a second time. How had the bandy-legged little man walked all that way and, with his aversion to speech, managed to sell their wares? She was off her chair in a flash, wrapping her arms around him. He beamed with pleasure. Then she hugged them all and kissed them until she thought her lips would fall off.

"How much it is?" Mattie demanded.

"Enough for a king." Ruby laughed. "Or a queen." She counted out the change in little piles, straightened the crumpled dollars to lie flat on the table. "I do believe there is forty-two dollars and twenty-five cents here. Lord in heaven, how can I ever thank you?"

"You stay. We go in car, eh?" Rosie laughed.

"You bet we go in the car. Tomorrow we'll go. No house-work, no cooking, no nothing tomorrow. Tomorrow is St. Andrew's day, according to Ruby Blue."

"Not charity," Nelie said, wagging her finger as they trooped out of the kitchen, Joshua in their wake.

Ruby was wiping the last of the dishes when Father Joachim knocked on the screen door, a letter in his hand.

The pastor's eyes were sad when Ruby related the story of the money for Martha's milk. "I don't know what they'll do when you leave. They've grown so attached to you and your daughter. I knew what they were doing, and I gave them my blessing. Perhaps this letter will have your answers. Thank you, Ruby, for being so kind to my little flock."

"Father, if it weren't for you, Martha and I would be living on the beach without a roof over our heads. By now we'd have starved to death. It is I who should thank you. You must believe me when I tell you I will never forget this, and somehow I'll make it all right. It might take me a while, but I'll do it."

"Bless you, child. It's time for evening service. We'll talk again. I hope this letter has good news. Good night, my dear."

Ruby sat down at the table with the last of the coffee to read her husband's letter.

Dear Ruby,

What the hell is this goddamn shit you're feeding me that you're living in some fucking mission on charity with our kid? If that's the best you can do, you better try again, and don't go giving me that crap that the Corps put you out on the street with a kid. The Corps doesn't do things like that. You must have done something to have them move you out, if that's really what happened. Who did you rub the wrong way? I bet anything you stuck your nose up in the air and didn't play the game. That's right, isn't it, Ruby?

All I can say to you is you damn well better not be living at some mission on the cuff. How could you be so damn stupid! How's this going to look? The fact that Mrs. Frankel hasn't been in touch makes me believe you really screwed up. And don't think for one minute I believe that crap about mixed-up orders. I'm sure there was a mixup, but they would have caught it in a matter of days.

When I get back, all I can say is you better be living on base or off, but not in any goddamn mission. Now, get off your ass and do something about it before I get back. In the meantime I'll do what I can from here.

I have only six more weeks to go and then I'll be home. I'm real disappointed in the way you're handling things. With the exception of that Dixie thing, you got off to a real good start. I thought you could handle motherhood. What's the big deal? If you stop and think about all that's gone wrong for you, you should realize how many mistakes you've made along the way. The Corps has a long memory. Delivering the kid on your own for starters is so out of whack we'll never hear the end of it. That stunt you pulled ripping up your I.D. and PX cards will stay with us, too. Things like that don't go away.

I wanted you to make me proud of you, not ashamed.

Andrew

Ruby folded the letter and then ripped it into tiny shreds. She did the same thing with the flimsy air mail envelope. She

watched, dry-eyed, when the tiny little pieces fluttered into
the trash barrel.

"Go to hell, Andrew," she snapped.

He hadn't even asked how Martha was. Nothing on this earth
could make her move now. This was where she would be when
her husband returned, housing or no housing.

Ruby hated herself two weeks later when she walked out to
the avenue to try to call Mrs. Frankel. A steward answered the
phone and said the Frankels were back in the States, visiting
their children and weren't due to return until after Thanksgiving,
but no later than the first of December. She didn't know why
she felt relieved at the words. Now she could stay. She'd given
up calling the base. They had the number at St. Andrew's. Father Joachim would have given her a message if they'd called.
Let Andrew fight with them on his return. Let him see how the
Marine Corps took care of its own.

She hadn't responded to Andrew's letter and had no intention
of doing so. She was still angry and would probably remain angry for a very long time. Andrew had a lot of apologizing to do.
A lot.

Ruby was scrubbing the kitchen floor when she noticed
movement by the screen door. She looked up to see her husband
towering over her. He looked so sharply creased, she wanted to
throw the bucket of dirty water all over him. She sat back on her
haunches, her hands full of soapy water. She knew she looked
awful. She needed a permanent and her skin was rough and
peeling. Her nose was red from standing in the sun, hanging out
the wash. Even her ears were red. The hostility that had been
building steadily since Andrew's last letter exploded. "You're
standing in my way. I have to finish this. Move!"

"What do you mean, move? Get up, Ruby. You look like a
damn scrubwoman."

"You're wrong, Andrew. I don't look like a scrubwoman, I
am a scrubwoman. And when I'm done with this floor, I have
to scrub the bathroom, and then I have to take the clothes off the
line and fold them, and then I have to cook dinner. Move,
please, you'll make me run late. I'm on a schedule. You should
understand that, being a marine."

"I told you I wanted you out of here," Andrew blustered.

"I guess you're aware I didn't pay any attention. I didn't bother to write back because I had no intention of moving. Do you have a place for us to live?"

"For Christ's sake, I just got in, not three hours ago. Do you think I'm some kind of magician?"

"Do you think I'm one?" Ruby retaliated.

"We'll go to a hotel. Get the kid."

"The kid's name is Martha, or did you forget? She's napping, and no, I won't wake her. I'm not going with you, Andrew. When you have a place for us to live, and it better be decent, then and only then will I think about leaving here. Not before. There had better be decent furniture, too. You know, you could have sent me some money. As I understand it, there isn't a whole lot you could spend money on in Korea. Did you want me to beg?"

"C'mon, Ruby, I just got back. Give me a break. We haven't seen each other in so long, I can't remember how many months it is. I just want my wife and ki—Martha. Jesus, what's happening to us? I thought you'd be glad to see me."

"Why? So you can tell me how ashamed you are of me? No thanks. Why don't you leave now, before we both say things we can't take back. I have to finish this floor."

"I'm not leaving here without you and the kid. Now, let's go!"

"I told you my terms," Ruby said stonily. "Take them or leave them." She dropped to the floor and dipped the scrub rag into the bucket. She sloshed soapy water all over the floor. "Move, Andrew!"

"Damn you, Ruby, I'm not going to put up with this." He reached down to grab hold of her arm, but Ruby slid out of his way. His face full of rage, Andrew moved to the door.

"Andrew, wait a minute," Ruby called. She was on her feet in an instant, the bucket in her hands. She swung it upward, the dirty water hitting him square in the chest. He sputtered and bellowed.

"Now you can leave. But I think it's only fair to tell you I may decide not to return with you. I've been thinking a lot about going back to Washington with Martha. Be warned. My decision will be based on your attitude, and let's hope for both our sakes that it improves a great deal. Don't come back here and . . . *em-*

barrass me again. Just bring an apology from you and one from the Corps. Close the door on your way out."

Well outside the door, Andrew spat out, "Give me the keys to the car. I can't go back to the base looking like this."

"The car isn't working. As you can see, I have no money to get it repaired. It's *my* car, and don't you forget it."

"Paid for with my money. That makes it half mine. You're going to regret all of this, Ruby. This was supposed to be a happy homecoming," he yelled, stalking off.

Ruby filled the scrub bucket a second time. She should be feeling something, but she wasn't. She hadn't wanted to touch him, to kiss him. She hadn't even wanted him to see Martha.

It took Andrew a full two weeks before he returned. He looked humble, but Ruby knew it was a temporary state of affairs. He even went so far as to look misty-eyed when he was introduced to his daughter and she wouldn't go near him, but ran to Mattie, who picked her up and cuddled her against her ample bosom.

The good-byes were tearful. Ruby was so choked up, she could barely speak. "I'll come back every Wednesday. I promise." She was rewarded with wet eyes and tremulous smiles. Joshua howled his displeasure, his tail between his legs as he stalked Andrew. Ruby wondered indifferently if the dog would bite her husband. Instead, in front of everyone, the dog boldly lifted his leg and peed down Andrew's smartly creased uniform. Ruby laughed, she couldn't help herself. The grandparents smiled and Martha giggled, wanting to be part of the fun. Even Father Joachim did his best to hide a grin.

"Thank you, Father, for everything. I'll come back and visit."

In the car on the way back to Pearl, Andrew unlocked his jaw long enough to say, "I don't want you to ever go back to that place again. Do you hear me?"

"Stuff it, Andrew, and don't ever make the mistake of telling me what to do again. We might be married, but you don't own me."

"Can you shut that kid up? All she's done since you got in the car is bawl."

"You're strange to her, Andrew, she doesn't know you. And you've just upset her life. Babies and children don't like change.

It's going to take her a few days to get used to you. Can't you at least be a little understanding?"

"That's almost funny, coming from you, Ruby. When I asked you to be understanding, you tossed a bucket of water at me. Dirty water."

"That's not the same thing, and you know it. I'm not in the mood to fight, so if you don't mind, let's make the rest of the trip in silence. I'm still a little raw."

"Ha!" Andrew snorted.

Ruby mimicked her husband, her last show of defiance. Once they were settled in their apartment she would have to be a dutiful marine wife again if she wanted her marriage to work. Martha needed a father. She wasn't sure anymore if she needed a husband. Like it or not, for the time being, she had one.

The apartment in Pearl City was dingy and dark, but it was clean enough, she decided. All their furniture was there. At least the Corps had done that much for her. Nothing appeared damaged.

While Ruby made up Martha's bed so the child could nap, Andrew went to the grocery store for food. Martha was still wailing for her grandparents, calling for them by name, one after another, to Ruby's dismay. She was off the bottle now, and the promise of juice, a cookie, or a sugar stick didn't work the magic she thought it would. She was also old enough to crawl over the bars of her crib. Ruby's nerves were twanging at an all-time high when Andrew walked through the door, both arms full of groceries. He was stony-faced when he strode into Martha's room. Ruby watched as he picked up the child and put her into the crib but not before he swatted her on the rear end. "You will not climb out of that bed again. You will not even think about it. When I say it's time to get out, your mother will take you out. Do you understand?" When Martha sobbed harder, Andrew took her thumb from her mouth and said, "Say 'yes, sir.' " Martha hiccoughed and struggled to get her hand free from her father's tight grasp. "When you say 'yes, sir,' you can go to sleep."

"That's enough, Andrew, you're scaring her out of her wits. Enough, I said!" Ruby screamed.

"I can see you're weak in the discipline department. That isn't going to work here. When she says 'yes, sir,' she gets to go to sleep, and not before. We might as well train her now. Untrain her is more like it. You botched it up, Ruby. Go make dinner. I'll handle this."

"Andrew, for God's sake, she's just a baby. She doesn't understand."

"She understands enough to keep bawling. She's holding her breath. She's spoiled. Don't worry, nothing's going to happen to her."

A long time later, or an eternity later, Ruby thought, Martha ceased her screaming. Andrew returned to the kitchen, a triumphant look on his face. "She said it. Patience is all it takes. She'll probably go through that act for a few more days, and then we'll have some peace."

"I hate you for that, Andrew," Ruby said. "Just what did you accomplish in there? Now she's going to sleep through dinner and be all wound up when it's time to go to bed for the night. You're a brute."

"My kids are going to learn respect."

"What's happened to you, Andrew? You weren't like this before you left for Korea. She's not a damn soldier and neither am I. She's just a baby. I can't forgive you for this."

"You better try. And nothing happened to me in Korea. Martha is no longer a baby. She walks and she talks, so that makes her a little person, and little persons are little soldiers. All military men feel that way about their children. Wise up, Ruby. I'm serious about this, so don't even think about undermining me. If you do, it will be twice as hard on the kid."

Ruby turned her back on her husband. She removed the scrambled eggs and bacon from the stove and handed Andrew his plate. Her own was untouched when Andrew pushed back his chair. "C'mon, let's go to bed, I waited long enough."

Ruby's stomach churned. Making love was the last thing she wanted to do. Especially with this man standing next to her. Something must have showed on her face, because Andrew grabbed her by the arm and dragged her to the bedroom.

An hour later, Ruby left the bedroom to take a shower. She felt like she'd been raped. She'd tried to be responsive, to smile. She did her best to feel something, and when she couldn't summon the passion she'd felt previously for her husband, she lay still and succumbed to his hunger.

She faked her orgasm.

In the days to come, Ruby lost all sense of who she was. Andrew confiscated her car for his own use, deliberately making it difficult for her to go to St. Andrew's. Once she suggested she drive him to the office, but he read her intent. He gave her one excuse after another. Determined to go to St. Andrew's, she took three buses and didn't return till after eight in the evening. Just in time to feel Andrew's wrath. She didn't care.

She no longer tried to make him happy. A week after his return, she knew it wasn't possible. She started making plans to leave, to return to Washington with Martha. She'd written a letter to the bank, one to Rena, and one to Opal, asking for advice. Opal generously offered to send her the money she'd saved by living rent-free, and Ruby accepted the offer. She had enough for a plane ticket back to Washington, when she discovered she was pregnant.

She carried the baby till the seventh month, certain all along that something was wrong because she felt no movement. The baby, a boy, was stillborn. She settled into a fit of depression that lasted three months. She postponed her trip back to the States and returned the money to her sister.

Every chance she got she returned to St. Andrew's to do whatever she could to help her friends. She suffered through Andrew's blistering confrontations because she always felt good about herself and happy when she returned from a long day at the parish.

A year and a half later, Ruby discovered she was pregnant again, just after new orders came through. They were being transferred to California. At least California was closer to Washington than Hawaii was, she told herself.

She cried bitter tears when she said good-bye to all those she'd come to love at St. Andrew's. She vowed to never forget them and promised to do whatever she could to aid them, a promise she intended to keep.

Martha was four when the new baby was born, a roly-poly boy named Andrew, Junior, Andy for short. Andrew doted on his new son and totally ignored Martha, to Ruby's relief. Fortunately, Andy was a good baby who mostly ate and slept.

She loved California. So did Martha. It was always sunny, and somehow the days were better when the sun shone clear and bright.

She wasn't exactly happy, but she was content in what she considered the summer of her life.

Andy was two years old when Andrew made rank again, still

under the command of General Frankel. Being a major's wife
demanded she become involved in the military social scene. She
could afford baby-sitters now, as well as new clothes, and her
own car. She still wasn't happy, but she was content.

The day Martha turned seven, Ruby opened the door in the
middle of the afternoon to what she thought would be Martha's
party guests, only it wasn't a gang of seven-year-olds standing
on her doorstep; it was her sister Opal.

"I wanted to surprise you. We just transferred to Miramar. I
told my husband I was coming here and he'd just have to get
along without me. He's a great guy, Ruby, you'll like him when
you meet," Opal cried, swinging her sister off the ground. "God,
it's good to see you. I really missed you. Letters aren't enough,
if you know what I mean. And speaking of letters, I haven't had
one from Amber in almost a year. Last time I heard, she had
seven kids. How's that possible, Ruby?"

Ruby laughed, never happier in her life. "If I have to tell
you, then you better file for divorce. My God, Opal, it's so
good to see you. Look, you're going to have to help me with
this party. Marty has ants in her pants. She can't wait to open
her presents. That's what this party is all about, you
know."

"I didn't come empty-handed."

After the party, while Martha played with her presents and
Andy whirled around the back patio on his little bike, the sisters
talked, laughed, and cried.

"How's Mom?" Ruby asked hesitantly.

"I don't know. I invited them to the wedding, but they didn't
come. You should see my in-laws, Ruby, they're wonderful.
Real parents. They laugh and talk a lot and tell jokes. Mac's father is always clapping him on the back, and his mother is forever kissing and hugging him. He pretends to be embarrassed,
but he isn't. You know, when he calls his family he never hangs
up till he says I love you both to his mom and dad. We really
bummed out, didn't we?"

"Victims," Ruby said sadly. "Just like Mom."

"C'mon, I want to hear all about Major Blue and Calvin," she
said slyly. "Everything, Ruby, and don't leave out one word. We
have years to catch up on. Swear, every word."

"Okay, you got it. You better sit back. You see, it was like this . . ."

Three hours later Opal said, "Are you telling me you never, as in *never*, heard from Calvin? Ruby, how can that be? I thought . . . what I mean is, you loved him heart and soul. Your marriage doesn't sound like it was made in heaven. Why don't you try and contact him again? It will put some spice in your life. I dare you!" Opal said devilishly. "*I* would."

"Would you really?" Ruby said.

"Yep. Life's too short not to be happy. I say go for whatever makes you happy. Think about all those miserable years we had growing up. We're never going to get them back, not that either one of us wants them. But we should be compensated somehow, don't you think?"

"Well . . ."

"Well what?"

"I'm married," Ruby said lamely.

"You could get a divorce if you wanted to. We don't have to answer to Mom and Dad anymore."

"Opal, I . . . I'm afraid I can't sustain any kind of relationship. Everything always goes sour. Only at St. Andrew's, where I worked like a dog, was I *happy*. Why is that? I felt like I was just beginning to find out who I was and then bam, we moved, and I'm back to the same old me. Does any of this make sense to you?"

"Sure, you're nuts like the rest of us." Opal giggled.

"Aren't you ever serious?" Ruby demanded.

"I try not to be. I had enough of that back in Barstow. I like it on the edge. I guess I get that from Mac."

Ruby looked at her sister. She was pretty, in a wholesome way, with her large blue eyes and soft golden curls. She was tiny, size six, maybe a four. Petite. But she was nervous, her hands and head seemed to be in constant motion, her feet tapping the floor in rhythm with her moving hands. She smoked too much and she was already on her fourth drink.

"I guess you're a free spirit," Ruby said.

"Pretty much so. Now, what are you going to do about Calvin what's his name?"

Ruby laughed. "Well . . ."

CHAPTER NINE

Ruby felt as if a piece of her life were being cut away when Opal left four days later. They'd had such a wonderful time trading gossip and memories. Pop was still peeing through a tube; no one had heard from Grace since she'd moved to Pittsburgh; and Rena now had four holes in each ear for her jewelry. She had become quite a real estate tycoon, now owning a dozen properties. Of the three Connors sisters, Opal had come out of Barstow the health-iest. That she was happy showed on her face. Ruby had felt more than one twinge of envy as she talked to her sister. She felt shame now, though, when she remembered the way they'd sliced Amber up in little pieces and their father as well.

They'd cried and blubbered, hugging each other as their mem-ories, at least some of them, were laid to rest.

They'd promised to keep in touch, to call once a week, and to write every two weeks. Tears flowed at the airport as Ruby, with her children at her side, watched until the plane was a speck in the sky.

Ruby dropped Martha off at a friend's before she returned home with Andy, who was asleep in the backseat. Andrew wouldn't be home; he never was on a Saturday. On Sunday ei-ther. Or most nights.

She had her own life now, and it was full and rewarding. She and Andrew lived in the same house, ate at the same table oc-casionally, and slept together rarely. Their married life had gone straight downhill after Andrew's return from Korea. She'd taken the full blame for it. Sometimes she didn't feel anything for her husband. The rest of the time she detested him.

In true military fashion, according to Andrew Blue, she had to keep lists and charts. Even Martha, young as she was, had a list—one for chores, one for personal hygiene, and one for the children she played with. And little Andy had a chart, which

Ruby was forced to maintain. Saturdays, before Andrew left to play golf with his friends, he made a point of checking off the charts. The first time he'd done it, Ruby had been flabbergasted; he'd made a sloppy star at the top with his dull pencil. Martha lived in fear of the stars, or lack of them. When she didn't see the squiggly pointed design, she knew her father would threaten her with loss of privileges. The child was a nervous wreck, trembling and shaking in her father's presence. A bicycle was the prize she'd been striving for, but so far it eluded her. She needed, according to Andrew, four stars in a row, or a whole month of perfect behavior. To date, she'd fallen off the flagpole six times in her try for the bicycle.

Last month Ruby railed at her husband when he checked the list on the last Saturday of the month. Martha would have earned the bicycle but for a stray sock found under her bed. Andrew had looked triumphant when he stared down at his daughter and told her she had to start over. Not only had she railed at her husband in defense of her daughter, she'd actually given him a shove that sent him sprawling across the kitchen, and then she called him a son of a bitch in a voice that dripped venom. He'd laughed as he gathered up his golf clubs and hadn't returned till three-thirty in the morning, reeking of liquor.

Time and again she questioned why she stayed in her loveless marriage. The best she could come up with, as she'd told Opal, was that she didn't want to fail and deprive her children of a father. Opal had looked disgusted and told her in her own way she was no better off than their mother. And it was true.

Andrew was having affairs, one after another. She'd seen the pitying looks on the faces of the few friends she'd made, but she didn't care who he shacked up with, as long as he left her alone.

Andy woke as soon as the car pulled into the carport. He scrambled on chubby legs to the back patio, where he started to tinker with his little bike, yelling at the top of his lungs that he was going to "fix it." Ruby smiled indulgently. He was so normal in every way because Andrew hadn't gotten to him yet.

A packet of letters had arrived in the afternoon mail. A thick one from the bank in Washington drew a frown. A letter from Amber with the same postmark made her clench her teeth. What was Amber doing in Washington? The third envelope sent her heart thumping: it was from Dixie Sinclaire. The last had been forwarded twice. The original postmark was months old.

She ripped at the envelopes of the three letters, though she knew in advance she wasn't going to be able to handle the news in any of them. If she had been a drinker like her husband, she would have headed for Andrew's liquor cabinet and swigged straight from the bottle.

The letter from the bank was simple but full of surprises. George and Irma Connors had contacted the bank (because that's where their monthly checks came from) and asked that the bank forward their letter to Ruby. It really wasn't a letter at all, but a demand for housing in Florida because Mrs. Connors was suffering from severe arthritis and Mr. Connors had retired from the monument works. Ruby laughed hysterically when she read it. She tossed it on the floor and sifted through the other pieces of paper. One, written on crisp French Embassy letterhead, was an outright offer to buy her house on Poplar Street at a price three times what she'd paid for it. A note from the bank clipped to the French offer, recommended doubling the rent and offering an option to buy with a lump sum settlement up front. The note went on to say Washington was now in a supply-and-demand cycle. If, the note said, you decide in the future not to honor the option, the option monies will be returned to the French Embassy. The second form was for the renewal lease on O Street. The bank's recommendation was to terminate the current lease when it came due in thirty days because the present tenants were behind in their rent payments and owed back late charges. Embassy personnel would snap up the property at twice the rent. The bank's final recommendation was so startling, Ruby felt light-headed; if you decide to honor your parents' request, we recommend you take the option on Poplar and let us see if we can get the same kind of deal for O Street. The option monies, along with the one-month advance, will give you sufficient money for a down payment on a house for your parents.

Ruby's eyes were wild as she fought to quiet her breathing. She'd paid off her debt a year earlier and now this. As far as she was concerned, she didn't owe her parents anything. What in the goddamn hell were they doing with their money? Between her two sisters and herself, they'd paid out almost eighteen thousand dollars. Opal said she'd paid for a few years and then stopped. Mac, she'd said, had forbidden her to send another cent. If her parents sold their house in Barstow, they would have more than enough to pay for a house in Florida or, at the very least, to make a down payment. Of course, if her father wasn't working, no bank would give him a mortgage. She wasn't working, so where did they think she'd get a mortgage? Why me? she grated.

"I fix, Mommy," Andy said, tugging on her skirt, his red plastic screwdriver clutched in his chubby fist.

"Honey, I wish you could," Ruby said, hugging the little boy. "Mommy has to read the mail. Fix your wagon now and make it run, okay?"

"I fix," the little boy chortled as he attacked the rubber wheel on his wagon.

Ruby unfolded the letter from Amber. She'd probably gotten the same letter from their parents and wanted to know what to do.

The letter was short and to the point. They'd been wiped out by a typhoon and lost everything. Saipan, she said, had been virtually washed away. Nangi had appealed to Calvin, who pulled some political military strings and managed to get them all to Washington. With what little money they had, they rented a house in Arlington, Virginia, but the seven kids had to share bedrooms, and they were so cramped, she couldn't stand it. The bottom line was that they needed a loan of five hundred dollars. Calvin had loaned them two hundred to see them through. If she could find a competent baby-sitter, she was going to go back to work. Nangi was looking for a job. She could live for a year on what they had to pay out for one month in the D.C. area. "I know what a major's pay is, Ruby, and I know you're a saver. Lending me five hundred dollars won't kill you. I'll pay you back."

Ruby crunched the letter into a ball and tossed it across the yard. "My ass," she muttered. There had been no mention of their parents, so that could mean only that Amber hadn't been asked to contribute. She didn't even want to think about Calvin's contribution to her *sister's* welfare.

She unfolded Dixie's letter. Her hands trembled as she smoothed out the single sheet of paper.

Dear Ruby,

I imagine this letter is going to shock you. I'm sorry for that. If I knew where you were, I would call. I put out a few feelers to see if I could locate you, but nothing came back. I can only hope this letter will be forwarded, and in true military fashion, I am prepared to wait at least six months for it to catch up to you and for you to respond.

Ruby, I'm sorry I didn't say good-bye. I wanted to, more than you know. I wanted to write, too, but I was too ashamed. A day didn't go by that I didn't think of you. It wasn't fair to you. We were such good friends.

By now I know you must have heard the rumors about Hugo. Yes, they're true. How often I wanted to confide in you, but my pride wouldn't let me. I didn't want to see pity in your eyes. You were the sister I always wished for.

I never blamed you for Hugo losing out. He did, though. When Andrew got his promotion, I was really happy for you. I wanted to write to you then, but Hugo was watching me like a hawk. I was so afraid.

Hugo made captain this year, and we both know he won't go any further. Of course, he blames me and takes it out on me. He doesn't beat me anymore because he knows the military is watching him. I don't love him; I'm afraid of him. I'd leave, but have nowhere to go.

We're stationed at Quantico, and I think we'll be here until Hugo puts in his twenty years. He says we're going to retire to Rumson, New Jersey. Last year he put a deposit on a piece of land, and he says we'll build our own house there.

Thanks to you, Ruby, I've gotten a little gumption this past year. I've rented a post office box and that's where I want you to write me if you decide to reply. I'm also working part-time, for all the good it does me. Hugo takes my money so fast, I don't even get a chance to count it. Once in a while I stand up to Hugo just to hear the sound of my own voice. I truly believe the Corps turned him into what he is. He was never like he is now until he started with all that Semper Fi stuff. Maybe I'm being unfair, but I no longer care. It's all baloney, if you want my opinion.

Please write to me, Ruby, a long letter, and tell me everything that's gone on. I'd like to hear everything from the day we left. Did the others miss me, even a little bit? We really had a good time fixing up that rat's nest you moved into. I think about that all the time.

It's time for me to go to work, so I'd better close. That's funny, isn't it, me working? Once Hugo got it through his head he wasn't going to get any more promotions, he decided I could work. You want to hear something else that's funny?

I wish he'd cheat on me so he'd leave me alone. I'll say good-bye on that note.

> All my love,
> Dixie

Ruby blew her nose and wiped at her eyes. This wonderful letter canceled out the other two by a mile. Seven years to retirement. Rumson, New Jersey. She said the words over and over like a litany. She now knew where she would retire, and if Andrew had no desire to go to Rumson, she'd go alone. Seven more years. Seven more years.

Ruby fixed herself a glass of iced tea, gathering her writing materials together before she rejoined her son on the patio. First she wrote to Amber. It was a short letter. She apologized for not having any available cash to send. She wished her luck on her new move and said she was confident things would work out. She included a recent picture of Martha and Andy.

The letter to the bank was carefully worded; the letter she enclosed to her parents was even more so. She instructed the bank to sell the house on Poplar Street and to pay cash for her parents' house in Florida. The deed was to be in her name alone. Her parents could stay in the house for their lifetime and pay her one hundred dollars per month rent. It was a take-it-or-leave-it offer, and she fully expected her parents to reject it—not that she cared one way or the other.

Her conscience pricked her as she walked around to the front of the house to put the letters in the mailbox. She could have offered Amber the house on O Street until she got on her feet financially. She could still offer her five hundred dollars if she wanted to tap the money the bank would get for the option on her remaining house. She didn't owe Amber anything. Not one damn thing. She had to keep reminding herself that she hated Amber.

All afternoon she stewed and fretted about her curt response to her sister. At six-thirty she called Opal in San Diego to ask for advice.

Ruby read Amber's letter over the phone. Opal laughed. "You know you're going to do it, you just want me to agree with you. If it was me, I'd do it. What the hell, Ruby, you're the only one of the three of us who's solvent. Jeez, you must have felt great when you wrote to Pop and the bank. You finally got your pound of flesh."

"Is that what it is—my pound of flesh?" Ruby asked in a hushed voice.

"You bet. Actually, if you stop and think about it, it's a double whammy. You're socking it to old Amber and at the same time you're helping her. I'm not sure if Pop will realize you got him by the short hairs. Go for it, Ruby, but you were too cheap on the rent. Think about that!"

"I'm thinking about the way you talk," Ruby said sternly. "Where did you learn such things?"

Opal whooped with laughter a second time. "From my navy flier husband." Opal's voice turned serious. "It makes you the better person, Ruby. Just do it. The reasons don't matter. Listen, my husband is due any minute now, and while he was generous in allowing me to visit you, my time is his once he walks through the door. I love you, Ruby. I'll write. Hey, I hear Mac's car; he drives the way he flies. See you."

It took Ruby an hour to rewrite the letter to Amber. She didn't experience any wild rush of elation when she closed the mailbox. Obviously, only one wild rush of elation was allotted to her on any given day, and she'd gotten hers with Dixie's letter.

A week later she received a letter from Amber, chastizing her for not forcing her tenants to move a month ahead of schedule. She said she wasn't going to be responsible to some damn bank and an Egyptian Gypsy. Ruby scribbled off a reply that told her sister to take it or leave it. Amber didn't respond, but the bank informed Ruby that Amber and her family had moved in an hour after the tenants moved out.

A week later she received a telegram from the bank confirming that her parents had agreed to her terms. Three days after that, she received a hateful letter from her father, which she tore into shreds.

Nothing, not even Andrew, could dampen Ruby's spirits now that she had Dixie's friendship again. She wrote twice a week and called as often as she could from one phone booth or another. Both women were determined to keep their friendship secret. Men, they agreed, simply could not be trusted or depended upon. Their last conversation still rang in Ruby's ears; she had confessed to Dixie how she'd been filing amended tax returns every April and keeping secret all her business dealings. Dixie giggled and said if she was ever in serious trouble, Ruby was the one she'd go to.

Ruby's spirits were so high that she found herself being more tolerant of her husband. She went out of her way to be accommodating and responsive. Andrew's reaction was to accuse her of having an affair, which he used as an excuse to withdraw even more from their family life. Ruby hardly noticed.

Her life these days was her children, Dixie, and her sister Opal. Once again Ruby Blue was happy.

{{{{{{{{{ CHAPTER TEN }}}}}}}}}

It was a dreary, stormy afternoon. Rain slashed at the windows, and Ruby hated the sound. Today, she hated everything. Dr. Ainsley, the base shrink, had just called to render his current evaluation of Martha, who had been seeing him for over a year. God, what was it he'd said? She needed continued therapy, but therapy could go only so far. If Andrew wasn't prepared to come in for counseling, treatment would take years. Martha, it seemed, was seeking her father's approval. He'd also suggested that if she was certain Andrew would not make the effort, she should think seriously about taking the children and leaving her husband. Her own sessions with the doctor always left her feeling morose and withdrawn. She'd done everything she could for her child. She'd argued and tried to assert herself for Martha's sake and Andy's, too. Andrew's response was that Martha needed her ass whipped, and this psychological shit was from Ruby's kooky side of the family. "Go ahead, Ruby, tell that jerk about your old man and then come back and tell me I'm to blame." She had talked about her father, with tears streaming down her face. The doctor hadn't said her daughter's problems were her fault or that anything was hereditary, but neither had he again asked to see Andrew after that session. That was two years ago.

She was smoking these days, something she swore she would never do. It gave her something to do with her hands. It also seemed to help her twanging nerves. She used cigarettes the way

Martha still clung to her security blanket. That blanket was another thing. Andrew had forcefully ripped it from Martha's arms on the first night she'd wet the bed at the age of seven, which happened to be also the first time she'd come close to winning her first star. Ruby had fought him like a wild woman. She'd even gone so far as to pick up a butcher knife from the table, and in a voice so terrible she still remembered it, ordered her husband to give Martha the blanket and never to touch it again. He'd thrown it at the child and advanced with his hand raised to strike her, but Ruby had whipped the long blade upward, murder in her eyes. She doubted now that she would have had the guts to lash out at her husband; she wasn't a violent person. But Andrew obviously believed she was capable of harming him.

At least she had some power over him. In general, she wasn't strong anymore; she was weak, jelly in her husband's hands. She even found herself getting upset over his extramarital affairs. Because she wanted to blame someone, she blamed Calvin for her present state. In the end, though, she put all the responsibility on her own shoulders.

Martha and Andrew weren't her only problems these days. In the three years Amber and her family had lived in her house on O Street, Ruby had heard from her twice. Both letters were full of complaints. Now, according to a letter she received from Rena, there was a problem. Ruby was behind in her mortgage, and the bank was threatening to foreclose because Amber hadn't paid the last six months' rent. The house was a shambles, according to Rena, with holes in the walls and stains on the carpets that would never come out. Dog and cat stains. She'd underlined that sentence. The same animals had chewed the molding and door frames. There were six broken windows, and the cellar door was off its hinges. They never mowed the grass, and the flowers and shrubs were all gone. Two of the boards on the back porch were missing, and the house smelled like cat piss. She'd underlined that sentence, too.

Ruby burst into tears that came out in hard, racking sobs. Her shoulders shook and her stomach heaved. She jerked upright when she felt a gentle hand on her shoulder.

"What's wrong, Mom?" Andy asked in a shaky voice. He'd never seen his mother cry, and he was scared. "Did I do something wrong? If I did, tell me and I'll fix it."

"I'm just having a bad day, honey. Sometimes mothers get

weepy and things bother them. It has nothing to do with you, Andy, or Martha, either."

Not satisfied, Andy demanded, "Is it Dad? You know, Mom, he has demons in him. Not real ones, but . . . when people act the way Dad does, that means he can't handle things. I learned that in Bible class. You can't let Dad get under your skin. You have to learn that his bark is worse than his bite."

Ruby stared up at her seven-year-old son. He was a handsome, sturdy little boy with blond curls and incredible blue eyes. A smattering of freckles danced across the bridge of his nose. These days all he worried about was how long it would take for his two front teeth to come in. "How did you get so smart?" she asked playfully. "How is it you are so in tune with me?"

The little boy pondered the question and then shrugged. "You're my mom. I'm always going to be a good boy so you'll be proud of me."

"Oh, Andy, I am proud of you. I think I love you more than life. Martha, too."

The phone rang and Andy raced to answer it. The call was for him. He started to jabber excitedly about tin cans tied to strings that could be stretched between houses. Ruby smiled.

Ruby squared her shoulders. Andy was okay, and she would keep him that way. Martha would heal. Martha would be fine. Whatever she had to do to ensure that end, she would do. Now, though, she had to deal with the problem of Amber.

She left at seven o'clock, the moment Andrew walked through the door. She babbled some lie about a family emergency and did her best to avoid looking him in the eye. Not that he was able to focus. There was alcohol on his breath.

Andrew followed his wife out to the carport, squawking at her the whole way: she was crazy like her old man, and who did she think she was, taking off in the middle of a rainstorm?

Ruby closed and locked the trunk. She felt revolted when she stared up at her drunken husband. Thank God she'd sent Andy to sleep over at a friend's house. Martha was at a friend's, too, something Ruby always arranged carefully so the child wasn't home on weekends when there was a chance Andrew would be home.

"Who am I, Andrew? Your wife, but then, you seem to have forgotten that these past years. I'm the person who cleans up after you when you vomit your guts out and you miss the bowl. I'm the person who bore you the two wonderful children you're bent on destroying. I'm the person who cooks and cleans and goes to your shitty meetings so you can get ahead. *I'm the reason you're where you are.* I didn't know that for a long time, but I know it now. Do you want to know how I know, Andrew? Martha's doctor told me. You're the one with the problem. We're normal, you aren't. I tried, Andrew, my God, how I tried. I gave one hundred and ten percent. I don't care anymore. When I get back, you and I are going to have a long talk, and if we can't bring this marriage together, for us and for the children, I'm leaving. I want you to think about that this weekend. Think about it *all* weekend and not with your snoot in a bottle. I mean it, Andrew, I'll leave."

"Over my dead body," Andrew blustered.

"If that's what it takes," Ruby snapped. God, why was she even talking to him? He wouldn't remember any of it once he slept off his drunk.

"You aren't leaving. I'm up for promotion. I'll grind you to a pulp before I let you leave," he slurred.

Ruby climbed into the car and rolled down the window. "Don't threaten me, Andrew. And always remember what happened to Hugo. That's something else I found out about. The same thing can happen to you, and I'm the one who can do it." Ruby stuck her head out the window. She enunciated each word carefully. "I will do whatever it takes to make our daughter healthy. I will make her well, with or without you. Now, get the hell out of my way before I run you over."

The car roared backward with such force that Ruby was certain she had given herself whiplash.

As she drove across the state on Route 10, she muttered under her breath. She was still muttering hours later when she swung the Pontiac north on Route 95. She wasn't tired. In fact, she felt exhilarated. She drove with the windows wide open and the radio at full blast.

It was six o'clock the following day when Ruby carefully maneuvered the Pontiac down the narrow alley behind Rena's house on Monroe Street. She had driven all day and night without stopping. She smiled tiredly when she saw the garbage cans. The old metal ones had been replaced with large heavy plastic but were still flowered and beribboned. She blinked at the long white Cadillac. Rena was doing well.

Five minutes later she was wrapped in Rena's small arms with

Bruno waiting impatiently for his turn. "Oh, it's so good to see you. I've missed you both. Ah, more diamonds." Ruby giggled when she noted a rather small stone, by Rena's standards, studded into her pinky nail.

"Never mind. Come inside. You look tired. When did you leave?" Rena demanded as she pranced about the kitchen, opening and closing drawers while Bruno fussed with uncorking a wine bottle.

"About seven-thirty last night. I am tired, but I had to come," she said, a note of apology in her voice.

"Of course you did. That sister of yours . . . she is so ungrateful. She is also rude, and her children are like little savages." The tiny woman threw her hands in the air to indicate there was no describing them. "Eat, eat. Leave nothing. Tomorrow we will go to your house and you will evict that ungrateful wretch. Make her pay for the damages. Bruno will fix everything, for a small fee. The cat piss . . . I don't know if you can ever get that out . . . it's a disgrace."

"I wish you had written sooner," Ruby muttered as she bit down into a delicious chicken sandwich.

Rena forced a second sandwich on her while she consumed two glasses of wine. A slice of banana cream pie that was still warm completed Ruby's meal.

"Who lives upstairs?" Ruby asked, lighting a cigarette.

"A nasty couple from Alabama. Can you believe this, Ruby? They had the gall to change the locks on the door so I couldn't go in to check on my property. They took me to court, and the judge said they had to give me a key. I want to evict them. They talk like they have marbles in their mouths. Just last week they said they were changing the wallpaper. Out they go the minute their lease is up!"

Ruby sighed wearily. She was so tired, she had barely heard a word Rena had said.

"You are asleep on your feet, little one. Come, I have your bed all ready. Bruno has just given me the signal that he has turned down the covers."

Ruby stumbled down the hall, twice lurching against Bruno's broad shoulder. She sat down on the bed fully clothed. Bruno removed her shoes and covered her with a blanket. "Sleep, Ruby," he said gently. "Tomorrow my wife will help make things right for you."

* * *

Nothing Rena said prepared Ruby for her first look at the house on O Street. She drew in her breath in a sharp hiss. The doorbell was hanging by a wire, and the door itself was scuffed and dirty. Even the brass kickplate was streaked and tarnished. Tactfully, Rena said nothing.

Ruby knocked. She was forced to stand back in order not to be trampled when a horde of children exited, screaming and yelling. Then a dog streaked through, skidded to a stop, sniffed at Ruby's and Rena's shoes, and bolted down the steps.

Rena pushed Ruby inside. A thirteen-inch television blared from the living room, while strains of music echoed from the kitchen area. Rena was right, Ruby thought as she started to breathe through her mouth. The cat urine was so strong, it made her eyes water. She walked gingerly through the toys and clothes that littered the floor.

Ruby looked around in amazement at the holes in the walls, at the dirty drapes and curtains and the stains on the beige carpet. The parquet floors were scarred; all signs of the finish were gone. The furniture sagged and was filthy; the slipcovers were full of holes and stains. The watercolors on the wall hung askew, giving the living room a drunken appearance. Ruby shuddered.

From somewhere upstairs a baby wailed. Ruby's eyes widened. Amber hadn't said anything about a new baby.

"And she's pregnant again," Rena said under her breath.

Ruby felt her eyes roll back in her head. By sheer will alone she forced herself to calmness. She would deal with this as she dealt with everything.

"Is Nangi working?" she whispered. Where was Amber? Certainly she wasn't cleaning, she thought nastily. The dog was back, along with a cat, circling like vultures. Ruby was suddenly afraid to move.

"Yes. Bruno himself checked out the downtown firm he works for. Your sister told me they're saving all their money to return to Saipan."

"Not at my expense," Ruby grated.

"Amberrrrr!" she shrilled at the top of her lungs.

This couldn't be Amber, not this slovenly, unkempt, pregnant woman with a dishtowel in her hands. This creature couldn't be the persnickety, meticulous girl whose wardrobe matched, right down to her underwear and the bobby pins in her hair. Upstairs, the baby continued to wail. Amber seemed oblivious as she stared at Ruby. There was no hello.

"What are you doing here?"

"I own this house, or did you forget? The door was open, we walked in. I did knock."

"You could have closed it," Amber snapped, kicking at the door with her foot. Ruby winced.

Out of the corner of her eye she noticed movement on the stairway. She turned to see Nangi impeccably dressed in a navy blue suit and white shirt. He was carrying a lizard-skin briefcase.

"Ruby?"

"Yes. And I guess you know Rena. I have to talk to both of you. I'm sorry if it will make you late for work."

"I can make up the time. Is something wrong? Amber, offer our guests some coffee. Please, come and sit down," Nangi said, indicating the sagging couch. Surely, he wouldn't risk sitting there, Ruby thought crazily. He'll get dog and cat hairs all over his suit. She shook her head.

"This won't take long. I'm sorry about all this, but the bank that holds my mortgage notified me that you and Amber haven't been paying the rent this past year. They're ready to foreclose. I've charged you only two hundred dollars a month, and that's more than fair. I thought you would still be able to save a little. I didn't know about the baby"—she waved her hand toward the ceiling—"or that Amber is pregnant again. I don't want to lose this house, so we're going to have to do something."

"What? You want us to move, is that it?" Amber whined.

"That's one solution. The other is that you come up with six months' back rent, and you start taking care of this place. I sold my other house so that Mom and Pop could move to Florida, and I gave you this one in excellent condition to help you out. Now look at it. The dog and cat have to go!"

Nangi's briefcase snapped open. "You have my apologies, Ruby. I thought Amber had been paying you all along. You've been more than generous. I don't know what we would have done without your help. It seems no one wants to rent to people with children. I told Amber a while back that we should be paying you at least three hundred dollars a month. Your previous tenants told me when they moved out that they had been paying five hundred. That makes me appreciate all the more what you've done for us."

Ruby felt giddy; her heart thumped in her chest. She watched as Nangi wrote out a check and handed it to her. "You have my sincere apologies. From now on the rent will be on time, and it will be three hundred dollars. Is that satisfactory?" Ruby nodded dumbly as she looked at the amount on the check—eighteen hundred dollars. Dear God, she was off the hook; her only other alternative would have been to sell the czarina's ring.

Nangi bowed low. "It was nice to see you again, Ruby. I'm sorry it was under these circumstances. I'll be seeing Calvin in a few weeks. Would you like me to say hello for you?"

"Yes, say hello for me." She had to ask, she had to know. "Where is he these days? How is his family?"

"He has two handsome sons. He is now what you Americans call a full bird colonel. He says he's had "below the zone" promotions, which I think means he's advanced very quickly. He's stationed in Colorado. He always asks about you, but I never have anything to tell him. Amber says she never has any news of you."

A tiny, tinkling arm snaked out to steady Ruby. "Tell him . . . tell him I think of him often. You can tell him I, too, have two children, and we're stationed in Pensacola. Tell him . . . I look forward to seeing him someday. Wish him well and congratulate him on his rank. My husband is up for his silver oak leaves."

"I'll be sure to tell him, Ruby. Do you by any chance have a picture of yourself and the children?"

Thank God he'd asked. "I think so," Ruby murmured as she searched through her wallet. A small stack of pictures fell out and fluttered to the floor. Both she and Nangi dropped to their knees. It was Nangi who picked up the old picture of her and Calvin smiling into the camera. He pretended not to see the tears swimming in Ruby's eyes. She handed over a glossy photo of herself and the children sitting on the sofa. It was an old picture, taken when they were stationed in California.

The moment the door closed behind Nangi, Amber snarled. "I hope you're happy. That money was supposed to pay for our trip back to Saipan. You haven't changed at all; you're still a bitch. Go to hell, Ruby."

Ruby wanted to kill her. "You better clean up this place. I'll ask Bruno to come and do the repair work. I was hasty about the animals; you can keep them, but you get that cat neutered. I want this place cleaned up. And while you're at it, clean yourself up. Soap and water cost very little, but if you don't have the money for it, I'll give it to you. Get it through your head, Amber, I don't owe you anything."

Amber brushed impatiently at the straggly hair falling about her face. Overhead, the baby was still wailing. She had the good sense, at that point, to look embarrassed, and Ruby saw a vulnerability she hadn't known Amber possessed. Her heart fluttered. The moment she saw Amber's eyes fill, she turned to Rena. "Go back, I'm going to stay here for a while and . . . help my sister. I'll take a cab back to your house."

"What happened, Amber?" Ruby asked gently, leading her sister to the sagging couch when Rena had gone.

Amber threw her hands into the air. "God, I don't know. The kids, one after the other . . . Saipan . . . it's so hot over there . . . no one does housework . . . I was always tired, always pregnant . . . Mom and Dad . . . not enough money. I couldn't get back into the swing of things when we moved here. Look, I'm sorry I let the house go . . . I'll find a way to pay you back for the repairs . . . honestly, Ruby. I just didn't have the energy to discipline the children, and Nangi works late hours. It isn't easy raising so many kids. God, I don't even know if we have enough money to pay the doctor to deliver the next one now that Nangi paid you. It's right that he paid you. Ruby, I'm just so damn tired."

"Do you really want to go back to Saipan?" Ruby whispered.

"We don't belong here. I guess you can see that."

"Were you happy over there?" Ruby asked curiously.

"Yes, I was. There were no pressures. Nangi didn't let you see it, but he's tied up in knots at work. They don't treat him the way they treat the others. He gets all the shitty jobs, and he's the one who always has to stay late with no overtime. This should give you a laugh. He thought I was a miracle worker because we saved all that money. He didn't know I paid you only the first year. He's a wonderful husband. He's never once complained about my housekeeping. I don't know how I'm going to face him when he comes home tonight. I don't know how to make it right."

"Well, I do."

Ruby was a whirlwind. She worked nonstop scrubbing, scouring, and sweeping. She had sent Amber upstairs to wash up and to look after the baby. By noon she had the worst of the kitchen done. The stove was so bad, she knew she would have to get a new one, but for now, she covered the burners with tinfoil. Roaches by the hundreds scurried for safety as she scoured the oven. When she was satisfied with the condition of the kitchen, she opened every window in the house. It took her an hour to dust and vacuum the living room and dining room. It took her another hour to collect the trash and lug it outside. It was one o'clock when she called to Amber to come downstairs.

Ruby eyed her sister critically. "That's not good enough. Go back and put on more makeup and some stockings. Surely you have a better maternity dress, at least one that's been ironed." Amber burst into tears.

"Okay, okay. Stop with the tears. Look, take your time. Really fix yourself up. I'm going out; there's something I have to do. When I get back I want to see a smile on your face."

Ruby sat back in the taxi, wondering if she was doing the right thing. She'd come prepared with the czarina's ring in case things were so bad she couldn't save the house. It was time to sell it. If she was lucky, she could maybe get five thousand dollars for it. If she haggled, she could get it up to sixty-five hundred. That would pay for Amber and her family to return to Saipan, and she would have enough left to refurbish the house and rent it out again.

The jewelry store was alight with winking gems. The man coming toward her was so austere and formidable-looking, Ruby wanted to turn tail and run.

"May I help you?" the man asked in a nasal voice.

"Perhaps," Ruby said coolly. "I have a ring I'd like to sell."

"We don't buy used goods, madam. We're in the business of selling. Try a pawn shop," he said, looking her over from top to bottom.

"This isn't the kind of ring that's pawned," Ruby said icily. She opened her purse and walked over to the counter, where she laid the ring down on a square of black velvet. She smiled when the man's eyes bulged. From somewhere in the back of the store two other men appeared, their eyes widening in surprise.

"Make me an offer, and if it's satisfactory, I'll consider it. If it isn't acceptable, I'll go somewhere else. I want the money now. A bank check will do."

One of the men picked up the ring and was about to walk to the back of the store. "No, no, no. Look at it here. I don't want that ring out of my sight." The man harumphed and huffed but followed her order. Ruby tapped her foot impatiently. What was taking them so long? She looked at her watch. If she hurried, she would have enough time to make the bank and cash the check. Perhaps she could call and make an appointment and explain the situation. She interrupted the hushed conversation behind the counter. "I need to know *now*." She reached out to pick up the ring.

"What do you want?" the first man asked.

Ruby's heart fluttered. She didn't want to name an amount in case she was too low. If she went too high, they would think she was a fool. "I said to make me an offer. I'll let you know when your offer is acceptable."

"Six five."

Ruby shook her head. So she was right. That's what she would accept, but if she held out, she might get more.

"Seven."

Ruby shook her head again.

"Eighty."

She liked the perspiration beading on the men's faces. She shook her head again and made as if to pick up the ring.

"Ninety."

Ruby shook her head again, her hand poised in midair. Wait. He'd said *ninety*, not *nine*. It was *eighty*, not *eight*. She felt the blood rush to her head.

"A hundred thousand. That's as high as we'll go." Ruby swayed dizzily. She was offered a glass of water, which she drank greedily. "Very well, madam, our final offer is one hundred twenty-five thousand dollars. I will go next door to our bank and secure a draft if that is agreeable to you."

"I think that will be fine, gentlemen." Ruby said in a voice she didn't recognize as her own. She wouldn't think about the amount, not now. She almost laughed. That little dizzy spell had driven up the price twenty-five thousand dollars. Oh, Bubba, do you have any idea what you did for me?

Ruby made the bank with five minutes to spare. "Give me ten thousand dollars, no, make that ten thousand five hundred. I have some shopping to do. I'll be back in the morning to pay off the mortgage on the house. In the meantime, apply this," she said, producing Nangi's check, "to the overdue mortgage." She was out of the bank in a flash.

When she returned to the house on O Street, it was almost five o'clock. The taxi driver carried in the bundles; she carried the bag from the butcher. The money was secure in her purse.

They were waiting for her, the children lined up, solemn and serious, their eyes full of questions. It was hard to believe they were the same rambunctious children who had barreled through the door earlier that morning. Amber introduced them one by one. Ruby shook hands with each one. To her surprise, there was a George, an Irma, and an Opal, and the baby was named Ruby. The dog at the end of the line offered his paw. Ruby giggled and the children laughed. It was a shame she would never get to know these little honey-colored, dark-eyed children. So many mouths to feed, so many to clothe and buy shoes for.

Ruby looked down at the oldest. "I want to talk to your mother for a little while, so how would you all like some ice cream and candy? Here's ten dollars. Buy some soda pop, too. Shoo." She laughed as the children ran through the door.

"What's all this?" Amber asked, shifting the baby from one hip to the other.

"One bag has steak and stuff for dinner—a celebration dinner you and I are going to cook. The rest of the stuff is for you. New maternity clothes, underwear, and shoes. I know your size, since I borrowed your shoes once. And this," she said, handing Amber an envelope, "is ten thousand dollars. Enough for you to go back to Saipan. When things are straightened out, I'll send you another five thousand so you'll have a little nest egg. If you start to cry, Amber, I'm leaving," Ruby said hoarsely. Amber sniffled as she handed baby Ruby over to her aunt.

"Where did you ... how ... ?"

"I suppose I could lie to you and say I saved it, but I'm not much of a liar. I sold the czarina's ring. Bubba gave it to me when I left for Washington. She wanted me to have it, and she didn't say anything about sharing. I'm going to give some to Opal, too. I think that's fair." Please, she prayed silently, don't let her ask me how much it was worth.

"How much was it worth?" Amber demanded.

"They offered seven, but I held out. Twelve five." God would forgive the extra zeros. She held her breath for Amber's response. Amber merely shrugged.

"I'm surprised you got that much. I always thought that ring was a joke, you know, that it wasn't real. You're giving me most of it. Why?"

"You need it the most. Bubba always said I would know when it was time to sell it. I guess this is the time. I brought it with me. I sort of thought you might be in financial trouble, and I didn't want to lose the house. Let's just say we both needed it. Amber, this baby is so funny-looking, she's cute. Why does her hair grow straight up in the air?" Ruby asked, chucking her little niece under the chin. The baby gurgled happily.

"It lays down about the same time they start to walk." There was more than a hint of annoyance in Amber's voice when she said, "Are you trying to tell me my kids are funny-looking?"

"No. Well, sort of. Different, Amber. Is that why you feel you don't fit in here anymore? They're yours and I'm sure you love them as much as I love mine, but we can't pretend they don't look different."

"If you'd married Calvin, your kids would look like mine. Is that so terrible, Ruby?"

There was a catch in Ruby's voice. "No, it isn't. I'm sorry I even brought it up." She hugged the baby to her until she squealed. "I think it was nice of you to name two of your kids after Opal and me. I'll take care of the baby while you get all duded up for Nangi and start supper. Call him and tell him to come home. Better yet, tell him to tell those . . . people he works for what they can do with their job; you're going . . . home. Go on, Amber, do it. Is it okay to put Ruby on the kitchen floor?"

"Sure, now that you scrubbed it. I won't be long. Jeez, I hope my hair is dry. Nangi is going to be . . . he's so good, Ruby, he never, ever complains. He's like Calvin in that respect. Calvin isn't happy, Ruby," Amber called over her shoulder.

Ruby wanted to call her back, to demand to know why Calvin wasn't happy. She wanted to know everything, every detail. Perhaps at dinner something would be said. "Amber," Ruby called up the stairs, "yell when you're finished talking to Nangi. I have to call Andrew and tell him I'm staying over another day."

Dinner wasn't the zoo scene she thought it would be. In their father's company, the children were well-mannered and quiet, speaking only when a question was asked. She did notice that they had trouble cutting their meat, and the baked potato seemed to puzzle them.

Amber laughed. "We mostly eat rice, Ruby, but you couldn't

know that. Usually, I make something in one pot. That's what they're used to. This is a real treat for Nangi and me. We haven't had steak in a very long time."

Ruby found her eyes going to Nangi, drinking in the sight of him. He reminded her a little of Calvin. She wished someone would bring up his name so she could ask questions. Nangi had seen the tears in her eyes and the picture she still carried in her wallet. Good manners would prevent him from bringing up Calvin's name. Nangi would never embarrass her. She was stunned to hear Amber say, "It's a shame Ruby won't be here when Calvin arrives. It's always nice to see old friends."

"I know he will be disappointed at missing you," Nangi said quietly.

"Why is he coming to Washington?" Ruby asked in what she hoped was a nonchalant voice.

"Something to do with his next tour. He said he had business at the Pentagon. I think he's going to train pilots or something like that. Calvin is usually vague when it comes to specifics. He did say he would be here for a week. He usually stays with us, but now that we're going to return to Saipan, I don't think we'll wait around for his visit. I gave my notice after Amber's call. Why don't I ring him up after dinner and you can talk to him? I have to call him anyway. I can't let him arrive thinking he's going to stay with us if we aren't going to be here. Or would you rather not talk with him?"

In one motion Ruby knocked over her water glass, while her elbow went into one of the children's plates, causing a baked potato to sail across the table and land on Nangi's plate, splattering butter on his snowy white shirt. She tried to say something, but her tongue was too thick in her mouth. Amber saved the moment by jumping up to wipe up the spill and declaring in a brisk voice, "Of course she wants to talk to Calvin, just make sure what's-her-name doesn't know it's Ruby on this end. I swear, Nangi, sometimes I have to think for you."

Ruby found her voice. There was nothing wrong with speaking to an old friend. She wasn't betraying Andrew or even being disloyal. Calvin was in Colorado, she was in D.C., and Andrew was in Florida, miles and miles apart. Still her conscience pricked. "Well . . . I . . . it probably . . . what I mean . . ."

". . . is that she'd love to. Go do it now. We can have our dessert after I clear the table." Ruby watched as she handed out Popsicles to the kids, who were going to watch cartoons before attacking their homework.

"We'll call from upstairs. It will be much quieter."

Ruby perched on the edge of the bed, her nervous hands busily pleating and unpleating the folds of her skirt while Nangi made small talk with Calvin in their native language. Nangi's eyes apologized. He scribbled on a pad near the phone, "Calvin always switches to our language when he asks about you. I've told him nothing." He held out the phone and mouthed the words "I just told him someone was here who wanted to say hello. I'll be downstairs." He closed the door softly behind him.

"Hello, Calvin? It's Ruby. How are you?" The silence on the other end of the phone drove the color creeping up her neck to her cheeks. They burned. "Calvin, are you there?"

"Yes, yes, I am." It was the same voice that she remembered. "It's . . . I can't believe . . . how are you?" The voice was suddenly sad. Ruby's heart fluttered.

"Surviving. I think of you often, Calvin. I . . . I tried to get in touch with you. I called, I wrote . . . and then Nangi said you got married. I thought . . . I waited . . ." Damn, the tears were spilling over, and here she was acting like some damn lovesick adolescent.

"It was my fault. I had too much pride. Nangi explained what happened that day, but it was too late by then. I tried to reach you when I returned to . . . it was my fault."

"And mine," Ruby said softly. "Are you well? Are you happy?"

"Yes. No. And you?"

"Yes. No. We screwed up, Calvin, big time."

Calvin's voice dropped several octaves. "I've thought of you every day since . . . even when I'm flying I think . . . it's best then, up there all by myself. Sometimes I dream . . . Nangi has kept me aware of you and your whereabouts. I always ask. And I always feel good for a week or so when he tells me news of you."

Ruby strained closer to the earpiece. She didn't want to miss a word.

"Calvin . . . I . . ." The tears were falling, choking off her voice. "I have to hang up, Calvin, and not run up Amber's bill. I . . . oh, Calvin, why couldn't you have trusted me, believed in me a little more? Damn you, I did everything, I tried to kill you

emotionally, and I . . . it didn't work . . . I did everything I could
think of . . . I got married for all the wrong reasons, and now I'm
stuck. And all because of you." She couldn't take the feelings
anymore. She slammed down the receiver. God, what if he called
back? She lifted the receiver once she was certain the connection
had been broken. She stuffed it under the pillow and closed the
door on her way out of the room. Now he couldn't call back.
Now she wouldn't make a fool of herself again and further bare
her bleeding soul.

In the bathroom she sprinkled cool water on her face and ran
her fingers through her hair. Now she had to get out of there before she started to blubber all over the place again.

"Thanks, Ruby," Amber said, pecking her on the cheek. Nangi
hugged her and whispered, "It will be all right in the end." She
nodded miserably, refusing to meet his gaze. She kissed and
hugged each of the children. They smiled shyly.

"They're beautiful, Amber," she said sincerely.

When Ruby had climbed into the cab, she stared back at the
house. Amber was happy now. She, Ruby, had made Amber
happy. Opal was happy, too. By God, she wouldn't cry, she just
wouldn't.

{{{{{{{{ CHAPTER ELEVEN }}}}}}}}

With silly little smirks on their faces, Martha and Andy Blue
watched their father's inept efforts at the stove. Andy kept nudging his sister and whispering, "This is the third day we're eating
eggs, and if the grape jelly gets on them, they turn green. I don't
like green eggs, do you?"

"I looove green eggs," Martha purred. "I even love Dad's
black toast. He said I could set the table," she said importantly.

"Yuk. You never liked to set the table before Mom went away.
All you did was whine and try to get out of it." He felt rather
than saw his sister shrug her shoulders. Her eyes were glued on

her father. It was okay, he decided, because these past few days their father had paid more attention to Martha than to him.

He adored Marty. It was good to see her giggle and joke with Dad. She'd gotten a kiss on the cheek today after school when she showed him her big red A on a math test. She was smart, the smartest one in her class—everyone said so. "Keep that up, and they'll give you a scholarship to Harvard or Princeton," his dad said. Marty beamed from ear to ear. She said she'd love to go to Princeton someday, but Andy hoped she wouldn't because it meant she'd go away, and he wouldn't have a sister anymore.

"Go wash up, Andy," his father ordered briskly. Andy trotted off to the bathroom. Boy, did he ever hate green eggs. He counted to sixty-five times as he lathered and rubbed his hands together, the way his father taught him. If he got to the kitchen one second earlier, he got a check mark on his list, which was pasted to the cabinet door. He dried his hands thoroughly, then hopped from one foot to the other and counted out another twenty seconds just in case he'd counted too fast the other five times.

The little boy took his seat, folded his hands, and waited for his father to say grace. He eyed the eggs and the mound of grape jelly on his plate. The eggs were green all around the edges. There wasn't any bacon or sausage, either. He liked bacon and sausage. He hated eggs. He thought the toast looked like tar paper, the kind they were putting on the roof down the street. If he ate it, he was going to get little black specks in his milk. He hated black specks in his milk. He hated this whole supper. He sucked in his breath and blurted out, "I don't want to eat this. I like Mom's eggs better. You're supposed to push the button on the toaster so it doesn't get like . . . tar paper."

Andrew laid down his fork and stared across the table at his son. "Did I hear you correctly?" he asked in a calm-sounding voice, one the little boy recognized as the tone he'd always used on Marty.

"Yes, sir," Andy said defiantly.

"If it's good enough for your sister, it should be good enough for you. Do you find anything wrong with the eggs or toast, Martha?"

"Oh, no, sir," Martha said, stuffing her mouth. "I like it this way. It's better than Mom's," she lied. Suddenly, she wanted to strangle the little brother she dearly loved. Now their father was going to change from the kind, sweet, gentle father he'd been since their mother went away. "He ate cookies before," she tattled, and immediately hated herself for the look of betrayal in her brother's eyes. "Well, maybe he didn't eat them, but he was looking at them. I didn't eat any."

"Andy, did you eat cookies before supper?" Andrew demanded.

"Yes, sir, I did. I ate four. I'm glad I did, because you're going to make me go to my room without supper, and if I didn't eat them, I'd starve. I don't care. I hate this," he said, jamming his fork into the now-cold eggs.

"Tell me exactly what's wrong with this supper," Andrew said quietly.

Andy swallowed past the lump in his throat. "Mom always makes bacon or sausage and the toast is kind of brown and yellow, and there aren't little black things floating in my milk. I don't like jelly on my plate. I don't see any dessert."

"Well, why didn't you say so when I started to cook? If I don't know what your mother does, how can I duplicate her efforts?" His eyes swiveled to his daughter's clean plate. "I think you . . . fibbed to me, Martha."

Martha looked terrified. She would have eaten slime if her father asked her to, Andy thought. Didn't Dad know that?

The room suddenly boomed with their father's laughter. "Okay, kids, let's see if we can't cook up a supper like your mother does. Martha, you get the bacon; Andy, you crack the eggs. I'll clean up this mess. Martha, do you think you can eat anything else, or are you full?"

She stared at her father with wide, adoring eyes. "I could eat some bacon, and if we're having dessert, I think I have enough room for that."

"Okay, let's go for it. On the count of three, fall in and hut to."

His father was neat, Andy thought as he slopped the eggs and bits of shells into the mixing bowl. Mom was right. If you tell the truth, no one is going to punish you. Jeez, he wished she'd hurry and get home. "When's Mom coming home, Dad?"

"Sometime tonight. You'll probably be asleep. She'll be here to cook your breakfast."

"I hope it isn't eggs," Andy muttered. Andrew laughed uproariously, nudging Martha and winking at her.

"Oh, Daddy, I love you," Martha said, throwing her arms around her father's waist.

Andy looked at his sister and father, who was still in uniform. Martha's hands were greasy from the bacon. He was aware suddenly that the moment was too quiet after Martha's exuberant outburst. Her father had not answered. "Hey, you jerk, I love you. Do you love me?" Andy demanded, poking the egg-dripping fork he'd been beating the eggs with at his sister.

Andrew stared at the little boy in a way Andy wasn't used to. It was a *nice* stare.

"Hey, none of that name-calling stuff around here. Your sister is your sister, not a jerk. I love you guys. I love you, Martha, and I love you, Andy. I guess I'm supposed to say that more often, but I thought you both knew. I guess I'm not real good at this father business. I'll try to do better, how's that?"

"Sure, Dad," Andy mumbled. Jeez, he was hungry. All this talk about being a father. For crying out loud, his dad was the same as Billy's dad, and he didn't go around promising to be a better dad. He didn't have to do that. He was already a good dad. Who cared anyway? His father never kept his promises. Like the time he said he'd be home to go to his soccer game and they waited so long for him to get home from work he'd missed half the game. Martha believed him, he could tell. Girls were so darn dumb. But she was happy. Her eyes were all sparkly and she looked so sappy, he wanted to swat her.

Andrew twirled the bottle of Schlitz beer between his hands. He'd been nursing it for the past three hours, and it was warm and flat now. He could get a fresh one from the fridge, but he felt too lazy to get up. It would be just his luck to be in the kitchen when Ruby pulled into the carport. If he stayed where he was, he'd at least have surprise on his side. She wouldn't expect him to be up, and that would give him an advantage. He was going to need every trick in his bag to get Ruby to do what he wanted. Getting on the good side of the kids had been the first step up the ladder. He knew Martha was still awake, waiting for her mother. She'd gone to the bathroom three times in the past two hours, but that was better than her wetting the bed.

The pounding at the base of his skull was a trip-hammer gone berserk. He needed a drink to make it stop. It was starting to worry him that alcohol instead of aspirin cured his headaches. His mind played around with the word *alcoholic*. He rejected the word. He hadn't had a real drink for four days. One or two beers a day didn't make him anything but what he was—a marine. Marines weren't alcoholics. The Corps wouldn't tolerate it.

He leaned back against the sofa cushions. He was uptight and had been in this condition for the past week. It began the day he had heard that old man Frankel wasn't going to get his third star. The rumor mill said he wasn't considered lieutenant-general material and that he was too old. That was bad enough, but when he heard a second rumor in the latrine, he'd all but puked his guts out. He would be under a new commanding officer, but then, not so new, as he'd served under him once before. And this commanding officer was headed for Vietnam. There was no way in hell he was going to another stinking, rotten Asian pest-hole. He'd kissed too much ass along the way for that shit. What the hell good was having a wife with connections if you didn't use them?

Ruby was on a first-name basis with Arlene Frankel. If she cozied up to her a little more and had her put in a word or two to the general, and if she called the Querys and did the same thing, he might get off the hook and stay stateside. Christ, was it so much to ask? He'd sweet-talk her, promise her anything. Martha was the key. Ruby would do anything for Martha.

He had realized that five days ago, when Ruby, pissed to the teeth, had sailed out of the carport. She'd threatened to leave him, and Ruby, he knew, never made idle threats. A warning bell sounded in his head. He'd pushed her too far. He'd told himself that night to fall back and regroup, and that's exactly what he'd done. Yes, Martha was the key.

It was five minutes to midnight when Ruby arrived. A lamp burned in the living room, but the kitchen was dark.

Obviously, everyone was asleep. She felt relieved. Now she wouldn't have to talk to Andrew. Still, if he was in bed but awake, he might be waiting for the talk she said they would have on her return. She was tired now, but not the same kind of tired she was when she had arrived in Washington. Then she'd been tired *and* worried.

A hot shower was going to feel good, but first she had to check on the kids. God, she'd missed them. A peek, that's all.

Ruby was halfway down the hall when she heard her husband call her name from the living room. So he *had* waited up. She squared her shoulders. Now was as good a time as any to talk.

Postponing would only make her more miserable. She'd never been one to let anything simmer if she could bring it to a boil. She walked back to the living room.

"Would it be too much trouble to ask you to make me a cup of tea?"

"Be glad to. Do you want anything to eat?"

She did, but Andrew's efforts in the kitchen left too much to be desired. "Maybe a cookie," she called over her shoulder.

Andy was sound asleep, sprawled across the bed, his pajama legs hiked up above his knees. She pulled up the sheet. He didn't stir when she kissed him on the cheek. "I love you," she whispered.

Martha was sleepy but awake. "Mom, oh, Mom, I'd glad you're home. Wait till you hear." She babbled on and on until Ruby thought she would scream. The smile she was offering her daughter was sickly at best. "He means it, doesn't he, Mom? He was so nice. He kissed me and hugged me and he apologized. Isn't it just the greatest thing? I knew Dad loved me! He said he has a hard time saying it, but we should know because he's our father. He's really going to try harder. That means he's going to be better and nicer to you, too, isn't that right?" Ruby nodded, she didn't know what else to do. "I think this is the best day of my life, Mom. It was better than two Christmases and Easter, too. Nothing will go wrong, will it?"

"No, honey, it's time for sleep, it's late. Tomorrow is a schoolday. We'll talk about it over breakfast."

"Mom, don't make eggs, okay? Make oatmeal. Andy wants farina. I can eat farina, too. No toast, either," Martha said, snuggling under the sheet, both arms wrapped around her pillow. "Dad tucked me in and kissed me good night. You wait and see, I just know I'm not going to wet the bed tonight. I know it."

"I know it, too, sweetie."

Ruby's shoulders slumped. Her feet dragged on the way down the hall to where her husband was waiting for her. It was magic as far as Martha was concerned. Ruby had never seen Martha this happy, but she suspected she would pay for her child's happiness. She wondered what it was going to cost.

"Hi, honey, how was the trip? You look tired," Andrew said quietly, handing her the cup of tea. "This will fix you right up. Sorry there are no cookies, the kids ate them all."

"I am tired and the trip was okay. I hope you managed without me," she said wearily.

"Hey, we had a ball. I don't think the kids are going to want eggs for a while, but no one starved. I think you taking that trip was the best thing you could have done. Martha and I really got to know one another. She's a great kid. I'm going to let up on her. Andy, too. I'll even bet you fifty cents she stops wetting the bed," he said playfully. "You're much too protective of them, Ruby. I'll make a deal with you. You let up and I'll back off. Is it a deal?" Andrew nuzzled his wife's neck. "What do you say?"

"I'll try. You haven't exactly lived up to your word of late, Andrew. How do I know you'll . . . you'll be decent to Martha?"

Andrew straightened up. "I resent what you just said. I have never been anything but decent to that kid. Strict, yes. Children need discipline. You coddle them too much. How in the hell do you expect them to grow up to be independent?"

Ruby cringed. "What about love, Andrew? When was the last time, except for these past few days, you were within a foot of your daughter? Never, that's when. What is it you want, Andrew? I know there's more, so you might as well tell me now. Let's get it all out in the open before you break Martha's heart."

Andrew's voice was harsh. He hated it when Ruby nailed him to the wall. Damn her anyway. "Rumor has it that Frankel is going to be passed over, and if that happens, I don't get promoted. It also means I'll get another commanding officer, namely, my old one, who is a real pain in the ass, among other things. He likes young girls, Ruby. Real young ones, like Martha. I can't work under Lackland again. If I do, I'll end up killing the son of a bitch. What this means to you is that I want you to go to the general's wife and plead my case and then hit on the Querys. I could do it myself, but if you do it, it will be better. They like and respect you. You're personal friends. He still has pull and clout. If you don't I'll have to go to Vietnam with that bastard. Remember what it was like when I was in Korea, and all the shit that went wrong for you because I wasn't here? You have two kids now. It won't be any easier."

"Little girls like Martha?" Ruby whispered. "Why didn't you turn him in? What kind of man are you? You knew . . . know . . . and aren't doing anything about it? Then I will," she said, jerking free of Andrew's pleading hand.

"I'll take care of him; don't you worry about it," Andrew said in a panic. "Don't even think about sticking your nose into it like you did with Hugo and Dixie. That, Ruby, whether you know it or not, was why I had to go to that rat hole Korea." There was edginess, a wariness in Andrew's voice she'd never heard before. Everything he said was untrue, and it sounded untrue. She felt herself stiffen.

"I had nothing to do with Hugo and Dixie. You know it, Andrew. What you just told me is so low, so . . . so unbelievable, I cannot just sit still and do nothing."

"I said I'd handle it, Ruby, and I will." There was such desperation in her husband's voice, Ruby knew she wasn't getting all the facts. "I want you to talk to the general's wife and the Querys. Will you do it?"

"I can't. Mrs. Frankel told all of us we were never, ever to ask her to intercede with her husband concerning our husbands. Never, ever. She said if we did, it would be a black mark on our husbands' records. Be thankful he did what he did for you, Andrew. The answer is no. As for the Querys, the admiral is in the hospital. He's very ill, and I refuse to bother him with your problems. Do your own dirty work," Ruby said angrily.

"You really want me to go to Vietnam with that pervert, is that it?" Andrew shouted.

"No, I don't want that. Go to his commanding officer and tell him what you told me. If this Corps is as wonderful as you seem to think it is, they'll handle it quietly and he's out."

Andrew's stomach scrunched into a tight ball. A drink would unknot it. Ruby could unknot it, too, if she'd just go along with him. "I don't stand a chance if you don't help me, and you know it. You have to, Ruby. That's a goddamn order, and I expect you to obey it!" He let his eyes slowly circle the room and zero in on Martha's bedroom door.

"You louse, you'd turn on your own daughter! I knew it was too good to be true. It was all a game to you. Well, you know what, Andrew? You're going to play alone, because I don't like your rules. I've had enough. I'm leaving."

"You try it, and you'll never see those kids again. I'll tell everyone you're an unfit mother—that you sleep around. There's a hundred guys on this base who will lie for five bucks. I made a deal with you—I give you something and you give me something. That's the way it works."

"You're sick, Andrew. And you're rotten. How could I have been such a fool to believe you were—"

"—a nice guy? I am. Ask anyone."

"Who? Your cronies? Maybe I should ask their wives."

"Only glowing testimonials." Andrew grinned.

Ruby surrendered. There was nothing else to do. She knew her husband meant every word he said.

For three days Ruby tried to reach Arlene Frankel but was told by one of her stewards that she was out of town. Ruby thanked God on an hourly basis. The phone went unanswered at the Query house in Chapel Hill. She refused to call the local hospital, where the admiral was recuperating.

While Ruby tried to make her calls, Andrew was upholding his end of the agreement by watching Martha roller-skate and ride her new bike, a special present he'd bought her for not wetting the bed for four days in a row. He played Monopoly with both her and Andy. Martha blossomed, while Andy went about his business, sneaking glances at his mother when he thought she wasn't looking. He was full of suspicion where his father was concerned. At night, when he buried his head in his pillow, he muttered, "I just know something awful is going to happen."

On the fourth day Andrew's patience with Ruby ran out. "You're stalling. I'm going to stand right here while you call." The response was the same. Andrew stalked out of the room. Ruby heaved a sigh of relief.

On the sixth day Ruby came to the conclusion that the general's wife was avoiding her. She believed the same of Mrs. Query, but she didn't tell Andrew. Because of Martha, she kept calling, praying the steward would say the same thing.

By the end of the tenth day Andrew wasn't fit to live with. Ruby no longer made a pretense of trying to call the admiral or the general's wife.

"She's on the goddamn base, I saw her myself," Andrew raged on the eleventh day.

"That should tell you something," Ruby snapped. "She knows why I'm calling, and this is her way of saying she won't get involved. Are you trying to make fools of both of us?"

"Call the admiral again," he ordered. Ruby did as instructed. The phone rang twenty-three times before she hung it up. She was careful to keep her face impassive.

The days dragged on. The new month arrived, twenty-three days from the day she'd arrived home from Washington.

Andrew charged into the house by way of the kitchen door at midday, his face contorted in rage. "That bastard sailed right out the door, said good-bye, and had the goddamn gall to say he hopes I make rank. He didn't say good-bye, go to hell, or drop dead. He's out and I'm stuck. He knew I wasn't going to make it. He didn't go to bat for me. Why should he? He's out. He doesn't give a good rat's ass about me, and his wife doesn't give a shit about you."

Ruby digested the information at the sink, where she was cleaning vegetables. She was so relieved, she felt like singing. "I'm sorry, Andrew, that it didn't work out. The admiral is too sick to help you, even if I could have gotten through."

"Some goddamn friends you have," Andrew snarled.

"I don't judge my friends by what they can do for me. You should be thankful they ever did anything. You could still be out there, floundering, waiting years to move up in rank. Be grateful, please, for all our sakes."

"That's pretty easy for you to say. You aren't going to Vietnam. So fuck you!" Andrew roared as he stomped from the house.

Ruby buried her face in her hands. What should she do? Did she dare take a chance and leave? Or should she wait until Andrew shipped out for Vietnam? Whatever she did, there was no telling how Andrew would retaliate.

Overnight, the Blue house turned into a war zone. The battle lines were drawn, and Andrew was the enemy. Ruby viewed herself as a field marshal who left no stone unturned to prevent that same enemy from claiming the ultimate prize: Martha.

Ruby knew she was teetering on the edge of a nervous breakdown. She couldn't eat and dropped fifteen pounds from her slim frame in three weeks. Dark smudges underlined her eyes. She looked gaunt, almost skeletal. Whenever possible, she avoided looking in the mirror. Over and over, as she wrung her hands in despair, she asked herself how her life had reached this point. What had she done wrong? When had Andrew gained so much power in their marriage? When he had returned from Korea? Maybe she had overplayed her hand during the fiasco at St. Andrew's in Hawaii. Staying in touch with her friends at the parsonage was one of her few pleasures left in life. If she had to do it over again, she'd do nothing different.

Now all she wanted was for Andrew to be gone before he could do any more emotional damage to Martha. His port call was in less than twelve hours. If she could get through that time, she could survive.

Ruby made the decision to absent the children by arranging a Girl Scout trip for Martha and taking Andy to a YMCA swim meet.

It was best for everyone. Martha was wetting the bed again and spending too much time alone in her room, staring at the walls.

She was going to try one more time to reason with her husband. She didn't want him leaving with things so hateful between them, but until now, he'd refused to discuss anything except to repeat that she had refused him when he really needed help.

She wished she loved Andrew, and she wished he loved her, even a little. So many years lost, she thought sadly. Maybe now was the time to see if things couldn't be made right. They would be apart; each of them would have time to think.

Ruby looked stunned an hour later when Andrew walked into the kitchen and poured himself a cup of coffee. He sat down at the table with her and cupped his hands around his mug.

"I was sitting here thinking about some of our happier times, trying to figure out what went wrong," Ruby said quietly.

"Did you reach a conclusion?" Andrew asked just as quietly.

"Sort of. You were different when you came back from Korea. I was angry and hurt. I blamed you for all the things that went wrong for me. It wasn't easy for me, but I survived. You wouldn't let me get close to you. You didn't seem interested in Martha. I know it must have been difficult to be thrust into the role of a father so suddenly. Martha was a little person who made demands on me . . . on us. I was too protective, you were right about that. For a long time she was all I had to hang on to. I was all she had. I know I tried. I'm not really sure if you did. It didn't seem like you did. You didn't like the diapers, the crying, the attention I gave our child. I tried to understand that. What I couldn't understand was why you didn't want me to go back to St. Andrew's. You fought me every step of the way over that. I went anyway because it was important to me. You refused to let me go to Kalo's funeral. I went anyway because it was important to me. Just as I sent a ten-dollar donation at Christmastime, even though you said no to that, too.

"I'm tired of this house being a battleground. Our children are supposed to come first, but they don't. If it's important to place blame, then I'll take it all. I'm a nervous wreck. I can't handle it anymore. It's getting to the point where I can't seem to help myself, and if I can't take charge of my own life, how can I take care of the children? We have to have some kind of understanding and go on from there. We have to put all the hateful things we said to each other, all the threats, behind us and look to our future. I'm willing to try if you are. The only alternative to trying is divorce," she said bleakly.

Andrew's shoulders slumped. His voice was almost gentle. He was facing the inevitable, so there was no point in fighting it anymore. He was going to Vietnam, and there was a good chance he wouldn't come back alive. It was the first time in his life he'd ever really had to face death. And even if he survived, he didn't want to be like the other guys who returned from an overseas duty to find their wives and children gone. He hadn't had a drink in over two weeks, and he was thinking clearly for a change. Everything she said was true, so true it smacked him in the gut like a mule kick. He felt his insides shrivel when he remembered the demands he'd made on her. He should apologize. She was right about the kids, too. He wondered if there was any way he could make things up to his family. Words, he knew, weren't going to do it this time. Ruby wouldn't accept words or promises, but that was all he could give her. He nodded, his voice a hoarse croak when he spoke.

"You're right. As much as I hate to admit it, you're usually right about everything. I was wrong to order you to intervene. I was a real bastard. I never thought about you. I cared only about myself. I'm sorry. You were right about Korea. I did change. I broke the rules, Ruby. I guess you already know that. *Sorry* is such a trite word sometimes. Saying it as often as I do makes it trite.

"Look, I'm scared, I admit it. Korea was a nothing situation. This ... this is different. I've never been this scared. Marines are not supposed to harbor fear, but anyone who goes over there and says he isn't scared is a liar. As for my commanding officer, what I'm going to tell you now is perhaps ... it's terrible, but you have a right to know. I lied to you when I said he liked young girls like Martha. He does like young girls, but he prefers them to be around sixteen and virgins. I helped him when I served under him. I can't . . . turn him in because he . . . I'm not proud of that, Ruby; in fact, I'm downright ashamed. That's why I had to get out from under. He scares me more than Vietnam. If I bring him down, I bring myself down. I want to put in my twenty years and get out. If you can live with all this, and if you're willing, I'd like to give it all a second go-round when I get back. We'll pack it in and settle down in a real town; we'll buy a house and I'll get a job. We'll have my retirement pay, and if you want, you can get a job, too. Financially, we'll be okay. What do you say?"

Tears rolled down Ruby's cheeks. She'd heard promises before. "The kids?"

"If I drive like a bat out of hell, I think we can make it up and back from the campgrounds in time to see Andy do his minnow swim." He reached across the table for Ruby's hand.

Ruby didn't know if she was doing the right thing or not, but for the children she had to try. Martha would be so happy. Andy would grin and shake his fist in the air. As for herself, this was better than a hateful parting and years of recriminations. For now it was best. Best for their family.

{{{{{{{{{ CHAPTER TWELVE }}}}}}}}}

*Andrew Blue looked at his pocket calendar and ticked off an-*other day. Just thirty-three more and he was leaving this hell-hole, this cesspool of the universe and going home. Every day he thanked God that he was still alive. Every day he thought about Ruby and the kids. Every day that passed made it one day closer to the time when he could return to his family.

He was one goddamn lucky son of a bitch. Twice he'd almost bought it on a night patrol. He'd lost three good men, men he'd come to call friends. The kind of guys you would look up after you got home. The kind of guys you could have a beer with and not lie to to make yourself look good. Of course making friends had been a mistake. Now they were gone. Jesus, he hadn't been prepared for that. Dave Harkness had stepped on a land mine. There wasn't enough left of him to identify. And then Bic Nexus had gotten it right through the throat from a sniper's bullet. He'd held Charlie Duvalier in his arms and felt him expire. He'd talked to him, told him all about Ruby and the kids and his football days in high school. He'd bawled like a baby when Charlie drew his last breath. They had to pry Charlie's body out of his arms. He'd carried blood on himself for days. If Charlie hadn't been ahead of him, he would be the one who was dead. Jesus, how he prayed after that. He made promises to God, to the angels, to every priest and minister he could remember. And he damn well meant to keep them.

And if it was the last thing he did, he was going to stick it to Lackland. Because all Andrew could think about was the look on Ruby's face when he had told her about his part in his C.O.'s past. He'd damn well let the chips fall wherever they were meant to fall, but he was going to report everything when he got stateside. Ruby would be with him every step of the way.

Andrew swatted at the bugs bent on sucking his blood. He hated this fucking place, hated the smell, the humidity, the fighting, the dying. Charlie, Bic, and Dave had given their lives and left their families fatherless for this godforsaken place. It wasn't right. Nothing about this fucking place was right.

He wished there were a way to line up all the Cong in a long single file. He'd pull the trigger of his M-16 until his fingers fell off and then he'd stomp the rest of them to death. Fucking bastards.

Every damn day when he wasn't busy trying to save his life and the lives of his men he thought about his past and all the things he'd done wrong. He thought about judgment day and how he'd be called to account for his sins. He'd vowed to lead a better life, to correct those mistakes that still needed correcting. Maybe this was his hell, he thought, his punishment for all the wrong he'd done in his life.

Lackland had seen the change in him and had started to sweat. That made him dangerous. Andrew started to watch his own back. He confided his fears to a young lieutenant and wrote them all down. He told him to get in touch with Ruby and to tell her to get the sealed package out of their safety deposit box if anything happened to him. He wasn't leaving this earth without owning up to his part in Lackland's perverted activities. Ruby would be able to live with the shame he'd create because she loved him and they had kids to think about. Ruby was loyal and loving. Christ, he owed her so much, and he'd been such a bastard.

Andrew patted his thick breast pocket, which held letters from his family. He knew their contents by heart, and when he was scared like he was now, he ran the words over and over in his mind.

Sniper fire ripped through the thick humidity. One shot, two, three. Foliage rained down on him when his men responded with automatic weapons fire.

"I got the bastard! Jesus H. Christ, I ripped his fucking head right off his neck!" It was Stanapopolus, and his voice was hysterical.

"You want a medal?" someone barked.

"You're fucking right I want a fucking medal. Oh, Jesus, sir, you better come see this."

Andrew joined his men and looked at where Stanapopolus was pointing. "He got it on the second pop, sir."

"Lackland!"

"Yeah, right through the back of his head. Clean shot. He didn't suffer, sir."

"Too bad," Andrew said.

"Sir?"

"Too bad he bought it. He had his whole life ahead of him," Andrew said curtly. "You know what to do," he said, ripping Lackland's dog tags from his neck.

"This guy had six kids, did you know that, sir?"

"No. No, I didn't. I didn't know ... I'd heard he was divorced," Andrew said.

"He was, twice. The kids were with his first wife. He showed me their pictures. He was a good soldier. It's important for kids to know their old man was okay. You going to write a personal letter, sir?"

"You're sure he had six kids?" Andrew said.

"Yes, sir. Six little towheads. It was an old photograph. They were all spruced up and in a line. He seemed real proud of them. What should I do with his letters, sir? There's two in his pocket."

Andrew held out his hand. Later, when it was his turn to sleep, Andrew read one. It started out the same way his did:

Dear Dad,

We all pray for you every night. Mom made us a special calendar and we check off the days until it's your turn to come home. It's my turn to write this week and everyone has something they want me to tell you. Jamie got two stars on his spelling paper. Abbie fixed the wheel on her bicycle by herself. She said you showed her how to do it. Carrie made fudge, the kind you like with marshmallows and nuts and peanut butter. Mom is wrapping it up to send you so your sweet teeth will be satisfied. She said to share it with your friends. Stan is pitching his second game. He walked everybody last week, but the coach doesn't have another pitcher. Everyone has chicken pox. Mary Ann got a job and is working in a bakery. She brings home cupcakes every night. I'm last since I'm the oldest. I'm graduating third in my class. I got my class ring last week. I wish you could be at my graduation, but I understand. We all want you to be careful and to take care of yourself. We miss you and we send our love.

The letter was signed by all the children. Andrew folded the letter neatly and replaced it in the worn, tattered envelope. It, along with Lackland's other gear, would be returned to his family.

Damn, he wasn't prepared for this. If he went through with his plan, he would be destroying the trust of six children who loved and believed in their father. Better to forget it. It wouldn't take away his guilt, but it might make him a better person. The guilt he carried would be his punishment. He nodded, it seemed appropriate.

"Lieutenant!"

"Yes, sir?"

"Lieutenant, we are going to forget everything I told you. There's no reason to destroy this man's family. I want your word as an officer that it will go no further."

"You got it, sir," the lieutenant said, snapping off a smart salute.

CHAPTER
{{{{{{{{{ THIRTEEN }}}}}}}}}

When Andrew Blue returned from Vietnam his family met him at
the airport, wearing smiles. Their arms were waving frantically
to gain his attention.

Andrew took a full three minutes to take the sight of his family
in. Martha was Ruby's look-alike; even from this distance, they
looked like sisters instead of mother and daughter. And Andy, he
was taller than Martha—eleven, going on twelve. How mature he
looked. Ruby had said he took his position as man of the family
seriously. Ruby looked different, too. She'd put on weight, but it
wasn't unbecoming. Her hairstyle was different—soft and wispy.
She looked more womanly, certainly no longer girlish. His family.
He felt choked up. They were glad to see him. Damn, he was
glad to see them, too. He ran then, his long legs pumping. He
leapt the Cyclone fence and gathered them in his arms.

Things were on track. He was glad now that he'd put in his
time by writing once a week to each of them. He knew who they
were. He knew all about Martha's corn on her little toe and how
she hated her period and loved her first training bra. He knew that
Andy was scared when he got up to bat at Little League, knew
that he included his father in his prayers every night. Only things
a father would know. But he didn't know any more about Ruby
now than when he left. Oh, she'd written faithfully, twice a week,
but the letters contained nothing about her. She always closed by
saying she missed him and was looking forward to the day when
he returned. That was as personal as she got.

"We're having turkey in honor of your homecoming," Martha
said happily. "I made the stuffing. Mom said it came out good."

"Can't wait to taste home cooking," Andrew said, hugging her.

"How about you, sport? What did you contribute? Tell me
you made an apple pie," he said, ruffling his son's hair.

"Aw, c'mon, Dad, guys don't cook. I set the table." He grinned self-consciously.

"That's good. It used to be my job."

Ruby smiled warmly. The anxiety she'd felt building up the past month began to ease. Andrew was trying; the children were happy. They were a family now. It was going to be all right. She leaned against her husband, enjoying the smell of his aftershave. He was as handsome as ever. She felt a tingle of desire for him. It must have showed in her eyes, because Andrew whispered, "I can't wait, either." She laughed then, a sound of pure delight. She caught the wink he gave Martha and saw the way he poked his son's shoulder.

It was wonderful. She said a prayer that it would last.

It did. For a while.

Two years and two months later the Marine Corps packed up all the Blues' belongings and moved the family to Rumson, New Jersey. Ruby was so thrilled, she thought she would burst on the drive up the Atlantic coastline. Martha chattered all the way about the scholarship to Princeton she was sure she would get. When she took a deep breath, Andy plunged into a long discussion about cars. Would he have one when he was old enough to drive? Andrew yessed them to death as he concentrated on the sandy roads. Sand was as treacherous as ice, he told them. Ruby smiled. She'd never been happier.

They were really going to buy a house, one with an upstairs and a basement. A garage, too, and a yard with trees. A nice, residential neighborhood that she hoped wouldn't be too far from where Dixie lived.

Her eyes sparking, Ruby Blue marched into the autumn of her life, certain her happiness would last forever.

PART THREE

AUTUMN

CHAPTER FOURTEEN

{{{{{{{{{{ }}}}}}}}}}

1975

Andrew Blue sat behind the wheel of his new Buick Special, his eyes glued to the greasy windows of the Knife & Fork Diner, where he'd just had his breakfast. It was the same diner he'd eaten breakfast at for the past five years. The waitresses called him by name; the owner always poked him on the shoulder playfully when he paid his check. Routine. His routine.

He should move along. Sitting here like this was out of character for him. He knew the waitresses were watching him through the steamy window. The thought was enough to make him turn the key in the ignition. He backed out of his parking space in front of the building and drove around to the back, where the produce trucks were already lined up for their morning deliveries. He cut the engine and slumped against the seat. Today was not going to be a good day, he thought shakily.

Until this very minute, he hadn't really noticed how chilly it was, but then he saw steam escape the mouths of the truck drivers as they hefted crates of lettuce and eggs. He turned on the heater. A blast of stale air hit him in the face. He turned off the heater and rolled down the window. The cold air felt good against his freshly shaven face. He felt perspiration bead his forehead and wondered, not for the first time since getting out of bed, if he was getting sick.

Andrew lit a cigarette and blew smoke out the window. Christ, how he hated New Jersey. He hated this frigging diner and he hated the Sears, Roebuck store, where he was supposed to be this very minute, getting ready to take inventory.

With the cigarette clamped between his teeth and the smoke spiraling into his eyes, Andrew took stock of his hatreds for the day: his job, his home life, his routine, the bucket of bolts that he was sitting in, the waitresses in the diner, Ruby, Martha, his job selling Rototillers and garden supplies, his boss who reminded him of his last commanding officer in the marines, New Jersey, Rumson in particular, the house on Ribbonmaker Lane, his thinning hair, his four root canals, his paunch, his age, and his gambling. The last two were the kickers. Ruby would divorce him on the spot if she ever found out about his gambling problem. On the other hand, she didn't seem to care that he was within a hairbreadth of turning fifty. Fifty goddamn years! And what did he have to show for it? A house that was mortgaged to the hilt because he'd forged Ruby's name to a second mortgage and used the money to gamble. There was every possibility they could lose the house in the next few months if he didn't come up with some ready cash. He'd even gambled away young Andy's college tuition. Come August, when the bills came in, Ruby would find out there was no money in Andy's account. He ticked off the months on his fingers—seven and a half to come up with the kid's money. He could feel the sweat rolling down his back. He started to shiver, not with cold, but with fear. He owed Stan three grand and another two to a bookie in Asbury Park. They were starting to crowd him, making noises he didn't like. The jungles of Vietnam hadn't evoked the kind of fear he was feeling now.

He'd never gambled in Vietnam. Oh, maybe a little poker once in a while, but nothing like what he'd been doing the past two years. He couldn't even remember how it started. A bet on a football game, then two bets, then on to baseball and basketball. Finally the horses. Inside of three months he was betting on anything that moved.

Andrew risked a glance at the Rolex on his wrist, the only thing he owned of any real value, and it wasn't his in the sense that he bought it or even earned it. He'd taken it off a smelly little Vietnamese who probably didn't know what it was. Sometimes it bothered him that he was wearing a dead officer's watch. It was top of the line, an eye-catcher, a real conversation piece when he was rolling dice or propping his arm on the bar. Maybe if he had it cleaned and polished, he could pawn it and get enough money to keep the sharks at bay until he could fall back and regroup. But he was kidding himself and he knew it. There was no way he could come up with enough money to keep the house and pay Andy's tuition.

Fifty goddamn years old! Jesus, wait till Ruby found out he'd borrowed on their life insurance. He started to sweat again. His hands were trembling, too, something he noticed lately when he lit his cigarettes. He wondered what his blood pressure was right now, this very second. Sky-high, even with the pills he popped every morning with his orange juice in the diner.

What he should do, what he should have done four years and nine months ago, was go to Sears and slit his boss's throat. Beady-eyed Alvin Demster had promised him the managership of the entire store within a year of hiring him. "You'll start out in the garden department, and we'll move you steadily every six weeks or so." Alvin had been a marine, so Andrew had believed him. Rototillers and lawn mowers were big sellers, Alvin said. So were lime and fertilizers. What it boiled down to was he was selling shit by the truckload. He should have quit, but jobs had been hard to find and the commission checks weren't that bad. Ruby banked the money, paid the bills, and managed to save enough to send Martha to Rensselaer, where she graduated with top honors. He'd wanted to kill his own daughter when he calculated the cost, and kill Ruby, too, when he saw her cutting their budget six ways to the middle just so the ungrateful kid could have what she wanted. It didn't matter that she graduated summa cum laude. He couldn't attend her graduation because he'd had to work that day. A lawn maintenance company was sending one of its men to order a dozen sit-down lawn mowers along with leaf blowers and Rototillers. He'd made a couple of thousand on commissions alone that day, enough to buy Martha a Gucci watch, which she thanked him for and never wore.

Andrew burrowed deeper into the car seat. He was in some deep shit with nowhere to turn. Nowhere but to Ruby. Somehow Ruby would find a way to get him out of the mess he'd put them in. Rightly so. If it wasn't for Ruby, they wouldn't be in this stinking town, and he wouldn't have this stinking job.

It had been so easy to take over the bills and the checkbook. All he'd said, in his best military-sounding voice, was, "I can do this better, and I don't want to hear another word." The first checks to stop were the ones to St. Andrews'. He gave her food and gas money every Friday, the same day he banked her check from the card and gift store where she worked part-time. He remembered how her eyes filled with tears when she handed over the household bills in their neat folder along with the checkbook. The whole shebang was in the trunk of his car. The only things Ruby cared about these days were her friend, Dixie, and young Andy. That was another thing, the kid. He'd expected Andy to be a chip off the old block, and he was, but off Ruby's block. The kid had ethics and morals and a streak of decency equal only to his mother's. He worked, too, all through high school, in a supermarket, and during summers for a construction company. The kid's bank balance had stunned him. What stunned him even more was the fact that the boy had paid cash for his first car, paid for his own insurance, paid his own taxes, bought his own clothes, and paid half his tuition and room and board to Rutgers University. There was only one name on young Andy's personal bankbook and it was his own. Ruby had opened a separate account for him when he was eight or so, but all that was gone now, thanks to his own father. The kid would forgive him, Andrew thought irritably, because Andy was just like Ruby.

Fifty years old. Over the hill. Half a century. Shit!

Andrew backed the car away from a produce truck and inched his way through assorted milk crates and garbage cans to the side street that would lead him onto the highway and the Sears store. If he took the U-turn, he could head for Asbury Park and a pawnshop or a jewelry store to see if he could sell the Rolex. Or, he could cross over the highway, return home, confess to Ruby, and hope for the best. He pondered his options for a full five seconds, as long as it took for the red light to turn green. He crossed over the highway. He really loved his Rolex watch.

Ruby hung up the dishtowel to dry and stepped back to view her sparkling kitchen. She loved all of its green plants and copper pots. The solid oak table and chairs, which she polished every day, gleamed. The red checkered place mats with their delicate fringe matched the checkered curtains on the window and back door. All had been made by her. The braided rugs by the sink and refrigerator had been made the first winter after they moved into the house. The entire contents of the house had been purchased with Andrew's discount. She remembered how she'd chortled with glee when she tabulated the savings. They'd been like two kids just starting to keep house.

It had started off wonderfully, this move to New Jersey. Andrew had gotten a job almost immediately, and he'd given his okay for her to work in the gift store, the same store Dixie worked in. She'd saved money, kept the house looking beautiful, and managed to send Martha to the college of her choice. She'd done well and felt proud for almost three years. Then things started to sour. Andrew began complaining about his boss and the long hours he put in. She saw a pattern emerge, but she was too wrapped up in her part-time job, her friendship with Dixie, her children, keeping up the house that she dearly loved, and Andrew to pay much attention.

Andrew was drifting away from her. He had his nights and Saturdays out with the boys from the store. Sundays he either slept the day away or put in extra hours at work. It was an easy, comfortable life, and neither of them complained. Occasionally they slept together, but it was obvious to both that the passion was gone, and neither tried to activate it. They were pleasant to one another, pecking each other on the cheek from time to time or patting one another's shoulder in passing. They settled without complaint into complacency.

Ruby described it to herself as contentment, while Andrew saw it as sheer boredom.

Ruby looked up at the kitchen clock. She had exactly twenty-five minutes till it was time to leave to pick up Dixie for work. All she had to do was put on her makeup, brush her hair, and write a note to Andrew, telling him there was a casserole in the refrigerator if he got home before she did.

The house was always tidy these days, she thought as she bent down to pick up a white thread from the staircase. With the kids gone, there was little housecleaning to do, except for the daily vacuuming and dusting.

Twelve minutes later, Ruby locked the back door to the kitchen. She was raising the venetian blind over the sink so that the thin winter light would aid her windowsill plants, when she saw her husband swerve into the driveway. Her heart thumped twice before it settled down to its normal beat. Andrew never came home for lunch. Andrew never came home in the middle of the morning. Andrew never looked the way he looked now, haggard and drawn. Maybe he was sick. Ruby's heart thumped again. Something was wrong, very wrong. She knew without talking to Andrew that whatever it was, it was going to change her life. She had been relying on her gut instinct for so long where Andrew was concerned, she'd honed it to a razor-sharp edge.

Ruby unlocked the kitchen door and opened it just as Andrew turned the knob. "What's wrong?" she asked anxiously.

"Is there any coffee left?"

"No, I washed the pot. You know the doctor said you were permitted only one cup a day, Andrew. Is your blood pressure up again? Did you have a doctor's appointment this morning? Is that why you're home?" Her eyes went to the calendar on the side of the refrigerator, but the date was clear of appointments.

"In the space of five seconds you've made two statements, asked three questions, and checked out the calendar at the same time," Andrew said sourly. He smiled, as if to take the sting out of his words. He shook his sleeve down over the Rolex. "I'll have a glass of juice. It's fresh, isn't it?"

Ruby nodded and swallowed past the lump in her throat. "Here," she said lightly, setting the glass in front of him. "Sorry I can't stay around to chat, but this is my week to drive, and I have to pick up Dixie. If I don't hurry, I'm going to be late, and Mrs. Harris doesn't like to fiddle with quarter hours on our time cards." She had her coat on and her hand on the door leading to the garage, when Andrew spoke. Damn, what made her think this was going to be easy?

"I need to talk to you, Ruby. Not later, *now.*"

"Andrew, can't it wait till this evening? Mrs. Harris specifically asked both Dixie and myself to come in early to help take inventory. I promised, and Dixie is waiting."

"You always have something to do. You never have time for me. So what if I want to discuss the weather or the price of pork bellies? It's your job to listen to me. If you made a fortune working in that crappy store, I could see it, but you make only minimum wage. I think it's time you got a real job, like selling real estate or something."

"Is that why you're home in the middle of the day? Do you want to talk about me getting a full-time job? If so, Andrew, we can discuss it this evening. I really have to leave."

"Let Dixie walk to the store. Call her and tell her you can't pick her up. After we have this little talk, you won't feel much like going to work anyway. Have her tell that old biddy you're sick. Dixie is a good liar, or have you forgotten?"

Ruby didn't like the look on her husband's face. She called Dixie and said, "Andrew's home and needs to talk to me. I'm sorry, Dixie. Tell Mrs. Harris I'll be late." She took off her coat and tossed it on one of the oak chairs. She sat down, her back stiff, her hands folded in front of her.

"We're going to lose the house. There's not enough to pay Andy's fall tuition. That's it, Ruby."

Ruby felt the color drain from her face. She didn't ask her husband to repeat his words; she'd heard him quite clearly. She wondered why she felt so calm, so detached. She knew she was supposed to say something. She couldn't think of a thing. They were going to lose the house. They'd have to move. How could she have been so stupid as to believe that her life on Ribbonmaker Lane in this wonderful old house was going to last forever? She could feel her eyes start to burn when she thought about Andy and how hard he was working at college. Her part-time wages had been going into his college fund from the first day she started to work. There had been more than enough to cover his tuition. But suddenly, she didn't want to know why there was no money. She got up, her movements awkward, and slipped into her coat. She was at the door leading to the garage when Andrew said, "Don't you want to know the reason?" She shook her head. "Goddamn it, Ruby, that's just like you."

Ruby was walking through the door when he shouted, "I gambled it all away. We're ten months in arrears on the mortgage. We got our last notice yesterday. I used Andy's money to try and get it back. Jesus, Ruby, will you say something?"

Ruby slid into the driver's seat of her car. In a trance she got back out, opened the garage door, and climbed back into the car. She drove to the gift store with tears rolling down her cheeks. She parked next to Dixie's beat-up Mustang.

Just like that. One minute she was singing and humming and feeling pleased with herself and her world, happy and contented in the house she'd worked so hard to make a home for her family, and the next minute it was all being ripped away from her. Evicted. They were going to lose the house. There was no money for Andy's college. Gambling. In a million years she would never have thought of her husband throwing away their hard-earned money. This couldn't be happening to her, but it was. Damn, why had she come here to the store? She wouldn't be able to concentrate on the numbers and the time-consuming hours of inventory.

"Like hell," she muttered, grinding the gears as she backed out of her parking spot.

In her frenzy to get home before Andrew left, she cut the corner too close and plowed over her prize rosebushes. She hardly noticed. She slammed the kitchen door so hard, one of the square panes broke, and glass tinkled about her feet. She crunched it as she marched into the kitchen, shouting her husband's name at the top of her lungs.

"You bastard! You miserable, rotten, stinking bastard. You stole our money. You stole from your own son. Do you have any idea how hard Andy's worked so you wouldn't have to pay all his bills? How could you? What kind of person are you? I've had it with you, Andrew, with all your smutty little affairs, your drinking, your lousy me-first attitude. I want a divorce and I want it now. I'm going to a lawyer. No more! I can't take any more!" she shrieked.

Andrew blanched. The word *divorce* wasn't in his present vocabulary. A divorce wasn't going to help him one bit. His tone of voice was so oily and slick, it surprised him. "Stop talking nonsense, we aren't going to get a divorce, and you know it. Sit down and let's put our heads together and see if we can't get out of this mess. I swear I won't do it again. I learned my lesson. Once I get out from under these bookies, I swear I'll never make another bet. I quit drinking when you hassled me, didn't I? I can quit this, too. Think of something, Ruby. That's what you're good at, coming up with solutions."

Ruby's voice was icy cold when she responded. "You're wrong, Andrew. I will file for a divorce. You stole from our son. You begrudged the money we spent to send Martha to Rensselaer. You never even congratulated her. I'm surprised you haven't hit her up for a loan. My God, you did, I can see it on your face. What kind of man are you? This is our house, our home, and you gambled it away. If I let you get away with this, if I stay married to you, that makes me no better than my mother. I won't do it, Andrew. Sell your watch. And while you're at it, sell those expensive golf clubs and your membership to the country club. Sell everything you can get your hands on. Your car, too. Ride Andy's bicycle. No more, Andrew!"

"There's no money to pay for a divorce," Andrew said snidely. "You can't leave, you have no place to go."

Ruby laughed. And laughed. Andrew cringed at the sound. Ruby continued to laugh.

She told him then. All about the house in Georgetown and the amended tax returns. "So you see, Andrew, I do have a place to go. I can go there anytime. Years ago, just to be on the safe side,

I put the deed in Andy's and Martha's names. The house my parents live in is in their names, too. I'm glad I did it. If I hadn't you would have used it somehow against all of us."

Andrew's face registered horror. "You sneak. You let me bust my ass at that lousy Sears, Roebuck store when you could have made life easier for us. Amended tax returns! I'll goddamn well turn you in to the Internal Revenue Service myself. That's not legal," he sputtered.

"Yes, it is, it's so legal, it's pathetic. We had enough money, Andrew. With your retired pay from the marines and your salary, plus my part-time job, we had enough. When I was handling the money, I even saved enough to make things a lot easier, and no one did without a thing. I wanted to get a full-time job; I even begged you to let me work for that law firm in town, but you said no. You said you wanted a clean house and dinner on the table. You said you wanted me home. So I did what you said. Now you fault me. You're a louse, Andrew," Ruby shrieked, her face contorting with rage.

"You should just see yourself, Ruby, right now this very minute. So what if I did something wrong. You're my wife, you should be thinking of ways to help me instead of threatening me. You act as if I killed somebody. You just admitted you own property, so you can sell it and everything will be just fine. You're overreacting," he said virtuously. "I can't believe you'd really pay out money for a divorce, money I could use to pay off these sharks, instead of helping me. God help you, you are your father's daughter. Don't think for a minute that I'll forgive you for not telling me about those houses. I won't." His voice was pious-sounding now. He even looked shamed . . . for her.

She wondered if it would do any good to defend her position concerning the properties. Would he even understand that for so many years he threw it up to her that she was stupid, a hick from the sticks, and that she had tried to prove her own worth? Was it worth mentioning that she secured the properties before she married? What difference did it make now? She had a tidy little nest egg, thanks to her astute management. She could bring the mortgage up-to-date. She had many options, she realized, and if she did exercise those options, Andrew would walk away without a backward glance and show no remorse while she buckled under. Not this time, she fumed. She had plans for the nest egg, plans to go into business with Dixie. If she told Andrew about her plans, he would belittle her, say it was all a pipe dream and she'd never make a go of it.

"I know that. And you know something else, Andrew? I don't really care. I still want a divorce."

"On what grounds?" Andrew snorted.

"I don't love you. You don't love me. That's grounds enough."

"Not in a court of law." He wondered if his words were true. "This is half my house, you can't make me leave, and besides, I have no place to go and no money. I suppose you're going to take back the bills and give me an allowance." He sneered to make sure she knew what he thought of that idea. "Now, how soon can you come up with the money?"

Ruby turned her back on her husband and walked to the bathroom. She slammed and locked the door. She sat down on the edge of the tub and dropped her head into her hands. She'd said it out loud. She'd actually told her husband she didn't love him. Damn him.

Ruby cried, then. For the would-haves, the could-haves, the should-haves. She was splashing cold water on her face when she heard the kitchen door open and close. She leaned closer to the mirror over the sink. Surely the creature staring back at her wasn't herself. She turned and sat back down on the edge of the tub; her feet scuffed the pearl-gray carpet alongside the claw feet.

How long, she wondered, was she going to sit here like a ninny? She should be angry, and she was to a point, but what she was feeling more than anything was shame and guilt. Shame that once again she hadn't seen the signs, or, if she had, she'd subconsciously chosen to ignore them because her life was on an even keel, and she hadn't wanted to disturb it. She should have known, suspected, the day Andrew said he was taking over the bills. Instead, she relinquished the annoying job, gladly, as a matter of fact, because it freed some of her time.

Ruby blew her nose in a piece of toilet paper. She flushed the toilet just to hear sound in the quiet house. She straightened her shoulders, put one foot in front of the other, and walked out to the kitchen. There was no sign that Andrew had been home. She closed her eyes, hoping it was all a bad dream.

She was making coffee when the phone rang. She reached for

it automatically and burst into tears when she heard Dixie's concerned voice.

"I'll be right there," Dixie said. "Put on coffee, and don't think about anything until I get there. Shift into neutral, Ruby, and we'll work it out together."

Ruby cried harder.

Why was it, Ruby wondered when Dixie was done soothing and crooning to her and patting her on the shoulder, that only a woman, a mother, had the right words, the right touch to make things bearable? Dixie's plump arms were a haven, her soft voice so peaceful-sounding. Ruby hiccoughed as she sipped the strong coffee.

"Listen to me, Ruby. I just got fired. You did, too. Mrs. Harris said nothing was more important than her inventory. I told her what she could do with it. You're important, I'm important. You told me that so many times these past few years, it's burned into my brain. You were entitled to cry and you've done that, so let's get down to business here. We're jobless, and that means we're going to have to forge ahead with our idea. You are not, I repeat, you are not a failure where Andrew is concerned. My God, Ruby, no one could have done more. You've kept this family together. You are not like your mother. You have to believe that or you're lost. Your circumstances are totally different. And you were right in keeping your real estate dealings secret. If Andrew had known about your tax returns and the properties, he probably would have used that money, too. Gambling is a disease, Ruby. It's not your fault. And there are things you can do if you are prepared to do them. It's not as if you have no choices."

"But . . ."

"There are no buts. I don't think it gets much worse than this, so that means you've hit bottom. There's nowhere to go but up, unless you want to wallow in your own misery."

"It's this awful guilt." Ruby whimpered.

Dixie's voice grew stern. "I want you to think about something. What if you didn't have the houses in Georgetown, what if you didn't have the house in Florida, what if you didn't have the money from the ring? What if . . . you really were going to lose this house, what if you really couldn't pay the bills, what if there was no food in your refrigerator? Did you forget about that time you were in Hawaii with Martha when things got so fouled up? What if Andy really couldn't go back to school in the fall?

None of that is going to happen because you can make it right. You make it right, you cut your losses, and go forward. Without Andrew. You have the guts, Ruby, use them. How's that for a pep talk?" she said cheerily. "Hugo is going to have a fit when he finds out I got fired. What the heck, it will just go to prove that I'm as worthless as he says I am. You know what? I don't care anymore. Do you think we're screwed up, Ruby?" She giggled.

"About as screwed up as you can get." Ruby sniffed. "God, what would I do without you, Dixie?"

"Does that mean I'm up there with your old friend Nola?"

Ruby's eyes popped open. "Up there with her! For God's sake, Dix, you are so far ahead of Nola, she's . . . what brought that up?"

"I was always jealous of your friendship with her. I thought I could never measure up. I wanted to be your best friend."

Ruby hugged Dixie. "You are my best friend. Nola was . . . Nola. All these years she never bothered to . . . it only takes a few minutes to scratch off a note or a few dollars to make a phone call. I don't know what her reasons are. I did my best to try and keep in touch by staying in contact with Mrs. Quantrell. Nola isn't the person you are, Dixie. As far as friends go, I couldn't ask for a more wonderful one. I truly treasure our friendship. I thought you knew that. The day you wrote me all those years ago was one of the happiest days of my life."

It was Dixie's turn to burst into tears, which she did, with gusto.

"Now that's all behind us. Let's get on with my problem," Ruby said briskly.

Dixie rummaged in Ruby's sink drawer for paper and pencils. "I have a sort of running tally in my head, so we can compute within a few hundred dollars. We have enough to go on."

It was four o'clock when Dixie leaned back in her chair and bit into a glossy red apple. "I have to hand it to you, Ruby, I don't know if I could have been as generous as you were with your sisters. Or your parents."

"They were debts of honor," Ruby mumbled. "The ring was given to me, but my grandmother didn't know how valuable it really was. I truly believe if she knew, she would have wanted me to share it with my sisters. She meant to make my early years a little easier, but I did it on my own. I had to share."

"With Amber getting the lion's share. I wish you'd show me the justice in that," Dixie snorted.

Ruby shrugged. "It's expensive to raise kids. Amber has eleven. Nangi's salary goes only so far. Opal has a house that's hers. My grandmother had a saying: When you get you give, otherwise it will never mean anything. If there's one thing I'm proud of, it's that I paid back the debt to my father and provided a home for them in their last years. If you don't understand, don't worry about it. I don't understand it, either."

Dixie laughed. "It's like the seasons of your life, right? What are we in now?"

Ruby propped her chin in her cupped hands. Her eyes were serious. "The down side of summer. Any day now it will be autumn. That's when you're settled into your marriage, the kids are grown, and you go back to work to provide for the winter of your life. Big things can happen in the autumn."

"You could be right," she grinned devilishly. "You might have a chance at the man of your dreams."

Dixie looked as if she wanted to bite off her tongue the minute the words came from her mouth. Tears had come to Ruby's eyes. "Ruby, I'm sorry, I didn't mean . . . no, I'm not sorry. Once you're free, you can do whatever you please."

"He's married, Dixie. I can't . . . I wouldn't . . . I'm not that kind of person. Calvin is like Nola. They aren't the people I thought they were."

"Okay, if you say so," Dixie muttered.

"I say so," Ruby said through clenched teeth.

A while later, when Dixie had gone, Ruby realized she had to tell the children. She called Martha first.

"Mom, is anything wrong?" Martha asked anxiously. "You never call at this time of day. Aren't you working anymore?"

"As a matter of fact, I got fired today. I didn't realize I was such a creature of habit and routine that you had my calls fine-tuned to a certain time of day, and yes, Martha, something is wrong, depending on your point of view. Should we go through the how-are-you, you-don't-call-often-enough amenities first?"

"Mom, I'm sorry. I know how you loved your job. I spoke to Andy last night and he was fine, so that leaves Dad. Are you calling to tell me something in particular or to discuss whatever it is that's bothering you?" Ruby hated the way her daughter's voice turned reverent when she mentioned her father's name.

"A little of both, I guess. Your father and I are going to separate. We're not going to get a divorce right away. At least I don't think so. This is . . . I came to the decision . . . your father doesn't know I'm planning all this, but he will when he gets home."

"Do you want to tell me why?" Martha asked softly.

"Yes, I do, Martha, but I don't want to upset you."

"Mom, when it comes to Dad, you can't upset me. I'm not a kid anymore. Tell me what he did to make you reach this point."

Ruby told her. Once or twice she thought she heard her daughter gasp, but it was probably her imagination or, worse yet, her own guilt.

"It doesn't surprise me," Martha drawled. "I thought it was kind of funny when he called and asked if I could lay my hands on eight hundred fifty dollars real quick. Don't panic, Mom, I didn't give it to him. I called Andy and asked if he had any idea why Dad would need money. Andy said he bet on sports events and the horses. He told me not to give it to him."

"Martha, I'm sorry. I didn't know. This whole thing just socked me between the eyes. I guess I've been living in my own little dream world too long."

"Are you gonna be all right, Mom?"

"I'm fine, honey. Don't worry about me."

"You want to know something, Mom? You are the most together lady I know."

"Thank you, Marty," Ruby said proudly.

"Listen, I have a date, but I can call you later tonight, and we can have a real gab session. You probably want to call Andy now, since it's suppertime and you'll catch him in."

Ruby laughed. "You could always anticipate me."

"One more thing, Mom. Don't let Dad buffalo you. Stand firm. I'm behind you, and Andy is, too. I love you. Bye, Mom."

Ruby smiled. It was good to know she had the support of the children. She dialed her son's number.

"Yo, Ma! How's it going?" Andy boomed.

"Some days good, some days not so good. This is one of those not-so-good days, Andy. I'm filing for a legal separation from your father. I wanted you to know. Your father is going to move out of the house, probably tonight. I'm going to pack his things after I hang up."

"What'd he do this time?"

She told him.

"You okay, Ma?"

"I'm fine, Andy. That's not exactly true, but I will be fine. I got fired today, and Dixie and I are going into business."

"Do you want me to come home? I can be there in forty-five minutes."

"Absolutely not! Andy, don't lend your father any money. Marty told me you knew he was gambling. Is that true?"

"Yes and no. I suspected. I heard him a couple of times on the phone. Everyone lays down a bet at sometime or other, but when you gamble the homestead, that's something else. Do what you gotta do, Ma. And if you need money, I have a little put away . . ."

"Andy, no. I'll be fine. Once I sell the house in Georgetown, things will be fine. Promise me you won't worry about me."

"You got it, Ma. I love you. Call me if you need anything, or even if you just want to talk. I'm a good listener. Be tough, Ma. That's the best advice I can give."

"I love you, Andy. Talk to you later in the week."

Ruby wished for a dog, something warm and snuggly that she could hug. Animals were loyal and they loved unconditionally. She had asked Andrew for a dog once, and Andy had cried for weeks after his father refused to be swayed. She should have stood her ground.

In a little less than an hour, Ruby had neatly packed her husband's bags, dusty Gucci luggage he'd purchased without her consent and took on his golfing jaunts, where he said he won prizes of money. She lugged the four matched suitcases out to the hallway. She looked back at the room they'd shared and would never share again. It looked the same. It was as if Andrew had never slept there.

The first time she walked down the stairs, her shoulders were slumped. The second time, her head righted itself. The third time, her shoulders were back. A lone tear trickled down her cheek when she made the last trip down the stairs.

Andrew wouldn't see the bags unless he went into the living room. He wouldn't know that he wasn't going to sleep in this house ever again until she told him. Of course, if he argued with her, didn't take her offer to pay off his debts in exchange for a divorce, he would sleep upstairs, but she wouldn't be in the bed.

She knew he'd take her offer because it was his only salvation. Tomorrow she would have the locks changed on all the doors.

The minutes and hours crawled by. Eight o'clock ticked onward to nine, ten, eleven. She stopped watching the clock then and started to pace the kitchen. She stopped to drink two cups of tea. At twenty minutes to one, the Buick's headlights flashed on the window. Ruby drew in her breath and put her hands in the pockets of her robe so her husband wouldn't see them tremble. She clenched her hands into balled fists and gritted her teeth. She was ready.

"Here," Andrew said, tossing a paper shopping bag full of bills onto the table when he came in. "It's all yours."

"On one condition," Ruby said quietly.

Andrew sneered. "You aren't in any position to make deals. Filing late tax returns, forging my name, keeping money that should have been ours, paying that crazy coot of a father with money I could have used. Uh-uh, that won't work. I haven't forgotten St. Andrew's either."

"I never forged your name. Any time your attorney wants to see the tax returns, he can contact my attorney," Ruby said in a level voice. "You have no grounds to fight me on, Andrew. If you want to pay a lawyer to find out what I'm telling you is true, then be my guest. It's your money. I don't want anything from you."

Andrew snarled and stormed about the kitchen. "*Now* you don't want anything from me. What about before?"

Ruby ignored him. "I have a proposition for you. Would you care to hear it?"

"Not likely. You just get the money together you've been keeping from me and pay off these bills before we lose the house. I never thought you were a sneak like that, Ruby."

Be tough, Andy'd said.

"Andrew, I'm going to ask you just once more if you want to hear my proposition. If you don't, you can go under with this house, and I'll move back to Washington."

"You are a living, breathing bitch, do you know that? Okay, what's this proposition that's going to make up for the lies *you've* told all our married life."

Andrew listened, his eyes narrowed, his face going from red to white and back to red. He raised his hand. Petrified, Ruby remained still. Her mother must have felt like this. Be tough, Andy said.

"If you strike me, I swear to God I'll make you regret it. Please, Andrew, don't be like my father."

Andrew's hand dropped to his side. He licked his lips. Then he slammed his fist into the wall. He looked pleased when little bits of plaster and paint showered down on the floor.

"You're right, Ruby. As usual," he said bitterly. "I'll sign whatever you want, but—"

"But what?" Ruby said stonily.

"It seems to me I'm giving up a lot here. You, on the other hand, have some pretty nice cushions to fall back on. Let's not forget the dirty dealing you did behind my back all these years. I should be compensated for that. I could make a lot of trouble for you legally; but, like you said, why go through all that and pay a lawyer to tell us what we already know? A piece of the house your parents live in in Florida when they kick the bucket. I keep my military pension. Andrew makes it on his own. You don't hit me up for tuition. And," he said craftily, "if you do decide to go into some kind of business with that cripple, I get a percentage if it gets off the ground. These are *my* terms."

Ruby's head reeled. She'd been expecting something, but this was almost more than she could comprehend. She nodded numbly, knowing she was probably making the biggest mistake of her life by giving in. But Andrew was the father of her children. Actually, it would be the second biggest mistake. Marrying Andrew had been her biggest.

"Okay," she said hoarsely. "Tomorrow I'll go to a lawyer and have him draw up an agreement and file for a separation. I want this legal."

Andrew smiled. He would be affable now, Ruby thought, even charming. It was after two in the morning when they finally had hammered out an agreement satisfactory to both of them. Andrew would receive semiannually, if the business got off the ground, one and a half percent of the gross. She would pick up all the car insurance premiums, and when the house in Florida was finally sold, he was to get another five percent.

"Okay, I'll need you to write some checks," he demanded. "To pay off my debts."

"Not on your life," Ruby grated. "You get them tomorrow, when you sign the agreement, and not one second before. I want a legal opinion on all of this. Your bags are in the living room. I'll stop by the store tomorrow or you can meet me at the lawyer's office at five o'clock. If there's a change, I'll call you at the store."

"Jesus Christ, it's three o'clock in the morning. Where am I going to go at this time of night?"

"Try the parking lot at Sears, or an all-night diner," Ruby said callously. "Out! Now!"

"By God, the nut doesn't fall far from the tree! You really are like your crazy father. You better watch it or you'll end up just like him."

"What's that supposed to mean?" Ruby screeched.

Andrew laughed. "Did I hit a nerve, Ruby? You figure it out."

Ruby's throat constricted. Her voice, when she managed to speak, was little more than a hoarse croak. "Andrew, why did you marry me?"

"I needed a wife. You were a virgin. You were available."

If ever Ruby had held any illusions about her marriage, at that moment they shattered. Until now, this very second, she would have gone on with her life just the way it was, and settled for whatever little happiness she could find. Tears blurred her vision as she watched the taillights of Andrew's car until they were tiny red dots in the night. Almost instantly she saw a full set of headlights spring to light down the street. She frowned as the car drew closer and then swerved into her driveway. "Dixie!" she cried, running out the front door.

Dixie laughed. "Jeez, I'm almost frozen. I've been sitting out here since midnight. I thought you might need me. Hugo is dead to the world and I couldn't sleep. Are you okay?"

"Yes, no, oh, hell, Dixie, I don't know . . ." Ruby began to sob.

"You sit right there and don't move. I'm going to turn the heat up, it's freezing in here. You didn't eat, did you? I'll make some eggs and coffee. I'm staying right here till I talk some sense into you. While I'm doing all this, you tell me everything he said and what happened. Exactly as it happened," Dixie ordered.

When the sun crept over the horizon, neither woman seemed to notice. All night Ruby had talked and Dixie had listened.

Now Ruby eyed the shopping bag Andrew had left. She gave it a kick with her foot and then bent down to pull it closer to her. "I have to go through this. I have a feeling things are worse than Andrew let on. You'd better go home, or Hugo will take a hissy fit. Come back after he goes to work. I'm going to take a shower and go through this stuff. I can't make any decisions until I know how deeply in debt Andrew's put us."

"Okay," Dixie said sadly. "But remember to do what your son said. Be tough. You'll make it, I'll be here for you. Together we'll work it out."

Ruby cried all the way through her shower and while she dressed. She was still crying when she walked downstairs. She managed to fight her tears while she made her phone calls and scribbled notes. Then she made plans.

The very first thing she was going to do when she had money to spare was make a sizable donation to St. Andrew's in Hawaii. She was going to go back there, too, maybe take Martha, if she wanted to go. She'd go to Chapel Hill, too, to see Mrs. Query. She would do all the things Andrew objected to. All the things that were important to her. She'd track down Mabel MacIntyre from the Navy Annex and do something nice for her, too.

Ruby raised the blind at the kitchen window. January was always so cold, and it looked bitter outside. She wondered where Andrew had spent the night.

"Look out world, it's my turn now," Ruby whispered.

{{{{{{{{{ CHAPTER FIFTEEN }}}}}}}}}

It took the entire month of January and part of February for Ruby to get her emotions under control and begin her new life. She hunkered down and refused to leave the house for days at a time. She used the bitter cold as an excuse. When the January snows came, she said she was afraid to drive in hazardous conditions. Dixie did her shopping and ran her errands.

The day before Valentine's Day, when most of the snow was gone and the roads were clear, Dixie stormed into Ruby's kitchen with a beribboned box of chocolates and announced in no uncertain terms that six weeks was long enough to be in a funk.

"Either you get your shit together or I'm leaving and not coming back," she thundered at a dumbstruck Ruby. "I'll give you time to open your mail before you make your decision."

In that one heart-stopping moment, Ruby knew Dixie was more serious than she'd ever been. It was time to get on with her life. She'd come to the same conclusion on waking when she realized it was the middle of February. "I've got it under control, Dix. I woke up this morning and realized that all I accomplished in a month and a half was to run up an enormous fuel bill. It'll take me till August to pay it off."

The phone rang. "I'll get it," Dixie said, rising half off the chair. "On second thought, answer your own phone. I'll just sit here and eat this wonderful candy I was thoughtful enough to buy for you."

When Ruby came back, she announced, "I've just had an offer on the house in Georgetown from a Brazilian diplomat. The real estate agent said he's so hot for the house, he wants it right away. Rena said not to sell right now, so we hiked the rent and gave him an option to buy. I have cash flow now. My God, I can breathe again," Ruby said, popping a chocolate-covered caramel into her mouth. "I feel like a ton of weight has been taken off my shoulders."

"Does this mean we're ready to sit down and make some concrete plans in regard to this business venture we were dumb enough to promise ourselves we would undertake?"

"Damn right," Ruby said, reaching behind her for a fat notebook stuffed with scribbled notes.

"The first thing we have to realize is that we don't know diddly-squat about going into any kind of business. We don't even have a product to sell and we don't have any customers. We have limited, and I do mean limited, working capital. I don't think a bank will lend us money, since we don't have paying jobs or a means to repay the loan. The only definite is we need money. I need seventy-five dollars a week to live on and so do you, so whatever we sell has to give us a one-hundred-fifty-dollar return. That comes to six hundred a month every month of the year. Maybe we should try and get by on less," Ruby said, her brow furrowing with worry.

"I need only twenty-eight dollars a week. Hugo is satisfied with what I was earning at the gift shop. If I take only twenty-eight dollars, what does that come to?" Dixie asked anxiously.

"If I cut back to sixty dollars and you take twenty-eight, that's—Ruby's pencil flew over the paper in front of her—"three hundred fifty-two dollars a month. That sounds a lot better."

Dixie finished the last of the chocolates. She patted her lips and groaned. "I wish I hadn't eaten so much, but they were so good. Sweets are my downfall," she said happily.

"This business," Ruby said, throwing the empty candy box into the trash basket, "whatever it turns out to be, will have no overhead. We can operate it here in the kitchen or use the garage. The only problem, as I see it, is that we don't know how to do anything." She threw her hands in the air. "It's true, Dixie. We've been wives and mothers all these years. Working part-time in a gift shop hardly qualifies us to go into business. Obviously, we have to sell something we make ourselves, but we're not craft people, and even if we were, homemade things take so much time to make, and people don't want to pay for labor. Where does that leave us?"

Dixie shrugged. "The same place we were before you threw away the candy box. We don't know how to do anything, and we have nothing to sell."

"We can't be negative, Dixie. If we're negative, we're beaten before we start. *Think.*"

"You think. I have to go to the bathroom. Your phone's ringing."

Ruby grinned as she looked at the calendar. "I'll bet that's Andy. He calls every Monday morning. He's in need of another Care package. Want to bet?"

"Not me. You know your son better than I do."

"I'm mailing it out today," Ruby said before her son had a chance to announce himself.

"That's what I like about you, Ma. You anticipate me. Listen, this cafeteria food is so bad, I've been thinking of asking you to send me double batches of your great cookies so I can sell them and use the profits to buy my meals on the outside. Want to go into business?"

Ruby's heart thumped, pumped, and almost leapt out of her chest. "Say that again, Andy," she said in a strangled voice.

"What? The part about sending me more cookies or the part about me eating on the outside?"

Ruby laughed, a sound of pure delight. "Andy, could you really sell the cookies?"

"Well, yeah. Actually, I did sell a few last week, that's why I'm all out. I sold them for ten cents each. It was enough for a slice of pizza and a Coke. I ate the rest. Some girl asked me to ask you to make her some peanut butter cookies. I told her your speciality is oatmeal raisin and chocolate chip. Next time send some peanut butter ones. Her father is a doctor, and she has a huge allowance. Go for it, Ma. I think it's a great idea. Have to run. Don't want to be late for class. Love you."

"Oh, Andy, I love you, too. I mean I really love you. I'll call you tonight, honey. Bye."

"Dixieeeee! We're going into the cookie business!" She repeated her phone conversation with her son. Dixie's eyes sparkled.

"I love to make cookies. I love to eat cookies. Your grandmother's recipes, right?" Ruby nodded.

"Let's figure it out. Cookie sheets, baking supplies, another stove, maybe two. Sears. Andrew will get us a discount. A whole garage full of stoves. Not right away of course. Mixing bowls, all from Sears. A relatively small investment. We can bake the cookies early in the morning or late at night and deliver them before noon. Andy can sell them for us until we get established. Kids love homemade cookies. Reasonably priced. This is it, Dix, I can feel it in my bones. That kid is so smart. If he hadn't called, we'd still be sitting here, sucking our thumbs. You know what, his best friend, Jeff Larsen, goes to Princeton. I'm going to call his mother, Jeannine, and ask her if she'll ask him to do the same. Princeton isn't far from Rutgers. We can deliver to him after we hit Rutgers. And Monmouth College isn't far from here, either."

Dixie clapped her hands in delight. "We'll put them in paper sacks, brown for now, with a ribbon. Packaging is as important as the product. When we start to show a profit, we can have our name printed on the sacks. Except that we don't have a name," she said in dismay.

"Sure we do. Back in Barstow there was this lady named Constance Sugar, and she made the best brownies. Her daughter used to bring them to school on her birthday, and the teacher gave one to each of us and put a candle in it. We always called them Mrs. Sugar's brownies. How about Mrs. Sugar's Cookies?"

"It's going to work, isn't it, Ruby? I mean really work."

"Show me a kid that doesn't like fresh, homemade cookies. There is no such kid. We are going to make a *fortune*."

"Let's start now, to get the feel of it. We'll bake all day and drive up to Rutgers tomorrow with our first delivery. We'll get an idea of the cost for one day.

"I can go home and bake in my kitchen and bring what I've done over here before Hugo gets home. I have six trays and two oven racks, same as you. It's going to take us a long time. We have to go to the store, too." She looked down, as if embarrassed. "I hate to bring this up, but I need money. All I have is three dollars, and it has to last me till Thursday, when Hugo gets paid. I have to buy milk and bread."

"I don't have much, either, but I do have some put aside for my electric bill. I'll hold off paying it. I'll have to write you a check, though."

"How many cookies do you think we can bake between now and tomorrow morning?"

"Hundreds. Maybe a thousand."

"God. We're entrepreneurs!"

The two women looked at each other for a moment. There didn't seem to be any need for words. Ruby reached out and hugged her friend. "That's just for being you, Dix."

Dixie dabbed her eyes. "I think it'll help your baking if you turn on the oven first." She was out the door before Ruby could throw the dishtowel at her.

Dixie was back two hours later, her nose wrinkling in delight at the fragrant-smelling kitchen. "Tantalizing," she groaned. "How many have you made?"

"I tripled the recipe and made the cookies a little bigger because we're selling to kids and we want to give them their money's worth. I think I made about ten dozen so far. The last batch is in the oven. Deduct five or six. I ate three and you're on your third one. What'ja get?"

"Lots of stuff and some information. The manager of the A&P told me where to buy ingredients wholesale. I knew Mrs. Harris at the gift shop wouldn't tell me what time it was, much less where she buys her sacks and ribbons, so I asked the cashier and she said she'll go through Mrs. Harris's records when she

leaves to go home for supper. She'll call us tonight with names
and phone numbers. Did I do good, Ruby?"

"You did just great. Oooohhh, you got colored bags. And
matching ribbon. A class operation, Dix."

"She was out of the plain brown ones, and these shiny little
bags were so pretty. They look like little satchels. Girls will love
them. The guys won't care." Dixie gurgled as she stuffed another cookie in her mouth. "There is a down side to this," she
grumbled. "We're going to get fat."

"Who cares, as long as we make money. Anyway, three days
from now neither one of us will be able to eat one of these
cookies. Trust me."

When Dixie left the house on Ribbonmaker Lane with her tri-
ple batch of oatmeal raisin cookie mix, Ruby was in such high
spirits, nothing, not even a visit from Andrew, could have soured
her outlook. Over and over she kept whispering to herself, "Oh,
Bubba, you did it for me again. If it wasn't for these old country
recipes of yours, I wouldn't be doing this. You must be watching
over me." She stopped what she was doing, her hands frozen in
the air. "It's true," she whispered. "Every time I trip and fall,
when things get so bad there seems no way out, somehow, because of you, it's made right. You get, you give. That's it, isn't
it?" She raised her eyes upward, fully expecting to see a sudden
burst of white light shower down on her kitchen. "Okay, so you
aren't giving off clues or signs, but I know. Andy's call today,
the cookie conversation . . . that didn't come out of thin air.
There's a reason for everything." Her voice dropped lower
still. "It's nice to know, to feel there's someone watching over
me. Don't stop, please, don't stop."

She didn't feel silly at all when, as she went on with her
cookie baking, from time to time she patted her shoulder. Everyone knew guardian angels perched on your shoulder.

It was almost midnight when Ruby and Dixie dried the last
mixing bowl and tidied up the kitchen. "We're done." Ruby
sighed. "Lord, it's been an exhausting day, but I don't think I've
ever felt better in my life. Doesn't it look beautiful, Dix?" Ruby
pointed to the neatly beribboned cookie bags lined up all over
the kitchen floor and counter. Dixie nodded wearily.

"Everything is taken care of. If we leave at six-thirty, we
should make Rutgers, even with commuter traffic on Route 1,

by seven-thirty. Andy has a class at eight o'clock. We'll drop the cookies off at his dorm and head for Princeton. Andy said he'd sell them between classes. He said he had an idea but wanted to check it out before he gets us all worked up, whatever that means. Now, for the paperwork. We have to stay on top of it no matter how tired we are. You work behind me in case I make a mistake."

At one-thirty the two bleary-eyed women looked at each other over their spiral-bound notebooks. "*If* we sell all the cookies, we should show a profit of . . . Lord, this can't be right." Ruby dithered. "All this work for fourteen dollars, and we have to deliver the cookies ourselves! Using our time and our gas. If we sell cookies every day for a week, we'll make only seventy dollars and we'll be killing ourselves." Ruby groaned.

"It's the bags and ribbon. They're pretty, but we paid retail prices for them. We won't bake tomorrow . . . I mean today. We'll go to all these wholesale places and get prices. We'll have to buy in bulk. That will drive the cost down and our profits up," Dixie said wearily. "You were right, Ruby, I don't want to look at another cookie."

"I can't believe the trimmings cost more than the ingredients. And that's not the only problem we have to correct real fast. We also need to get in touch with a chicken farmer in Freehold and buy our eggs direct. Obviously, we jumped into this a little too quickly. My fault, Dix, and I'm sorry. I'm not usually this impulsive. If you're half as tired as I am, you must be upset with me."

"Nah, I didn't have anything else to do."

Ruby grinned. "We're learning. The real test is going to be seeing if these cookies sell. You should go home, Dix, and get some sleep. By the way, how are you going to get out of the house tomorrow? Hugo is going to wonder why you're leaving at six o'clock. You have to help me load the car."

"I pretty much covered that at dinnertime. Hugo wanted to know why I was making so many cookies. I lied and said they were for the church and they were made with donated ingredients. I said I had to have them over at the rectory for a breakfast cake and cookie sale. Since he doesn't go to church, he had no reason not to believe me. I'll be here. 'Night, Ruby."

"It's going to work, Dixie."

"I know. See you in the morning."

* * *

Ruby stared at the colorful bags of cookies for a long time after Dixie left. So much work. And where, she wondered, was she going to get the money to buy the next load of supplies? Ruby looked at the clock. It was midnight in California. She dialed Opal's number. She didn't realize she was holding her breath until Opal's cheery voice came over the wire. Ruby straightened her back, her shoulders hurting with the effort. She'd never asked anyone for anything before. "Opal, I need a favor. A big one."

"Whatever it is, you got it. Listen, I was sorry to hear about you and Andrew, but when something doesn't work, it doesn't work. Now you can go on the prowl and find a new man. Hey, listen, I can fix you up with some buddies of Mac's. Great guys, they love a good time. Real jolly guys. What's the favor?"

"I need money. A loan. Just for a little while. I got an offer on the house in Georgetown today, and I'm taking it. I should close on it real soon, before the end of March. I can pay you back then. I need three hundred dollars."

Opal's voice changed. "That's a lot of bread, Ruby. Mac and I are only one step ahead of the bill collectors now. The most I could come up with is a hundred dollars. When did you say you could pay it back? I don't know how Mac . . ."

"Never mind," Ruby said quietly. "Look, I'm sorry I bothered you so late."

Opal's voice was cheery again. "No problem. Sorry, Ruby, I guess I better start to save, huh?"

Ruby didn't bother to respond. She replaced the receiver in the cradle. She would not think about the money she'd given Opal for a house. Why drive herself crazy?

Suddenly, Ruby didn't care about the time. She flipped open her address book and called everyone she could possibly think of to ask for a loan, leaving Rena till last. She drew a big fat zero on a piece of paper when she dialed Rena's number and a management service operator told her Rena was out of the country. She drew another fat zero. She felt like crying. So much for friends. She was about to close her address book when she saw the name and phone number on the last page.

Grace Zachary. As she dialed the number, she was glad she'd always sent a Christmas and Easter card to the Zacharys. At least she'd kept in touch.

Grace's sleepy voice became alert the moment she heard Ruby identify herself. "Ruby, is that really you? Paul, wake up, it's Ruby. I don't care what time it is, get up. Go pick up the extension. Ruby honey, how are you? Something's wrong, I can tell. Lord, child, Paul and I talk about you all the time. What is it, Ruby, how can I help you?"

The dam inside Ruby burst. She babbled and prattled, wiping the tears trickling down her cheeks. She sobbed when she got to the part about Calvin. She could hear Grace cluck her tongue in sympathy. She heard Paul chuckle when she told them about the houses in Georgetown. When she asked for the loan in a shaky voice, both Grace and Paul said in unison, "How much?"

"Three hundred, five if you can spare it. I'll sign a note, whatever you want. I'll pay whatever you think is fair in interest."

"You'll do no such thing," Paul said briskly. "We'll send you out a check first thing in the morning. You pay us back when you can. No interest. Now, let me tell you where to go for your wholesale products. Don't pay any attention to what that manager at your supermarket told you. I'm the eastern seaboard manager for the chain. You call this man and tell him I told you to call him, and this is what he's to do for you. Get a pencil, honey, and copy all of this down. If you get this off the ground, we'll buy from you. You can't sell to college kids forever, and for Christ's sake, fifty cents a dozen is not nearly enough to charge. A buck, Ruby. Trust me." She did. They talked for an hour.

"You listen to Paul, Ruby," Grace said, "he knows what he's talking about."

"I will, Grace. I'll pay you back as soon as possible. Thank you both."

"That's what friends are for. Go to bed and get some sleep. We'll talk again, honey."

As Ruby was replacing the receiver, she fidgeted on the kitchen chair and raised her eyes upward. Always, when she was at the bottom, things like this happened. In a sudden flash of insight, she knew it wasn't her grandmother at all. It was someone else. A Higher Being. She remembered the way she'd ditched her Bible on the train. It had been a long time since she'd gone to church.

Instead of going to bed, Ruby climbed the stairs to the bathroom. She showered and washed her hair. She was never more awake than she was right now.

Whoever would have thought the Zacharys would be the ones to come to her aid? If she hadn't flipped the last page in her address book, she'd probably be giving up at this very moment. She laughed as she danced under the needle-sharp spray.

She was smiling as she fried herself some bacon and eggs. She could hardly wait for Dixie to arrive. Wait till she found out they could get the ingredients for the cookies cheaper than wholesale. Paul had even given her a name of a firm that dealt in paper products. He'd said the man would make her bags to specifications as long as she told him Paul Zachary would consider doing business somewhere else if he didn't give her the same kind of break he got for his stores. She would have to buy in the thousands, though. The thought didn't bother her at all. It didn't bother her that she was going to buy her flour in three-hundred-pound sacks and her shortening in fifty-pound cans. There would be no problem with picking up the supplies, since the wholesaler delivered. The same thing would apply to the egg farmer. Free delivery would save her time. The only hitch, and it was a big hitch, was the wholesaler had to be paid up front, by cash or check. No credit to a first-time customer, especially a woman, Paul said. Well, she could live with that, too.

"Someday," she said, sliding the eggs onto her plate, "they'll beg me for my business."

As she ate, Ruby ran her conversation with Paul over again in her mind. "You're dealing in a cash-and-carry business, Ruby. Don't be tempted to skim off the top. It's easy to do, but the Internal Revenue Service frowns on such things. Keep accurate records, down to the penny, and make sure you keep all your receipts. This is technically a cottage-type industry, where you're going to be hiring people. Make it clear that you are reporting to the government what you pay them. As independent contractors, they pay their own taxes. You're going to have a lot of headaches, but it will be your own business, and if I can help you, call me. Anytime."

She would, too. How wonderful it was to have caring friends.

Dixie and Ruby talked all the way to Andy's dorm at Rutgers in New Brunswick. A sleepy Andy walked out to the car, his hair tousled, his feet in slippers, his pajama legs sticking out from his jeans. Thick, muscular arms wrapped themselves around Ruby. He tried to whisper, but his voice carried across the street. "Good to see you, Ma. Let me carry those. You two carry those little shopping bags. One trip is all it will take."

"I swear that kid gets handsomer and handsomer every time I see him," Dixie stage-whispered. "He gets bigger, too. He must be six-two by now."

"Three." Ruby giggled. "His eyes are bluer than Paul Newman's. He said he gets teased about it all the time. He's such a good kid. And," Ruby said proudly, "he's doing well. He's going to make a first-rate architect."

"Okay, Ma, just set them over there and I'll unload them sometime today. How much should I charge?"

"A dollar a bag," Ruby blurted out, remembering Paul's words. Dixie gasped and then closed her open mouth. "Send us a money order. I'll call you when we're ready to do this again. The little purple bags are peanut butter. Thanks a million, Andy."

"Ma, for you, anything. Drive carefully."

"Hey, Blue," a voice down the hall roared, "can you lower the volume a little?" The voice was good-natured. Andy grinned. "They tolerate me." He mouthed the words in a harsh-sounding whisper.

Ruby hugged him.

"How many can I eat?" he whispered again.

"The ones in the green bag are for you and your roommate. We have to get going, Andy. Call me." Andy nodded.

Back on Route 1, on their way to Princeton, Dixie chortled gleefully. "We quadrupled our profit. Whatever made you say a dollar a bag?"

"Paul Zachary. Hey, if it doesn't work, we'll come down to seventy-five cents. Twenty-eight dollars for yesterday's labor sounds a lot better than fourteen. I can live with twenty-eight. I just have such a positive feeling about all of this."

Jeff Larsen, Andy's friend, was standing on the curb outside his dorm with two of his buddies. In the blink of an eye they whisked the cookie boxes from the backseat and had them over their shoulders. Like her son, he said, "Which ones are mine and how much?"

Back on Route 1 South and headed for Route 202, the women sat back and relaxed. "By tonight we'll know if our cookies are worth our asking price. I have a hunch the kids will sell them all."

"I think so, too. What time do you think we'll get home, Ruby?" Dixie asked anxiously.

"By three, if we don't get held up. Are you going to have a problem?" she asked, concerned.

Dixie shrugged. "Hugo has been acting very peculiar. For a while now he hasn't really kicked up a fuss about anything. He still asks questions about what I'm doing, when I'm doing it, and why, but he's acting so out of character in other ways. I don't know how to react to it."

"And you're complaining?" Ruby grinned. "This is what you always said you wanted."

"I know, but he's not doing it in the right way. It's probably just my imagination." Ruby nodded. She wasn't going to let Hugo ruin her day or Dixie's either, if she could help it.

Abe Saltzer of H & R Wholesalers was a giant of a man. He was taller than Andrew and beefier, with a pot belly under a stained shirt that was missing two buttons. He had the reddest hair and beard she'd ever seen. The evil-smelling cigar clamped between his teeth made her eyes water. His hands, which were big as ham hocks, were directing huge semis to the loading docks as he tried to pay attention to the trucks and her at the same time. "You got business here or just taking up air other people need to breathe?"

Ruby worked her tongue around the inside of her mouth. "I'm here to place an order. Paul Zachary said I should ask for Mr. Saltzer. Are you Mr. Saltzer?"

"I was when I got up this morning. Paul, eh? You know Paul?"

"He and Grace are friends of mine."

"My sister married Paul's brother," Abe said, rolling the cigar from one side of his mouth to the other.

"Oh, that's nice. I'm sure Paul's brother is just as nice as he is."

"Yeah, yeah, yeah. Why'd Paul send you to me?"

"He said you'd give me a good deal. My friend here, Dixie Sinclaire, and myself, I'm Ruby Blue, are going into the cookie business, and we need to buy wholesale. Paul said you would deliver. See, I made notes. This is what he said. You can call him if you want," Ruby said, handing over the slip of paper.

"He said all of this about me?"

He seemed pleased, Ruby thought.

"Would you like a cookie?" Dixie offered. "I have some right here . . . somewhere . . ." She reached into her oversize shoulder bag and drew out a little yellow bag full of assorted cookies. To Ruby she said, "I thought we might not have time to stop for lunch, so I took two of each."

"No credit," Abe said with his mouth full of cookies. Ruby nodded. "Delivery is Tuesday where you live. We unload. You tip the driver, since this is all Paul's idea. That okay with you?" Ruby nodded. "Where did you get this bag?" he demanded.

Ruby blinked. She couldn't even see the little lemon-colored bag in his hand. "In a gift store. They cost nineteen cents each."

"It's worth only two cents. Three buildings down is the guy you want to see. Listen, if you have a mind to, you could slip the driver some of these cookies when he delivers. Tape the box. I'm partial to the peanut butter ones. Taste like my mother's."

"Well, sure. It's a deal. How many?"

"Surprise me. Let's go inside and I'll give you an account number, and when you're ready to order, you call, ask for me, and I'll make sure you get the first delivery of the day. See this squiggly number at the end? That means you get preferential treatment. Thanks to my generous brother-in-law's brother. You want to order now or wait?"

"We don't know how much to order and we need to ask some questions. Like how long will flour keep?"

"Tightly closed you can keep it forever. The butter and shortening need refrigeration once the cans are opened. Get your eggs from a local farmer. I hate dealing with eggs. No money in eggs. Everybody bitches when they get cracked. Brown eggs are the best. Anything else, ladies? Oh, yeah, I need forty-eight hours' notice for an order unless it's an emergency. I been in this business a long time, and I only had one emergency and that was when the Red Cross needed food for disaster relief."

The honest, honorable streak in Ruby made her blurt out, "Mr. Saltzer, will you still make a profit selling to us at this price? We don't want charity, even if Paul was good enough to . . . to agree for you . . . what I mean is . . ."

Abe rocked back on his heels. He shook his head, the cigar

wobbling in his mouth. "Ladies, you don't ever ask a question
like that. Now, what kind of businesswomen are you going to
turn out to be if you go around asking dumb questions?"

"Honest ones," Ruby said forcefully.

"Well, as one honest businessman to another, yeah. I'm still
making a profit, but for Christ's sake, don't go blabbing this to
anyone, okay?"

"Okay. We'll be in touch, Mr. Saltzer."

"Cash!" Saltzer called after her.

"Cash," Ruby called over her shoulder. "And the cookies."

"Yeah, don't forget the cookies."

"He's practically *giving* it to us, and he's still making a
profit," Dixie said in awe. "We're being robbed at the grocery
store, you know that?"

"I've known that for a long time," Ruby muttered.

After they had made a similar deal for their bags with a man
named Petrocelli, they headed for home.

When, forty-five minutes later, Ruby swerved into her driveway, she ran over the same rosebushes she'd mutilated in January. She didn't care. All she wanted was to sleep. She made it
into the house on her own. Dixie led her to the couch, turned up
the heat, and covered her with an afghan. She turned the phone
down to ring low before she let herself out of the house by way
of the garage so Ruby would be locked in.

The garage was huge, oversized. Dixie closed her eyes and
tried to visualize the place filled with thousands of colored bags
of cookies, waiting for delivery. It was such a pleasant picture
that she smiled. Success. She was glad she was going to share
in it. Her only misgiving was she had no money to put into the
business and yet Ruby was willing to split everything fifty-fifty.
Her own eyes closed wearily. What she couldn't give in the way
of money would have to be made up in work. That she knew
how to do.

The first thing she was going to do when she got some money
was go to a doctor and see about getting some stronger pain
pills. The arthritis the last doctor said was going to set in was already entrenched. Some mornings she could hardly get out of
bed. A hot, steaming bath was the only thing that helped, along
with four or five aspirin.

Already, she could feel the beginnings of stress and strain.
She'd been blithe about Hugo with Ruby, but she somehow sus-

pected that he was working up to a nasty mood, one she would suffer from if she didn't try to head it off. "If he would just die, I'd be so happy," she whispered. She was filled with shame immediately. Hugo wasn't going to die, and she wasn't going to leave him because she was tied to him in a sick kind of way. She wished she had Ruby's guts. Ruby always managed to land on her feet even when things were at their worst. This business venture, if it got off the ground, was proof. One minute she had nothing but an idea, and the next minute they were in business. It would get off the ground because Ruby said it would. Her last-minute decision to sell the cookies for a dollar a dozen instead of fifty cents had already netted them, providing they sold, twenty-eight dollars each. Just what she'd made working in the gift store. If she worked hard, right alongside Ruby, she could net one hundred forty dollars a week. Once she handed over twenty-eight dollars to Hugo, she would have one hundred twelve dollars to bank. In a month she'd have four hundred and forty-eight dollars. If Ruby agreed. She'd been stupid to say she'd settle for twenty-eight dollars. But Ruby was fair, she thought uneasily. If she worked hard, banked her profits, she might be able to shed her husband.

Wearily, Dixie struggled to her feet. "I wonder what it's like to live by yourself and not have to answer to anyone. It must be a kind of heaven." She closed and locked the garage door.

She hated going home, hated making dinner for Hugo, hated sitting across from him. She hated the silent meals and the silence in the house after meals, when Hugo read the paper. She wondered if Hugo would be the same married to someone else. Maybe she was the problem. Maybe she was too plain, not educated enough. Maybe, maybe, maybe. So many times she'd gone over the same things in her mind. She'd tried so hard, even harder after her accident, but there was no way she could camouflage her deformity. She knew he hated it. He'd called her a damn cripple so many times, she'd lost count. She could feel his eyes on her when she moved about the house, and she'd read the disgust in his eyes. Her eyes sparked momentarily. He'd made her this way, and then had the gall to look disgusted. "Die already and make me a widow," she muttered. This time she felt no shame. None.

Hugo was waiting for her in the kitchen when she walked

through the door. She cringed when she saw the look on his face.

"Where were you?" he demanded.

To lie or not to lie. Dixie felt like a cornered rat. Had he gone by the church or, worse yet, stopped by the gift store? She realized in the split second it took him to ask his question that she could turn around and walk out the door and go to Ruby's house. Ruby would let her stay in one of the kids' bedrooms. Ruby could make it right. Thank God for Ruby.

"I was out," she said curtly. "You could have started dinner," she added, walking toward the refrigerator. She didn't take off her coat. She removed a bowl of leftover spaghetti and set it on the counter. Vegetables for a salad were next. She reached for the salad bowl with one hand while the other picked out a knife from the knife holder, a sharp, pointed knife. She still made no move to take off her coat. She turned around, knife in hand. It's coming, she thought. He'd going to tell me he knows I wasn't at the church and that he knows I was fired. He's going to tell me I can't see Ruby anymore. Her grasp on the knife tightened as did her lips.

"Is something wrong, Hugo?" she asked coldly. The strength in her own voice stunned her. Hugo, too, she could tell. It must be the knife, she decided.

Hugo Sinclaire was a tall and intimidating man. Something he drew on every day of his life. He was attractive in a way, but getting jowly. The beard and mustache he was growing gave him a sinister look, something Dixie didn't like even though he kept both well trimmed. He dressed nicely, much more so than she did. Right now, Dixie thought, he looks pitiful. She'd never seen him uncertain, never seen him back down. She was almost giddy with the pleasure of it.

"You're over an hour late. The church was closed and locked and so was the gift store. Where the hell were you? You know I like my supper on time."

"I told you I was out. The longer we stand here talking, the longer it's going to be till dinner. Do you want rolls?"

"Out doesn't tell me where," Hugo blustered. His eyes never left the knife in her hand.

"Actually, I was driving around for a while. I stopped by Ruby's but she was . . . busy. Now, do you want rolls or not?"

"No, bread is good enough. Aren't you going to take off your coat?"

Dixie thought about the question for a full thirty seconds. "No. I'm going to warm this dinner that you could have warmed yourself, and then I'm going back out. Do you," she said, enunciating each word carefully, "have a problem with me going out after dinner?"

He would have a problem with it, she knew. Dixie never left the house after dark. His voice took on a singsong quality when he said, "It depends on where you're going and why. I don't see any need for you to leave the house. We have milk and bread, so you don't need to go to the store. The church is closed and so is the post office, and you don't have any letters or bills to mail."

Dixie's voice took on the same quality as her husband's. "I'm going over to Ruby's. She's helping me make a quilt. For your mother for Mother's Day." She was stunned at how easy the lie rolled off her tongue. "I'll be over there a lot from now on. It takes a long time to make a quilt. Of course, if you'd rather spend the money to *buy* a quilt, that's fine with me. Your mother said that's what she wanted." She waved the wicked-looking knife in the air to make her point.

"All right, all right, get supper on the table and don't be all day about it," Hugo said resignedly.

Dixie turned, the knife still in her hand. "Set the table, Hugo. You can do the dishes, too. I don't have time." This must be what Ruby meant by asserting yourself. She shivered and shook at her own brazenness. Hugo had never once in their married life set the table or washed a dish. For a moment she thought he wasn't going to do it. Her eyes were as narrowed as her husband's. You can be intimidated only if you allow yourself to be intimidated. She'd read that in a magazine in the dentist's office last month. So far she'd made no move to put the spaghetti in a saucepan. "Don't set a place for me." God, I'm really pushing it, Dixie thought. Going into business was heady stuff, but she felt ready to deal with anything, even Hugo.

Still wearing her coat, but weaponless, Dixie ladled out the spaghetti onto her husband's plate. She filled his glass with milk and set his salad and bread just so. She felt as if she should unfold his napkin and tuck it under his chin. "Will there be anything else, Hugo?" She was out the door a minute later with no place to go.

Dixie drove aimlessly until she saw a crowd of women heading toward St. Jude's Catholic Church. Bingo night. She pulled into the parking lot and gambled away her milk and bread money. When she left the church basement at ten o'clock, she had seven dollars. She'd won the round robin but had to split it with four other women.

Dixie elected to drive past Ruby's house. There was a light on in the kitchen. That had to mean her friend was awake. She stopped, tooted the horn lightly. The outside light flashed as the front door opened.

"I'm hungry," Dixie said, shrugging out of her coat. "Wait till you hear how I . . . what I did was I asserted myself. I could never have done it before." She shrugged. "For want of a better word, today was a milestone of sorts for me. I think the knife helped. Can you believe it? Hugo set his own place at the table, and I told him to do the dishes. You should have seen me, Ruby. I had backbone. I actually stood up to him. God, it felt great!"

"Listen, Dixie, I don't want you taking chances where Hugo is concerned. He's not exactly predictable. I think it's wonderful that you got the confidence to stand up to him, and I'm glad that our business venture gave you that confidence. But please be careful. I don't want him to forbid you to see me, and I don't want to have regrets later."

"Ruby, that could never happen. No matter what, you and I will always be friends. You're the sister I never had. If it ever came down to choosing between you and Hugo, I'd . . ."

"No, no, don't say that. You are not going to have to make a choice, so don't even think about it." The phone rang. "Oh-oh, that's Andy."

"Yo, Ma! I have good news!" Ruby smiled as she held the phone away from her ear. Dixie giggled as the boy's voice boomed over the wire. "Wait till you hear this. I sold all the cookies except one bag that my roommate ate by mistake. I could have sold more. Zack and I took them over to the student union and we were sold out in an hour. I sent you out a money order this afternoon. I called Jeff down at Princeton, and he said it took only forty-five minutes. He's sending his money order tomorrow morning. But that's not the good news. You ready, Ma?"

I m ready, Andy." She winked at Dixie and mouthed the words "Is this kid on the ball or what?"

"One of the guys from the Fiji house bought a bag of cookies. His girlfriend was with him. The Fiji house is a frat and they have a sun porch. He said you could sell cookies from there. His girlfriend said she'd handle the concession. She belongs to a sorority. She said she and her sisters could sell three hours every afternoon. The brothers want enough cookies for the frat house and so do the girls. Nine guys in Fiji and there's thirteen in the girls' sorority. No money paid out, but I said you'd kick through with something if sales are up. Whatcha think, Ma? Super, huh?"

"That's wonderful, Andy!" Ruby said weakly. "When do they want us to start?"

"Next week sometime. We'll put it in the paper and the guys said they'd make a sign for the front yard. I'll oversee it. You want I should call Jeff and ask him if he can make the same kind of deal?"

"Do you want to run that last sentence by me again, Andy? I thought you went to college to learn proper English. And yes, tell Jeff to go ahead. This is so unbelievable." She told him about her and Dixie's trip to Easton.

"Ma, that sounds great. Listen, I have another idea. I know a couple of girls over at Douglass, freshmen fifteeners. They'll go for it in a big way. You want I should . . . I mean would you like me to call them and present the idea?"

"Why not?" Ruby said giddily. Dixie was already adding columns of numbers on a piece of paper. "What's a freshmen fifteener?"

Andy's laughter boomed again. "Freshman girls usually put on fifteen pounds their first year. Us guys work it off, they sort of hang on to it until their sophomore year and then we have a new batch to watch. Did I do good, Ma?"

"Andy, you are the marvel in marvelous. Guess we'll have to cut you in for a percentage. On the other hand, if we get Mrs. Sugar to the stage where we have to have a building, you can design it for us. Think about it, okay?"

"You got it, Ma. I want to call Jeff now. Talk to you tomorrow. I love you."

"I love you, too, Andy."

There were tears in Ruby's eyes when she turned to Dixie. "Guess you heard all of that."

Dixie shook her head. "My ears are still ringing. That kid is something else. I guess we're in business," she said carefully.

"Looks like it," Ruby said just as carefully. "Can we do it, Dix?"

"Not with one stove. Or even two. We need three, or else we need a commercial oven. I don't know what they cost. A lot, I think."

"Look," Ruby said, reaching for a pencil, "we don't have to move on this right away. Let's look at it as a business opportunity, fine-tune it, and see if we can handle it. Tomorrow we'll go to a restaurant supply house and see how much an oven costs. We owe it to ourselves to give it a try, but I don't think we can bake enough cookies to sell every day, even if we have a commercial oven. Maybe three times a week. Our other alternative is hiring someone to make our deliveries. Then we'll have to pay for gas, tolls, and wear and tear on our cars. I had no idea going into a business of your own had so many problems. I have to start thinking about health insurance, too. Andrew said he's cutting me off his. Can we do this, Dixie?" Ruby asked worriedly.

"Of course. We both knew, we talked about this, Ruby, that we might have to work around the clock till we got established. I'm prepared. I know you're worried that I won't be able to hold up my end, but I can. I won't let you down."

"Dixie, I know that. It's me I'm worried about. We aren't twenty years old and living in Camp Lejune anymore. In those days we could go all day and night and not wipe out. We're forty now. I get tired, so do you. I can't handle more than a fourteen-hour day. We have to think logically and hire someone. And we have no money. We already know we can't get credit. The five hundred from Grace and Paul isn't going to last very long. And I can't take out a mortgage on the house my parents live in. If we flop in this business, I won't have any means of paying it off, and now that I don't have a husband or a steady job, a bank is going to be leery about lending me money."

"Do you have anything you can sell at a flea market? I have some old stuff in the attic I could sell. You must have the same things I have. We might be able to get fifty or seventy-five dollars for the lot and use it to pay a driver and that will free us to bake. We'd have to do it on a Saturday, because that's the only day the flea market is open. I can bring my stuff over here during the day and Hugo will never know.

"It's the practical thing to do. All that stuff isn't being used, will probably never be used, and is taking up space. We can pay for a lot of hours and tolls, not to mention gas, if we net seventy-five dollars. And on that note I think I'll leave."

Ruby spent the next several hours adding, subtracting, and multiplying. She scribbled and tossed wads of paper into the trash. She longed for an adding machine. Finally, in disgust, she picked up the phone and dialed her husband's number. She was surprised to hear his sleepy voice. "I need to talk to you, Andrew," she said briskly. "Wake up."

"Ruby! For God's sake, it's quarter after two. If you're calling to tell me the house is on fire, tough, that's your problem. You kicked me out. Call me at the store tomorrow."

"Andrew, I have to talk to you now. I need a commercial oven, maybe two. Does Sears sell them? Do you know where I can get them at a good price?"

"You called me in the middle of the night to ask me something so stupid?"

"Think of it in terms of your percentage, Andrew. Dixie and I are going into the cookie business and I need commercial ovens."

"You're what?" Andrew exploded.

"You heard me, the cookie business. We have too many orders and can't fill them with our home ovens. Andrew, are you listening to me?"

"You're nuts, Ruby, and I'm nuts for listening to you."

Ruby clenched her teeth and then crossed her fingers. "I have orders."

"I don't believe you." He sounded interested.

"You're a dipshit, Andrew. This is going to work. I told you to think in terms of your percentage. You'll be a rich man."

"Three percent," Andrew said craftily, fully awake now.

"Two," Ruby said coldly. "Providing you get me two ovens at wholesale prices."

"Four," Andrew said coolly.

"Two and a half. That's my only offer. Two and a half is not shabby."

"When do I start getting my share? When can I quit this lousy job?"

"When I'm rich and famous. Don't quit your job, Andrew, I could fall flat on my face, but it won't be because I haven't given it my all."

"Is that you talking, Ruby? The Ruby who can do anything? The fixer-upper Ruby I was married to? Nah, she never fails. She can do anything."

Ruby could feel the tears spring to her eyes. "I never said I was all those things. That's the way you thought of me. It wasn't fair to me, Andrew, then or now. I'm trying, so give me some credit, okay? If I succeed, so do you. I won't ever cheat you. I think you know that."

"Okay. How soon do you need to know about the ovens?"

"Tomorrow morning, before ten. Call the manager of the appliance department before you go to work, and get back to me. By the way, Andrew, you left a lot of stuff in the garage—tools and things. If I clean them up, do you mind if I sell them at the flea market? I need the money to pay a driver for a while. I've already borrowed everywhere I can."

"You aren't signing my name to anything, are you?" Andrew demanded, a hard edge to his voice.

"No, I wouldn't do that. Can I sell the stuff or not?"

"How much do you think you can get for it? Those tools are top of the line."

"Rusty tools. Twenty-five dollars, maybe thirty-five. Enough for me to pay a driver for a few days."

"That's piss-away money. Okay, but if you get more than that, I want a share. I trust you, Ruby, not to cheat me."

"I'm flattered, Andrew. Good night."

"Ruby?"

"What?"

"Aren't you going to ask me how I am?"

"The kids said you're fine. I'm glad you're okay. I'll talk to you in the morning."

It wasn't until she was halfway up the stairs that she realized he hadn't asked how she was. Some things would never change, she thought wearily.

{{{{{{{{{ CHAPTER SIXTEEN }}}}}}}}}

The brand new, ugly commercial ovens were turned on for the first time at 7 Ribbonmaker Lane the day before St. Patrick's Day. The time was 8:01 A.M. They were turned off fourteen minutes later by the town's health inspector. A representative from the gas company arrived at 9:25 and disconnected the gas he'd turned on the day before.

Dumbfounded, Ruby and Dixie could only stare with their mouths hanging open as they listened to the health inspector tell them their operation didn't meet the sanitary codes of the town. "And," he said coldly, "you don't have a license to operate a business in your home. This is a residential area. It isn't zoned for business. Furthermore, you need a fire wall behind the ovens and a fire door. You are not up to code," he said, slapping a bright orange sticker on the wall behind the ovens. "What all this means, ladies, is you are to cease and desist until the town council can meet two weeks from tomorrow. I would suggest you at least apply for a license. Your presence is requested at the meeting. There's a fine for operating a business in a residential area without the proper authorization. Licenses and Permits will tell you how much it is. Today," he said, tongue in cheek, "would be a good time to pay it. Good day, ladies."

"Drinking on the job." The inspector clucked his tongue to show what he thought of two women with wineglasses in their hands at nine-thirty in the morning.

"Now, just a minute," Ruby said in a hoarse, crackling voice. "We didn't know we needed a license. What's wrong with my garage? It's clean. I cleaned it myself. And we aren't drinking. This is ginger ale!"

"Ignorance of the law is no excuse. Leave it up to a woman to make a mess of things," he muttered.

"You come back here," Ruby yelled, emerging from her daze.

"Are you saying we messed up here because we're women and women are stupid?"

"That about covers it," the inspector yelled over his shoulder, ignoring her order to return to the garage.

"You can't do this!" Ruby screamed.

"I just did it! We take our laws seriously in this town," the inspector shot back.

Andrew took that particular moment to waltz through the side door. He was smacking his hands gleefully, demanding to see the first cookies roll out of the oven.

"Shut up, Andrew. Just shut up!" Ruby fumed. "We're out of business."

Andrew craned his neck to stare out the side window at the departing health department car and gas company truck. "I should have known this was a harebrained scheme; you can't do anything right, Ruby. I bought these ovens under my name. Who's going to make the payments? They can't be taken back. They're goddamn used!" he bellowed.

"There's not a crumb in them. They were turned on and turned off."

"They're used!" Andrew continued to bellow. "And who's that kid?" he said, pointing to a young man dressed in a three-piece suit and carrying an imitation leather briefcase. Dixie met him at the front door.

Ruby's eyes rolled back in her head when she heard the young man ask for Mrs. Sugar. He took a scarlet bag from his briefcase. Out of the corner of her eyes she saw Dixie lead the young man into the kitchen and close the door. She was back five minutes later, her face drawn and white. In a hoarse croak she said, "He wants to order fifty gross of cookies, assorted, every week, for the school cafeteria at Monmouth College. How many is fifty gross?"

Andrew's eyes popped. "One hell of a lot of cookies, and you have no way to make them."

"I hate your attitude, Andrew. I mean, I really hate it!" Ruby said, sticking her face right up against her husband's. "Please leave so I can tend to business."

"Ruby the screwup. I should have known better than to go along with this cockamamie idea. You damn well better come up with a way to make the payments on these ovens," Andrew snarled.

"I'll remind you of your attitude when it's time to write out your first check. I'm going to deduct. Do you hear me, Andrew? I'm going to deduct for every miserable, negative word you said here this morning. I want you out of here. Now! This is my house and I want you off the property. I'll take a broom to you if you don't move right now!"

Andrew leaned against the wall. "It's not yours yet! You don't get the deed until you get fully caught up with the mortgage and give me my money, and, by the way, when is that going to be? Exactly?"

Ruby picked up the long wooden paddle that was to be used to remove the cookie trays from the oven. She swung it wickedly. "You've pushed me too far, Andrew. Out! Call your lawyer, call mine, but get out of here!"

Andrew's Buick Special roared out of the driveway. He was shaking his fist at Ruby as he barreled down the street.

Inside the sweet-smelling kitchen Ruby found herself gaping at an array of papers spread out on the kitchen table. These papers belonged to the young man. Business papers, probably contracts. He was serious. Well, by God, so was she. She smiled and held out her hand. "I'm Ruby Blue, half of Mrs. Sugar. I'm sure Dixie introduced herself. I hope it's not too much trouble to ask you to explain your offer again."

Kevin Sandler pushed his glasses closer to his eyes. "I represent the food concession for the Monmouth College cafeteria. My sister is matriculating there and she dates a boy from Rutgers. It seems her boyfriend bought a bag of your cookies and shared them with her. She said they were excellent, and now that Mrs. Sinclaire has given me one of each to try, I'd say I agree. We'll pay seventy-five cents a dozen. We'll pick up ourselves. The bags, while nice, aren't really necessary. Since we'll be buying by the gross, you can pack them in baker's boxes, which we'll return, so you'll need two sets. We also supply the food for Rutgers, Princeton, Rensselaer, NJIT, and quite a few of the community colleges. It's just a matter of time before we're under contract for *all* the community colleges."

"Ninety cents," Ruby said briskly.

"Seventy-seven," Kevin said just as briskly.

"Eighty-five."

"Eighty. Don't counter, it's as high as I'm authorized to go."

"Agreed," Ruby said coolly. "However, we can't make delivery until the first of April."

"That's fine. It will take that long to get the paper work under way. This is our agreement. Show it to your attorney. I'll be in touch. You don't have any extra cookies I can take along with me, do you?" he asked, snapping the briefcase closed.

Dixie handed him two bags. He thanked her politely and left as quietly as he'd arrived.

"He said we need business cards," Dixie whispered, "and he gave me the name of a printer. Ruby, what are we going to do?"

"I don't know. I really don't know. I hate to admit this, but I think Andrew's right. I am stupid. How could I have forgotten something as important as a license?"

"Then I'm just as stupid, because I didn't think of it, either." Dixie groaned.

"What are we going to do with all this dough we made last night?"

Ruby looked at the huge stainless steel bowls full of cookie dough. It had taken them hours to mix. "We're not throwing it out, that's for sure. One of us has to stay here and bake and the other one has to go down and get a license they won't let us use. Do you have any extra money? All I have is eight dollars."

"Ruby, you know I don't have any money."

"You keep saying that. Look, I've been robbing from Peter to pay Paul. You're going to have to do the same thing. Look at me, Dixie. There's no place else I can get money. I am tapped out. I can't come up with a dollar extra. It's your turn. I'm sorry, but that's the way it is. Otherwise, we have to pack it in and call it quits."

"What . . . what do you want me to do?"

"You told me you and Hugo have a joint savings account. That means whatever is in that account is half yours. If you want to, you can draw out money; all you have to do is sign a withdrawal slip. I'd hoped it wasn't going to come to this, but I can't carry all the burden. As it is, *I* owe Andrew for the ovens. *I* owe Paul and Grace. *I've* juggled my own bills to pay *our* bills. The money I get from my closing next week is already spent. We have to get a lawyer, too. *I've* covered your part-time salary these past weeks so Hugo won't find out what we're up to."

"What about the quilt? If we have no money and can't make

any until we get the town's okay, where am I going to come up with a quilt? He'll kill me if he finds out," Dixie blubbered.

"The quilt is taken care of. I wrote to Nola's mother and asked her if she'd make one for you. She said she would and promised it for Mother's Day. She agreed to wait for the money."

"Okay, I'll do it!" Dixie said in a shaky voice after a long moment of struggling with her fears. "How much?"

Ruby swayed dizzily. "At least a hundred dollars. We'll find a way to put it back before the bank computes the quarterly interest. If Hugo gets nasty and finds out, tell him the price of materials for quilts has gone up."

Dixie wiped her tears. Ruby blew her nose.

"We survived this hurdle," Ruby said. "I'll stop by and see that lawyer, the one who's on the corner of Main Street. You get the money and meet me at the town hall in half an hour. While I get the license and fill out the papers, you come back here and take some of the dough home and bake there. I'll finish up here with the rest of the dough. Is that okay with you?

"Hugo Sinclaire, if you so much as touch a hair on her head, I will personally kill you," Ruby hissed in her quiet, empty kitchen.

Ruby dropped her head into her hands. She cried, her shoulders shaking uncontrollably. What right did she have to tell Dixie to steal from her husband? What if something happened to her friend? She shouldn't be expected to carry the whole load—workwise and financially. Partners meant a fifty-fifty split in every sense of the word. Business was business. Time was money. "What about friendship and endangering one's life?" She wailed. It was Dixie's decision in the end. Dixie didn't *have* to do it. Sure she did, her conscience pricked. You goaded her. "It's fair," Ruby shouted. Financially, it's fair; morally, it isn't. You know it, Ruby Blue. You know it!

Ruby reached for the phone. She dialed Dixie's number. Her heart pounded as she listened to the ringing phone. Finally, Dixie's breathless voice came over the wire. "Don't do it, Dixie. Don't go to the bank. I'll think of something else. Come back here for the cookie dough. I'm sorry, Dixie. I had no right to put you in a position like that." The relief in her friend's voice was obvious. My God, what kind of person was she turning into? Fall back and regroup.

The something else came to Ruby after she had paced out of the kitchen, into the hall, through the dining room, into the living room, and back to the dining room.

The first used-furniture dealer she called said he would stop by with his truck at four o'clock. "I won't take a penny less than five hundred dollars. If you aren't interested, don't take up my time. This is solid cherrywood and has two hutches and eight chairs, plus two table extensions in perfect condition. It seats twelve comfortably. Bring the money."

It took a long time for Ruby to soothe the sobbing Dixie when she found out what Ruby had done. "You don't need me, Ruby. I'm more of a problem than I'm worth. When we needed my help the most, I didn't come through. I'm so sorry."

"You were willing to do it and that's all that matters. We're friends, I thought you knew that. Later, when we get some cash flow, you can put some back in the business if you feel that strongly."

"But, Ruby, you love that dining room set. I'm so sorry."

"One should never get attached to material objects. Besides, now we'll have a nine-by-twelve room to fill with cookies. Wall to wall." She laughed then because she didn't want to cry.

The rest of the day passed in a blur for Ruby. She had a license to operate Mrs. Sugar's Cookies, but it was temporary, pending council approval. She'd paid a fifty-dollar retainer to the law firm of Spitzer and Spitzer to handle their case at the council meeting, and she had five hundred dollars in her purse from the sale of her dining room set. But the best thing that happened was her realization that friendship was more important than material things, or even the business, when it came down to the bottom line. She felt now as though her friendship with Dixie was carved in granite.

The days until the council meeting were hectic. Ruby tramped the streets with a petition for permission to operate Mrs. Sugar out of her garage. It took her ten days to cover the five-block radius the town required. She had no objectors. While Ruby trudged the streets, Dixie oversaw the sketchy work that was going on in the garage to bring it up to town code. A white tile floor was installed. A fire wall and fire door took two full days of work. Two coats of fresh white paint were added to the new plasterboarded walls. Even the secondhand refrigerator gleamed with a fresh coat of enamel. The effect was so sanitary-looking, it blinded the eye.

Ruby called for an inspection the day after the work was finished.

To Ruby's delight, the health inspector slapped an approved sticker on the wall. "This doesn't mean the town is going to let you run this business. All this sticker means is it's up to code. You have to pass the zoning code before you can turn those ovens on again." He looked at the crisp dimity curtains on the garage window and door. He snorted. "It figures; women think curtains will fix up anything."

Ruby gnashed her teeth together. "Good-bye, Inspector."

"Two more days, Dix, that's all, and we'll be back in business. Mr. Spitzer said he didn't think there would be a problem. His cousin is on the town council."

Joel Spitzer was wrong; there was a problem. The town council voted to allow Mrs. Sugar to operate for ten months at number 7 Ribbonmaker Lane. Their thinking, Spitzer told Ruby the night of the meeting, was that the business would mushroom and bring too much traffic to the street: delivery trucks, drivers making cookie deliveries, and customers who walked in off the street.

"Look at it as a vote of confidence, Mrs. Blue," Spitzer said. "The men on the council are businessmen, and if they feel your business is going to grow, it probably will. Ten months is plenty of time for you to find a suitable location downtown. You're going to need a parking area and a loading dock. You're probably going to need a bigger refrigeration system, more ovens, and shelves. In other words, more room. I consider this a win for you, Mrs. Blue. I hope you do, too. And, my wife, who considers herself one of the better cookie bakers in our family, said your cookies are the best she's ever eaten. Congratulations!"

Ruby walked on air as she relayed the news to a jittery Dixie. "He's right, Dix, it's a win for us and . . . a real plus that those men think we're going to make it. We can look for a new location on weekends. Now we have to start mixing dough for Monmouth College. We have four days till our first delivery. You did find us a driver for our other customers?"

"Two. One who is on call. He's a retired public service man. It's a good way for him to supplement his income. His wife took the job for him, but he agreed. The crossing guard downtown gave me his number, and they're both nice men. They won't let us down."

The following morning the ovens were turned on five minutes after the gas company hooked up the gas—for the second time. The women virtually worked around the clock, taking catnaps every four hours or so until their first order for Monmouth College was completely filled.

Kevin Sandler balked at Ruby's demand for cash when she wouldn't hand over her cookies to his driver. "A check will do nicely, Mr. Sandler. Because I'm a woman, I can't get credit for my supplies, so that means I have to deal on a cash basis. I'm sorry, but that's the way it has to be."

"This is a major problem, Mrs. Blue. I wish you had told me this before we signed our contract."

"Why is that, Mr. Sandler? Were you planning on stiffing me? I pay cash, you pay cash. From here on in, it shouldn't be a problem. The cookie business is not like most businesses. You eat the cookie, it's gone. If you haven't paid by then, it's only human nature not to want to pay."

"Okay. I'll write it in my report, and I'll be out there sometime this afternoon with a check."

"I'm sorry, Mr. Sandler. These cookies don't leave here till I have a check in my hand. Your driver is waiting. What should I tell him?"

"Tell him," Sandler said through tight lips, "a special messenger is on the way with a check. He should be there in thirty minutes."

Ruby smiled. Dixie smiled. The driver munched on cookies.

Mrs. Sugar and her cookies thrived. Three part-time housewives were hired to bake in four-hour shifts. At the end of three months, Ruby and Dixie hired a night crew to bake until the early hours of the morning. Three more drivers were added to the payroll, and still there wasn't enough help or enough ovens to fill the demand for the sweet confections.

In the fifth month they purchased two more commercial ovens and hired more housewives. They now had a list of women waiting to be hired for the night shift. Retirees knocked on the door constantly, asking for jobs as part-time drivers.

By the end of the sixth month Mrs. Sugar was forced to move from the cramped garage into new downtown quarters. Ruby and Dixie no longer actively baked, but they did mix the dough; they didn't want to give away Ruby's grandmother's old country recipes. Their time was suddenly filled with paperwork, visits to Joel Spitzer's offices, scheduling, handling phone calls, and seeing to the distribution of their cookies. Thanks to Kevin Sandler, they now held the exclusive contract for every college and university in the state of New Jersey, although they'd had to reduce their unit price by fifteen cents.

By the time Mrs. Sugar's first anniversary rolled around, the company was operating in the black. They put their first five-dollar bill of real profit in a frame and hung it in Ruby's kitchen over the stove, as a symbol of both their success and the strength of their partnership. All bills were paid and a prestigious accounting firm was hired to handle finances. Joel Spitzer relinquished their account to the even more prestigious firm of Friedman, Farren, and Armenakis, saying he could no longer do them justice, but keep sending the cookies, please.

Both women gasped when the twinkly-eyed Friedman said they should give some thought to expanding and possibly offering franchises at some point. He handed them a list of colleges and universities in the Manhattan area. Ruby was at a loss for words. Dixie smiled happily. "A retainer will be required," Friedman said. "I'd like you to meet my associate, Alan Kaufman. He'll be handling the franchising if you agree."

Ruby studied the urbane Kaufman and made an instant decision. "Okay, but not yet. I want to lock in a certain supermarket chain's account first. I have this friend . . ."

On the first day of May, two weeks after filing her personal income tax return, Dixie, with Ruby's help, filed an amended return, and rented a post office box and a safe deposit box. The keys were kept in a locked drawer in their new offices.

The second major event on the first day of May was the contract the two women signed with a trucking company to move their cookie dough to a Mrs. Sugar at an as yet undisclosed location.

The third was the arrival of heavy-duty mixing machines, which would free Ruby and Dixie from their long night's labor. In a little less than two hours the machines did what it took Ruby and Dixie eight hours to do.

On the eve of their second anniversary Mrs. Sugar moved to

a converted warehouse in Asbury Park, which they rented with
an option to buy. Mrs. Sugar now employed close to a hundred
people, most of them housewives, and ran three full-time shifts.
The twelve-thousand-square-foot building had wall-to-wall
ovens, islands of refrigerators, and six double sinks. Paper products were stored in an adjacent building, which they had also
rented with an option to buy. The refrigerated trucks were now
moving Mrs. Sugar's cookie dough to New York and Pennsylvania.

"We're going out on the town," Ruby said when the two
women returned to her house in Rumson. "We're driving into
New York, and Mrs. Sugar is picking up the tab. We'll wear
those fancy outfits we bought in Bloomingdale's last month
when we were in New York. I called the Four Seasons and made
a reservation this morning."

Dixie's eyes sparkled. "A real New York restaurant! I've
never been to one."

"Neither have I. You use the downstairs shower and I'll use
the one upstairs. Your clothes are all in the front closet."

"I feel like I have two identities. I'd love to go," she said de-
jectedly, "but I have to make Hugo's dinner. Some other time."

"Oh, no, that isn't going to work. You want me to come up
with an excuse or a way out for you. This time, Dix, you're on
your own. But I'm telling you this, I'm going, with or without
you. We've done nothing but work round the clock for two full
years. We are never going to have another second anniversary.
I'm celebrating! This is my night!" Ruby called airily over her
shoulder as she made her way up the steps.

Ruby waited at the top of the steps. She let her breath out in
a loud swoosh when Dixie called, "Okay, okay, I'm going, but
I have to go home and leave a note for Hugo. I'll be back in ten
minutes, or as long as it takes me to come up with a plausible
explanation."

"A suitable explanation would be to tell him to drop dead,"
Ruby muttered under her breath. "Barring death, tell him to take
a hike and never darken your life again." She stopped short. She
was interfering in Dixie's life again, even if in a different way.
She was about to reach for the phone to call Dixie and cancel
the evening, when the phone rang. "How's this sound?" Dixie
chortled. "Hugo, I'm going out to dinner with Ruby. I'm probably going to be very late, since we're going to New York. If I

get back after twelve, I'll sleep over at her place. I'm sorry, but if I don't get back, you'll have to make your own dinner and breakfast."

"It's the truth!" Ruby squalled in delight.

"Exactly. I'm tired of telling lies. I'll be there in ten minutes."

"I was just about to call you and cancel. I don't want to make trouble for you, Dixie."

"Fat chance. You aren't celebrating our second anniversary without me. We're a team."

They were a team with plenty to celebrate, Ruby thought happily as she stepped into the shower. Right now she had more money than she knew what to do with. Seeing an investment counselor was on the top of her priority list. Everyone was happy, even Andrew. Young Andy was ready to go out on his own with a friend and open his own business. She'd promised, with Dixie's approval, to have him design a new building that would be the Mrs. Sugar corporate headquarters.

CHAPTER SEVENTEEN
{{{{{{{{ }}}}}}}}

It took seven long years of working fourteen to sixteen hours a day before Mrs. Sugar's Cookies were sold on virtually every college campus in the United States. The cookie lady, as Mrs. Sugar was called, became a household word by the middle of the sixth year, and franchises were offered to the public at half a million dollars each.

On a bleak, snow-filled day two weeks before Christmas, in their seventh year of business, Ruby opened her front door to greet Marty Friedman, Alan Kaufman, and her investment banker, Silas Ridgely.

"Oh, uh, come in. Gee, it's snowing . . . ah, whatever it is you've come for will have to wait till Dixie gets here. Sit down . . . no, not here, I hate living rooms, in the kitchen. I'll make coffee. There are some cookies on the counter . . . I have to get dressed . . . it's Andrew, isn't it? No, don't tell me . . . someone got sick from the cookies and is suing me. I'll be right back. The . . . ah, the coffee is over there in the can. Six scoops, seven cups of water . . . I'll be right down," she said, racing up the steps.

Damn that Andrew, he must want more. Wasn't he satisfied, living in her condo in Hawaii, having her pay his bills, driving a Mercedes-Benz she was paying for, and accepting his damn two and a half percent? She'd even paid for his outrageous trips to Europe and for the bimbo he was squiring around—although she hadn't known that until after the fact. I'll kill you, Andrew, really kill you if you think you're getting one more penny out of me. I mean, that damn Marine pension of yours, you aren't sharing that with me, are you? Damn right you're not. "Oh, shit!" She dithered.

She wasn't going down those steps until Dixie arrived. God, maybe it wasn't Andrew at all but Hugo. Hugo would . . . Hugo would. Oh, shit!

She could hear voices now. God, she hadn't washed her face yet. "Who cares?" she muttered. She slapped a wet washcloth against her face and dried it. She looked at herself in the mirror. She'd grabbed the first thing she could lay her hands on. A Rutgers sweatshirt with a hole in the sleeve and her well-worn jeans. One foot was covered in a green sock, one in yellow. "Oh, shit," she yelped again as she looked for the mate for either pair. She ended up settling for a pair of plain white socks with a hole in the heel.

Dixie's eyes were the first to meet hers in the kitchen. They held fear. Obviously, she'd been thinking along the same lines Ruby had. She inched her way over to the counter and stood next to her partner. In a raspy voice she demanded, "Which one is it, Hugo or Andrew?"

The men laughed. And laughed. No one said anything.

"It can't be the kids, they're too decent," Dixie said in a twin of Ruby's voice.

The men laughed and laughed.

"Ladies, all the franchises have been sold. As you know, we still have a waiting list. The last of the money arrived yesterday, according to Silas. We've come to offer our congratulations. You are now among the Fortune 500." Marty beamed.

"I closed the last deal personally." Alan grinned. "Well done, ladies!"

Not to be outdone, the austere banker, Silas Ridgely, smirked happily. "Investing your profits at twenty percent interest these past few years helped to boost you over the top. I would like to offer my congratulations, too. As Alan said, 'Well done, ladies!' "

In a daze, Ruby clutched Dixie's arm for support. She licked her dry lips. "My ... my husband stood right here in this kitchen, looked me square in the eye, and said, 'You have ... you have two chances of pulling this off ... slim and none.' "

Silas Ridgely's back straightened. He said prissily, "I'd live with that if I were you, and advise against sending him a quarterly financial report." The attorneys concurred.

Ruby risked a glance at Dixie, who was clutching her arm so tightly, Ruby knew she would have black-and-blue marks.

"More coffee, gentlemen?" Ruby squeaked.

"Thanks, no, Ruby, we have to drive back to the city. We wanted to deliver this news in person. We're going to leave you ladies now since we know you must have a lot to discuss. What can we say but congratulations?"

"That's good enough," Ruby said, her head bobbing like a puppet. Dixie still looked like she was carved from stone. She hadn't moved at all.

The round of handshakes was firm and hearty.

Back in the kitchen, after seeing her guests out, Ruby snapped her fingers under Dixie's nose. "Hey, lady, wake up. I hope you took all that in, because I can't remember half of what they said. What's the matter with you?" she demanded uneasily.

"I have to tell Hugo now. It's still a mystery to me how we've managed to keep my real name out of it for so long. Do you realize he still thinks I'm your bookkeeper? He's been content with my one-hundred-ten-dollar check every Friday. How will I explain that I locked in certificates of deposit at"—her eyes glazed over—"and didn't share it with him."

"Dixie, you knew this was going to happen someday. You said, you told me more than once, that the minute you were solvent you were leaving your marriage. You had your chance to do that, and for whatever reason, you didn't take it. We could have gone round and round over this, but I didn't want to stick my nose in and prod you. Now you have to tell him. There's no way we can keep you out of it any longer. The media loves stuff like this. Two housewives . . . I don't have to tell you the rest." All the joy was gone from her eyes.

"I'm going to go home now, Ruby. I need to be by myself for a while so I can think. I spoiled it, didn't I? I'm sorry, Ruby. This . . . I still can't comprehend . . . don't worry about me, you bask in our success, okay? Will you forgive me?"

"There's nothing to forgive. We're partners, friends forever. You said that, remember? If I can help . . . do you want me with you when you tell him? Can you handle it, Dixie?"

"I hope so," Dixie said, struggling to her feet. "Give me some time. There's nothing really pressing at the office, is there? If I take off a day or so . . ." She let the rest of what she was about to say hang in the still air of the kitchen.

"Take as much time as you need. We own this company. We can take off whenever we want. But don't let any moss grow under your feet. We have to start giving some thought to going worldwide, the way Marty suggested. That means a lot of travel. Imagine, Mrs. Sugar in, say, Greece, England, Paris. Lord!"

"All that money," Dixie said listlessly. Ruby's eyes clouded over as she held Dixie's coat for her.

"Call me, okay?"

Dixie nodded.

Dixie was right, it hadn't been easy keeping her part of the business from Hugo, but like Dixie said, all he was interested in was her check on Friday night. In the early days, when she had been working virtually around the clock, Dixie told him she was getting double time. As the business smoothed out and knowledgeable people were hired, both women were usually able to leave at six o'clock, though Dixie often worked at home at night when Hugo was asleep.

Amended tax returns hid her income. There was a way around everything, Ruby thought. It wasn't her fault that Hugo Sinclaire was a stupid, greedy monster of a man. She hadn't twisted Dixie's arm to deceive her husband. *You aided and abetted her to insure your own success,* a worrisome voice whispered. Her own success, too, Ruby argued. But now what?

"Now," Ruby said, "Dixie stands up to her husband and whatever happens happens."

Suddenly she felt guilty. Her desire to run after Dixie was so strong, she dug her heels into the rug by the kitchen sink. The hell with it. Dixie would have to deal with it. She could stand up for herself.

I should be doing something, Ruby thought. Calling the kids, Grace and Paul, her sisters . . . maybe even her parents. Calvin. Andrew. Yes, Andrew.

Ruby reached for the phone. Andrew's voice sounded alert even though it was the middle of the night in Hawaii. Ruby thought of warm, fragrant breezes wafting through the penthouse apartment. And she could never think about Hawaii without also thinking about St. Andrew's.

"Are you on the balcony, Andrew, staring out at the ocean?" she asked quietly.

"As a matter of fact, I am. Why are you calling in the middle of the night?" he asked suspiciously.

"Because I want half of your military pension," Ruby snapped irritably. She heard her husband's squawk of outrage. Ruby ignored him. "Actually, Andrew, I called to ask you something. Do you remember the day you stood in the kitchen and told me I had two chances of making Mrs. Sugar's Cookies work? Do you remember that, Andrew?" She heard another squawk and ignored it, too. "You said my two chances were slim and none. Slim and none. I want . . . I'm calling you to . . . to thank you. Every time I was down, every time something went wrong, every time I thought I wasn't going to make it, I thought about those two words." Her voice turned reminiscent. "Remember the time we made fifteen thousand cookies, had them ready for delivery to Rutgers and Princeton, and found out the schools were on spring break? You told me if I was dumb enough to screw up like that and not check my dates, then I deserved to go in the hole. You also told me to stand on the street corner and give them away. I did that, Andrew, and you know what? To this day, Rutgers, Princeton and the towns themselves remain our biggest customers. I want to thank you for that, too."

"I don't get it," Andrew barked. "Are you going through the change of life or something? What's with all this . . . this thank-you stuff?"

"This stuff, Andrew, is what kept me from buckling under, from quitting. Today, Mrs. Sugar made the Fortune 500." The complete silence on the other end of the line brought the first smile of the day to Ruby's lips. She was still smiling when she hung up the phone. "I really meant it, Andrew," she murmured, "thank you."

Ruby's next call was to Opal, who picked up on the first ring. She sounded sleepy. It was almost noon. "Hi, Opal, how's it going?"

"Ruby? Lord, why are you calling so early? Is anything wrong? I'm not real up this morning. I have a hangover. Mac and I partied all night."

"No. I just thought I'd call and share some good news. At least it's good for me and Dixie. We made the Fortune 500 today." *Hangover. Partied all night.*

Ruby could hear Opal yawn. "That's great, Ruby. What does it mean?" She yawned again. "I see your cookies all over the place. I bought some one day. They taste just like Bubba's cookies. Mac said they were too sweet, but he ate them. Hey, Ruby, I've been meaning to write you and tell you I met that guy you used to be so hung up on, what's his name . . . the one that's related to Nangi. Mac and I were at the Officers' Club one night, and he was there. He's a general now. I was a little tipsy, so when we were introduced, I didn't place him. It wasn't until the next day that I realized who he was. He kept looking at me that night and saying I reminded him of someone. You, probably. Anything else, Ruby? Hate to cut you short, but I have to shake it. Write me. I love getting letters, and you're the only one who ever writes."

"Okay," Ruby whispered. Her knuckles were as white as the sheet on her bed. *Don't think about what she just said, Ruby. Block it out. You're real good at that. Break the connection and make your next call.*

Nangi's voice sounded far away, as though he were talking from inside a drum. He was shouting. She shouted back her news.

"Ruby, that's wonderful! Congratulations! I would not be averse to selling your cookies in Saipan. The children love them. I bought some when I was in San Francisco last year. If you ever decide to open an Asian division, count me in."

"Are you serious, Nangi?" Ruby shouted.

"Absolutely. I'm not getting any younger, and it would be nice to work for myself for a change. I think Amber would be receptive to the idea."

"Then it's yours. Just today my attorneys suggested we go

worldwide. They mentioned England and France. Asia now . . . Tell you what, let me check out a few things, and I'll make a trip over there. It'll be nice to see you again."

"Ruby, I can't come up with franchise money," Nangi shouted.

"You don't have to. I'll give you a share of the profits and you can run the operation, if we can get it going. I'll call you back later in the week. How's Amber?"

"She's fine, but she isn't here right now. She'll be sorry she missed your call. I know she's going to be delighted when I tell her your good news."

It was time to say good-bye. She had to ask. She wanted to ask.

"Have you heard from Calvin?" she blurted out.

"He's up for his second star, but he said he doesn't think he'll make it. He says he's the Air Force's token minority general. He was here about six months ago. Didn't Amber write you?"

"No!"

"As always, he asked about you. I made sure I told him about your thriving business. He couldn't believe it. He said . . . his wife buys your cookies all the time. He's still at the Pentagon. I took him aside and told him you and Andrew were legally separated, and I suggested that he write to you. He feels . . . he failed you. Actually, the word he used was *betrayed*. If you ever want to see Calvin, Ruby, you will have to make the first overture. I don't think I'm out of line by saying he spoke of getting a divorce. I'm going on too long here. You're going to have an enormous phone bill, Ruby."

"Give my love to Amber. Thank you, Nangi, thank you very much. I'll be in touch.

"Don't think about that, either," she cautioned herself as she dialed Grace Zachary's number at the store. Their conversation was long, wonderful, and uplifting. Ruby felt happy when she hung up the phone.

The next call was to Martha, who was at work. Ruby waited while she was paged. Her daughter's voice crackled over the wire. "Is anything wrong, Mom?" Martha asked anxiously. "Dad's okay, isn't he?"

"Nothing's wrong, Martha. Your dad is fine, I spoke to him half an hour ago."

"You called him in the middle of the night? Mom, how could

you do that? Just because you're estranged doesn't . . . was he mad?"

"Not at all. As a matter of fact, he was sitting on the balcony. I had the impression he had company. We had a very nice conversation. I told him the same thing I'm calling to tell you. Today, Mrs. Sugar made the Fortune 500. What do you think of your mother now?"

Martha's voice sounded flat when she replied, "I think it's great, Mom. How did Dad take it?"

Ruby's shoulders slumped. They shot upward almost immediately. "Very well. We had a civil conversation." She bit down on her tongue. There was so much she wanted to say to Martha concerning her father. Martha was still seeking Andrew's love and approval. Ruby hoped someday he would give his daughter what she needed.

"Dad invited me to Hawaii for Easter. Andy, too. He said he would send the tickets. I'm really looking forward to it," Martha said with a lilt in her voice. "Andy isn't sure yet. I think he thinks you might be upset. He also said that if he went, he'd buy his own ticket." Martha's voice turned flat again. "Andy said the money for the ticket came from you. Indirectly, of course. Andy is so . . . protective of you, Mom. I keep telling him you have to be a barracuda to survive in the business world and you've survived very well."

"Is that how you think of me, Martha, as a barracuda?" Ruby whispered.

"Sort of. But, Mom, that's a compliment. Do you like *shark* better?"

"No," Ruby said curtly.

"You aced out Dad real neat. You got rid of him, paid him off, and now you're on easy street. I think that falls into the fast lane of traffic. Hey, Mom, I'm not saying there's anything wrong with what you've done. This is a man's world, especially for design engineers, as I find out each day I come to work. You gotta do what you gotta do to survive and make it. You made it and I'm proud of you."

"I better let you go, Martha. I don't want to get you in trouble. We'll talk next week, okay?"

"Bye, Mom."

Stung to the quick, Ruby bit down on her lower lip till she tasted her own blood. A barracuda. She hated the word. Don't think about this phone call, either. Get on with it, Ruby. Two down and one to go.

Andy's voice roared through the phone. "Yo, Ma, what's up? You call during the day only when something good is happening. How'ya doing?"

Ruby's spirits lifted the way they always did when she was talking to her son. Nothing ever got Andy down. "I've got news for you that will lift you right out of your shoes," she said. "Sit down!"

"I'm sitting, Ma! Come on, come on."

"Mrs. Sugar made the Fortune 500!"

Andy's whoop of pleasure forced Ruby to rear back and hold the phone away from her ear. "Hey, everybody," she heard her son yell, "my mother and her friend made the Fortune 500! Ma, that's right up there with General Motors! Jeez. I'm taking you out tonight. Get all gussied up. The best restaurant in town. Hey, I'll even shave, and if you don't mind sharing me, I'd like to bring Nancy."

"I can't think of anything I'd like more. You know I adore her."

"Okay," Andy boomed. "We're on. She can quit work early and be here by seven. Then we'll come and pick you up."

Andy always came through, she thought as she said good-bye and hung up. If it weren't for Andrew and Andy, she wouldn't be sitting where she was. She must never lose sight of that. Never.

One last call. How sad she felt that she had to look up her parents' phone number in her address book. Ruby sucked in her breath as the phone started to ring. Her father answered on the fourth ring. "Pop, it's Ruby. I'd like to talk to Mom."

"She's weeding the garden. What do you want, girl?"

Ruby's back stiffened. "I want to talk to Mom. I want to talk to her now. Please call her."

"Call back later, after she's done."

Ruby planted her feet firmly on the kitchen floor. "No, I want to talk to her now. Fetch her. Please."

"You giving me orders, girl?"

"Yes," Ruby said bluntly. The click in her ear didn't surprise her. She waited ten minutes, her eyes on the clock, before she dialed the number a second time. Her father answered.

"Let me put it to you another way, Pop. Either you put Mom

on the phone now or your ass, not Mom's, will be on the street in as long as it takes me to call the police. I mean it, Pop, and I'll do it."

"Worthless, no-good bitch. The television set is broken."

"Ask me if I care, Pop. Get Mom." Ruby waited and waited. She was still waiting fifteen minutes later when she finally heard her mother's voice, all trembly and shaky-sounding. As trembly and shaky as she felt.

Ruby's voice was tear-filled when she spoke to her mother. "Mom, it's Ruby. I ... I'm calling to ... to ... tell ..." She couldn't tell her mother about the Fortune 500; she wouldn't know what it was and it wasn't important right now. "Mom, would you like to ... to come and live with me? Or if you don't think we can live together, how would you like to move to Hawaii without Pop? I have a house in Maui I would like occupied. Amber and Nangi can visit you; they'll only be five hours away. Mac and Opal can fly there anytime. I can visit. You can finally see your grandchildren. Mom, whatever you want, I'll give you. Maui is beautiful. This house is beautiful. It overlooks the Pacific. It's like a big jewel in a setting of flowers. You could garden. I'll get you a housekeeper and you'll never have to do another thing. I'll get you a car and have someone teach you to drive, or better yet, get you a chauffeur and he'll drive you. Mom, are you still there?"

"I'm here, Ruby. That's very generous of you, but your father needs me here. If you really want to do something for me, give us the deed to this house."

Ruby's head jerked upright. It was a minute before she could make her tongue work again. "I can't do that. If it were just you, I'd give it to you in a heartbeat. You know that."

"That's what I want, Ruby."

"No, it isn't. It's what Pop wants. He's making you say that. You don't need to have the deed. I pay all your bills. I haven't asked you to pay me rent in five years. And I've sent you money, lots of money. Having a deed is not important to you, but it is to Pop, and I'm not parting with it. Ask me for anything else, I'll give it. Gladly. But not that house. If you change your mind, call me. It's a forever offer, Mom. Bye."

This was another thing she wasn't going to think about.

Ruby dialed Dixie's number, but there was no answer. She let the phone ring seventeen times before she hung up.

The biggest moment of her life, and here she was with no one to share it. "Oh, yeah, we'll just see about that!" She reached for the phone, dialed the long distance operator, and placed her call. "Person to person, operator, to General Calvin Santos. This is Ruby Blue."

Ruby poured the remains of the coffee into her cup. It looked as black as tar. She gulped at it. It tasted like mud. She finished what was in the cup. Her sinuses cleared immediately.

"Ruby. Ruby, is it really you?" Calvin asked quietly.

"In the flesh, Calvin. Listen, I know this call is a surprise, but I got some good news today, and I've been calling around to share it with someone. Nangi was happy for me and so was my son. That was important to me, but I'm ... I'm all alone here ... my partner can't seem to handle it and she went off.... Oh, Calvin, I just need someone to talk to."

"I'm listening, Ruby," Calvin said gently.

Ruby talked, Calvin listened. Then Calvin talked and Ruby listened. For ninety minutes. And then she promised to come and see him on Friday morning. Calvin.

After the call, Ruby tore through the house in a frenzy. She had nothing suitable to wear. What was appropriate? There was disgust on her face as she ripped through her closet, tossing out one outfit after another. Nothing! Damn! She needed everything from the skin out. What would a CEO wear? Something stylish, something sophisticated. Something feminine. Something gorgeously outrageous. Calvin would notice. He'd always complimented her on her simple wardrobe. He liked crisp, neat attire. She'd give him crisp and neat and soft and feminine.

"It's my turn now. Mine!" She rolled over on the bed and howled like a coon. After all these years the sparks were still there for her. She'd heard them in Calvin's voice, too.

Just three more days. Seventy-two hours and she would see Calvin—if she didn't count the rest of today and the early morning hours of Friday. "Oh, God," she moaned happily. It's finally happening. After twenty-eight long years, she was finally going to see Calvin again.

The Fortune 500 and Calvin. Ruby rolled off the bed. She laughed until she cried.

While Ruby was rolling off the bed, Dixie Sinclaire was limping up and down the boardwalk in Asbury Park. She was numb with cold and her hip was so painful, she was actually dragging her leg. She looked for a bench to sit down.

How angry the ocean looked. And Lord, it was cold, but she didn't want to go home. She was afraid to go home. She wasn't afraid of Hugo's abuse anymore. What she was afraid of had been haunting her for a very long time. Once or twice she'd tried to talk to Ruby about her fear, but something always held her back. She didn't want to destroy their success, and telling Ruby would have been tantamount to the ultimate betrayal in Ruby's eyes. She should have left the moment she knew the good times were here to stay. Instead, she'd banked the money and confided in no one.

She knew exactly what her husband was going to say. She could probably say it for him and save him the effort. God, why hadn't she left? She was certainly solvent, she could have bought a mansion at any point in her life during the past few years. Her old age was taken care of, thanks to Silas Ridgely. If she walked out and filed for divorce, there wasn't a thing he could do. And yet she hadn't done it. She hadn't done anything but coast along and exist. Hugo wasn't the problem. *She* was.

Dixie shrugged deeper into her coat, which wasn't nearly warm enough. Hugo was going to say she'd shortened his life by making him work so hard these past years when he could have retired and taken life a little easier. He'd start off by calling her a cripple, then a liar and a thief. He would throw every little thing in her face that had ever made him unhappy. He would say they could have been eating steak and roast beef instead of casseroles and hamburger. And of course he would say that the money should have been in his name, too. In his eyes, she would be nothing but a cripple and a criminal.

Overhead, a sea gull swooped down on the rocky beach below where she was sitting. His mate joined him to scavenge for food.

Finally, she said the simple truth out loud, as if Ruby were there to listen. "I didn't want to be alone. Hugo gave me something to do, something to worry about. I had to make his meals, wash his clothes, clean his house. A woman is only half a woman without a husband."

But Ruby wasn't half a woman. Ruby was as whole as they came. For three years she'd lived in a house with no furniture. She'd sold off the dining room set first, then the sofa from the living room, and then the television set. Ruby had survived. She hadn't worried about cooking meals, dusting, and doing laundry. And she'd gotten through her breakup with Andrew. If Ruby could do it, why couldn't she? Now it was too late. She couldn't leave Hugo. It wouldn't be right. He was dying. And because of that, she knew she would give him whatever he wanted.

"Oh, Ruby, I'm so sorry. So very sorry."

The gulls swooped upward, their cries shrill against the slapping waves. Dixie sobbed.

It was almost dark, time for her to return home . . . to return somewhere. She really didn't want to go home, so where? To Ruby's, of course. Who else could make sense of what she was going through? Hugo could ruin everything. Everything. No, that wasn't true, she'd already ruined it. She'd allowed things to get to this point, and only she could make them right.

Ruby's house was dark when Dixie arrived. She shouldn't have stopped at the diner for a supper she hadn't touched. She'd had five cups of coffee, and now she felt strung out. She reached down under the mat for the key Ruby kept for emergencies. She let herself into the dark house, heading for the kitchen. Ruby still kept her shopping bags of receipts behind the table. Her briefcase was there, too.

All she needed was a piece of paper and a pen. Ruby's briefcase yielded both. She wrote steadily for a full minute. Satisfied with the wording, Dixie put on her coat and went next door to the Mastersons. She asked them to witness her signature. She headed back to Ruby's and removed the framed five-dollar bill from its frame over the stove. Her eyes were dry when she removed the brittle bill. It was Ruby's money. She'd earned it as of today. Dixie choked on a sob when she laid the bill alongside the note. She'd just sold her shares of Mrs. Sugar to Ruby for five dollars. She would not allow Hugo to ruin Ruby's life. It was all she could think of to do to protect Ruby.

The front door was open to the dark night. She'd just made a decision no one in her right mind would make. Well, she could certainly justify that. She hadn't been in her right mind since the day Hugo crippled her. But maybe she was being hasty. Something, instinct perhaps, told her this wasn't the time. She drew a five-dollar bill from her purse to put into the frame, then returned the frame to its place over the stove. The single sheet of paper and Ruby's five-dollar bill crackled when she folded them into a neat square. She'd hide it under the floor mat in her car. If the Mastersons mentioned it to Ruby, she would have to come up with a suitable story. The elderly couple hadn't read the paper, just signed and dated it.

Dixie looked around Ruby's neat kitchen. Nothing had changed over the years in this house. Ruby had replaced the furniture she'd sold off, but that was the extent of her personal spending. Nothing had changed in her own house, either. Life had become easier, resting on a velvet cushion of money, but neither of them had gone out and bought fancy cars or mink coats. On Silas Ridgely's advice, Ruby had invested heavily in real estate. She had bought two condos and a house in Hawaii, which she rented out. She'd also invested in a ski resort in Vail, Colorado. She had a fortune tied up in stocks and bonds and funds, with a total yield of twenty-four percent. She doubted if Ruby had any idea how rich she really was.

She, on the other hand, had been ultra conservative, putting all her money into certificates of deposit, which Silas rolled over when they came due. She wasn't diversified. She had turned down flat the offer to invest in a Dallas shopping center. She'd also turned down one that was being built in Pennsylvania. Ruby had simply nodded and told Silas to "do it." She'd also jumped in with both feet when the proposal came through to buy into a Mercedes-Benz distributorship. The only time Dixie had ever really felt a twinge of envy was when she turned down an offer to buy two office buildings on Madison Avenue in New York. Ruby had been angry with her that time. "What if Mrs. Sugar goes down the tubes one of these days, Dixie? You have to be diversified." But she wouldn't be budged. She had, however, followed Ruby's advice and taken out a monstrous insurance policy on her husband six years before. Ruby had taken one out on Andrew, too, but with his approval. She'd had to pay through the nose so Hugo wouldn't have to take a physical. Now she felt like a ghoul. Five million dollars was a lot of money. She wondered what she would do with it when Hugo died. And he *was* going to die. Life expectancy with liver cancer was short. If the gods smiled on Hugo, he had a year, the doctor said. If they didn't, less than a year. The news had overwhelmed her. It affected everything she did. She had even decided to postpone hip surgery at the Mayo Clinic, because she felt guilty about getting better when Hugo never would.

Dixie's fingers drummed on Ruby's kitchen table.

She looked at the kitchen clock. It was eight-thirty. She had to go home and talk to Hugo.

{{{{{{{{{{ CHAPTER EIGHTEEN }}}}}}}}}

Ruby was up with the sun the following morning. She fixed and ate an enormous breakfast and, for the first time in her life, left the dishes in the sink. Today she was taking the company limo into New York, where she was going to shop till her feet fell off.

She thought about Dixie. Her friend was so withdrawn these days.

Things just weren't the same anymore, Ruby thought sadly, because Dixie wasn't the same. That made all the difference. She herself had taken the call from the Mayo Clinic and spoken to the orthopedic surgeon who had scheduled Dixie for a hip socket replacement. He'd called because Dixie hadn't shown up for her preliminary tests. Ruby had promised to give Dixie the message, but she'd had one of the office girls write it out and swear not to tell Dixie who had actually taken the call. That was the first she knew that Dixie's deformity could be corrected, and it had hurt that Dixie hadn't confided in her. Neither had Dixie confided in her about Hugo's illness. Ruby had seen Hugo only once in recent weeks, but he was obviously sick. His skin had turned a deep yellow, and he'd lost so much weight, his face looked skeletal. Only once before had she seen anyone with that particular look: an employee who had died of a liver tumor.

Ruby sighed as she pulled up the zipper of her gray flannel skirt. Maybe she would give Dixie a call when she got home tonight. She looked at her reflection in the mirror. For God's sake, I look like a Brownie leader, she thought in disgust. She made an instant pact with herself not to buy a thing that was beige or gray. Color—bold and beautiful. Colors with zip. First chance she got she was trading in her gray Oldsmobile for something

that would turn people's heads. Clearly it was time to move out
of the shadows and into the sunshine.

That night, Ruby returned with an enormous pile of packages
from Bergdorf Goodman, Saks, B. Altman, and Bloomingdale's.
She tried to call Dixie—she'd been missing her all day—but
there was no answer, so all alone, she tore into the bags and
boxes, yanking out the clothing and throwing the bags and boxes
out the door into the hallway. She was panting when her bed
was finally loaded with her purchases. All about her were colorful scarves, designer handbags, soft leather gloves, dresses in every color of the rainbow. Thirteen pairs of shoes were scattered
all over the floor. Boots so soft they felt like velvet were on the
chair. How, she wondered, had she gotten through her life without all these gorgeous things? She pulled out a turquoise wool
dress from the pile and held it against her, twirling round and
round in front of the mirror. It was so perfect, the lines so stunning, she blinked. It was almost as though it were meant for her.
It had been a perfect fit and worth every outrageous cent.

Ruby looked at the label inside the dress. Nq LTD. Ruby's
eyes widened. It couldn't be! Yet, they were such odd initials.
Nq had to be Nola Quantrell.

In a frenzy Ruby pawed through all the clothes she'd purchased. Time and again she'd gone back to the same racks looking for skirts and blouses with the same clean, stark lines. Her
hands were feverish as she flipped back collars, pulled down
zippers to look at the seams where some of the labels were
sewn. All of the garments bore the same label, Nq LTD. Ruby
dialed New York information. Seconds later she scribbled a
number on the pad by the phone. She placed her call, holding
her breath. A nasal-sounding operator much like the one back in
Barstow said, "Nq Limited, how may I help you?"

"I'd like to speak with Nola Quantrell," Ruby blurted out.

"You and half the fashion world," the operator quipped.
"Would you care to leave your name and number?" Ruby's
mind raced. Answering services protected their clients from the
kind of call she was making. And it was after hours. If she said
she was Ruby Blue, the operator would write down her name
and she would get lost in the shuffle. "This is very important,
ma'am," Ruby said briskly. "Please tell Miss Quantrell that Mrs.
Sugar of Mrs. Sugar's Cookies called and needs to speak with

her immediately. Tell her Ruby Blue wants to deliver a dozen to her personally. This is my number, where I can be reached all evening." She rattled off her number in a daze.

"Are you really that cookie lady?" the operator demanded.

"I really am." To tell her she was only half of the famous lady might stall the call. "Nola knows me, so please tell her I'm waiting."

"You better be on the up-and-up," the operator fretted. "She gave strict orders I wasn't to put through any calls. I could get fired. Nq Limited is a big account for my boss."

Damn. "Operator, Mrs. Sugar isn't too shabby, either. If you find yourself out of a job, call me and I'll hire you on the spot. You have my home phone number. Is it a deal?"

The operator giggled. "Okay, Mrs. Sugar. If she's gone for the day, I'll call you back myself. It is late, but she usually stays till nine or so."

"I really appreciate it, thank you."

Mrs. Quantrell hadn't said anything about Nola's business in her yearly Christmas card, but there had been *something* peculiar about that card, now that she thought about it, something that brought a smile to her face. She laughed aloud when a vision of the card materialized behind her closed lids. It had been signed in red crayon with a lot of Xs and Os. It was the first year Mrs. Quantrell hadn't added a personal message. She'd stopped sending thank-you notes years earlier for the weekly batch of cookies that was shipped to the Michigan farmhouse, but she'd always managed to scribble a message of sorts. She should have called Nola's mother more often.

When the phone shrilled to life moments later, Ruby smiled from ear to ear.

"Don't tell me *you're* the famous Mrs. Sugar," Nola trilled. "For God's sake, Ruby, is it really you?"

"It's me all right. Nola, I can't believe . . . yes, I do. I always knew you'd be rich and famous. And today I made you richer. I think I bought one of everything you've made. Your own label. How wonderful for you. Tell me everything, but not until you tell me why you never got in touch with me. How's your son and Alex?"

"Alex and I went kaput right after we got to Europe. I married him only because of Mom and Dad. They didn't want to see me live in sin for the baby's sake. But he's fine. In fact, he's my partner. He handles the selling end. I do the designing. It wasn't easy at first. I was all mixed up. I had to work and leave my son with sitters. Alex wasn't father material. Mom was on my back in a nice kind of way, but she was still on my back. Dad was, well, he was acting like a father. I got a little huffy and thought I knew more than they did. For a long time I didn't stay in touch with them. I worked for Dior for a while, but that was a no-where job. The pay was lousy. Then I met some people who offered to front me and I made it. Can you believe I'm on the stock exchange? NASDAQ."

"Well, I can top that, old friend. On Monday Mrs. Sugar made the Fortune 500." Ruby pretended not to hear the note of envy when Nola congratulated her. "I'm planning on going worldwide. I almost have the Asian market tied up. My God, I'm proud of you, but I won't forgive you for not keeping in touch. Your mother, how is she?"

"Fine, I guess," Nola said airily. "She has a housekeeper now. I made sure of that. She still has the orphans, at least I think she does. She gets a new batch every other year. I got a card signed with a crayon this year. I haven't been back there in, oh, probably five or six years."

"You call, don't you?" She didn't want to hear this, didn't like the way the conversation was going.

"Time gets away from me. Hey, what is this, the third degree? Do you call your folks and go visit them? As I recall, you didn't put yourself out very much. Did you ever pay off that stupid debt?"

"My situation was a lot different, Nola. And, yes, I paid off that stupid debt." Her voice was curious when she asked, "I bet all those orphans have designer clothes now, huh?"

"Well, not exactly. I don't do kids' clothes."

"You send material and stuff like that, don't you?"

"No, I don't. You sound like you're accusing me of not caring about my mother and father and all those pissy rejects they have living with them."

Ruby's heart thudded in her chest. Suddenly it was hard to breathe. "I thought you loved all those little guys. What's happened to you, Nola?"

"I grew up, for God's sake. I don't owe them my life. I send money."

"No, you don't. Last year your mother said she hadn't heard

from you. And I bet you five dollars that if I'd called as Ruby Blue, you wouldn't have bothered to return my call. Mrs. Sugar made a difference, didn't it? It was nice talking to you, Nola. Good-bye." She hung up.

"Another chapter of my life over and at rest," Ruby said sadly as she started to fold the clothing on the bed. Tomorrow she would call Goodwill to come and get it. Not for all the money in the world would she wear Nola Quantrell's designs.

"Grew up, my ass," Ruby snarled as she tossed the pile of clothing into a plastic garment bag.

Ruby cried then, great racking sobs shaking her shoulders. She cried for the wonderful friendship she'd treasured all these years. "It must be me." She sobbed. "I expect too much from people." She cried herself to sleep.

CHAPTER NINETEEN
{{{{{{{{{   }}}}}}}}}

Ruby spent the night before her departure to Washington, D.C., prowling her house on Ribbonmaker Lane. She'd gone to bed after the eleven o'clock news, but sleep eluded her. She had tried calling Dixie several times, but there was still no answer. Twelve o'clock found her in the kitchen making black rum tea and a fried egg sandwich. The tea tasted like dishwater, the sandwich like fried rubber. She tried smearing ketchup over the egg, but it didn't help. She tossed both the tea and sandwich out and opted for a bottle of Coca-Cola. For two hours she smoked, a bad habit she'd developed to help her get through some of her more stressful times. When her soft drink was finished, she popped another bottle. She continued to smoke as she paced the rooms, creating circles in the pile carpet.

Tomorrow, today actually, was a turning point in her life, her meeting with Calvin. Unfortunately, she hadn't been able to book a room at either the Holiday Inn or the Guest Quarters. Frustrated with her inability to secure a room anywhere close to the Pentagon, she'd finally resorted to trading on her company name and booked a room at the Twin Bridges Marriott in the name of Mrs. Sugar.

Shortly before the sun came up, Ruby made a pot of coffee and ate some toast. Her hands trembled so badly, she could hardly hold the cup. The toast tasted as awful as her egg sandwich. Her eyes kept going to the kitchen clock and then to the framed five-dollar bill over the stove. She felt herself frown. It looked askew. In all the years since she'd hung the bill, it had never shifted, not once, mainly because she'd fashioned Silly Putty on the corners of the frame. She reached up to straighten the memento, but the frame refused to right itself. Annoyed, she tugged and yanked it off the wall. She could have sworn that Abraham Lincoln's somber face had been staring back at her all these years. Now she was looking at the Lincoln Memorial. It wasn't possible. Or was it? When was the last time she'd actually looked, really looked, at the bill? Just a few days ago when the New York attorneys were sitting in her kitchen. Silas had commented on it. She wasn't imagining things. An uneasy feeling settled between her shoulder blades. Someone had been in her kitchen, and that someone, whoever it was, had tampered with the five dollars. The Silly Putty was still stuck to two of the corners of the frame. "Damn," she muttered. Well, she couldn't worry about this now. She had to shower and be ready when Anthony arrived to drive her to the airport.

Today was her day, and nothing was going to spoil it. She looked down at her packed bag and smiled. She was going to see Calvin. They were going to sit across from one another and talk and talk. They would stare into each other's eyes and possibly touch hands over the table. Old friends meeting after a long separation. She *wouldn't* allow the conversation to drift to "you should have, I'm sorry I didn't, why did you do what you did." It was all behind them. As far as she was concerned, today was the first day of her new friendship with Calvin. She was older and wiser now. She was sure she could handle it.

Ruby dithered and fretted as she applied her makeup. What would Calvin think of her? How much had she changed? How old did she look? She wasn't a young girl anymore, but Calvin wasn't a young man, either. The word *seasoned* flitted through her mind. Her hand slipped as she applied lipstick to her puckered mouth. She wiped the red streak with a tissue. Her heart beat faster as she tried to imagine the look on Calvin's face when he saw her in just a few hours. He would approve of the neat gray suit with the pearl pin on the lapel. The soft yellow silk blouse with the small black tie at the throat made her look like the CEO she was. The streaks of gray at her temples showed maturity, she told herself, as did the fine wrinkles around her eyes. She'd always had good skin. There wasn't a pimple or blemish to be seen. "Thank God," she muttered. She smelled good, too. She loved the scent of Nocturne, a perfume she'd purchased in St. Croix several years ago when she'd forced herself to take a vacation. It was the same bottle and almost empty now. Later, right before she was due to meet Calvin in the lobby of the hotel, she would dab some more behind her ears so he would have something to remember her by. He'd always said he liked the way she smelled of vanilla. She giggled. Lord, what was the name of that shitty perfume that sold by the gallon? Another memory.

She was ready. Her plane ticket was in her purse. Her best clothes were neatly packed. If Calvin suggested dinner, she had a black dress that was suitable for any occasion, as long as she dressed it up with jewelry or a scarf. She wondered how Calvin would look in his general's uniform.

"In just a few hours you'll know," Ruby told herself.

Nothing to do now but twiddle her thumbs until Anthony arrived, unless she wanted to use the time to dial Dixie again. Her arm reached out for the phone at the same minute the front doorbell rang.

Ruby opened the front door. It was the limousine driver. "I'll just be a minute. I have to make a call."

She dialed Dixie's number. The line was busy. Home at last! She broke the connection and dialed again, and again and again. Who in the world was Dixie talking to so early in the morning? Maybe the phone was off the hook. Or maybe something was wrong. Ruby dialed the operator, her eyes still on the clock. They'd hit rush hour traffic on the turnpike. God, what if she missed the plane? Telling Anthony to drive like a bat out of hell would be like telling a turtle to pick up speed. She swallowed past the lump in her throat. Nothing was more important than Dixie, not even Calvin. She dialed the operator and asked her to check Dixie's line to see if it was out of order. The operator came back on the line and said there was conversation on the wire and the phone was in working order.

I'll call her from Washington, Ruby decided as she slipped into her coat. As soon as she reached the hotel.

Calvin wasn't in the lobby when she arrived at the hotel. She'd asked at the desk if she'd had any calls. The answer had been no. Relieved, Ruby used the bathroom and fixed her makeup. She dabbed with the perfume stopper. She was ready now. All good things come to those who wait, she thought giddily. She was almost out the door when she remembered the call she wanted to make to Dixie. She closed the door, read the instructions on the phone, and called the desk to place the call. Her foot drummed impatiently. Her eye twitched. Her nose itched. Her ears felt red and hot.

"That number is busy, ma'am," the operator said briskly.

"Thank you, I'll try it later."

Now. Now it was time to go out to the lobby and meet Calvin. She was forty-five minutes late. Please let him be there, she said over and over as she walked down the long, carpeted hallway. Her heart stopped when the only person she saw was a bellboy. She told herself Calvin was late, just the way she was late.

With nothing better to do than wait, Ruby headed for the hotel gift store. As she walked around and idly examined the tacky merchandise, she had a clear view of the lobby. She'd just paid for a clear plastic cube filled with coins and was reading the verses on a rack of greeting cards when she noticed in the lobby a tall figure in a dark brown overcoat and Russian fur hat. Calvin? Was this man Calvin? Where was his uniform? She felt disappointed, cheated somehow. If he would just turn, she'd know for sure.

He was turning, so slowly Ruby wanted to scream. His eyes stared past her for a moment and then came back to the rack where she was partially hidden. She stepped forward and raised her hand slightly as their eyes met. She saw him take a deep breath. She did the same. She smiled then, a wide smile of pure delight. His own smile was just as wide, echoing her delight. She moved, he moved. They met in the doorway.

"Hi, I'm Ruby Blue," Ruby said softly.

"I would have known you anywhere, Ruby," Calvin said gently. "I don't think you've changed at all."

Ruby moved, her eyes hooked greedily on his. He seemed nervous and fidgety. She wanted to tell him he'd changed and not for the better. This Calvin was gray, almost bald, and he looked thin, too thin. The smile on his face wasn't in his eyes. He was supposed to be delirious with joy. It was so hard to read Calvin.

They were walking, side by side, down the hall to the coffee shop.

In the red leather booth sitting across from each other under the bright fluorescent lighting that was giving Calvin a ghostly pallor, Ruby felt her heart flutter.

"It's good to see you, Ruby."

How sweet his smile is, Ruby thought. But he's staring at me so intently, almost as though he's trying to memorize my features.

She felt a sudden rush of fear. "I never thought I would see you again. I've thought of you so often, Calvin." She leaned across the table. "Are you okay?"

He laughed, at least Ruby thought the sound escaping his lips was laughter. "I'm all right now. The day you called, I . . . I'd just gotten back to work. I was in the hospital. Do you believe a bleeding ulcer? Me with a bleeding ulcer." His eyes widened as though he himself couldn't believe what he'd just said. "The review board meets in March. I don't think I'll make it. It pays to have a clear health record."

"Do I understand this right?" Ruby asked, feeling a second rush of fear, "You're concerned you won't be promoted because you've been ill? I know you, Calvin. You . . . you probably had this problem before, maybe for a long time and you didn't get treated. Or if you did, you went to a doctor on the outside so it wouldn't show up on your military record. Am I right?" Damn, what kind of reunion was this? She wanted smiles, hand-holding, and yearning looks.

Calvin nodded. "I collapsed in the office one day and was rushed to Walter Reed Hospital. They say I need an operation. But I didn't come here to talk about my health, Ruby. Tell me, how have you been?"

"I'm fine. Well, sort of . . . actually, I am fine. And yes, you do want to talk about your health and the Air Force because you know you can trust me and you have not confided this to anyone. You need to talk. I'll listen, Calvin. Let's get it out of the way. And all that other stuff, too, so we can just be Calvin and Ruby again, even if it's just for a little while, okay?"

Calvin threw back his head and laughed. This time the smile reached his eyes at the same moment he reached across the table to take her hands in his own.

"I don't understand," Ruby said at four-thirty when the shift of waiters changed, "why you didn't get out? The military has given you ulcers, your wife hates the Air Force, your kids want no part of it, and still you stayed in. Was becoming a general that important, Calvin?" Ruby asked gently.

"To me it was. I knew I made a mistake marrying Eve. All I could do was channel my energies into work. It was the only life I had, Ruby."

"And now the military is going to turn on you. You said yourself you won't make major general, that you're their token minority general and that's all they owe you. You must believe it, or you wouldn't have told Nangi the same thing."

"I could be wrong," Calvin said in a faraway voice.

Ruby squeezed his hand. "But you're realistic enough to know you aren't wrong. Get out, Calvin, before they can tell you that you aren't good enough. You can make it in the corporate world. You should do it. But you won't, will you?" Ruby said sadly.

"Probably not. I guess I need to have my nose rubbed in it before I'll understand. I thought, I believed I could go all the way. How'd you get so smart?" he asked playfully.

"From baking cookies. It's kind of a dumb-witted job. You can actually think while you're doing it. I've had a lot of years to do that, Calvin."

Calvin's voice was suddenly shy. "Did you think of me?"

"More than I should have. Especially when things weren't going right. My God, Calvin, I tried so hard. And when that wasn't good enough, I tried harder. Nangi said you were thinking of getting a divorce. Actually, he said you mentioned the possibility. Is that true?"

"I brought it up once when things were really bad. I felt like I couldn't take it another day. Eve . . . converted to Catholicism, and she takes our religion seriously. I suppose that's good. What she didn't take seriously was our marriage. She hated it from the beginning. She hated sex; she hated sharing a bed with me; she hated doing my laundry, and she hated cooking the foods I liked; she particularly hates the military life. Some years ago she said that if I didn't put in for a job at the Pentagon, she'd take the children and leave. You know how the military feels about divorce. She never helped me, not once. All she did was bitch and moan and grumble and then she'd bitch and groan and grumble some more. From morning till night."

Ruby thought she'd never heard such bitterness in a human voice before. "So you endured, but by your own choice." She felt a sudden empathy for the faceless Eve.

"It's been a piss-assed existence. I traveled a lot just to be away. I hate going home at night, especially in the winter. The house is dark and cold and there's no dinner. Eve is always out with her friends, going to some opera or ballet. She has her own life, her friends, and she keeps her money separate. She's a good mother," he finished lamely. "I cook for myself, do my own laundry, and sleep in a rollout bed in part of the basement I converted into an office."

Ruby's eyes grew moist. "How awful for you, Calvin," she whispered. "I wish one of us had had the nerve to call the other, to try and keep our . . . our . . . we could have talked, bolstered the other . . . you know what I'm trying to say."

Calvin pulled his wallet from his pocket. "See this?" he said, pulling out a creased, yellowish piece of paper. He unfolded it carefully. The paper, Ruby thought, looked as though it had been handled a lot. "These are all your different phone numbers over the years. Nangi gave them to me. I just didn't have the guts to call. I wanted to, a hundred times, a thousand times. Sometimes I even placed the call and cut it off before the operator could make a connection. I was too ashamed." Calvin cleared his throat. "One time," he said hoarsely, "I sat outside your house in Pensacola all night. I saw you have an argument with your husband on the carport. At least it sounded like one. You took off, rubber squealing. It was pouring rain. I tried to follow you, but somehow I lost you in traffic. I went back to your house to wait, but you didn't come home that night. I left Pensacola to go back home, and a day later you called from Nangi's house. I never did figure that out," he said ruefully.

Tears trickled down Ruby's cheeks. "That night I left for

Washington. I drove all night and most of the next day. What in the world were you doing in Pensacola?"

"Checking on a flight program. I was there only two days. I had planned to show up at your door and"—he shrugged— "I never got beyond showing up at your door in my thoughts. I didn't know how you would react. How would you have reacted?"

"I don't know. You broke my heart, Calvin. For a while I hated you. It's my turn, want to see something?" Calvin nodded. Ruby showed him the faded snapshot she'd carried for twenty-eight long years. He threw back his head and laughed. Ruby smiled.

"Did I really look like that? Was I ever that young? You were so pretty, Ruby. You're still pretty," he said, flushing.

"Thank you for that, Calvin," Ruby said shyly.

"Listen, I have to go back to the office, but I can come back around six or so. We can have dinner. There's a very nice restaurant here in the hotel. Please say yes."

"Of course I'll say yes. Do you have a curfew?"

"Believe it or not, I do. Eve likes to know where I am. I have no idea why. But this evening is too important for me to worry about Eve. We have a machine at home that takes my calls. The office has to know where I can be reached twenty-four hours a day. It's a piece of mechanical wizardry that I can turn on and then turn off. Eve can't tap into it. We won't be found out," he said, a devilish look in his eye.

"I never gave that a thought, Calvin," Ruby said, slipping out of the booth. "Obviously, you have, though." The thought bothered her.

On the long walk down the hall to the lobby, Ruby wondered what Calvin would do if she gave in to her crazy urge to grab him and kiss him till he fell out of his shoes. Unable to stop herself, she blurted out the question. Calvin stopped in his tracks. "Why don't we save that question for after dinner?"

"Consider it saved." Ruby grinned. "I have a few others I'd like answered, too."

"Aaaah," Calvin said softly. "I just might have the answers for you."

They were in the middle of the lobby now with people milling about. Calvin extended his hand. His face was impassive, revealing nothing of his feelings. Ruby felt foolish standing in the center of the room with what she knew was a stunned, unbelieving look on her face. Her cheeks flaming, she turned on her heel and marched down the hall to her room.

Back in her room, Ruby told herself there was a protocol of sorts Calvin had to follow. He was, after all, in the military, a high-ranking officer, and it wouldn't look good if he'd kissed her on the cheek or even patted her shoulder. There might have been someone in the lobby who recognized him. At dinner tonight she would mention how she felt. It was Calvin's idea for her to come here. Calvin was such a stickler for right and wrong. So was she, for that matter. Damn.

She was annoyed, she realized, when she took a quick shower and changed into her black dress. The meeting had been rather flat. Calvin had problems. Did she want to get involved in them? After all, Calvin was still married. She'd expected too much, she told herself.

Ruby stared into the steamy bathroom mirror. She looked as if she were dressed for a funeral. Maybe dinner *was* going to be a funeral—hers and Calvin's.

Defiantly, Ruby reached for a crimson scarf and looped it through a huge gold and pearl pin. She clipped on matching earrings and added a gold bangle bracelet to her arm. Now she was dressed for an assignation. She was ready. The rest would be up to Calvin.

If he was going to be as late as he usually was, she had time to try Dixie again.

This time Dixie answered. Her voice sounded strangled. Ruby wondered wildly if Hugo had his hands around her neck.

"Dixie! I've been trying to call you for days. I was starting to get worried. Is everything all right?"

"Of course everything is all right," Dixie snapped. "I've been busy, that's all."

"Your voice sounds terrible."

"If this is why you called, you wasted your dime. Now, would you mind if we cut this short? I'm expecting another call."

"I've never heard you like this, not even in the days when it was bad. Something is very wrong. You might as well tell me now. Spit it out."

"Very well. I'm going to have surgery on my hip, and I'll be away for a while. Hugo is going to handle my end of the busi-

ness. I'm signing over my power of attorney to him." Ruby had
to strain to hear the terrible words.

"In a pig's eye you are! That wasn't part of our deal," Ruby
exploded. "I'm glad you're going for the operation, take as
much time as you want. The business can take care of itself.
You don't need anyone to look out for your interests. That's why
we have all those professional people on retainer. Unless, of
course, you don't trust me." Ruby held her breath, waiting for
Dixie's reply. When it came, she wanted to lay down and die.

"Hugo has some ideas; he'd like to make some changes."

"No way, Dixie. Our operation is running as smooth as
silk. Hugo doesn't know diddly-squat about the cookie business.
No. Absolutely not. Ask me anything else, but not this. This is
our business. Why are you doing this, Dixie?" Ruby cried.

"To protect my interests," Dixie replied.

"From whom?" Ruby screamed into the phone.

"Outside interference," Dixie said flatly.

"You're going to have to do better than that. Who? Listen to
me, Dixie, I didn't bust my ass all these years working sixteen
and eighteen hours a day for you to turn on me just when things
peaked. I all but promised Nangi the Asian franchise. The attorneys are working on it. I'll fight you, Dixie. If I wouldn't give
my own husband a say in the business, what makes you think
I'll give your husband a say? If you want to give him a percentage, I'll split that percentage, but I'm not letting him become a
full partner. You think about that, and I'll call you when I get
home."

"I'll get a restraining order. I'll stop our operation. No business conducted until we come to terms."

"You'd really do that to me, Dixie?" Ruby whispered in a dis-
believing voice.

"It's what I want to do."

Ruby wiped her eyes with a tissue. "You do what you have
to do and I'll do what I have to do," she said coldly. "Good-bye,
Dixie."

Ruby's head was in a whirl. She blew her nose. She repaired
her makeup. She dabbed perfume behind her ears. She blew her
nose again and then she flushed the toilet. She wondered why
she always flushed the toilet when she was under stress.

The need to breathe fresh air was so strong, Ruby reached for her coat. If Calvin didn't want to go with her, she'd go alone. Maybe she should be alone right now.

Ruby's eyes raked the lobby for Calvin. She was through the revolving door in a second. She didn't look to the right or the left as she started down the circular driveway. She turned when she heard her name called.

"I'm going for a walk. I need to clear my head. Want to come along?" Ruby said hoarsely.

"What's wrong?" Calvin asked, concern in his voice.

Ruby told him as she walked along, hunched into her coat. "I meant it, Calvin, I'll fight her every step of the way," Ruby said bitterly.

"I don't understand. How . . . why would she do this to you?" He sounded angry.

"How the hell should I know? Why did you do what you did to me? Why did Amber always treat me like a pariah? Why did Nola forget about me? What's wrong with me? It must be my fault, because I'm the one who keeps getting kicked in the teeth. And let's not forget about Andrew. Do I care too much, or don't they care enough? That person on the phone wasn't the Dixie I know. That was some stranger. The Dixie I know . . . knew, would cut out her tongue before she'd say something like that to me. My God, twice in one week. I must be the world's worst judge of character."

"No, you're not. You picked me a long time ago, and look, almost thirty years later, here we are. That has to mean something." Calvin chuckled.

"What? Tell me what that means, Calvin. I need answers not riddles."

"It means there is a reason for everything. We're together, and I guess it's meant to be, unless one of us walks away. I don't know about you, but I'm not walking away. I want to take you to dinner, Ruby. I want to sit across from you and look into your eyes and tell you all the things I should have told you years ago. I want to tell you how many times I've thought about you, how many dreams I've had of you. I want to tell you, over and over, how sorry I am, and I want to hear you tell me you forgive me. I want us to hold hands and smile at one another. I want to laugh with you. I want to be with you."

Ruby stepped into his arms. She let her head fall against his chest. He smelled faintly of aftershave and mint. She closed her eyes wearily, hardly realizing they were standing in the middle of the dark street. She felt as though she belonged there, in the safe haven of Calvin's arms. She pushed Dixie and Nola far back into the recesses of her mind.

"What if someone sees us, Calvin?" Ruby murmured.

"We'll talk about that inside, where it's warm. Are you ready to go back to the hotel?"

She wasn't ready, but she allowed Calvin to lead her.

Inside the restaurant, their coats on the chairs next to them, Ruby leaned across the table, her eyes dark and imploring. "What are we going to do, Calvin?"

"I don't know. What I mean is right this minute I don't know. What I do know this minute is I love you. I never stopped. Eve was . . . Eve is . . . someone who lives in my house like an unwanted guest. I imagine she probably feels the same way about me. I can't lie to you. I won't lie to you. I won't make any decisions where Eve is concerned until I know for certain what the future holds for me. I want this all out in the open. You must understand that as long as I'm in the Air Force, I cannot get divorced. If I get passed over, when I'm tired of licking my wounds, I'll make the decision. That doesn't mean Eve will agree to it."

"What about your children? If you get divorced, will they understand?"

"I don't know. Ted is . . . I think Ted will understand. Steve is totally different. He wants to learn the hardware business. He says he doesn't want to go to college. He's got this van he fixed up and he has a girl. He's a rebel. I know he smokes pot. I think I've been too strict with them. Eve was too lenient. So, to answer your question, I just don't know, and I don't think that's something we have to worry about right now."

"Calvin, are we . . . are we talking about having . . . are we talking about having an affair?" Ruby asked in a whispery voice.

Ruby could see Calvin's Adam's apple bob up and down as he worked his throat muscles. Instead of speaking, he nodded, his eyes dark and twinkling. Ruby felt faint.

"I don't know. How are we going to manage it? Washington isn't exactly around the corner from New Jersey. Hiding out in hotel rooms . . . I don't think I could handle that, Calvin. I'd always be worried your wife or someone you know would show up and knock on the door."

"I thought about that, too. I travel a lot. You could travel if you wanted to. You leave from position A, I leave from position B, and we meet at position C. This way my office will be able to reach me if need be. You'll have your own room, so your family and your office can reach you."

"Where *do* you travel?" Ruby asked. This was all happening so fast.

"Texas, California, the Mojave Desert ... you'll love that. Kansas City, St. Louis. You name it."

"It sounds as if you planned this all out days ago." Ruby smiled wanly.

"I did. The minute I hung up the phone from talking to you. I stayed late and made out a schedule. Want to see it?" He grinned.

"You're fitting me into your schedule?" Ruby's eyebrows shot upward.

"Now, why did I know you were going to take it that way?" Calvin admonished her. "No, I'm not doing that at all. I'd like to see you as much as possible, so I will arrange to take a trip whenever you agree you can get away. What do you think?"

"I think I should see that schedule." Ruby's eyes went to the first name on Calvin's list. "Have you ever been to Kansas City at Christmastime?" she asked curiously.

"I think it's one of the nicest places on earth at that time of year. All you have to do is come up with a time, and I'll arrange the trip."

Ruby's heart fluttered. "I think," she said carefully, "it's a wonderful idea, but I would like us to get reacquainted first. We can call one another and write. I can't run away from the problem I presented to you earlier. And I have several things I have to deal with at home before I can ... well, before I can make a commitment to you. And it *is* a commitment, Calvin. At least for me."

"Logical Ruby. Why is it you always have the right answers? You always seem to know the right thing to say at the right time. Friends first. I understand. God, I'm glad you called me, Ruby. I don't want us to get lost again."

"I don't either, Calvin."

"Then would you be interested in going back to your room and spontaneously hopping in the sack?"

A stifled yelp escaped Ruby's lips. Calvin laughed, a sound of

pure delight. "We're going to do it eventually, aren't we? Look
me in the eye, Ruby, and tell me you haven't been thinking the
same thing." He laughed again, enjoying Ruby's blushing.

Damn him, she *had* been thinking about it. "In my thoughts
I never got beyond this meeting," she lied. "We can't just jump
into this. And for God's sake, Calvin, I wish you'd stop making
this sound like a . . . like a business deal."

"Oh, Ruby, I'm sorry," Calvin said, instantly contrite. "I was
trying for levity. I guess this wasn't such a good idea. You have
other things on your mind right now. I'm just so damn glad to
see you."

"And I spoiled it. It's me who should be sorry, and I am. We
found each other again, that's what important. As my son says,
we'll go with the flow. I'd love to meet you in Kansas City. No
one will know either one of us, and we can do as we please.
Let's write, too, okay? Do you think you could rent a post office
box?"

"Hell yes, that's a great idea, Ruby. This way my aide won't
be opening my mail. You can call me at the office if you want,
but let's give you a name. My secretary is a bit of a busybody."
He thought for a moment. "Paul Farano. I actually know somebody by that name. When you want to call me, say you're his
secretary. How does that sound?"

Ruby found herself giggling. "Devious and sneaky. Why
aren't you wearing your uniform? I was looking forward to seeing you in it."

"Next time, okay? I wear it only a couple of days a week."

"Calvin, about your medical problem. I know it's *your* health,
but going under the knife is serious. I read an article in a health
magazine that said if you drink sauerkraut juice, it will heal
bleeding ulcers. Before you make a decision to be operated on,
why don't you try it? I can send you the article if you want."

"Send it." He grinned. "Although sauerkraut juice sounds
more likely to kill you than cure you."

Ruby propped her elbows on the table. "Who are you going
to believe, Calvin, me or some doctor who went to medical
school for twelve years? Have you seen a specialist outside of
the military?"

"I've been thinking about it. I already have three opinions
from military doctors."

"Drink the juice for a few weeks and then go see the outside specialist," Ruby suggested. Calvin nodded.

Calvin poked at the rice on his plate. "What will I do with my time if I have to get out? I'm not a youngster. Who's going to want to hire me at my age?" The stress and worry were back on his face.

Ruby smiled. "First, you will spend a great deal of time with me. And then you can do all kinds of things. Calvin, you have all of Washington at your disposal. You could lobby, you could do consulting work. You were a pilot. What about Lockheed or Boeing? Or how about running for political office? As a last resort, you could go to work for a fast-food joint."

"Just like that."

"That's pretty much the way it works. You get out and you get a job. What does your wife say?" Ruby asked curiously. She wondered what Eve looked like.

"I really haven't talked to her about it. She hates the air force just the way you hated the marines. She's not a sympathetic person unless it involves the kids, and even then she doesn't dole out a lot of caring."

"What are we going to do tomorrow?" Ruby asked brightly to change the subject.

"Tomorrow?" Calvin asked stupidly. "Tomorrow is Saturday."

"Yes, I know. That means you have all day off, right? So, what are we going to do? I'd like to drive up to Mount Pleasant and perhaps stop and see Rena and Bruno. I lived in their house after I left Kilbourne Place. Why are you looking like that, Calvin? Don't you feel well?" she asked in a panicky voice.

"No, no, I'm fine. It's just that on Saturdays I do certain things. I've established a routine over the years, and if I break that routine or step out of character, Eve will know something is up. She has her routine on Saturday, too. Please, Ruby, try to understand."

"Oh, I do, Calvin," Ruby said in a dangerously cool voice. "Do you think I flew to Washington only to have lunch and dinner with you? I can't remember exactly what you said, but you implied we would spend the weekend together. Obviously, I misunderstood you."

Calvin's lips compressed. "Let's clear this up *right now* before it blows up into something we're both going to regret. I take the blame, I thought . . . and I admit it was wrong, that it

was just for today . . . your visit, I mean. I assumed that you
would want to get back home to your business. I thought we'd
talk, make plans, and go on from there. I'm sorry, Ruby."

"For someone who says he's contemplating a divorce, you
certainly appear overly concerned about what you do and when
you do it. Or was that just talk, Calvin? I don't get it."

"Eve and I maintain civility in our relationship. We go for
weeks without speaking to one another, but we're always home
on the weekends doing what has to be done to make the house
work."

Ruby blinked. She listened to all the words. It was another rejection. Three in one week. Not on your life. She had her coat
and purse in her hand and was halfway out of the dining room
before Calvin comprehended he'd done something to make her
leave. He stared at the twenty-dollar bill she'd thrown on the table.

"For my dinner," she'd said before she flounced out.

He caught up with her just as she rounded the corner to the
corridor leading to her room.

"Ruby, wait."

"Aren't you late? You did say you have a curfew. Isn't your
wife going to send someone looking for you? Go away, Calvin.
I made a mistake coming here. When you get your life together,
call me. I assumed you led your own life and your wife led
hers. I think you want your cake topped with ice cream. But I'm
not your ice cream, Calvin. Good night. It was nice to see you
again."

She slammed the door in Calvin's face.

She had already kicked her shoes off and was on her way to
the bathroom when she heard Calvin softly calling her name.
Then he knocked quietly. She opened the door a crack. He
squinted at her through the links of the chain that prevented him
from entering the room.

"What is it, Calvin?" Ruby asked miserably.

"I just wanted to tell you I'll be by to pick you up for breakfast. Is nine o'clock too early? I'm going to tell Eve I'm taking
an old friend out for the day. I'm going to do a lot of things,
Ruby, make a lot of changes. We can talk about it tomorrow."

Ruby bit down on her lower lip. She'd forced him into making a decision, one *she* could live with. But only if his marriage
was really over and if he was prepared to act on it would she

spend the day with him. She refused to be a party in the breakup of his marriage. Calvin would have to make that decision. "All right, Calvin, I'll have breakfast with you, and if we can agree on certain things, we can spend the day together."

"I'll see you in the morning. Good night, Ruby."

It was ten-thirty when Calvin entered his house through the kitchen. It took him a long time to fit his key into the lock in the dark. Eve never left a light on for him. He cursed under his breath.

He turned on the light and glanced around for the cat. Slinking about somewhere or pissing on the couch. Christ, how he hated the smell. He'd wanted to have it neutered, but Eve had refused. Dishes and crumbs covered the counter. The toaster was still out. He couldn't remember the last time Eve cooked a real meal. Usually, he cleaned up the place, but he wasn't going to do that tonight. He wasn't going to clean the cat's dish, either. He turned out the light.

Calvin walked through the living room, hating the sight of furniture clad in sheets. Cat hairs. The house revolved around Eve's cat. It was curled up on the corner of the sofa. He turned on one of the lamps. The white sheets, as usual, had been sprinkled with yellow spray. He was the one who washed them. No more. He turned off the light and headed for the family room, where Eve was staring at the television, a magazine open in her lap.

"I'm home," he said to hear his own voice more than anything else.

"So am I," Eve said curtly.

Calvin stared at his wife, comparing her to Ruby. It wasn't fair, but he did it anyway. Eve's hair was gray and frizzy. He told himself she'd taken a shower and that's why it was standing at attention in little spiky sections. Her face was lathered with cold cream. Ruby probably did the same thing. Eve wore white cotton gloves. Once he'd asked her why and she said her hands were rough and she was trying to get rid of the brown spots. It wasn't till later that he wondered why her hands would be rough; she didn't do dishes or scrub floors.

Ruby's hands were soft, the nails clipped short and covered with a pale pink polish. She had freckles on her hands, too. Eve popped a handful of peanuts into her mouth. Even from this distance he could see the little salt sprinkles dust the fine hairs over her lips. He thought about telling her the salt was there. She was addicted to eating peanuts and guzzling diet soda. On nights when he couldn't sleep, he could hear her tripping to the bathroom every thirty minutes. Eve didn't sleep any better than he did. Now he wondered why.

She shifted from her position in the recliner, his favorite chair, which she sat in when he wasn't home. They had an unspoken agreement concerning the chair. Whoever got to it first stayed in it for the evening. "Is something bothering you, Calvin?" She sounded as though she didn't care one way or another. She shook the peanut can. It must be empty, Calvin thought. She fished around for crumbs.

"No. I wanted to tell you that I won't be home tomorrow. I'm having breakfast with an old friend who's in town. I'll be out most of the day." Eve shrugged as she shifted her position in the recliner. He stared down at her slipper socks. She would have on wool socks underneath. Eve's feet were always cold. She jerked at the robe she was wearing. Calvin frowned. He could have sworn the robe was pink. Ted and Steve had given it to her one year on her birthday. It wasn't pink now, and it had little balls of fuzz all over it.

Calvin was the first to admit he knew almost nothing about females, but if men could make themselves presentable, why couldn't women? True, it was time for bed, and people tended to get comfortable, but Eve.... Eve didn't seem to care. There was nothing fashionable about his wife; there never had been. He wanted to be kind. She was older than Ruby, older than himself. That had to be the answer.

"Eve, I'd like to talk to you. This is the first time for a long time we're in the house at the same time. We need to talk about a few things."

"Like what?"

"Like I'm probably going to get passed over when the selection board meets. I'll be out of a job. I could resign now and get out in June, when my thirty years are up. What's your feeling?"

Eve shrugged, her eyes still glued to the television. Just as Calvin gave up on the thought that she might express an opinion, she said, "I think you're right. You were passed over once, so there's no reason to think they'll view you any differently this time. You'll have to get a job. I'm certainly not going to work. And your retirement pay won't stretch to meet the bills."

"We might have to move. This is an expensive place to keep up. The kids are gone; we don't need all this room."

"I'm not moving, Calvin. I told you that when we settled here. You dragged me from one end of the country to the other, uprooting the kids every time we got settled. You'll have to find a way to keep up this house. Close off the rooms we don't use, rent out the basement. It's your problem," she said flatly.

The program changed. Eve cranked the handle on the recliner, was out of it in the blink of an eye, changing the channel. She was back in the chair, tugging and yanking at her robe to get comfortable.

Calvin leaned forward. "Let's discuss a divorce, Eve."

Eve turned. "Let's not."

Calvin sighed. "You aren't happy with me; I'm not happy with you. Your parents are dead, so you can't use them as an excuse."

"It was your idea for me to convert to Catholicism. The church forbids divorce." She smirked to show what she thought of his idea.

"I could walk out. Then what would you do?" He had her attention now. An ugly look crossed her face.

"You've been saying that for the past fifteen years, and you haven't done it. You won't do it now, either. Your precious air force frowns on divorce."

"Ah, but you're forgetting, I'm probably going to get out. Then it's just you and me. I don't care anymore, Eve. I'm sick and tired of this empty existence. You don't contribute, financially or emotionally, you never have. You've never tried to make things easy."

"You're supposed to be the man in this house. It's the man's responsibility to provide for his wife and family," Eve said flatly.

"You were never a wife to me," Calvin snapped.

"And you were never a husband," Eve retorted.

Calvin stood. He stared down at his wife. "Did you ever love me? Did you *ever* care, just a little?" He waited for her response, holding his breath.

"No."

"Then why in the goddamn hell did you marry me?" Calvin roared, his voice full of pain and anguish.

Eve laughed. "Because you were the only one who ever asked me. I wanted to get away from my parents and my dizzy sister before I ended up just like her. A woman born and bred in the South is brought up to believe she isn't complete unless she has a husband, a protector. You were a means to an end. You've known this all along. I never made it a secret. Why are we going through it again? All you wanted was a body. You didn't want to be alone. You settled for me; I settled for you."

"I told you, I want a divorce. I'll stay till June, and then I'm going to a lawyer. We'll sell the house; you'll get half and I'll get half. We'll go our separate ways. If you trench in, I'm still leaving. We'll let the lawyers handle things. You can have the cat," Calvin said, marching stiffly from the room.

Eve turned completely around in her chair, spotted a stray peanut on the end table, and popped it into her mouth. Her eyes narrowed.

"There will be no divorce," she muttered as she marched into the kitchen in search of a fresh can of peanuts. "I didn't put up with you all these years to go it alone now when I'm due to go on Medicare. Think again, Calvin."

{{{{{{{{{ CHAPTER TWENTY }}}}}}}}}

The following morning, over a breakfast of ham and eggs, Ruby Blue and Calvin Santos began an affair that was to last five years. They were young again, in one of the most romantic cities of the world, a city where they'd met long ago and fallen in love.

Ruby stared across the table, her eyes starry, at Calvin, who wore an identical expression. They talked steadily until the waiter asked them if they were staying for lunch. They were laughing like two children; Calvin paid the bill and left a generous tip.

Outside in the parking lot, Ruby turned to Calvin. Her voice was serious. "What did we eat, Calvin? I want to remember this breakfast. I'm in such a dither, I feel as if I should take notes."

"Waffles and bacon," Calvin said promptly as he ushered her into the front seat of a VW Beetle which had seen better times. Ruby scribbled down waffles and bacon on the back of her checkbook, certain she'd had pancakes and sausage.

They drove off, whooping and laughing, sillier than teenagers, happier than newlyweds.

They drove all over Washington, to Mount Pleasant, past the house on Kilbourne Place, and down the alley behind the house on Monroe Street to see if the flowered trash cans were still in existence. They weren't. Rena and Bruno now lived in Arlington, Virginia, in a magnificent colonial house. They drove past the zoo. Ruby's eyes grew misty. Calvin cleared his throat huskily.

"Let's go to the park," he said, executing a wicked turn. "I want—"

"What?" Ruby asked softly.

"We had some of our happiest times in the park. We picnicked, we necked. We talked about our future, our plans, and how we'd be together for the rest of our lives. Remember how we talked about growing old together?"

"We are old, Calvin." Ruby giggled. "Yes, let's go to the park. You should have carved our initials in a tree so we could look for it."

"I wish I had," Calvin said softly, reaching for her hand. "I'm going to do it right now!" he said, steering the little car at break-neck speed into a parking space. He was out of the car a second later and opening Ruby's door.

They ran over the frozen ground, laughing and shouting each other's names over and over. Breathless and winded, Ruby collapsed against Calvin. How wonderful it is, she thought, being here with Calvin's arms around me. She knew he was going to kiss her; she wanted him to. She felt the softness of his fingers as he cupped her face in his hands; she heard his strangled sigh—or was it her own—and felt his lips on hers. It was like the first time he'd kissed her, sweet and gentle, until she'd demanded more. She demanded now and he responded the way he had that very first time.

When they parted, Calvin said in a choked burst of laughter, "I'd drag you off to my lair if I had a lair."

"I have a lair," Ruby whispered.

"I know. Jesus, Ruby, I never wanted anything so much in my life."

"What are we going to do about it?" Ruby continued to whisper.

"Not much if we stay here. My balls are almost frozen." Calvin grinned.

Ruby linked her arm in his. "Then, General, what I think we should do is head for my lair and do whatever comes naturally." She was smiling; Calvin was grinning from ear to ear.

Calvin tossed his overcoat onto a chair. Ruby's coat followed. She kicked off her shoes, hardly noticing them flying across the room as Calvin removed his suit jacket. She shed her jewelry; he did the same. She untied her scarf as Calvin jerked at his tie. It was a nice tie, she noticed. His shirt was on the floor as her dress slipped down about her ankles. She reached for his belt buckle as he reached to undo the clasp of her bra.

Wings of fear and apprehension beat in Calvin's chest as he stared at Ruby's breasts. She leaned into him, one hand trying to slide her half slip down over her hips while her other hand continued to loosen his trousers.

"Jesus," Calvin murmured. "Help me, Ruby. Why do you wear so many clothes?"

"So you'll appreciate me more when you finally—" She toppled him onto the bed, her breathing as ragged as his. Her head was spinning. The raw, aching need she felt transferred itself to Calvin as he crushed his body against hers. She felt the strangled sigh build inside him. She drew away and buried her face into the crook of his arm, her hand busy, creating little trails up and down his chest. She listened to his heartbeat, wondering if it would leap out of his chest, the way hers was about to.

Her fingers moved again, stroking the wiry hair on his chest in little circles and then moving, slowly, in a straight, tantalizing line toward his navel. She inched away from the crook of his arm, whispering. "Let me, I want to do this. I want to drive you to the brink and back again until neither of us can stand it. Lie still."

As if he could move. He was dead, halfway to heaven. The excitement he was feeling was unbearable. His eyes rolled back in his head when he felt Ruby's soft hands move downward. He pushed himself into the pillows, against the headboard, waiting for the surge of passion to ease. Instead, it built and he cried out her name—again and again.

And then it began in earnest. He knew he was being driven out of his mind as Ruby used every bit of her body to bring him to that one last excruciating moment. How could a soft tongue, an equally soft breath, be driving him to the point of insanity? He'd never been licked, never been tasted. And then the wonderful, tantalizing ministrations ceased and she was straddling him, staring deeply into his eyes. "Do you want me to do it or do you want to do it?" she asked breathlessly.

He rolled her over and was exploding into oblivion a moment later. He was crushing her, he knew, but he couldn't move. He loved nestling his head between her sweet-smelling breasts. He felt her inch out from under him, her breathing as harsh as his own.

He drew her to him, kissing her damp forehead, her eyes, the tip of her nose. "My God, I love you." He groaned. He stared deeply into her eyes, waiting for her response that he needed to hear. He sighed happily when she whispered the same words. God in heaven, she truly did love him. He wished there were a way to measure love to see which one of them loved the most. He voiced the thought. He felt her smile against his chest.

He allowed her to see his vulnerability then, the words rushing out, his wedding night, the subsequent tries at making love with his wife. His dreams of her. "Shhh, don't cry for me, Ruby. That's past. We're here now. We're together," he whispered, tightening his hold on her.

"I can't help it, Calvin, no one should be able to count the times they made love in thirty years on both hands." She squirmed in his embrace, propping herself on her elbow. He wiped at her tears with a corner of the sheet.

"Smile, Ruby, and please don't pity me."

Ruby smiled. "I have an idea," she purred, "if we try real hard, between now and when I leave tomorrow, I think we might be able to set a new record for you." She nibbled on his ear, her tongue soft and moist as her hands charted, explored, and conquered once again.

They slept, they made love, they showered, and made love again. It was almost dawn when Calvin slid his legs over the side of the bed. He felt like a bull. He pawed at the carpet before he got dressed. He scribbled a note and propped it up next to the phone. He was going home to change his clothes. He'd be back by ten. He'd drive her to the airport at five o'clock. "I love you," he whispered. He leaned over to kiss Ruby on the cheek before he let himself out of the room. He whistled all the way to the car and on the twenty-minute drive home. He was still whistling when he let himself into the kitchen. The same dirty dishes stared up at him. The cat hissed angrily that his dish was empty. He was still whistling softly as he made his way down the steps to his office bedroom. He almost burst into song when he stepped under the needle-sharp spray of the shower.

"That mustache you're trying to grow looks stupid," Eve said when he walked into the kitchen for a cup of coffee.

Ruby liked it; said he looked distinguished. He liked it himself. Another few days and it would be fully grown and ready to be trimmed. Calvin ignored her. He walked away, down to the den and the chair he could commandeer until it was time to leave. He turned on the television. A moment later he realized he had two choices: he could either watch a religious program or cartoons. He was laughing uproariously when Eve walked into the room dressed for church.

"I'm ready, aren't you going?" Eve demanded, brandishing her prayer book under his nose.

"No," Calvin said, watching a cluster of mice attack a big black cat on the screen.

Eve sniffed. How dowdy she looked, Calvin thought. "You should get a new coat," he said generously. "I don't see coats like that anymore." Ah, good, the cartoon mice had the cartoon cat tied to the table leg. "You'll be late if you don't hurry." He wanted her out of the room so he could be alone.

Eve turned on her heel. "Don't forget we're playing bridge with the Olivers at four o'clock."

"Can't today," Calvin said, slapping his thighs when the mice struck a match under the cat's foot. He howled when Eve's cat hissed his displeasure at such goings-on. "I have plans."

"What plans?" Eve shrieked. "We always play bridge on Sunday afternoon. We have to keep up appearances."

"I told you a friend of mine is in town. I'm having breakfast and lunch with that friend and then I'm driving that friend to the airport. End of discussion." Damn, the cat was free and chasing the mice. Calvin finished his coffee and turned off the television.

"Then I can't play, either. Why didn't you tell me this last night? Now I'll have to call and cancel."

"So call and cancel. You always said I was a lousy player. You're a good player, so you should find a good partner. In fact, I think I won't be playing anymore. And I'm not shaving off this mustache," Calvin declared. With Ruby in his life he'd finally found the courage to rail back at Eve. God, how he hated the Sunday afternoon bridge games.

"You can't just go and change everything in our lives whenever you feel like it," Eve shouted.

"Oh? Did you forget that talk we had last night? I meant every word," Calvin said airily.

Both Ruby and Calvin stared at the digital clock with the bright red numbers. Calvin shifted the pillows behind his head. Ruby squirmed to a more comfortable position in the crook of his arm. "We have to get dressed," Calvin said quietly.

"I feel sad," Ruby said, snuggling deeper. "I don't want to go home. There's no one there for me."

"I don't want to go home, either," Calvin muttered as he smoothed Ruby's damp hair back from her brow. She smelled so sweet, so musky, so like himself. "I'll call you tomorrow, and you can tell me when you can get away so we can meet in Kansas City. What's a good time to call?"

"Before you leave the office or on your way home. Six, six-thirty."

"Okay. I'll rent a post office box on my lunch hour. You'll write every day even if we talk on the phone?"

"I promise."

Thirty-five minutes later the green Beetle roared to the curb at Washington's National Airport. "You'll have to run, Ruby, you have only ten minutes. Don't say anything."

She nodded. On the curb, suitcase in hand, she turned, "You forgot to carve our initials in the tree." She grinned.

"A small matter for this general. I'll drive over to the park and do it now with my official Air Force pocket knife."

"It's dark." Ruby laughed.

"I'll use my official Air Force flashlight. The next time you come back, it will look like it's been there for twenty-seven years. Go, now, before one of us does something stupid."

Ruby ran. Calvin drove to Rock Creek Park and kept his promise.

Calvin was so absorbed in this thoughts when he came home he barely noticed that the outside light was on or that his place was set for dinner. A pot of spaghetti, one of his favorites, was on the stove. He discovered Eve sitting on the sofa in the den. "You can have the chair," he said magnanimously. "As a matter of fact, you can have the whole room." It was hard not to smile, not to shout out how happy he was. It was a weekend he would never forget.

He left the room and closed the door behind him. He locked the door to his own room when he went inside. Funny, he thought. In all the years they had been married, this was the first time he had ever locked that door.

CHAPTER TWENTY-ONE
{{{{{{{{{   }}}}}}}}}

Ruby backed her car out of the driveway before she turned on the headlights. Twenty minutes yet till dawn. She was going to bang on Dixie's door until it was opened to her. If she had to break a pane of glass to get into her friend's house through the garage, she would do it. She wasn't going to let one more minute pass until she knew what was going on in Dixie's life. Five days with no word from her meant big trouble. Dixie owed her a satisfactory explanation if nothing else.

The drive was short. Seven minutes according to the watch on her wrist. Now what? she thought as she doused the lights and cut the ignition. Now you get out of the car, walk around to the kitchen door, and you bang hard enough to wake the dead. There was that word again, the word she hated the most in the English language. Dead. Or was it *good-bye*? *You're stalling, Ruby.*

The night-light in Dixie's kitchen cast a yellowish light on the furnishings. For a second she almost didn't see her friend sitting at the breakfast table in the corner. She could tell Dixie was crying by the way her shoulders shook. She felt her eyes widen when she noticed the bottle of whiskey and the short, squat glass near her elbow. Something was wrong. Dixie never drank. She'd never seen her take more than a few sips of anything. Hugo didn't drink at all.

She had second thoughts now. Did she have the right to intrude on her friend? She argued with herself. Friends and family were what life was all about. Whatever was wrong now had something to do with that awful phone call and the words that passed between them. She knew the door wasn't locked. Dixie hardly ever locked the kitchen door. She turned the round brass knob and the door opened without a sound. Ruby tiptoed into the kitchen.

"Hey," she said softly, "I was in the neighborhood and saw your light."

Dixie turned, tears streaming down her cheeks. "I was just thinking about you, Ruby. Oh, Ruby," she wailed.

"Shhh," Ruby said, wrapping Dixie in her arms. "Whatever's wrong, and I know something is wrong, we'll make it right together. Two heads are always better than one. Now, tell me."

"Hugo is dying. He absolutely refused to go to the hospital. He slipped into a coma last night. The doctor was here. He stops by twice a day. I couldn't burden you, Ruby. This was . . . is something I have to deal with. That . . . that phone call . . . it was a horror. Hugo . . . well, what happened was I finally told him I was half of Mrs. Sugar. I came right out and said the words. If he hadn't been so sick, I know he would have killed me right on the spot. He's been getting some kind of bootleg drug from Mexico. He used almost all the money in our joint savings account. I don't care about that. He refused to go to the Navy doctors. The truth is, I think he refused to believe he was as sick as he was. Then, when I told him about all the money I had, he went into a rage. He said he could have gone to Switzerland, to France, to all these places where they have miracle cures. He even said he wanted to go to Lourdes. I was getting all set to call and make arrangements to take him, when you called. Hugo was being . . . Hugo. Then he went into this whole thing with his family and how he was the only one who never measured up. He said . . . Ruby, he said he married me only to spite them."

Ruby's heart thumped in her chest. She wanted to go to wherever Hugo was and drive a stake through his heart for the way he'd treated her friend.

"Do you know what he did then, Ruby? God, you are never going to believe this. He made me sign over a power of attorney. Then he called his family. He . . . he had this absolutely insane conversation with them. He said . . . he told them he was half of Mrs. Sugar. He said it was the same as being a famous heart surgeon, a judge, a big-time lawyer, or owning a famous antique store. Then he told them he was dying. He had this . . . this terrible look on his face. I think it was the first time he . . . admitted to himself that he . . . that he wasn't going to make it. Then he said . . . he . . . he said he was making a will and leaving his half of Mrs. Sugar to his family. My God, Ruby, he really said that! He was going to give away half of what I've worked for all these years."

"Oh, Dixie, how terrible for you. It's all right. Everything is going to be all right. We'll *make* it right. Now, go wash your face. I'm going to cook us some breakfast and then we're going to do whatever has to be done."

A fierce protective surge rushed through Ruby. She cradled Dixie in her arms as if she were her own child. She murmured comforting, soothing words, stroked her hair while she patted her back.

"Oh, Ruby, what would I do without you?" Dixie sobbed. "You're the only good thing that ever happened to me. I'm sorry I upset you. I'm sorry about the phone call. Sorry I put you through even one moment of anxiety. I wish . . . sometimes I wish I were dead."

Ruby stiff-armed her friend. "Do not, I repeat, do not ever let me hear you say that again. Do you hear me, Dixie?" she said harshly.

"I didn't mean it, Ruby. It's just that sometimes I—Look, let's start over. I was going to wash my face and you were going to make breakfast. I'm really hungry. I don't think I ate last night. I can't really remember. Just one egg, though."

"You got it," Ruby said, giving herself a mental shake.

Everything was going to be all right. She was almost sure of it.

* * *

Ruby shifted in the redwood chair she had brought into the sickroom. Dixie was dozing, something they took turns doing. It was so hard to stay awake. She tried to think of other things, tried not to listen to Hugo's labored breathing. Somewhere she'd heard the term *death rattle*, a sound that came from a dying person's mouth right before he took his last breath. She wondered what it would sound like. There was something different about Hugo's breathing now, but she didn't know what. She shifted again, her dress sticking to the plastic seat cushions. She had to go to the bathroom. She wanted a cigarette, too, and a cold drink.

"What's wrong?" Dixie said, jerking to wakefulness.

"Nothing. I have to go to the bathroom and I want something to drink. There's no change. Let's go downstairs to the kitchen, where it isn't so hot."

Dixie nodded. She walked over to the bed, checked the IV, straightened the sheet, which didn't need straightening, and brushed a nonexistent wrinkle from the collar of her husband's pajama top. Satisfied that nothing had changed, she followed Ruby from the room.

It was cooler in the kitchen where a gentle breeze puffed through the window. It occurred to Ruby to wonder why neither she nor Dixie had installed air-conditioning in their houses. Just as they hadn't moved or remodeled. Did they try to keep things the same out of fear? Someday she was going to sit down and do nothing but think about it all.

"We should have gotten a nurse," Ruby said, sipping from the soda bottle. "If you're half as tired as I am . . ." She let the rest of what she was going to say hang in the still air.

"I like this time of day," Dixie said quietly. "The day is over. Either you did well or you know that tomorrow you can do better. The sun is going down, the leaves on the trees rustle. It's a nice sound, trees rustling, don't you think, Ruby?"

Ruby turned on the oven again. She nodded. "Why are you whispering?" she whispered.

"I don't know."

"Hugo is in a coma, he can't hear us," Ruby continued to whisper. "Why *didn't* we get a nurse, Dixie? I'm so tired, I can't remember."

"Because I'm stupid, that's why. I'm all mixed up. When I go

on after Hugo's death, I want to know I, personally, did everything I could to make his last days comfortable. I didn't want
some person who didn't even know him washing my husband.
I signed up for until death do us part, and I'm still on the books.
I guess it's stupid and foolish, because I couldn't have done all
this without you. I'm sorry if I haven't thanked you."

Ruby turned the oven on. She didn't know why. Maybe for
the same reason she always flushed the toilet when things were
bothering her. She turned it off again.

"We should eat something."

"What?"

"Cereal, tomato soup, that's about all you have."

Dixie shook her head. "Not for me." She thought for a moment.

"I don't think Hugo will make it through the night. His
breathing sounds different to me."

"Are you going to call Hugo's family?"

Dixie brushed at a fly circling in front of her. "There's a hole
in the kitchen screen. Isn't it amazing how a fly can find that
tiny little hole and get through? No."

Ruby turned on the oven. "Where's the fly swatter?"

"Under the sink." Dixie turned the oven off.

"Have you given any thought to . . . to . . . you have to get his
clothes ready, call the minister, go to the funeral home, all that
. . . stuff. Pick out a . . . or else they do it . . . die!" She
screamed shrilly as she swatted at the fly, missing by a foot.

Dixie turned the oven on. Ruby turned it off. They looked at
each other helplessly.

"Where are you going to . . . wake him?" She dreaded the
three-day ordeal looming ahead of her.

Dixie opened a second can of soda. She sat back down at the
table. It was a long time before she replied.

"I'm not. I'm gonna nuke him," she said, her eyes wild.

Ruby choked and sputtered, swallowing the smoke she'd been
about to inhale. "What?"

"You know, cremate him. You get the ashes in a cup or something," Dixie said, her lips barely moving as she talked.

"Or something? Then what? What are you going to do with
the . . . cup? Keep it on the mantel? My God, when did you
come up . . . when did you decide this?"

"This morning. If there's a place, a grave, I won't be able to get on with my life. It will never be over if there's a place."

Ruby felt weak. Cremation was something she'd never thought about. "The ashes . . . the cup . . . they'll be there . . . in a place. They have rooms for . . . stuff like that. I saw it in a movie once. A place is a place. How can that be different?"

"It isn't. That's why I'm not going to keep the ashes. I believe in ashes to ashes, dust to dust."

Ruby swayed dizzily before she reached down to turn the oven on. Her tongue refused to work. The bluebottle was in front of her. She reached up, caught it in both hands, walked to the screen door, and let it loose. She pinched off a corner of a paper napkin and stuffed it in the miniscule hole in the screen. She felt Dixie's eyes boring into her back.

"The only way there won't be a place, the only way I can end it is to . . . you know that bridge on the way to Point Pleasant? You can walk across it. I'm going to dump . . . pour the ashes into the water. The current will carry them away. Hugo will be . . . out there somewhere, but there won't be a place where . . ." Her voice turned stubborn, unlike anything Ruby had ever heard.

Ruby worked her tongue around the inside of her mouth, trying to work up enough saliva so she could talk. "That's illegal! My God, kids fish there," she said stupidly. "What if some kid's mother doesn't clean his fish well enough?"

"It's the only way."

"The pine barrens, you could go there and . . . and sprinkle . . . dump, unload . . ."

"The river is the only answer. The river will wash him away."

"But what if someone sees you, what if you get caught? Picture the headlines, Dixie. Picture the headlines!" Ruby said desperately.

"I'll do it at night, when it's dark. No one will ever know but us."

Ruby knew when to give up. "All right, all right, but it's the dumbest, stupidest thing I ever heard of. I'm sorry I brought up the subject."

"I'm not. I needed to say it out loud, to talk it through."

The fly was back. How did it get in? Ruby reached for the fly swatter, taking a wild swing. She lost her balance when Dixie said, "I'd like it if you'd go with me when the time comes. You don't have to go on the bridge with me, just sort of stand at the end and warn me if ... if anyone is coming. Think about it, Ruby, you don't have to give me an answer right now."

Aiding and abetting. She nodded, too rattled to do anything else. No, no, she could never do it. Not even for Dixie.

When the new sun crept over the horizon, both women watched Hugo Sinclaire take his last tortured breath. Ruby cried; she didn't know why. Relief, she thought.

"I want you to go home, Ruby. I need to be alone with Hugo for a little while. It's going to be awful when ... when they take him away. I don't want you to see that. I have calls to make, things to do. Thanks for being here all these weeks. I couldn't have gotten through this without you. I'll call you later, I promise. There are some things you can't help me with, and this is one of them."

Ruby stopped in the bathroom. She flushed the toilet.

Two days later, on August 25, Mrs. Sugar's corporate doors were closed for the first time in the company's history. The reason: a memorial service for Hugo Sinclaire.

Four days after the memorial service, on a sticky, unbearably hot day, Dixie called Ruby. "I picked *it* up today. Tonight is the night. I just have to transfer the ... the contents into something less visible. I thought a mayonnaise jar would be good. What do you think?"

"Why the hell not?" Ruby snapped to cover the horror she felt. "A mayonnaise jar is as good as anything else. What are you going to do with the ... the urn and the jar ... after?" God, oh, God, she wasn't having this conversation.

"Toss it in the first Dumpster I come to on the way home. Do you think it's gonna rain?"

"Will that stop you?" Ruby shrilled, her stomach curling into a knot.

"No. Who's going to drive? You are coming with me, right?"

Ruby's fuddled brain struggled to come up with an answer. If she agreed and Dixie drove, that meant she would have to hold the remains. She shivered. "I'll drive. What time do you want me to pick you up?" She wasn't saying all this, wasn't agreeing, it was a nightmare, and she'd wake up as soon as she hung up the phone.

She wished she'd gone to the office, but she hadn't been back since Hugo's death. Dixie hadn't either. She did call once a day, though, to see if anything out of the ordinary was going on. She always felt disgruntled when she was told everything was under control.

She couldn't stand around there sucking her thumb like some ninny. What she needed to do was something physical that required the use of both arms, both feet, and all of her attention. She opted for the garden and her flower beds.

Pruning shears, trowel, shovel, spade, and watering can in hand, she marched to the yard and the borders that lined the house. She looked at everything with a critical eye and could find no fault with any of the flower beds, rosebushes, or evergreens. Obviously, the money she paid her gardener was not wasted. "Shit," she muttered, dumping her tools on the ground. Damn, she'd come out here to do something and she was damn well going to do it. Within ten minutes she hacked her rosebushes to a stub, whacked six spreading yews to nothing, and decapitated two white birch trees. She tramped through a bed that was supposed to resemble an English flower garden. Obviously, her talents weren't needed in the garden.

Inside the house she decided to scrub the kitchen floor with a brush. She was about to lather the floor, when she remembered the time she'd thrown the bucket of scrub water at Andrew when he returned from Vietnam. "Oh, shit," she cried, scrambling to her feet.

Five minutes later she was in her car, heading for the shopping mall, where she bought forty-one towels, two shower curtains, and a purple plastic wastebasket. When she returned home she dumped the bags in the garbage. The linen closet couldn't hold one towel more, and she had a tub enclosure with no need of shower curtains. She kicked the bag with the purple trash basket.

She was sweating profusely when she popped her first bottle of beer, which she kept for Andy's visit. She stuck two more bottles under her arm along with the bottle opener. She drank until all three bottles were empty, giving her a delightful buzz. She dozed in the shade of the sycamore in the backyard. She woke an hour later to the distant toll of thunder. A streak of lightning slashed across the sky. *Thank God, now maybe it will cool off.* Tomorrow, by God, she was going to call for central air-conditioning.

Ruby left the beer bottles on the grass and stomped into the house, muttering over and over, "I don't want to do this, I can't do this. I don't know why I agreed. I understand, I really understand what Dixie is going through. There just has to be a better way, and I don't know what it is." She shivered violently. "Anything, I'll do anything, but I can't do this."

At eight-thirty Ruby climbed out of her sports car. She was so jittery she could barely make her legs function. She rapped on the screen door, something she never did, and called Dixie's name. For some reason she didn't want to go into Dixie's house; she didn't want to be here in the carport, either. She didn't want to be anywhere near Hugo Sinclaire, and yet she was going to be driving with him in her car. She shuddered, hating the thought. Her heart pounded in her chest.

Dixie appeared at the door, a two-pound sky-blue Mrs. Sugar bag in her hand. Ruby knew what was inside. "For God's sake, couldn't . . . you have put the jar in something else?" Her voice quivered. Her arms felt weak as she held the screen door for Dixie. I'm not doing this. I'm not standing here. This is someone else. This is all a bad dream and I'm going to wake up any second now.

"It's a throwaway bag. I left my briefcase at the office. I haven't done any shopping lately, and didn't have a grocery bag. Hugo's favorite color was blue. It seemed . . . fitting," Dixie said tightly.

"It's going to rain . . . soon," Ruby said, sliding into the driver's seat. She tried not to look at the shiny blue bag in Dixie's lap as she backed the car out of the driveway.

"We should be back here in an hour. I practiced . . . what I did was fill the jar with sugar and counted the minutes . . . seconds really, while I poured it down the drain." Her voice was still tight and strained. Ruby clenched her teeth.

"One more time, Dix: this is not a good idea. You should have rented a boat and . . . you know. God, what if . . . Listen, why don't you put him in the trunk, I'm having a real hard time with this, in case you haven't noticed," Ruby said hoarsely.

"I will not involve you, Ruby. All you're going to do is be the lookout. When you give the signal that traffic is . . . is . . . I'll do it.

"I stapled the bag," Dixie said quietly.

"That's real good, Dixie, now he can't get out. What difference does it make if you stapled the bag or not?" Ruby fretted.

"I thought it would make you feel better. Let's talk about something else. Are you ready to go to Saipan? Have you heard from Calvin? Did you get all new clothes? Are you planning on staying at a hotel or with your sister?"

"I wish I were there right now. I wish I were anywhere but here. Calvin called last night. He says he can hardly wait to make the trip. We're going to meet in San Francisco, spend a few days there, then go on to Hawaii and three days of . . . you know, and then on to Saipan. I'll be staying at a hotel. Calvin will have his own room. Amber pretty much told me not to count on staying with her because she won't be a party to an illicit relationship. One of these days I'm going to belt her right between the eyes," Ruby said in a brittle, shaking voice.

"Are you going to see Andrew?"

"No. Well, maybe. I might call him from the airport when I'm leaving. I'll have to play that one by ear."

Overhead, a low rumble of thunder could be heard. Ruby blinked as the sky temporarily lit up and then darkened. Ruby hated storms because they reminded her of the night she'd given birth to Martha all alone. A second streak of lightning slid across the sky, bathing the road in a bright light. Ruby shivered in the warm car.

"There's absolutely no breeze," Dixie complained. "I've never seen humidity like we've had the past few days. I hope the rain cools things down. I think it will, don't you?" Dixie babbled.

Ruby slowed the car. "We're approaching the bridge. This is your show, Dixie, what do you want me to do?" Ruby whispered. She was insane, out of her mind for coming along. It was harder and harder to breathe.

"Find a side street and park. We'll walk to the bridge. Listen, I've been thinking. If you just stand there at the end of the bridge, you're going to look suspicious. If a patrol car comes along, it will stop sure as anything. They'll want to know why you're standing there. You know what the shore police are like. Maybe you should stay in the car," Dixie said wistfully.

"And get picked up for loitering! Yes, I know what the shore police are like. We look like criminals, I feel like one, and it will show. We can still ... change our minds," Ruby said desperately.

"Does that mean you're coming?" Dixie asked.

"Move," Ruby snapped as she withdrew the key from the ignition. "Let's get this over with." My God, she really was going to ... help.

"I didn't think there would be much traffic at this time of night, especially in the middle of the week," Dixie whimpered.

Cars whooshed past them, one after the other, as the women approached the bridge.

Dixie squared her shoulders. It was right what she was doing. She took first one hesitant step and then another. She looked over her shoulder at Ruby, whose eyes were on the oncoming traffic. In the bright headlights she could see the sheen of perspiration on her friend's face and neck. Ruby was to whistle when there was a break in traffic. Fifteen seconds, that's all it took to pour the sugar down the drain. Fifteen seconds and Hugo was history. She ripped the bag, pricking her fingers on one of the staples. She tried to appear nonchalant as she leaned against the rail, the shiny blue bag in front of her. Cars continued over the bridge, bathing her in the yellow glow of the headlights. She could feel herself start to tremble. In a few minutes she would be free and Hugo would cease to exist. Just a few more minutes. She risked a glance over her shoulder and she saw Ruby walking slowly toward her. Once again she squared her shoulders.

The jar was in her hands when Ruby whistled. She twisted and twisted, but the lid wouldn't yield. She tried again. Ruby's voice thundered in her ears, but she knew it was no more than a whisper. "Do it!"

"I can't get the lid off. It's the jar ring. The suction is too tight!" Dixie wailed.

Ruby was alongside Dixie now, her eyes on the traffic approaching the bridge. "You put a jar ring on there!" she said, incredulous. "For God's sake, why?"

"So he ... so it would be tight and not ... I didn't want it to spill out. Here, you try it," Dixie said, passing the jar to Ruby.

Ruby backed up a step. She didn't mean to reach for the jar, didn't mean to try to unscrew it, but she did. She felt the pressure seal give and at the same moment she thrust the jar back at Dixie. Her eyes on the traffic, she whispered hoarsely, "Start to walk, there's more traffic. We've been standing here too long already."

They were halfway across the bridge before another break in traffic occurred. "There's a car coming quite a way back. Do it *now*," Ruby ordered. "For God's sake, hurry up!" she said, her voice filled with panic.

"I can't," Dixie whimpered. "I want to do it, I need to do it, but I . . ."

"Then let's go home," Ruby said, backing away from the railing.

"I'll do it, I'll do it, just wait a minute."

Ruby turned her eyes on the car approaching the bridge. In her panic she misjudged the distance of the RV, which was pulling a pop-up trailer and using only its running lights. She saw it all in slow motion: Dixie removing the lid, the RV rushing closer and closer and creating a gust of wind. Her jaw dropped open in disbelief as the RV rushed past just as Dixie upended the jar she was holding. She sucked in her breath in a loud gasp, ready to yell "Run," when Hugo Sinclaire's ashes swirled upward in a swoosh of air caused by the RV. The ashes rained over her.

Ruby shrieked, her hands moving in a frenzy as she batted and swatted her face and arms. She lost control completely as she fought with Hugo's remains on her damp, perspiring skin. "Get him off me, damn you, Dixie, get him off me!" she shrilled. "Oh, God, oh, God, he's in my hair, my nose, I swallowed him! Did you hear me? Do something! Help me!" she continued to shriek as she ran off the bridge. Dixie ran behind her, crying and sobbing.

"You said to do it. You were supposed to be watching the cars. You said to do it!" Dixie bleated as she followed her friend off the bridge and down the embankment to the river's edge. She watched in horror as Ruby lost her footing and slid all the way down, rolling over and over, screaming all the while. She followed carefully, but she, too, lost her footing and slid the way Ruby had, all the way to the bottom. She watched as Ruby rolled into the river. For a moment her shrieks were silenced but started again the moment her head appeared above the water. "He's in my eyeballs, I can feel it! Don't come near me. I'll kill you, I swear to God, I'll kill you!" Screaming, she dove into the water again and again.

* * *

A long time later Ruby dragged herself to the water's edge and crabbed her way to dry land. She lay exhausted, her breathing harsh and irregular.

"I didn't force you to come with me," Dixie bleated. "I wanted you to and I did ask you, but I didn't force you. You were supposed to be watching the lights. You said do it and I did it. It's not my fault the RV was using running lights. You were watching," she accused her friend.

"That's right, blame it on me. Your fucking husband is all over me, and now it's my fault. Get away from me! Oh, God, oh, God," she wailed as she turned and rolled back into the water.

The rain came then, torrents of it bucketing downward as streak after streak of lightning whitened the sky.

"Get out of the water!" Dixie screamed. She reached out her hand. Ruby grabbed it and pulled herself upright, hardly aware of the storm raging overhead.

"I want to go home," Ruby blubbered. "I have to go home."

"I'll drive," Dixie said in a shaky voice when they approached the car. She helped Ruby into the passenger seat. Rain pelted her as she walked around to the driver's side of the car. She was crying as hard as Ruby was when she backed the car out of its parking space to make a left turn. It was all her fault. She couldn't do anything right. Hugo had always said she was stupid. Her shoulders were shaking as violently as Ruby's. He was in the car with them. She knew he was still stuck to Ruby. Some of the ash had flown at her, too; she'd felt it. Now she'd never be rid of him. He was all over the damn place. She'd never be able to drive over that bridge again.

Dixie squared her shoulders with effort. She wasn't stupid; she was emotional, dealing with a situation the only way she knew how. Ruby was out of control, and all because of her. She had to take charge and make things right, but she didn't know how. She tried to imagine how she would feel if the situation were reversed and it was Andrew Blue's ashes all over her. The thought nauseated her. There was nothing she could do to make *this* right. Nothing.

"We're home," Dixie said a long time later. "I'll bring the car back in the morning, unless you want me to come in with you. Ruby, I'm sorry. I'd trade places with you if I could. I mean that."

Ruby got out of the car. In a voice that wasn't hers she said,

"Don't ever bring this car back here. Junk it. Give it to the sanitation department, paste a sign on it that says Hugo Sinclaire's remains are in here, but don't you ever bring it back here. Leave me alone. Get away from me," she shrilled as she ran up the driveway and into the garage, where she ripped at her clothes. She was about to kick off her sandals, when she realized she was barefoot.

She ran then, sobbing hysterically, through the kitchen, around the table in the dining room, down the hall to the stairway, where she took the steps two at a time to the bathroom and turned on the water in the shower.

She didn't bother with a bar of soap; instead, she poured shampoo over her entire body and let the scalding water bubble and froth. She rubbed and scrubbed, her eyes burning. She had to clean her eyeballs, soap her ears, clean her nose. She stuck her finger down her throat and forced herself to throw up. She watched the dinner she'd eaten swirl down the drain. She poured more shampoo until the bottle was empty. She cried and sobbed as she bubbled and foamed, her fists pummeling the tiled walls. When the water turned cool, she got out of the shower and reached for a towel. Shivering and shaking, she walked into the bedroom for her robe. She was trembling so badly, she could hardly fit her arms through the sleeves.

Back in the bathroom she dropped to her knees by the toilet and again stuck her finger down her throat. She gagged and retched, but Hugo refused to erupt. Ruby beat at the toilet seat.

She was crazy, she knew it, and she didn't care. She struggled to her feet as she tied the belt of her robe so tight, she squealed in pain.

She ran, she paced, she stormed about the upstairs rooms, going first to Martha's old room, then to Andy's room and back to her own. Looking for what, she didn't know.

Coffee. Coffee was what she needed. She walked jerkily down the stairs, holding on to the railing for support. In the kitchen she measured out the coffee, filled the pot, her eyes glazed and blank.

Ruby leaned against the stove, staring at her puckered fingers. They looked dead, all shriveled and white. Her eyes went to the clock—ten-fifty. The phone rang. Dixie? She reached out a trembling arm to pick up the receiver. She listened to the operator say she had a collect call for a Miss Ruby Blue.

Ruby's jaw tightened. Her eyes narrowed to slits. "Collect!" she shrilled in the voice she'd heard herself use earlier, the voice that wasn't hers. "Collect! No. Now, hang up this phone. I don't want any collect calls, tonight or any other night. Get off my line!" She slammed the phone into the cradle so hard, her ears popped with the sound.

Five minutes later, when the coffee bubbled double time, the phone rang again. She stomped her way to the counter, yanked at the phone, and screamed, "I said no more collect calls!" She was about to rip the telephone wire from the wall when she heard Andrew's crystal-clear voice say, "What the hell are you screaming about?"

Ruby blinked. Andrew. She told him, sobbing and sniffling.

"Jesus!" Andrew said softly.

"Oh, Andrew, what am I going to do? My skin is crawling. I can't . . . oh, God, I can't believe this happened to me. I have to hang up, I need to take another shower, there must be hot water by now."

"Ruby, I can take the next plane out if you need me. I can be there in eleven hours if I can make connections."

He sounds worried, Ruby thought. Worried about me. "That's silly," she said, "what are you going to do, scrub my back? Did you call for a reason?"

"If I did, I can't remember what it is," Andrew grated. "Go take your shower and I'll call you later."

Ruby replaced the phone and stared at the coffeepot. She poured the coffee, drank it in three gulps. It bubbled out of her throat almost immediately. Her hands flat on the countertop, Ruby braced herself to stop the wild shaking that was turning her into a puppet. She drew in her breath, backed away, and reached under the counter for a can of Drano. She poured half the contents down the drain.

In the pantry she looked around wildly for a bottle of shampoo. She had everything but shampoo. When the kids were home she always had five or six extra bottles, but these days she went to the beauty parlor and rarely bought shampoo. Her frantic eyes raked the pantry shelves. She reached for a box of Tide and carried it upstairs with her, the Drano under her arm.

Ruby showered again, this time with Tide. She did more than bubble and froth with the strong detergent. She foamed, she itched, and she burned. Her scalp felt as though it were on fire.

Her eyeballs ached and burned. She danced under the shower, trying to rinse herself off. Foam spilled over the sides of the tub onto the tile floor. When the toilet was completely covered in suds, she climbed from the shower and dried off. She marched down to the bathroom between Andy's room and Martha's and stepped into the bathtub. She continued to suds up. "Oh, God!" she wailed. "Oh, God!" She got out of the tub and into her robe.

She was sitting in the middle of the bathroom floor when she heard the kitchen door open and close. Dixie?

"Yo, Ma, you up there?" Andy called as he rushed up the stairs.

He dropped to his knees and gathered his mother into his arms. "Pop called me, he said to get over here, that you needed me. He told me what happened."

Andy stroked his mother's wet head as he whispered soft words of comfort.

Mother and son were still sitting in the middle of the bathroom floor, asleep, when the sun came up. Ruby awoke and tried to open her eyes, but they were too swollen. Her face felt twice its normal size, and she itched and burned. Andy. Andy was with her. Then she remembered. Trembling violently, she tried to free herself from her son's tight grasp. She had to take a shower.

"Ma?" Andy said groggily. "Wait, let me look at you. Oh, Jesus," he said, his eyes filling. "What the hell . . . what did you do?"

Ruby sighed. She tried to shrug, but she itched too bad. "I took . . . I poured Tide all over me. I had to . . . I tried . . . I have to take a shower."

"I'm calling a doctor for you. Can you stand up?"

"If you help me. It's . . . he's . . . all over me . . . I can't . . . I know he . . . God, I had my mouth open . . . I threw up once and then the coffee came up . . . oh, Andy, what am I going to do?" she cried.

"Sit down here, Ma," Andy ordered. "I'm going to . . . what I'm going to do is see if anything is . . . stuck to you."

"Oh, Andy," Ruby cried, "I don't want you to . . . touch me."

"Listen, Ma, I'm going to do it, so sit still," he said with forced cheerfulness. His thin fingers at first were merely going through the motions, but as he parted the strands of her hair, he realized how serious the situation was. He stared at her red, blistered scalp, trying to see any signs of Hugo Sinclaire. He checked his mother's ears, looked up her nose, and made her open her mouth. He pressed down her tongue with a toothbrush. He leaned back on his haunches. "You're clean, Ma. It's all gone."

"Andyyyy," she whimpered.

"Ma, I have never lied to you."

"Oh, Andyyyy," Ruby continued to wail.

"I'm getting you to bed. Come on, Ma, up and at 'em." Ruby did her best, but she was so weak, she stumbled. She felt herself being picked up and lowered gently onto her son's bed. "You wait here, I'll be right back."

Nick Palomo, M.D., an old friend of Andy's, whistled soundlessly when he ushered Andy from the room. "Go make us some coffee, because I'm going to give your mother a shot. Then I can spend seven and a half minutes with you."

Andy had the cups on the table, the pot of coffee on a hot plate, when his friend walked through the door. "She did a number on herself, I can tell you that. But she'll be okay. I left some ointment on the dresser and a prescription you'll have to have filled. I've given her a shot, so she'll sleep through the day. Best thing for her. Three days, four, and she'll be right as rain. Twenty-five bucks, Blue, and I don't take checks." He cackled. "Were you bullshitting me or did she really . . . you know . . ."

"Yeah, they did it. Look, it's a long story, and hey, you know mothers. They gotta do what they gotta do. Remember that time your mother took the trim off the garage and we fixed it for her so your father wouldn't know? Mothers . . . hell, you can forgive them almost anything."

Nick's round chocolate eyes warmed. "Yeah, I know."

{{{{{{{{{ CHAPTER TWENTY-TWO *}}}}}}}}*

When the ornate clock on the mantel struck twelve, Ruby shifted her weight in the cocoon of blankets to get more comfortable. She felt so alive, so wonderful, so satiated. She was curled in one of the back-to-back sofas so she could bask in the warmth of the fire. A monstrous cherry log was still burning and would continue to burn for another hour or so. It smelled woodsy and fragrant. The television was playing softly, had been for hours. All Ruby was aware of was muted voices. It was sound, nothing more.

Ruby jumped in her cocoon when the cherry log snapped in two, sending a shower of sparks up the chimney and against the fire screen. She wished Calvin were there enjoying the fire with her. Calvin was alone in the daybed he said he slept on, and here she was, curled up on the sofa, just as alone as he was. It didn't seem fair.

The phone on the table at the other end of the sofa rang. "Calvin!" Ruby cried. She almost killed herself getting untangled from the blankets she'd wrapped herself in. She was certain she'd pulled a tendon in her arm when she struggled to reach the ringing phone. "Hello!" she said breathlessly.

"Ruby, is that you? You sound delirious," Andrew said jovially.

"Andrew, it's midnight. What's wrong?"

"Nothing's wrong. I just called to talk. The way you do sometimes. I don't give you the third degree when you call. And no, no woman's husband is gunning for me. That was last week." He laughed at his own joke. Ruby made a face at the phone.

"What do you want to talk about?" Ruby asked carefully. With Andrew, talking could mean any number of things. "I'm glad you called. I planned on calling you this week myself. Also to talk."

"About what?" Andrew asked suspiciously.

"You called me. You go first."

"I flew over to Maui last week and I think I can make a deal with one of the big hotels going up there for a concession to rent out Jet Skis to their guests. It's big money, Ruby. I checked around and the rental on a ski is sixty-five dollars for half an hour. I think I can make deals all down the strip. Three or four other hotels are going up. I have to lock it in now, though, and place the order stateside for the skis. I'll need some trailer hitches, a van or a truck of some kind, and a couple of prefab buildings on the beach. The hotels won't go for anything crappy-looking. What do you think, Ruby?"

"Are you asking for my advice or for money?"

"Both," Andrew answered promptly. "Well?"

"Are you going to be the exclusive ski rental? If so, I'd say it sounds good. I presume you've really thought this through. How much?"

"I can send you the paperwork. I'm not really sure how much yet. I might have to come back to take a course in maintenance so I can train people over here. Usually maintenance contracts boost the price. You think it's a good idea?"

"What about insurance?" the ever-practical Ruby demanded.

"Hotel property, they pick up the tab. I'm just providing the entertainment."

"Then it sounds like a good idea. Does this mean you're actually going to work? And by the way, why aren't you using your own money?"

"Aw, Ruby, you know I live beyond my means."

"I know this is a silly question, but what do I get out of this?"

"You're the beneficiary on my insurance policy. I never took you off," Andrew said smugly.

"Get off it, Andrew, I pay the premiums. I'll tell you what. I was going to sell a block of stock tomorrow. Instead, I'll sign it over to you and you tap it as you need money."

"Thank you, Ruby. And listen, I have something else to say. I'll probably never get up the nerve to say this again, but when you called me and told me your good news about the Fortune 500, I was stunned. I was honest-to-God happy for you. I truly didn't even think what it meant to me until a few days later. When you thanked me for being such a louse, I had to sit back and take a good, long, hard look at myself. And the real reason I called you tonight wasn't the business with the Jet Skis, it was to tell you I'm sorry about everything, the whole ball of wax. I'm sorry you had to go through that Hugo business. I'm splitting the profits on the business with you. I'll be as fair with you as you were with me."

This can't be Andrew, Ruby thought crazily, not this gentle-sounding, fatherly voice she was hearing. "Well, thank you, Andrew." She couldn't think of another thing to say.

"I know that tone." Andrew laughed. "You're wondering what I'm up to and you think I'm out to put one over on you some way, but you're wrong. Of course, only time will prove what I've just said. You're okay, Ruby, and I'll punch anyone in the nose who says differently."

Tears pricked Ruby's eyes. "Thanks, Andrew."

"Hey, that's what ex-husbands are for," he responded huskily.

"We aren't divorced. What's your feeling on that, Andrew?"

"Whatever it's worth to you. Ask me when you're serious. We'll discuss it."

"Good night, Andrew. Stay well," Ruby said softly.

"You, too, Ruby. Regards to the kids."

Ruby added another log to the fire before she wrapped herself back into the colorful afghan. Regards to the kids. Ruby shook her head to clear it. Andrew had been nice. He'd been considerate and he'd warmed her heart when he mentioned the kids. He'd sounded happy, too. These last years they'd had a testy, long distance relationship that had gotten steadily better. The old animosity was gone. They were actually friends these days. She knew in her gut he would make a success of the Jet Ski business simply because it was as cockamamie as her and Dixie's going into the cookie business. She felt good that she could help him.

A long time later, when the logs were glowing embers, Ruby dozed off, a smile on her face. She dreamed of a forest of trees with Calvin running from tree to tree, carving their initials. In her dream she smiled and clapped her hands ecstatically as each tree was finished. She shouted over and over in a loud, clear voice, "I'm happy! I'm happy!" Calvin worked faster, muttering, "Me, too, me, too!"

Monday, a new day, a new week, Ruby thought as she backed into her private parking slot. She sat for a moment, the way she did every morning, and stared at the building her son had designed. She always smiled, and she smiled now.

Mrs. Sugar, Inc., was a long, low, sprawling brick building that resembled a Hansel and Gretel house, complete with flagpole and flag. Andy had had the company flag made to order. It was a heavy sailcloth and carried the company logo—a baker's hat and rolling pin. Andy had even designed the landscaping and oversaw its planting. Tasteful and cozy. She often observed people slow their cars just to stare at it.

The parking area was virtually empty with the exception of the night guard and janitors, who left at seven-thirty just as the office staff arrived. Dixie had been the one to institute an early start to the day, saying people liked to get home early to do things in their homes, especially in the winter, when it got dark early. She'd always been an early riser, so she'd enthusiastically endorsed Dixie's idea.

William, the night guard, held the door for Ruby. "You're early, Mrs. Blue. Your fire is ready and the coffee is on. Cold this morning, isn't it?" he said respectfully, doffing his visored cap.

"Thank you, William. It certainly is cold. Mrs. Sinclaire isn't here, is she?"

"You're the first one," William said, locking the door behind her. It would be another forty minutes before the building was officially open for the day's business.

Ruby walked down the corridor to the wide center door marked PRESIDENT. Her office was on the left, Dixie's on the right, separated by a foot-high brick planter filled with plants.

It was a beautiful office, and Ruby felt more at home there than she did at her own house on Ribbonmaker Lane. She loved the butcher-block desk, the fieldstone fireplace which blazed with warmth, and the huge copper cauldron that held simmering vanilla and cinnamon. It was William's job to add fresh water and spices when he started the fire. It was also his job to fill the cavernous hole in the spring and summer, when the damper was closed, with fresh, colorful flowers.

Solid-oak rocking chairs with red-and-white checkered cushions beckoned invitingly. Soon the matching oak table would hold plates of freshly baked cookies, which were brought in three or four times a day. The bow window at the end of the room was diamond-paned, allowing for the early morning sun. The low, wide window seat held colorful checkered cushions in the same red and white motif that was a Mrs. Sugar theme. All around the office were green plants in shiny copper pots. Dixie watered them every Monday morning. An alcove to the right of the fireplace held a small television, a stereo, and a coffee machine. Underneath was a portable bar and refrigerator.

The oak floor, so shiny that it gave off one's reflection, was partially covered with an original hooked rug Andy had commissioned in the Amish country.

What delighted Ruby more than anything was the specially designed wallpaper Andy had installed. Fat little gnomes wearing bakers' aprons and hats scurried across the walls with trays of cookies and wide, happy smiles on their faces.

Ruby walked around the planter to Dixie's side of the office. She found herself smiling sadly when she looked down at the low wicker basket on the hearth. Inside was a family of calico cats that looked so real, she'd bent down to pick one of them up the first time she'd seen them. Dixie had hooted with laughter. Everyone commented on them at one time or another. This time she did pick up one of the stuffed animals. She brought it close to her face. She imagined she could smell Dixie's cologne. She replaced it in the basket, tweaking its spiky whiskers as she fought her tears.

Ruby walked back to her own side of the room to pour herself a cup of coffee. She sat down in the rocker to enjoy her first cigarette of the day. She wanted to think about all the things Andrew had shared with her the night before.

Ruby's private telephone chimed behind her. She'd deliberately picked a chime instead of a loud, ringing bell; it was more in character with her cozy work area. She reached behind her to pluck the receiver off the old-fashioned wall phone, the kind her grandmother had had in her kitchen long ago.

Fully expecting to hear Andy's or Martha's voice, she put a smile into her own and said, "Hello, we're all out of cookies."

"That's not why I'm calling," Calvin's voice drawled. "Good morning, Ruby. I wanted to start off my day hearing your voice."

"Calvin! How wonderful of you to call. I was thinking about you just a minute ago." She lowered her voice to a whisper. "I dreamed about you all night."

"I hope it was a nice dream."

Ruby laughed. "Ah, *mon général*, it greatly pleased me," Ruby said lazily. "Where are you, Calvin, it sounds noisy."

It was Calvin's turn to laugh. "I'm at the Marriott. My car sort of headed here on its own. I can't talk any longer, Ruby, I have to leave. I'll call you around five-thirty. I love you Ruby," he said softly.

"And I love you. Bye, Calvin."

Her day was off to a wonderful start.

Her secretary, Olga Peters, poked her head in the door to announce her arrival.

"Did you get all the messages I left on your desk, Mrs. B.?"

"I saw them, but I didn't go through them. Is there anything important?"

"A man named Conrad Malas called eight times. He wouldn't tell me what he wanted, just that it was personal. I told him you'd be in the office today, and he asked for an appointment. He's due shortly. I can say you're still out of town if you don't want to see him. I wasn't sure if I should make the appointment or not. He sounded so mysterious. He didn't leave a phone number, but I had the impression he was elderly. His voice kind of quivered."

Ruby hesitated only a moment. For some reason, she had a good feeling when she heard the man's name. "When he arrives, bring him in. Did Dixie call, Olga?"

"She called on Thursday and again on Friday. I told her you'd be back Monday. She sounded like she had a cold. She hasn't come in this morning. She hasn't called in, either."

"She's probably under the weather. I don't think I'll be here all day myself. If I don't get to the grocery store, I'm going to starve," Ruby said lightly. "Close the door when you leave, Olga."

The secretary's eyebrows shot up. Her eyes twinkled. "Yes, ma'am."

Behind her desk, Ruby leafed through the stack of messages. There was nothing urgent. She wished Dixie would come back. It had been two weeks since Hugo died, and Dixie had yet to make an appearance. Ruby felt terrible about all the things she had said to her friend on that awful night with the ashes, but she couldn't help herself at the time. She prayed Dixie would forgive her.

Ruby's fingers drummed on the desk as she watched the hands of the clock creep toward nine. Damn, she'd forgotten to ask Olga what time she'd set for Mr. Malas's appointment.

Ruby managed to fritter away an hour doing absolutely nothing. She felt as if she were waiting for the proverbial other shoe to drop and didn't know why. Maybe it was all the coffee she'd been drinking. She was ready for any kind of diversion, when Olga opened the door just wide enough to inch through.

"Mr. Malas is here, Mrs. Blue."

"Already?"

"He seemed very eager to see you. He's carrying a paper bag, you know, one of those waxy kind you get in a bakery."

"Bring him in," Ruby said, her curiosity piqued.

Conrad Malas looked like a skinny Santa Clause with his curly hair and beard so fine and silky, the color of iridescent pearls. She motioned him to one of the rocking chairs near the fire. She had an impulse to reach out and touch his beard.

"I used to be heavier," Malas said as if reading her mind. His faded blue eyes twinkled. "People constantly mistook me for the famous gentleman. Thank you for seeing me." He accepted a cup of coffee. "My wife would have loved a room like this. She's in a nursing home in Atlantic City. Her mind is gone, though her doctors tell me she has the heart of a twenty-year-old." His puzzled, faraway expression said he didn't understand how that could be.

"I'm sorry, Mr. Malas. Would you like us to send cookies to the nursing home? We can, you know."

"Lord love a duck, no, that's not why I'm here, Mrs. Blue. I came here to offer you something. This," he said, extending the waxy bag to Ruby.

"Brownies?"

"I made them myself at six o'clock this morning. My wife and I operated a bakery in Atlantic City for forty years. I had to put it up for sale in order to keep my wife ... comfortable. It was just a small bakery, what you might call a mom-and-pop operation. My two sons helped us. They have families and needed more money than I could pay them and still take care of my wife. They work for Nabisco now," he said tartly.

Ruby bit into the brownie. Normally, she didn't taste anything a stranger brought to the office. So many people came over the years with cookies and cakes for her and Dixie to sample. All of them wanted their products test-marketed. Ruby had always politely declined with the explanation that Mrs. Sugar was strictly a three-cookie operation. She finished the brownie and looked into the bag for another to give Olga. She wished Dixie were here. "Mr. Malas, this is delicious," Ruby said sincerely.

"Thank you, Mrs. Blue. In the bottom of the bag is a cookie. Please, taste it."

Ruby withdrew a small oatmeal raisin cookie and bit into it. Her eyebrows shot upward in stunned surprise. "This is a Mrs. Sugar cookie!"

"Yes, in a manner of speaking, it is. But in Atlantic City we call them Mr. Malas's Cookies. Both my wife's mother and my own made those cookies for us in the Ukraine when we were little children. When we came here to America, we wanted to be Americans, so we changed our name, but we wanted to retain something of our homeland, so we started up our little bakery."

"My father changed our name, too," Ruby said thoughtfully

as she tried to anticipate where the conversation was going. "What is it you want me to do for you, Mr. Malas?"

"I would like to sell you my brownie recipe. I talked it over with my two sons and they agreed. Mama . . . Mama, she would approve if she was thinking clearly."

"I'm sure she would," Ruby murmured.

Mr. Malas waited, his bright eyes twinkling.

Ruby smiled. "Mr. Malas, how would you like to bake me a batch of these brownies here in our test kitchen?"

"I'd like that very much. By a batch do you mean a dozen or twelve dozen?"

"How about six dozen?"

"Six dozen it is," the old gentleman said as he followed her from the room.

"Well, here it is," Ruby said pointing to a gleaming, white kitchen. She hesitated a moment before she opened the door. "Mr. Malas, why did you come to me?"

"Because I didn't want to go to those other cookie people. They make dry, hard cookies and then put them in cellophane bags. Then they put them in a box. My sons work for Nabisco. I don't think they make brownies. They would put so many preservatives in them they wouldn't be fit to eat. I can't pronounce the ingredients. If I can't pronounce it I don't want to eat it. Other people shouldn't eat it either," he said spiritedly.

"I hear you," Ruby grinned. Damn, he really did look like Santa Claus. She said so. He laughed in delight.

"I'm ready," Mr. Malas said.

"Then I guess you should get started. I have to go back to the office so you'll be alone here. As a matter of fact, I have to come back here to make some phone calls. Tell me," she said, looking over her shoulder, certain she was going to see eight prancing reindeer following her, "are you available to go into New York? When the brownies are done, of course. I'll send you in a company car, and my driver will wait and bring you back here. My attorney will be prepared to make you an offer."

"I understand, and yes, I can make the trip, but I must call the nursing home and tell them I won't be there today. I don't like this kitchen," Mr. Malas said, looking around at the antiseptically white room.

Ruby smiled. "I don't like it, either, but the health codes say it must be sterile. All the supplies are fresh, stocked daily before the start of business. I'll turn on the oven for you. Don't worry about cleaning up, we have people who do that. See that buzzer, just press it when you're ready to come back to my office. I'm sorry, but when the kitchen is in operation, the door locks automatically. Will that be a problem for you, Mr. Malas?"

"Not at all, little lady."

Ruby's heart went out to the old man as he handed her his shabby topcoat. She swallowed past the lump in her throat when she saw the neatly darned elbows of his cardigan. Mrs. Malas must have been a superior needlewoman. The seat of his pants, she noticed, was as shiny as his bulky-toed shoes.

"You must wear this . . . this wraparound coat and hat," Ruby said, pointing to the items in a drawer beside the sink. "Health codes," she muttered. "Mr. Malas, how much do you want for your recipe?"

The old man's shoulders slumped. He threw his hands in the air. Ruby smiled.

"It will be a fair offer, Mr. Malas."

The two attorneys thought her offer was too fair. "A half million dollars," Alan squawked. "You're out of your mind," Marty shouted.

"You're probably right, both of you. Let's just look at it as my good deed for the decade. Listen, I'm not a fool. Mr. Malas's two sons work for Nabisco. If I'd turned him down, he would eventually have gone there. Who knows? They might have offered him more. I don't want to take that chance. I want the recipe. He has it with him. I want all the family members to sign an agreement that they are giving up all rights to the recipe."

"We're lawyers," Alan said testily.

"Right." Ruby laughed. "Sorry, I didn't mean to tell you how to do things. I just bake cookies."

Ruby curled up in the chair near the fire that Olga had replenished while she, Ruby, had walked Conrad Malas to the car. She called the nursing home, left Mr. Malas's message, then dialed Silas Ridgely. She presented the morning's happenings. He squawked louder than both attorneys. "This is not good business sense. First you hand over a small fortune to your husband to buy Jet Skis, and now this. You aren't even sure you will ever use this recipe. I really don't see the point. And before you can ask, I'm booked on a six o'clock flight out of Kennedy. I've already called your husband, who has promised to meet me at the airport. He said he liked the way I do things and that my personal touch won't go unnoticed, whatever that means. Ruby, this is not a good financial move for you," he said sternly.

"Only time will tell. Listen, I want you to apprise Mr. Malas of the tax laws. Make sure he understands, Silas, that if he takes all the money at one time, he will be paying out a great deal to the government. Give him a payment schedule of some kind out of an escrow account in his name. Make it all clear to him, Silas. Oh, one more thing: think of me curled up here by the fire when you step off that plane in Hawaii and some pretty girl throws a lei around your neck. Bye, Silas."

Ruby poured still another cup of coffee even though her hands were shaking from the six cups she'd consumed earlier. Thank God, the pot was finished. Dixie should have been here for this. Where was she?

Every nerve in Ruby's body was twitching when she picked up the phone to dial the Sinclaire house. She let the phone ring twenty times before she hung up. Where could Dixie be? Then a thought struck her. Maybe Dixie wasn't at home recuperating after all. She called the travel agent the company used for corporate travel. She identified herself and said, "I'm calling to see if Mrs. Sinclaire picked up her ticket. It seems the secretary forgot."

"Oh, yes, Mrs. Blue, Mrs. Sinclaire picked it up Friday afternoon. She was booked for an early flight this morning. I think it was for seven A.M. I can check if you'd like."

"No, that's not necessary, as long as she picked it up. What I need to know is, is it an open-ended ticket?"

"Yes, it was. Direct to Rochester, Minnesota, and the return was open. Is there a problem, Mrs. Blue?"

Ruby laughed ruefully. Rochester, home of the Mayo Clinic. "It looks like I may have to join her. I'll call for my reservation as soon as my plans are firm. Thank you, Joan."

"My pleasure, Mrs. Blue."

Dixie was finally going to get her operation. Why else would she be going to Minnesota? They'd discussed it for hours while they watched over Hugo. Still, it would have been nice if Dixie had told her she was going through with it now. Ruby felt a lump settle in her throat. She hoped it was a success. Dixie would do what was right for Dixie. Ruby wouldn't call her. That would only upset her. Ruby dozed, her half-sleep filled with

Calvin. An hour or so more and he would call. Then she would go home and have a solitary dinner, just the way Calvin would do. It wasn't fair. They should be together.

Ruby was jarred from her fragile sleep by a knock on her door. She felt groggy when she opened it to Conrad Malas, who was beaming from ear to ear.

"What can I say?" The old man fretted.

"Nothing, Mr. Malas. I only bought what someone else would have bought from you. I believe Nabisco would have given you the same amount."

Malas shook his head. "They are too big, too impersonal. They would have packaged it in a dry old box, filled the recipe with preservatives and things I can't pronounce. It wouldn't be the same. My Inga would like you, Mrs. Blue. She would understand all this. My Inga was always better at the business than I was. I just know how to bake."

Ruby pretended not to see the faded eyes fill with tears.

"The lawyers explained everything to you?"

"Oh, yes, and other man, too. The lawyer said if you ever decide to market the brownies, I would get one and a half percent. I told them that wasn't necessary, but they said it was. They said it might never happen, but if it did, and Inga and I are gone, my two sons will receive the money."

"That's right, Mr. Malas. It's fair."

"More than fair. Tomorrow I will tell this to my Inga, and maybe . . . there will be a little spark, a glimmer that she understands. Sometimes that happens."

"I hope so. It's snowing again, are you sure you want to go all the way to Atlantic City? The roads aren't good at this time of the day."

"The nice man who drove me to the city had two of your people put the chains on my tires. I'll be just fine. Thank you for everything," Malas said formally.

"Come along, Mr. Malas. I'll walk you to the door."

When Ruby returned to the apartment, the receptionist buzzed to say a Paul Farano had called.

"What did he want? Did he leave a message?" Then she remembered Paul Farano was Calvin's alias. "Did he say he would call back?"

"No, Mrs. Blue, he didn't."

"Did he ask me to return his call?"

"No, Mrs. Blue, he didn't. I'll be leaving now myself, unless you want me to stay longer."

"Good night, Maria."

"Good night, Mrs. Blue."

Ruby felt her spirits sag. There would be no call from Calvin now unless he called her at home, which she thought unlikely. She brightened when she remembered her promise to write. That's what she would do this evening after dinner. She'd build a fire, curl up on the sofa, and write a long letter to Calvin. Her spirits lifted almost immediately. Outside, with the snow falling, Ruby realized she was more than content. She was almost happy.

After dinner, Ruby showered and got comfortable for the evening. Then she walked back to the kitchen to call the Mayo Clinic. She couldn't bear not knowing how Dixie was. She said she was Dixie's sister and wanted an update on her sister's condition.

The young voice on the other end of the phone informed her that Mrs. Sinclaire had gone through preliminary testing. Tomorrow the doctors would decide if they would operate on Wednesday. "Would you care to leave a message for your sister?" the young voice asked.

"No, no message. My sister wants to go through this alone, so we all promised not to bother her with calls."

"Some patients are like that," the young voice said cheerfully. "If you want to call back tomorrow, ask for me, Dawn Baker, and I'll be glad to give you an update."

"Thank you, Miss Baker. I'll do that."

"I have the early shift."

Ruby didn't know if she felt better or worse after the call. The blank paper stared up at her. How was she going to write a letter to Calvin when Dixie was on her mind like this? Dixie was about to go through a serious operation. Somebody should be there, somebody who cared. But maybe Calvin would know what to do. Maybe that's what she should write to him about.

Ruby's pen literally flew over the lined paper. Writing about Dixie was easy. Occasionally a tear dropped, puckering the yellow paper. She didn't care. Calvin would understand.

At nine o'clock, when she had sealed the letter in an envelope, the phone rang. An operator told her she had a person-to-person collect call from Paul Farano. Ruby blinked. *Collect.*

Person to person. She felt a surge of something she couldn't identify. She accepted the call as she sent the blank envelope sailing across the coffee table.

Calvin's voice was hushed and whispery as he identified himself. "I'm sorry to call collect, but I wanted to talk to you and there's no way I can get out at this time of night without Eve getting suspicious. As it is, she's been looking at me strangely all evening. I must be giving off something. I'll give you the money for the call when I see you."

"I thought you said you didn't care about Eve, Calvin. What difference does it make if you make long distance calls or not? She doesn't know who I am. You really didn't have to make the call person to person, either. No one is here but me."

"Listen, Ruby," he whispered, "I thought we talked this through. You know I can't put these last months in jeopardy. For now, this is the best I can do." His whispering made him hard to understand.

"You're going to have to talk louder, Calvin, I can't hear you," Ruby complained.

"If I talk louder, Eve will hear me. Turn off your television set or turn the volume down," Calvin said.

"I can't talk to you and enjoy our conversation if you're trying to . . . if your wife is close by. I can see how the phone calls can add up, so why don't you find a phone booth somewhere, get the number, give it to me, and we'll take turns calling at an agreed time. What's wrong with getting a legal separation the way I did?"

"There's nothing wrong with it, but Eve won't do it. I told you about that religion thing."

Ruby felt the beginnings of a headache. She'd looked forward to this call all day. It wasn't supposed to be like this. She should be feeling elated, loving. "I have a blinding headache," she said. The blinding headache became a reality the moment the words were out of her mouth.

"You're unhappy with me, aren't you? You're having second thoughts. I'm picking up something in your voice," Calvin whispered.

"No, Calvin, I'm not unhappy with you, but I am unhappy with your situation. I didn't think it would bother me, but it does. No, I'm not having second thoughts. How could I? I love you. I didn't plan this headache, it just happened. When will you call me again?"

"On Friday, when I leave the office. Five-thirty or so. Is that okay?" Ruby shook her head, them remembered he couldn't see her. She gritted her teeth. "I'll look forward to it, Calvin."

"I should have my schedule set by then, so we can make some plans. I love you Ruby, I truly do. Dream about me, okay?"

"Okay," Ruby whispered in return.

"What did you say? Why are *you* whispering?"

"So you'll know what it sounds like," Ruby said. "Good-bye, Calvin."

{{{{{{{{{ CHAPTER TWENTY-THREE *}}}}}}}}*

*The first thing Ruby did after she dressed on the following morn-*ing was to call the Mayo Clinic. It was still hard for her to accept that Dixie had just up and gone without telling anyone. She was probably scared to death and knew talking about her operation would only make her more anxious. Even so, Dixie simply didn't do things like that.

"Miss Baker? This is Ruby Blue, I'm calling for an update on my sister, Dixie Sinclaire," Ruby said into the phone. She could hear the worry in her own voice.

"Mrs. Sinclaire's surgeon has scheduled surgery for eight A.M. tomorrow," the young nurse said cheerily. "It's a very long operation, Mrs. Blue. You can call tomorrow evening. Ask to be put through to I.C.U."

"Thank you. I will."

Dixie must be frightened out of her wits, Ruby thought after she hung up. How could she go this alone? Ruby made her decision to fly to Minnesota in the time it took her heart to beat twice.

Ruby called Northwest Airlines, booked a seven P.M. flight to Minneapolis, where she would change planes for Rochester.

"Your arrival time is eleven P.M.," the reservation clerk said briskly.

Good. She could put in a full day at the office and leave for the airport at closing time.

Ruby stepped off the plane at Rochester Municipal Airport at eleven-fifteen. She had a sour stomach, a miserable headache, and she had to go to the bathroom.

She found a ladies' room, then went outside to look for the taxi stand. She thought she would die when the twenty-below temperature whacked her body.

The warm, steamy taxi felt like a sauna. "Take me to the nearest hotel or motel," Ruby gasped.

"Won't do you any good," the driver said, leaning over the backseat.

"Why? Please don't tell me there's a convention in town and all the hotels are booked. Please don't tell me that," Ruby pleaded.

"Worse than that. You have to make reservations months in advance. Mayo Clinic patients and their families always have the rooms sewed up tight."

"What do people do?" Ruby demanded irritably. Damn, why hadn't she thought about this?

"They look for boardinghouses, bed and breakfast inns." He shrugged.

"Can you take me to one of those places?"

"Ain't any."

"Then take me to the clinic. I'll stay in the waiting room."

"Okay," the driver muttered as he swung his hack onto the hard, crunchy snow. Ruby hated the snow, the cold, Minnesota, her fatigue, and the place the driver was taking her to.

The lobby of the clinic was warm, but not as warm as the taxi. Ruby sank down on one of the imitation leather chairs. She would not look at the other people, who were either talking in hushed tones or crying. She thought she heard someone say a Hail Mary as she closed her eyes. She fought the urge to tell the person to stop. When push came to shove, people always turned to prayer. If you do this for me, Lord, I swear I will never do another wrong thing in my life. Did they think God was stupid?

Her eyes still closed, Ruby searched her own life. So often she'd felt the presence of a higher power giving her direction and hope when she needed it. This higher power she called God. And at times, like now, she spoke to him, but not to ask for anything.

You don't owe me anything, she thought. It is I who owe you. She'd tried over the years to repay what she thought of as her emotional debt. She funded scholarships, corporate and personal. She donated to the poor, both corporately and personally. She donated huge sums of her own money to Greenpeace and to various animal shelters in the state. She'd personally seen to it that the newest batch of Quantrell orphans, as well as the earlier children, were provided with tuition for the colleges and universities of their choice. Just because Nola had turned her back on them didn't mean Ruby was going to do the same thing. She'd provided for Nola's parents, too, sending them a twelve-passenger Dodge van to transport all the children in. Twice a year she sent truckloads of toys, clothes, food, and bedding to three orphanages in New Jersey. And always, she sent huge monthly donations of money to St. Andrew's. She called every other week to speak with the new parish priest, who said he remembered her in his daily prayers. She always felt so good, so wonderful, so up and on top of things when she did something charitable. Maybe she should have done more, given more. Maybe she should have gone back to the Church. Maybemaybemaybe, she thought wearily. You couldn't second-guess God. If she hadn't done enough, he would let her know somehow.

She was so tired. Maybe she should go back to the desk and ask where Dixie's room was. Maybe they'd let her see her. In the middle of the night? Unlikely. Her eyes snapped open when she heard more than one voice say the words to the Hail Mary. Across from her was a family; at least they all looked alike. A mother, a father, and three children, all wide awake with rosaries in their hands. Their voices were soft, almost indistinct. She couldn't help but wonder who they were praying for. Someone who meant a lot to them. There were tears in the parents' eyes. She closed her own. She didn't want to know, didn't want to get involved in their grief. They looked poor, but neat and clean. That much she did notice.

Like it or not, she was going to hear all about it. The elderly couple sitting behind her were discussing the praying family with another couple sitting next to them. "They're the three oldest Denzel boys. Twelve, ten, and nine years of age. They were in the family barn with their grandfather. The two older boys were milking cows while the youngest was gathering eggs. The grandfather was forking hay into the stalls. A huge semi, one of those eighteen-wheel things, skidded around a curve and went out of control. It plowed across a snowy field and headed straight into the barn. They're all in critical condition. And no insurance," the elderly woman said.

This sounded like one of those slim-to-none chances life doled out. Ruby leapt off her chair as if she'd been stung by a bee. She walked aimlessly down one hall after another in search of a bathroom. She looked around the sterile whiteness, hoping to see a chair or stool. It was so quiet here. There was no stool or chair, just a huge trash can with a sloppy-looking plastic bag draped over the side. Ruby pulled out the bag, tied it into a knot, and upended the can. She sat there with her back against the white tile wall, smoking one cigarette after another until six o'clock.

She splashed water on her face, ran a comb through her hair, and brushed lint off her dark sweater before she slipped back into her coat.

She headed straight for the coffee shop, where she ordered breakfast. She wondered what the Denzels were going to do. Children were always hungry. Did they have money for breakfast, or would they go home? The food, when it came, looked appetizing, even tempting, but she couldn't eat. She nibbled on toast and drank coffee.

The shop was filling up. The elderly couple appeared first, and then some of the others she'd noticed when she bolted off the chair. She looked over her shoulder, through the glass partition. The Denzels were alone, huddled together. The two smallest children were on their parents' laps.

The poor were always so proud. How could she possibly offer them breakfast?

Ruby called the waitress over to her and spoke in low tones. The woman smiled and nodded. A bill changed hands.

It was a few minutes to seven when Ruby walked up to the nurses' station to inquire about Dixie.

"She's been sedated, and she's being prepped for surgery. I'm sorry, but you can't go in now. Are you a relative?"

The lie rolled off Ruby's tongue. "Yes, her sister."

"Mrs. Sinclaire indicated no one from the family would be here," the nurse said, puckering her mouth. "If I had known you were here, I would have told her."

"I wasn't sure if I could make it," Ruby said lamely.

"There's a waiting room down the hall with a television and magazines. We have a coffee shop on the first floor. It's a very long operation. I do wish you had come sooner. Mrs. Sinclaire was so frightened."

"When they're done prepping her, can I see her? She might be . . . she might . . . or you tell her I'm here. Sedatives don't . . . they won't knock her out completely . . . it would mean so much to me . . . to her."

Ruby's heart fluttered in her chest as she watched conflicting emotions cross the nurse's face: the well-being of the patient, the rules, doctor's orders, the patient's wishes. The rules won out.

"I'll tell her you're here if she's awake. I'm sorry."

Ruby waited while the nurse walked down the hallway in her soundless rubber-soled shoes. Nurses' uniforms didn't crackle with starch these days. They swished and clung with static.

Ruby wondered where the Denzel children and their grandfather were. She couldn't even begin to imagine what the family was going through. Did prayer help? "God, if I only knew," she muttered.

The nurse was back, her face puzzled, the front of her uniform hiking up with static cling. There was something on the market for the condition, but for the life of her Ruby couldn't remember what it was. You sprayed it. Maybe she would tell the nurse to look for it. The thought popped out of her head. In the scheme of things, it wasn't up there with death and prayer.

"I'm sorry," the round-faced nurse said. "For a few seconds I thought she was awake and understood me, but she's out. She muttered something about giving you her purse. Of course I can't do that. You understand?" Ruby nodded. "I don't seem to recall a purse when she checked in. Now, I wonder why that is." The nurse was still talking to herself when Ruby turned to leave.

Ruby yelped in fright when she felt a hand on her shoulder.

He was tall, six-foot-four, pencil-thin. The battered Stetson pushed far back on his head allowed a nimbus of red-gold curls to dominate the long, angular face, covered by an army of freckles. He had compassionate, soft brown eyes. His eyelashes were thick and double-fringed. The slender body was cloaked in street garb, faded jeans, cowboy boots, and an oversized sweatshirt that had seen far too many washings and proclaimed him a member of the Harley-Davidson Club.

Until she saw his hands, Ruby wondered who the brash young man was. Then she knew. Beautiful hands with long, slender fingers, the nails clipped short. A piano player's hands or a surgeon's.

"Sorry," the man said, stepping back, "I didn't mean to startle you. I'm Kyle Harvey, Mrs. Sinclaire's surgeon. Is your name Ruby Blue by any chance?" More than capable. His voice was deep with an underlying chuckle threatening to erupt at any moment.

"That's me. Yes, yes, I'm Ruby Blue. You don't look like a doctor. How old are you? Did you ever do an operation like this before? How long is the operation? Will Dixie be all right? You . . . you look like Huckleberry Finn. Oh, God, I'm sorry, I didn't mean to say that. I'm just nervous," she twitted. "I didn't get much sleep. No hotel vacancies."

"Let's see if I can answer in order. I'm thirty-six. I've done many operations like the one I'm going to do on Mrs. Sinclaire. Let's say ten, maybe twelve hours for the operation. I've got lots of degrees that say I'm capable of doing surgery, but I imagine the one you're most interested in is Mrs. Harvey's testimonial. My mother says I'm the best in my field. As for looking like old Huck, well, I'm flattered. I cut my teeth on Tom Sawyer. And although doctors, like lawyers, never commit, there's every reason to believe Mrs. Sinclaire will be fine after a period of recuperation."

As long as it took to blink, Dr. Harvey whipped off the shirt he was wearing. Ruby stared at the paper stuck to his chest with adhesive tape. IF ALL ELSE FAILS, I PROMISE TO READ THE INSTRUCTIONS. Ruby burst into tearful laughter.

"I did it as a joke for Mrs. Sinclaire. She laughed. I mean, she really laughed. She was scared out of her wits. I wanted her to drift into sleep with a smile. That's what's important to me. I hope you understand." Ruby nodded. "She had herself worked up pretty good until the nurse came in and said you were here. Then she calmed right down. Nurse Adderly won't take responsibility for handing over the purse, so I have to sign it out for you. Dixie made me promise to give it to you. All we have to do is find it. Hey, you aren't going to cave in on me, are you?"

"Probably," Ruby sniffled.

"Atta girl." The doctor grinned. "If you'd said anything else, I'd have committed you. Now, let's find that purse, so when

Dixie comes out of recovery I can tell her I gave it to you. It will be the first thing she says because it was the last thing she thought about before conking out."

Ruby was aware of nurses scurrying to and fro as they searched for Dixie's handbag. The doctor beamed with pride when he handed it over. "We can do anything around here when we put our minds to it. Why don't you go down to the waiting room. I'll find you when it's all over. Curl up on the sofa and take a nap. I slept for two full days so I'd be rested up to do this." He grinned.

"I'm glad you're here. Dixie needs someone. Yesterday I asked her to call you, and do you know what she said?" Ruby shook her head. "She said you'd be here; she didn't have to call you. I sensed she didn't believe her own words, that it was more a wish than anything else, but here you are."

"Dr. Harvey?" It was the doctor who turned this time, the soft brown eyes full of worry he hadn't had time to mask. "The Denzel family . . . I saw . . . how, how are the children? Do you know?"

"Sometimes, Ruby Blue," he said, laying his hand on her shoulder, "we get a miracle around here. In this instance, we need four of them." All signs of humor were gone, to be replaced with a hopeless look of inadequacy.

"I'll tell you what, Dr. Harvey, I'll pray for one. Howzat?" Ruby asked tiredly.

"You got my vote. See you in a bit."

A bit turned out to be nine hours. Ruby spent them pacing, drinking coffee, and smoking cigarettes. She felt grungy and dirty. Twice she trekked down to the lobby to see if the Denzel family was still there. The children were stretched out on the plastic sofas. The parents were huddled together, the husband's arm around his wife's shoulders. Ruby felt like crying.

Ruby found her way to the chapel. How hushed it was. The scent of candle wax was almost overpowering. "Either you do it from the heart or you don't do it at all, and you never do it for yourself," she murmured.

Ruby slipped into the polished pew and dropped her head into her hands. The words were stilted at first, because she hadn't prayed for a very long time. "Listen," she whispered, "I know You haven't heard from me in a very long time. I can't promise I'm going to do this again real soon, either. That crazy-looking doctor up there on the fourth floor said they need four miracles. I'm not in the miracle business, but You are. At first I was going to pray for Dixie, but I know in my gut she's going to be okay. We're two of a kind, she and I, and that would be kind of like asking for something for myself. Instead, I'd like it a whole lot if You'd shift into second and direct it all to that little family. I'll pick up the tab if You do Your part." She prayed then, all the prayers she'd learned as a child and never forgot.

A long time later, a weary Dr. Harvey found her asleep with her head in her hands and leaning over the pew. He shook her shoulder gently. Startled, she toppled sideways. He reached for her, his surgeon's hand comforting and strong.

"Is she okay?" Ruby asked groggily.

"The operation itself went well. She's in I.C.U., down the hall from where we spoke earlier. You can see her in the morning, but only through the glass partition."

"You look tired, Doctor," Ruby said softly.

"When I was sixteen and learning to drive, my father made me drive in reverse through his homemade obstacle course for hours on end. When I wanted to quit because I tensed up and you had to be alert, he made me keep at it till I thought I would drop. That's the kind of tired I am right now."

"You should get some sleep," she said, patting his shoulder. Of course, *she* was wide awake and uncertain what she should do now that the hospital was asleep for the night.

Her travel bag in hand, she said good night to the doctor and headed for the lavatory down the hall, where she gave herself a sponge bath. She changed her underwear and stockings and put on a clean blouse. She brushed her teeth three times. She felt like a new person when she searched out an all-night cafeteria, where she ordered a grilled cheese sandwich and a cup of hot chocolate. While she waited for her sandwich, she opened the local newspaper that had been left on one of the tables. The Denzel catastrophe captured the headlines. She read it word for word before she turned to the life-style page and Ann Landers, Heloise, and her helpful hints. She learned that an open can of ground coffee would destroy, ab-so-lute-ly destroy, any kind of odor in a refrigerator or freezer. White vinegar, Heloise said, would open a drain if mixed with baking soda. Everybody in the world knew about white vinegar and baking soda, Ruby snorted. She read on: use toothpaste against the grain of wood to erase nicks and scratches.

She'd known that, too. She wondered when the famous lady would come up with something to get the gooey, sticky price labels off glassware and dishes. She put the newspaper down.

Then she remembered Dixie's purse. Why had her friend given it to her? Was she supposed to open it? Ruby undid the zipper. How neat Dixie's purse was, so like herself. Her own was a jumble of keys, papers, makeup, loose change, and paper money. A pack rat's paradise. Dixie's purse held a wallet with two hundred dollars, a change purse full of quarters, a comb, lipstick, and a small compact along with a sealed envelope bearing Ruby's name.

Ruby slit the envelope with her nail. The single sheet of paper and the five-dollar bill brought tears to her eyes. She had to read the simple agreement twice and then a third time before she fully comprehended what she held in her hands. Dixie had sold her her shares of the business for five dollars. Ethical, honest Dixie had removed the five-dollar bill that belonged to her from its frame and substituted another to make the deal binding. Dixie had protected her the only way she knew how in case . . . in case she didn't make it. She blinked away her tears. She would not cry.

Ruby's eyes popped at the array of medical equipment in the I.C.U. Two of the nurses, their eyes on the monitors, were eating chocolate-covered cherries. A smile tugged at the corners of Ruby's mouth when she saw the sky-blue Mrs. Sugar bag sitting on the end of the desk. She cleared her throat to gain the nurse's attention.

"Can I see Mrs. Sinclaire? I'm her sister." The lie was getting easier.

"Only through the glass. She's sedated. She was awake a few moments ago. Stand directly in front of the bed, and if she's awake, she'll acknowledge you. The doctor's already made rounds, and she's doing just fine."

Ruby pressed her face against the glass. How white her face was, how still her hands. Her eyes were closed. Ruby risked a glance over her shoulder at the two nurses who were now devouring the contents of the Mrs. Sugar bag. She tapped lightly on the glass with the tips of her nails. Dixie's eyelids fluttered and then stilled. Ruby tapped again. She could see her friend struggle to focus her eyes. She tapped again. This time Dixie raised her hand slightly. Ruby almost whooped, but remembered where she was. She offered a thumbs-up, her face splitting into a wide grin. She mouthed the words "You're okay." Dixie's hand moved a second time to show she understood. Ruby reached into Dixie's handbag and withdrew the letter. She held it up and nodded her head. Dixie smiled before her eyes closed.

Back at the nurses' station, Ruby asked if she could write a note, as she had to return to New Jersey. "I'd appreciate it if you'd read it to her when she's awake. She saw me, so she knows I was here." The nurse agreed.

"I think you should keep this," Ruby said, handing over Dixie's purse minus the letter that was now in her own purse. Of course, she had no intention of keeping Dixie's half of the business.

On the way to the elevator, she saw the Denzels sitting on a bench in the hallway. She wanted to say something to them, to tell them she knew how hard it was, but she didn't feel she should intrude on their grief. She did wonder where the rest of their family was, their neighbors and friends. Probably taking care of things back at the farm. Someone must be taking care of the little girls. She smiled at the Denzels, her eyes misty.

Downstairs in the lobby, Ruby looked around at the overhead signs for one that would lead her to the billing office. She followed the arrow.

Checkbook in hand, she approached a middle-aged woman with frosty hair and wire-rimmed glasses. She explained what she wanted to do.

"This is very generous of you, Mrs. Blue. It will lift a heavy financial burden from the family. That's not to say they're worrying about it at this time. I'm sure this is more than enough. What should we do with the remainder if there is a remainder?"

"Give it to the Denzels. I'm leaving now for the airport. Is there any way you can find out what ... how ..."

"Of course. I'll just be a moment." She was back a minute later. "They're holding their own. I wish it were better news, but this is ... wonderful things happen here."

"Someone told me the same thing yesterday. I'll hold on to that." Ruby smiled. She knew in her heart the slim-to-none chance had escalated to a more positive outlook.

At the airport, Ruby called Calvin's office at the Pentagon and identified herself as Paul Farano's secretary. Calvin's voice was cautious when he came on the line. She explained where she was and gave him an update on Dixie's condition.

"I've been counting the hours until tomorrow when I was scheduled to call you," he said. "I'm all clear for the second week in February. Can you imagine being together on Valentine's Day?"

"It sounds wonderful. I'll make a reservation when I return to the office. I should have it all set when you call me tomorrow. I'm so tired, Calvin. I feel as though I could sleep for a week." His voice is so soft, so soothing, Ruby thought. She told him about Dr. Harvey and his Harley-Davidson shirt and the sign underneath.

Calvin clucked his tongue. In disapproval, she thought. "It worked, Calvin, it made Dixie laugh. Me, too, even though I didn't want to admit it. Lighten up, and don't be so serious all the time. By the way, did you take the sauerkraut juice?"

"I mentioned it to my doctor, and he said it's an old wives' tale," Calvin said defensively.

"I hear something in your voice. You're all tensed up and your stomach isn't behaving. Am I right? I'll bet the doctor you spoke to is a surgeon, right?" Again there was no reply. "Well, naturally he's going to say that. He wants you under the knife. They couldn't print that sauerkraut-juice thing in a medical journal if it weren't true. You aren't a patient to me, Calvin, you are the person I love, and I don't believe in surgery until all other possibilities have been eliminated. Furthermore, if you have an operation, I won't be able to see you for a long time. Think about that."

"All right, I'll buy a bottle of sauerkraut juice tonight on my way home. I got your letter. I read it five times already. I'm writing one to you, too. I'll mail it in the morning. I spent half the day and all of the night thinking about us, Ruby. Did you think about me while you were there?"

She hadn't, not really. "Of course," she replied.

"I have to go, Calvin, there are people waiting to use the phone, and I'm about out of change. I'll talk to you tomorrow."

"I love you, Ruby," Calvin whispered.

She hated whispered conversations.

CHAPTER TWENTY-FOUR

Calvin Santos was operated on for his bleeding ulcers when he collapsed and was rushed to Bethesda Naval Hospital a week before the Memorial Day weekend. His recovery was slow due to his depression, his doctor felt. The general had been passed over for his second star. The nurse and doctor who attended him thought it strange that a man of his stature had no visitors, but they closed ranks and didn't let the fact go past the surgical floor. At the bottom of his hospital chart the words *extremely depressed* were underlined twice.

On July 1, General Calvin Santos would be officially referred to as General Calvin Santos (Ret.). His wife, under protest, and his two sons would be with him when he exited the building for the last time. A picture would be taken for *Stars and Stripes*, the only reason his family agreed to take time out of their personal schedules to keep up appearances.

The first thing he did when he entered the house was to call Ruby collect at the office to apologize for not allowing her to escort him on his last day, away from the only life he'd known for thirty years. He begged her to understand, begged for assurance that she still loved him, begged her to forgive him. In return he assured and reassured Ruby that he would now think seriously and plan for his divorce. In September he said he would be going to Saipan and would meet Ruby there. "I need you, Ruby," he said in a choked voice.

On the very same day Ruby drove to Newark Airport to pick up Dixie. She felt anxious, jittery, and yet exhilarated to be seeing her friend again.

She was at the gate, a single rose in one hand, a bag of Mrs. Sugar's cookies in the other, and the agreement and five-dollar bill stuck between her teeth.

As the passengers trickled past her, Ruby scanned their faces.

Did Dixie miss the plane? Had she changed her mind? Maybe she still had trouble walking and would be one of the last off. She *really* didn't know much about Dixie's progress, only what Dixie wanted her to know. "I'm coming along. The doctor is satisfied with my progress." That was all she'd had to go on during the past five months.

Then she saw her. She was taller. Her back was straight. She looked like an arrow. Ruby grinned from ear to ear.

Dixie stopped, threw her arms in the air, her face alive with joy, and shouted, "Taaa-daaah! No, no, wait there, Ruby! Get ready!"

"I'm ready, I'm ready!"

Dixie took a deep breath and sprinted down the hall, falling into Ruby's arms, tears streaming down her cheeks. "Kyle said I could run, but I've been afraid to put it to the test. I probably won't do it again for a while."

"God, you look great, Dixie. I'm so happy for you." Ruby gurgled. "And ... is that rouge on your cheeks? Your hair is lighter. I looove that dress. I didn't know they sold stuff like that in Minnesota."

"This dress was a going-away present from Kyle. He picked it out himself. He said it was for the new me. He's so wonderful, and no, it's not what you think. He's just one of those doctors who really cares. He's getting married in September. Okay, I'm ready, I want to go to work. Give me a rundown on what's been going on. Is Nangi working on the Asian end?"

"It's off the ground. Smooth as silk. I'm going over in September. Want to go with me?"

"Naah, I have this wedding I have to go to." Dixie laughed. "Tell me about Calvin. How's all that going?"

Ruby told her about her noonday call.

"I know you, Ruby. What's really bothering you?" Dixie asked, her face full of concern. "Are you having second thoughts?"

"Dixie, you wouldn't believe the stories he told me about the way he lives with his wife. I think they hate each other, but he can't bring himself to leave her."

"How awful for Calvin. How awful for you. How's he doing now? I mean, really doing? With being passed over and his operation?"

"He says he's come to terms with it all."

"Let him get through this the best way he can."

"I just wish I could be there with him. But he still can't bring himself to stand up to his wife. I didn't think he was so ... so ..."

"Weak?" Dixie said, supplying the missing word. Ruby nodded. "Is there more?"

"That's it," Ruby said, putting on her blinker and inching into the fast lane.

"Okay, we're down to two topics. I *like* this car. I want one!" Dixie laughed, hoping to wipe away the miserable look on her friend's face.

"It's parked in the parking lot. Arrived three days ago. Yours is yellow, since that's your favorite color. The top comes off, you know."

"Oh, yeah. Did you get me one of those fancy license plates?"

"Yep. Says Sugar 2."

Dixie clapped her hands in glee. "We should have done this a long time ago. I'm never going to drive a station wagon again."

"Okay, Dixie. It's your day."

Twenty minutes later Ruby pulled the car to the curb outside the office. "Listen, I'm going to park this bonbon on the other side of the lot so no one bumps into it. You go in alone. Thumbs-up, Dix."

Dixie swung her legs over the side of the seat. "I had to learn how to do that all over again." She giggled. She turned back and leaned over the side of the open window. "You hire any new men while I was away?"

"A sixty-five-year-old retiree who pinches ass better than a twenty-year-old." Ruby laughed.

"Uh-huh. Won't do. I want a Kyle Harvey–type."

"Should have snatched him up when you had the chance," Ruby called as she swung the car around. "Until he says I do, he's up for grabs. Remember I'm the one who said it."

"Thanks, Ruby."

"Go on, your public awaits. If you can strut, Dix, this is the time to do it. You've earned it."

Dixie strutted.

In September Ruby returned from Saipan, angry as a wet hornet. Calvin hadn't met her as he'd promised, and she had a vicious head cold she was nursing with a steam tent, rum toddies, and chicken soup.

Seven full days passed before Ruby was back to normal. She was dozing off in front of the fire when a knock sounded at her door. She opened it, expecting to see Dixie, but it was Western Union with a telegram. She signed for it. Who in the world would send her a telegram? People picked up the phone and called. Then she remembered that she'd disconnected the phone and answering machine several days before.

Ruby read the printed words, her eyes widening at the message. She walked in a daze over to the phone and dialed Opal's number. Her father was dead. Dead.

"Opal, it's Ruby."

"Your phone isn't working," Opal said shrilly.

"I had it turned off," Ruby said wearily. "I was under the weather for a week or so and I didn't want to be bothered. When did it happen?"

"Early this morning. Listen, I don't want to go. I don't think I should have to go. What are you going to do?"

Instead of answering the question, Ruby asked one. "Who's taking care of things? Mom. Does Mom know how to handle stuff like that?"

"Well, how the hell should I know? Maybe it's time she learned to do what has to be done to live in this world. What's with you, Ruby?"

"More to the point, what's with *you*, Opal? If Mom is waiting for us to get there, I guess we have to take care of it. And before you can say it, Opal, I know I said I was never going back to that house, but I didn't ever say I wouldn't go to their funerals."

"That's being a hypocrite. You hated Pop. I did, too. Why should I go now?"

"You don't have to justify anything to me, Opal. Do what you want. Not paying your debt off . . . does that have anything to do with you not wanting to go?" Ruby asked quietly.

"No, it doesn't. We haven't seen them for twenty years. They didn't want to see us. Mac said if I felt this strongly, I didn't have to go. I'll send a Mass card. God will forgive me. Just send me my share of the money," Opal snapped.

"And I thought Amber was the bitch in the family," Ruby muttered. "By the way, did you call her?"

"Yeah, and it's on my bill. It costs at least fifty dollars to call over there. I think I should be paid back out of the estate."

Ruby wanted to ask her what estate she was talking about. "I guess I won't see you there, then."

"You're really going?" Opal asked incredulously.

"Yes, I'm going. Shall I give Amber your regards?"

"Hypocrites, both of you," Opal said sourly.

"Bye, Opal." She's drinking, Ruby thought. Somehow she'd figured that out a while ago. She'd gone so far as to confront her sister, who in turn told her to mind her own business. If nothing else, it explained Opal's mood swings, her churlishness, and silliness. Her sister a drunk. She shouldn't be surprised. With the childhood she and her two sisters had survived, it was a miracle they hadn't all ended up hitting the bottle.

Ruby wanted to cry when her mother opened the door. Words whirled around her head. Her tongue felt glued to her mouth. She didn't know what she was expected to do. Her mother stared at her. She stared at her mother.

"Come in, Ruby. It's so hot out there. I made some lemonade and there's chocolate cake. Would you like some?"

Ruby swallowed hard. Her mother had just uttered four whole sentences. All of them directed at her. She nodded because she didn't know if her tongue would work.

It was a pretty little house, sparkling clean and tidy, and, like the house in Barstow, empty of all personal little touches.

Irma sat down opposite Ruby, a glass of lemonade and a slice of cake in front of her. "It happened this morning. He died in his sleep. He's gone, so you don't have to feel uncomfortable. The wake is tonight. I decided one day was enough for all of us."

"Did you call Uncle John and Uncle Hank?"

"I did, and they won't be coming. They never liked your father, but they said they would send Mass cards out of respect for me. They're good men. God will forgive them."

"That's what Opal said," Ruby blurted out.

Irma swallowed a forkful of cake. She washed it down with a sip of lemonade. "Does that mean Opal isn't coming?"

Ruby nodded. "If you have the wake tonight, Amber won't be here. I think you should change it to tomorrow evening. It's a long flight from Saipan."

"I can do that," Irma said seriously. "I didn't think about that. Why did you come, Ruby?"

"I don't know. Why did you bother to call us?" she demanded. She lit a cigarette. She saw her mother frown as she blew out a stream of smoke. "I'd like an ashtray."

"I don't have any ashtrays. I'll get you a saucer. Your father didn't like cigarette smoke. I called you because it was the right thing to do," Irma said, setting the saucer next to Ruby's cake plate.

"For who, Mom? It wouldn't have bothered me if you wrote after the fact."

"It was my Christian duty," Irma said seriously.

Ruby's fork crumbled the chocolate cake as she remembered how many slices of thick, rich cake she'd been forced to eat over the years. "What are you going to do, Mom?" she asked curiously.

"Die," Irma said flatly.

"No, I mean now . . . after . . . after the funeral."

"What do you think I should do?" Irma asked curiously.

Ruby stared across the table at her mother. Once she'd been pretty. She was still pretty, Ruby thought, but then, a child always thinks that of her mother. But she looked world-weary. Ruby wondered if she would be able to function without her husband. She voiced the thought aloud.

"It will be different. Yes, it will be different." Irma finished her cake and carried the plate to the sink.

They were strangers instead of mother and daughter.

"Did you ever think of me after I left?" Ruby asked.

"Every day."

"And Amber and Opal, did you think of them?"

"Every day."

Ruby was on her feet. "I cannot believe, I will not believe, that somewhere, somehow, you couldn't have written to one of us. When you went to the market, you could have called. Something, anything, to show us you cared. I don't believe you cared for any of us."

"I can't change what you think, Ruby. Do you want me to say I'm sorry?"

"Only if you really are sorry. I'm all grown-up now. *Sorry* is just a word people use when they can't think of anything else to say. In our case I don't think it will make any difference. I tried.

You cut me off every time. You cut us all off. You don't even know what your grandchildren look like."

"Of course I know. Your uncles always stopped by to show us pictures. Your father didn't look at them, but I did. I remember their names, too."

"Now, isn't that nice," Ruby said sarcastically.

"We shouldn't be talking like this. There's been a death in the family."

Ruby snorted as she shoved the cake plate across the table. "I have a lot to get off my chest, and I'm going to get it off."

"I always knew you were the strongest of the three. I knew your anger would make you a survivor, and I was right."

"That stinks," Ruby said succinctly.

"It does, doesn't it?" Irma smiled. "Each time you stood up to your father, even knowing you would be punished, I cheered you on. All that . . . bullshit with the Bible, that's when I really knew."

Ruby burst out laughing. "Mom, did you hear what you just said?"

Irma giggled. "I *always* thought it was bullshit. Not the Bible itself, but all that . . . that bullshit your father put us through. But now we're here and he's . . . done for." She giggled again.

A strange, prickly feeling washed over Ruby. Something wasn't right.

"I can forgive you, Ruby. You were justified. I don't expect you to understand how it was with me, and I don't want to talk about it. Is it possible for us to go on from here?"

"What exactly does that mean, Mom? Twenty years is a very long time. I don't know you and you don't know me. You don't know my children. I can't slough that off. They should have had grandparents. Every child should have grandparents," Ruby said in a choked voice.

"I can't change the past, Ruby. Today is a new day—for both of us. I would like us to have one or two days. I can try to be the mother you didn't have."

There was such sadness in her mother's voice, Ruby almost cried. She wished she could feel something for the woman standing by the sink, but she didn't. Was it possible she'd never felt anything, even as a child? Or had she felt so deeply, she'd buried all her feelings and couldn't resurrect them now? For one crazy moment she wanted to say something smart and nasty, but she was instantly ashamed, though not ashamed enough to keep from blurting out, "My husband and I are separated and I'm having an affair with a married man."

"Are you happy, Ruby?" Irma asked in a voice that sounded as if it hadn't been used for years.

"I don't think I know what the word *happy* means. I do think my inability to *really* feel something has a lot to do with you and Pop. I worried so much about ending up like you, I didn't let myself give one hundred percent. I blame you both for that."

"And I'll take the blame," Irma said softly. "I'll take *all* of the blame. Now, do you think we can have those two days, Ruby?"

"Sure, why not," Ruby said tiredly.

"I'll change my dress and we'll go out to dinner. I've always wanted to go to this restaurant downtown called . . . *Ruby Tuesday's*. It will be my treat. I believe there was money in your father's pockets. We'll use that."

Ruby thought about Hugo Sinclaire. "Why are you having Pop embalmed? Why don't you fry him to a crisp?" she said bitterly.

Irma turned and walked over to Ruby. She cupped her face in both her work-worn hands. "Let it go, Ruby. It's done, he's gone, and that's the end of it."

Now she understood what Dixie meant when she said she didn't want a place, a final place for Hugo to rest. She nodded miserably.

Irma returned in ten minutes, wearing a dress that was so outdated, Ruby cringed. She looked ethereal somehow, alive but not alive. I'm going nuts, Ruby thought.

"I learned how to drive," Irma said proudly as she got behind the wheel of a Ford Galaxy that was so clean, it looked new.

"Is this Pop's car?" Irma nodded. Defiantly, Ruby lit a cigarette and wanted to clap her hands in glee when the cigarette ash dropped all over the seat and floor. She hated the car. Hated the fact that she was sitting in it, hated the fact that she was here for *his* funeral.

Irma was an expert driver, Ruby noticed, weaving in and out of traffic on A1-A.

With a luscious green fern dangling down her neck in the restaurant, Ruby leaned across the table. "How do you really feel now that you're free and alone? I'm not asking out of curiosity, I need to know."

"I think I'll have one of those cigarettes, and I want a drink, too. A whiskey sour. A double," she said matter-of-factly. "I feel afraid."

Irma blew a mouthful of smoke in Ruby's direction. She leaned back and puffed contentedly. She looked ethereal again, kind of wispy, as though there were a veil covering her, a thin veil of gossamer. It was eerie. She didn't ever remember her mother looking like this. Maybe she was getting cataracts. She whipped open her purse, scrambling for her glasses, which, for the most part, she was too vain to wear. She perched them on the bridge of her nose. Her mother looked the same, though clearer somehow. The drink was at her lips and she was gulping it the way she drank lemonade. She wondered wildly if her mother was a secret drunk and smoker. And then for no good reason she could name, a word popped into Ruby's mind: *Alzheimer's.*

"Do you know when Amber is due? The time, I mean."

"I'm not even sure she's coming. You said she was. I called Opal because there was no answer on your phone. You said Opal isn't coming."

"Maybe she'll change her mind at the last minute," Ruby said lamely.

Irma continued to puff on her cigarette, which was almost down to the filter. She stubbed it out. She gulped the rest of her drink. Ruby hadn't done more than sip her glass of white wine. She slid it across the table. Irma drank it.

"We have plenty of room for all three of you. I put clean sheets on all the beds after they took your father away."

"I'm sorry, Mom. I'm not staying anywhere that man lived. We passed a Howard Johnson's on the way. I'll stay there. You can drop me off on the way back. I'll rent a car and then call Nangi to see what time Amber is due in. I'll pick her up. You must be eager to see her."

"No more eager than I was to see you."

"You used to talk to Amber; you never talked to me. You never even said good-bye when I left."

"In my heart I said good-bye. In my heart I cried. Please don't be cruel, Ruby."

"Okay, I won't be cruel. What do you want from me, Mom?"

Irma leaned across the table. "Nothing, Ruby. All I ever wanted was to see my three little jewels again. I'm sorry you don't want to stay at the house. It is yours, after all. Your father didn't like that. He thought he could break you, but he couldn't.

He was awful when you wouldn't hand over the deed. I'm glad you didn't give it to him."

"You asked me to give it to him. You said it was all you really wanted."

Irma attacked her cajun food with gusto, her eyes watering at the sharp, hot spices. "I lied," Irma said matter-of-factly. "What will you do with the house now, Ruby?"

Ruby stopped eating. "Nothing. Is that what's bothering you? It's yours for as long as you want it. I'll send you money. If you want to move to a condo, we can do that, too, or you can come and live with me if you want. The offer I made will always be open."

"When I found out you were Mrs. Sugar, I was so pleased, Ruby. Your father . . . he wasn't happy. It disproved everything he ever said about you. I am so proud of your success. A mother is always proud of her children."

Damn, she still wasn't feeling anything for the woman sitting across from her. She tried, she rubbed her chest, at the spot where she thought her heart was, hoping she could shake something loose, some feeling, some kind of emotion. It was just a person, a strange person sitting across from her. She had to try harder.

"I don't think I'll need your house long. I'll know in a few days. Will that be all right, Ruby? Goodness, that was good. I never ate anything like this before."

Ruby stirred the mess on her plate. "Are all the arrangements made? Do you need me to do anything, Mom?"

"My goodness, no. Everything has been taken care of. I changed the sheets on the beds for you girls, did I tell you that?"

"Yes, Mom. Do you want dessert?"

"Chocolate Thunder Cake. Yes, I'll have dessert and coffee."

Ruby watched her mother while she ate. "Did you ever love Pop?"

"In the beginning I did, then I hated him. Why do you ask?"

"Now that he's dead, do you still hate him?"

"Of course not. He's gone. There's nothing left to hate." She finished the Chocolate Thunder, drank the last of her coffee. "How much do you think I should leave for a tip? It's been a very long time since I've eaten in a restaurant. Is it more than ten percent?"

"Leave fifteen," Ruby said gently. She watched as her mother counted out the exact amount of money for the bill. She pocketed the rest. "This is the first time I've had money in my pocket for years and years," she said cheerfully. Ruby swallowed past the lump in her throat.

In the car on the way to Howard Johnson's, Irma said, "Ruby, I don't want you fretting about me or the way you feel. I understand and I truly do not blame you. My goodness, here we are. Shall I call you tomorrow or will you call me? We should decide now so we don't get all mixed up. Would you like to come for breakfast?"

"I'll call you in the morning, Mom," Ruby said in a strangled voice. Irma waved cheerfully as she drove away.

While Ruby was bawling her head off in the motel room, Irma parked the car along the sandy strip of beach on the A1-A. She sat watching the waves for a long time. "Just give me these two days, that's all I ask. I swear I'll never ask for another thing." Her eyes grew puzzled. "I don't believe I ever asked You for anything. It was understood between us that You would look out for my little jewels. I turned them over to You. You did real good with Ruby. I'm pleased."

A rush of young people ran past her, surfboards under their arms. She was aware of young, tanned, healthy bodies whooping and shouting to one another. She tilted her head to stare at the youngsters, wishing she were young again. Had she ever laughed like that? Had she ever looked like that? She couldn't remember. She couldn't remember if her own children had ever looked like these laughing youngsters. How sad, she thought.

In a little while it would be dark. She fretted then that Ruby would think she was strange for having dinner at such an early hour. Ruby wasn't going to forgive her, she could see it in her eyes. She didn't blame her. She understood, but she felt sad that Ruby was trying so hard. She had to remember to tell her it wasn't important anymore. Or did she tell her that? She couldn't remember.

She'd never driven with the lights on. Never past six o'clock in the summer or past three-thirty in the winter. George wouldn't allow it. She wondered if she would have an accident, if the lights would confuse her as she drove up A1-A. If she stayed in the right-hand lane and watched the taillights of the car in front of her, she shouldn't have any problem. She wasn't stupid. George was stupid for thinking she was stupid.

Irma turned on the headlights, pleased that they cast such a bright glow. She would be fine. The cigarettes lying on the console caught her eye. She felt giddy when she pushed in the cigarette lighter. She puffed on the cigarette the way she'd seen Ruby do it. When she finished it, she lit another one. "George, I don't care what you think," she muttered as she tooled along in the right lane, one arm resting on the door.

When Irma expertly drove the car into the garage, she made the decision to sit up all night and watch television, all the shows George said were sinful. And for breakfast . . . well, she simply wasn't going to make breakfast. Maybe she'd have a beer . . . and a cigarette. George's beer.

Delighted with her decisions, Irma tripped into the house and headed straight for the refrigerator. She popped a bottle of beer, made a face as she swigged. She'd never had beer before. "So there, George," she said, holding the bottle aloft. "So there."

Ruby hated the orange and brown decor of her room. Motel rooms were so impersonal, just like the house her parents lived in. In five minutes she had her bag unpacked and her toilet articles on the vanity in the bathroom. She'd thrown two dresses into her suitcase, a black jersey with a boat neckline and a vibrant red silk, sleeveless dress with a mandarin collar. At the last second she'd tossed in a black lace scarf for her head. She shook it out and hung it over the shower rack so the wrinkles would fall out.

There was nothing else to do except turn on the television and call her children, something she should have done before she left Rumson.

She placed a call to Martha first, explained where she was and why. She waited a long moment for Martha's reaction.

"I can take a seven A.M. flight out of Philadelphia, Mom. Don't worry about picking me up. I can take a taxi if you give me the address."

Ruby felt her eyes burn. How awful it was that her children didn't have their grandparents' address. It was her fault, all of it. She rattled it off along with the phone number.

"Are you okay, Mom?"

"I'm fine. It's a bit of a shock. I guess I thought your grandfather would live forever. The truth is, I don't feel anything one way or the other. I'm just angry with myself that I don't feel anything. I want to."

"I don't understand any of this. Maybe someday you'll take the time and explain it to me, adult to adult," Martha said, a hard edge to her voice.

"Someday, Martha. I'll see you in the morning. I love you."

Her call to Andy left her feeling more depressed. His response was much like Martha's.

"I'll take the first plane. Don't worry, I can find my way if you give me the address."

Ruby's next call was to room service to ask for two gin and tonics. A glow might help her to think clearly. If she managed to get a real buzz on, she might be able to relax enough to figure out what was wrong with her.

The fourth call was to Saipan. Calvin answered the phone. How like Calvin to arrive after she had left. Ruby's heart thumped at the sound of his voice. His voice was cool and strained. She wondered if she should apologize for refusing his last series of collect calls. In the scheme of things, she decided it really didn't matter much.

"I guess Nangi explained what happened."

"Yes, and I'm sorry. I wish there were something I could do for you. Why wouldn't you take my calls, Ruby? What did I do?" Calvin asked miserably.

"I'll explain it all when I see you, Calvin," Ruby said wearily, "but I'm not sure I can accept your reason for not going with me to Saipan as we agreed."

"I couldn't. There was ... Eve ... I'm sorry, Ruby. I told Eve I planned on staying two weeks. I have to start looking for a job. She's on my case."

Ruby felt her back stiffen. "Please," she muttered, "make it right. If you must tell me about Eve, tell me you're leaving her."

"I want to see you so desperately. I know you've been upset with me. We need to talk ... I need to talk to you. If we don't sit down and discuss all this, things are going to go from bad to worse, and we'll be lost to one another."

"This is September, Calvin. You told me you were going to get a divorce when you got out of the service. Have you filed for one?"

"That's what we have to talk about, Ruby. Look," he said, his voice desperate, "you're running up your bill. It's outrageous how much it costs to call over here."

"You never worried about my bill before. Why are you worrying about it now?"

"Ruby, please . . . let's wait and discuss this in person. Right now you're upset with your father's death, and I understand that."

"I'm not upset, Calvin. How's Nangi? Do you by any chance know what time Amber's plane gets in?"

"I have it right here. If there are no delays, she should arrive in Fort Lauderdale at ten o'clock, your time, tomorrow. I miss you, Ruby. I sent you something via Amber. I hope you like it. I can't wait to see you. I've thought about nothing else. God, Ruby, if you only knew how much I love you."

Ruby smiled, for the first time in weeks. "I needed to hear that, Calvin. I love you, too, very much. I'll think about you when I fall asleep, and I'll dream about you all night."

"Bye, Ruby."

"Bye, Calvin."

She didn't think about Calvin, and she didn't dream about him, either. She dreamed about her mother taking her on a picnic under the plum tree in the backyard. Her mother was holding a buttercup under her chin and tickling her, telling her she was pretty as a picture, calling her her precious little Ruby. In her dream she was smiling and giggling. So was her mother . . . until a dark shadow loomed overhead.

Ruby thrashed about, kicking at her covers, her arms swinging upward to cover her face. She woke, drenched in perspiration. The green numerals on her travel alarm said it was twenty minutes past three. "Damn." She hated dreams like this; they always ended at a crucial moment. She'd had hundreds of them, maybe thousands. Some she remembered, others she forgot on awakening. She'd had this one before, many times. She didn't need a dream book to tell her what the dark, looming shadow was—it was her father, and he must have done something so horrible, so terrible, she'd blocked it out. The part with her mother, well, that was wishful thinking on her part. What child didn't want to picnic with its mother using a tea set, a tin tea set with little flowers. A tea set with a real teakettle and tiny little spoons.

Just another bad dream.

It was raining when Ruby woke again at seven-thirty. She'd hoped for sunshine, since she knew the day wasn't going to be a good one. Not with Amber arriving full of . . . what, she didn't know. In her gut she knew Martha was going to be a problem if Andy couldn't head her off. She didn't know the why of that, either; it was just something she felt.

She pressed her face to the wide pane of glass. It must have rained all night the way the cars were sloshing through huge puddles. There was no one on the beach. She could see heavy fog rolling inward. She backed away from the window. The raindrops reminded her of tears. Hers. She turned on all four lights in the motel room. She had to remember to book rooms for Martha and Andy. Amber would stay at the house.

As Ruby stood under the pelting shower, she wondered if she should call Opal and try to convince her to come to Florida. Opal had showed such promise. She'd changed so much, she felt she hardly knew her at all. A party girl obsessed with travel, keeping up appearances, and buying all the latest fashions. Once she'd thought Opal the healthiest, mentally, of the three of them, but not anymore. Now she knew Opal was sick, maybe the sickest of the three of them. It was sad, sad for Opal and sad for her. She wanted a sister so desperately. Shame filled her when she realized she'd tried to buy Opal's affection, first with the down payment for her house, the birthday gift of a new car, other handsome gifts for Christmas, and other birthdays. It wasn't that Opal wasn't appreciative; she was, she called and gushed all over the place. What she didn't do was visit or ask Ruby to visit. She never called unless there was a reason, such as to borrow money she would never pay back. She never wrote and she always forgot Ruby's birthday, although she usually sent Christmas cards from places like Bangkok, Singapore, Hong Kong, or Japan that arrived around Eastertime. She'd never sent a present of any kind. The hell with it, let Amber handle Opal; she was, after all, the oldest, as she was fond of pointing out to anyone interested enough to listen.

Ruby stepped from the tub and patted herself dry.

At eight-thirty she was sitting in the motel's restaurant, eating a breakfast she didn't want. She couldn't remember if she was supposed to call her mother or if her mother was going to call her. It didn't matter, she'd take a taxi to Sunrise. If she was careful and paid attention to the clock, she could time her arrival to coincide with her children's.

At nine-fifteen Ruby left the restaurant. She returned to her room to add fresh lipstick, use the bathroom, and brush her teeth. She arrived at Sunrise ten minutes ahead of her daughter.

It wasn't until she was sitting at the kitchen table that she remembered she was going to rent a car and pick up Amber. She shrugged. Amber would just have to find her own way.

"Mom, I hope you aren't frying that bacon for me. I already ate."

"The children might want to eat when they get here. No, I wasn't making it for you," she added as an afterthought.

Ruby wanted to say something, to cut to the quick. "I had an awful dream last night," she blurted out. "I've had it before, often. Do you dream, Mom?"

"No. It's a waste of time."

Ruby's eyebrows shot upward. She decided not to comment.

"Did we ever have a picnic under the old plum tree? In my dream I had a tin tea set with little flowers on it and it had a teakettle." Ruby saw her mother's shoulders twitch. Her eyes narrowed. "Did we, Mom?"

"Once. I made little sandwiches to fit on the tiny plates. We had real tea in the pot. Yes, it had flowers on it. Your uncle John gave you the tea set for your birthday. I think your Bubba bought it for him to give you. It had spoons, too."

"In the dream we were laughing. You had a buttercup under my chin. You said I was pretty like the flower and I was your precious little Ruby," Ruby said in a choked voice.

"You were so pretty and you were my precious little Ruby," Irma said, wiping her hands on her apron.

Ruby was on her third cup of coffee when her daughter arrived. She sat in stunned surprise as her mother and Martha talked as though they'd known each other all their lives. Her jaw dropped when she listened to her mother recite a litany of Martha's growing-up years, right down to her very first pimple. Martha's eyes glowed. Ruby wanted to slap her.

Andy was next. He dived into his breakfast, specially prepared by his grandmother, his eyes wide and wondering as his grandmother referred to his first skinned knee, his first date, and the first fish he'd caught. He pushed his plate away, asked for a second glass of orange juice, and leaned back in his chair. He beamed with pleasure until he saw his mother's tight face. His chair righted itself almost immediately. It wasn't just his mother's tight expression that made it so tense in the room; Marty's speculative looks at her mother predicted trouble.

"I think I'll take a walk around the block and work off that breakfast. It was good, Grandma."

"She's had a lot of practice cooking huge meals," Ruby said tightly.

"I think I'll join you, Andy. I don't ever remember you eating such an enormous breakfast." Marty shot her mother a suspicious look as she followed her brother out the kitchen door.

Amber was the next to arrive, Opal right behind her.

"Look who I ran into at the airport," Amber said, pointing to Opal. "Hiiii, Mom," Amber said happily. "How are you? Gee, it's good to see you again." She wrapped her mother in her arms, laying her head on her shoulder.

She looks as if she's in ecstasy, Ruby thought. Opal followed suit, hugging and kissing both her sister and mother. She waved to Ruby.

"What time is the wake?" Amber asked. "Are we chipping in for flowers, Mass cards, or what? Is everything taken care of, or did you wait for me to do it, since I'm the oldest?"

"Mom took care of it," Ruby said.

Opal poured a cup of coffee. "What time is the funeral? I have to go to a . . . I have a commitment tomorrow evening."

Irma bustled about the kitchen, opening and closing the refrigerator. "I don't know what to make for lunch." She fretted. "I think I'll make a turkey for dinner. It's thawing. A real nice dinner for the children."

"Why didn't you tell me you were bringing your kids?" Amber hissed. "I could have brought mine."

Same old Amber. She'd hoped their cordial relationship would continue. She should have known better. Ruby could feel the anger start to build. "This isn't exactly a social event. Why should I have to tell you to bring your kids? You're their mother. My kids made their own decision to come here."

"The wake is at seven o'clock. The funeral is at nine. Do any of you object to that?" Irma asked as she piled vegetables on the counter. No one answered.

"Did Pop leave a will?" Opal asked.

"My goodness, I don't know. Carrots or peas?" When there was no response, she shoved the carrots back in the refrigerator.

"Well, what about his life insurance?" Opal persisted.

"I don't know anything about it." The carrots were back on

the counter. "Green peas and carrots make a nice contrast. We'll have both."

"Would you girls like to discuss your father?" Irma asked. "I think I'll go out on the patio and drink my coffee. This way you can say whatever you want, and I won't be able to hear you. I think that's fair, don't you?"

No, it isn't fair! Ruby wanted to scream, but she didn't.

"You," Ruby said, jabbing her finger in Opal's direction, "have about as much finesse as a bull in a china shop. For God's sake, he isn't even in the ground yet." She jabbed again. "You're the oldest, straighten her out!" she snapped at Amber.

"Why?" Amber asked blandly. "I'd kind of like to know myself. Just because you have money to burn doesn't mean we do."

Ruby snorted. "Money has nothing to do with this. Lower your voices. She can hear you out there. Listen, Mom is . . . she's acting strange. We have to decide what we're going to do . . . leave her here living alone or what. I mean, suppose she has Alzheimer's or something."

"I don't have any extra room, if that's what you're leading up to," Opal said sourly. "If you think she's losing it, you take her. If I take her, that means I have to take Mac's father, and he wets himself and stinks up the whole house."

"Is there anything to drink around here?"

"I'm willing to take Mom if she wants to come to Saipan," Amber said generously, "but you'll both have to kick in financially. When we sell this house and divide it up, we can all kick in. I don't think she should be alone. She's always had Pop. What's she going to do, get a job?" The look on Amber's face said that was just too ludicrous for words. "She doesn't look like she has . . . what you said."

"I'll take her, and it won't cost either one of you a cent," Ruby said quietly. "I don't think she'll come, though. I asked her back in January and she said no. I offered her the condo in Maui and she didn't want that, either. As far as I'm concerned, she can live here as long as she likes, and if she gets to the point where she can't take care of herself, then we can get a companion or a nurse. It's important for older people to be independent."

"I'm not paying for a nurse. I don't have that kind of money," Opal said coldly.

"You keep saying that, Opal, but I happen to know what an

aviator makes and I know Mac's rank. You aren't hurting for money."

"It costs a fortune to live in California," Opal whined. "You all know we live beyond our means. I say we sell the house and let Ruby take Mom. It's settled as far as I'm concerned," she said jerkily.

Ruby took a deep breath. "Yesterday you said you weren't coming to the funeral, and yet here you are. I want to know why. What made you change your mind?"

"Well, Miss Moneybags Sugar, I didn't want to be aced out. I wanted to see with my own eyes that the bastard is really dead. I want what's coming to me, that's what I want. Pop made a will, I know he did. I want my share."

"Share of what?" Ruby demanded.

"This house, whatever he has in the bank, his insurance. It should be a tidy little sum. You certainly don't need it, so why don't you divvy up your share with me and Amber. It's a payback for our miserable childhood."

"You bitch!" Ruby seethed.

"Wait a minute, Ruby," Amber said coldly, "I happen to agree with Opal. When he was alive, he never gave us anything but grief and heartache. Now that he's dead . . . well, we're entitled. I want what's mine, nothing more."

"I don't goddamn believe this," Ruby said, banging her fist on the table. "My memories aren't any fonder than yours. But that's our mother out there on the patio, not some lump. You disgust me, both of you."

"I knew it was going to come to this," Opal screeched.

"So did I," Amber retaliated. "As soon as you stick your nose into something, Ruby, it gets screwed up."

Ruby pursed her lips, her temper rapidly reaching the boiling point. "I seem to remember sticking my nose into your business because you were going down the drain. Does that count as screwing up? And you, Opal, you'd be living in a damn tent if it weren't for me. You owe me so much money, I've lost count already. So don't either one of you stand there and tell me *I* screw things up. Do what you want. I don't care. Remember this, though. I won't be a party to anything you two come up with."

Opal sidled up to her sister and pulled at her arm. "Did I just hear you right? You're complaining because you gave me money for a house? You want the money I owe you? Fine.

When Pop's estate is settled, I'll pay you. You want my blood, too, say so now and I'll drain it right here in the sink."

"Why bother, she'd just sell it," Amber said sourly.

Ruby closed the refrigerator door, a bottle of soda pop in her hand. She shot both her sisters a murderous look.

All hell broke loose at that moment. Opal reached for Ruby's arm and demanded, "Well, what do you have to say?" Ruby dropped the bottle she was holding. She closed her fist, shooting it upward just as Andy and Martha walked through the door. Opal toppled backward, knocking Amber off balance.

"Motherrr," Martha shouted. "What's going on?" She hurried to Opal to help her to her feet.

"Stay out of this, Martha. Andy, take your sister out of here. Now!" Ruby shouted furiously.

"You're crazy," Opal raged. "You broke my jaw, my nose, too!"

"You should be so lucky!" Ruby continued to rant. "We're going to settle this right now. First of all, *there is no estate*. This house is *mine*. Neither one of you contributed when they wanted to move here to retire. I took a second mortgage on my house in Georgetown so they could come here. I paid all these years. Me, not you, not Amber. The deed is mine. As for any money, well, let me tell you a thing or two. Amber and I paid our debt, so that makes it part of the estate. You weaseled out. Now you want part of what we busted our asses to pay off? No way, Opal. As for insurance, there's a thousand-dollar life insurance policy from the monument works, and you know what? It's not enough to bury Pop. *We* have to pay it. Money in the bank . . . there's six hundred forty-three dollars. Do you want a third of that? Mom inherits, not any of us. So get it through your head, there's nothing to inherit!"

Breathless, Ruby took a step backward. Amber's mouth hung open as she stared first at Opal and then Ruby. For once she was at a loss for words.

Opal staggered to the table, a strange look on her face. Time stopped for Ruby. She'd seen that look before so many times, she had no trouble identifying it now. It was her father all over again. Amber saw it, too. She whimpered as she clutched the side of the table for support. When she found her voice, she muttered, "If I'd known all this, I wouldn't have spent the plane fare to come here. It cost me fourteen hundred dollars. I should get that back. I want it back."

"Tough," Ruby snarled.

Ruby whirled when she heard Martha's voice behind her. "I thought you said this house was in my and Andy's names. How can you turn on your sisters like this? Is that what you did to Pop? Is that how you aced him out? God, now I understand."

"Shut up, Martha," Andy ordered.

"Don't tell me to shut up," Martha fumed. "Sure, you'll side with *her*, you were always the favorite, you were the goody-goody. Can't you see what she's done? All these years she told us our grandparents didn't want us. Twenty years, maybe more, and she hasn't seen them. Grandpa dies, and here she is like nothing happened. Twenty years! Try explaining *that*!"

From that point on, it was a cat fight—sister against sister, brother against sister. They yelled and screamed, punched and shoved, rolled and tussled on the floor. Hair flew, clothes ripped, breathing was labored, and harsh curses rang in the kitchen.

Andy struggled to get to his feet. His sister grabbed him by the neck of the shirt and pulled him backward. He swung. She toppled to the floor. He reached for the bowl of ice water his grandmother was soaking vegetables in and tossed the contents over all the combatants. Peas and carrots sailed through the air. The silence that followed was worse than a violent peal of thunder.

"Enough!" he roared.

"Oh, Jesus," he said as he helped his mother to her feet. Her face was covered in blood from deep scratches on her cheeks. He reached for the dishtowel as he helped his mother outside, where his grandmother was rocking placidly on the aluminum rocking chair. Martha stayed behind with her aunts.

There were no winners, only casualties.

"Did you all decide what you want for lunch?" Irma chirped. Andy's jaw dropped. Ruby's eyes rolled back in her head.

"String beans," Andy said, remembering where the peas and carrots were. To his mother he whispered, "Marty didn't mean it, Ma, she was scared. Hell, I was scared. Don't worry about Marty. I'll straighten her right out."

"No. No, leave Martha alone. She's old enough to make her own decisions. If this is the way she feels, she has a right to say so. Promise me, Andy," Ruby gasped as she held the dishtowel to her bleeding ear. Amber had ripped her earring right through the soft flesh.

"Ma, I think you better tell me what this is all about."

"Not now, Andy. Please, not now. Go inside, I want to talk to Grandma."

"Okay, but I'll be watching out the window." Reluctantly Ruby's son entered the house. He started to clean the kitchen.

"Mom, I'm sorry. You heard all that, huh?"

"For heaven's sake, the whole neighborhood heard it. You girls should learn to be more quiet. You didn't have to go through all that if you didn't want peas and carrots. All you had to say was you preferred string beans."

Ruby dropped to her knees, much the way she'd done with her Bubba when she was young. "Mom," she said quietly, "don't you really know what that was all about? I know this is too soon, but you're going to have to decide where you want to go."

Irma rocked gently. "Right here. I'll stay right here."

"Good. That's good, Mom. It's definite, then."

"Yes, right here."

"Mom . . ." Ruby licked her dry lips caked with blood. "Mom . . . in there . . . just for a moment . . . in the blink of an eye . . . I thought I saw . . . what I mean is Opal scared the hell . . . how did that happen? She's like Pop. Amber saw it, too," Ruby said miserably.

"I know," Irma said gently. "Send her away. Can you do that, Ruby? Do you have enough money to send her away? I have twenty dollars left from the money in George's pocket. You can have that if you need it."

Ruby dropped her head into her mother's lap and howled. Andy came on the run. Irma motioned him away.

The sun was high in the sky when Irma said, "I think I should make some Jell-O. Strawberry. You always liked strawberry, Ruby. When it's nice and firm it looks like a big red ruby. I have lime, too, if you'd rather have lime."

"Strawberry is fine, Mom," Ruby said, getting to her feet. She felt stiff and sore, her knees bruised from the concrete.

"Mom, would you like to go back to Barstow?"

"That sounds nice, Ruby. I don't know if I have enough string beans."

There was panic in Ruby's voice when she said, "Why don't we just have sandwiches. Egg salad or tuna."

"That's a wonderful idea. Now, you run along, Ruby, and I'll fix it all. It will only take half an hour."

Ruby left her mother in the kitchen. Andy trailed behind her to the living room. There was no sign of her sisters or daughter.

"Did you see my purse, Andy?"

"Is that it?" he asked, pointing to the hat rack by the front door. Ruby nodded. "Fetch it here, please," she said wearily.

Andy stood aside, his eyes worried as his mother rummaged in her purse for her checkbook. He watched as she squared her shoulders before she climbed the stairs. She shook her head when he started to follow her.

Twenty minutes later there was a parade down the stairs and out the front door. Andy watched bug-eyed as his sister followed his aunts. From the window he could see all three of them getting into a cab. What the fuck was going on? What kind of family was this?

"Lunch is ready," Irma said behind him. Andy jumped a foot when he felt his grandmother take his arm and lead him to the kitchen.

"Egg salad. Celery sticks and tea," Irma said brightly.

Andy looked at the table. His knees turned weak. "I . . . ah . . . I have to . . . to . . . wash up, Grandma . . . you . . . you wait here for me."

Andy bolted up the stairs. "Ma, where the hell are you?" he croaked hoarsely.

"Here," Ruby said from the bathroom.

"Ma . . . they left in a taxi! Does that mean they won't be here for the funeral?"

"That's what it means," Ruby said through clenched teeth. "Does your grandmother know?"

"Ah, I'm not sure. You bought them off, didn't you?"

"Yes, I bought them off. All except Marty. That's the only reason they came. I gave them what they wanted. I asked them to stay. They declined."

Mother and son walked into the kitchen. If Andy's grip wasn't steady, Ruby would have toppled to the floor.

"You're late, children," Irma said, wagging her finger at them like errant little children.

"I'm sorry," Ruby mumbled as she took her place at the table. She stared at the blue flowered tea set with the tiny little sandwiches.

"Tea?" Irma smiled.

"Pl-please," Ruby said, holding up the tiny cup. She stared at the minuscule flakes of rust around the rim. She began nibbling on the postage-stamp-size sandwich.

"Mom, Amber and Opal left," Ruby said miserably.

"Yes, I know. Do you think it matters, Ruby?"

"I guess not," Ruby mumbled.

"That's how I feel. Your father will never know," she sing-songed.

"I'd like you to come home with me and Andy tomorrow . . . after the funeral, until you can decide what you want to do."

"All right," Irma said agreeably.

"Atta girl, Grandma," Andy boomed.

Irma beamed. "I'm hardly a girl," she said coyly.

"I think I'll go for a walk," Ruby muttered, excusing herself.

"You go along with your mother, Andy. I have to clean up and start the turkey."

They walked for a long time in silence, up one street and down another until they approached the highway. They crossed A1-A and walked across the sandy beach to the water's edge. Ruby slipped off her shoes, as did Andy.

"I don't know what to do," Ruby said.

"You always tell me when I don't know what to do to do nothing," Andy muttered.

"I guess you want to know . . . I hate talking about it." The words, so long suppressed, tumbled out. Andy listened with no expression on his face. "Well?" she said when she had finished.

"Do you want advice, an opinion, what?" Andy asked, plopping down on the sand.

"No, nothing like that. I don't think I did anything wrong. If I did, it certainly wasn't intentional. Opal is right in one respect. I may be a hypocrite to come here and attend Pop's funeral. I came for Grandma. I didn't know she was . . . unwell. I'm glad I came. I'll get through the wake and the funeral because I have to. I hated him all my life. I still hate him. I won't lie about it.

"What we did back there in the kitchen, it wasn't sister against sister. We were all lashing out at Pop. That's who we were fighting, whether we admit it or not. I tried to tell them that, but they wouldn't listen. We never got the chance to lash out, you know, tell him what-for. He died before we got the chance. Each of us, in our own way, thought the time would come when he'd either come to us and ask forgiveness or we'd go to him and really let him have it. Marty looked so ... I wanted her to understand ... she chose sides. I find that so hard to accept. I feel like my heart is broken. How could she turn on me like that?"

"Marty is a horse's patoot," Andy said sourly. "She can be a real little snot when she wants to. She'll come around. Don't worry about her, Ma."

"I'm glad you're here, Andy. Really glad. I don't think I thanked you for helping me with the—"

Andy laughed. "Which just goes to show you you can survive anything. No thanks are needed. I got to read half of *Atlas Shrugged* again."

"We should be getting back. Let's take a taxi, my legs are killing me."

"Mine, too. I worked up an appetite, I can tell you that."

"You came to the right place. If there's one thing my mother knows about, it's food. She's making a turkey with all the trimmings. There's going to be a chocolate cake, too, you wait and see."

While Andy was paying the driver, Ruby walked around to the back of the house. She stopped when she heard the sounds of laughter coming through the kitchen window. Her mother must have company.

"Dixie! Dixie, my God, is it you," Ruby cried. "Oh, Dixie, I'm so glad you're here. How ... when ... ?" Tears streamed down Ruby's cheeks as Dixie gathered her in her arms.

"Andy called earlier this morning. How did I get here ... well, let me tell you how I got here. I chartered a plane. I felt so ... wicked. Money is a powerful thing."

"Tell me about money," Ruby said bitterly.

"Your mother and I have had a very nice visit. I cleaned the vegetables and she stuffed the turkey. It should be ready soon."

"I think I'll leave you young people and get ready for this evening. I'm not wearing a black dress," Irma said, a stubborn note in her voice.

"I'm wearing a red one." Ruby smiled.

"I brought a yellow one." Dixie giggled.

When they heard the water gurgling in the pipes overhead, Dixie said, "Tell me. I heard your mother's ..."

"Did she make sense?" Ruby asked anxiously.

Dixie nodded. "Enough so I got the drift of what was going on. I guess I just need to know what it's done to you."

"It's whittled down my bank account, but that doesn't matter. What matters is I was able to buy off my sisters. They didn't say thank you, go to hell, and they didn't look back. Jesus, Dix, we had such a fight. We were actually bloody. I had a whole fistful of someone's hair. If Andy hadn't doused us with ice water, we'd have killed one another. My daughter . . . she said terrible things. I swear I could feel my heart break."

"It's done. You'll go on. It's their loss."

"Marty . . ."

"Marty is a big girl. She made an impulsive decision. She's been trying to blame you for years for the breakup of your marriage. She needs to get rid of her anger, and this is how she's doing it. She'll come around if you give her some space."

"It hurt so bad, Dixie. I saw Amber in her all over again. And I saw Pop in Opal. Boy, is she screwed up. Boy, am *I* screwed up."

"A hundred years from now it won't make a bit of difference," Dixie said cheerfully.

Ruby snorted. "We'll be dead in a hundred years!"

"Exactly." Dixie slapped her leg and doubled over laughing. "You know what else?" Dixie continued to laugh. "I told the pilot of that private charter to *wait* for us!"

"No!"

"Yep, I did. A fortune, Ruby. It cost a fortune. It's the single most wicked, most outrageous thing I've ever done in my life. I loved every minute of it. You will, too. Isn't it wonderful we have the money to do it."

Ruby nodded. Her world was right side up. Dixie was here. Andy was here and so was her mother. Now she could get through the coming hours and keep her sanity.

George Connors's funeral was uneventful. It was attended by four people, none of whom shed a tear.

On the way back to the house, Irma turned to Ruby. "Do you think your father is in hell?"

"Wouldn't surprise me a bit," Ruby said.

"That's pretty much what I thought," Irma said cheerfully.

Dixie looked at Ruby. Ruby shrugged. Andy put his arms around his grandmother.

"Let's have some coffee," Ruby said when they all trooped into the kitchen. "I'll make it. Mom, you go sit on the patio, and Dixie and I will wait on you, just like in a restaurant."

"I'll join you, Grandma, as soon as I get out of this suit," Andy said.

"All right," Irma said agreeably. "Put some cinnamon in it, Ruby."

"Okay, Mom."

"Real cream, too."

"Okay, Mom."

"Use a tray."

"Okay, Mom."

"Put some cookies on a plate for Andy."

"Okay, Mom."

Irma sat in the aluminum rocker. It was a pretty garden, she thought. She didn't much care for the spiky grass they had here in Florida, though. She rocked contentedly. Once she looked upward and shook her head. When she did it a second time, her lips started to move. "No, I don't think so. Stop being so impatient, George, you just got there. Give me one good reason why I should?" Irma sighed. "*All right*, George, but I'm going straight up, not down."

Andy barreled into the kitchen. "What time is liftoff, Aunt Dixie?"

"Whenever," she said airily. "Today, tomorrow, whenever."

"Here, let me carry that," Andy said, reaching for the tray. "You guys bring the coffeepot."

Andy's shrill cry was not of this earth. Dixie and Ruby sprinted for the door when they heard the tray he'd been carrying clatter on the concrete patio.

Ruby's hand flew to her mouth to stifle her own screams. Dixie's face drained white. Andy was shaking his head from side to side, his face as white as Dixie's.

Irma Connors's funeral was simple and attended by three people, all of whom cried tears of genuine grief.

"It should be more. A person's life should never be this tidy," Ruby said as she looked down at the cardboard box at her feet. It had taken her only forty minutes to pack her mother's belongings in the carton. Her eyes brimmed when she looked at the

box. Her mother's things and the tin tea set. That's all there was
to carry away.

Andy nodded to the steward to take the box and their luggage
onto the plane.

Before she stepped into the plane, Ruby stared off into the
distance. "I'm glad there's a place. I'll be back, Mom. As often
as I can."

CHAPTER
{{{{{{{{{   TWENTY-FIVE   }}}}}}}}}

Dixie looked across the kitchen at the wall calendar. Five years
since Hugo's death. How was that possible? she wondered.
Where had the years gone? Why was she sitting here, waiting
for the dawn to arrive? Because, she answered herself, it's what
you've been doing since Hugo died, and old habits are hard to
break. Please help me, God, she prayed.

The kitchen was dark, but she didn't care. Right now she
wouldn't care if the house blew up with her in it. Dixie raised
her head to stare across the kitchen at the small night-light over
the kitchen stove. The bulb had wavered, flickered, and then
gone out. She had no idea of the time, since she couldn't see the
clock on the stove.

Dixie leaned back on the kitchen chair. In front of her was a
cup of cold tea. She really didn't care for tea, especially the flavored kind, but Ruby said tea always made things better. This
time Ruby was wrong. Her hands reached toward the table.
They didn't fumble, they slid right to the terrible piece of paper
she'd gotten earlier in the afternoon. An admitting slip to the
hospital. She hated the word *biopsy*. Hated the meaning that
went with it. God, why was she being punished like this? All
those years of being a cripple. Then the miraculous operation,
and now this. She knew, no matter what they said, when she
woke from the operation, one of her breasts would be gone.

This period in time was supposed to be the best of their lives;

Ruby had said so. Actually what she'd said was "We're going to march right into the winter of our lives and start to live. It's our time, Dix. We can do what we want. We have no worries. That's what the winter of your life is all about. You start to embrace life, you slow down, you smell the roses, you travel, you don't catch any more colds, and for some strange reason your feet stop hurting." She'd laughed herself silly when Ruby said that.

Ruby was set. She had two wonderful children—Martha soon would come around and make things right between her and her mother. Ruby had Calvin—although Dixie had watched the recent election returns and wondered where Ruby would fit into Calvin's new life.

A slash of pale pink invaded the dark kitchen. I've sat here all night, Dixie thought. Where was Ruby? She'd willed her to come, in her mind, all through the long night. She'd willed her to come the night Hugo slipped into his coma, and she had. She'd willed her to figure out that she was at the Mayo Clinic, and she had. Now, when she needed her more than she'd ever needed anyone, she wasn't there. Pick up the phone and call her. *Ask,* Dixie. That was the problem. She couldn't ask. Pride, her other self said, is a deadly sin. You need her now. Ruby will understand what you're going through. Yes, maybe, but Ruby was . . . things had never been quite the same after . . . after she . . . after Hugo. They had both put so much effort into their friendship it had become a chore. She was the one who backed away, not going to the office, not answering the phone or the doorbell when it rang. She'd hurt Ruby and she could never, ever make what happened right again. She was too weary, too heartsick to try anymore.

Now that it was full light, Dixie looked at the piles of papers on her kitchen table, at the brown accordion folder with its sturdy thick rubber band. Her fortune, thanks to Ruby. Her hand drew a thick stack of government bonds toward her. A memo under the rubber band said there were five hundred ten-thousand-dollar bonds in the stack. She had four stacks. Two thousand all together. Ten million dollars. Twenty million when they matured. She could fit them all into her purse if she wanted to. Such flimsy paper. They should be thick and maybe make a crackly sound or something, she thought. The CD certificates were on thin paper, too, a kind of onion skin. Even if she folded the stack in half, she could fit them into her purse, too. The memo under the paper clip said she had over five million dollars tied up in CDs, at over fifty banks, that she just kept rolling over when they came due. She had accounts in four brokerage houses. She hadn't wanted to do that, but Ruby had insisted and in the end she'd gone along with it. She looked at the totals on the front page of each account. So much money, thirteen million dollars. An unlucky-sounding number. Then there was Hugo's insurance, the insurance she'd taken out on herself after her operation. Again at Ruby's insistence. It was all in a trust to pay the inheritance tax if and when she . . . died. There was also a five-million-dollar partnership policy that both of them had taken out on each other's lives.

She could see the clock on the stove now. Where was Ruby? She stared at the yellow wall phone. If she called her, Ruby would be there in less than seven minutes. "Not this time," Dixie whispered. "Not this time."

How swiftly they'd secured a bed for her at the hospital. *That's because . . . they think I'm going to die.* First the operation, chemotherapy, maybe radiation. It will depend, the doctor said, but he hadn't said depend on what, and she hadn't asked. She was supposed to check in at ten o'clock, they'd run a few last-minute tests, she'd be prepped, and be operated on at seven A.M. She looked at the clock again. In exactly twenty-four hours she'd be under the knife.

You died in the winter of your life. Well, she was on schedule, she thought sadly. "Don't even think about not having this operation, Dixie," her doctor had said. She recalled that moment so well. It had been such a shock, and she'd started to babble about the seasons of life. The doctor had looked at her as if she'd suddenly sprouted a second head. Then she'd repeated one of Ruby's favorite expressions: "Is this one of those operations where my chances are slim to none?" He'd replied that there were no guarantees in life, and a bunch of other stuff Ruby would have called pure doctorish crap.

Slim to none. The winter of my life. Ruby, where are you? We're so attuned, how can you not know what I'm going through? Call her. Do it now. You need her. Call her. "No, not this time." If Ruby hadn't come, then perhaps she wasn't *meant* to come this time. "Maybe I've used up all my credit with her. Maybe I've been a burden to her once too often." Ruby deserved to go through the winter of her own life without shouldering her, Dixie's, problems one more time.

But to face an operation—to face death—all alone was something she couldn't do. Ruby always said, "When you don't know what to do, do nothing." And to Dixie, doing nothing meant only one thing: run. Run away as fast and as hard as she could.

Dixie raced down to the first floor and then to the cellar, where she kept her strongbox. Inside was sixty thousand dollars in cash. She took all the bundles to the kitchen and stuffed them in her new bag. She ran back to the cellar with the accordion file and stuffed it behind the cushions of an old rocking chair. Back in the kitchen, she stared at the admitting slip to the hospital. She looked at the clock. Two hours before she was to check into the hospital. She tore the admitting slip into little pieces and put it through the garbage disposal. She emptied out the refrigerator and threw sheets over the furniture. She called the airline and the telephone company and the post office.

Ruby knew what she was feeling was grief, she'd felt it once before, after her mother died. This time, though, there was nothing to bury, no one place to go where she could say something profound like here lies . . . forever more . . . no more . . . over, end . . . *fini*.

It was so cozy by the fire. She'd deliberately lighted the fire even though the temperature outside was only down to forty-four degrees. She liked to watch the flames from the cherry logs dance and sway. Without any lights on in the living room the jiggling flames created all kinds of wonderful patterns on the walls. Not that she was really noticing them. She was *really* sitting there because she couldn't sleep. For months now she hadn't been sleeping well.

The list of things she hadn't been doing these past months was endless. She hadn't been going to the office. There was no need. She hadn't been in touch with Dixie for . . . she didn't know how long. She didn't even know where Dixie was right now. She squeezed her eyes shut, trying to remember when she'd spoken to her last. At least a month. She'd called once recently and left a message, but Dixie hadn't returned the call. Ruby hadn't bothered to call back. How long ago was that? She couldn't remember.

Ruby's eye fell on the scratch pad on the end table. She always kept it near the phone in case she wanted to write something out in detail. Seeing something in black and white always made it clearer somehow. Maybe that's what she should do, write everything down that she was thinking, and then maybe this awful feeling would go away. She'd look at it in the morning, shrug her shoulders, and tell herself none of it was important.

Ruby huddled into her thick robe, her legs curled under her. Tears brimmed in her eyes. From the smoke, she told herself. A log crackled, split, and fell against the fire screen, making a shower of sparks that reminded her of shooting stars. She smiled sadly as she remembered another time—in her ski lodge in the Poconos with Calvin. They'd spent two whole hours lugging in logs for the fire because Calvin said they weren't going to move for three full, wonderful days. They had, though. They'd played in the snow like kids, rode Andy and Martha's snowmobiles over the vast acreage, chasing one another until both machines ran out of gas and they had to walk back, giggling and laughing all the way. They feasted on lamb chops three times a day because they were Calvin's favorite. When they weren't cooking, eating, or romping in the snow, they made slow, lazy love on a pile of soft yellow blankets.

It was a beautiful memory she wouldn't trade for anything.

Their five-year affair was something she wouldn't change, either. She'd seen the world with Calvin: the Holy Land, Egypt, Greece, most of Asia. They skied in Austria, drove the autobahn—to their horror—and she'd pointed out two banks in Zurich where she had numbered bank accounts. When Calvin had wanted to see how it worked, Ruby had entered the bank and taken out money. They'd spent it immediately. He'd been so impressed, it was all he talked about for days.

They'd gone to Paris and did all the things lovers do. He'd bought her flowers, shasta daisies, from a sidewalk vendor who smiled at them because they were in love. She still had one of the flowers pressed inside her passport.

They'd made love in New Orleans, San Francisco, and on Maui under the stars.

At the end of five years she thought she knew everything there was to know about Calvin Santos.

Ruby squirmed inside the warm robe when she remembered how it had all been possible. Mrs. Sugar, with Dixie's approval, had hired Calvin as a consultant, a traveling consultant. Off the books, of course. She'd never allowed the word *gigolo* to enter her mind except for times like now, when things were all wrong. She had always managed to justify the situation to Dixie and herself by saying she could not, would not, take anything from Calvin's family. She could take him, his love and passion, because his wife didn't want those things.

Ruby added a huge log to the fire. It would last till morning. She threw in an empty orange juice carton to give the sparking log impetus.

She was back on the sofa, her thoughts again on Calvin. He had made an unsuccessful bid for the United States Senate, unsuccessful because he hadn't been prepared, mentally or financially. She'd hardly seen him that year, surrounded as he was by advisers who didn't seem to know what to do with him. Calvin had refused to listen to them anyway. At first he'd called Ruby often to tell her how things were going and ask for her input, which he ignored. At the end, when things grew black, he stopped calling. She'd watched the election returns and cried for his loss.

Now he was making a second try, and this time she thought he'd make it. She tried to be an asset to him by contributing handsomely to his campaign fund. Beyond that, she lent him huge sums of money. Still, she knew without being told that his new advisers had her down on their books as a liability.

He still called once in a while, but his voice was always full of shame. He promised they would get together as soon as he had a free moment. She felt like calling him now, this minute, and telling him . . . what? You broke my heart? I believed in you? I trusted you? She snorted. She'd done all that in a letter, and he hadn't answered. He was probably too damn busy even to go to the post office box to pick up his mail. Out of sight, out of mind. She hadn't written for three weeks now. Up to that time she'd written twice a week, sometimes three times, but for months there had been no response.

"Fuck you, Calvin Santos," Ruby whispered.

She cried then, huge, gulping sobs that shook her shoulders. Once she'd told herself she had no regrets about anything in her life. It wasn't true now, though. There was plenty to cry about.

All her old friends were gone. Grace and Paul were dead. She'd gone to their separate funerals just months apart. Paul had gone first with a heart attack. Lost without her love, Grace had managed to hang on for several months and then took an overdose of sleeping pills.

Then there was Mabel McIntyre. On a bright October day
with the leaves all bronze and golden she'd called the number in
her address book and was told the number was disconnected.
She'd known what that meant and hadn't tried it again. Mabel
was gone. So, too, were the Quantrells. God, so many times
she'd wanted to go to Michigan to see them, but she hadn't. The
year the Christmas gifts came back was one of the hardest things
to bear. She'd made them part of her life. Now they were gone.

And Rena and Bruno. Rena had called a year before and said
they were liquidating all their assets and going back to Egypt.
She'd written again six months later from her homeland and said
Bruno had passed away. The letter was long and rambling, but
only in the bottom line did she finally get around to saying that
she, too, was dying and had perhaps three months to live. It had
taken that long for the letter to reach her. She'd called right
away, but she was told Rena had already passed away. She'd
truly grieved for Rena and Bruno.

Her uncles were gone now, too. It was only her immediate
family and Dixie that were left to her. She was still estranged
from her daughter and sisters, even now, four and a half years
after their parents' deaths.

Betrayed by her own daughter. It had hurt so unbearably,
more than she thought possible. Andrew's intervention and con-
fessions hadn't swayed Martha at all. "She's just like you, Ruby,
stubborn as hell. Even when I told her how I cheated on you and
gambled away everything, she told me I was making it all up
because you support me and I didn't want it all to come crashing
down on me."

As for her sisters, the only information she had was what
Andy got from Martha. Amber was the same. Opal had gone to
a detox center to dry out, but she was back on the bottle again.

That left Dixie, who had been acting peculiar for some time
now, and Ruby didn't know why. She hadn't wanted to stick her
nose into her friend's affairs.

She was half a century old, and she hadn't done half of what
she wanted to do. Mrs. Sugar now was like a shiny red bicycle
that was getting rusty on the fenders. She needed things to oc-
cupy her time, to challenge her. Ruby reached for the pencil and
pad and started scribbling furiously.

Move Mom and Pop back to the cemetery in Barstow. Check
to see if Amber and Opal have to give their approval. Go back

to St. Andrew's in Hawaii. Go to Michigan and see the Quantrell farmhouse. The list went on and on.

A pilgrimage. That's what it all added up to. She'd go on a pilgrimage.

Tomorrow she would go to a travel agency and make arrangements. After she did that she'd go to Nick Palomo and have a complete physical. Maybe he could give her something for her hot flashes. Fifty-two years old, going on fifty-three, was time to start taking care of herself. She should drop the twenty pounds she'd put on and quit smoking. She should do a lot of things. Death had begun to scare her. Maybe she should start thinking about going back to church, too.

Maybe she should start to think about moving. She'd never decorated her bedroom the way she wanted. If she moved, she could do that. It wouldn't be the same if she did it here in this house. She didn't know why, it just wouldn't be. Maybe because Andrew had once lived in the same room. Maybe she should go back to Barstow. With her parents. Never alone.

"Where did I go wrong?" Ruby cried into the sleeve of her robe. "What's wrong with me?"

Ruby fell into a tortured, uneasy sleep that lasted till four o'clock. Then she got up, dressed, and walked out to her car.

Dixie's house was dark. Usually, there was a night-light burning in the kitchen, but not tonight. She lifted the flowerpot by the front door, but the key was gone. There was another in the carport under the milk box. It was gone, too. She walked back and forth, ringing one doorbell and then the other. Twice she threw a pebble at Dixie's window.

Ruby picked up a rock from the flower border and carried it back to the carport, where she tapped at the small pane of glass in the kitchen door. She reached in to unlatch the security chain and turn the button on the doorknob. *Breaking and entering.* She didn't care. She didn't care about a whole lot right now. She wondered what she would do if the police came. "Well, hey, now, this is my best friend's house, and I'm free to do whatever I please." Sure, sure, lady. And off to the police station she'd go.

The night-light *had* been on, Ruby decided when she pressed the switch. The bulb was burned out. She rummaged in Dixie's junk drawer for a new bulb and fitted it in. The kitchen glowed in dim yellow light.

The refrigerator was empty, as was the freezer. It took her a minute to realize it had been disconnected. The cabinets held nothing but canned soup. All the staples, the flour, cereal, and coffee, were gone.

There was nothing of Dixie left in the house. Not a hair ribbon, not a grain of talcum powder, nothing. The closets were empty, all of them. Dixie's strong box, which she kept under a pile of pillows in the closet, was gone, too. The beds had all been stripped and covered with dust sheets. The same with the furniture in the dining room and living room. Ruby sat down with a thump on the shroud-covered sofa. When had this happened? How had it happened without her knowing about it?

Dixie was gone, but the power was still on in the house. She ran to the phone in the kitchen. There was no dial tone. Standing where she was, she could see the thermostat in the hallway. It was set at fifty-five, just enough heat so the pipes wouldn't freeze.

Ruby made a mental note to call a glazier to repair the window she'd broken. What was going on? Where was Dixie? Ruby began to worry.

Her whole body was trembling when she let herself into her own house. She went immediately to the fire and threw on another log. She sat on the hearth, shivering as she waited for the log to light.

Her head was pounding so badly, she couldn't think. Under the shower she took stock of her situation. She'd lost nearly everyone—even Calvin, if she was honest with herself. And now Dixie. Dixie was gone. Just like that. No good-byes. Dixie's M.O. When things don't work out, take off. Dixie hated dealing with problems. Dixie hated change of any kind. Had she neglected Dixie? No more than Dixie had neglected her. Though at first they'd pretended otherwise, their friendship had never been the same since that night she . . . since Hugo. For a while, Dixie had seemed like a prisoner set free, doing all sorts of adventurous things, but after a few weeks, she had fallen back into her old ways. Dixie had never fully recovered from Hugo's death. That was the bottom line.

Ruby stepped from the shower, wrapped her hair in a towel, and slipped into her terry-cloth robe. She sat at her makeup mirror and slashed lipstick across her lips. She grimaced at her reflection. "Fuck you, Dixie, fuck you, Calvin. It's me now. The hell with both of you. The hell with Mrs. Sugar and Martha, the hell with you, too. As for you, Amber and Opal, kiss my butt, dead center."

Ruby patted her hips as she sat down to an enormous breakfast of ham, eggs, toast, mounds of jelly, croissants, and coffee laced with thick, rich cream. She knew she was eating too much, and all the wrong foods, but she seemed unable to stop herself. What else was left? she wondered miserably.

Long fingernails tapped on the tabletop. The idea of going for a physical today was stupid. First of all, she had to make an appointment and fast the night before. At some point during the course of the evening, she recalled having inhaled half a cheesecake.

Today she was going to make travel arrangements and check on Dixie. Regardless of her previous intentions, she couldn't take off not knowing what happened to her friend. Before she did anything else, she had to call the glazier and have Dixie's back door repaired.

Ruby dumped the dishes in the sink. She looked at the pile of dishes that were days old. It would take her five minutes to put them in the dishwasher. She didn't feel like it. She snorted. One of the fringe benefits of living alone was that she could do whatever she damn well pleased whenever she damn well pleased.

When Ruby returned to the house at four o'clock, she was so disgruntled, she ate the other half of the cheesecake, wolfing it down in six bites. She slammed her way around the kitchen, angry with Dixie, angry with herself.

As she paced her way around the dining room, she realized the only concrete thing she'd accomplished was having the glass on Dixie's door repaired. The travel agency had said they needed several days to coordinate all the stops she wanted to make. In disgust, she'd told them forget it, and stomped out. She'd had absolutely no luck in tracing Dixie. The post office said there was no forwarding address, that mail was still delivered to Dixie's house. She'd stopped by to see if there was mail, but the only things in the box were flyers and circulars, which could mean only that Dixie had notified anyone she dealt with that she was moving on and had given them her new address. *She thought this through and covered her tracks. Why?*

As a last shot, she called the Mayo Clinic and asked to speak to Dixie's doctor.

"I'm sorry," Kyle Harvey said gently when she had explained

why she'd called. "I haven't seen or heard from Dixie for several years. She came back twice, as you must know, for checkups. I recommended a doctor in New York."

She laughed, a funny little sound that stuck in her throat. "You forgot to mention Dixie's trip out there for your wedding. She said it was beautiful. Any children?" She was being polite, nothing more.

"Being on call twenty-four hours a day doesn't make for a good marriage. No children. Someday," he said brightly.

"Yes, someday." She hated those words. "Thanks, Doctor."

"It was nice talking to you again, Mrs. Blue."

So what she had was zip, as Andy would say.

In a fit of helplessness Ruby picked up the dishes and threw them in the trash. She washed her hands before she called the attorneys in New York. Dixie hadn't been in touch. They hadn't called her because there had been no reason to call. "Well, don't bother; the number has been disconnected. She's moved out." No reason to tell them she'd broken into Dixie's house. She wasn't in the mood for a lecture. Her anger was starting to build again.

Ruby's third phone call was to Silas Ridgely, who said he didn't know a thing. He reminded Ruby that Dixie handled her own investments.

"Shit," Ruby said succinctly. She peeled the paper off a Milky Way bar and started to chew. She sat down on the chair, too tired to sustain her anger. She started to cry. In the deep recesses of her mind a warning bell sounded. *You're on overload, Ruby. One more thing, just one more and you're going to snap.*

"Oh, yeah?" *Yeah.*

On the edge or not, she had one more thing to do. One more thing. Something she should have done weeks ago, but hadn't had the guts.

Her shoulders stiff, her jaw clenched, Ruby picked up the phone and dialed Calvin Santos's campaign offices in Washington, D.C. She didn't bother making the call person to person. A voice that sounded barely pubescent answered the phone.

"This is the Oval Office calling for General Santos," Ruby snapped. What the hell, if she was going to jail, she might as well go big.

The voice gasped, and Ruby heard her squeal, "It's the Oval Office! That's the President's place, isn't it?"

Good luck, Calvin, how can you lose with people like that working for you?

"General Santos speaking," Calvin said, coming on the line.

"Sorry to disappoint you, Calvin, it's Ruby."

"Oh."

"That's it? Oh?"

"Well, I . . ."

"Remember, you're talking to the President. I'm going to ask you some questions and all you have to do is say yes or no."

"I can do that . . . sir."

"I've written you a dozen letters, you haven't responded. You aren't going to write, are you?"

"That's not necessarily true. I've been busy, sir."

"Calvin, go to another phone, where people can't hear you. I'm not hanging up till I get some answers from you. And don't *you* think about hanging up, because if you do, I'll come to those offices."

"It isn't possible. There's just this one big room." Calvin's voice lowered till Ruby had to strain to hear him. "Everyone will be gone in thirty minutes. Call me back then."

"Calvin?"

"Yes?"

"If I had called and told that girl who I was, would you have taken my call?"

"I couldn't . . . sir, not at that time. I expect to be here another hour, sir."

Ruby's shoulders drooped. "Good-bye, Calvin."

The same internal voice she'd argued with before attacked her again. You really accomplished a lot. You know, of course, he won't be there when you call back. "*If* I call back." Oh, you'll call back, you need to have your nose rubbed in it. The truth hurts. Only a fool ignores the truth. You just don't want to admit you made a mistake with Calvin. In the beginning you had all those doubts, but you pushed them out of the way. You knew way back then that Calvin wasn't who you wanted him to be. He's weak. He lies. He's selfish. He's sneaky. He cheated on his wife, and you helped him. Wise up, Ruby. Remember, he was never there for you when you needed him, but you were there to pick him up and dust him off time and time again. He wouldn't be running for the Senate if it weren't for you, but now he can't afford to have it come out that he's been seeing you. He's just going to let it fade away because he has no guts.

Ruby took up the other side of the argument. I'm not blameless here, she whispered to herself. If Calvin was sneaky and cheated on his wife, I helped him. I'm as guilty as he is. Once Andrew had said to her, "You aren't God, Ruby, you aren't even a saint, so don't try and make other people guilty when it's you who started the whole mess." She couldn't remember what he had been referring to, but she supposed it didn't matter. She took charge, issued orders like a general. She always believed her way was best, and if . . . Calvin . . . if people didn't do it her way, she always blamed them, never herself. That's what Andrew had been trying to tell her.

Tears dripped down her cheeks as she listened to the phone ring in Washington. She let it ring twenty-six times before she hung up.

Ruby was never more aware than she was at that moment of how alone she truly was. All her reserve was gone, there was nothing more to draw from. She wept then, her head buried in her arms, for yesterday, today, and all tomorrows yet to come.

{{{{{{{{{ **CHAPTER TWENTY-SIX** }}}}}}}}}

November 6, 1984. The date was circled on Ruby's calendar.

Ruby told herself it was morbid curiosity that was making her sit there in front of the television watching the election returns. Tomorrow she was going to go for the physical that was eleven months overdue. Then she was personally going to pound, with a sledge hammer, the For Sale sign into her front yard.

She'd decided months ago that she wasn't going to make the trip to St. Andrew's or any of the other places she'd planned on. She was too tired, and it no longer seemed to matter. Nothing mattered anymore. What she was going to do was time her arrival in Barstow to coincide with the mortician she'd hired to bring her parents' bodies back to the town where they were born and married. Then she was going to get in the car and drive, and wherever she ran out of gas would be the place to which she would move. In approximately fifty-three hours, she would be gone from this place, just the way Dixie was gone. The thought of her friend made her eyes brim over. She didn't know what hurt more, Dixie or Calvin. Neither was she yet over Martha's heartbreaking betrayal.

All she did these days was go through the motions of living. Going someplace else the way she planned was her only way to survive. She'd been teetering on the edge for too long.

Ruby finished the bowl of popcorn just as the television anchor announced that Calvin Santos, Democratic candidate for the U.S. Senate, had won his state.

"Bravo, Calvin," she whispered before she shut off the television.

Her eyes glistening with tears, Ruby made her way upstairs. Calmly and methodically, she packed her bags, two huge ones and one long garment bag. She was surprised to discover that she had so little in the way of personal possessions. Andy had been by earlier in the day, his face long and sad when she told him to take whatever he wanted from the house. The rest was to be given to the Salvation Army.

She'd tried so hard to make her voice light and motherly when she said that he would be the first person she would call as soon as she found a tent to camp in.

"You talked about this with Dad, huh?"

"For hours. You know what he said?" Andy shook his head. "He said, 'do whatever the hell pleases you. You paid your dues, Ruby, and you don't owe anybody anything. Reach out. Do what you want for a change.' " She laughed then with a genuine mirth that surprised Andy as well as herself. "He said, 'just tell those lawyers of yours not to screw up the payment schedule.' End of quote."

"And Marty? Did you tell her?"

"As a matter of fact, I did. She was outraged that I would sell the old family homestead. She said a lot of things, half of which I don't want to remember," Ruby said in a choked voice.

"She'll come around one of these days," Andy said miserably.

"She betrayed me, Andy, at the most vulnerable time of my life. It's not important anymore. Your father is right, she's as stubborn as I am. Who knows? In time, none of this will be important."

"What about the business?"

"It runs like clockwork. My secretary told me last month that I got in her way. She said I add to the confusion. Do you believe that?"

"And Aunt Dixie?"

Ruby shrugged. "She wasn't the person I thought she was. It's that simple."

"You were like sisters, you know, attached at the hip." Andy threw his hands in the air. "Women!"

They said their good-byes then, and with much effort, both managed not to cry. Ruby watched until her son's Jeep was out of sight.

The following morning Ruby showed up at Nick Palomo's private clinic and went through seven hours of testing. "I want the works, whatever the works are," she'd said briskly. "And, yes, I fasted."

From the clinic she drove by Dixie's house. She pulled to the curb but didn't cut the engine. She stared at the house for a full five minutes before she gave a jaunty middle-finger salute. She drove home and pounded the For Sale sign into the front yard. She hoped Andy wouldn't be swamped with calls. It occurred to her then that the neighborhood had recycled itself. She really didn't know anyone anymore. From time to time she nodded and waved to her neighbors, but she couldn't come up with a name to put to a face.

After a quick dinner Ruby sorted through the papers she thought she would need to take with her. The rest were filed into huge cartons, which Andy would take back to his house and store in the attic. The last things to go into the box she was taking were the Rolodex from her desk at the office and her personal address book. Her checkbook and wad of traveler's checks went into the zippered compartment of her purse. All nineteen credit cards were safe in their special compartment. With what she had in her purse, she could probably live out the rest of her life in luxury if she wanted to.

At nine-thirty Ruby went to bed and slept straight through the night. It was her first full night of restful sleep in over five years.

Since there was no food in the house, Ruby went out to breakfast and passed the time with the owner of the diner. Then she headed out to the highway and the shopping mall, where she walked around for two hours. She bought two books, one by Helen MacInnes and one by William Goldman. She prowled through the five and dime, marveling at the array of costume jewelry that smelled like burned popcorn.

Ruby killed another hour by stopping for an Italian hot dog, French fries, and a milk shake. If she took the long way home instead of the highway, she'd only have an hour or so to wait till Nick Palomo called with the results of her medical tests. She could read one of the new books while she waited.

It was almost four o'clock when Ruby picked up the phone to hear Nick identify himself. They made small talk for a few minutes and then Nick said, "I want you to sit down, Mrs. Blue." Ruby sat, her face draining. So, there *was* a reason she'd been feeling so lousy lately. It wasn't all nerves and emotionalism. She drew in a deep breath and held it while her son's friend talked.

Ruby immediately picked up on the seriousness in Dr. Palomo's voice. She wondered if he were going to tell her she needed a life-saving operation or if she was going to die.

"First things first, Mrs. Blue. Your blood pressure is high. I'm sending over a prescription. Follow the instructions on the label. You're thirty pounds overweight. The weight *must* come off. The urologist who administered your kidney and bladder tests says you have a kidney infection of long standing that hasn't been treated. The medication for that will be delivered, too. You also have the makings of an ulcer. Diet will aid you there and some additional medication. That's the *good* news."

Ruby's eyes rolled back in her head. She drew a deep breath to steady her nerves. How was she going to handle what came next?

"The *bad* news is what we found out from your blood work. Listen to me, Mrs. Blue. You are a *prime*, and I do mean prime, candidate for a heart attack or a stroke. . . . You do know what cholesterol is, don't you?"

"Vaguely," Ruby whispered, her eyes twitching so badly she could barely see.

"Well, yours is so high, I don't know how you're still walking around. I *am* trying to scare you. With the medication I'm sending you, there are some medical pamphlets for you to read. Your HDL and your LDL have to be controlled as well as your triglycerides. Do you know what they are?"

Ruby shook her head. She realized Nick couldn't see her. "No," she squeaked.

"By tonight, if you read what I've sent along to you, you'll know everything. You're a smart woman, Mrs. Blue. Don't ignore any of this. I made out a special diet for you, and I want you to stick to it to the letter. *Most* important, you must exercise."

"Wait a second, Nick. Someone's at the door."

On legs made of Jell-O Ruby opened the front door to the delivery boy from the clinic. It took her five minutes to extract the right amount of money from her wallet along with a tip. With her thumb and forefinger clutching the bag as though it held poison, she made her way back to the kitchen.

"It was the delivery from the clinic," Ruby muttered.

"Good. I'm not finished, Mrs. Blue."

"Am I going to die, Nick?" Ruby whispered.

There was a pause on the other end of the phone line. "There's always that possibility, Mrs. Blue. It's all up to you. You can't cheat, Mrs. Blue. You don't have that luxury. Is there anything you want to ask me?"

"Yes," Ruby mumbled. "You won't tell Andy, will you?"

"Of course not. Are you alone, Mrs. Blue? Do you want me to come over?"

"I think I've been alone all my life, Nick," Ruby said sadly. "No, I don't want you to come over. I'll do as you say. Thank you, Nick."

Ruby stared at the calendar on the wall. For some reason it looked ominous. Dates. Numbers. She was moving into the winter of her life. She felt like crying.

Death. Die. Dead. Other people died. You died when you got old. How much time do I have? Will I just drop over or will I die in my sleep? Will I struggle to breathe? Will I turn blue?

The prescription bag from the clinic was heavy. Nick said there were pamphlets and articles. Prescription bottles weren't heavy. She wondered if she would die if she got up from the chair for a glass of water. She was afraid to move. Did she dare move? Maybe she shouldn't exert herself. *When you don't know what to do, do nothing and nothing will happen.*

If I die here in the kitchen, how long will it be before I'm found? Everyone thinks I'm leaving tomorrow. I can't call Andy and tell him. I'm ... it might be weeks. They'd have to tear down the house because they wouldn't be able to get the smell of her decomposed body out of it.

Ruby quivered and shook, her legs like straw as she minced her way to the kitchen sink for a glass of water. She carried the water and the bag from the clinic to the living room. If she was going to die, she'd damn well die in a comfortable chair. She flicked on the television as she passed it. She needed sound.

Ruby read the instructions carefully, trying desperately not to make her eyeballs move. She shouldn't move. Once she took the pills she would hunker down and never move. Ever.

Stroke. She could become a vegetable. *Phffftt,* and she could go like that with a heart attack.

Her life flashed before her then, the way the books said it did. She tried not to cry. She didn't want to cry. All she had in her pocket was one used tissue.

Who, she wondered, would come to her funeral? Andrew, of course. And Andy. But Marty, would she attend? Dixie wouldn't even know. Neither would Calvin.

She sniffed, unable to stem the flow of tears. Andrew would give her a hell of a sendoff. Top-of-the-line casket, the whole works. He'd probably give the eulogy. "Say something nice, Andrew," she whimpered.

Is this what I worked for all my life, to die now, when I'm at the top? "Oh, God, I don't want to die, I don't want to die," she sniveled into the sleeve of her sweater.

The only thing left was to pray. Pray not to die or pray to live? She wished then for the Bible she'd left on the train so many years ago. A rosary to pray. All she had was her fingers. Make do, Ruby. Maybe an act of contrition, if you can remember the words.

Her voice was thin, frail, when she started to pray, but it grew stronger with each Hail Mary. She dozed during the fourth decade, between the fourth and fifth Hail Mary.

When she struggled to wakefulness later, she stared wild-eyed at her living room. The television was still playing, and it was at least an hour past dawn. She was *alive.* She'd made it through the night; that had to mean something. Maybe she did have time, time to rectify all the damage she'd done to herself.

Ruby finished the rosary, said the act of contrition, blessed herself, and got up from the chair. She looked upward. "I didn't ask for anything. I just prayed. I'll take it from here. If You have the

time, look out for me, okay? Last night . . . yesterday.. . . was . . .
to get me to this place in time. I needed to hit bottom. I think I
cut myself a little slack. Whatever . . ."

Ruby showered and dressed in the clothes she'd laid out the afternoon before. She made a cup of tea just to have something to
do, then sipped her tea as she read Nick Palomo's instructions. It
took her a full hour to read through the pamphlets. When she had
all of the information secure in her mind, she folded the papers
and stuffed them into her purse. "I can handle all of it," she muttered as she washed down the pills with a glass of water.

When she reached Barstow she would stop in the library and
photocopy every article ever written about high blood pressure,
cholesterol, and all those other things she never knew about. She
allowed a smile to tug at the corners of her mouth when she
looked at the three bottles of pills. Yesterday she hadn't noticed
that one of them said estrogen.

"What the hell." She grinned. "I'm alive, and if I have anything to say about it, I'm going to stay that way."

Ruby left the autumn of her life behind in Rumson, New Jersey. None of that slim-to-none stuff for her this time around. The
winter of her life was hers, to do whatever was best for her. A
time to look back, a time to make new inroads if she so chose.
A time to come to terms with everything in her life. A new beginning. The last season of her life. When she drove away from
the house on Ribbonmaker Lane, she didn't look back.

PART FOUR

WINTER

CHAPTER TWENTY-SEVEN

{{{{{{{{{{   }}}}}}}}}}

1985

It was a ramshackle office, the decor early junk, consisting of aluminum lawn chairs and a plywood desk covered with artificial wood-grained sticky paper peeling and curling at the edges. Prints of Whistler's Mother and something by Grandma Moses hung askew on a mustard-colored wall. Everything was old and dusty, including the man sitting across from Ruby. The sign on the door said the offices were inhabited by Angus Webster, Realtor. Even the man's name sounded old, Ruby thought.

Angus Webster looked old. The word *wizened* popped into Ruby's mind. Pale blue eyes hid behind smudged spectacles. Never eyeglasses, for eyeglasses denoted something modern, whereas spectacles denoted a period gone by. He was a slight man with puffy pink cheeks that huffed and puffed when he spoke. Rather like a squirrel eating a nut. He wore a battered baseball cap that said he was a member of the Knights of Columbus. It covered a full head of wiry white hair that matched his thick eyebrows, one of which trailed down the left side of his face. A gold tooth winked when he spoke.

"We're a mite off the beaten track here in Lords Valley. I'd be interested to know how you found your way here," he said in a voice that sounded as if it were made of gravel and molasses. Sort of sticky. Ruby sat back in the rickety lawn chair.

"Does that mean you don't much care for outsiders in . . . these parts?"

"Not at all," he mumbled. "Not much call for property by outsiders around here. Might be one or two pieces, but that's it."

"I'd like to see . . . both of them. Now if possible."

Angus nodded, the baseball cap bobbing on his head. The brim was greasy and a leaf was stuck to the visor. It had probably been there for a very long time. "You didn't say how you found Lords Valley," he complained as he struggled up from his

chair. It creaked and groaned. Or maybe it was Angus Webster's
joints creaking.

"I developed car trouble and ran out of gas at the same time.
The man at the Mobil station fixed the fan belt and filled my
tanks."

"That's a spiffy vehicle you're driving, Mrs. Blue. Don't see
cars like that in these parts. We're simple folks. We drive
trucks," he said, spitting into a spittoon, dead center. "You need
a vehicle with four-wheel drive around here."

Ruby nodded as she gathered up her purse. She slid behind
the wheel of her car, a duplicate of the one she'd sold after the
fiasco on the Point Pleasant bridge. She waited a full five minutes before Webster settled himself and started the engine. She
noticed *his* vehicle had a running board.

The trip to the first piece of property that *just might be for
sale* took thirty minutes of solid driving—up hills, down hills,
around corners, and across a field because it was a shortcut.
Ruby bounced along behind, keeping up with the old man with
the lead foot. Twice her head hit the visor as she jounced over
ruts big enough to bury a bear.

When the ancient truck ground to a halt, Ruby had to swerve
to avoid hitting it. Mr. Webster didn't believe in signaling.

"Here 'tis," Webster called. Ruby watched as he put both feet
on the running board before he stepped gingerly onto the
ground.

Ruby's heart fluttered.

"A real fixer-upper," Webster cackled. Ruby's heart fluttered
again before it started to pound.

"You said there were two properties."

"What I said," Webster said, wagging a finger, "was there
might be more than one, but there ain't. T'other one doesn't
have a clear title. Probably won't ever have a clear title, not
leastaways in my lifetime. This is the only one available. Comes
with a right nice parcel of land. Hundred acres. Taxes ain't bad.
Septic tank in the back. You got your own pond for fishing.
Deer run right through here."

Ruby's eyes widened. The house looked like an antebellum
mansion gone to seed. "There's a hole in the roof," she sputtered.

Webster snorted. "One in the back, too, bigger. Porch floor is rotten, front and back. Told you it was a fixer-upper. Price is right for a fixer-upper."

In its heyday it must have been beautiful, Ruby thought, with its wrap-around porch and floor-to-ceiling multipaned windows. Over the front door that Webster said was solid oak was a fanned window of stained glass.

"Seven fireplaces, all with solid oak mantels. Staircase is in bad shape, but it's oak, too. Oak costs a fortune today. Price is right," he muttered.

"Who owns it?" Ruby asked.

"People," Webster said curtly.

"Why are they selling it? How long has it been for sale?"

He shrugged his shoulders. "Maybe five years, maybe more."

"I don't need a hundred acres. It's all woods, mountains."

"Goes with the house. Price is right," he repeated.

"It will cost me twice the price of the house to fix it up. If I were considering buying it," she blustered.

"Has a barn, a chicken coop, toolshed, and watering troughs."

"I don't need any of those things," Ruby said in a jittery voice. "Are you sure this is all you have?"

"Yep. You want to see the inside?"

"I'm here. Why not."

"Has sixteen rooms."

"Sixteen!" Ruby yelped.

"Yep, and that don't count the pantry or the garage or the cellar and attic."

"Heat?" Ruby asked just to hear her own voice.

"Ain't none, leastways no central. Franklin stoves. Blast you right out of the house. Chimneys work good. You step where I step so's you don't go through the floor."

This is crazy, Ruby thought. *There's no way I'd buy this nightmare.* Andy would kill me. Still it wouldn't hurt to look.

The ceilings were high, twelve feet or so, and they were water-marked. Rusty chandeliers hung in all the rooms.

The bathrooms were quaint, their size alone intimidating, bigger than her bedroom on Ribbonmaker Lane. When she got to what Webster said was the master bedroom, she closed her eyes and tried to visualize a fire blazing in the baronial hearth. The room was furnished with a four-poster with a handmade quilt, ruffled curtains, a dressing table, rag rugs on the oak floor, and a rocking chair with bright red cushions. The kind of room she'd once promised herself.

There was no way she was going to buy this dump. No way at all.

"I want to see the kitchen," Ruby said as they trooped down the long staircase. She did like the carved banister and the newel post at the bottom of the curved stairway.

"Won't like it. Needs work."

He was right, Ruby thought in dismay when she stepped over the cracked linoleum. The stove was a horror, the sink a nightmare. The shelves lining the wall were ugly and rotting. "What's that?" Ruby said, pointing to a rusty fixture at the sink.

"Pump. You have well water here. You have to prime it."

"Oh, God," Ruby muttered. She closed her eyes again and imagined a Sears, Roebuck kitchen. A bow window with a window seat. She'd put a rocking chair next to the fireplace, and a basket of logs on the oversize hearth. Fieldstone was beautiful. *Only a lunatic would buy this dump.*

Ruby screamed when she saw movement out of the corner of her eye.

"Just a rat," Webster said in disgust. "A couple of cats will clear them right out." Ruby shuddered.

"The floor's rotten," Ruby said.

"Yep. Window's rotted clear through, too."

There was no way she would even think about buying this monstrosity. No way at all. Andy would commit her.

"Want to see the root cellar?"

"No."

"Peach trees, apple trees and some pear, all over."

"I like plum trees. Those sweet green ones."

"Might be one or two. Can't be certain. You want to see the outside buildings?"

"Might as well."

She should have known better. The barn was little more than a roof and floor. Parts of several stalls remained. The garage didn't have a roof, but it did have two sides and part of a third. There was no door. Ruby knew if she pushed real hard, it would tumble down. The chicken coop seemed to be intact for some reason, but it was an eyesore.

A dimwit with no brains at all would pass this one up, Ruby thought.

"I don't need a hundred acres," Ruby said again stubbornly. "Where's the pond?"

"Fed by a natural spring. A real beauty. You can swim in it. Good exercise, they tell me, swimming." He pointed off into the distance. "Down there. You don't have on the right shoes, Mrs. Blue."

"Who does the carpentry work around here? Who does renovations?" She was asking only out of curiosity.

"The Semolina brothers. Fine work they do. Craftsmen. You don't find real craftsmen these days." His face wore a disgusted look when he said, "And they don't wear hard hats the color of canaries, either."

"If they're craftsmen, they must be in demand." She was nuts, why was she even talking about this? She had no intention of buying this nightmare. None at all.

"They take their time. You young folks, everything has to be done yesterday. You can't speed up the Semolina brothers."

"I don't need a hundred acres," Ruby said for the fifth time, or was it the fourth, she couldn't remember.

"I hear you. Fifty."

"No."

"Thirty-five," Webster said.

"Twenty-five. Wait a minute, I didn't say I was buying. This house should be torn down and rebuilt."

"Yep. Better to have the Semolina Brothers fix it. You want to buy this house, don't you?"

Ruby wanted to say no. She meant to say no, but what she said was, "I'll take it, but only twenty-five acres." They would lock her up and throw away the key. She felt light-headed with the words.

"Contingent on the Semolina brothers doing the work and Sears, Roebuck putting in a new kitchen."

"They won't like that, Sears, Roebuck doing their work." Webster spat three feet, tilted forward to see if he hit the mark he was aiming at. Satisfied, he climbed into his truck. "Get in, we can negotiate inside, where it's warmer."

Ruby's head buzzed as she tried to recall exactly how much she had in her purse.

"What's your offer?"

"Offer?"

"What do you want to chew me down to?"

Ruby rattled off a price that was fifteen thousand dollars less than the asking price.

"Done." He scribbled out an agreement, in pencil, on a crumpled piece of paper. The pencil was barely two inches long and the eraser was worn down to the metal cap. He spit on it first, his gold tooth winking.

"Shouldn't you be drawing up a contract? Shouldn't I sign something?"

"No need. I'm a man of my word. You look like a lady of your word. We can do business. I seen that right away when I saw you close your eyes in that upstairs bedroom. That was my mother's bedroom."

"You own this!" Ruby said, startled.

"Yep. Me and my brother, but he's senile. I handle his affairs."

"I need to move in now. I can pay rent till we close."

"No need. We can close when we go back to the office. I'm selling and you're buying. That's how we do things. Tomorrow you can have the deed. How you paying for this here property, Mrs. Blue?"

"Cash."

"That's a fine way of doing business. I accept."

"And the Semolina brothers, when can they start to work?" This was all moving too fast for her. She'd never done business in such a crazy way. No warning bells were sounding, so it was probably all right. Still, she wouldn't tell anyone until it was official. It was an adventure. That's how she had to look at it.

"Tomorrow morning. Bright and early. You can move in today."

Ruby nodded. All she needed was some food, a sleeping bag, and a car full of cleaning supplies.

"If I'm going to come back here, I think you'd better draw me a map of some kind. I don't think I could find my way without one."

Angus Webster spat out the car window at some invisible target. "No need. Two lefts, a hill, a right, another left, and here you are."

"What about the field?" Ruby gaped at the man.

"That's your last left. Can't miss a field, lessen you're blind."

But she did miss it, and it was six o'clock when she returned to the house on Orchard Circle. One of these days she was going to find out why her driveway was called a circle. There wasn't a house for three miles in either direction.

Ruby sat in her car for a long time with the heater running. Once she entered the house, she had to lug in wood and then lug it to the upstairs bedroom, if she was going to sleep up there. On the other hand, she could lug the wood as far as the kitchen and sleep on the floor in her brand-new down sleeping bag.

She kept her coat on while she built the fire. The minute the dry wood caught and spewed out warmth, she removed her coat and began to rummage in her bags for something to eat. She chomped down two apples, an orange, and a container of bullion she'd picked up at the pharmacy that doubled as a cafe. She was so hungry she wanted to cry, but the thought of being laid out in a coffin was frightening. She ate another apple.

In her spacious tote bag, she kept all the literature about her blood problem. She knew she had to eat a lot of salmon and other fish, a lot of beans and broccoli. The only sweet she could have was angel food cake. She would stick to the diet Nick gave her or die in the attempt. The only thing she really hadn't done was exercise, but she had that under control, too. She'd run up and down the steps a few times for starters, and tomorrow after the Semolina brothers arrived, she'd go for a long walk and explore her twenty-five acres. If they could get the old stove to work until she got a new one, she might be able to cook.

An adventure. Andy was going to have a fit, she thought as she started to run up and down the steps. She made it twice before she collapsed into the sleeping bag. She thought about the rats as she started to doze off, but flashlights she'd placed all over the floor might scare them off. Tomorrow she would set traps. Right now, her only concern was her health and the fact that she'd followed the doctor's orders for three full days. She thought she felt better. Most likely it was wishful thinking on her part. She didn't care about that, either.

Ruby slept deeply and dreamlessly. She was wakened promptly at seven A.M. by a sharp rapping at the door. The Semolina brothers chose not to be formal so early in the morning. They opened the door, walked in, and introduced themselves. Ruby gaped at them. They were as old as Angus, maybe older. They doddered.

"I'm Dick, and this is Mick, my brother. Tell us what you want done," they said in unison.

Ruby told them. They nodded until she got to the part about calling Sears, Roebuck for a new kitchen.

"No need for that, missus. We can put a kitchen in here in two days' time. One you won't be ashamed of. We can have this pump primed in thirty minutes, and Dick here can jerry-rig some e-leck-tricity until the power company comes out. We can fire up them Franklin stoves if you bring in the wood."

"Okay," Ruby said, flustered. "I want you to do the whole place. The roof first." God, she hoped they lived that long. "For now I can get by with a kitchen and bedroom and bathroom that work. Is that . . . is that okay with you gentlemen?" Both men nodded. She wondered if they were twins. And she would have bet her last five dollars they were related somehow to Angus Webster.

"We know this place like the back of our hand. We played here when we wuz youngsters with Angus. We're cousins. We know what to do to make this old place livable. Didn't think anyone would be fool enough to buy it. Gonna cost you a poke of money, missus."

"We should . . . we should discuss just how much it is going to cost," Ruby said.

"No need to worry, missus. We buy on tic from the lumber mill. We'll give you all the receipts. We wouldn't cheat a fine woman like yourself, even if you is fool enough to buy this place. It was grand in its day. Just grand."

"Let's . . . let's do one room at a time."

"We wuz going to suggest that, missus. First thing we're going to do is fix the back steps so you don't go breaking your legs. We have the lumber on the truck. You start fetching in that wood and we'll have you cozy warm soon."

There was no need for further exercise for Ruby after she'd carried in her last armful of wood.

The Semolina brothers ignored her when she said she was going to Port Jervis to order the things she needed for the house.

It took most of the day to pick out furniture. She bought a kitchen set the proprietor of the store told her had been hand-crafted by the Semolina brothers and would last a lifetime. The table was round, with big claw feet that jutted from the center of the pedestal. The chairs were heavy and the back intricately carved. Ruby knew right then and there her dilapidated house was in good hands. She bought a gorgeous four-poster with a stool to climb into bed. The mattress was firm but comfortable, though it was so high that if she ever fell out of the bed, she'd break every bone in her body. She bought two double dressers and two rocking chairs, one for her bedroom and one for the kitchen. Her last purchases were a washer-dryer combination, a refrigerator, and a stove that worked on propane gas.

Ruby was so pleased with her accomplishments, she headed straight for the nearest diner and ordered a broiled salmon steak, rice, broccoli, and a huge salad with lemon juice. Then she drove to a motel, where she rented a room, showered, changed her clothes, and headed back to the house.

It wasn't until she was driving across the field that thoughts about Dixie, Calvin, and her health began to pester her, but now she knew the secret to dealing with those thoughts: keep so busy that you don't have time for them.

The Blue project, as they called it, proposed a challenge to the Semolina brothers. They debated for all of fifteen minutes before finally deciding that they had to call in reserves if they didn't want to go over their deadline. They allowed themselves only two weeks a year to work on renovations. The rest of the time, they built furniture. Elias, Eggert, and Eustace, the Semolinas' cousins, were recruited to put in a roof, new windows, and a new floor on the front porch.

Not to be outdone, the Semolina women, consisting of Hattie, Addie, Erline, and Delphine, brought basket lunches to their men, clucking in approval at their handiwork. When the picnic baskets were repacked, complete with red-and-white checkered napkins that were washed and ironed on a daily basis, they cleared the flower beds, raked the yard, and stacked firewood.

While all the pounding and hammering was going on, Ruby whiled away her time with trips to Port Jervis, buying whatever struck her fancy. Each merchant was told the same thing: delivery in two weeks. Ruby thought it an impossible deadline, but the merchants didn't seem to think so when she told them who was doing the work on the house. She could hardly wait for delivery day. This would be the first time she had full control of decorating a house that belonged solely to her. She didn't have to consult anyone.

The first weekend after the house was completed she would invite Andy for a look-see. Andy would be the final judge.

The roof had been repaired, and she now had electricity and

an electric pump as well as a generator in case the power went off, which Mick said happened real often. She had a telephone and answering machine hooked up in one of the empty rooms.

Ruby had no idea how they did what they did. After one day she had a new roof, after another, a brand-new kitchen. It didn't take a day to sand all the floors. The new windows went in so quickly, she was dazzled. Eggert said that when you knew what you were doing, things ran smoothly.

The cousins, who admitted to being on the shady side of seventy, hung new chandeliers, bopping up and down the ladders like youngsters. Elias said they were sure-footed.

Eustace, the only cousin with a wife, was the plumber of the group. With Hattie handing him his tools, he had all the drains working and the toilets flushable. They squabbled often and loudly, with Hattie calling her husband a horse's ass more often than she called him darlin'. Eustace called her his buttercup, and it was easy to see who wore the pants in the family.

Ruby wondered what would have happened if she'd said she didn't like oak. The brothers and cousins probably would have departed en masse because they said oak was the only wood worth using, as it lasted a lifetime. Ruby wasn't sure whose lifetime they were referring to.

"Missus," Mick said on the morning of the thirteenth day, "you won't be able to stay in the house today. Today we varnish all the floors and lay the new floor in the kitchen. Tomorrow afternoon you can return. We want to be paid then."

"Of course," Ruby said. "What time?"

"Afternoon," Mick said out of the corner of his mouth.

"Need to talk about the barn and outbuildings," Dick said. Ruby waited.

"We can do it next year. It will take two weeks." Ruby nodded again. "House is good as new."

"It's beautiful," Ruby said sincerely. "You do magnificent work."

"We know. Big house for just one lady."

"I've been thinking about a pet."

"Used to be square dancin' in the big room years ago." It was the first casual sentence Mick had volunteered. The big room was the living room, which ran the whole length of the house. Seven thousand square feet of living space. What *was* she going to do with this big old house after she furnished it, and who was going to *clean* it? She gave voice to the thought.

"Tsk, tsk," was the only answer she got.

"I guess I might as well get my stuff together. I'll be at the Holiday Inn if you need me."

"Why would we need you?" Dick asked.

Ruby shrugged. "You never know," she said lamely.

"Four o'clock tomorrow," Mick said.

Ruby looked at Dick, or was it Mick? "You said afternoon, you didn't say a time."

"I did now. Four o'clock."

"Okay."

When Ruby returned the following day, promptly at four, the Semolina brothers, their male and female cousins, and Angus Webster were waiting for her on her new front porch. She felt curious as to how much it was all going to cost. For days now she'd kept a running tab in her head. Somewhere she'd zeroed in on a hundred thousand dollars, probably when she'd seen the loads of lumber arrive, or maybe it was when all the new windows and sliders appeared. She also wondered if they made out receipts or if they worked like Angus Webster, on a handshake.

She noticed something different about them today. They weren't in their working clothes; even Hattie had a dress on. God, she dithered, it must be closer to one hundred fifty thousand dollars.

Mick handed over three sets of keys to brand new locks. "Front, back, and side."

"Wood for the rest of the winter is piled up on the back porch and covered. 'Nuff wood upstairs to last a week or so for your bedroom," Dick said.

"Stoves all fired up. Got a real good blaze in the kitchen going for you," Eustace muttered.

"Brought you a picnic supper," Hattie said. "A bowl of lemons, too."

"You want to look around, missus, before you pay us?" Mick asked.

Ruby nodded. She fit the shiny brass key into the lock of the heavy oak door. She blinked, first at the shiny floors and then at the braided rug she was standing on.

"I made the rug," Addie said. "One by all the doors."

"Thank you. Thank you so very much."

For twenty minutes all she said was thank you—over and over again—as she trooped from one room to the other. She'd saved the kitchen till last.

She was speechless, tears brimming in her eyes. She clapped her hands in delight. The bow window was beautiful, and one of the cousins, probably Erline, as she said she had a green thumb, had hung a monstrous, lush green fern in the center of the overhang. Bright green pillows lined the window seat.

She now had a solid oak counter and magnificent oak cabinets that were to die for. She touched them reverently. "It's beautiful," she said softly.

"Never said we didn't do good work."

"No, you never said that," Ruby said in a hushed voice.

"That be my present to you, missus," Angus said, indicating a solid oak rocking chair. "Was my mother's. Mick and Dick fixed it up and now you got it. Used to sit where it's sittin' now. 'Course the cushion was different then. Addie made the new cushions. Do ya like it?" he asked gruffly.

"Like it! I love it! How can I thank you?"

"By paying us," Mick said. Clearly the social end of things was at an end.

"It will be my pleasure," Ruby said, opening her purse. "How much does it all come to?"

Dick handed her a slip of paper. "This is on tic at the lumber mill. They take checks." Blinking in stupefying amazement, Ruby wrote out a check for seventeen thousand dollars. "This is what you owe us. We don't charge for these here gifts we brought. They're grat-tus," he said, handing her a second slip of paper.

Ruby's eyes popped. Eight thousand dollars. It couldn't be right. He must have left off the first number. "Are you sure this is right?"

"Now, missus, we don't haggle. That's it. That's what we charge. Not a penny less."

"That's not what I meant. I thought . . ."

". . . you were gettin' us cheap. We don't work cheap. We do quality work at quality prices. You unhappy with somethin', missus?"

"No, sir, not at all. I thought you would charge me more. I expected to pay more, not *less*."

"How much more?" Eggert asked craftily. Ruby shrugged.

"A fair day's work for a fair day's wages, that's our charge. Be obliged, missus, if you'd pay us now, so we can be on our way."

Ruby counted out ten thousand dollars and handed it over. Mick spit on his fingers and counted the bills behind her. "Too much here, missus." He handed back a sheaf of bills.

Ruby watched her guests leave, a helpless look on her face.

Andy was *never* going to believe this. Hell, she didn't believe it. *No one* would believe it.

With every light burning in the house, Ruby trooped through the rooms again. She toed off spaces where her new furniture would go.

It wasn't until she was dozing off in her sleeping bag in front of the kitchen fire that she wondered how she was going to spend her time in this monstrous house.

"Like Scarlett said, I'll think about that tomorrow," Ruby murmured sleepily.

Ruby woke with the roosters. She replenished all the fires, poking down the wood with a fire tong. She replenished the water in the old iron pots on all the stoves to add moisture to the air. She added extra logs to the fireplace in the kitchen. While she waited for the kitchen and bathroom to get warm, she fixed her daily bowl of bran cereal. Soluble fiber. It supposedly would help cleanse her clogged arteries. She wolfed it down along with a banana and an apple and two glasses of water. She took her pills neat. She rocked contentedly until the kitchen felt just right. The bathroom, she knew, would be just perfect. Toasty really.

At seven-thirty she was ready for her new day in her very own house. Her first delivery was scheduled for eight-fifteen. Her bedroom was the only room in which she was installing carpet—a deep apple-green, thick pile. The drapery people were due at eleven to hang the custom-made curtains for the wrap-around windows in her bedroom. They'd also custom-made a bedspread and a vanity skirt to match. Just the way she had always said she would someday. Well, her someday was here. She was finally going to have a frilly, feminine bedroom. She'd earned it.

It seemed to Ruby all she did all day was yell at the delivery men, "Be careful, don't scratch the floors." The rest of the time she was running up and down the steps, checking on her bed-room and the placement of the second-floor furniture.

At three-thirty, when the last delivery truck drove away, Ruby smacked her hands in glee. Now the house was hers, fully fur-nished, complete with several radios and televisions. Her dinner, a stew made with chicken was cooking. The radio was playing. The table was set for one on a bright green place mat with her new dishes and silverware. And she was warm.

Now that everything was done, what *was* she going to do with her time? The days were long, the nights longer. Her eye fell on the wicker basket near the fireplace. There was one in every room of the house, filled with all the books she hadn't had time to read over the past years.

Sleep, eat, exercise, and read. It sounded like a prison sen-tence. Maybe she could do some kind of volunteer work. In the spring she could garden; she'd always loved digging in the soft earth. She knew how to prune. Maybe she'd plant some rose-bushes. She'd do a garden, a real one, with all kinds of vegeta-bles, since that seemed like all she could eat these days.

She thought then about the dressing room off her bedroom, which she'd carpeted but not furnished. Maybe she would go to town and order some exercise equipment, a treadmill and an Exercycle to start. She'd take care of that tomorrow.

She could look into joining the church. Looking into it wasn't the same as joining. That would need a lot of careful thought.

Ruby felt like an old lady when she sat down on the rocker. "This is just temporary, this rocking," she mumbled. "Just until I get myself together. I'm not going to turn into a recluse. What I'm going to do is live quietly for a while, get well, and then I'll jump back into the mainstream of things."

But that wasn't what she did at all. She bought a huge freezer and installed it in the pantry. She stocked it with fish and chicken and frozen vegetables. The first year she froze her own fruit and vegetables and felt like a true farmer. The freezer, along with a pantry full of every kind of staple known to man, eliminated the need to drive into town.

The only thing she joined were three book clubs; she would order a dozen or so books each month from each of them. For hours on end she watched the home shopper's channel on her television, buying everything they flashed on the screen. When she wasn't watching and dialing the 800 number to order everything from cubic zirconias to cordless screwdrivers, she read until her eyes gave out. And she slept.

She also used her exercise room on awakening, walking three miles and pedaling five every day. Occasionally she walked over her property, but two sprained ankles from gopher holes convinced her the treadmill was the way to go.

The doctor to whom Nick Palomo had referred her was pleased with her lab tests but cautioned her that she wasn't out of the woods. Convinced that she wasn't going to die ... yet, she started to experiment with recipes to make them more tasty, less unappealing.

Ruby Blue was neither happy nor miserable: She was existing.

On the day of her fifty-fourth birthday, when she burst into tears for no apparent reason, Ruby knew she had to do something.

The word *depression* bounced through her head like a basketball shot out of bounds. She had no responsibility. Nothing to strive for. God, how had she allowed this to happen? A year was gone out of her life, and now, when she looked back, all she had to show for it was hundreds of books and a cellar full of merchandise she hadn't unpacked. She also had a stack of mail on her dining room table that she hadn't looked at for six or seven months.

She would be celebrating her birthday alone this year. Andy was off on a jaunt somewhere, and Marty, well, Marty was still upset with her. Andrew might call to wish her a happy birthday, if he remembered.

Ruby swung her legs over the side of the bed. "I'll make myself a cake and go into town and buy myself a present. What the hell, why not?"

Ruby burst into tears. They continued to overflow all day long.

She was angry now. With herself.

In the middle of the living room, her hands on her hips, she screamed at the top of her lungs, "Happy birthday, Ruby!" She cried again, sniffling into a tissue.

Ruby was about to walk out the door in the middle of the afternoon, when the phone rang. She debated about answering for so long, it stopped ringing just as she picked it up. She shrugged. The best thing she'd ever done was to disconnect her answering machine.

In Port Jervis she stopped at a bakery and bought the richest, creamiest cake she could find. At the drugstore she purchased two boxes of candles. Because there was a shoestore next to the drugstore, she bought herself a pair of Reebok sneakers—her present to herself. She ignored the strange look on the salesman's face when she asked to have the box gift-wrapped.

The last stop was the local bookstore, where she bought seventy-two dollars' worth of books.

On the ride home in the Range Rover she'd bought months ago, she decided it was time to call on the Semolina brothers to have her outbuildings done. If she was lucky, she might be able to entice them, or maybe *cajole* would be a better word, to build her some bookshelves in one of the downstairs rooms. She now had a library, something she always wanted, and more than enough books to fill it.

As she bounced over the field, Ruby started to feel sorry for herself. Her eyes filled. It was true she'd said at first she wanted to be left alone. But now, a year later, she longed for someone to talk to. She needed a friend, a confidant.

It was all her own doing. She'd allowed herself to turn into a recluse, to become depressed. Half the time she walked around in a fog. She relied on Valium to take the edge off her misery.

Always, the fear that she was going to die loomed on her horizon. *That* was hard to deal with. She could have died at any time here in the woods and no one would know.

Ruby slammed the car into gear as she rocketed across the back end of the field. She hated what she'd become, hated herself for her lack of initiative. Once she'd had guts. Where did they go? Her back stiffened as she bounced along.

Well, by God, she was going to come up for air. She was tired of wallowing in her own self-pity. Enough was enough.

Ruby pulled up so short, the cake on the seat beside her slid to the floor. "Oh, shit!" She wasn't going to eat it anyway so what the hell difference did it make? None, none at all.

She might have sat there until it got dark if the phone hadn't rung at that precise minute.

"Yeah," she bellowed into the mouthpiece.

"For Christ's sake, Ruby, is that any way to answer the phone?" Andrew complained.

"What do *you* want?" Ruby snarled.

"You got a bee in your undies or did the squirrels finally get to you? You want me to call back? I just called to wish you a happy birthday."

"That's it, happy birthday?"

"Okay, I'll bite, what else? How are you? Have you heard from the kids? You do get mail out there in the wilds, don't you? Listen, you told me not to call, so I didn't call. Is that what you're pissed about, or are you upset that you're a year older?"

"Shut up, Andrew. I'm having a real hard time today."

"Do you want to talk about it?" Andrew asked more sympathetically. "You always told me it's better when you talk it out."

"No. Yeah. Maybe. I don't know. It's crazy. Here I am, a very rich woman, living alone in a farmhouse, miles from anywhere. All I do is eat, sleep, order crap from the shopper's channel, and read. I exercise, too. I lost thirty pounds. I'm kind of scrawny now. I pop Valium like aspirin. I have no friends. I fucked up, Andrew. Bigtime."

"Then do something about it. Why in the goddamn hell don't you practice what you preach? It bothers me that the mother of my kids is a loser, Ruby. How'd that happen?"

"You bastard! How dare you say something like that to me!" Ruby shrilled.

"So take a Valium and it won't matter that I said it," Andrew challenged.

"Shut up, Andrew!"

"Sounds to me like you have an acute case of cabin fever." Andrew laughed. "Jesus, Ruby, what's the good of having money if you don't spend it? Spend it on something that will make you happy. Go out on the town, buy some new duds, go back to the office. Jesus Christ, do something! You probably need to get laid," he said tritely.

"That's it, Andrew! I don't need any more of your advice!"

Andrew pressed his advantage. "That gook shaft you? I tried to tell you, but would you listen? Oh, no, you had all the answers."

"I don't know what to do," Ruby sobbed. "You're right about everything. I hate you for being right, Andrew," Ruby blubbered.

Andrew's voice changed. It was soft now, even worried when he said, "Sometimes, Ruby, you have to stand up and say fuck it all! Then you go on. You were always such an expert at . . . at picking up the pieces and forging ahead. Do it now. Pull up your socks, get it in gear, and go on. Other people are losers, Ruby. Not you. Never you. Listen, have a wonderful birthday! Bye, sweetie."

Sweetie. In his life Andrew had never called her sweetie. Now, when she was in her own private pit of hell and when she was fifty-four years old, he called her sweetie. She felt like calling him back to tell him to go to hell.

Ruby ate her dinner, her body rigid, her mouth grim as she chewed her way through a filet of sole and brussels sprouts. Then she turned to the mail, which by now had filled the dining room table.

She'd lived in a vacuum for months. How could she not have looked at her mail? She was nuts; there was no doubt about it. Soon she had put the first class mail in one pile and the junk on the floor. It reminded Ruby of a flea market at the end of a busy day.

The house in Rumson had been sold, but then she knew that. What she hadn't known was that a check for two hundred seventy-five thousand dollars was in the mail and had been on her dining room table for over six months.

There were seven notices from American Express threatening to sue her for nonpayment. Her eyes started to water when she saw she'd bought sixteen thousand dollars' worth from the shopper's channel. She riffled through the other credit card bills, sorting them into piles—first notices, second, third, collection agencies, finally lawyers. All the final notices said she now had a bad credit rating. All nineteen of the credit companies wanted their cards cut up and returned by certified mail.

"Ha!" Ruby snorted.

Deposits from the utility companies were in other envelopes. She'd forgotten about that, too. Enough there to buy books for at least a year. Six appeal letters from Greenpeace, three from the Sierra Club, and two from an animal activist organization. Ruby's eyebrows shot upward at a gilt-edged invitation to a private Nola Quantrell showing in New York. Ruby looked at the date. A week from tomorrow. She flipped over the invitation. On the back was a handwritten note from Nola.

I'd like it very much if you could attend, Ruby. I want to—actually I *need* to apologize to you. If you can make it, I'd like us to have dinner so we can talk. I think I had a nervous breakdown this past year. I had something that knocked me out of the game for seven months or so. I'm not really on my feet yet, but the show goes on. I'd really like to see a friendly face in the audience. And for whatever it's worth, I'm sorry about that phone call. I'd like to explain and make it up to you. I live at the Dakota in Manhattan. Either way, will you give me a call?

Nola

The word *friend* ricocheted around and through Ruby's head. Nola was sorry. She looked at the phone number. Did she dare stick her neck out again? She slid the invitation to the side in the "must answer" pile.

Ruby slit the envelope from Saipan with her nail. It was written by Nangi and was more an invitation than a letter.

Dear Ruby,

Amber and I would like to take this opportunity to invite you to Saipan to share in our upcoming anniversary. All our children will be here, and we'd like it if you, Andy, and Martha can see your way clear to joining us.

Calvin and Eve will be here. They more or less invited themselves. Amber and I will understand if this is a problem for you. I want to take this opportunity to tell you how badly I feel about the way Calvin treated you. I told him I could never forgive that sort of shabbiness. I think the reason he's coming here is because Eve knows about you, and she won't let him out of her sight. I no longer write to him, and when he calls, our conversations are strained and bitter. He's not a happy man. He asks about you each time he calls. I won't give him the time of day anymore. It hurts me that I was wrong about Calvin.

Stay well, Ruby, and keep in touch. Amber sends her love.

Nangi

Ruby snorted, a very unladylike sound. She looked at the date on the envelope. Scratch one anniversary party; the letter was four months old. "Fuck you, Calvin," she muttered as she went on with her mail.

Ruby held her breath when she got down to the last two pieces. She crossed her fingers. Please, let one of them be from Dixie or Calvin. Of course it wasn't. One of the letters was from the Rumson Volunteer Fire Department and the last piece was a personal note from her secretary wishing her a happy birthday.

Ruby spent the next hour writing out checks, filling out deposit slips and writing a short note to Nangi. She left the invitation from Nola till last. Should she or shouldn't she?

Her inner voice sent out a cautious warning. Stick your neck out, and they will chop off your head. But I can listen, I don't have to get involved. Friends are too precious to lose, she argued back. She's not your friend, she proved that. She *was* my friend. It won't kill me to meet her again, to have dinner. I can walk away afterward. Not you, Ruby, the voice continued, you jump in with both feet. You expect too much and then you can't handle it when people disappoint you. Think about Dixie.

No, *don't* think about Dixie. Do something. Don't leave time to think. First she would go to see Angus Webster. It had to do with something Andy had said when he came to the house several months ago.

"Who are the Semolina guys, Ma? I'll sign them up right now, pay them whatever they want. Jesus, I've never seen such work. Do you know how much this house would go for at home?"

Ruby said she had no idea.

"A half mil, easy. And twenty-five acres. What the hell did you say you paid for this?" He'd gaped at her, at a loss for words. "I have clients that would pay anything, anything, for a retreat like this." He'd been bug-eyed at her pond as he pointed out ways to spruce up the area, taking away the brush, making it look more like nature had planned it to look.

"You made a mistake, though, Ma. You should have taken the whole hundred acres. If it's not too late, make an offer."

She'd meant to do it, wanted to do it, and even planned on doing it a week or so after Andy left, but the shopper's channel, a good book, and her cozy kitchen had stopped her.

It was almost noon when Ruby shook Angus Webster's hand and started home. Andy was going to be so pleased. Finally, she'd done something right. What she would do with one hundred acres of timberland she had no idea, but if her son said she needed it, that was good enough for her.

If she hadn't been thinking about Andy, she would have paid more attention to the road. It finally dawned on her, at around twelve-thirty, that she'd taken the wrong turnoff.

The road was narrow with deep ditches filled with fire bushes on both sides. There was no way she could turn around until she came to a turnoff or a fork. She looked at her gas tank. Almost full. She breathed a sign of relief.

Five miles down the road, she saw a sign that said ANIMAL SHELTER. Ruby's eyebrows shot upward. She had an inspiration. She'd get a dog. Finally, she would have someone to share her life with, someone who would look at her with adoring eyes, someone who would love her unconditionally, someone whose tail would wag, someone who would listen but wouldn't answer back. Man's best friend. She knew what it took to be a best friend. It was other people who didn't understand. She'd train the dog. He'd come to love Neil Diamond and Chuck Mangione the way she did. She could even read aloud to him. She'd cook T-bone steaks for him, give him vitamins. Responsibility. The dog would force her to get up in the morning, force her to take care of him, force her to get out more.

Do it! her inner voice ordered. "Okay, this time you're on the money," Ruby muttered. She steered the Rover over the steep rise and she coasted down the incline to a wide apron of gravel outside the shelter.

Arthur Bidwell, Biddy to the locals, watched the green Rover grind to a halt in a spurt of gravel. The ricocheting pebbles told him the driver of the car had made up her mind she wanted a pet. Those that couldn't make up their minds drove slowly, uncertain if they *really* wanted the responsibility of an animal.

Biddy resembled a gnome, but no one was sure exactly what Biddy was. A little person, four-six or so, that was certain. It was *good* that Biddy was little, the locals said, because he didn't intimidate his charges. He was as round as he was short.

The sheriff had said Biddy reminded him of a harvest moon. Biddy's face was round, his eyes were round, too, because of a thyroid condition, and his mouth was round, sort of a rosebud mouth that was constantly puckered, as though he were waiting to be kissed. Even his nose was round on the end, full and fleshy. His ears were funny, though, half-moons stuck close to his head.

Everyone loved Biddy, even though he was crochety and cantankerous. The town knew the critters were in good hands with him. They had no strays, no roaming packs anywhere. Agatha Penny had donated the money to build the shelter, and she had kept it going as well, sending checks once a month to Biddy for food, vet bills, his salary, and the salary of the boy with Down's syndrome who worked for him. It was an excellent arrangement and worked fine—until Agatha died.

Everyone in town had thought that Agatha had money to burn. It turned out she had barely enough to bury her once the house was sold to a slick real estate salesman from Harrisburg. Biddy and the animal shelter were left to fend for themselves.

Biddy did the best he could, going into Stroudsburg every Saturday afternoon to stand on street corners and beg for handouts. The two chimps, his constant companions, did tricks, though nothing strenuous because they were getting old. Sometimes he made enough to buy food for the week for all the animals. Sometimes he didn't. Sometimes he and Mikey ate dog food, too. Mikey was a castoff just like the animals they cared for.

He didn't mind eating dog or cat food, but he hated giving it to Mikey. He liked Mikey as much as he liked the animals.

Next week they were going to move into the shelter with the animals because the smart-ass real estate salesman who bought Agatha's property said he was tearing down the trailer and putting up a ga-zeeb-bo, whatever the hell a ga-zeeb-bo was. What that meant was the nine dogs, seven cats, fourteen rabbits, and ten other assorted creatures would have to move back into a space that was meant for twenty-five animals.

Biddy rubbed his chin as he watched Ruby Blue crunch her way over the gravel apron. He knew who she was. Everyone around these parts knew about her. A reck-loose, they said. Didn't like people. Must have been done dirty, Biddy decided. That he understood. He was a reck-loose himself; so was Mikey.

He'd found Mikey sleeping in a ditch six or seven years ago. It was after the Fireman's Carnival, which was the highlight of the year for country folks. The little guy, as Biddy thought of him, was dirty with stinky pants. Mikey couldn't talk right or walk right, either. The sheriff said he had Down's syndrome.

The sheriff was a smart man, but not smart enough to find out who dumped Mikey in the ditch. The best he could come up with was that someone who'd come with the carnival had left Mikey behind. He'd tracked the Soja Carnival people through their booking agent, but all the carney people said there were no kids with their outfit. For a year the sheriff sent out notices and pictures of Mikey, but no one came forward to claim him.

Agatha Penny had offered to pay for Mikey's keep if Biddy wanted to take over the responsibility. Biddy didn't have to think twice. Mikey had been dumped, just like most of the animals he tended. Mikey was a stray. It didn't matter, Biddy told the sheriff, if the boy was in an animal shelter or a children's shelter as long as he was sheltered. The sheriff had made him put his hand on the Bible and swear to God he would do his best to take care of Mikey.

Biddy wasn't a learned man. In fact he'd only gone to the fourth grade, though he could read and write enough to get by. He'd been castoff, too, down in Delaware, by people who had been paid to take care of him. They *hadn't* taken care of him, though. They used the money to buy liquor and they played cards for money. He'd struck out on his own when he was eleven years old and worked at the racetrack until he found his way to Lords Valley, and he'd been here ever since.

Ruby eyed the paper sign pasted to the desk. Arthur Bidwell.

"Mr. Bidwell?" she said hesitantly.

Biddy nodded.

"I want a dog," Ruby blurted out.

"Why?"

"Why? I just do. I always wanted a dog, but the time was never . . . right. Now it's right. Do you have any?"

"Yep, got a lot of dogs. What you got in mind?"

"Well . . . I don't know a lot about dogs. Maybe a girl dog. One that will . . . you know, *love me*."

Biddy's heart pounded in his chest. "A dog's a big responsibility, ma'am. They need a lot of care. You prepared to clean up messes, throw sticks, walk it? Dogs need a lot of exercise. You look to me like a real lady. You sure you can clean up a dog's mess?"

"I'm sure. Do you want my social security number, too?" Ruby asked fretfully.

"Yes, ma'am. I never give out animals until I'm sure they're going to get a good home. A lady like you, well, I'm not so sure. You'll be going off and doing things and leave the animal behind. Who's going to take care of it?"

"I'll do no such thing," Ruby blustered. "I'm not going anywhere. I thought you wanted to get rid of these animals."

"You thought wrong," Biddy said huffily. "I don't want to get rid of any of them. I love them," he said vehemently.

"I can love one, too. Now, what do you have?" Ruby said just as huffily.

"Might have one that will suit you. Mikey, fetch Sam," he bellowed.

Mikey trotted out a gorgeous springer spaniel. Ruby watched as the boy dropped to his knees to rub the dog's belly. He was making strange sounds in the dog's ears. Ruby's eyes were questioning.

"The dog's hungry, ma'am. We don't have enough food to feed them. Mikey rubs their bellies so they'll forget how hungry they are."

"No food? Isn't this a public . . . you know . . . doesn't the town pay you to care for the animals?"

"No, ma'am." He told her then all about Agatha Penny. He showed her around the kennel, calling the animals by name. Like Mikey, he stopped to rub bellies.

"I don't know what's going to happen to all these animals." He told her about the trailer and having to move. He told her about Mikey. He hated to see her cry, to know he was the one responsible for her tears.

Ruby couldn't write out the check fast enough. "If you take it to my bank in town, they'll cash it right away and you can buy food."

Biddy told her how he hated giving Mikey dog food. Ruby added a zero to the check.

"I'll take the dog," Ruby blubbered.

"Listen, Mrs. Blue, there's something I haven't told you. That dog, Sam, well, he would die without his buddies. Agatha raised them all together and she . . . they can't bear to be separated. When I first got them, they raised holy hell here until Mikey here figured out they had to be together. You can't separate them. It wouldn't be right," Biddy pleaded.

"How many are there?" Ruby asked anxiously.

"Well, there's Fred. Fred's a girl, Sam is a boy. Then there's

Doozie, he's a cat. Likes to fight. Charlotte is a parakeet and she sings. On command," Biddy said proudly.

"What . . . what does she sing?" Ruby asked stupidly.

"Mostly the national anthem. Sometimes 'Ninety-nine Bottles of Beer.' Gets a little loud at times. All you have to do is cover her cage. They loved Agatha Penny."

Ruby's heart fluttered. "Does that mean they won't . . . maybe they're one-person animals. Maybe it isn't such a good idea . . . me taking someone else's pets. Maybe I should take a stray."

"Nosiree, ma'am, these animals will love you the way they loved Agatha so long as you give them love back. They're *starved* for love," Biddy said dramatically.

"Mikey, fetch the others," he ordered.

Ruby dropped to her knees and rubbed Sam's belly the way she'd seen Mikey do. In a heartbeat she was hooked on the dog's sad brown eyes. He licked her face and she laughed.

Fred was a fluffball whose coat was matted and dirty. She held back, staying close to Mikey, who was rubbing her belly. She growled low in her throat when Ruby reached out to scratch her ears.

"She's just hungry. Once you feed her, she'll be all over you. Once you feed an animal, it belongs to you."

The cat eyed her disdainfully as if to say, "Oh, sure, you're going to feed me. First I want to see the food. Then maybe I'll purr for you."

The bird was fluttering wildly, feathers flying all over her cage. She wasn't singing. Ruby asked why.

"She's feeling strange. Once you put her in her space, a window is good, she'll sing her little heart out for you. I do have seed for her. Doesn't eat much."

Ruby left the shelter with the two dogs, the cat, and the bird Biddy said would sing on command.

Once the animals were settled in the Rover, Biddy leaned in through the window. He had to ask; he couldn't let her drive away until he knew for certain. "Will you be taking over for Agatha?"

Ruby thought about it for thirty seconds. "Yes. Yes, I will, Mr. Bidwell. The first of every month, how does that sound?"

If she hadn't called him Mr. Bidwell, he wouldn't have believed her.

With eyes as wet as his dogs', he watched Ruby drive away.

He put his arms around Mikey and said, "Tonight I'm going to make us hamburgers and macaroni and cheese. You take care of things, Mikey, and I'll be back in a little while with some food for all our friends. You just keep rubbing their bellies. We'll have a regular party."

Mikey smiled, understanding perfectly.

Ruby drove away, the dogs hopping and jumping all over the seats. Doozie, in her cage, hissed and spit her displeasure. The bird was screeching something that sounded like "ninety-nine bottles of beer on the wall . . ."

Had she been snookered? She doubted it. Nothing, not even paying Conrad Malas for his brownie recipe had given her this much pleasure.

Though Ruby drove slowly over the country road, the dogs yelped and slid to the floor every time she put her foot on the gas pedal. In between times they barked in hatred of the ride. Next they would start to fight. The cat snarled, and his claws tried to reach the squabbling dogs. The parakeet was still singing. Not to be outdone, Ruby joined in with the bird. The dogs silenced immediately and lay down on the backseat. The hissing cat grew quiet. Ruby sung on lustily, the bird right along with her. So that was the secret to silence. The tension in her shoulders eased.

When Ruby swerved the car to a halt in her driveway, Sam flew over the front seat. Fred landed with her paw tangled in the space between the headrest and the top of the seat. Ruby untangled her and was rewarded with a ripe red scratch on her hand. The cat hissed and spit when Ruby picked up the carrier. The bird fluttered her wings wildly.

It was a goddamn menagerie, Ruby thought when she had let the cat out. She stood by helplessly as the animals raced and tore about the house. Her helplessness turned to horror when Sam lifted his leg four times on various table legs. The cat pawed through the junk mail on the dining room floor before it relieved itself. Ruby squealed, the cat froze, then hissed and continued.

"Oh, shit!" Rub hissed back.

Fred took her word literally and crapped between the dining room and kitchen doorway. The bird was starting on the national anthem, feathers flying all over the kitchen, her cage rattling ominously.

Ruby want to choke the life out of Arthur Bidwell.

It was a full ninety minutes before she had thawed enough chicken for the two dogs. She added some gravy and vegetables from a bowl of leftover stew in the refrigerator. She carefully cut the meat into small pieces and mashed the vegetables to disguise them.

The animals were watching her like vultures. A lump settled in her throat as she wondered when they had had their last meal. When the dogs' food was ready, she set it aside. She opened a large can of tuna, flaked it with her fingers, added some of the stew gravy and vegetables, and warmed it.

Ruby almost lost her arm when she set the plates on the floor. Charlotte sang her heart out as the animals devoured their food. When they were done, they backed away and looked at her expectantly.

"What's that look mean?" she muttered. "Do you want more?" She filled their plates a second time. Charlotte continued to sing.

Ruby developed a headache. An hour later she threw a dishtowel over Charlotte's cage. Fred cocked one ear from her position half on top of Sam by the fireplace. Sam squirmed. Doozie was between Fred's legs. They looked like a giant pretzel, Ruby thought.

A smile tugged at the corners of her mouth. How long would it take, she wondered, for the animals to become hers? When would they jump on her, lick her face and hands? When would they view her as their master? When, if ever, would she take Mrs. Penny's place? Her heart thumped. What if Mrs. Penny weren't replaceable?

Confident that the animals would sleep for a while with full bellies, Ruby drove into town. Her first stop was a pet store, where she bought three wicker beds with bright red plaid cushions and a litter box. She purchased three leashes, three collars, assorted dog and cat toys, catnip, chewies, and cat treats. A spiky brush, dog shampoo, and a complete grooming kit was added to the pile.

In the supermarket she purchased fifty dollars' worth of canned dog food, along with moist packets and a large bag of dry food. She added another twenty dollars' worth of cat food to her basket alone.

In the checkout line Ruby stared at the contents in the basket. The word *family* popped into mind. Her new family. Commitment. Responsibility. Love. The animals would love her. Unconditionally. Forever. For all their lives. And she would shower them with love in return. They were *hers*. They would never go, and no one would ever take them away from her.

People . . . people trampled all over you. People disappointed you. People caused pain and broken hearts. Damn you, Dixie, damn you to hell. Damn you, Nola, damn you, Calvin. Who needs you? Who fucking needs you?

From the market she went to the bookstore and bought two books on dogs and cats. When the salesclerk asked her what breed the dogs were, she shrugged. At the last minute she asked for a book on birds. If she was going to do her best for her new family, she needed to be prepared.

"Would you be interested in reading some of James Herriot's books?" the saleswoman asked. "They're wonderful if you like animals."

"Why not?" Ruby muttered.

All Things Wise and Wonderful, The Lord God Made Them All, and *All Things Bright and Beautiful* were added to her order.

Fifteen minutes later she was convinced you never left animals alone. There was something wrong with every room in the house. When she finally located her new roommates, she could only gape. Sam had tugged the bedspread down to the middle of the bed. He was on one pillow, Fred on the other. The cat was asleep on the mantel between a picture of Andy holding his first fish and Marty riding her bicycle for the first time without training wheels. All three animals ignored her.

Hands clenched into fists, her thumbs pointing backward, she yelled, "Out!" The cat hissed. The dogs barked. None of them moved.

"Listen up. I don't care if Mrs. Penny lets you sleep on her bed or not. You aren't sleeping on *mine*. Out!" When they still didn't move, Ruby shouted again. "Oh, shit!" She stormed out of the room and stomped down the stairs.

Obviously, she was doing something wrong or else the animals didn't like her. It was their first day. She was a stranger.

Maybe she had to change her attitude. Maybe she needed to be more patient . . .

Something strange was happening to her, something that was within her grasp. All she had to do was open up, reach out. The moment was gone a second later. Her heart pounded in her chest. She wasn't sure why.

In her life Ruby would never understand how three animals could drop so much poop. They must have been house-trained. How could an old lady clean up after three animals?

For five whole days Ruby tried her best to fasten the collars and leashes on the animals so they could be walked. They refused to come within a foot of her. Neither would they go near any of the doors in the house. She spread newspapers all over the place, hoping the animals would hit one once in a while. They didn't. She'd gone through two bottles of liquid cleanser and almost a gallon of bleach. The new beds hadn't been slept in. The dog and cat toys were in a red basket by the fireplace and hadn't been touched. The litter box by the pantry door was used, but that was it. The only thing the animals permitted her to do was feed them.

She'd read all the books, tried all the tricks. Nothing worked. She called Arthur Bidwell and said she had to bring the animals back. "I've done everything, Mr. Bidwell, they won't cooperate. I'm so tired of cleaning up their messes. If you can't come up with something, I really will have to bring them back."

Biddy shook his grizzled head. "They should have come around by now. They love to go for walks. Fred especially. She knows how to get the leash off the hook. She gets it when she has to go. Maybe they're afraid you're going to bring them back here. They don't like cages or pens. No animal does. Now, wait a minute, I seem to recall hearing Agatha call them by special names. Let me think now so I get this straight. Fred was honey button, Sam was her honey bunch, and Doozie was her sweet honey. Try that. Hell, ma'am, it might work. They're scared is all. I'd stake my life on it."

"I don't think they like me." Ruby wanted to cry. No one liked her anymore, except her son.

"That's not true, Mrs. Blue. Animals are smart. I think they're afraid you're going to go away. Why do you think they picked *your* bed to lay on? You said you have other beds. That means something to them."

Ruby brightened considerably. "Okay, I'll give it a few more days."

"How's Charlotte?"

"I now know most of the words to the national anthem, what does that tell you?" Biddy allowed himself a small chuckle when he hung up the phone.

Ruby felt silly as hell when she walked upstairs to her bedroom that wasn't her bedroom anymore. The animals didn't acknowledge her in any way. She walked to the center of the room, where they could all see her. She called them by names Mr. Bidwell suggested. Fred opened one eye; otherwise she ignored her. Sam's tail swished, but he, too, ignored her. Doozie lifted her head at the sound of the familiar name and then lowered her head to her paws. It wasn't working.

She found herself pleading; her eyes filled with tears. "I thought we could be best friends, that you would like me. Don't you understand? I don't have anyone, and neither do you. Mrs. Penny is gone. I know you loved her. Can't you love me just a little?" Ruby asked brokenly. "Mr. Bidwell couldn't keep you. You were hungry and you were dirty. You were sleeping in a cage. Now you're sleeping on pillows, eating steak and chicken. I don't rub your noses in the messes you make. I've been more than fair, haven't I? All my life I've been fair, and what happens? They stick it to me every damn time. Now you're doing the same thing."

The dogs stared at her. The cat leapt to the back of the rocking chair, her eyes on Ruby. Her plumed tail swished.

"I don't think it was too much to ask. I never had animals before, so maybe I'm doing something wrong. Don't you understand? I *need* someone to love me, someone to care about me. Somehow, I screwed up everything. Well, you know what? I don't care anymore. I don't care about you anymore, either." She wiped her eyes with the sleeve of her shirt.

Sam inched closer to Fred, nuzzling her furry neck. Doozie stared with unblinking eyes at the distraught woman.

Ruby called the animals by Mrs. Penny's pet names. She stayed with it for a full hour. Finally her shoulders straightened, her eyes sparked. "I cannot believe I am standing here, talking to you, begging and pleading with you."

The two dogs were huddled into a tight ball, their eyes on the cat, whose tail was swishing furiously.

"Okay, that's it! You hear me? That's it! I'm sick and tired of your crap. I've had it!" Ruby screeched at the top of her lungs. "I did my best. I cooked for you. I goddamn cooked for you. *Real* food. I sneaked in that dog food only once in a while. I bought you toys, beds, leashes. And what the hell do you do? You sleep in my goddamn bed, that's what! *I* sleep in the guest room! No more! Get your goddamn asses off my bed. You're going back to Mr. Bidwell. Live in a stinking cage, see if I care. Ungrateful, stinking animals. I hate you! You're supposed to be my goddamn best friends, and what are you? Takers. That's what you are, just like everyone else in my life. I give, you take. *Bullshit!* Get out of here! Now! I don't ever want to see you again! You hear me, dammit, get out of here!

"You're just like Dixie and Nola and Calvin. They didn't care about me. I did everything, went out of my way to be the best friend I know how to be. For God's sake, I practically did their . . . thinking for them. I was always there for them, but were they there for me? Hell, no, they weren't. Time and again they . . . they . . . disappointed me. I expected . . . I expected . . . Oh, God, it wasn't them at all, was it? It was me. I *expected*. If they didn't measure up to . . . my standards, to my way of doing things, I copped an attitude. The way I'm doing now with you. I was so damn busy blaming everyone else but myself." Andrew was right, she thought. She was stupid for not seeing it. Well, she was going to . . . to . . . bawl her damn head off.

Ruby dropped to her knees and howled, her shoulders shaking with sobs. She had the animals' attention now, but she didn't know it. Fred crept to the edge of the bed, Sam alongside her. They looked at one another. Both of them looked at Doozie, who was standing at attention on the rocking chair. As one they leapt, knocking Ruby off balance. They licked her, they pawed her, they snuggled against her, pushing at her hands and arms so she would pet them.

Hiccoughing with pure joy, Ruby was a child then, rolling and tussling, tickling and scratching, yelping and hollering. Doozie purred. The dogs woofed. Ruby cried some more. The animals backed off, waiting to hear the strange sounds they heard before. They crept closer, gentler this time as they licked daintily at her tears, pawed her more carefully, woofing softly.

"Okay, you can stay." Ruby hiccoughed. She blew her nose loudly. They were on their haunches now, lined up like little soldiers. It must mean something, Ruby thought wildly. What? "You want to go for a walk? I want to go for a walk. Get the leashes." Doozie streaked ahead of the dogs and had the leash in his mouth. Fred couldn't seem to make up her mind if she wanted the red or green one. She finally settled for the red one. Sam was left with the green one. Once again they lined up.

"You little devils," Ruby muttered. "You knew how to do it all along. You put me through hell this past week," she cried happily.

Like a Park Avenue matron walking her prize show dogs, Ruby sailed through the open kitchen door with her two mutts and her stray cat. They walked beautifully, even the cat. They all did what they had to do in record time. As one, they turned. They wanted to go back. Doozie's back was up, Sam's tail between his legs.

"Okay, we're going back. You did real good. We'll do it again after supper. I'm going to give you a special treat tonight, real liver and bacon. For you, Doozie, I'll split my salmon steak." She thought she saw Fred nod.

"I'll be dipped," Ruby mumbled as each animal went to the red basket to pick out a toy and chewie. They carried them back to their beds. She watched, a wide grin splitting her features as Doozie and Sam waited for Fred to make her choice. "So, you're the boss." She laughed. "Now I know who to defer to." With a wild flourish she removed the dishtowel from the bird cage. "Ninety-nine bottles . . ." Ruby threw the towel back over the cage.

"Tomorrow you're learning a new song or you're heading back you know where."

Ruby chirped happily as she set about preparing a gourmet dinner for her new family.

Her world was right side up.

The following morning Ruby called her attorney. He came on the line and wished her a good morning. "Alan, I want you to hire the best private detective in the country. I don't care what it costs. I want him to find Dixie. Tell him to use all his operatives."

"Ruby, I thought . . . are you sure you want to do this?"

"I'm sure. Someday I'll explain, not right now, though. And, Alan, that check Amber sent back after my parents died? Deposit it. It was important to Amber to send it. If we've held it too long, write to her and ask her to issue a new one. I have a feeling that check was a milestone for Amber, and it needs to be acknowledged. I'm sorry it's taken me so long to do it. I'll write her a letter myself as soon as I get some things straight in my mind."

"Sounds like you're clearing away a lot of mental cobwebs."

Ruby beamed. "Alan, that's exactly what I'm doing. Thanks for saying it out loud."

"So, what's on your agenda?"

"First, I'm going to get myself duded to the nines and attend *the* fashion show of the year. A very old, dear friend personally invited me."

"Good for you, Ruby. I'll do as you ask. By the way, I suggest you turn on your answering machine. Detectives call in their reports and you won't want to miss them."

"Good point, Alan. Thanks for everything." Ruby happily hung up the phone.

CHAPTER TWENTY-EIGHT

{{{{{{{{{ *}}}}}}}}}*

Ruby weighed her options as the day of Nola's private showing drew near. Part of her wanted to go, to see Nola again. They could compare nervous breakdowns. She'd never seriously given a name to what she'd gone through the past year and a half. The doctor hadn't given it a name, either. A breakdown was so . . . so unstable. When you had a breakdown, you lost control. Other people couldn't depend on you.

She had turned tail and run. She had thought it was to her credit that she went off, alone, to lick her wounds and not subject other people to her fits of melancholy and depression. Now she wasn't so sure. But at least she'd turned herself around and

gotten her health back. She was almost the old Ruby again. Seeing Nola again might make her feel even *more* like the old
Ruby. It was at that moment that she discovered she didn't *want*
to be the old Ruby any longer. But she did want to see Nola.

Ruby settled herself at the kitchen table to pen off a note to
Nola. She scribbled furiously and then read the letter several
times to make sure it said exactly what she wanted it to say.

> Dear Nola,
> Of course I'm going to attend your showing. Thank you for
> inviting me. I'll be the friendly face in the front row in a blue
> dress, designed by Nq, sewed by Hattie Semolina. I'll explain
> when I see you.
> I've missed you, Nola, and no explanations are necessary
> regarding that old phone call. I'm the one who needs to do the
> explaining, if you have the time to listen.
> Good luck, or do I say break a leg or something like that?
> Whatever, consider it said. I can't wait to hug you, Nola.
>> Affectionately,
>> Ruby

She had other unfinished business to attend to. She ripped a
sheet of paper off the tablet.

The letter was short, instructing her attorneys to file a law suit
against Calvin Santos for money he owed her. He had borrowed
much over the years and had never paid any of it back, including the loans she had given to him for his campaign. She included copies of canceled checks and itemized lists. She also
included two letters Calvin had sent, in which he mentioned his
intention to repay the money he owed her.

"You deserve to be sued, Calvin," Ruby muttered, "but
maybe you don't deserve to be hit between the eyes." She wrote
a second note. On her seventh draft she decided it sounded right.

> Dear Calvin,
> I instructed my attorney to file suit against you for money
> you owe me. I had hoped to avoid doing so and believed you
> when you said you would repay me when you were solvent.
> I'm sure it simply slipped your mind, so if you would like to
> pay me, let's say, within thirty days, we can avoid litigation.
> I'm sorry about everything, Calvin. I'm willing to take the

blame. I expected too much from our relationship. When you didn't measure up, didn't do what I expected, I reacted. I guess if I have to say there was a bottom line, it was that you broke my heart twice, once back in Washington and then again when you were elected. The affair was wrong for both of us. I'm not willing to take all the blame for that, though. You *did* say you were getting a divorce. I guess all men say that when they enter into an affair, and I guess all women believe it.

What I would like, Calvin, is for you to square off your debt to me so we can look each other in the eye if we ever chance to meet. I think it's the honorable thing to do.

Part of me will always love you, Calvin. From this point on, I wish for you what I wish for myself, the best. My son gave me a plaque to hang in my kitchen. I'd like to pass it on to you, Calvin. It pretty much says it all. If you have a mind to be open, that is. JUDGE YOUR SUCCESS BY THE DEGREE THAT YOU'RE ENJOYING PEACE, HEALTH, AND LOVE.

You, Calvin, are someone I used to know.

Ruby

Ruby read the letter over twice before she scribbled her phone number and address at the bottom and again on the envelope.

Ruby called Federal Express and asked to have all three letters picked up. She gave directions to her house and listened while the operator said the letters would be delivered by ten o'clock the following morning.

More unfinished business. She called Martha. Her office said she was out on a site and offered to take a message. Ruby declined to leave one.

The last of her unfinished business. She called Andy. Ruby smiled, as she always did, when her son's voice came over the wire.

"How's the troops?" he chuckled.

"We're a team these days. Not one accident and Charlotte is learning a new song today."

Andy whooped with laughter, not because of the bird but because of the lilt in his mother's voice. She was finally coming around. He wished he were with her so he could hug her.

"Listen, Andy, about that acreage. I have an idea. Can an access road be put in from the top of the hill to the back end of the property?"

"Don't see why not. Why?"

"Do you think you could come up this weekend and take a look? The Semolina brothers are working on the outbuildings. They should be done any day now. I've been thinking about building a larger animal shelter, one that can accommodate more animals, and a wildlife preserve of some kind. A small cottage for the caretaker. I mean caretakers, plural."

"It'll cost you some bucks, Ma. You want to spring for a whole bunch or a little bunch?" He laughed.

"Whatever it takes. I'll ask Mr. Bidwell and Mikey to come by while you're here. They might have some ideas. I want it to be . . . a . . . ah, a sanctuary for them and the animals. Like this place is for me."

"I hear you, Ma," Andy said softly. "How about Saturday? And will you make me a pineapple upside-down cake?"

"You bet. I might even throw in some whipped cream to top it off."

"Now you're cooking. I'll see you Saturday."

"Andy, do you have the time to take on a project like this?"

"Ma, I'll make the time. I'm in business for myself, remember? By the way, speaking of business, how's yours?"

Ruby threw back her head and laughed. "I have no idea. Okay, I guess."

"No word on Dixie?"

"Nope, but I'm hiring a private detective to find her."

"That's great. They're paging me, Ma. I love you."

"I love you, too, Andy."

"*You're* gonna love him, too," she said to the snoozing animals.

While the animals slept, Ruby went through the file folder in which she kept the design Nola had given her so many years ago. Her eyes puddled up as memories engulfed her.

The past.

Two hours later Hattie Semolina was taking Ruby's measurements.

"Can you have it ready in a week?"

"Don't see why not," Hattie muttered around the pins in her mouth.

"Is this going to be a creation?"

"Everything I sew is a creation," Hattie said.

"Do you think the fabric is ... it has to be special. This is very important. It has to have a one-of-a-kind look," Ruby said anxiously.

"It's going to be one of a kind. I'm only making one. Stand still, Mrs. Blue."

That was all she was going to get from Hattie Semolina by way of assurance.

Ruby's hand was on the doorknob when Hattie said, "Miss Quantrell won't find fault with my sewing."

"You know Nola?" Ruby said in amazement.

"I can read." Hattie pointed to Nola's signature on the design.

Ruby smiled. Nola's design was in good hands. She was never more sure of anything in her life.

Ruby climbed out of bed. Today was the day she was driving into New York. She'd made reservations at the Plaza. She would change into Nola's creation after she showered and put on fresh makeup. She wanted to look as good as she could when she saw Nola again. God, she was excited.

She moved faster than usual. She walked the dogs, fed them, and ate some breakfast. She dressed in a pair of slacks and a pullover sweater. She looked good enough to walk through the lobby of the Plaza. She'd even hired a limo to take her from the hotel to the show.

Promptly at two o'clock, Ruby entered the showroom on Seventh Avenue. She marched to the front row of seats where Nola had said she was to sit. A young man pointed to the middle of the row and whispered, "Nola said she wants you in her direct line of vision. I don't know who's prettier, you or the dress," he said, his eyes full of admiration. Damn, she felt good.

Ruby looked around. She knew diddly-squat about the fashion business, but if this turnout for Nola was any indication of success, then Nola was a success.

"And now, ladies and gentlemen, Miss Nola Quantrell," the young man said to the audience. Everyone clapped, Ruby the loudest.

And there she was, done up in feathers and combs, her dress made from something that looked like handkerchiefs all sewed together at crazy angles. She looked wonderful, Ruby thought.

The show moved swiftly, with Nola introducing each outfit.

Ruby risked a look around. The buyers were all scribbling furiously. That had to be good; they were going to buy. She looked up and gave Nola a jaunty thumbs-up, which Nola returned.

"And now, ladies and gentlemen, my last design. I was going to show you something else entirely until . . . until the beginning of the show when I . . . bear with me a minute, ladies and gentlemen." Ruby frowned, as Nola walked off the stage. Was something wrong?

The touch on her arm was feather-light. "Come with me, Ruby," Nola said quietly. "I can't believe you saved . . . God, Ruby, I'm going to bawl right here any minute."

"Like hell you are," Ruby said, following Nola to the back of the makeshift stage.

Her arm around Ruby's shoulders, Nola led her to the center of the stage. "Ladies and gentlemen, this is Ruby Blue. For those of you who don't know Ruby Blue, let me tell you she is half of Mrs. Sugar, the famous cookie maker." She had the audience's attention.

"Years ago, when I only dreamed about being a designer, I met Ruby Blue. Of course, she was Ruby Connors in those days. I worked hard, but I couldn't make it. I found myself in dire straits and Ruby . . . Ruby gave me all the money she had for me to get back home. I couldn't just take her money, so she told me to sign a design I'd *given* her. She said . . . she said she knew one day I'd be a famous designer. She believed in me when no one else did. And here she is, ladies and gentlemen, in that same dress I designed more years ago than I care to remember. What I do remember saying is that if she ever had it made up to be sure and use blue material." Then Nola whispered, "Strut, Ruby, around and around, and when you come to a stop, cross your ankles."

Shaking and trembling, Ruby strutted.

The audience clapped loud and long as Ruby took up her stance next to Nola. The buyers' hands went in the air, a sign they wanted to purchase the dress Ruby was wearing. Nola smiled at Ruby before she said, "Sorry, this is not for sale. It's the only one-of-a-kind Nola Quantrell design in the world, and this lady, this friend, deserves the best I have to give. Thank you all for coming today."

Nola pushed and shoved Ruby free of the models and the people clamoring backstage. "C'mon, we're getting out of here.

Other people can handle all this. It's just you and me, kiddo, so let's move. We have a lot of catching-up to do. A lot of I'm sorry to get out of the way. Jesus, Ruby, I cannot ... I will never forgot ... how in the hell ... God, I'm glad to see you."

In the middle of Seventh Avenue, with the vendors moving their wares while delivery trucks inched their way around them, Ruby and Nola hugged one another, tears streaming down their cheeks.

"I think this is the second best day of my life," Nola said tearfully.

"My second best day, too," Ruby said.

Neither woman asked the other what *the* best day was. It simply wasn't important.

In Nola's apartment, over glasses of wine, the two women curled up on the floor on piles of cushions. "Tell me everything," Nola said. "I wasn't sure you'd come. I prayed, Ruby, that you would."

"I wasn't going to at first. I mean, part of me wanted to come, but I don't think I would have. I was a different person then. I expected too much, couldn't accept other people for their weaknesses as well as their strengths. They could never be brave enough, strong enough, fair enough, good enough. They could never do enough to prove they really loved me. It's all mixed up, but I'm sorting it out. Part of it, I know, stems from my childhood and my parents, and I'm working on that, too. It seems," Ruby said, "my only happiness, my only peaceful times, my only contented times, are when I'm doing something for other people. It's when I start insisting other people do things for me that I screw up. That's when I start making demands on everyone to live up to *my* expectations. I want the world to love me my way, and that's not always possible.

"What made me figure it all out was ... I got these pets that used to belong to someone else and they didn't ... they didn't like me. God, I tried so hard to make them like me. I let them shit all over the house, I cooked special food for them, and gave them the best of everything, and still they wouldn't have anything to do with me. I needed someone to ... love me. And I blamed them when they couldn't. I was blind to the fact that they were frightened. ... That was when I took a good long look at myself. Soul-searching is not an easy thing to do. The only times I didn't screw up was when I was giving without expecting anything back. I got such ... Lord, I can't describe the feelings ... I just felt good that I was able to make someone happy. That's why I loved giving to the orphans at your parents' house. In fact, I thought *your* parents were perfect. And always in the back of my mind was the thought that I might end up completely unloved and unloving, like *my* parents. I couldn't let go, it was always there. When you seemed to turn on your parents I ... I just couldn't understand. But now I'd like us to be friends, Nola. I mean real friends, like we used to be. If we start over, I think we can do it. If you're willing, that is." Nola nodded, her eyes glistening. Ruby beamed from ear to ear. "Now, tell me about Nola Quantrell."

"Nola Quantrell is a liar, Ruby. She lied to you from the git-go. The Nola you thought you knew hated those orphans, hated the farm life, hated doing without, hated going home pregnant. I don't know who I thought I was that I should have had something better. You want to talk about guilt, that's my middle name. I wanted to write you so many times, but I knew you wouldn't be able to accept who you thought I was. One summer, Ruby, we didn't have anything to eat except fried potatoes, cucumbers, and bacon. Everyone got one slice of bacon. Sometimes the potatoes were baked or mashed. Sometimes the cucumbers were creamed, sometimes they were in vinegar. I swore to myself I would never eat those things again. One whole summer, Ruby. My father got laid off that year and they wouldn't take welfare. I made up all those stories about how wonderful it was and you ate it up and then I couldn't tell you the truth. I'm glad you sent those things. I mean that. But my parents weren't all that wonderful, either. They never forgave me for having my son out of wedlock. It was my father who tracked Alex down. It was my parents who insisted on the marriage. They wanted to make an honest woman of me and to get me and the baby out of the house. I had no choices at the time. At least I didn't think so. I've learned since that you always have choices if you have the guts to act on them.

"Years later, when I started to earn money, I did send it home. Grudgingly, I admit. I tried to keep track of everyone, but every time one batch of orphans left, another one came in. At one point there were twenty-one. For so long I didn't understand. All those kids, the simple life, was what made my parents happy.

You're like them, Ruby. I was selfish. I'm still selfish. I guess I will always be selfish," Nola said, miserable.

"No, you're not. If you were selfish, you would have sold my dress right off my back," Ruby giggled.

"You better hang on to it," Nola said, wiping her tears.

"We fucked up, Nola."

"Where did you learn to use such language?" Nola demanded.

"Andrew. You should hear the words I know."

"How is Andrew?"

"Andrew is fine. We're actually friends these days. With Andrew you know where you stand. I know now that he'd go to the wall for me if I needed him to. For a long time I didn't know that. We're honest with each other. What about Alex?"

"He's dead. I cried a lot when I found out. We never should have gotten married. It was a sexual thing with us. Better to have left it at that. My son is great. We're good friends. He's in California. He pretty much runs Nq Ltd. He does a hell of a job, too."

"What about your nervous breakdown?"

"One day I couldn't get up. I didn't want to get up. I was carrying around all this guilt, and that day it finally got too heavy for me to carry. I've been seeing a shrink for a long time now. I need ... Ruby, I need to share something with you. I haven't told anyone. I haven't even told the shrink and I know that's stupid, but ... I'm one of the orphans. I was never a real Quantrell. My parents never had any children. I never knew until my parents died. There were seventy-two children at my mother's funeral. My dad died first. My sister, the girl I thought was my sister, was four years older than me and she said she remembered the day they brought me home. I wasn't real, Ruby. I wasn't me. I felt so cheated. And then I tried to justify my attitude by saying somehow down deep I knew it all along, but I didn't know. I thought I belonged. I thought I was their child."

Ruby stretched out her arms. Nola laid her head on Ruby's shoulder. "I know, I'm going to tell the shrink. You're working through your problem and I'll work through mine. Do you think we can call one another with progress reports from time to time? You'll listen, won't you, Ruby?"

"Only if you listen to me." They sniffed and cried, and blew their noses together, smiling through their tears. "I knew we'd always be friends. We got sidetracked for a while, but I think we're both going to make it," Ruby said.

CHAPTER
{{{{{{{{{{   TWENTY-NINE   }}}}}}}}}

Andy sat in his makeshift trailer on the sanctuary building site, looking at the guest list for his mother's surprise birthday party. He'd dragged his butt finishing the sanctuary to make it coincide with the party. He'd called just about everyone: the attorneys in New York, Silas Ridgely, Nola, his father, the entire work force at Mrs. Sugar's, and all the names he'd gotten from his mother's address book, which he'd snatched. He'd delayed calling Martha, but his father said, "Go ahead and just do it, Andy." Still, he wasn't sure. He wasn't sure about his two aunts, either, but he had called them. Neither had confirmed they would attend, but they hadn't said they wouldn't. The Semolina brothers and cousins, including Angus Webster, would definitely be there.

His biggest problem right now was getting his mother away from the house a few days before the party so the new barn could be decorated. He'd been flirting with the idea of an emergency call from the corporate headquarters, saying the workforce was going on strike. *That* alone would mandate his mother going down to check it out. He could rig a phony picket line with no sweat. The minute things got sticky, they would march off in disgust, hop on a bus he would provide, and head for the party. Olga would stay behind to tell his mother there was an emergency back at the farm. If there was one thing his mother had always been good at, it was doing two things at once.

His slender fingers drummed on the Formica desktop in the grungy work trailer. It was hard to believe a whole year had gone by since his mother had first approached him with the idea of the sanctuary. It was almost as hard for him to believe his mother was fifty-five.

He thought about Biddy and Mikey when they saw the cottage last week. Biddy had almost cried; Mikey did cry. The boy couldn't believe he was going to have his own room. Andy had felt tears mist his own eyes.

The new furniture was being delivered today, and his mother was straw-bossing the installation of everything. He'd seen her whiz by several hours ago, the dogs yapping in the back of the car, the cat perched on her shoulder. The way the tail end of the Rover had been dragging, he knew it was loaded with staples, people food, and at least a quarter ton of dog food.

She'd been so excited when she told him how she was decorating the room for Mikey. She'd ordered custom-made wallpaper with all the woodland characters and some of her personal favorites: the Lady and the Tramp, Tom and Jerry. In the center of the ceiling, a sappy-eyed cow jumped over a moon. "For the nights when Mikey can't sleep," his mother had said.

The small kitchen was a compact marvel, the family area held a stereo, a television, VCR, and shelves of VCR tapes for Mikey and Biddy.

There were new clothes in the closets and drawers. For winter, warm down jackets, flannel shirts, long underwear, heavy boots, and shoes. Also warm caps and gloves for Mikey. Summer wear was bright and colorful; Mikey and Biddy both liked bright colors.

Andy found himself laughing aloud. Once his mother got into something, she went all the way. He looked at his watch. Time to get over to the cottage. He'd told Biddy and Mikey to meet him there at noon. He thought he could hear Biddy's ancient truck rattling across the field. He could hardly wait for Biddy to see the spanking-new truck that had been delivered forty minutes earlier.

This time they did cry, all of them. With Sam under his left arm, Fred under his right, and Doozie on his shoulder, Mikey walked around his new home, tears streaming down his cheeks. They watched him from the doorway while he bounced on his new bed; he touched his new robe hanging over the bottom, smiled when he poked at his new slippers and sneakers alongside the night table. They giggled when he looked in his own mirror, preened for a minute, pointed to himself, and said, "I hasmome."

"You sure are handsome." Ruby smiled. His head bobbed excitedly.

"Mine?"

"All yours!" Ruby agreed.

Mikey pointed to Sam, Fred, and Doozie. "Mine?" he grinned devilishly.

"No way." Ruby grinned.

"Ish joke," Mikey said, falling back on the bed, the dogs on top of him.

"Some joke. I think they like you, Mikey. They remember the way you rubbed their bellies when they were hungry. They didn't forget you," Ruby said quietly.

"Not forget." It was said so clearly, Ruby's eyebrows shot upward.

She tousled the boy's hair before she bent down to kiss his cheek.

"No one ever forgets the things that are important, Mikey."

Mikey sat up on the bed. "Im-ptant. No cages."

"Damn right, kiddo. There aren't going to be any cages in our place," Andy said, slapping Mikey on the back. The boy poked him playfully.

"You did real good, Ma," Andy stage-whispered.

"I'd like to second that," Biddy said gruffly. "I don't know what to say. It's like a dream come true."

"Do you think Agatha Penny would approve, Mr. Bidwell?" Ruby asked anxiously.

"Agatha would approve, most definitely. You've always called me Mr. Bidwell, Mrs. Blue. Everyone calls me Biddy. Don't you think it's time for you to call me Biddy, too?"

Ruby was about to say yes until she saw Biddy's eyes. "Oh, I can't do that, Mr. Bidwell. I have too much respect for you." She *knew* no one had ever called Biddy Mr. Bidwell but her. "I hope it doesn't offend you."

"Not at all, Mrs. Blue. I rather like it." The little man grinned.

Ruby looked discreetly away, pretending not to see the old man's glistening eyes. "So, Mr. Bidwell, what do you think of the other building, the one where you and Mikey will be spending most of your time? Andy did a wonderful job, didn't he?"

"Yes, ma'am, he sure did. I didn't know too much about arke-teks until he explained what he was trying to do. Me and

Mikey, we like it a lot. Folks around here are sure going to be surprised when we open up."

"Folks around here are already surprised." Andy guffawed. "The Semolina brothers and cousins come by at least once a week to check on our progress. They told me, mind you they told me this to my face just a few weeks ago, that for a city whipper-snapper, I knew my business, even though I never lift a hammer. It was a real compliment."

Ruby smiled. "Well, I guess I better get back to the house. I want to put a roast in the oven for you guys and I promised my menagerie I'd make them cheeseburgers for dinner."

"Ma," Andy whispered, "aren't you forgetting something? The barn," he whispered a second time.

"Oh, yes, the barn. Mr. Bidwell, there's something in the barn you might want to take back to the shelter with you."

"Do you think he'll like it?" Ruby said anxiously while she waited for Biddy to open the barn doors.

"Ma, he's going to love it. Especially the sign on the door. Now, *that* was a good idea."

Biddy walked back into the sunshine and stared at Andy and Ruby. "Is this vehicle for me and Mikey?" he asked, a catch in his voice.

"Yes, it is, Mr. Bidwell. I think it goes well with that brand-new building, don't you? Since none of us knows what Mikey's last name is I . . . I hope you don't mind if his name is first."

"I like it. Mikey would, too, if he could read. Has a ring to it. THE MIKEY/BIDWELL ANIMAL SHELTER, LORDS VALLEY, PA."

Andy tossed Biddy the keys.

"We put a block on the gas pedal and brake," Andy said.

"I feel like a kid with a new bike. Mikey!" he bellowed.

Andy and Ruby watched till Biddy and the new truck disappeared behind the rise.

"I just figured out something a little while ago," he said. "Most people give because they get something in return. You aren't going to get a thing for this, no writeoff, no nothing."

"Oh, but you're wrong, Andy. I've got *me*."

{{{{{{{{{ CHAPTER THIRTY }}}}}}}}}

They were all gathered, all the friends Ruby thought she didn't have. The four-piece band stood ready to blast its way into "Happy Birthday," the caterers stood behind their long tables filled with chafing dishes. Other waiters and waitresses circled the huge barn with trays of drinks and finger foods.

Andy felt pleased with himself as he looked around the barn, decorated by a local florist with summer flowers and colorful streamers.

A table by the door was piled high with gaily wrapped presents.

"The dogs are getting jittery. That means Ma's close by," Andy said to his father. "She's going to be mad as a wet hen, you know that, don't you?"

"Only for a second. The minute she sees everyone, it will be all over. Your mother . . ."

"Is kind of special, right, Pop?"

"Yes, she is. I tell her that all the time. Lately, I think she might be starting to believe me."

"She's gonna be real surprised to see you. I didn't think Marty would come, but she did. The aunts are here, too. I hope there aren't any fireworks."

"I won't allow it," Andrew said firmly. Andy believed him.

"Everyone, quiet! I think she's here," Andy said, running to the side door where Fred and Sam were scratching furiously. "Listen, I'll bring her through the big doors, so get ready." He slipped out with the dogs and Doozie.

"Yo, Ma! How'd it go?" he demanded nervously.

"They want a union. Can you believe that!" Ruby sputtered. "They wouldn't even talk to me! They walked off and left me standing there. The place is closed!" Ruby fumed. "This is the worst birthday I've had in my entire life!"

"Okay, okay. Listen, I hate to ask you to do this, but could I have a minute of your time? There's something in the barn I have to show you. I think the Semolina brothers screwed up and the roof is . . . is coming down."

"What?" Ruby squawked.

"They're going to stop by tomorrow, so you have to see it now. You know the brothers, they arrive at the crack of dawn."

"Andy, I'm so tired, can't I see it in the morning?" Ruby pleaded.

"You gotta see it now, Ma. It will only take a minute."

"Okay, but only a minute. You'll have to deal with the brothers. I have to worry about this damn union . . ."

"Happy birthday!"

It was the grandest party of her life. Ruby cried all through it. She cried while she square-danced with her husband, while she waltzed with Mick and Dick Semolina, and while she cuddled with Mikey in his new suit. She really bawled when her daughter looked her in the eye and said, "I'm so sorry, Mom." She sniffed when Nangi wrapped her in his arms and Amber patted her head. She was dry-eyed when Opal tried to meet her gaze but failed. Ruby patted her on the shoulder before she walked over to her husband and straight into his arms.

"Happy birthday, Ruby."

"Thanks, Andrew. Thanks for coming. It's good to see you. I mean that. It really is good to see you."

"Does that mean you finally got your shit together?"

"Does it ever?" Ruby gurgled. "You're lookin' good, Andrew. How many bimbos you dangling these days?"

"Meow," Andrew said good-naturedly.

Ruby leaned closer, her eyes wide and guileless. In a husky voice she whispered, "Does that mean you can still get it up?"

Andrew laughed till the tears flowed. "I can still get it up. Since I'm staying at your house, I can show you later, if you want."

"No, thanks. How old is she?"

Without hesitation Andrew replied, "Thirty-three. A willowy blonde. How about you?"

"Dead in the water, Andrew."

"It's a shame." His voice grew quieter when he said, "I know a couple of guys who could really rough him up for you. He had no right to treat you like that."

"I went into it with my eyes wide open. I deserve what I got for being so stupid. But I'm filing a suit against him for the money he owes me."

"You mean he owes *us* money?" Andrew asked, outraged.

"I guess you could put it that way. Yes, he owes me a chunk of money. I'll handle it." Damn, he did look good with his bronze tan. He was fit, too, just as lean as he'd been when he left Rumson. His hair was attractively gray at the temples. "I'll be dipped, you're wearing a rug. Andrew! Are you *that* vain?"

"It's not a rug. I had that hair-weave thing done. It's my own hair. They use what they cut off the back. Costs a fortune," he said happily. He turned serious for just a moment. "I wish you were happy, Ruby, I really do."

"I am, Andrew. Hey, that's my favorite song, let's dance."

They did, to the strains of "Blue Moon." They smiled at one another. They were friends now, she thought, who could accept each other for what they were, not what they wanted each other to be. Neither was aware that the dance floor cleared until the end of the song and the round of applause that rang in their ears. Andrew bowed, Ruby curtsied.

"I'll see *you* later," Andrew whispered.

"No, you won't. Those four-legged creatures let no one, and I mean no one, not even Andy, past the door in my bedroom. I will see you for breakfast, though. Thanks for the dance, Andrew." She was halfway across the barn when she turned to shout over her shoulder, "How much did you say you get on social security?" Andrew laughed so hard, his daughter had to pound him on the back.

She was jostled then, her face mashing against someone's fragrant-smelling chest. "Nola!" she squealed. "Is this a party or what?"

"It's a party," Nola laughed. "From the looks of things, it seems as if half the world is here."

"It's missing two people, but that's okay. I'm living with it. What's up with you?"

"All kinds of good things. I'm catching a midnight flight to France, so I have to leave early. I'm sorry, Ruby. I have some heavy-duty ... I'm thinking of selling out my interest in the company, and I want to see what the French will offer. These plans were made long before I knew about the party. I gotta go, Ruby. Happy birthday and all that jazz. I left your present on the table. I hope you like it."

"I'll like it no matter what it is," Ruby said sincerely. "Thanks for coming, Nola."

"Ruby, I wouldn't have missed it for the world. I hope you have many happy birthdays to come. Say good-bye to Andrew for me. He told me that for an old broad, I looked pretty good. I took it as a compliment."

Ruby hugged her friend. "Have a safe trip and call when you can."

"Will do."

The door had just closed behind Nola when Ruby felt someone touch her arm. "Happy birthday, Ruby." It was Amber.

"It would be if you meant it," Ruby said quietly.

"I remember telling you once back at the Y that you and I would never be friends. I meant it at the time, and as much as I try, I can't really feel anything for you, Ruby. I try to do the right things because Nangi gets so disappointed in me when I don't. He's very fond of you. If they had shrinks in Saipan, I'd probably go to one, but I know what my problem is, and no amount of counseling is going to take away my childhood. I don't even want to try. I don't want to spoil your birthday, but I felt I had to say these things. Nangi says I'm jealous of you. Maybe I am. But I don't think so."

"I don't think you are, either. You're who you are, and I'm who I am. I appreciate your honesty, though. I guess we'll both get on with our lives. We're in the winter now, you know."

"Ruby, that's just rubbish." Amber grimaced.

"That's because you don't want to believe it. There's no one standing in front of us, Amber. We have to stare at our own mortality now. You do that in the winter of your life. Mom and Dad are gone. We're next, if you're counting."

"Well, I'm not counting," Amber said tartly.

"Okay," Ruby said lightly. "Do we kiss each other or do we shake hands?"

Amber leaned over and pecked Ruby on the cheek. "That was for Nangi. For being good to him. For giving him a chance. *That* I appreciate."

"I'll accept that, Amber," Ruby said. And she would. "I'm glad we had this little talk."

"Me, too. Nice party. Good food. Great music," Amber said.

"Then go partake." Ruby grinned.

The band was playing "Happy Birthday" again. Ruby

marched over to the bandstand, where her son joined her. She stood back while Andy asked one of the musicians to make the birthday announcement. He obliged.

Ruby looked around at the smiling faces. It was all for her. They were *her* friends. She noticed Mikey and Biddy were standing next to Andy.

Ruby opened her presents. She cried, she smiled, she laughed as she thanked everyone. She was about to get up from the orange crate she was sitting on when Mikey approached, carrying a box. His head bobbed as he offered the huge sneaker box to Ruby.

"Ishsay."

Ruby peered into the box. Once again Ruby's eyes brimmed. "Stray puppy, huh?" she said, hugging the boy. "Does he have a name?" Mikey shook his head. "Okay, tomorrow we'll come up with one." Mikey beamed when she kissed him soundly on the cheek. She hugged Biddy.

When all her guests were gone except for her family, Ruby walked back into the barn. They were all gathered around the table with glasses of champagne in their hands. Andrew held one out to Ruby.

"It was so good of all of you to come," Ruby said. "I'm glad we're all here together again. The last time . . . that was unfortunate. We're all we have, one another. Except for Amber, of course, who has that wonderfully huge family." There was a tinkle of laughter in the room. "What happened before . . . that's history, we can't go back and make it right. If I did something wrong, I'm sorry. If it's at all possible, I'd like us to start over.

"Hey, the band is packing up. Stop them, Andy. I want us to sing and dance, just us. Just us."

The sun was creeping over the horizon when the family walked back to the house. Ruby's arms were linked in her son's and husband's. Martha was tripping ahead, backward, giggling and laughing.

While the others trooped off to take showers, Andrew and Ruby sat at the kitchen table, waiting for the coffee to perk.

"Ruby," Andrew said, "do you plan to live the rest of your life here in the boonies alone with your dogs and cats?"

Andrew looked as if he found it impossible to believe anyone would withdraw from life the way Ruby had. He looked tired, Ruby thought. Jet lag and alcohol, probably.

"I don't see anything wrong with what I'm doing," Ruby said quietly. "So what if this is the life I prefer? So what if I don't want to go back to the rat race? So what, Andrew?"

"Nothing," Andrew mumbled, "as long as you aren't *hiding*. As long as this is what you *really* want. I thought I knew you. You were a mover and a shaker for so long, it's hard for me to . . . to accept this. Are you happy?"

"If you can give me a definition of happy that I'm comfortable with, I can answer you. This concern you're showing comes a little late, don't you think?"

"It was always there, I just never verbalized it," Andrew said wearily. "I'm not going to . . . it's your life. Do whatever the hell makes you happy. That's my motto."

"Mine, too." Ruby grinned. "I think there might be a shower available now. The pipes aren't gurgling."

"This is a hell of a nice place, Ruby," Andrew said grudgingly. "Listen, do you think you could whip me up some breakfast before I leave? I hate airplane food."

"You're leaving?" Ruby asked, shocked.

Andrew stopped in his tracks. "Well, yeah. We're all leaving. Martha is . . . I'm going back with her, and she's going to drop me off at Newark Airport. Your sisters . . . I think Andy is driving them into Kennedy. I thought . . . jeez, Ruby, did you think we were staying?"

"Well, you all came so far, I just assumed you'd stay a day or so."

"Those beach bums I left in charge will rob me blind if I don't get back. But if you want me to stay, Ruby, I will."

"No, that's okay. This was all such a surprise," she said lamely. "Eggs and bacon okay?"

"Fifteen minutes," Andrew called over his shoulder.

Marty was next to enter the kitchen. She hugged her mother before she bent down to scratch the dog's ear. "I missed you, Mom."

"I missed you, too, Marty," Ruby said, cracking eggs in a large yellow bowl.

"Did you mean what you said in the barn, about the past being history and all that?"

"Of course. You should know I never say anything I don't mean."

"Then why do I feel this strain between us?"

"It's been a long time, Marty. People change. I love you, that will never change," Ruby said, her heart thumping in her chest.

"Have you forgiven me?" Martha asked in a shaky voice.

"Of course. I thought we weren't going to talk about this. It serves no purpose. It's history."

"I want it to be like it was before. I want yesterday," Marty sobbed.

"It's gone," Ruby said sadly. "We still have today, though. Maybe it can be better than yesterday."

"I didn't mean any of those things I said at Grandma's house."

"At the time you meant them. You said what you felt. I . . . for a long time I thought you had betrayed me. I'm past that now. I hate to see you cry, Marty. Please don't." Ruby took her daughter into her arms.

"Can I come back here?"

"Anytime you want. I'm not planning on going anywhere. I'll always be here for you."

"Do I have to call first?"

"No, of course not. The door will always be open. You don't even need a key. I don't lock up," Ruby said, her own eyes filling with tears.

Ruby knew that Marty wouldn't pop in any old time. And she'd always call first. She thought, for just a second, that she should tell her daughter her own heart wasn't healed yet, but she kept quiet. The day would come when her heart would heal, she was certain of that.

"I'm going to try to talk Dad into staying with me for a few days. What do you think my chances are?"

"Slim to none," Ruby laughed. "He thinks he's being robbed blind by staying here. He's probably right. When you're in a cash business, you're at other people's mercy. But your father is a constant surprise, so who knows? Would you like me to speak to him?"

"Would you, Mom?"

"Sure. Listen, how about taking the dogs for a walk. Are you sure you don't want some breakfast?"

"I'm sure. Mom, was Aunt Amber telling the truth when she said she . . . said she sent back the money?"

Ruby's eyebrows shot upward. "Yes. But it's not important anymore, Marty, so don't worry about it."

Marty snatched two pieces of bacon, sharing one with the dogs, before she left the kitchen.

"Right on the dot, Andrew," Ruby said, pouring the eggs into the fry pan. "Listen, Andrew, I want to ask a favor of you. I've never asked you for anything really . . . really important. I want a yes out of you before I ask you."

Andrew pretended to think. "I guess you're entitled to one favor. Okay. This better not be something like asking me to become celibate."

"I want you to spend a few days with Marty. Will you do it?"

"If you make up whatever I lose with those bums running things back on the island."

"Take it out of my share. You'll do it, then?"

"Yeah, it's not a problem. Forget making it up. She's our kid. I'll do it. Just don't go making a big deal out of it, okay?"

"Okay." She set the plate of eggs in front of her husband. "You know, Andrew, right now I'd kill for those eggs."

"You want half?" he asked, stuffing his mouth.

"You want to see me laid out? What color, Andrew, purple, green, what would I look best in?"

Andrew frowned. "Why don't you tell me exactly what that means?" he said in a strangled voice.

His eyes popped, his jaw dropped as he listened to her recite her medical history.

"That's it! I've had it, Ruby!" he said angrily when she had finished. "This must be a big year for assholes. I cannot believe, I will not believe that you . . . why didn't you tell me . . . tell Andy . . . Martha . . . I would have told *you*."

Ruby laughed, a genuine sound of mirth. "Then there would have been four of us worrying. I did what I thought was best. For me, Andrew. I handled it."

Andrew attacked his eggs again. "When was the last time you had a physical? Are you okay now?" Andrew pushed the plate away. He sounded so concerned, Ruby laughed again.

"Almost. Another six months and I should be back to normal. So, you see, Andrew, this is the best place for me to do what I have to do."

"You could have told me. What the hell do you *do* here to pass the time?"

"Come here, I'll show you." Ruby led him to one of the downstairs garden rooms and pointed to the bookshelves which lined the walls. "I read every one of those books. Come on, you'll have to see this or you won't believe it. Be careful, the steps aren't all that good," Ruby said, switching on the cellar light.

"What the hell . . ."

Ruby waved her hands about. "This is what I did for the first eight or nine months. I only watch one television station, the shopper's channel. I shopped. I bought everything," she said expansively.

"It looks like a goddamn warehouse. They aren't even opened."

"I know. Every time a package came, I just booted it down the steps. I considered it therapy. I spent seventeen thousand dollars. American Express canceled my card. So did all the other companies. I didn't open my mail for six or seven months. I now have a bad credit rating!" Ruby said proudly.

"No shit! Wow!"

"Every one of those credit card companies started law suits against me. The lawyers are handling it. Twenty lawsuits. What do you think of that, Andrew?"

"I'll be damned." Andrew laughed. They slapped one another on the back, both of them hysterical as they ripped and gouged at the boxes. From time to time one or the other would say something funny and they'd go off into peals of laughter. "Bet there's all kinds of stuff here you can take back to the bimbette in Maui." They collapsed on a pile of cardboard cartons, laughing their heads off. Neither of them noticed their children at the top of the steps, or Amber and Opal, who were staring at them as though they'd lost their minds.

Exhausted with their efforts, Andrew put his arm around his wife's shoulders. "I have to get the hell away from you before this kind of stuff starts rubbing off on me. You did okay, Ruby," he said, kissing her lightly on the cheek. "You really did okay. Jesus, I haven't laughed like that in years. I'm glad I came."

"I'm glad, too, Andrew. What say we throw you a soiree when you hit the big six-five?"

"You're on, but let's do it on my turf."

"You ready, Dad?"

"I've been thinking, Marty, how would you like to spend a few days with your old man?"

"I'd love it!" Martha beamed.

"But," Andrew said, holding up his hand, "I want to drive that Testarossa."

"Okay," Martha said happily.

"Bye, Mom. Bye," she said to her aunts and uncle. Ruby winked. Martha ran back to her mother. "Thanks, Mom."

When the sounds of the Ferrari faded away, Andy drew his mother to the side. "You're the best, Ma."

Later, when Amber said good-bye, Ruby thought, *I'm never going to see her again. And I don't care. She means good-bye in the true sense of the word.* "Good-bye, Amber. Good-bye, Nangi," she said, holding on to her brother-in-law a moment longer than necessary.

A minute later, Opal was half out the door, waving airily. "Nice party, Ruby" was all she said.

Ruby stood on the rise, the dogs at her feet, watching till Nangi's rental car was out of sight.

"I think, mind you, this is just my opinion," she said to the dogs, who stopped squabbling long enough to listen, "but I think I just leapt another hurdle." She dusted her hands dramatically to show what she thought of her latest effort.

On the way to the barn Ruby carried on a running conversation with the dogs. "Don't you just love it when the party is for you and you have to clean up?" Suddenly she bolted as she remembered the tiny puppy in the sneaker box. "God, how could I have forgotten!" she shrieked. He was asleep, curled into his paws, prettier than any diamond, more gorgeous than a spring bouquet. A smile spread across her face.

The phone rang. Ruby scooped up the receiver as she poured detergent into the dishwasher. She heard a strange voice say, "This is Eve Santos."

Ruby sucked in her breath, her eyes frantic as she pulled a chair out from the table.

"Yes?"

"I know all about the lawsuit," Eve Santos said coldly. "I also have all the letters you wrote to Calvin. I'll make them public if you go through with this . . . this circus. What do you hope to gain? We don't have any money. Not the kind of money your attorney is demanding."

The dogs were at attention at her feet, Doozie on her lap.

They watched her face, their eyes wide and unblinking. "It's no longer in my hands, Mrs. Santos. You shouldn't be calling me. If you have something to say, have your attorney speak with my attorney."

"You want my husband, don't you? That's what this is all about," Eve said nastily.

"Where did you get my phone number?"

"In a letter you wrote to Calvin. He doesn't even know you sent it. I open the mail at the office."

"Why is that, Mrs. Santos? What are you afraid of? Certainly not me."

"I've known about you for a long time. I told Calvin I knew. I told him I would tell our children if he did something stupid."

Ruby had her wits about her now. "Are you eating peanuts, Mrs. Santos?"

"What?" Eve sputtered.

"Don't threaten me, Mrs. Santos. I personally don't care what you do or who you tell. I'm perfectly happy to let everything come out if this case goes to court. All the things I know about you, I'll say them, too. So remember that when you threaten me. You should be discussing this with Calvin, not me. All I want is the money due to me, which, by the way, he admits he owes in a letter I have in my possession."

"I'll give you back your letters if you give me the ones Calvin wrote you."

Oh, Calvin, what do you have here? "I'm sorry, Mrs. Santos, I can't do that. I don't make deals."

"I know who you are. You think money can buy anything. Well, it can't buy Calvin."

"I know who you are, too, Mrs. Santos. And I never tried to buy your husband. I wanted Calvin's love, yes, because he said it was his to give. But I never bought it. I'd like it if you'd hang up now, Mrs. Santos."

"I'll never give him a divorce. You'll never get him," Eve said venomously.

"You know what, Mrs. Santos? I think you and your husband deserve each other. Do what you want. We'll see one another in court. And don't call me again. Good-bye. Oh, yes, give Calvin my regards." Ruby slammed the phone down. Doozie hissed.

Ruby carried on a running conversation with herself as she snapped the dogs' leashes onto their collars. She continued her discussion as she walked the dogs to the pond and back. She played the conversation over and over in her mind. She should have said this, shouldn't have said that. "The hell with it!" she muttered as she returned to the house. Calvin and Eve Santos were history.

To Ruby, the seasons of her life seemed to leapfrog ahead of her. Nineteen eighty-six was a blur, 1987 blurrier still.

The chrysanthemums were gone now, replaced with holly, a sure sign that winter was ready and waiting to settle on the valley. Christmas was less than ten days away.

What had she done these past two years to make the time go so fast? At times she felt as if she were on an out-of-control treadmill, racing ahead to what she didn't know. What she did know was that there weren't enough hours in her days. She went full-tilt from morning to night.

The kitchen was sunny and warm, just the way she liked it in the early hours. She hadn't changed anything in the farmhouse; lemons were still on the table, the fire still blazed, the dogs still snoozed, Charlotte still sang her heart out most of the day, Doozie still sat on top of the refrigerator. She, Ruby Blue, hadn't changed, either.

But Dixie still hadn't been located and Calvin had managed to stall her lawyers and the lawsuit, but he'd finally given up and paid. She wondered if she would ever hear from him again. Somehow she doubted it. And she doubted that she would care.

There was something ominous about today, Ruby thought from the kitchen window as she watched the snow fall. She couldn't explain her feelings. She thought about calling Nola to invite her and her son for Christmas. Maybe, just maybe he and Marty would hit it off. She didn't want to talk, though. She couldn't explain that to herself, either.

Andy was fine, working on the ice-skating rink he was designing for a hockey player who lived twenty miles down the road. She'd never seen Andy as happy as he'd been this past year. Hockey had always been his first love, when it came to sports. Marty was fine, too. Ruby had called her earlier in the day. There had been a letter from Nola in the mail. Nothing wrong there. It was her. The fine hairs on the back of her neck started to prickle. Somewhere, something was wrong. Something that involved her somehow.

Because she didn't know what else to do, she called Andrew. She could hear the sound of the surf when he spoke on the portable phone he carried with him everywhere. "Andrew, it's Ruby. Listen, I'd like it if you'd come for Christmas. It will be just us and maybe Nola and her son. How about it?"

"Send me a ticket and I'm yours. First class, Ruby. Yeah, I'd like to see snow again. Hey, thanks for asking. I'll look forward to it. I'll start to make plans. Is anything wrong?"

"No, of course not. I just thought you'd like to spend Christmas with your family."

"You sound a little strange."

"I don't know. Today is kind of strange. I feel . . . like something is going to happen. It's snowing, but then, I love snow. Maybe I'm . . ."

"Getting eccentric in your old age?" Andrew chuckled. "Make yourself a drink and say the hell with whatever is bothering you. That's what I do. Gotta go, Ruby, I got some cash customers waiting. Thanks for the invitation."

"My pleasure, Andrew." Suddenly she didn't want to hang up. She needed to keep talking, needed to hear another voice, but Andrew was already gone. She called the office, but her secretary couldn't talk either.

She loved the snow, had always loved the snow. Maybe if she went for a walk by herself, her head would clear and she could shake off this ominous feeling settling between her shoulders. Or she could go back into the living room and finish her Christmas wrapping. She decided on the walk.

Ruby returned two hours later, her legs aching, but she felt good, less tense. She hung up her coat and set about making some vanilla hazelnut coffee. She loved the smell of it. The dogs were on their feet the moment the coffee grinder whirred to life. She carried her steaming cup into the living room, the animals on her heel. The Christmas tree was up, but unadorned. Ruby brought out the ornaments.

By five o'clock the huge living room was fragrant with balsam. A fire blazed, the Christmas tree lights twinkled, the mistletoe and the huge wreath, with its red velvet bow, proclaimed that the Christmas season had arrived at Orchard Circle. Ruby dusted her hands dramatically as she closed the last box of ornaments. She'd done it all herself. For the first time in many years, she felt the Christmas spirit.

She was humming to herself, the stereo was playing Christmas songs, the dogs were tramping through the pile of wrap and ribbons she'd left in the middle of the floor. Doozie was hopelessly tangled in a skein of red ribbon.

Gaily wrapped presents were piled as high as the branches of the tree in a wide half circle. They were also piled in corners, on tables, and under tables, on chairs and sofas. They were piled in crazy angles at the base of the stairs and into the alcove. Mounds of presents stood like sentinels on each side of the front door. The dining room contained the overflow, as did the room she called the library. Hundreds of presents, maybe thousands, for all she knew. She shopped daily and wrapped nightly. She had presents for everyone: Mikey, Biddy, the Semolina brothers and cousins, her children, and Andrew. The dogs had their own pile, as did Doozie.

She'd been baking for days now and the smells in the house were so delightful, she walked around sniffing and smiling to herself.

Charlotte was singing a chorus from "Jingle Bells" when Ruby walked into the kitchen to toss a pile of crumpled papers into the trash. Her front doorbell rang just as she was pulling the vacuum cleaner from the closet. Doozie's back went up. Sam snarled as he raced from the kitchen to the living room and the front door. Fred growled low in her throat. The only person who ever rang her front doorbell was Rob Frazier, the woodcutter.

Surely it wasn't Rob, not in this weather.

The bell rang a second time. "Okay, okay, I'm coming. Stay!" she ordered the dogs. When the bell rang a third time, Charlotte started to sing again.

Ruby opened the door, fully expecting to see Rob Frazier.

"Dixie!" Ruby did the only thing she could think of. She slammed the door shut. Doozie hissed as she circled Ruby's trembling legs. Sam's ears flattened against his head. Fred continued to growl. Number Five was tramping through the Christmas wrap. Ruby watched her squat and pee. She felt her eyes roll back in her head.

The doorbell rang again and again.

Ruby opened the door a second time.

"Please Ruby, can I come in?"

"Why?" Ruby demanded.

"Because I need to talk to you."

"Lately everyone needs to talk to me. Well, I don't need to talk to you. Get the hell off my property, Dixie. I don't want to see you, and I don't want to talk to you, either."

All the old anger and hurt rushed to the surface. She completely forgot about the private detective and the soul-searching she'd done in regard to Dixie.

"Then I'll stand out here and freeze, because I'm not leaving until you talk to me."

"Suit yourself," Ruby said, slamming the door a second time.

The animals were in a frenzy, sensing their mistress's distress.

Ruby felt out of control, much the way she'd felt the night Hugo Sinclaire's ashes had rained over her. In her heart of hearts she'd always hoped Dixie would come back, but the logical side of her believed she'd never see her old friend again. How many times she'd rehearsed different scenarios, from wrapping Dixie in her arms and saying, "Whatever it is, it's okay, I forgive you," to "Get the hell out of my life, drop dead, go away, I never want to see you again." The ornery streak in her said Dixie had to pay for all the hurt and anger. Standing in the cold and snow was a small payback for the anguish she'd suffered.

The time was here. She could play out whatever scene she wanted.

Ruby parted the sheer curtain on the slim pane of glass in her front door. Dixie was sitting on the steps, her arms wrapped around her knees. A stubborn woman. Dixie would sit there till she took root or froze to death. She owed Dixie nothing, not even the time of day. Then why did you hire the private detective? she argued with herself.

It was Christmas, for God's sake, couldn't Dixie have waited till after the holidays to come around and upset her life? Now everything was different. She thought she was past the anger, past the hurt. She felt dizzy with the thoughts ricocheting in her head.

Ruby sat down; the animals sat next to her. She inhaled the fragrant balsam twined around the banister, her eyes on the six-foot Christmas tree with its twinkling lights. Tears burned her eyes as she stared at the mountains of presents. Not one for Dixie. "Oh, no, I'm not playing *that* game."

How long would Dixie sit out there in the snow? She knew the answer. Forever. Ruby didn't move. Her stomach churned. Why now, after all this time? Dixie must want something.

You're being cruel, Ruby. Open the door. Dixie is like a sister. Better than a sister. You love her. It doesn't matter what happened before. It's the now that counts.

Ruby scratched behind Sam's ears. "I'm not in the life-saving business anymore," she muttered to the dogs. "I'm fresh out of absolution. You want absolution, go to church." Her eyes continued to burn. How had Dixie found her way here? Obviously, the private detective had located her.

Fred was on her lap, nuzzling her neck. Number Five was back in the pile of Christmas wrap. He was pooping on a piece of red wrapping paper that said Noel. It was her fault. She hadn't let the animals out in a while. Maybe she should sic them on Dixie, let them chase her off the property. *Grow up, Ruby. Be kind. Forgive whatever you think her sin is. Listen to her. Give her a chance.*

Ruby looked at her watch. Twenty minutes had gone by. Dixie hadn't been dressed too warmly. Ruby gently eased Fred off her lap and walked jerkily to the door. She parted the sheer curtain. Dixie was huddled on the steps. She was covered with snow.

Her face grim, her lips narrowed into a thin, tight line, Ruby yanked the door open. "Okay, I'll give you ten minutes. I don't want your death on my conscience."

Dixie struggled to her feet. Ruby noticed she wasn't wearing gloves.

Dixie shook herself the way animals did when they were wet. She stomped the snow off her shoes. Stupid shoes. Sling backs with open toes.

Ruby didn't offer to take her coat, but she said, not unkindly, "Come in by the fire."

"This is pretty," Dixie said, looking around. "It smells good, too. You were always big on smells. I'm kind of cold, Ruby. Do you think I could have a cup of coffee or something?"

"All right, but it's going to eat into your ten minutes," Ruby muttered.

In the kitchen she poured the coffee, then put it into the microwave to heat it. While she waited she rearranged the lemons. When the coffee was steaming, she added an extra spoon of sugar to it. At the last second she bent down to pick up her slipper-socks by the rocking chair.

"Put these on. When your feet are cold, the rest of you can't get warm."

"Thanks, Ruby," Dixie said gratefully. "Are all these animals yours?"

"Yes. They're better than *some* people." Number Five, the new puppy, was by Dixie's feet, wiggling and squirming. She was rubbing her belly.

"Let's cut to the quick, the social part is over. What do you want? I know you want something, otherwise you wouldn't be here. Just for the record. You broke my heart. Now I'm just starting to get it back together, and here you are. As far as I'm concerned, you're yesterday's news."

"I want yesterday back," Dixie said quietly.

"Well, it's gone," Ruby said quietly. "So if there's nothing more, you should be on your way. You can keep the socks."

"Ruby, please, I need to talk to you. I want to try and explain ..."

"Now, where have I heard those words before? We don't have anything to say to one another. You're just someone I used to know."

"When did you get so bitter?" Dixie asked quietly.

"When? You have the nerve to ask me that?" Ruby raged. "Why don't you just kick me in the gut and stomp me to death? I don't understand. I *never* understood."

"I had some problems. I had to handle ... I don't know. I panicked. I had to run. It was either that, or once again lay everything in your lap, and that just wasn't fair."

"Oh, no, you don't. You aren't laying this one on me," Ruby grated as she paced the living room. She was almost dizzy with the scent of the evergreen in her nostrils. "Nobody forces anyone to do anything. You had a free will. You chose to disappear. You chose to cut me off. I don't want to hear it. It's over, it's history. I want to sell you my half of the business, not that there's much left to sell. Business is down. Those upstarts snapping at Mrs. Sugar's heels should have been nipped in the bud, but I couldn't do anything because you weren't around to agree. What's their names—Mrs. Field and David? They now have the corner on the cookie business. Now they want to buy *us*. I was always there for you, Dixie," Ruby sobbed.

"I seem to remember being there for you, too," Dixie sobbed in return.

"You ran away. You sold your goddamn house. All you had to do was make one phone call, send one letter, a fucking note, telling me you were okay, that you had a problem you had to deal with. Five minutes out of your life, but I wasn't worth the effort. Get out of my face, Dixie. I'm sick of you and your excuses," Ruby said shrilly. "You said we were a team, better than sisters. You said we were going to grow old together and sit in rocking chairs and reminisce. That was all bullshit of the worst kind, because you knew it was a lie. I believed in our friendship. You didn't and that's the bottom line."

Ruby sat down on the sofa and dropped her head into her hands. She couldn't stop the flow of tears. The dogs inched closer, eyeing Dixie warily. Doozie was on the mantel, hissing and snarling.

Dixie walked across the room. She dropped to her knees, careful to stay far enough away from Ruby so the jittery dogs wouldn't spring at her.

"I couldn't handle the success, Ruby. That's what my shrink said, anyway. I couldn't seem to get a handle on anything after Hugo died. All I did was exist, mark time. Even when I got sick, I couldn't bring myself to go to the hospital for two years. I just didn't care. I didn't want any more troubles, any more problems. When you don't know what to do, do nothing, right? I was so damned tired of being a burden to you and to myself."

Ruby raised her head, tears rolling down her cheeks. "You expect me to buy that bullshit? You marked time for five goddamn fucking years? Stuff it. I'm not stupid. You hung me out to dry. I'd appreciate it if you'd leave now," Ruby said wearily, the tears drying on her cheeks. *Sick? What did she mean?*

"I was never as tough as you, Ruby," Dixie said sadly. "I couldn't stare it down and pull up my socks."

"I would have helped you. That's what friends are for. Why now, after so long?"

"Well, I thought if I came here now, at this time of year, you might feel more charitable toward me. At least I hoped so. Because I need you. I need someone to take care of me. I'm dying, Ruby. I have breast cancer. I had a mastectomy three years ago, but the tumor has come back."

Ruby's head whirled. She felt faint, sick. "Who told you you were going to die?"

"I've been to five different specialists. It's not spreading,

Ruby, it's galloping through my entire body. Each day I ... I don't have long, Ruby. A month at the most. I'm taking massive ... Look, I don't want to die alone, and you're all I have. I didn't mean to come here and spoil your Christmas. Ruby, I am so sorry."

Dixie was dying and she was apologizing for it. Ruby looked at her old friend, really looked at her. She opened her arms and Dixie stepped into them. All the bad was gone, the years wiped away. Ruby swore later that she felt her broken heart snap back together.

"I wanted to tell you ... so many things," Ruby said. "About myself. About us, our friendship. I wanted to clear all the negative out of my life. I spent a lot of time being angry with you. The reasons I came here aren't important, but this place, these animals and some very nice people, helped me to get back on track. And Andrew has been wonderful. Hard to believe, huh? My God, of course I'll ... take care of you. I'll do my best, but are you sure you don't ... wouldn't you be better off in a ..."

"No, Ruby. This is right for me, if you can handle it. If you can't, I can walk away. As you always say, I'm good at that. Only promise one thing. I don't want a *place*. You have to agree to that."

"*No place!* Oh, no, Dixie, I can't agree to that."

"No place, Ruby," Dixie said stubbornly. "I know you. You'll go there all the time and weep and wail, and before you know it, you'll be blaming yourself for my death. No place. Promise me."

Ruby sniffed, the tears rolling down her cheeks. She nodded.

"Everything is taken care of legally. I'm not leaving you a mess to deal with. Ruby, I think I love you more than anyone on this earth. I'm not just saying that because ... I'm saying it because it's true. Do you think I could lie down for a little while?"

"Lie down," Ruby said stupidly. "Oh, lie down. Yes, yes, of course. Can you make it up the steps? I can help you. Lean on me, Dixie."

In the guest bedroom, Ruby turned on the electric blanket. "Sit here and don't move."

Ruby ran to her room for one of her long flannel nightgowns and a pair of heavy wool socks. Within minutes she had stripped off Dixie's clothing and bundled her up in bed. Dixie was so emaciated. Skin and bones. Tears rolled down Ruby's cheeks.

"Don't cry for me, Ruby. I cried enough for both of us. I hate to ask this, but could you get me something warm to drink? I have some pills I have to take, and they go down easier with tea. That's silly, isn't it?"

"No, not at all. Just tell me what to do and I'll do it. I'm going to make a fire for you. The room will be toasty in a few minutes. The wood is really dry. It's cherry, and it smells so nice. See, it's sparking. Oh, Dixie, I wish there were something more . . . you should have come sooner," she babbled. "I'll be right back with the tea. Do you like the flavored kind? It's all I have."

"It's fine, Ruby. Hot water would be fine, too."

In the hall and on the way down the steps Ruby cried. For all the would-haves, the could-haves, the should-haves. She was still crying while she waited for the water to boil. Without thinking why, she picked up the phone and called Andrew. She sobbed in misery as she told him what happened.

"Andrew, I need you to come here," she told him. "I need someone nearby, someone I can count on to . . . to pick me up if I . . . if I falter. I know it's asking a lot. You can help Andy with the ice-rink project he's working on for that hockey player. I need a friend, Andrew."

"I'm packing as you speak. I won't be able to get a flight out till morning, unless you want me to charter one. It's your call, Ruby."

"Go for it, Andrew. Just get here as soon as you can."

Andrew walked into Ruby's kitchen the following afternoon looking haggard. "Jesus, you could have told me you had two feet of snow," he blustered good-naturedly. The animals circled his feet, yapping and barking to be petted. He obliged, his eyes on Ruby.

"Coffee?" she asked.

"Hell yes, and something to eat."

Ruby broke down. She started to shake, tears rolling down her cheeks. Andrew wrapped her in his arms.

"Jesus, Ruby, what can I do?"

"I don't know, Andrew. Maybe nothing. Just be here for me, okay? If you see that I'm . . . you know . . . not cutting it . . .

kick me in the shins, anything to get me . . . I have to do this, but I'm all screwed up. There's one little part of me that won't let go of the hurt and the anger. Say something, Andrew. Help me."

"Ruby, you can't save the entire world by yourself. You are a born giver, but you're not perfect. No one is. You've told me yourself the reason you failed in your relationships is that you expected too much from other people. But you haven't figured out that you also expect too much from yourself. You're allowed to falter now and again. It's no big sin, Ruby. I think it's okay for you to hang on to that little bit you don't want to let go of. It's who you are."

"But, Dixie . . ."

"There is no doubt in my mind that she loves and trusts you more than anyone in the world. She knew you would come through for her. She knows you better than you know yourself. Don't worry about forgiving her. Just open your heart all the way to her, Ruby, even if you're still angry. All the way or you won't get through it."

"Andrew . . . Andrew . . ."

"Yes," Andrew drawled.

"I never . . . I never thought about it like that. You mean that I could be so angry with her and still love her? How did *you* . . . how did you get so smart?"

"How the hell should I know? We both know I'm a selfish bastard. I don't want to talk about this, Ruby," Andrew said.

A long time later Ruby said, "It's almost Christmas. What kind of holiday is this going to be?"

"It's going to be whatever you make it. I hope you bought me a great present."

"What kind of present are you giving me?"

"Something you will treasure the rest of your life."

Ruby snorted. "I'll believe that when I see it. Marty told me you started watching the shopper's channel. You better not be giving me something you bought over the TV, Andrew."

"It's a meaningful present," Andrew said.

Sam took that moment to appear in the kitchen. He tugged on Ruby's pant leg before he raced back upstairs. "Dixie's awake. All she's done is sleep. Sometimes she doesn't . . . she's back in the past . . . this morning she didn't know me for a little while. I called the local doctor and he came by earlier. He said he was sending over a stronger painkiller. I feel so helpless. I need to *do* something for her."

"You are. What you're doing is making her last days as good as you can make them. You, Ruby, not some nurse, not some stranger."

"Come with me, Andrew. I know Dixie would like to see you. We'll say you came early for the holidays."

"Look who's here, Dix," Ruby said cheerfully when they came into her room.

"Dixie, it's good to see you," Andrew said, leaning over the bed to kiss her cheek. "Sorry you're under the weather."

"Andrew, it's nice to see you. Are you here for the holidays?"

"Yep. You're stuck with me for a while. For now, though, I'm going to let you ladies talk. I think if I want to be fed, I'm going to have to do some snow-shoveling. You do have a shovel, don't you, Ruby?"

"It's on the back porch."

"Can I try one of the new pills?" Dixie asked when Andrew had gone.

"They didn't get here yet, Dixie. There's a lot of snow out there. I don't know if the main roads have been plowed."

"Then can I have two of the others? The pink ones."

"Sure." Whatever it takes, Ruby said to herself. Did it matter now if Dixie got two or three pills instead of one? "Can I get you a book, or would you like me to turn on the television? Are you warm enough?"

"I'm fine, Ruby. I think I might like some sound, though."

"Music? I can bring in my portable radio. Would you like that?" Dixie nodded.

A little while later Ruby was back in the stifling bedroom, trying to make Dixie comfortable.

"Ruby, don't try so hard," Dixie whispered.

"Am I doing that?"

"I think so. Talk to me, okay? Tell me everything from the time . . . from the time I left. Don't leave anything out."

Ruby talked until her voice grew raspy.

It was late afternoon when Dixie said, "What will you do if you sell the business?"

"I don't know. I'll think about that when the time comes. I do know one thing, though. I'm never going to leave this place. I might go away, but this is the home I've always wanted. I belong here. Money isn't an issue for me, my children, their children, or their grandchildren. I've provided for generations still to come. If I said I was going to do good deeds, would you laugh at me?"

"No. I'd say good for you, Ruby. If you ever get tired of doing that, you'll have the brownie recipe. Maybe you can do something with it. I wish I'd tasted one."

Ruby broke down then and howled her grief. "It's not fair," she bellowed. "Why does it have to be you? Why not some criminal, some person who deserves to . . . why you? You never did anything wrong. You're a good person. It isn't time for you to go. I need more time with you!" Ruby cried out, totally losing control.

Down below, on the first floor, Andrew knocked over his coffee cup and then took the stairs two at a time.

Inside the bedroom Ruby was screaming, tears flooding her eyes. She'd flung herself on the bed, her hands clutching Dixie's.

"What the hell . . ."

"Shut up, Andrew. Just shut the fuck up," Ruby wailed.

Andrew watched then as Dixie comforted her friend, mouthing words he'd heard Ruby say to their children. His wife calmed almost immediately under Dixie's gentle touch. He continued to watch as the Yorkie licked her tears. He was seeing something here he'd never seen before, something he knew he would never experience no matter how hard he tried. True, loving, devoted friendship. The kind that comes along once in a lifetime.

"Now, Andrew, you can speak," Ruby said, sliding off the bed.

"Ah, the man from the drugstore dropped off Dixie's prescription."

"Would you please fetch it?" Ruby said calmly.

"Sure. I just made coffee, can I bring you some?"

"Yes, coffee would be nice. Dixie?"

"Thank you, but just half a cup."

"Dixie, I'm sorry, I didn't mean to go off on you like that."

"It's okay, Ruby. You feel better now, don't you?"

"Yes, I do."

"To answer your question, since God isn't here to answer it for you, it's my time, Ruby."

"I know," Ruby said, biting down on her lip.

"I made a decision today," Dixie said. "I decided that it's okay to have a place, but there are . . . certain conditions. Promise me you'll give me a hell of a sendoff."

"The biggest and the best," Ruby said. "Are you agreeing to this because of me? If so, don't, Dixie. I can handle it."

"No, not for you, Ruby," Dixie lied. "For me."

"Okay, but just so you know I can handle it," Ruby lied in return.

"All the big things are settled, then," Dixie said tiredly.

"I think so. Okay, open up, here's your new pill. Easy now, just a little sip."

Dixie fell back against the pillows. "Ruby, tell me again about Biddy and Mikey and the preserve you had built. I think that's the most wonderful thing I've ever heard. You should do one in New Jersey, maybe down by the pine barrens. It's your way of giving back, isn't it? I'd like to contribute if you do. Why don't you decide now so I can sign . . . you know, while I still can."

"You got it. Andy should be finished with his skating-rink project in January. I'll get him started on it right away. I think I'm his best client." Ruby could deny nothing to this woman she called her friend.

"Tell me about Biddy and Mikey," Dixie said.

"Well, it was like this . . ."

A new routine was established in the Blue farmhouse the day after Dixie's arrival. It was Andrew's job to walk and feed the animals. He prepared sketchy meals for himself and Ruby and even dusted and wet-mopped the kitchen floor. Ruby's duties consisted of caring for Dixie, changing her bedlinens, washing her, combing her hair, changing her oversize diaper, and singing lullabies that made her friend smile.

Ruby sat in a deep, comfortable chair that Andrew had carried upstairs. She talked constantly while she held Dixie's hot, dry hand. Her monologues started with her earliest memory and worked forward. She spared herself not at all. Often Andrew found himself listening before entering the room with coffee or a cup of tea. More than once he walked downstairs with tears of frustration in his eyes. He worked out that frustration with the wet mop and the dustcloth. He broke so many dishes, he went into town to buy a new set.

Ruby's devotion was total, all-consuming.

Christmas and the New Year passed quietly. Dixie grew weaker, until she was unable to lift her head from the pillow. On the tenth day of the new year, with Ruby holding one of her hands and the old local country doctor holding the other, Dixie Sinclaire took her final breath.

Ruby walked dry-eyed down the stairs to her kitchen, Andrew's arm around her shoulder.

"Let me make the arrangements, Ruby."

"I have to do it, Andrew. Thanks for offering, though."

"Are you okay?"

Was she? Would she ever be okay again? Yes, in time. "She didn't deserve the heartache she suffered. I contributed to that, and for the rest of my life I will carry that around with me. She is ... was a better person than I'll ever be. I'm going to miss her, Andrew. She told me to bury her here in Pennsylvania so it would be easier for me to ... visit. I will, too."

"I know you will, Ruby," Andrew said, hugging her.

The Oliverie and Son Funeral Home was a two-story, pale-pink brick edifice with four white columns supporting a stark white portico. Small circular flowerbeds, barren now, dotted the half-acre of frontage along with beds of holly and shrubbery which looked as if it were pruned and clipped with manicure scissors.

Two hearses, one white and one black, sat in the driveway.

Ruby's movements were like an old woman's when she climbed from the Range Rover. Andrew stumbled behind her. Together they made their way to the gleaming white door. The interior was cool and dim. She was aware of dark colors, somber colors, dull-looking brass, and the sickening scent of flowers. Music of some sort was playing softly in the background. Maybe it wasn't music. Chirping birds and the sound of a waterfall wasn't really music. Paradise. Eternity. It was a crock.

A woman dressed in a three-piece suit was sitting at the neatest desk Ruby ever saw. She rose to greet them. She looked, Ruby thought, like one of Oliverie's customers, with her waxy makeup and round circles of rouge. She smiled a greeting that barely stretched her facial muscles.

"I'm Ruby Blue."

"Yes, of course you are. We've been waiting for you. Follow me, please. She turned smartly, the skirt of her gray suit fussing about her knees. It hiked a little. Ruby fought the urge to bolt and run.

"Easy, Ruby," Andrew said under his breath, sensing Ruby's need to escape.

"And this is our showroom," the three-piece suit said quietly. The moment she closed the door, the birds stopped chirping and the sounds of the waterfall ceased, to be replaced with flute music. Ruby shivered. "Mr. Oliverie will be with you in a moment."

It *was* only a moment when Pasquale Oliverie, Sr., turned on the bright fluorescent lights. "Mrs. Blue, you have my deepest sympathy. Such a tragic loss." He shook his head. "Tragic," he said in his somber, professional voice. "Walk around, Mrs. Blue, take your time. Ask me any questions and I'll be glad to answer them. This is our moderate to high, the last row, of course, is quite simple and economically priced." His voice clearly said no one, but no one, picked from the last row.

Ruby swallowed past the lump in her throat. She looked at Andrew, who half-heartedly pointed to the second casket in the deluxe row.

"May I say you have discriminating taste, Mr. Blue. That's our most popular choice. Airtight. Double lock. I'm partial to bronze myself. The crepe de chine coverlet is a work of art. The pillow is down-filled. Mrs. Sinclaire will look lovely in it."

The birds chirped, the waterfall gurgled, and Andrew yanked at Ruby's arm.

Ruby nodded numbly.

"You won't be sorry. I always say one's final journey should be made in style. Now, if you'll follow me into the office, we can conclude this sorrowful chore."

When the trio reached Pasquale Oliverie's office, Ruby noticed a serving cart with an elaborate silver service. A plate of danish on a lace paper doily. Fine china cups with silver rims and sterling silver spoons were passed around. Ruby's hand trembled when she accepted a cup. It rattled against the saucer. She tried to balance it on her knee. It still rattled. She handed it to Andrew, who set it on the tray. "I feel as if I've been put here by mistake, Andrew," she whispered. Andrew nodded.

"Now, Mrs. Blue, about the viewing," Oliverie said briskly. "Tomorrow at two o'clock and again at seven o'clock. Three hours each."

"Viewing?" Ruby gawked at the funeral director.

"Yes, viewing. Your friends will want to pay their respects. Three days is customary."

"No," Ruby said in a voice she didn't recognize as her own. "No viewing."

"Very well," Oliverie said huffily. "Did you bring the clothing?"

"What clothing?" Ruby said blankly.

"The clothing you want your friend laid out in," Oliverie said patiently.

"It . . . it will get here by Federal Express this morning."

It was eleven o'clock when Ruby and Andrew left Oliverie and Son. "It's expensive to die," Ruby muttered.

"Sure seems that way," Andrew said. "Now what?"

"Now what *what*?"

"What do we do now? What about flowers? Who calls the minister?"

"Doesn't Oliverie do that?" Ruby asked harshly. "My mother had everything written down. What kind of flowers she wanted, who were to be the pallbearers, where she wanted to be buried. She even had the plots ahead of time."

"Some people do that," Andrew said.

"Yeah. Okay, drive over to the church and then the flower shop."

The pit loomed in front of her. She closed her eyes behind the oversize black glasses, refusing to look ahead at the opening directly in her line of vision. It was a hole, a very large hole, the biggest damn hole she'd ever seen. A sound bubbled in her throat. A giggle? Relief? The sound threatened to erupt again. Instead, she concentrated on the Astroturf she was standing on, which was greener than any grass, and the thin winter sunshine filtering around the edges of the faded matching awning.

Where were her tears? She should be riddled with grief, not feeling this all-consuming panic. Maybe this numb feeling *was* grief. Ruby's gaze moved behind the dark shades, first to the right and then to the left. Who did all these shoes belong to? Her children, a few friends, reporters. The man in the white collar wasn't saying any of the things she'd written down. Ministers, Unitarian and otherwise, were not supposed to say stupid, meaningless things about dead people who deserved to be honored. The list she'd handed to the reverend had been long, detailed, and so carefully written. Here lies a gentle, caring woman, a woman born to laughter and warmth. A generous woman not only with her life but her time as well. A woman who could laugh at herself, a woman whose eyes filled at the sight of the tin cans the Humane Society placed in stores for contributions. A gourmet cook, a wonderful friend, a forgiving friend. She'd wanted all these things said. This damnable idiot was mumbling about good neighbors and helping hands.

Ruby's head inched up slightly. She stared at the casket she'd chosen. Top of the line. Fifty big ones. That was okay; it was the least she could do, but where was the lock the mortician promised? It was supposed to have a lock with the combination taped inside the bronze coffin. Never mind that he'd looked at her as though she was crazy, which she was at the time. Vaguely she recalled saying, "It isn't necessary for you to understand, just do it!" It had been Dixie's request. "In case my spirit wants to get out," she'd said. Goddamn it, he'd promised. She wouldn't pay, that's all there was to it. She wouldn't pay the damn penguin, either. Oh, God, oh, God, she was really dead. Gone.

"Ashes to ashes, dust to dust . . ." Over. Done. In another few minutes the mourners, complete with long-stemmed roses, the same kind she was holding, would file past the casket to pay their final respects. She dropped her rose and ground it to a watery pulp in the Astroturf. She didn't have to pay her final respects.

Was the casket *really* waterproof? Maggots and worms . . . what would they attack first? The toes, the ankles . . . oh, God, she was really dead. Dust to dust, ashes to ashes . . . what about the skeleton? In the movies, bones lasted for hundreds of years. Ashes to ashes. Ashes were thick, dust was dry, almost as thin as air. Oh, God, oh, God . . . she was really dead.

Ruby's eyes snapped open. She thought about moving but didn't. They were all watching her, all the pairs of shoes, waiting for her to throw herself on the casket.

They were going to be disappointed. Six Valium in as many hours didn't allow for sudden moves. A hand touched her elbow.

"You don't have to leave, but you must stand over here," the minister said, motioning to the brick walkway to her left.

"You didn't say any of the things I wanted. I wrote them down so you would . . ."

"My dear, they simply weren't appropriate," the minister said quietly.

"Reverend," Ruby said just as quietly, "I don't give a good rat's ass what you think is appropriate. I paid for this funeral and all you . . . you made her sound like a stranger, someone I didn't know . . . when someone is dead she has the right . . . I have the right . . . get away from me . . . I'll say the words myself. You should be ashamed, Reverend."

"My dear, you're upset . . . it's only natural for you to feel . . ." the minister tried lamely, knowing he'd forfeited her donation.

"Don't placate me, Reverend, not now," Ruby said icily.

In the end Ruby found it impossible to summon forth the words she wanted. She looked around for her children, certain they would have disobeyed her instructions to leave her alone at the end. Instead, they were following them to the letter and driving off.

She was alone now.

{{{{{{{{{ CHAPTER THIRTY-ONE }}}}}}}}}

Ruby longed for spring, wished for it fervently, but it seemed intent on eluding her, and no amount of wishing was going to make it arrive one day sooner than March 21.

It was raw and cold with patches of snow still on the ground. Ruby found herself ticking off the days on the kitchen calendar. Another week. She wondered if the flowers would magically poke their heads through the hard ground on the morning of the twenty-first. That, she decided, would take a miracle, or at least an immediate warming trend. The calendar said it was 1989, which meant she was still on the sunny side of sixty. Two and a half years to go till she hit the big six-zero. The thought didn't depress her at all. If she had any regrets these days, it was that she had never had one completely euphorically happy day. Other than that, she was content with her life.

Last year she'd finally allowed the friends she'd made over the years to get a little closer. She now belonged to the Garden Club, was an active member of the library reading group, taught a Sunday School class, and belonged to the little white church in the town square. She was active in environmental issues and constantly wrote her opinions and letters to the local newspapers. She headed a recycling drive and gave a speech at a town meeting about the hazards of plastic containers on the environment. Any extra time she had was devoted to animal rights. It was not unusual at all for her to spend every waking hour of her weekends campaigning with animal rights activists.

Ruby Blue became a "rights and causes" person.

She was disgruntled on the morning of March 24 when she returned to her kitchen from walking the dogs. There hadn't been one sprout, one green blade poking through the heavy mulch.

She was home today, with a heavy, thick, head cold she couldn't shake. She felt listless, out of sorts, poor company for anyone who called or stopped by. Better to stay by herself and be miserable alone.

Ruby had her head in a steam tent, trying to unclog her stuffy nose, when a news bulletin blared on the kitchen television. She removed the towel.

Her eyes widened as the commentator gave details of an oil spill in Alaska. Eleven million gallons of oil. A tanker, the *Exxon Valdez*, had run aground. Prince William Sound. Ruby tried to picture the state of Alaska in her mind. She couldn't bring it into focus. Eleven million gallons of crude oil was something she couldn't comprehend. What she did understand was that it was a disaster for the Alaskan environment.

She forgot about her cold as she stayed glued to the television all evening and for the next ten days. Then she made a decision.

After the dogs were fed and walked and she'd cleaned the kitchen, Ruby called Nola.

Nola sounded happy to hear from her. "How are you, Ruby?

I've been thinking about coming up for the weekend. Can you use some company?"

"Normally I'd jump at a visit from you, but I won't be here. I'm going away. That's why I'm calling. I was wondering if maybe, if your calendar is clear, you might want to go with me."

"A vacation! I'd love it. Where are you planning on going?"

"It isn't exactly a vacation. I'm going to Alaska to help with the oil spill. I'd like it if you could see your way to come along."

"Are you serious?"

"Never more serious in my life. I've been thinking about this for days. I need to give back, Nola, for all the good in my life. It's that simple. I want to do this. I *need* to do this. Do you think it's something you might want to do?" Ruby held her breath, as she waited for her friend's answer.

"You know what, Ruby? I think this is the best idea you have come up with yet. I've been watching the news myself. The only problem is my dog."

"Hey," Ruby said, her breath exploding in a long swoosh, "hop in the car and bring him here. Mikey and Biddy are going to take care of my animals. I'm sure they won't mind one more. I'll wait up for you. It's okay to go ahead and make all the arrangements, then?"

"More than all right. I need to give back myself. Thanks, Ruby, for thinking of me."

"I always think of you, Nola. You're my friend," Ruby said happily.

"I'll see you in a couple of hours. God, Ruby, this is going to be so wonderful. Just me and you, like in the old days. God."

"Yeah. God," Ruby whispered as she hung up the phone.

On the eleventh day Ruby and Nola were standing in front of 1436 U Street in Washington, D.C. Ruby pushed through the door marked GREENPEACE.

A tired-looking man raised his eyes from his desk.

Ruby laid the newspaper detailing the Alaskan oil spill on the man's desk.

"My name is Ruby Blue. This is Nola Quantrell. What can we do?"